# FOUR COUNTRIES

# FOUR COUNTRIES

*by*

WILLIAM PLOMER

'. . . and life delights in life'
BLAKE

JONATHAN CAPE
THIRTY BEDFORD SQUARE
LONDON

FIRST PUBLISHED 1949

PRINTED IN GREAT BRITAIN BY BUTLER AND TANNER LTD.
FROME AND LONDON
BOUND BY A. W. BAIN AND CO. LTD.

# CONTENTS

# CONTENTS
## STORIES OF ENGLAND

6

# PREFACE

AFTER I had selected and arranged these stories, their present publisher asked me to provide some kind of introduction to them. If they were now making their first appearance I might have recoiled from this invitation, but they have all been printed and some reprinted, and have therefore been through a period of probation. Whatever I may say about them now cannot alter what has been said by others, and can hardly increase or lessen the likelihood of their being read — that must depend on the stories themselves.

I cannot pretend that when I began writing fiction I had any cut-and-dried theory about the nature and art of the short story. It seemed to me then, as it seems to me now, that the genesis of a good story may be not unlike that of a poem, and that a good story must have, above all things, cogency and point. In recent years there has been a cult of the short story, and some of its devotees have been solemnly self-conscious; some, indeed, have tried to fob off on us the feeblest trifles, mere notes and sketches that leave the reader none the happier and none the wiser, that leave him in fact quite unmoved, except to mild exasperation or a yawn. We rightly expect a story to have a point, and this generally means that we expect it to be dramatic. A short story must let us into the secrets of other people's lives, and unless it lets us into their lives at a moment of crisis, it is unlikely to have much point or to be dramatic. The crisis may be a small one, but a crisis there must be. This crisis must engage the reader's imagination, and it must illuminate some new or unfamiliar aspect of the human predicament, or some familiar aspect in a new way. As for the manner in which this is done, there are infinite possibilities, but it must be adroit.

7

Some exact and enlightening observations on the short story are to be found in the essay prefixed by Elizabeth Bowen to her anthology, *The Faber Book of Modern Stories*. She stresses the need for a short story to have a 'poetic tautness and clarity' and that amazement and awe which are part of poetry. It should have, she says, 'the valid central emotion and inner spontaneity of the lyric'; it should be 'as visual as a picture'; and she rightly believes that it can 'measure man by his aspirations and dreads and place him alone on that stage which, inwardly, every man is conscious of occupying alone'.

It will be seen that these stories are grouped geographically; each group represents and is an outcome of a phase of the writer's experience. This does not mean that the order is strictly chronological. *Thy Neighbour's Creed*, for example, was written long after the three stories with which it is here printed and with which it is linked, and long after those which follow it. It is often necessary for some time to elapse before an experience or an idea can become a story and not a mere piece of reporting. It may be like a photographic film awaiting a particular catalyst before it can be developed, or like a negative requiring a particular strong light before it can be printed. It may have to go through a process of maturing or transmutation, and I have found the length of time needed for this process extremely variable: in the case of *Thy Neighbour's Creed*, the situation it describes sprang suddenly into focus after nineteen years.

Looking over these stories, it occurs to me that few of my writing contemporaries were so far-flung at so early an age: I think I was twenty-two when I wrote *Ula Masondo*, which I certainly could not have written unless I had already spent some of my early years in Africa, and unless my father before me had done the same and had been professionally occupied with African natives. From Africa I went straight to Japan — an unusual transition: I will not say it was made at a still impressionable age, for a writer had better be impressionable at any age.

8

# PREFACE

When I returned to England I did not see it with the same eyes as if I had been there all the time. I had to re-adapt myself, and felt almost as if I had returned from another planet or from the dead. In the midst of this strange experience, I was absent for some time in Greece.

Let it be said that I was lucky to live when young in these different, distant and oddly assorted places. Perhaps I was; but, luck apart, it does seem to me that my transplantations have been not uncharacteristic of this age of dislocation, disorientation and exile, this age of the Displaced Person. In their way I think most of my stories reflect the age by isolating some crisis caused by a change of environment or by the sudden and sometimes startling confrontation of members of different races and classes. It is not uncommon nowadays to hear people say that they have 'no roots'; but for a writer to be effective in the present age it seems to me needful for him to be thoroughly conscious of his origin and at the same time adaptable enough to strike new roots as often as may be necessary. Displacement may be only necessary once, or it may not be necessary at all, but one cannot help noticing how many admired writers of the present century have either lived in exile from their native countries, or have divided their allegiance, or have adopted a new country, or have been made fruitful by travel or residence abroad. If fear and aggression, and the misery and stringency that result from them, do not do away with all freedom and all zest, it may be hoped that in time it will be nothing out of the ordinary for a man to get to know life in several different countries while he is still young enough to make the most of it.

Another thing that strikes me about these stories is that each group of them has more or less its own underlying theme. The African stories all touch more or less directly upon that conflict between white and black, which was, and is, and is going to be the most important of all human concerns in many parts of Africa. *Ula Masondo* treats particularly of the impact of industrialism (or whatever you like to call it) upon a detribalized native. The theme of detribalization and of transition from a village community to a great town, where the individual is apt to be exploited, recurs in the Japanese stories; and they are set in a whole civilization which had, so to speak, gone to town and lost its balance, retaining however a militant nationalism, the subjection of women, and other barbaric survivals.

The Greek stories are concerned with the pursuit of pleasure in spheres frugal, lazy and corrupt, haunted by the consciousness of ancient glory, and charged with vitality. They date from days when the Greeks were in general no less obsessed with politics than usual but when the obsession was less openly ferocious than it has often been since that time, and when the powerful charm of the national character was far more conspicuous (to me at least) than its less amiable aspects. In three of these stories, I notice, there is a chance impingement upon a Greek scene of individuals from ostensibly more sophisticated levels of civilization, and these sophisticates tend to appear ludicrous, for they lack the dignity, the freedom from fussiness, of the uninhibited and un-privileged persons with whom they come in touch.

The English stories are concerned, almost inevitably, with the comedy of class distinctions, and the two last of them give, I hope, a hint of that aura of slight craziness that may surround an individual at a time of national or general convulsion.

For the stories in the first three groups I can at least claim that intelligent natives of the three countries have felt that essentials had been seized upon and newly illuminated.

In case it is of interest, I may say that, to the best of my belief, the only two short-story writers who strongly affected me as a young man were Maupassant and Bunin. I do not think I should have written *A Piece of Good Luck* if I had not known the *Histoire d'une Fille de Ferme*. As for Bunin, *The Gentleman from San Francisco* came to me with the force of a revelation; it elec-trified me, and until I read it I had not known how much the short story could do; it still seems to me the best short story written in this century. If my own stories have any clarity of outline, it may be largely due to an early acquaintance with these two masters.

W. P.

# NOTE

SOME of these stories are taken from *I Speak of Africa* (1927), *Paper Houses* (1929), and *The Child of Queen Victoria* (1933). To Mr. Leonard Woolf and the Hogarth Press, which published the first two of these books, I tender thanks for permission to reprint stories from them here.

The other stories have appeared in periodicals, and certain of them also in anthologies, but they have not hitherto been collected together. Acknowledgments are made to the editors of the *Listener*, the *New Statesman and Nation* and *Penguin New Writing*.

# STORIES OF AFRICA

# ULA MASONDO

## § I

THE white storekeeper who sold Ula Masondo a blanket was a jovial-looking man. The morning had begun well, he thought, counting the money into the till: twenty-five shillings before breakfast.

'Good-bye,' he said cordially when the native turned to go. '*Ja, baas,* stay in peace.'

The white man wondered 'what that boy wanted with such an expensive blanket', for he fancied himself a little as a psychologist. He could not find a satisfactory reason, so he consoled himself with the thought that 'those Masondos are all alike, extravagant, improvident, but you can't help liking them all the same'.

It was breakfast-time. He took the keys off a hook and closed the door and locked it, and began to whistle and to rub his hands, which were not cold, thinking of steak-and-eggs, the steak underdone, like the one in the story of the clergyman who asked for a 'bloody steak'. The storekeeper chuckled.

'Yes,' he said musingly to his wife, 'those Masondos. That young Ula was in this morning for a twenty-five-bob blanket. At this time of the morning! And what does he want with that, I should like to know? What I like about that family is, they're not afraid to spend a bit of money, and they're so united. It's the old mother who keeps them all together, a fine old girl she is! Five strapping sons and four handsome daughters, and the old man not dead yet! The sons go out to work, and the daughters get married, but they all keep in touch with the old people. And so they'll go on, generation after generation. Ula's life'll be just like his father's. What is there to change? Except that the natives are getting to want more and more every year, and by and by little Freddy will be able to start a second Harrods here in Lembuland. Yes, they always come back to the old people, and you'll come back too when you're big, won't you, Freddy?'

And he patted the curly head of a child at his knee, a little blue-eyed boy with a bib under his chin.

§ 2

Away down the mountain path Ula Masondo was trying on his blanket in the sun, opening it, turning it, waving it, fluttering it. He held it up to the light. He ran his long straight well-bred hands across the glowing circles of black and rose and scarlet with which it was enflamed, as if with his slender and inquiring fingers he should find a flaw. Shifted by the wind, the brown paper in which the blanket had been wrapped rustled away over the long dry grass.

The whole valley was full of sunlight, and Ula Masondo's walk became a dance. For every three steps he took forward he took one back, and stamped his hard black feet in the soft brown dust. He began to hum a monotonous song, and soon the sound of his voice was drumming and vibrating, twisting and turning like a sombre serpent of sound. Out of his very nerves the hymn of the darkness of his happiness uncurled and uncoiled itself like a black and flexible snake.

Down he continued through the mealie field, where the last dry stalks, stripped of their cobs, scraped their bleached and pallid leaves in the wind, leaves and stalks bone-white like sticks and shavings in the sunlight. From the kraal his sister watched him coming down, stamping his feet, shuddering and jerking his spine and his hips and his shoulders with ecstatical movements swinging with circles of rose and scarlet and black.

She called out with astonishment, and others of the Masondos appeared to receive their splendid son. She snatched the blanket, and as she stretched her fat black arms there were dimples at the elbows. She swung it round her, and began, in the well-trodden open space between the huts, domes woven of grass, a grotesque dance. She threw herself about with the energy of a contortionist. It seemed that the blanket itself, furred and tigerish, was a skin to the supple and animated flesh with which it wobbled and waggled.

The voice of a herdsman from the next hill-top called out from the height and the distance:

'*Wé*, Ula, have you come back?'

'*Ehé*, I have come back!'

'You have got a red blanket!'

'*Ehé*, it is red!'

'It is very red!'

'Yes, like the blood of a white man!'

'Is it true?'

'Come down here.'

As the herdsman was descending, others joined in the dance. Four casual naked brats clapped their hands, and nodded their round blunt heads, and capered on tiny legs, their stomachs tight and shiny, distended with food. A youth was playing a mouthorgan, and a young girl played a jews' harp, with a tinkling of ornaments at her wrist. Two young married sisters-in-law of Ula Masondo got excited, jogging the babies on their backs, while all the loose fringes of beads at their wrists and hips made a chugging, swishing noise which could be heard between the thudding of many feet.

Even the old mother came out and waved her hands. No one noticed her, and she at once lost herself in the rhythm of the dance.

The blanket passed from body to body, and the herdsman arrived, with a pair of sticks in his hand, and cried:

'Oyoyoyi!'

His cattle could be seen drifting along the flank of the hill, as clouds go drifting across the sky.

§ 3

The thorn trees in the valley covered their shadows like cocks of fine plumage treading black hens, the bright branches extended like wings and quivering in the heat. Down near the stream the father of Ula Masondo was sitting, carefully combing his beard, picking his teeth, and pausing to take snuff out of a long spoon of horn. He could hear the dancing at the kraal, and he could hear the water running in the rocks.

He no longer works.

He will never go out again at dawn to work in strange places (as Ula Masondo will go to-morrow); he has his cattle, his cares, his tradition, his dignity, his gossip, his children, his grandchildren, his beer, his snuff, his old wife. A person of importance, he sits in the sun.

It is long since he went calling after his father's cattle. It is long since the rinderpest year, when the air stank with ruin. It is long since, with face daubed white, he suffered the proud privations of fasting and exposure and circumcision. It is long since he fought, in time of war or in time of peace, and was wounded and gave wounds. It is long since he went running to beer-drinks in the full moonlight, his feet beating faster than his heart.

It is long since he sat in the firelight of his second home, inside the hut, after work, with his young wife made a mother. He seems to see her again, stooping to bring for him a gourd of sour milk, he seems to know again the clicking of the thick swathes of small white beads at her ankles, the flapping of a skin loincloth at her thighs, and her familiar feminine smell.

He remembers her singing when her voice was young and tender; he remembers her small hands with pointed nails long,

long ago beating a tune with a reed on a wire, on a wire with a reed in the sun . . .

He went back to the family, and took the blanket. In a hubbub of conversation he solemnly held it up against the sun, while the lean brown hands of men and women and children began feeling all over its soft red surface, feeling sensuously, inquiringly, easily, slowly, nervously, fingers thick, fingers thin, fingers and thumbs.

A child stood apart, holding a mealie cob in one hand, and with the other scratching in its hair for lice with capable fingers.

## § 4

The train was crowded, and it took two days and two nights to get to Johannesburg from Lembuland.

In the excitement of the first day Ula Masondo and his fellow-passengers called out all sorts of pleasantries to the native people at the stations. And it was quite a long time before he forgot a girl he saw, whose figure was only half-developed; who smiled and said nothing, unlike her noisy companions; whose eyes were large and luminous like the eyes of a female antelope; and whose thin garments were waving in a fresh morning breeze.

After a time they ceased to call out, these travellers. They were benumbed by alternating sensations of heat and cold, and bewildered by the monotony of the journey. Often they fell asleep, sitting upright in their places. Sometimes they woke up with a start, sometimes they seemed to refuse to wake up even when shaken, their sleepy heads nodding almost as if their necks were broken.

It was the second day, and the train ran on through the cold bright air of a highveld afternoon. Quite suddenly appeared in the distance the first mine-dumps, sticking up beyond the horizon like the summits of snow-mountains. The passengers crowded to the window to see these peaks, on which the sun shone as it does on distant ships between a dark sky and a dark sea, and from round them, as from ships, stood out faint fumes of smoke, faint fumes in space. From the opposite window was visible a dump as big as a hill, quite near, rising sheer and white from the ground, with tiny trucks running along the top, against the afternoon sky. And on the other side of it the steel and iron and stone of the mine buildings stood drab and stern, bitter citadels of unreasoning industry.

The thin brown grass of the veld had already given way to dust. Natives stood about in groups, some in sordid rags, others in gaudy blankets. Or they could be seen walking singly or in pairs, with a confident but abstracted air, like followers of some unknown religion. They were all used to Johannesburg, but among their compatriots in the train was the silence of apprehension.

The train was now running parallel with the Great Reef Road, along which hurried an incessant traffic of cars, bicycles and pedestrians. Whole streets came into view, shacks of corrugated iron, varied with dingy plantations of gum trees, whose blue-grey leaves were powdered with red dust, and straggling hedges.

Some washing was hanging on a fence, flapping idly in a casual breeze. Dirty children were playing in a donga; they could be heard stirring with a stick among old tins in an ashpit. Some women were drinking tea on a veranda, and a fat old man with a very red face stood in his shirt-sleeves leaning against a gate. He was smoking a pipe, and his white trousers were braced up so high that the tabs on his brown boots were visible.

A native was playing a concertina. A dog lifted its leg against a lamp-post. A clanging tram hurried across an open space, and, although the sun had not set, all its lights were burning.

Rows of gaudy posters on a hoarding ran past as if on wheels, and a large white building was swinging into view with the easy grace of an acrobat. Trams, buildings, shops, many voices, and the train stopped in the great terminus like a cavern, like a nightmare, like a dread.

They were all hustled out. Jostling and unguided, as if they were sheep, they made their uncertain way down the platform, and the air was full of a strange and foreign newness.

'Here's an omen,' said Ula Masondo, who knew what he felt but not what he meant.

## § 5

As though he had lived through it all before, as though he would live through it all again, he suffered and never forgot the routine of work and rest at the Simeon and Steck Amalgamated, the sight of shivering groups standing in a darkening or a brightening air and waiting to descend at the skips, the voice of the shift-boss, the dampness and darkness below, the sensation in one's ears at the deeper levels, the dimness, and the moving lights, the hum of work in subterranean stillness, the stale fumes of gelignite and acetylene, and in the narrow stopes the loud staccato stutterings of the compressed-air drills, which men held in their hands like powerful animals that wanted to get away, jerked by a mechanical lust to fang the rock with steel.

When one came off shift at midday the sky was dusty grey like the pelt of a donkey, and the air was full of the perennial roar of the stamps rising and falling and roaring on revolving cams in the battery, whose walls were like cliffs scored with the sorrows of time; always roaring and shaking the ground, as the ground trembles to a war-dance of warriors, or summer thunder in the mountains of Lembuland.

When Ula Masondo came up out of the mine on a still, calm afternoon of winter he noticed, passing the engine-house on his way to the compound, the subdued and powerful humming of armatures, and saw a grey motor-car gliding down an avenue of gum trees to the manager's offices, and catching the sun between the shadows. A white borzoi dog was sitting at the back, and its long snout gave it a stupid and puzzled expression. As the car went past, Ula Masondo could hear its fat tyres treading richly on the gravel.

When he came up at evening the twin steel wheels of the headgear were spinning in an icy sky, and newly lighted fires were flickering in the dusk.

## § 6

Women were not allowed in the compound, a bleak building that was always being cleaned.

Ula Masondo, from the time he was born, had never slept by himself, so when he was found lying one night with a friend for warmth and company he was told that he was risking a flogging for sodomy. So he lay alone, and for a long time was afraid: the air was thick with ghostly visitors.

On Sunday afternoons life improved. One could, for example, put off the blanket and wear clothes instead: and the wearing of clothes was a permanent adventure for one who had been naked for the first decade of his life.

It was possible to get about and show off, or to do nothing, as one felt inclined. One had money, and ceasing to be a novice and assuming the airs of a man, one could have a good time.

The leisure of Ula Masondo was controlled by a man ten years older than himself, a moody and unprincipled *skebenga* who stood six and a half feet tall, and whose name was Vilakazi. It was he who directed how and where their time should be spent. As Sunday only occurs once a week he believed it should be spent in going recklessly from one debauch to another. It is a not illogical belief for a man who has no freedom for six days in the week.

If the two wanted drink, as they always did, Vilakazi knew

where to get it, sometimes from an Australian-German-Jew with a game leg who was generally in gaol, sometimes from a stout old Irishwoman who had come down in the world, and who, smiling gaily, was beginning to rise again behind the law by retailing methylated spirit at the price of French brandy.

If they wanted the fine fever of gambling Vilakazi arranged behind some obscure shanty a three-card-trick party.

On occasions of dispute Vilakazi gave blows where they were necessary, while Ula Masondo, loud with encouragement, danced at his elbow, and only took part when the scrap went against them.

When they wanted a woman, an appointment was arranged with Lu, a slightly coloured woman who existed for the arranging of appointments, or with Emma, a good-humoured young native woman, very smart with her tongue, who lived with a white man during the week and supported him by her earnings from black men on Sundays.

Vilakazi, in return for his great usefulness, expected a willing audience for his long speeches of advice and anecdote, companionship and constant flattery. He and Ula Masondo were always together.

## § 7

'*Wé*, Vilakazi,' said the younger man, 'I have a letter.'

'Where is it from, that letter?'

'From my home.'

'What does it say?'

'This letter? It says I am the chief of my father's people.'

'What!'

'It says I am the king of the white people.'

'What!'

'It says you must give me money. It says only ten shillings.'

'You are cheating me, my friend.'

'It is true. Read my letter.'

Vilakazi took the letter and looked at it vaguely, as though it did not matter whether one read it or not. It was addressed in the difficult and showy calligraphy of one who felt that the ability to write is the highest good of education. On the back was a hieroglyphic drawing of a train.

Slowly Vilakazi read the letter through to himself. Translated, it was as follows :

Greeting,

my child it is far to talk how can people talk when you are far. There is no rain, the Great-great one is unwilling to send rain, it is the same in every place, we are dead as to our stomachs, there is no food. It is the same at Ovuzane and Ovuzanyana, above and at the rivers, it is the same here. The children are crying, there is no money for food, there is no money to buy food. We are telling that you must send money to buy food for us, even if it is a pound only, or only two pounds. There is tax to pay, we shall hope to get money for tax, but if we get money for tax we shall be crying as to our stomachs. How is it my boy are you well? As for me I am old I am done for I am a husk that is chewed and spat out and I cannot sleep always always I am coughing and your father has fever he is sick and all the people send greetings but they are dead as to their stomachs send if it is a pound only o my child my beloved

greeting from your mother.

'Where does it come from, this letter?' asked Vilakazi without disclosing its contents.

'I am asking you.'

'You see this letter? It is the letter of a fool.'

'How is that?'

Ula Masondo stared at the letter, but it meant nothing to him; he could not even read his own name. The writing seemed to crawl across the page, a laborious puzzle with some significance hidden from himself.

'It is the letter of a fool,' Vilakazi repeated. 'It is only greetings.'

'Only?'

'Only.'

'But I want to hear. Read it.'

And Vilakazi read, pretending to spell out the words with great difficulty:

Greeting,

my child it is far to talk how can people talk when you are far. Here it is raining, the Great-great one has sent rain, it is the same in every place, the people are very glad, we have plenty of grain for food and beer. It is the same at Ovuzane and Ovuzan-yana, above and at the rivers, it is the same here. I think you are glad, I see you are glad, my boy. We do not want money now stay and earn money for yourself in the mines. How is it my boy are you well? We are all well my child my beloved and all the people send greetings and there are greetings from your mother.

'It is finished,' said Vilakazi.

'Is that all?'

'That is all. Yes, it is only greetings. Can greetings fill a person's stomach? You are the child of a fool.'

'O, silence,' said Ula Masondo. 'Give me the letter.'

'What! You tell me to keep silence! Do you think I am a liar, that you tell me to keep silence, my boy? Here, I will put your letter in my pocket. If you have it you will lose it, and it is safe with me. Some day we shall answer it; I will tell you when.'

Ula Masondo made no answer. It was Sunday afternoon, and he wanted an excitement of the blood, he wanted to drink and shout, to drink and forget.

27

§ 8

Ula Masondo put a cigarette in his mouth, and Vilakazi, with the gesture of a man who is sure of his power, held out to him a lighted match. A puff, two puffs of blue smoke rose in the windless air, and the two men turned to go.

Ula Masondo was wearing a red-brown suit: the short, close-fitting coat was fastened with a single button, and the trousers were cut with exaggerated fullness, drooping over silk socks and 'ox-blood' shoes with high heels. Round his waist was a cord of pink wool with swinging tassels. In the band of his hat was stuck a cigarette-picture of an American film star in her bathing dress. In his ears were gilt ear-rings, he had three brooches in his tie, and a silk shirt. For these adornments he owed several pounds at a store.

Emma was waiting at the usual place. She did not see the approach of her friends, being engaged in an exchange of repartee with a stranger on the other side of a wall.

Vilakazi pinched her plump arm, which was visible through a filmy blouse of lilac silk, cut low back and front to show an open-work camisole. Alternately pouting and using violent rhetoric she made out that she was offended. Ula Masondo took off his hat in the European manner, and there was a strong smell of pomade.

Finally the three went off arm in arm. Emma's heels were as high as those of Ula Masondo, and she walked with an easy abandon, swinging her hips. Round her neck she wore a string of metallized beads like swollen and tarnished pearls, and her ear-rings were flashing in the sun. As she walked, every nerve and muscle came into play, and even her clothes seemed part of her.

The three of them began to laugh. They were remarkably handsome, showing their teeth in a laughter that was not amusement.

§ 9

Before long Vilakazi induced the younger man to surrender
to him all his wages, and answered any protest by telling Ula
Masondo that he was a boy and did not understand the use of
money. Ula Masondo wanted to pay off some of his debt at the
store, where the white man was beginning to threaten him.

'Let him wait,' said Vilakazi, 'that little white man.'

They began to play a new card game, very intricate, which
Vilakazi learnt from an acquaintance, one Stefan, who belonged
to a gang of *amaleita* and was always boasting of his exploits.
At first they won steadily, and then continued to lose until they
were several pounds in debt. Stefan suggested that they should
join his friends, who knew a good way of making money, their
custom being to station themselves on a lonely road behind
the kopjes near the Simeon and Steck, and to lie in wait for
solitary cyclists and pedestrians, on whom they would rush out
with a volley of sticks and stones. After the assault there was
robbery, and after the robbery there was flight. The scene of
these operations had lately been changed, so there was little
danger of arrest.

In a series of conversations Stefan became eloquent on the
glories of crime. He related how certain ordeals were necessary
for a full initiation into the *amaleita*; what punishments resulted
from cowardice, disobedience or want of secrecy; the special
honours due to those who succeeded, single-handed, in robbing
a man or raping a woman; and how by committing a murder
and evading detection one became qualified for leadership.

He went into the technique of housebreaking, and disclosed
the methods of detectives and policemen. Having himself served
three terms in gaol he was able to give an extremely graphic
account of those secret prison-gangs which are far more cruel
than the *amaleita*. They consist of criminals, of all ages and of
different tribes and races, who have been mostly transferred from

29

that condition of unnatural celibacy, in which most natives are obliged to work, to one of closer confinement, in which by force of example they become abandoned, and by habit devoted, to the cultivation of various vices.

'There was a Chinese,' said Stefan, assuming an air of indifference, and speaking in a rich and modulated voice, 'who —'

And, at the history of the Chinaman, Ula Masondo laughed incredulously.

Finally, Stefan gave a generalized description of the character of the white race, a description so penetrating and analytical that it would have put to shame many of those pretentious Europeans who mix science with politics and hypocrisy with everything, pretending to be clean, and riding so smugly every morning to their classrooms and laboratories on the top of a tram, a newspaper in the hand, a cigar in the mouth, a pince-nez on the nose, and a worm in the brain.

Such a speech as Stefan's could only have been made by a native who understood the arts of conversation and oratory. Where there is intuition, what is the use of psycho-analysis? Where is the white man who can hide his character from a Kaffir?

Ula Masondo began to feel in himself, as the *leita* intended him to feel, slow stirrings of unreasoning resentment, the blending and brooding of deep agitations.

As for Vilakazi, he had been previously associated for a short time with other *amaleita*, and his brain, lately fuddled with excesses, was only waiting for some direct outside suggestion, like this of Stefan's, to become dominated once more by the idea of plunder.

And so, on a Sunday afternoon, when there was a sound of mission bells in the distance, when under a universe of clouds an angry and expanded sun was touching the horizon's rim, they walked back to the barrack-like compound with their hearts thudding in apprehension of dangers to come.

§ 10

In spare time Vilakazi and Ula Masondo now had nearly always the company of Stefan, the *leita* man-of-the-world, and also that of Emma, now unattached to her white man, lately convicted of forgery. She took to coming with a friend, called Smile by Europeans, and by his own people Isimayili.

It became the custom of these five to meet in a thicket of steenvrugte bushes on an unfrequented part of the kopje near the mine. Here, unseen by the rest of the world, they had a view of the road below them in the valley, and beyond, among the hills, a prospect of the roofs and dumps of the inner suburbs of Johannesburg.

Ula Masondo, youngest and most ingenuous of the five, now lived in a constant excitement, almost willingly giving up his money to buy drink, cigarettes and the goodwill of his elders, and quite willingly giving up all his attention to their talk. He had never felt so important, and was trying at the same time to flatter the giant Vilakazi, to imitate Stefan, and to make an impression on Emma, when he was completely distracted by the novelty of Smile.

Smile, short and powerful, never stopped smiling when sober, but when drunk he tried to bite. He had already at different times bitten a horse, a postman and a missionary, and when, on one occasion, he suddenly fastened his teeth in the arm of Emma, she uttered shriek after shriek as if her soul was leaving her body, and attracted the attention of a native policeman, who blew his whistle so near at hand, so unexpectedly, that Smile, drunk as he was, at once withdrew his incisive caress. The five of them lay flat on their bellies under the bushes, and Emma put her fist in her mouth to stop herself screaming, and nearly choked in consequence with pain, hysterics and anxiety. They could hear the policeman panting past them on his way up the hill. He stumbled, rummaging among the rocks, and even stopped to

31

beat the tops of the very bushes in which the party lay breathlessly hidden. When it was safe to speak again, Smile had begun
to snore in a drunken stupor, and Emma was nursing her bleeding arm. The tears gushed down her face, and in future, as soon
as Smile began to drink, she always sat as far away from him as
possible, in order to avoid his sadistic attentions.

To his masters Smile appeared simply as a cheerful houseboy.
He worked in a respectable slum for two small semi-detached
houses that shared one kitchen. One of his masters was a solitary
old bachelor, a retired sergeant-major with waxed moustaches.
The other was a Flemish carpenter who had formerly been in
the Congo and was so tolerant of Smile that he was ready to
treat him almost as one of the family, but his wife, a Danish-
Swiss, a lazy woman with a grudge against life, treated her husband like a child, her children like servants, and Smile like a dog.

On Sunday mornings Smile wore a black coat, and carried
in his pocket a Lembu Bible, for he belonged to one of those
innumerable native sects that make of Christianity an exciting
cult, and quote the Scriptures to their own purposes. In the
afternoons he still had the Bible with him, and used also to carry
a little cane, which he would wave like a wand, saying of somebody he disliked, in a tone of the utmost contempt:

'*Hau !* He's just a heathen!'

or, describing something he liked:

'Truly, this tobacco is Christian!'

There was in his character a considerable strength. With
little persuasion Emma would have allowed him to chew her
into rags. As for Ula Masondo, he even got the permission of
Vilakazi to buy a little cane, which he began to wave adroitly in
imitation of Smile.

§ 11

As for Ula Masondo, fascinated by the daring and sinister
insouciance of Stefan, obsessed with the Christian dandyism of

Smile, and infatuated with the over-ripe charms of Emma, he began to feel more independent than usual of his first patron and worldly guide. He and Vilakazi were, in fact, heading for a quarrel, when, in reviewing their debts, they found that some must be paid. Money they must have. While financial adversity kept them together, Smile, with a barbaric and original smile in which there was more naïvety than cunning, unexpectedly hinted at a sum that he supposed to be not less than £50.

It appeared that the carpenter and his family had decided to spend the next week-end visiting friends in the country, and Smile had already been told that he would be expected to guard the house.

'As if I was a watch-dog,' he explained. But if only his other, ex-military master could be temporarily transferred from one house to the other, the money would be theirs.

Vilakazi had lately been thinking more of getting Emma than of getting money, but now he sat up, stretched his arms and began to take notice.

'What money?' Stefan was asking with an air of tired dignity.

'The money we want!' said Smile, smiling.

'Where is it, this money of yours?'

'You say it's mine? The money of Shortlegs!'

'Who is Shortlegs?'

'My baas!'

'One of your baases, you mean. Where does he hide this money?'

'Under his bed.'

'Shades of my fathers! How do you know?'

'I've seen him.'

'What did you see?'

'I saw him put money in a box under his bed.'

'How much?'

'A lot! Pounds and pounds!'

'Fifty pounds?'

'Do I know?'

'Where were you, then?'

'Looking through the window.'

'Is it a big box?'

'No, small. So big.'

'Is Shortlegs married?'

'No.'

'Has he got a girl?'

'Do I know? Sometimes he goes out at nights. Do I know where he goes?'

'It is plain what we must do.'

'How, then?'

'Early on Sunday afternoon you, Isimayili, will be sitting in your outhouse talking to Emma. Then you will go and make a big fire of papers and sticks on the back stoep of the carpenter's house and start shouting: "Fire! Fire!" Emma will run through the kitchen and call to Shortlegs that the house is on fire. He will see that she is a fine girl and will come running with her to see what is the matter —'

'No!' said Emma vigorously, 'I don't want that!'

'What do you want, then? It is your work, I say, to bring Shortlegs out of his house.'

'I don't want! I don't want!'

'Shut up!' said Stefan. 'When Emma and Shortlegs come through the kitchen you, Isimayili, will be shouting and beating out the fire — make as much smoke as you can! — then Vilakazi will run into the kitchen to stop Shortlegs if he tries to come back. Meanwhile, I will run in for the box, and I'll throw it over the wall to you, Masondo, who will catch it on the other side. Then you must run. I shall run just after you, and Vilakazi must run after me. But each of us three must run a different way, and we will meet here afterwards. You, Isimayili, will stay in your outhouse with Emma and say you know nothing about anything.'

Ula Masondo was amazed at the ingenuity of this plan.

34

§ 12

When the time came, after many preliminary thrills, Ula Masondo heard a crackle of sticks and Smile's voice crying 'Fire!' and peeped over the wall just in time to see Emma leaping out of the back door with a jingle of jewellery, followed immediately by the ex-soldier, who had just been to sleep. With a scarlet face and moustaches like hat-pins, this veteran was trying to make haste slowly like an officer and a gentleman, though his beery eyes were goggling with panic. As soon as he had dashed into the kitchen, Vilakazi followed, and Stefan sprang out from behind a water-tank and darted into the house.

There was at once a smell of smoke, and sounds could be heard of excited voices, pattering feet and water hissing and sizzling.

Back came Stefan, hurdling over the wall, with the box under his arm. He threw it to Ula Masondo, and hearing a scuffle in the kitchen they both made off as fast as they could.

They were already crouching in the bushes, and trying to force open the box, when Vilakazi arrived panting and drenched with sweat.

'How was it, Vilakazi?'

'Hau! Isimayili put out the fire too quickly, and Shortlegs came back too soon. He isn't Shortlegs, he is Satane! He kicked like the devil and screamed like a pig. Can a person hold a screaming pig with a devil inside? There you are, I threw him under the table, and there you are, I have come!'

He wiped the sweat from his face with a handkerchief of magenta silk, and then lay down on his back to recover his wind, but Stefan succeeding at that moment in bursting open the lid of the box, he at once sat up again. The money only amounted to £23, and the three spent the rest of the afternoon in the frantic exhilaration of deciding how it was to be divided.

§ 13

Several times, during the week that followed, Ula Masondo felt uneasy at his work. The routine of the mine was becoming intolerable to him. He had a craving to go up and lie in the sun for days on end, doing nothing, saying nothing, nothing, nothing —

'Here, you!' said the shift-boss. 'What's up with you to-day? Get on with it!'

And as Ula Masondo turned his head, his teeth were even whiter than the whites of his eyes.

He suddenly wanted to provoke admiration, so he related to a man who was working on the same shift how a certain white man called Shortlegs had been thrown under a table and killed, and when they were going to put him in his coffin they found he had feathers in his brains, and also that he had a tail.

'You are lying,' said the man.

'Can I lie?'

'Can it be true?'

'I swear it's true!'

'There's an omen!'

'Yes,' said Ula Masondo, 'and then they found a doctor who had tried to cut it off when Shortlegs was alive, but every time he cut it off it grew again, and he always heard afterwards that one of his relations had died the same day.'

'No, no, no!'

But Ula Masondo felt confused and irritated, sick in his head, and fell silent.

§ 14

For the Sunday after the theft a party had been planned for the drinking of *skokiaan*. A quantity of that violent liquor had been prepared and hidden by Stefan in the bushes, and when Sunday came it was well fermented.

The five, reunited once more, settled down in their lair, and prepared to enjoy themselves, but the air was sullen and oppressive with foreboding. A thunderstorm was accumulating in the sky, and the hot blue clouds were collecting a sultry shadow over all the earth.

'I am going,' Emma said suddenly.

'What!'

'Why?'

'Not now! We are just going to drink,' said Stefan, whose breath was already thick with methylated fumes.

'I am going home to Lembuland.'

'When?'

'Soon.'

'To Lembuland!' exclaimed Ula Masondo. 'Is that your home?'

'Yes; didn't you know that?'

It turned out that she lived on the side of Aucampstroom remote from the home of Ula Masondo, and within two days' journey on foot from there.

'My time will soon be up,' said Ula Masondo. 'Wait, and we will travel together.'

'What!' said Emma. 'Shall I travel with a boy?'

'You will not go home, Ula,' said Vilakazi emphatically, 'when your time is up. You will stay here.'

'Are you both heathens,' said Smile, with a sarcastic and superior smile, 'that you should wish to return to such a place? It is more Christian here.'

'There is no money in Lembuland,' said Stefan. 'All the white people there are policemen or missionaries. How can you get money in such a place?' And he put to his lips the tin of *skokiaan*, and took a long and solemn drink. When the tin was passed round Vilakazi drank the most, because, as he pointed out, he was the largest.

'It is a drink for Christians,' said Smile, with a thirsty and Christian smile.

Stefan lighted his pipe. There was *dagga* mixed with the tobacco, and he puffed in silence, while there began to circulate dully in his veins the smoky blood of hallucination.

'I tell you, Ula, you will stay,' said Vilakazi, leaning forward aggressively. Ula Masondo felt too giddy to answer, so he put in his mouth a red steenvrugte, sucked its pink flesh and spat out the stone with deliberate vehemence.

'And you, too, Emma, you will stay.' Emma stared at him with intoxicated eyes, and made no answer.

'I am your baas.' Vilakazi laid a possessive hand on her knee. She made no move.

'I am your baas. You do what I tell you. You belong to Vilakazi.'

Emma seemed to gather herself together, like a cat that is going to spring.

'You damn fool, you boy, you bloody nigger,' she said, in the European manner.

She stood up, resting her hands on her hips. Below the waist she was in shadow, but Vilakazi, looking up, saw her eyes flashing, and the tawdry jewellery that glittered with the heaving of her bosom. He reached out a great hand and grasped her firmly by the ankle. As quick as thought she kicked him in the face with the other foot, sprang out of the bushes, and began to make her way, angry and graceful, down the hill.

Ula Masondo watched her stepping from rock to rock. Her short skirt was swinging from her hips, and her fat shapely legs curved down with the smoothest of curves to the smallest of ankles. He felt that so long as Emma stayed in Johannesburg he would be unable to return to Lembuland.

Vilakazi, slowly recovering from a stupor of surprise, got up and lurched after her, calling out clumsy threats and the most original personal remarks. Emma, still without hurrying, turned round, put out her tongue, spat copiously and proceeded.

Half-way down Vilakazi stumbled and fell. He got up cursing, and went lumbering on. There were several people in the road, and two natives, standing together, were watching his approach. When Emma reached the road they asked her a question, and seeming hardly to wait for an answer, rushed forward and closed on Vilakazi.

Ula Masondo wanted to make a move, but he was afraid of betraying the hiding-place. About to start up, he was restrained by the sight of Smile and Stefan lying face downwards, sodden and unconscious. He kept still.

When he looked down again, Vilakazi was standing between the two men. He held himself erect, his broad chest heaving, very dignified, although his pink shirt was torn and handcuffs were shining like silver bracelets on his wrists. The two detectives knew that others besides Vilakazi were concerned in last week's theft, and they looked up the hill, and seemed to be staring at the steenvrugte bushes. But apparently they thought better than to come and search, and turned to march away with their captive.

Emma, frightened out of her wits, could be seen running far along the road, escaping on her splendid legs.

At this moment there was a roll of thunder. The storm, which had been working up all the afternoon, was about to break.

Ula Masondo, full of lonely dread at the arrest of Vilakazi, began to try and rouse his companions.

## § 15

In the mine next day there was a fall of rock. In a narrow stope Ula Masondo found himself cut off from the world. Only by a few feet did he escape immediate destruction.

As it was he found himself confined in a small space without light, or air, or any sound save that of his blood singing thickly in his ears. A lonely terror, increasing every moment, confused his thoughts.

'I am dead,' he told himself at last; and to death he prepared to resign himself.

But after a time he was still breathing; after a time he could hardly breathe, his lungs seemed to be full of earth, he could see nothing, think nothing, feel nothing, know nothing . . .

But he could distinctly hear the voice of his brother, telling him that a cow was lost, and they must go up into the Mountain of the Bushmen to look for it.

'No,' said Ula Masondo, 'I am afraid of Bushmen.'

'There are no Bushmen there now,' said his brother.

'No,' said Ula Masondo, 'but I am not going.'

He could hear the voice of his father ordering him to go.

'Go, boy! The mother of my father was the daughter of a Bushman. The spirit of her father is calling you to find our cow.'

'There's an omen,' said Ula Masondo, who knew what he felt, but not what it meant.

'We shall see the pictures,' said his brother.

'What pictures?'

'The pictures of hunting. The cave-paintings of the Bushmen.'

Ula Masondo was afraid. He shuddered with apprehension, and struggled, breath by breath by breath, to breathe an air that was dying.

§ 16

The accident had hardly taken place when a rescue-party was at work. Light shone on sweating backs and driving arms, and the silence staggered with the echoing shocks of assault made on the entombing rock. The shift-boss himself, who had once been rescued from death in a Mexican silver mine, worked like a madman to dig out Ula Masondo, now with his brother, searching in the Mountain of the Bushmen for a cow that was lost.

## ULA MASONDO

It was in a krans titanic
Of that berg volcanic
That a dark cave was hidden
Where no foot could have trodden.

There the leopard and snake
And tawny partridge
Prey and are preyed on,
Unstartled by cartridge,
Where never a gun
Echoing shocks
The listening rocks:
Where in winter
When the flinty crags
Receive the sun,
Far down, far down,
In the sombre forest,
Under thin ice
The waters splinter
In flakes of fire,
And in shallow pools
The shadow of a hawk
(Tense above the tree-tops)
Quivers like a fish
Among the shadows
Of basking fishes.

When those parapets shimmer
In the morning in summer
The antelope turns
From the heat of the height
To a stream in the ferns,
Bounding unhurried
From sun to shadow.

There the lory wings scarlet
His way at noon; twilight
Flutters with bats;
And at dawn the cliff
Is crowned with eagles.
There the wild cats
Crouch and tremble,
And await the screams
Of the haunted jackal.
Has no foot trodden
Where the dark cave is hidden
In leaves and branches?

Not for centuries now
Cataracts, avalanches,
Have ruined the steep.
The cavern can keep
Its secrets in stillness,
In darkness, enfolded
In the wild fig trees,
Whose sinews are moulded
To the curves of the stone,
And whose roots are thrust
In a crevice of dust,
Clinging tightly within
To the nerves of the quartz,
And fed on the secret
And bitter, untasted
Dews of the desert;
While their leaves, unshaken
By wandering airs,
Are stirred by lizards,
A refuge for spiders,
An arbour for birds,

42

That gouge the soft fruit,
And swoop into space
With thin stabs of music
In a hollow of silence.
Has no foot trodden
Where the dark cave is hidden?

On windless nights
When it is deserted
By the last baboon
The shafted radiance
Of the risen moon
Illumines like a lamp
The vaulted roof,
Where the moss is damp
And beaded with black
Dews bled from the rock;
Illumines like the ray
White and deific
Of an enormous Eye
This tongueless place
With light terrific.

In the flare and the hush
Appear the painted
Walls that were frescoed
When the floor was last trodden
Of this cavern hidden.

Now the air is tainted
With a sudden whiff
Of distant carrion,
And the silence shrills
With the urgent quills

Of vultures soaring
From the soaring cliff.

But silence returns
And moonlight floats,
And the Eye returns
To men before men
In time before time,
Whose love and hunting
Are calcined in a blaze
Of light like chalk.
Life was their god,
And their god is transfigured.

Far down, far down,
Where are the savage
Cities of the future?

Where is steel?  Here is stone.
What are tombs?  Here's a bone.
What is science?  Declare,
Does it beat still, your heart?
What is life?  Here is art.
What are you?  Here is splendour.
O traffic and travel and trade,
Here rolls the thunder,
Ula Masondo,
Of hoofs and of hearts and of honour!

When these colours fade
And lichens hang in their places,
When these forms lose their graces,
When these lines are not lines,
Blighted and bitten
By the secret acid

Of rhythmic ages,
O up then and out
And over the placid
And fiery sky of midday
Will take their way
These gymnosoph hunters
With their slow-stepping women
Stained with rose ochre
Proudly proceeding
In prancing procession
With the eland and the gnu,
While each coloured
Courser canters
With the zebra and emu,
While the vulture
Waves them on like a banner,
Hunters and hunted
Flying forlorn,
Faint, faded and few,
To find fervour anew
Far ahead, far along
In the tranced and timeless blue.

What are you doing,
Ula Masondo?
Do you follow the Bushmen?
Do you travel to the valley
This side of the city?

Travelling to the valley, he found it was full of waving fields, green woods and flowering orchards. Beyond it there were hills, and beyond the hills there was a city deserted by its inhabitants, and beyond the city was the sky, where the sun was a flaming and a throbbing embryo.

The plantations of trees in the valley were threaded with the smoke of occasional trains, with telegraph wires and with random voices. And the houses of men of property were concealed in the trees, and even among the trees could be seen occasionally the movements of people of fashion, messengers on bicycles, or the fauna escaped from the cave.

In the orchards the women of the Bushmen were helping themselves to fruit, to *naartjes* and *perskies*; to the *pamplemoes* and the *spanspek*; to persimmons, pawpaws and pomegranates.

There were also gardens of zinnias and marigolds, with ferns and palms and plaster fountains; the air-plant, the egg-plant and the ice-plant; and lilies and orchids; the blood-flower, the eye-flower and moon-flowers of the dead-white datura, supernatural flowers that Ula Masondo dare not touch, for they were crying to him with maddening voices, and wanted to possess his nerves.

And among the trees and gardens were sun-wonderful spaces where humming motor-cars, shining and powerful, travelled over the grass with the men of property. Sometimes these men could be seen on stoeps in the shade sipping tea and beer and blood and water; or sprawling stoutly in unbuttoned ease at gluttonous picnics; smoking pipes of leisure but not pipes of peace, while the days and hours turned over like tremendous wheels, unhurried and colossal and compelling, dripping with the opulent waters of time, turning the hidden machinery of the Cosmos, and the revolving words of God.

And at both ends of the valley rose dry and sandy hills to heights of granite and basalt, steep and rocky and veined with unsuspected ores; hills where the red wind carried the sound of itself and its heat from desolate hill-top to hill-top, day and night, year after year after year, and carried the stink and bleat of shaggy goats mouthing for herblets in the broken kranses, goats with coarse hair matted with burrs and their eyes bulging with starvation.

The red wind carried and lost the groans of pregnant women

mounting and marching along the long and devastated path-
ways of parching precipices; with earthen urns of water on their
heads; water drawn cold, but bitter and tepid before the bearers
could get to the summit, their feet burning on the trodden grit
and bruised with purple pebbles.

Horrent with thorns, the aloe, the snake-apple, the poison
cactus and the century plant clutch the dry earth with tortured
roots, withering and sprouting and multiplying in the burning
waste, while on cool and distant beaches the sea-wind unwinds
a smoking iris from the spray, and somewhere gilded roofs
vibrate and vanish in a soothing or a harrowing triumph of
complaining pipes and prattling strings.

Here, in gullies and ravines, on arid flats, in scorched and
sullen places, on chill and barren ridges, and in damp and noisome
lairs, are human homes, coops of sticks that sag with dry-rot
and choke with fungus, hatching vermin. Here the valley-
dwellers never come, fearing infection of some hideous plague,
ulcered out of such filth. They stay safe in their green retreats
and suck stout through their moustaches, and marvel how these
beasts can exist like *dassies* in their crannies, these human vermin,
starved and swinking, scratching with hoes the scarlet sand, and
sowing seeds that sprout as willingly as stones.

Let the valley-dwellers condemn their drudges to a life of
deaths, but the soul screams out, and every sinew cracks.

Another whisky-and-soda? Thanks, I don't mind if I do.

Out of the strong comes forth sweetness, out of injury comes
forth power, and out of torture comes forth mercy.

Out of silence rise the songs of the oppressed, who fear not
thunder and lightning, for whom the sun has no warmth, the
rain not tears enough of pity, for whom the moon is a drug, a
promise, an echo, an Eye and a voice.

The phœnix flies, and fades, and only the wind is red, a
tornado in the Kalahari of sleep, a stormburst in the Stormberg
of patience!

Patience! patience! most dangerous of qualities, amplifier of the unknowable, tube of the trumpetings of a God tattooed with ten thousand moons!

A patient boy argues in the temple, and its foundations crumble.

The sun is an egg, and an egg is patient; the moon is an eye, and an eye is patient.

Woe to them who awake too early, when all others are still asleep!

Woe to them who sleep, when one is awake!

Woe to the dreamer, but disaster to the enemies of his dreams!

A voice, and it shall be inherited, and the prodigal father shall never return!

'The edict is writing in African blood,' announced the prophet, and the breath went out of his body.

'Europe cannot satisfy us,' announced the prophetess, and the breath went out of her body.

The toad, the rat and the scorpion howled with laughter, until they were driven to dance with death.

The pig and the spider grew fat, grew fat, until they were stabbed with the snake-tooth of a fountain-pen, from which outflowed as from a black storm-cloud the jetting poison of ink, and so they died.

And at their funeral was the frightful Cloacina, the squinting, the whey-blooded, who hunted for a husband till her elbows came through her skin, and she was left gorgoning gauntly in the Garden of Nunquam.

Death is sweet and transitory, and a dead face sometimes wears a smile, as if it knew a delightful secret.

A smile, a smile! Isimayili is smiling, Stefan is asleep, Vilakazi is bound, Emma is mine . . .

'Emma!'

'Here, look here!' exclaimed the shift-boss, flashing a light.

48

'Here he is! My God, he's smiling! I hope he's not out of his mind. All right, all right, boy, stop shouting!'

But Ula Masondo had swooned at the inrush of air, and heard nothing. He was removed to the hospital.

## § 17

Ten days later he walked out of the hospital with his hat cocked over one eye, and the other blinking in the sun. Although he moved with something of the natural style of his race, and although he was trying now to walk jauntily in the manner he most admired, an injury still obliged him to limp: it had been caused by an almost crushing weight that had lain on his leg while he was walled up in the mine.

The mine doctor had, as usual, entered particulars of his patient in the records: *Name, Date admitted, Symptoms, Treatment, Recovery*. He always enjoyed filling in the various details. He was still a young man, but he liked to be considered methodical. When he came to the section *Remarks* he paused a moment, the fountain-pen gleaming between his bloodless, soap-bleached fingers. Then he bit his lip with vexation, for he had almost forgotten his position so far as to write: *This boy's a bit queer.*

He was astonished at himself. He laid down his pen for a few seconds, and looked out of the window, from which he could see a cloud of red dust being blown along the Great Reef Road, obscuring and revealing the traffic like a dry and swirling fog.

The doctor left blank the space called *Remarks*, and turned over the page. In the evening he said to his wife:

'Such a strange thing happened this morning. We discharged a boy who wasn't quite right in the head. Partly shock, perhaps, and he was half suffocated. Fished out of that fall of rock Monday week. Lucky for him. Near thing. But he'll get over it. I actually found myself on the point of writing down in the records, under *Remarks*: *This boy's a bit queer!*'

'Well,' said she, 'I suppose the world wouldn't have come to an end if you had, so why worry? Shall we have coffee here or on the veranda?'

Discharged from the hospital, Ula Masondo, his time up on the mine, received his wages, paid his debts and went straight to Emma. She was in the family way, and did not know for certain who was the father of her child, but felt inclined to give birth to it at home; and having received letters from her relations urging her return, she was on the point of leaving for Lembuland. When Ula Masondo proposed to go with her she assented with an ungracious fondness that he found at once attractive and exasperating.

So after a few days they found themselves at the station, waiting for the train called the Kaffir Mail.

Ula Masondo was wearing as many of his best clothes as he could. The rest were contained in a suitcase of plum-coloured cardboard embossed to look like leather, which he carried in a hand resplendent with cheap rings. He was perched on high-heeled shoes which made him look as if he was standing on tip-toe. He wore voluminous tweed trousers fastened at the ankle with a buckle, and a wide scarf of purple silk under his coat.

Emma wore salmon-coloured silk stockings which cunningly suggested, at a close inspection, the blackness of her legs. Her underwear was visible through a thin silk dress, and its white mesh could be seen back and front against the blackness of her skin. She had made it herself with a crochet hook, as she had the two pillow-cases in her hand. These were stuffed with all her possessions, and both of them were worked with patterns of words in elaborate lace. The motto of one was *God is Love*; the other, *Forget-me-not*.

From her mouth dangled the ends of a pair of white silk shoe-laces, which she presently bent down to insert in her shoes.

Her movement provoked a salvo of interested comment from a group of her returning fellow-countrymen, who were standing in the background; they were clad in blankets; tall and statuesque, like figures in a fresco.

Still with one shoe-lace in her mouth, fat and breathless she watched her interlocutors between her legs, and although her face was upside-down they could see her handsome eyes glinting with the sparks of incipient repartee.

As soon as she stood up she flung round and struck a martial attitude. The speakers had the pleasure of bathing in a fountain of facetious abuse. When the fountain had played, it was succeeded by a captivating pout which at once gave way in the most disarming and feminine of smiles. But receiving, with a chorus of pleasantries, no less than three simultaneous proposals of free love, Emma fixed her face in a sneer. When she sneered there was a contraction of the muscles in the small of her back.

At this moment the train came in.

'Come along, my boy,' said Emma, and, with the complicated gait of a prodigal Bantu dandy, Ula Masondo, on high unsteady heels, followed her into the train.

## § 18

News travels quickly in Lembuland, and although Ula Masondo had sent no word to his relations they all knew of his return. His mother took on herself the task of meeting him, and on the day of his arrival set off for Aucampstroom before there was light in the sky. She was accompanied by a younger woman, a daughter-in-law with a baby on her back.

At first the long grass was wet with dew, but it rapidly dried as the sun rose in a cloudless sky. The old woman soon began to feel the heat. She was walking with a staff, and her steps became laboured. The travellers rested for some time near a stream, in the cool shade of some *umhlambamasi* trees, whose glossy leaves made a green and over-arching canopy. It was noon before they arrived at Aucampstroom.

The train was due and the station was crowded. The two women withdrew a little way, and sat down on the ground in the sun. The old woman took snuff. Her wrinkled face was eager with the rare exaltation of the aged. As for the countenance of the younger woman, it was calm with the rich calmness of early maturity. The child at her back was asleep. She sat like an image, heavy-lidded and smiling in stone, with worshippers a thousand years dust in the desert, but warm and brown and coming to life with a flow of reflorescent energy, warm and coming to life like a goddess that wakes on a carved and sunlit crag above the snow in Turkestan.

A screaming whistle grew louder, the rushing train was black, and its opening side broke into many moving forms of noisy and emerging humanity.

The mother of Ula Masondo saw him directly he got out of the train, and ran towards him through the crowd, clapping her hands excitedly against her scrawny thighs. She pushed her head forward and peered up into his face.

He looked down at her, recognized her, looked away without making any sign, and turned to Emma, flashy with jewellery.

'Let's go, let's go!' he said impatiently. The mother laid her hands on his arm.

'My boy, you have come back,' she said, nodding her head.

Ula Masondo turned on her.

'Who are you? What do you want?'

'What?' said the old woman slowly. 'Are you coming, my boy?'

She clutched at his coat, but he shook himself free.

'Who are you? Leave me alone,' he said, 'you bloody heathen.'

His mother saw him walk away with Emma, then she went back, quite stupefied, to her daughter-in-law, whose face was almost expressionless.

Ula Masondo and Emma went to an eating-house and bought food, which they sat down to eat on a crowded veranda. Afterwards, somebody played a desperate syncopated twangling tune on a zither, and Ula Masondo began to dance on his high heels, limply, slackly, clapping solemnly, suddenly, the upturned soles of his shoes, one-two, with the palms of his hands. His ear-rings were swinging and the streamers of pink wool at his wrist were describing flying curves in the air. There was a rash on one side of his face: it came into view as he turned in the dance.

When he had finished, he lighted a cigarette, and started off with Emma in the direction of her home.

The leaves of the station trees were applied in relief against a blank bright sky, and on the deserted platform the young woman sat impassively watching the mother of Ula Masondo beating the ground with her hands, nodding and nodding her withered head, her rheumy eyes screwed up in her dusty skin; refusing and refusing a consolation that was not offered; and crying again and again in a high small voice:

'Mayé, mayé, mayé, mayé.'

But after a time she was silent, like a bird ensnared, that gives up its crying and fluttering and lies quite still, knowing it cannot escape; its eyes set in a glassy stare and its stillness the still-palpitating annihilation of terror.

§ 19

The storekeeper, who had once sold Ula Masondo a blanket, was sitting at supper.

'You know those Masondos?' he said to his wife.

'Yes.'

'A shocking thing has happened. That boy Ula — used to be such a decent boy — came back from the mines about a week ago. Well, the old woman went down to meet him, and he refused to recognize her —'

'What!'

'Yes, refused to recognize her, his own mother, and told her that she was only a heathen. They say she came home in a terrible state, and they all thought she'd gone out of her mind. Two of the sons at once went off to see this Ula (the father refused to go) and found him at a kraal right on the other side of Aucampstroom, with some girl that he picked up in Jo'burg. He told his brothers that he wasn't coming home, and they couldn't persuade him, they couldn't do anything. Meanwhile the old woman surprised everybody by becoming unaccountably cheerful. They say she was laughing at everything for two or three days. Yes, and the day before yesterday, during a heavy downpour of rain that deadened all sounds, she hanged herself in an empty hut.'

'O, *Fred*! Hanged herself?'

'*Hanged* herself! Mind you, it's only the second time I've ever heard of a native committing suicide. By Jove, there's an example for you, of a boy going away quite all right, and coming back with all this Christian dandy business that I can't stand at any price. Give me the raw nigger any day, is what I have always maintained.'

'O, go on, Fred, you're the one that's always talking about increasing their wants, and getting the trade built up for little Freddy —'

'Yes, that's all very well, but if that Ula Masondo ever comes here again, won't I give him a piece of my mind!'

# BLACK PERIL

## § 1

A CAR stood outside one of the large white houses in the residential quarter of Dunnsport. It belonged to the doctor, who was making his third visit in twelve hours.

'Calm yourself,' he said irritably to the frantic husband of the young woman. 'I insist on your behaving calmly. Think of your wife.'

'Think of her! I can think of nothing else!'

'She won't recover from the shock unless you control yourself. Listen.'

He could hear his wife's voice. She was lying in the next room in a state of delirium.

'I want Charlie!' she was moaning in an unnatural voice.

The door opened, and a nurse came out. Her white clothes were slightly starched, and rustled as she moved. She beckoned to the doctor and they whispered together. The glare of the sun outside was reflected on the white walls of the room. The young man felt wounded by so much whiteness, the white suit of the doctor, the white veil of the nurse, the thought of his wife's white face on the pillow. In great anguish he heard again the unnatural sound of her voice, and covered his face with his hands.

'Come now,' said the doctor, 'she will recover from the shock.'

## § 2

In the dark bedroom the raving young woman, Vera Corneliussen, opened her eyes. She saw a view of the town as if she

55

had been standing on the flat roof of the house. It is a winter's afternoon, she can see the pale cubes and masses of square, modern buildings, the colour of sand and stone, under the faint blue of the sunny sky. Far away down there, their flat walls peppered with windows, they seem of archaic simplicity, awaiting or surviving events, unreal yet too real, like the buildings in a dream. On several pinnacles tiny flags can be seen flying at half-mast, for somebody is dead. On this fine, still, winter afternoon these are the buildings of Egypt, or the ruined cities of Asia.

It is night. She is two years old. They are staying at a farm in the summer. Her sister is dead, and she can hear her mother and her father weeping. The night air is full of the noise of frogs. There is a full moon. Her bath stands under the window and the surface of the water wavers in the moonlight. She is frightened and begins to cry. Suddenly the moonlight disappears, as if a curtain had been drawn. It is the black nursemaid who has come to see what is the matter. Her hands are hot, her voice is soft, she has a strange, friendly smell.

When the child sits at meals a native man moves noiselessly behind her chair. He wears loose white clothes that smell of soap and flap coolly against his warm, dark skin. When she looks up at his face she can see a rose-brown flush that suffuses his cheeks. The palms of his hands are pink.

At Dunnsport, sitting on the beach, she sees a woman pouring cold tea out of a dark-green bottle.

'O, he's devoted to Trixie and Stanley,' she is saying. 'Just look at him now.'

A native man is caressing the feet of her child. He smiles, showing his primitive white teeth.

'I was glad I got rid of that other boy I had. You remember that boy Isaac I had, eh? He was only fourteen, and do you know before he'd been with the kiddies a week they began to come out with the most shocking language. You wouldn't believe the expressions they came out with. I tell you, Mrs. Dawcock, really, my ears were burning. And the habits Trixie and Stanley learnt from that Isaac! I haven't got them out of them yet. Precocious little monkey he was, that Isaac of mine.'

There is a smell of straw. When she was twelve years old Vera Corneliussen was found in the loft with a native boy four years older than herself, and he was nearly flogged to death. Yes, of course, she is on the farm again. Smiling Morn is the name of the farm, but she remembers best the afternoons, the Sunday afternoons in winter. The long grass is dry and yellow, there is a low mud-house at the top of the slope above the river, whose bed is almost dry, with flat rocks under the silver-poplar trees which are only just losing their leaves, and in whose shade there is a damp, pungent smell. Somewhere the notes of a concertina are repeating over and over again a monotonous tune which makes her feel her heart could break, her heart could break in sobs, could break out sobbing, sobbing, sobbing.

And then, on the coast, she sees the train tunnelling through the feverish brilliance and glossy profusion of the foliage, and afterwards people walking along the line. All the trees are quivering in a hot steam of mist, all listening, all the nerves of trees listening to the funeral tom-toms of the Indians at the compound, all day, all night, quite slow, dead and dull, at intervals, like hammers thudding, tom-toms in the head, thud, tom-toms in the heart, thud. A young man of the Indians was beautiful. They called him the Jewel of Asia.

Tin bungalows in the hot, dry, dirty, loose sand full of bones, tins, papers, sticks, and the droppings of animals. Some towels are hung out to dry on the veranda. Inside, the furniture is yellowish, the food tastes like metal, the conversation is like stale beer. A pimply clerk gets out of the train. He lives next door. His wife, like a bedraggled cockatoo, runs down to meet him.

A tired actress, who travels with a concert party, is staggering back through the sand after bathing. She is still wearing her bathing-dress (to which some sand is sticking as if it had been thrown there); it fits tightly to her skin, and is wrinkled on her massive legs.

Vera Corneliussen feels herself travelling along the coast. As she goes she sees cape after cape, lagoon after lagoon, and the long horizontal seas combing in wave after wave. Inland, the slender curving bamboos, always waving in the air with gentle unvarying gestures, are like fishing-rods that have waited so long for a catch that they have long since broken into leaf, and yet they continue in every wind to wave with a forlorn, despairing hope. And there are groves of wild bananas everywhere, which on still days are green, but which on windy days are blown back so that they show their silvery undersides, like dead fish floating in a whirlpool, floating belly upwards in mockery of the lashed and straining bamboos.

Inland, there is a venerable old Arab storekeeper whose body is like biscuit-coloured marble. He has a white beard, and wears a coat of purple silk and a skull-cap embroidered with threads of silver tinsel. His son, they say, is on a pilgrimage to Mecca; he has a Zulu concubine; he has few customers; he lies on a couch and spits where he pleases.

After the banana plantation and the mango orchard there is a small tin house, painted pale blue, from which proceeds domestic smoke with an aromatic smell. It is raining softly, a steam of smoke is everywhere, and she can hear a baby crying. Under the trees with large leaves white and speckled fowls stand huddled together while drops of rain run down their tail-feathers.

Then there is a ploughed field with a path across it, and then a cemetery. In the warm tropical rain stands a group of natives round a shiny wet coffin, and an old German missionary in black is holding up with one hand a large black umbrella with a thick, knobbly handle, while the other supports a hymn-book. There is a nasal sound of singing. A black woman, under a wet white lace parasol, is wearing a pink dress which the rain has already spoilt: it runs with two colours, dark pink and light pink, in streaks.

Vera Corneliussen hears a motor-car, whirring with passionate and ecstatic compression like the respiration of some tremendous animal.

'It's a car! Mind you don't get run over!'

A cold sweat runs down her forehead, and the sun is sinking behind the hill. She can hear again the voice of the woman on the beach at Dunnsport:

'We took some bananas in a paper bag, but they weren't ripe, and a bottle of cold tea. There was a dead fly in it, and she had a shooting pain in her hip. It was very hot that day, and Steve's friend came, him that's been living with us, though time and again I've said to mother: "Let him go out and work, Steve has to go out and work," but he just stays on. Well, I said to Steve's friend: "Look here, my lad, don't think I'm going to let you get funny with me. O yes, I give him something to think about. Yes, trying to get funny, he was.'

## § 3

In Dunnsport Vera Corneliussen used sometimes to go and stay with her aunt Judith, a rich old maid, who lived in a house of which all the windows were sealed, and devoted herself to promoting the interests of the Fresh Air Fund. The house had a prickly garden, spiny with pointing palms as poisonous as fishbones, and in house and garden there was a deafening and hostile silence, and that air of secure and perpetual calm in which storms are born, in which they thunder and breed and die.

When Vera went out of Dunnsport it was nearly always to stay at New Havana, the home of her aunt Judith's brother, and once the centre of the social life of the commercial aristocracy of the coast. But even when she first went there times had changed.

The old white house was rotting in the bush. The road that once led to the old mill, through fields of coffee and arrowroot, was now a swamp, the building itself a roofless ruin. The vacant windows on the land side are full of branches tied and knotted to the walls and to each other by lianas thicker than ropes; the vacant windows on the shore side, like the lids of sightless eyes, are lighted by an upthrown glare from the dazzling white sand of the shore. From the beach, with savage constancy, comes the sound of the sea-waves pounding and sliding on an expanse of sand. In the tree-tops of the bush clatters the derisive laughter of monkey-birds. So perished the first glory of the Wesleyan conquistadors.

Now their fortunes are in plantations of sugar-cane that cover all the inland hills, which look in the distance like grassy downs. Yet near at hand the cane is tall and dry and sharp, deadly dry to every sense, dry green, dry leaves, papery metal rustling or grating, leaf against leaf, all those jointed stems full of hot, sweet sap.

In the canefields there are long, straight, earthy roads for fire-breaks, with the cane higher than her head on both sides extending out of sight with stiff and rustling monotony. At her feet a snake lies warming itself in the sun. There, in the distance, is an avenue of gum trees of a torrid greyness. Isolated *umdoni* trees, some dead and some leafy, are sticking up out of the cane: and occasional euphorbias, dark and fleshy and knotted and rigid, like many arms petrified in a moment of unanimous supplication to an unknown god.

At the new mill, as vast as a cathedral, the cane goes up and up in an endless everlasting elevator. She can hear the crunching sound of greedy and relentless jaws, and out runs the sap in astonishing quantities, as bright as vitriol and with the profusion of water. At the mill there are men running up and down steel staircases, men with red faces, men with brown bodies running along galleries, black men watching steaming vats with fumes of sulphur hovering over their surfaces, men pushing trucks, men feeding furnaces, men obeying machinery, machines obeying men, the inhabitants of a vast and noisy universe of sweat.

## § 4

It was at New Havana House that she first met George Corneliussen; it was there that she got engaged to him, it was there that they spent their honeymoon. This later house, which already has an air of slightly faded prosperity, is only thirty years old, and yet is completely hidden by the garden planted after it was built. It is at once forbidding and inviting, in a dark and ordered wilderness of firs and palms and eucalyptuses and flowering shrubs, and groves and groves of orange trees weighed down by masses of ripening fruit, that falls and rots with a rich and morbid odour in the damp shade, under firmaments and firmaments of hanging oranges. The house seems to be in a cave of permanent shadow, the sun is shining in some other world.

There is a dance. People are coming out from Dunnsport. It is dusk. She can see quiet and luxurious motor-cars following one another up the approach, with sombre regularity, like deadly thoughts succeeding one another in an unconscious brain. In the middle of the dance she is sitting out with George. He is smoking a cigarette. The trees are swaying in a wash of moonlight. A native servant comes to them with a tray and glasses.

'Here you!' It is the voice of George. 'What's your name? What? Charlie, you say?'

She can see the moonlight on his teeth and on the whites of his eyes.

She is going with George to the mill. It is just before they are married. The clerk in the office is rather sallow. He goes out of the room. She asks George:

'Is he white or coloured?'

'Hush, he's what they call a Coast European.'

Just at that minute the man comes in again: he must have heard what they were saying.

'After all,' she says afterwards to George, 'I suppose it isn't a sin to be coloured.'

'But it's a sin to look coloured,' he says in his pleasant voice. He is so kind and amiable, almost a boy, and he looks so delightful on a pony, his shirt open at the neck. He rides so well, and plays the gramophone so nicely.

'Quite enough people are touched with the tar-brush,' he says; 'we don't want any more. Just think, for instance, there's another of these Coast Europeans, also working in the mill, who can either go and have a drink in the European bar or in the Indian bar as he pleases. He's white enough for one, and dark enough for the other.'

'Dark enough, dark enough,' she repeats the words to herself.

It is the morning after her wedding-day. She is the first to wake. She is surprised to see that George's hair, always so smooth, so neatly parted, is all ruffled on the pillow. George, with his hair ruffled! It makes her laugh, but although the whole bed shakes with her laughing George does not wake up. She can hear the siren at the mill. It is seven o'clock.

After six months they are again staying at New Havana. She is always awake when the siren sounds at the mill. She is always the first down to breakfast. The servant Charlie waits on her at the table. He is taller and broader than George, and more grace-ful in his movements. His voice is deeper and more harmonious, his temper is better, he evidently has more character. Besides, he is magnetic. One morning she touches his hand as if by accident. He has an electric skin.

§ 5

She has been married two years. There is no child. The man Charlie has left New Havana and is working for her in Dunnsport. George is away. She has quarrelled with him for being irreproachable. She is satisfied that it is a good reason for a quarrel. George has gone away for the week-end to play golf. He tried to pretend that he was going to a woman, but he knew that she knew his pretence.

'You are content to leave me alone in the house?' she had asked him in the hall, as a servant was carrying his bag of golf-clubs out to the car.

'You aren't obliged to stay here. You can go to a hotel.'

At night, when she was in her bedroom, she rang the bell. There was only one servant in the house that night. She had arranged it. Charlie is standing in the doorway.

It is seven o'clock; she can hear a siren. It is afternoon, the light of the sun is pale. It is before dawn; there is lightning in the sky and frost on the ground.

## § 6

George Corneliussen takes his hands away from his eyes. It is midday. There is a cry in the bedroom. He opens the door. Vera has twisted her body out of the bed. Her head is hanging downwards, so that her ear-rings are hanging upside-down. The nurse runs forward, the husband runs forward, but the woman is dead.

*Frightful Outrage in Town, Society Woman Victim, Dies of Shock,* said the posters the next morning.

'What a shocking case,' people said, opening their newspapers on trams, trains and breakfast tables.

'Yes, these black brutes are all alike.'

'Have they caught him?'

'He'll be hung.'

'He ought to be lynched.'

'I remember once —'

'I must really buy you a revolver.'

Everywhere the same remarks were to be heard, but in an hour the outrage would be forgotten, and the wind would blow one of the posters into the gutter, where a half-caste peanut-seller, by shifting his feet, would, without knowing, partly obliterate the printed words.

# THE CHILD OF QUEEN VICTORIA

## § 1

A FORD car, rattling its way up a rough road in Lembuland in the most brilliant sunshine, carried two very different people — a hard-bitten colonial of Scotch descent, a trader, MacGavin by name, nearer thirty than forty, with a sour red face, and a young Englishman called Frant who had just left school. It was really very awkward. They did not know what to say to each other. MacGavin thought his passenger was despising him simply for being what he was, and Frant, feeling foolish and useless in contrast with this sunburnt, capable man, made a painful effort to be hearty, and looked inquiringly at the country. The road wound in and out, climbing through grassy hills, with patches of virgin forest here and there, especially in the hollows. There were outcrops of rock, and small tilled fields of red earth, and any number of beehive-shaped huts perched here and there in twos and threes. And there were always natives in sight, with herds of bony cattle and ragged goats. It did not need a specially acute eye to see that the landscape, though picturesque, was over-crowded, and that the whites, coveting the lowlands for sugar-cane, had gradually squeezed the natives up into these heights which were poor in soil, coarse in pasturage, and too full of ups and downs to afford space for any proper attempts at cultivation. Frant looked at the natives, naturally, with some curiosity. He wondered what they were like when you got to know them, and then he wondered if he couldn't say something suitable to MacGavin about them. At last he said:

'It seems a pity that the natives haven't got a higher standard of living, then there would be so much more money to be made out of them.'

MacGavin looked at him with the savage expression sometimes to be seen on the faces of the ignorant when confronted with what seems to them a new and difficult and rather mad idea.

'The black bastards!' he exclaimed. 'There's bloody little to be made out of *them*, as you'll pretty soon find out.'

And he violently changed gear. As the car began to strain its way up a steep hill, Frant, vibrating by his side, was glad that the noise of the engine destroyed what would have been a painful silence.

Sons of the 'new poor', young wasters, retrenched civil servants or Indian Army officers, and other mostly misguided wretches, they went to settle overseas — one even heard of suicides, because not everybody is tough enough to stand an absolute change of environment, or frightful isolation in some magnificent landscape. And Frant, lured by advertisements, driven by enterprise, encouraged by supposedly responsible persons, went out like them, only fresh from a public school.

His incipient relationship with MacGavin was not made easier by the practical basis on which it rested, for Frant came to him neither as a partner, nor as a servant, nor as a guest, nor had he paid one penny by way of premium. A committee in London had picked out MacGavin's name as that of a person who had declared himself willing to give a young Englishman free board and lodging and two or three years' training in the art of trading with the Lembus in exchange for nothing but that young stranger's 'services'. MacGavin was in some ways a practical man, and the chance of obtaining a responsible white servant who need be paid no wages seemed to him a good one. Frant had been brought up to be eager to oblige. And that was how they started.

Frant was young — so young that, bumping adventurously along into the heart of Lembuland, he could not help thinking of his former schoolfellows and of how they would have envied him if they could have seen him at that moment. A fatal eagerness possessed him. He was flying in the face of the world, as the young are apt to do, with the finest of ambitions. For some of us when young it does not seem so important that we should be successful in a worldly sense and at once enjoy money and comfort, as that we should try and become our true selves. We want to blossom out and fulfil our real natures. The process is complex, and is obviously conditioned by our approaches to the work we mean to do or have to do in life, by the way our heredity and upbringing make us react to our environment, and especially by our relations with other people. In the long run this affair of becoming a grown-up person, a real person (for that is what it amounts to) is, for most of us, an affair of the heart. We hear a great deal about sex nowadays; it is possible to overestimate its importance, because there are always people who pay it little attention or who apparently manage, like Sir Isaac Newton, to get along, without giving it a thought. But Frant came of a susceptible family. He arrived in Lembuland with a pretty appetite for life, and little knew what he was letting himself in for.

§ 2

The trading station at Madumbi occupied the top of a slope a little back from the road, or track rather, and consisted of two main buildings, the store and the house, about fifty yards apart, and a number of ramshackle outhouses. In front, there had been some attempt at a garden — not much of an attempt, for cows and chickens always roamed about in it, and it was now and then invaded by monkeys. At the back, there was some rough grazing land and a patch of forest that went with the place. The buildings themselves were made of corrugated iron, painted khaki and lined with deal boards, looking out, curiously hideous, on the land which sloped away from them on all sides with streams, and clumps of trees, and grassy spaces like a well-planned park. But Mr. and Mrs. MacGavin, in settling at Madumbi, had been little influenced by the scenery.

The store itself was lighted only by two small windows and the open door, and as you came in from the strong sunlight it was at first difficult to get your bearings. The place was so crowded with goods that it looked like a cave crowded with all sorts of plunder. Your head bumping against a suspended trek-chain or storm-lantern, you looked up and saw that the ceiling was almost entirely hidden in festoons of kettles and baskets, hanks of Berlin wool, enormous bouquets of handkerchiefs of all sizes and colours, bunches of tunics and trousers interspersed with camisoles, frying-pans, wreaths of artificial forget-me-nots, hatchets and matchets, necklaces and ploughshares. As for the shelves, they were entirely crammed with different kinds of goods, for the production of which a hundred factories had smoked and roared in four continents. All kinds of shoddy clothing and showy piece-goods, brittle ironmongery and china-ware, the most worthless patent medicines, the gaudiest cheap jewellery, the coarsest groceries, bibles, needles, pipes, celluloid collars, soup tureens, hair-oil, notebooks, biscuits and lace curtains rose in tiers and patterns on every side. Certain shelves were full of refuse left over from the war — grey cotton socks made in Chicago for American recruits who had never enlisted, khaki tunics and breeches, puttees, Balaclava helmets and so forth, all ugly and serviceable, made and carried by machinery to contribute to a scene of universal murder, produced in too great quantities, by contract instead of by necessity or impulse, and at last deposited here, so that a profit might be made out of the pleasure these things, by their novelty, gave to the blacks. The whole world seemed to have conspired to make a profit on this lonely Lembu hilltop.

Two doors at the back of the store itself gave access to two other rooms. One was large, and was used for storing reserves of bulky goods — sacks of salt, sugar and grain; ironware; boxes of sweets and soap; besides a profusion of bunches of Swazi tobacco leaves, at least two feet long, their fragrance preserved by an occasional sprinkling with water. It was the custom to give away a leaf or two of tobacco to each adult shopper, and to the young a handful of the cheapest sweets, their virulent pinks and greens and acid chemical flavours promising a quick decay to strong white teeth. The other and smaller room was used as an office, and contained a table, a chair, a safe, and a great accumulation of MacGavin's papers. The window, which received the afternoon sun, would not open, and was always buzzing with flies and hornets in various stages of fatigue. A flea-bitten dog was usually asleep on a pile of unpaid bills in the corner, while the ink, from standing so much in the sun, was always evaporating, so that when one had occasion to write one had to use a pencil.

But all that was only the background. The space before the counter was often thronged with Lembus of all ages and both sexes. The noise was overpowering. They would all be talking at once, some laughing, some arguing, some gossiping, some bargaining, while all the time a peculiarly strident gramophone was playing records of Caruso and Clara Butt. Sometimes an old black woman, nearly blind and nearly naked, her last peppercorns of hair grizzled to a pepper-and-salt colour, and her dry old dugs so long that she could comfortably tuck the ends of them into her belt, might be seen listening to it, with her head on one side, for the first time, uttering occasional exclamations of incredulity ('*Abantu! Inkosi yami! Maye babo!*') and slapping her scrawny thighs, as she demanded whether the voice was the voice of a spirit.

In another part of the room the only vacant space on the wall was occupied by a pier-glass, before which a group of very fat girls were fond of comparing their charms, to the accompaniment of shrieks of delight. Their main wish was to observe the reflection of their bottoms, partly out of pure curiosity and partly with a view to interesting the men present. Standing among the older customers there were always some children, patiently awaiting their turn to be served with threepennyworths of this and that. Some brought eggs or wild fruit to trade, which they carried in small bowl-shaped baskets on their heads. One might have a fowl under her arm, and a little boy of seven would perhaps bring an enormous scarlet lily, complete with leaves and root.

To say that all this was strange to Frant would be an understatement. It was a new world. Into this exotic atmosphere he was plunged; this was where he had to work; this was what he had to learn. What is called adaptability is little more than freshness and keenness and readiness to learn, and Frant, who had been brought up to obey, made himself completely and at first willingly subservient to MacGavin's instructions. He didn't like MacGavin, and it was plain that he never would do so, but it was also plain that MacGavin knew his business, and Frant's presence at Madumbi was, in theory, a business matter. So he rose early and retired late, working hours that no trade union would approve at a job that needed endless patience and good humour, with diligence and imagination as well. He struggled with a strange language, did accounts, avoided cheating or being cheated (he had been brought up to be honest) and toiled morning, noon and night, without haste, without rest, never for a moment questioning what he conceived to be his duty. And MacGavin, finding that he had to do with an honest and docile and responsible person, confided to his wife that the plan was succeeding beyond his hopes. Very soon, he felt, he would be able to leave Frant in entire charge of the proceedings, while he himself attended to other money-making operations out of doors. Mrs. MacGavin was pleased too, because she found she was less often required to help in the store, and could spend more time in the house. Though God knows the store was the pleasanter building of the two.

70

On his very first afternoon Frant had been given tea on the veranda of the house, in order to afford Mrs. MacGavin an early chance of sizing him up, but after that his tea was always sent over to the store. Apart from that he had meals in the house, and he slept in it, and spent part of his Sunday leisure in it as well. There were only four rooms. Frant's own room, nine feet by seven, was oppressively hot, was never properly cleaned, and had a disagreeable smell. The living-room, not large in itself, was so crammed with furniture that one person could with difficulty turn round in it, whereas three people were supposed to eat and sleep and rest in it, quite in addition to the fact that, the house lacking either hall or passage, it had to serve as both. Thus the pattern on the linoleum was in places quite worn away, and behind the front door was a rack bulging with hats, coats and mackintoshes, which gave off a greenish odour of stale sweat, cheap rubber and mildew. The middle of the room was occupied by a large table covered with a khaki mohair table-cloth with bobbles round the edges, and in the middle of that stood a large oil-lamp with a shade of crinkly pink paper. A sideboard held a load of worthless ornaments, and on the walls faded wedding-groups in bamboo Oxford frames alternated with dusty paper fans, cuckoo clocks and fretwork brackets supporting electro-plated vases containing dusty everlasting flowers in process of perishing from dry-rot. With difficulty it was possible to make one's way to a small bookcase which stood beneath a reproduction of a problem picture, showing a woman in evening dress in the fashion of 1907 kneeling on the floor before a man in a dinner-jacket, the whole suffused in a red glow from a very hot-looking fire in the background, and called 'The Confession'. Among the books were several by Marie Corelli, a brochure on the diseases of cattle, and a girlish album of Mrs. MacGavin's, in which her friends had written or attempted to draw personal tributes and pleasantries. Had this album been a little more vulgar, it might have been almost a curiosity, but the commonness of colonial schoolgirls in the second decade of this century has scarcely even a period interest. It must be admitted, however, that one contributor had written the following very appropriate wisecrack:

> Roses are red and violets blue,
> Pickles are sour and so are you.

'Fond of reading?' MacGavin, in an expansive moment, once asked Frant. 'No time myself.'

'Yes and no,' said Frant, who was trying to make up for his education and had a copy of *The Brothers Karamazov* in his bedroom. 'It depends.'

On the table in that front room there was nearly always a fly-haunted still-life consisting of a teapot and some dirty cups, for Mrs. MacGavin drank very strong tea seven times daily, a habit which no doubt accounted partly for the state of her complexion. But all day long and most evenings the double doors on to the veranda were open, and there was the view. As the trading station was on the top of a hill and partly surrounded with groves of mimosa trees, the outlook was very fine. Beyond the trees, it could be seen that every depression in the landscape had its rivulet and patch of forest, and that in every sheltered and elevated place there was a kraal of beehive-shaped huts with small fields of grain and roots; cattle were grazing here and there; and in the distance rose range upon range of blue mountains. At first sight it seemed, like so many African landscapes, a happy mixture of the pastoral and the magnificent, but those who lived under its influence came to feel gradually a mingled sense of uneasiness and sorrow, so that what at first seemed grand became indifferent or menacing, what at first seemed peaceful was felt to be brooding, and stillness and quietness seemed to be an accumulation of repressed and troubled forces, like the thunderclouds that often hung over the horizon of an afternoon. Those sunny hills seemed to be possessed by a spirit that nursed a grievance.

§ 3

Frant's approach to the natives was complicated by his character and education, which in some ways helped and in some ways hindered him. As a polite person, he treated them with a good-humoured consideration which they were quite unused to receiving from the whites, but then the whites in Lembuland are an unusually discouraging lot — the way they behave to one another is proof of that. A natural quick sympathy and warmth in his character immediately attracted the natives, who are uncannily quick at character, but at the same time they found a certain reserve in him. It was not that he stood on his dignity with them, but simply that he was a little too conscientious. There were certain vague ideas about the white man's prestige and so on which made him rather careful in his behaviour. He imagined that if he let himself go at all he might in some way damage MacGavin's standing and do harm to the trade, and of course MacGavin, in teaching him the trade, was careful to try and instil various principles about treating the natives firmly. And to MacGavin's credit it may be added that he insisted on the natives being treated as fairly as possible, though this was a matter of business rather than principle with him. And after all, there was no need to tell Frant to be fair — it was clear that though a trifle priggish, he was no swindler. This priggishness of his was easy to account for. It was partly in his nature, but also he had been brought up with certain rigid English ideas about being a gentleman, playing the game, and all that sort of thing, and until now he had had no reason to doubt that they were right. The effect of being abruptly transferred to a completely new environment; of being cut off from those familiar companions and surroundings which had enabled his principles to be taken for granted; and of associating with Mr. and Mrs. MacGavin, was not to make him doubt those principles but to convince him that they were right. And to be all by oneself and to think oneself right is really rather fatal, especially if one naturally tends to be both straightforward and severe. Already he would receive some of the opinions of MacGavin and his wife in a silence that was even stronger in its effect than the quiet and smiling 'Oh, I'm afraid I can't quite agree with you' which he often had to use in conversation with them.

'He always thinks he's right,' MacGavin remarked to his wife, 'but it doesn't matter about that. What's more important is that the niggers like him. There's a slight improvement in the takings this month, and I shouldn't be surprised if it's partly due to him. He does what he's told for the most part, and I shouldn't be surprised if he turns out a good salesman when he knows the lingo a bit better.'

The Lembu language presents no great difficulties, and it is surprising what good use one can make of a language as soon as one has a small working vocabulary and a few colloquial turns of phrase. Frant enjoyed speaking it, because it is one of those Bantu languages which, to be spoken well, have to be spoken with gusto, and it can be both sonorous and elegant. His progress in the language naturally made his work more easy and pleasant, but it had other effects — it drew him closer into sympathy with the Lembus, and showed him how little they liked the whites. In fact, he began to realize that the remains of the white man's prestige, in Lembuland at least, rested mainly on fear — fear of the white man's money, his mechanical genius and his ruthless and largely joyless energy — and not on love or respect. And since he himself had very little money, no mechanical genius and a certain joyful vitality, he felt that there must be something rather 'un-white' about himself. This discovery acted directly upon his pride — it made him resolve to treat the natives with as much kindness and dignity as were consonant with his odd position (the ruling race behind the counter!), as if to show that there were still white men who knew how to behave humanely. This made him think himself better than MacGavin and the few other whites with whom he came in touch, and shut him up in a small cell of his own (as it were) closely barred with high principles.

He did not pretend to himself that the Lembus were paragons of virtue. The very fact that as customers in a shop they had a certain right to order the shopkeepers about, added to the fact that these shopkeepers were nominally their 'superiors', was a temptation to some of the natives to be tiresome, cheeky or even insolent, and that was one reason why a great deal of persevering good temper was needed in dealing with them. By the time they had convinced themselves that Frant was both patient and cheerful he had already begun to get a good name amongst them. They were used to MacGavin, whom they thought of as a beast, but a just beast, and finding Frant just without being a beast, and youthful and personable as well, they undoubtedly began to come to Madumbi in greater numbers.

At first he had been much struck by the extreme suspiciousness and diffidence of the customers. They never entered the place with that air of cheerful confidence which, in the dreams of good shopkeepers, is found on every customer's face. On the contrary, they always seemed to come in expecting the worst. Many an old, wild woman, skirted in skins, smeared with fat and ochre, hung with charms, a bladder or an antelope's horn suspended at her neck, her hair dressed high and stuck with bone ornaments, a snuff-box at her waist, perhaps having about her too a couple of pounds, every penny of which she meant to spend, would pause in the doorway with a roving eye and an expression of extreme disillusionment and contempt, as though she found herself there unwillingly and by chance. After some time she would perhaps help herself to a cupful of water from a tank that stood at the door, and would then sit down in the shade and take a lot of snuff with immense deliberation, the expression on her face seeming to say, 'Well, here I am, and I don't give a damn for anybody. I haven't lived all these years for nothing. Experience has taught me to expect the worst of every

75

situation and every person, particularly if he or she happens to be white. If I condescend to do any shopping here, I mean to see everything, and to have exactly what I want or nothing at all. Don't think you can swindle me, because you can't. However, I shall proceed on the assumption that you mean to try, that all your goods are damaged, that you're a cunning profiteer, and that you think I'm a fool.' And when at last she deigned to enter the store, she would proceed accordingly.

But it was not only old women who were so much on their guard. Many and many a customer would show the same symptoms of a deep and cynical mistrust, walking in as if they were threading their way among mantraps all carefully set for them. Even children would show plainly how they had been forewarned, repeating innocently the last parental injunctions, and carefully counting their change from sixpence. And all this was not due to MacGavin but to the reputation which the white overlords of Lembuland had managed, in the course of two or three decades, to build up for themselves.

If for Frant this unpleasant relationship between the two races was one of his earliest and most enduring impressions, even stronger was that of the immediate physical presence of the Lembus. So many more or less naked bodies of men and women, coloured a warm brown, smooth-skinned and mostly graceful, with white teeth, straight backs and easy manners, do not leave one, when one is young and susceptible and unfamiliar with them, exactly indifferent.

'Don't worry about the stink,' MacGavin had said. 'You'll get used to it.'

Stink? The whites always say that the blacks have a bad smell. Well, there at Madumbi was a confined space usually tightly packed with natives, but although the weather was hot and the air sometimes scarcely moving, it could not have been said that the smell was much more than strange, though to Frant it was heady, like the very smell of life itself, and excited him with a promise of joys not yet tasted. The wholesome smell of an out-of-door race cannot in any case seem unpleasant, except to diseased nerves, and the lightly clad or unclad bodies of the Lembus are continually exposed to sun, air and water, while they are almost as vegetarian as their flocks and herds. If some of the old women were a little inclined to accumulate several layers of ochre and fat all over them by way of skin treatment, they were quite amusing enough in their manners and conversation, and had quite enough natural style, to make up for it. At Madumbi there was a far more oppressive smell than that of the natives, and that was the combined aroma of the dressing that stiffened the calicoes of Osaka and Manchester into a dishonest stoutness, and, to speak figuratively, of the sand in the sugar.

## § 4

In places like Madumbi, time seems more of a thief and enemy than in crowded cities or even in circles where the months are frittered away in useless leisure. In that part of Lembuland the changing of the seasons is less marked than in the highlands, and at Madumbi life was a packed routine; work began at half-past five or six in the morning; fatigue often precluded thought; and the tired eyes, turning towards clock or calendar, would close in sleep. Sometimes all sense of chronological sequence was lost; sometimes it seemed almost as if time were going backwards; and now and again Frant would realize with a shock how many weeks or months had slipped by since this or that trifling break in his existence. But he was not discontented, for he was interested in his work, not so much for its own sake as for the close contact with some of the realities of human nature into which it brought him.

There were certain things which he could never sell without a smile. Now and then a young Lembu would come in and say rather furtively, '*Amafuta wemvubu akona na?*' That is to say,

'Have you got any hippopotamus fat?' Whereupon Frant used to go to the small showcase in which the medicines were kept, and produce a small bottle with a label bearing a Lembu inscription, and underneath, in very small letters, PEDERSEN'S GENUINE HIPPO FAT. This commodity looked like ordinary lard, probably was ordinary lard, was put up by a Norwegian chemist in Dunnsport, and sold for a shilling a bottle. It was used for a love philtre, and helped the manufacturer to maintain his son at a theological seminary in Oslo. But other 'lines' were more lucrative than hippo fat. Love philtres, after all, were usually only required by the young and romantically inclined, whereas PEDERSEN'S BLUE WONDERS, as another Lembu inscription testified, were indispensable to both young and old. Certainly they were always in demand. Pills as large as peas and the colour of gun-metal, they were not merely an infallible, but a powerful aphrodisiac. When MacGavin happened to be asked for either of these medicines, he would never sell them without a clumsy pleasantry, a habit which had resulted in a falling-off of the sales of the hippo fat, for the younger natives, though their morals, according to some standards, were not above reproach, had their finer feelings. However, his misplaced humour did not much affect the demand for Blue Wonders, which were usually bought by customers of a coarser fibre. Mrs. MacGavin herself came to lend a hand in the store when business was brisk, and it would sometimes happen that she would be called upon to serve a customer with these things, which she would do with the grimmest face in the world — her expression might well have suggested a subject for an allegorical picture, 'Avarice overcoming Chastity'. But still, out of all the hotchpotch that the store contained, there was one kind of goods which she would neither buy nor sell. The male natives of those parts were in the habit of using a peculiar kind of *cache-sexe* made of the leaves of the wild banana. At Madumbi these were made, in assorted sizes, by an old vagabond of a native who sold them to MacGavin at wholesale prices. When he came to the store it was always at some odd time, when there was nobody else about, either on a very hot afternoon or just after the store had been locked up, or at dawn, or when the moon was rising. If he saw MacGavin, the business was soon settled. If he encountered Mrs. MacGavin, he would wave his bundle of unmentionables right under her nose, saluting her with his free hand and uttering all sorts of high-flown and wholly ironical compliments before crying the virtues of his wares. Nothing annoyed her more, as he very well knew. She always told him rudely to wait for her husband. If it was Frant he chanced to find, he would say with real politeness, '*Sa' ubona, umtwana ka Kwini Victoli!*' Greetings, child of Queen Victoria! This became shortened later to 'Child of the Queen' and at last simply to 'Child'. The very first time he had seen Frant he had said, 'Ah, I can see you're a real Englishman from *over there*,' and since England suggested Queen Victoria to him more than anything else it was not hard to account for the complimentary title. The old man, to whom Frant always gave an extra large leaf or two of tobacco, was also fond of saying that the *amaBhunu*, the Boers, were 'no good', which was partly his real opinion and meant partly as a piece of indirect flattery, though as Frant had not had anything to do with any Dutch people it was not particularly effectual.

'How can you allow that dirty old swine to call you "child"!' exclaimed MacGavin.

'Why, he's old enough to be my grandfather!' Frant retorted.

Frant's point of view seemed so fantastic to MacGavin that he laughed a short, harsh laugh.

'My advice is, don't stand any cheek from any nigger,' he said.

'He isn't cheeky to *me*,' said Frant. 'Only friendly.'

And with an irritable grunt from MacGavin the conversation was closed. It seemed extraordinary how full of prejudice the trader was. He was fond of generalizations about the natives which were not even remotely true, such as that they were incapable of gratitude (as if they had such a lot to be grateful for!) and he seemed to have a fixed idea that every black is determined to try and score off every white, under any conditions whatsoever. And when, as occasionally happened, a native addressed him politely in English, it made him so furious that he was no longer master of himself — it seemed to him a suggested assumption of equality between the races!

The MacGavins were amazed at Frant's continued progress, and if they welcomed his popularity with the natives as being good for trade, they resented a little that a stranger and a *rooinek*[1] should be able to beat them at their own game. As to what went on in his mind, they knew and cared nothing. They neither knew nor cared that neither work nor fatigue could prevent him from feeling at times an overwhelming loneliness and an intolerable hunger for experiences which his youth, the climate and the glorious suggestiveness of his surroundings did everything to sharpen, while its satisfaction was firmly forbidden by circumstances — or so it seemed to Frant. Already esteemed by the natives, he valued their good opinion of him too much to take chances with it, and in the background of his thoughts, in spite of the MacGavins, or perhaps because of them, there still presided that tyrannical spectre, the 'white man's prestige'. What it is to be an ex-prefect of an English public school!

§ 5

It was bound to happen that sooner or later his attention would become centred in some individual out of the hundreds he had to do with in the course of a week. One drowsy afternoon, when he was alone behind the counter and there was nobody in the store but a couple of gossips and a child, a young woman came in rather shyly and stood near the door, hesitating to speak. He couldn't see her very well because of the bright sunshine behind

---

[1] 'Red neck.' Dutch nickname for Englishman.

her, but he asked her what she wanted and she made a small purchase.

'Do you remember me?' she asked suddenly in a very quiet voice, looking at him gravely while she spoke.

He was surprised. He didn't remember ever having seen her before, but not wishing to offend her, he said in a slightly ironical tone of voice:

'Oh, when I've once seen people, *just once*, I never forget them.'

'Well!' she exclaimed, and uttered a little peal of laughter, partly because she was surprised at his ready answer and amused at his white man's accent; partly because, as a Lembu, she could appreciate irony; and partly because it made her happy that he should talk to her. But as soon as she had uttered that little laugh she grew shamefaced and cast down her eyes with the incomparable grace of a young woman with whom modesty is natural, and not a mere device of coquetry. There was more sadness than usual in her expression, because she had at once understood that he did not remember her, and no woman likes to be forgotten by any young man. She had moved now, and the diffused radiance reflected from the sunburnt hilltop outside shone full upon her through the open door. Her hair was dressed in a cylinder on the crown of her head, stained with red ochre, and stuck with a long bone pin at the broad end of which was a minute incised design; she wore no ornament but a flat necklace of very small blue beads and a few thin bangles and anklets of silver and copper wire. She was dressed in a single piece of dark red stuff which was supported by her pointed young breasts and fastened under the arms — it fell in straight, classical folds almost to her feet, and at the sides it did not quite join but revealed a little her soft flanks. From bearing weights on her head from early childhood she carried herself very erect; she was slender, and an awareness of her graceful nubility gave every movement the value of nature perfectly controlled by art. The fineness of her appearance may have been due to some remote Arab strain in her blood, for though unmistakably negroid, her features were in no sense exaggerated. Her nose, for example, though the nostrils were broad, was very slightly aquiline; her skin was unusually light in tone; and the modelling of her cheeks and temples could only be described as delicate. Her mouth was good-humoured, her eyes were lustrous, and though one side of her face was marked with a long scar, this only drew closer attention to its beauty.

'You don't come here very often, do you?' said Frant, leaning on the counter, partly because he did not want their conversation to be overheard by anybody else, and partly because he felt somehow weak in the legs. He was in the grip of an unaccustomed shyness, he felt unsure of himself, and so excited that his heart was beating very quickly.

'No,' she said, avoiding his eyes. 'I don't live very near.'

'Where do you live?'

'Down there — down in the valley,' she said, extending an exquisite arm and looking out through the open doorway with a vague and dreamy air. He noticed the light colour of the insides of her hands. 'Near the river,' she said.

'That's not very far away,' he said.

'You've been there, then?' she said. 'You know the place?'

'No, but I don't think it's very far.'

'The hill is long and steep,' she said.

Frant suddenly remembered two lines of verse —

> Does the road wind uphill all the way?
> Yes, to the very end.

'I don't know your name,' he said.

She looked at him quickly and uttered an exclamation of surprise.

'What's the matter?' he said.

'Why do you want to know my name?' she asked anxiously, for the use of names is important in witchcraft.

'I'm just asking. I just want to know it.'

'My name is Seraphina,' she said, with a mixture of modesty and seductiveness.

'*What?*'

'Seraphina.'

'How on earth did you get a name like that? It's not a Lembu name! You're not a Christian, are you?'

She laughed, as though the idea of her being a Christian was absolutely ridiculous — which indeed it was.

'No!' she said. 'A missionary gave it to me when I was a child. He made magic water on my head and said that Christ wanted me to be called Seraphina.'

This time Frant laughed.

'Christ chose well,' he said. 'But none of your family are Christians, are they?'

'No, it just happened like that.'

He laughed again.

'You don't know my name,' he said.

'Yes, I do,' she said, and pronounced it 'Front', and they both laughed.

Just then some noisy customers arrived, and he had to leave her. Suddenly bold, he said:

'Good-bye, go in peace. Please come again. I like talking with you.'

He couldn't possibly have dared to speak so directly of his feelings in English, but somehow in Lembu it was easier. Besides, he was stirred as he had never been stirred before.

'Good-bye,' she said, smiling. 'Stay in peace.'

She turned to go, and looked like some virgin in an archaic frieze saying farewell to the world. As for Frant, his hands were trembling, and there was a wild gladness in his heart.

§ 6

His tortures now began in earnest. His dreams and waking thoughts were haunted by the image of the black girl, tantalizing and yet infinitely remote. As his desire for her increased, so did its fulfilment seem to recede. He knew little or nothing of her; he knew little enough of her language and nothing at all of her situation in life. He had been so busy learning to make a profit out of the natives that he had had little chance of learning much about their customs, the way they lived and thought. Supposing, he said to himself, for the sake of argument, this girl were to become my mistress? First of all, is it possible? I am certain that to some extent she reciprocates my feelings, but to what extent? What would she expect of me? What would her family think of her? How would the affair be possible in any case? How am I to communicate with her? And then the MacGavins — presumably his success in his trading depends to some extent on the fact that he is not one of these white men who get mixed up with the natives; and if I were to become the lover of Seraphina, should I not damage his livelihood, besides ruining my own? Whatever happened, everybody would know about it, of course. And how could we live together? Are we to meet furtively in the forest? And have I the right to take this black girl? How can I pretend to myself that I love her? Is it not simply that I want to sleep with her, to touch, kiss, embrace and caress her? He found no answers to his questions, but the very fact that he could ask them was significant. His loneliness and his difficulties had taught him one of the very things that his education had been evolved to prevent — the habit of introspection. He was being Hamlet-ized by circumstances.

Of the numerous forms of anguish which Providence has designed for her creatures few can be more intense than the state of mind and body of a man who is young, sensual by nature and sexually repressed; and who, instead of yielding to the voluptuous provocations of his surroundings, tries to exorcize them with the public-school spirit. When he might well have acted with boldness, he found himself filled with doubts, scruples and equivocations, in addition to the ordinary fears of a lover. And he had nobody to turn to, there was nobody who would say to him what so much needed to be said, 'Well, go ahead and have the woman. You will have your pleasure and she will have hers, and you will both be a bit the wiser and possibly the happier for the experience. You will treat her with consideration, because it is your nature to be considerate. You are in no danger of "going native", because you aren't the sort of person who goes native. And as for worrying about the MacGavins, do you imagine they worry at all about you, or are likely to do so as long as you rake in the bawbees for them? Be a man! *Carpe diem*, etc.' Lacking such an adviser, Frant continued to torment himself.

Each day he got up with Seraphina in his thoughts. Day followed day, and Seraphina did not appear. Round the trading station, meanwhile, Africa unrolled her splendours and her cruelties. The seasons did not assert themselves overmuch. One waited for the rains to stop, or one suddenly noticed buds among thorns. One was aware, all too aware, of the spring, the season of trouble, when more people die, in all countries, than at any other time of the year. The sap was troubled, and the heart with it. All the mimosa trees at Madumbi broke into pollenous clouds of blossom, creaming in a light wind against the cobalt morning sky. Glossy toucans with scarlet bills nested in them, swooping among the boughs, and uttering the most touching mating-cries. Fireflies went through their luminous rites under a coral-tree; crested hoopoes, the colour of cinnamon, pursued their fitful flight across the clear green of dawn; on long, sultry after-noons a group of turkey-bustards, as grave as senators, would plod grumbling across some grassy plateau, looking carefully for the snakes which they could kill at a blow; raindrops pattered down on leaves as large as tables, magenta-veined; and on dry, tranquil afternoons, when the days were still short and some solitary voice was singing far away, an aromatic smell of burning sweet-grass sometimes drifted through the air, the clear light, and the music, and the odour all playing together on the nerves, and inducing an emotion inexpressibly painful and delicious.

When he was free, Frant could not bear to stay near the house: but in roaming about, which became his habit, he was none the less a prisoner. Fettered by scruples and afflicted with a kind of moral impotence, he wandered in a lovely world from which he was barred almost as effectually as if he were literally in a steel cage on wheels. His troubled eyes turned to the natural scenes around him but found no rest in them, and his repression might just have gone on increasing in morbidity had not a number of unexpected things happened.

Now the arrival of Frant at Madumbi had put a check on certain of MacGavin's habits. At one time, when the Scotchman was alone in the store, in the afternoons for instance, when the weather was hot or wet and business slack, or when his wife was busy in the house, he had not been disinclined for a little amusement at the expense of some of the coarser Lembu girls who came to deal with him. Joking with them in order to try and convert their apprehensive titters into abandoned fits of giggling, he had sometimes gone so far as to pinch their breasts and slap their behinds in order to win their confidence. The bolder ones had quickly taken advantage of his susceptibilities in order to try and get something for nothing, and pointing to this or that, had copied the horseleech's daughters and cried, 'Give, give!' When MacGavin so far overcame his sense of commercial fitness as to give them a string of beads or a damaged jews' harp, they immediately asked for more, determined to lose nothing for the want of asking. He would then refuse, but they would not go away, leaning on the counter and repeating their requests over and over again in a whining voice until he began to fear that his wife might come in. Whereupon he would suddenly fly into a raging temper. Purple in the face and trembling with anger, he would hammer on the counter with his fists and utter violent threats and abuse, and if that did not frighten the young women away he would hustle them out. One or two in particular loved to provoke him to the utmost, and then fly screaming with laughter down the road, their large naked breasts wobbling and flapping and tears running out of their eyes. But he had grown tired of these scenes, and even before Frant's arrival had abstained from inducing them. With the arrival of Frant he determined to behave himself, at least in Frant's presence, as he wanted the young man to concentrate on business and not begin his stay by getting obsessed with black women. But now that he had found Frant what he would have called 'steady', he was about to revert to his old habits, and it cannot be said that his wife, that freckled virago, with her ever-increasing indigestion and her less and less amiable moods, acted exactly as a strong deterrent.

But the first time Frant saw MacGavin behaving familiarly with a gross fat girl it gave him a shock — not because he was prudish by nature, but because it was something he was not used to, and the discovery that MacGavin did not always practise what he preached seemed likely to modify his own behaviour. The thought immediately occurred to him that MacGavin might abuse the modesty of Seraphina, and the idea that the trader's bloodshot and slightly protuberant eye might focus itself upon her natural elegance produced in him a most violent reaction. He said nothing. After MacGavin's wench had departed he came up to Frant and said:

'You'll excuse my saying so, Frant, but don't you feel you want a woman sometimes?'

The effect of this remark upon the young man was extra-ordinary.

'I do,' he answered at once in a quiet voice, 'but not a black one.'

And he launched into a flood of abuse! He said that he would rather do anything than touch a black woman; he said that they were dirty, that they stank, that they were no better than animals; he said that the blacks and whites were in his opinion races apart, and that on no account should they mix in any way; he said that white men ought to be respected by black ones, and that that could only be possible if they treated them as inferiors, absolute inferiors. He grew white with passion and the heat of his denunciation. His words almost choked him.

MacGavin was astonished beyond measure. He did not know whether to take it all as an attack on himself, or whether Frant had not gone a little out of his mind.

'Well, you do surprise me,' he said, in what was meant to be a sarcastic tone of voice. 'You've always given me the impression of being a bit too fond of the niggers, and treating them a bit too much as if they were really human beings.'

'I get a bit sick of the sight of them at times,' said Frant in a much quieter voice, not in the least meaning and indeed hardly knowing what he said. Then he turned away, and the incident was closed, except that MacGavin confided to his wife that he thought Frant was getting a bit restless, and perhaps needed a change or a holiday.

'He can surely wait till Christmas,' she said in an aggrieved whisper, for the walls of the house were thin. 'We could take him away with us then for a couple of days. But if you ask me, he's unsociable and disagreeable by nature.'

'Don't forget that the takings showed another increase last month,' said MacGavin.

'That's just why I don't want him to go away now,' she said.

It was a brilliant moonlight night, as quiet as the grave, and in his little room Frant was asking himself what on earth could have made him say a whole lot of things he did not mean, what on earth had made him lose control of himself. He felt he had come to the end of everything, that he could not bear this impossible kind of life any longer, and would have to go away.

His head was hot, he could not sleep, and he rolled uneasily on his bed. Suddenly, somewhere in a tree, a galago began to scream. Its screams filled the naked air and the heavy silence, the African silence; scream after scream, like prophecies of endless and unthinkable supernatural horrors, uttered by a furred and furtive little creature, hidden large-eyed among moon-drenched branches. Frant got up from his bed and drew back the curtains on a world chalk-white like the face of a clown or pierrot, silent and heartless, and with a sense of terror, of madness almost, let them fall back again.

And the next day Seraphina appeared.

§ 7

There she stood, balancing on her head a light bundle tied with grass. Her arms hung by her side, and when she turned her head authority and resignation, patience and sensibility were in the movement.

> Nowhere but here did ever meet
> Sweetness so sad, sadness so sweet.

Before the coming of the white man the Lembus lived under a system of strict discipline and formality, which did not, however, fail to allow various channels for the various passions of the Lembu heart. It was a system which recognized that some of life's best rewards are best appreciated by those who have not been able to win them too easily. In those days they were all warriors under a mad military autocrat, who believed that too easy an access to heterosexual pleasures might impair the morale and efficiency of his regiments; he trammelled them with a hundred taboos and would not allow them to marry young, while adultery was punished by pushing the guilty parties over

89

separate cliffs of no small height. As for the girls and women, they had a most clearly prescribed course of life, and each stage in their development was made to conform to strict rules. The later relaxation of tribal ethics, for which the white man offered little substitute but calico drawers and hyms A. and M., rapidly weakened the fibre of the race. But it still happened that there were members of it who managed to live lives not wholly devoid of order and dignity, there were still families 'of the old school' who from the force of heredity or a kind of good breeding managed to do homage to the ghosts of the beliefs of their forefathers. And such a family was Seraphina's. Both its ancient pride and its present obscurity had gone to the making of her features, and its vigour and vitality as well.

They were alone together in the space before the counter.

'Greeting, Seraphina.'

'Greeting, my white-man.'

Frant could hardly speak, he was so agitated. His heart seemed to fill the whole of his breast with its leaping, and he could scarcely recognize the sound of his own voice as he asked:

'Why have you been so long returning?'

'Do I know?' she said. 'Perhaps I was afraid.'

She had reason to be afraid — of gossip, of her family, of herself, of Frant, of consequences. With an unhurried movement she took down the bundle from her head and laid it on the floor without bending her knees. Then she untied the grass ropes that held it together and began to open it.

'A snakeskin!' said Frant.

It was a broad snakeskin, and crackled stiffly as it was unrolled. She put her foot on the tail to hold it down while Frant unrolled it. Fully opened, it was at least fifteen feet long, and a great part of it was quite two feet in width. It was the skin of a python, and there were two large rents in the middle of the back as if a spear had killed it. It was not often that the natives traded such things.

'How much are you asking for it?' said Frant in a caressing voice most unsuitable for a commercial transaction.

'I am not selling it,' said Seraphina without looking at him. 'I am giving it.'

'Giving it! To me?'

'To you.'

'I thank you very much indeed,' he said. In Lembu the same word means to thank and to praise.

There was a pause, then he said:

'Where did it come from? Who killed it?'

'I was hoeing in a maize-field near the river, and it disturbed me. Besides, two of the children were with me. So I killed it.'

'You killed it! What with?'

'With my hoe.'

When he had got over his astonishment he said, his face shining with admiration:

'But you mustn't give it to me. I must give you some money for it.'

'I don't want money,' she said, and looked at him with troubled, almost angry eyes.

'I thank you very much,' he said again, with the humility and the pride of a lover, and hardly knowing what he was doing he caught hold of her and kissed her on the mouth.

She uttered a cry of surprise and sprang away from him. She simply did not understand him, and was afraid. Natives do not make love as we do. She laughed, just a trifle hysterically.

'What are you doing?' she said.

'What's the matter?' said Frant, approaching again. 'I won't hurt you.'

'How do I know?' she said.

And he would have answered 'Because I love you' (which would have been so hard to say in English and was so easy in Lembu) had they not just at that moment been interrupted.

'Come again soon,' Frant said hurriedly. 'I want to see you.'

And he stooped down and rolled up his snakeskin. When he had finished she was gone.

In the evening he nailed up the skin on the walls of his bedroom. It was so long that it took up the whole of two sides. And very late, before putting out his light, he lay in bed looking at it. Like a banner it hung there to celebrate the intensity of his happiness; it hung like a trophy — the skin of the dragon of his misery, killed by Seraphina as she hoed her father's field of maize.

The next day at noon Mrs. MacGavin said:

'Oh, Mr. Frant, that skin in your room — it gave me such a nasty turn when I went in there this morning!'

'Isn't it a beauty? You don't mind my putting it up, I suppose?'

'Oh, I don't mind,' she said, 'though I couldn't bear to have such a thing over my bed. If there's one thing I can't stand it's snakes, alive or dead.'

It was nearly Christmas time and the MacGavins told Frant they thought a holiday would do him good, and that they would take him with them to the nearest town. The trading station would be closed for three days, and would be quite safe in the care of the servants. They were extremely surprised when he refused — not because he wanted to help to guard their property, but because the nearest town, of which he had had a few glimpses, did not attract him, and because he had other plans in mind. He felt no inclination to attend the gymkhana or the dance at which, in an atmosphere of false bonhomie and commonplace revelry, the white inhabitants tried annually to forget for a time all about the white man's burden. The MacGavins thought him almost mad for refusing.

'Whatever will you do with yourself?' they said.

'I shall be quite happy,' he said.

They felt that something was amiss.

'What, are you "going native" or something?' cried MacGavin. 'You need a change, you know.'

He always did his work well, and on account of his natural

air of independence they both respected and feared him a little. They gave up trying to argue with him and murmured to each other instead. Then on Christmas Eve the Ford car, newly washed, went rattling away, leaving behind it a cloud of blue smoke and a stink, both of which soon vanished. After the Mac-Gavins had gone Frant felt greatly relieved. It was such a blessing to be free to see and hear what was going on round him instead of being haunted by those harsh stupid voices, that sour red face and that pasty drab one, which had already got on his nerves. Unlike most white men alone in native territories, he had neither a gun nor alcohol in his possession. He did not feel the want of them. For the first time in his life he was to spend Christmas by himself. There would be no exchange of presents; no heavy meals; no forced gaiety; no stuck-up relations. His time, for once, was his own.

## § 8

On Christmas morning he stood on the veranda and stretched his arms, filled with a delicious sense of anticipation. Then he felt in his pocket for a cigarette, and failing to find one took a key and went to fetch a packet from the store. The atmosphere in that building, so closely shuttered at holiday times, was more than oppressive. It was a brilliant morning, and the heat of the sun on the corrugated-iron roof made the interior like an oven. He found some cigarettes, and paused a moment in the doorway to look round at the place where his days were spent. He shuddered slightly, then went out, locking the door behind him. Enjoying his cigarette, and the sun, and the shade, and the peacefulness of not having to look at *those* faces, of not having to listen to *those* voices, he took a path which led through a deserted garden, on the site of the first settlement at Madumbi, towards the forest. In the old garden the foundations of the earlier house remained, but the whole place was now a tangle of vegetation. The hardier growths had survived, and some still withstood the wildings that struggled to oust them. Thickets of ragged junipers and berberis made a forbidding fence which few ever sought to penetrate, and indeed the natives thought the place haunted. Snake apples, those cruel trees, with every bud a barb, and every fruit an ugly bulb filled with dry and poisonous powder, extended their angry foliage over crumbling brickwork. Rankly growing mimosas split with their coarse-grained roots what had once been a path, and month by month in the summer raised their smooth bark and feathery foliage perceptibly higher into the air. A solitary yucca, survivor of several, had produced a single spire thickly hung with white bells, which the mountain wind shook together as if they were made of paper. Tendrils of Christ-thorn put out here and there a few sticky scarlet flowers, and passion flowers hung in unexpected places, in the grass or high up among the junipers, together with the oval, dented granadillas into which they too would change.

Leaving the garden, Frant followed the path to the forest. Then, forcing his way through the undergrowth, parting lianas and monkey-ropes, breaking cobwebs so thick that their breaking was audible, being scratched by thorns, sinking up to the ankles in leaf-mould, he reached a glade he had been to before in times of unhappiness. In the middle of the glade there was a shallow stream of very clear water gliding over sand, and it was sheltered by the vast indigenous trees from the heat of the day.

Here, as he had done before, he threw himself on the breast of earth, surrendering himself to the trees, the water and the quietness. He lay on his back and looked up through half-closed eyes at the topmost branches, watching the fall of a leaf, hearing the call of a bird, the lapse of water, and the thin cries of insects. Under his hand lay a skeleton leaf, over his head a few epiphytic orchids lolled their greenish mouths open over the ancient, rotting bough that gave them life, and at times the wind brought a hint of the perfume of a hidden syringa or laurustinus. A clump of clivia lilies were blooming in deep shadow — they were living and dying in secret, without argument, and untroubled by eyes and voices. A humming-bird appeared from nowhere, and poising itself on the wing before every open flower, whirred there like a moth, gleamed like a jewel, darting its thin curved beak, as sharp as a needle, into each for honey. Nature is inevitable — this stone lies on that one, because it must; fronds uncurl from the hairy trunk of a tree-fern; each new growth and decay seems spontaneous and impersonal; there is a kind of harmony of conflict, and it may have been some sense of that harmony that brought Frant to a decision he might, had he not been so solitary, have taken long before. He was roused. He would act boldly. He would give up caution, discretion, doubt, hesitation, he would forget all about the Mac-Gavins, the trade, the future, he would give up all fear of gossip, of crisis, of reputation, he would break through the bars of his prison. He would go that very day down into the valley and visit the home of Seraphina. He would behave with candour, he would be open in his dealings. He had proved in commerce that he was 'a white man'; he would now be bold, and prove it in love.

Such was his resolution, but the enterprise was not entirely successful. He set out early in the afternoon, carrying a camera, and a stick in case he should meet snakes. He walked as fast as if he were in a more temperate climate, and felt the heat. The first part of the journey took him across an undulating plateau, through country much like that immediately round Madumbi. But after about an hour he came to the top of a hill which marked the end of an escarpment ('The hill is long and steep,' Seraphina had said) and he began to follow a downward path winding among rocks and thorn trees. This brought him out on to a platform or small tableland and before him lay suddenly open an immense view. Directly below lay the valley of the Umgazi river, where Seraphina lived, and he sat down under a bean tree to rest and to gaze at the scene.

Somebody was coming up the hill. It was a young man. He was a typical Lembu, naked except for a fur codpiece and some bead ornaments, upright, slender and vigorous. He came striding along, singing joyfully as he went, glistening with oil and sweat, his movements full of natural pride. He was holding a tiny shield, a stick and a knobkerrie in one hand, and in the other a large black cotton Brummagem umbrella, to shelter himself from the sun. When he saw Frant he looked surprised and then saluted him with a large and cheerful gesture. Frant knew him by sight and responded cordially.

'What are you doing here?' said the young man. 'Are you out on holiday?'

'Yes,' said Frant, 'I am just out on holiday.'

'Why aren't you riding?'

'I have no horse.'

'But white men don't walk!'

'I like walking.'

The native expressed surprise.

'Is that a camera?' he said.

'Yes, it's a camera.'

'Will you take my picture?'

'All right. Go and stand over there. But you must close your umbrella.'

'What, must I close my umbrella?'

So Frant stood under the bean tree with his feet among the open pods and little black-and-scarlet beans that had fallen from it, and took a photograph of the native, who stood smiling and glistening in the sun.

'Do you know me?' said the young man.

'Yes,' said Frant.

'Do you know Seraphina?'

Frant was startled.

'Yes,' he said, unable to conceal his surprise.

'She is my sister.'

'What! You're her brother?'

'Yes.'

'Fancy that!'

'Seraphina likes you,' said her brother. But, thought Frant, is he really her brother? The natives used such terms somewhat loosely. Was this perhaps a rival trying to warn him off? He put the thought out of his mind, for the native was so friendly. 'Seraphina likes you,' he said. But in Lembu the same word means to like and to love, so perhaps he meant 'Seraphina loves you'.

'I like Seraphina,' said Frant.

'It is not good,' said the native, 'when a white man likes a black girl.'

There was no condemnation in his tone, no threat, no high moral purpose. He smiled as he spoke what he no doubt regarded as a self-obvious truism.

'Why?' said Frant.

'Do I know? It is so.'

Frant wanted to say 'Would you be angry if your sister married a white man?' but he had no wish to suggest any such thing. And it seemed too crude to say 'Would you be angry if your sister slept with a white man?' So he said:

'We are all people.'

'Yes, we are all people, but we are different.'

'I like natives,' said Frant.

'I know you do. But you live in Lembuland, and there are no white people near here for you to like.'

This was really unanswerable.

'There are Mr. MacGavin and his wife,' said Frant.

Seraphina's brother (if he was Seraphina's brother) laughed. 'Nobody likes *them*!' he said.

'What is your name?' said Frant.

'Me? Umlilwana.'

'And where do you live?'

'Down there,' said Umlilwana, pointing to the valley.

The river Umgazi, which seemed to consist mostly of a broad bed of stones, with only a small stream of water in the middle, curved in a gigantic S-shaped bend just below where they stood. And on some slightly raised ground in one of the curves of the S were a group of grass domes, which were huts, and a cattle kraal made of thorn trees and brushwood, and a few patches of maize and millet and sweet potatoes. And that was the home of Seraphina. It looked the most peaceful place in the world.

'Will you take me there?' said Frant.

'Take you there! What would you do there?'

'I want to see your home. I want to see Seraphina.'

'Seraphina is not there.'

'Not there! Where is she?'

'She has gone on a journey to the mountains for several days with our mother and father to see our cousins. There's nobody down there but an old woman and some children.'

'Oh,' said Frant, and was silent a moment. 'I am sorry,' he said then. 'I wanted to see Seraphina.'

And suddenly everything seemed utterly remote. The view was like a view in a dream. Seraphina (*could* that be her name?) seemed only an idea and her cousins like characters in a myth. And even the friendly smiling Umlilwana seemed utterly strange and unapproachable.

'Yes, I am sorry,' Frant repeated in a dull voice. 'But I should like some day to visit your home and take photographs of Seraphina — and of all your family.'

Umlilwana was a little suspicious of this, but he said Frant would be welcome.

'Will you do something for me?' said Frant. 'Will you come and tell me when Seraphina returns? Tell Seraphina I want to see her. Tell her I want to see her again.'

'All right,' said Umlilwana in English and with great affability. It was about all the English he knew.

'Umlilwana, you are my friend.'

'All right, will you give me some cigarettes?'

Frant smiled, and gave him all he had. Umlilwana was loud in thanks.

Some children could be seen playing near Seraphina's kraal. They looked as small as ants. The distant mountains looked infinitely blue and remote, with the shadows of a few light clouds patterning their peaks. There was nothing to do but to return to Madumbi.

## § 9

Frant returned to Madumbi. So, a couple of days later, did the MacGavins, both with a touch of righteous indignation at Frant's oddness in not having gone with them, and Mrs. MacGavin with more than a touch of dyspepsia. Life then resumed its usual course. But things were not quite the same. First of all, Frant was in a far more cheerful frame of mind. Not only had he begun to act with some initiative, not only had he seen Seraphina's home and made friends with her brother, but he had told somebody of his love for her. As soon as she returned he meant to bring matters to a head, even though he and she were 'different'. And if her continued absence was a great trial to his patience, he got up every morning in hopes of a visit and news from Umlilwana in the course of the day. But day followed day, and Umlilwana did not appear. Frant played with the idea of sending him a message, but as it would have to be a verbal one, he thought it more prudent not to do so. And when he once ventured to inquire about Umlilwana, and to ask if he were really Seraphina's brother, the people he spoke to said they had never heard of either of them. And at night he lay naked and sweating on his bed, tortured continually with the image of Seraphina, remembering her gestures, her 'sadness so sweet', and the touch of her flesh.

'Frant should have gone away with us,' MacGavin remarked to his wife. 'He's quite liverish now at times.'

'This weather's enough to make anybody liverish,' said she. 'I always did say that January was the worst month of the year. It's bilious weather. But it's not his liver, if you ask me, it's his nerves.'

January was certainly a bad month at Madumbi, and that year it was more trying than ever. There had been no rain for weeks, and things were beginning to look parched. The heat was dry and intense. And then, day after day, clouds would collect in the morning and accumulate in the afternoon, thunder was occasionally heard and once even a few drops of rain fell in the dust, as if a few devils had spat from a great height. Every morning seemed to promise a thunderstorm, and one began to imagine how the earth would smell after rain, and how cool the air would be, and how the flying ants would come out in the twilight, but every evening the clouds dispersed and left a hot moon to glare down on the veld, or the glittering arrogance of the stars. And every morning Frant said to himself, 'Umlilwana will come, or Seraphina herself,' but every evening he found himself alone again, exhausted and restless. Even the natives, in their anxiety about their crops, were beginning to get on one another's nerves. The air seemed charged with electricity, it seemed to brace one's very muscles against a shock which was not forthcoming, and to leave them at once taut and tired. Even MacGavin took to glancing often at the sky, at the great cumulus clouds that hung in it all the afternoon, and he would say, 'It'll be serious if something doesn't happen soon.'

It was like waiting for an earthquake, a revolution, the day of judgment almost. There was an awful mixture of certainty that something was going to happen, and of uncertainty as to when it would happen. 'We only want a storm to clear the air,' Mrs. MacGavin repeated every day until Frant almost felt that he could murder her. The sweat ran down inside his shirt, his overheated blood inflamed his overstrained imagination, he found it more and more difficult to sleep and eat. Trade grew slack, because few could endure to climb up the slopes to Madumbi, and when the store was empty it was far less tolerable than when it was full. The morning sun beat down on the corrugated iron and the interior grew so hot that it failed to cool down during the night. Strange stories came in — that some grass had caught fire simply from the heat of the sun shining through an empty bottle, and several huts had been burnt in consequence; that a young crocodile had come right up one of the little tributaries of the Umgazi and had been found less than a mile from Madumbi itself, an occurrence never before known; and that a native woman had been arrested for killing a new-born baby with six fingers on one hand, in the belief that this deformity was keeping the rain away. Where was Umlilwana? Where was Seraphina? 'I will wait till next Sunday,' said Frant to himself, 'and if neither of them has come by then I shall go down to the kraal itself on the pretext of wanting to take photographs.' But he did not have to wait till Sunday, for the weather broke.

The worst day of all was the fourteenth of the month.

'Well, this is the worst we've had yet,' said Mrs. MacGavin at supper time.

'You've said that for the last four days,' observed her husband.

All the doors and windows were wide open. The sky was completely overcast and nothing was stirring but the moths and other insects which flew in from the garden and bumped against the paper lampshade, or against the glass which covered 'The Confession', or fell into the soup, the powder from their wings mingling with the film of grease which already covered that liquid. The rays of lamplight lay on the creepers of the veranda itself and on the path, but beyond them was utter silence and hot, heavy darkness.

'Hark! Was that thunder?' said Mrs. MacGavin.

'You always say that at supper time,' remarked her husband.

'It *was* thunder,' she said, her head on one side, as she pushed a stray wisp of hair out of her eye.

Yes, it *was* thunder. They all heard it. Low, continuous thunder.

'That's up in the mountains,' said MacGavin. 'It's a bad sign if it begins up there. If there *is* a storm, it'll probably miss us altogether . . . Ah, did you see the lightning? Yes, that's where it is. I bet it's pouring up there already. And I don't like a dry storm. It's much more dangerous. More likely to strike the trees.'

Frant's heart was beating loud and fast as if in anticipation of some personal, not a meteorological event. He walked alone to the bottom of the garden and stood there watching the play of lightning in the distance, but it did not seem much more than on previous nights. He came in and tried to read a paper, lighted several cigarettes in succession, throwing one or two away half-smoked, paced up and down in the garden, glancing up at the darkness, and then retired to his room where he lay on his bed without undressing. His hands were clenched, the nails dug into the palms, and he was conscious of little but the beating of his heart. He couldn't hear the MacGavins talking anywhere, or any natives, and had lost all sense of the time. He put out his light, and like a convict without a crime, in a prison that was not locked, for a sentence of indeterminate duration, he just lay there sweating.

At last he got up and went to the window. The moon was out again. It was almost full, and stood high in the sky, flooding the landscape with light. To the south, vast banks of cloud were ranged above the forest, and among them, now and then, a worm of lightning played, followed by a distant roll of thunder. Not a leaf seemed to be stirring, when he noticed that a light breeze was rising and feathering the tops of the distant trees. Very soon the tops of the mimosas near the house bowed, lightly swaying towards the moon, and a tremor ran through the grass as if an invisible hand had stroked it. The wind rose, the clouds towered and toppled upwards, the moon was caught in a web of flying mist, the thunder grew louder, and the flashes of lightning more frequent. A greenish light seemed to emanate from the moon, and as the sky grew more heavily loaded, the forest, by contrast, appeared more ethereal, the heavy boscage and the trunks of the huge indigenous trees appearing in great detail, all dry and luminous and lurid, the foliage beginning to churn and writhe slowly on the topmost boughs. The tenseness of the atmosphere, the expectancy of nature, and the way in which the whole landscape, the very buildings and their shadows, seemed to take part in the great symphony of the impending storm, combined to produce an effect so dramatic as to seem almost supernatural.

The rolling of the thunder was now continuous. All the mountain country was overhung with the incessant play of sheet-lightning, as if a curtain of fire, continually agitated by unseen forces, hung over half the world. The wind began to howl round the house, leaves and twigs to fly from the trees, a pile of timber was blown over, and the moon was half hidden in a swirl of clouds. Chains and forks of lightning, steely-blue and sulphurous red, larger and brighter and more frequent than Frant had ever seen, lighted everything with a continuous, shaken glare. Thunder pealed almost overhead, phalanxes of cloud advanced like avenging armies, the house shook, the windows rattled, and he put his hand to his burning and throbbing head. His pulses raced, sweat poured down his face and body, and he felt as if his veins would burst. Suddenly he caught sight of a white horse, which had broken loose from heaven knows where, and was careering madly, its mane and tail flying, its halter trailing, along the slope of the nearest hill. It seemed a creature of fire as it tossed its head, swerved at sudden obstacles, and galloped up to the ridge. There for a moment it stood, quivering with fear and exertion in the quivering glare of the lightning, and then, made splendid by freedom, disappeared from view.

'I can't stay in the house an instant longer!' Frant said aloud to himself, and taking up an electric torch, he stepped out into the garden. A strong refreshing breeze was blowing, but not a drop of rain had fallen. 'It looks as though MacGavin was right — the storm seems to have missed us altogether . . .' He wondered what on earth he had brought the torch for, since the lightning was quivering incessantly, like a network of luminous nerves.

'Is that you, Frant?'

It was MacGavin calling from the house.

'Yes. I can't sleep. I'm going for a walk. It's much fresher out now.'

'A walk! At this time! Don't go far. It's risky. And if it *should* come on to rain . . .'

'I'll be all right, thanks. Good night.'

He disappeared from view, and instinctively found himself taking the path he had taken on Christmas Day. He was frightened of the night, of losing his way, of the storm. He had at first no thought of going far, but when he paused to try and calculate how far he had already come he was almost as afraid to turn back as to go on, so he went on. He had got an idea that he must get to the bean tree, and he kept telling himself that it was not really very far. The wind was behind him now, and its freshness gave him energy. The glare and racket of the storm grew no less — it now seemed to be everywhere except immediately overhead. He hurried on, stumbling now and again, for the path was in places rough and narrow. He saw lights once or twice but did not meet a soul. And back at Madumbi MacGavin had grown anxious about him.

Before he came to the escarpment there was a loud detonation just overhead, and it began to rain. He had come too far now to turn back, so he hurried on, vaguely imagining that he would ask for shelter at Seraphina's. Near the top of the hill he realized that the worst of the weather was in front of him. The lightning revealed a thick grey veil of rain beyond the valley, and he could hear a tremendous steady downpour in the distance. The nearer he got to the top the louder the tumult grew, and he thought, 'The river must be a lot fuller by now than when I last saw it.' He was going downhill at last, but not so fast as he wanted, for it was raining pretty hard now and the paths were getting slippery. A feeling of terror seized him. He felt that he would never get down to the valley, that the storm would beat him, that it was no good thinking of turning back.

There was no doubt as to what he could hear now. The river must be in flood. And he suddenly thought, would the kraal be safe? Hardly . . . He was running now, to reach the bean tree. He was soaked to the skin, and his feet kept slipping. He missed the way twice and found it again, and then, waiting for the lightning to show him where he was, he found he was only a few yards from the tree.

And just at that moment, exactly as before, he saw a man coming towards him. Only this time the man was running. And this time it was not Umlilwana he saw. And this time he was terrified.

The man didn't see Frant until he almost ran into him, and he was too frightened.

'*Au!*' cried a familiar voice. '*Umtwana ka Kwini!* Child of the Queen! What are you doing here? Where are you going? Child! My child! Have you *seen*? Look, look!'

He dragged Frant over the slippery rocks to the very edge of the tableland.

'Look!' he cried.

A prolonged flash of lightning lit up the whole valley with a tremulous, pale violet glare like the light of some hellish arc-lamp, and in a few seconds Frant had understood. Gone was the S-shaped bend, gone were the grassy domes, the kraal and little fields! There was nothing where they had been but a gigantic swirl of greyish water, in which trunks of trees could be seen travelling, spinning and half raising themselves above the surface like animate things.

'Seraphina!' cried Frant. 'Do you know Seraphina?'

He had caught hold of the little old man, who was shivering with fear and cold and seemed the only reality left in the world.

'Seraphina!' cried Frant. 'Do you know her? Did she come back? Was she at home?'

'She was at home for two weeks, *umtwana*,' said the old man, shaking like a leaf. 'The cattle are drowned!' he cried in the voice of Job and of Lear. 'The houses, the people — all are drowned!'

'Drowned?' cried Frant, shining his torch full in the old man's face. 'Why? Why are they drowned?'

'The water came like a wall, my child,' said the old man, and the torchlight made the raindrops running down his face look as if it was covered with tears. He was shivering violently from top to toe, and his old tunic clung to his skin.

'Umlilwana,' said Frant. 'Was Umlilwana her brother?'

'Umlilwana?' said the old man. 'Umlilwana wasn't her brother! She was going to marry Umlilwana.'

In the lightning-glare he saw Frant's face.

'All is finished!' he cried, putting out a black and bony claw, as if to defend himself from some unknown danger. In Lembu the same word means to be finished or to be destroyed. 'Are you bewitched?'

Yes, all was finished, all was destroyed. Already the rolling of the thunder was increasing in volume, but the roar of the flood seemed to grow louder, and the rain was coming down like whips of ice and steel. It was like the coming of the deluge itself. It was like the end of the world.

Something in Frant urged him to leave the old man and run down the hill and plunge into those maddened waters and lose himself, but something stronger told him that he must return to Madumbi, to the store, to the MacGavins, to the making of a livelihood, to the fashioning of a way of life, to a roll of un-developed negatives, and to a python skin nailed to a wall like a banner, with two large holes in it cut by a girl with a hoe.

'I must go back!' he said to the old man, and gripped his shoulder for an instant. Then he made off in the direction of Madumbi, flashing the torch on the path. The old man called after him to take care, but he was at once out of earshot in the downpour. After he had stumbled a short way one spasmodic sob escaped from him, and he began to run.

# WHEN THE SARDINES CAME

Quite ordinary people sometimes behave in an extraordinary way. A sudden mood will possess them, and drive them to cast off their closest ties, which they find a hindrance to the attainment of new and mad desires. Lifted to the heights, they have no more use for comfortable valleys, and forsaking reality, they embrace the air. At any rate, that was the case with Mrs. Reymond.

On the South Coast of Natal, in the early nineteen-twenties, there was a charming and little frequented retreat which showed few signs of becoming so spoilt, or should one say developed, as it is now. A road, for instance, now runs past Reymonds, with quite a quantity of traffic, and houses are going up here and there. But at that time the only means of communication with the outside world (beyond one or two paths that led off through the bush into the native reserve) was the tiny station known as Reymond's Halt, which never figured in time-tables, but of which you caught a glimpse from the train. The line ran between the house and the sea, and everywhere was the characteristic thick bush. The house stood in a large clearing which had been converted into a pretty garden — a lawn, palms, poinsettias and so on. At the back were some grassy uplands called 'the farm', because Reymond ran a few cows, kept poultry, and maintained some fields of maize and a large vegetable garden, these things taking up much of his time. Yet he took things fairly easily. He was still under fifty, but the war had knocked him about rather badly. He was a quiet, harmless, equable sort of man, who took less interest in politics than most South Africans do — 'All governments are alike,' he used to say — and who, unlike many of his fellow-countrymen, treated the natives with fairness and even kindness, and had a good name among them in consequence.

His wife was rather younger than himself, and people had said that their marriage was romantic, though it was probably no more romantic than most. They were childless, but obviously very happy together, sufficiently alike (in their taste for a quiet life, for example) and yet sufficiently different to get on well with each other. Reymond sought for himself the quiet interests of the 'farm' as if to forget the strenuousness of his earlier existence. His wife, on the other hand, finding things a little quiet down there, made some effort to keep in touch with the outside world. She read a certain amount, played a lot of tennis and a little Chopin, and took an interest in all sorts of things. She was not very well educated, and had not very good taste. Rupert Brooke and Omar Khayyám were her poets, the dust having settled on Ella Wheeler Wilcox, but she enjoyed the efforts she made towards improving herself and enjoying herself. The contrast in the natures of husband and wife made a pretty balance. Sitting in a long chair on the veranda he would listen to her with his pipe in his mouth, and when she had done talking he would ask her advice or tell her about this or that happening on the 'farm'. She always made a point of spending a day in Dunnsport once a week, partly for shopping purposes and partly to see her friends there. Reymond went to town less often.

They might almost have been taken for a model married couple, until a slight restlessness in Mrs. Reymond's behaviour became noticeable. It seemed as if she no longer enjoyed her activities for their own sake but as an outlet for a kind of frustrated energy. As she was no longer a young woman, one might have expected her to be like her husband, contented and settled, but then she was not so old that there was really any reason for her to behave as if life had nothing more but repose to offer her.

No, she was lively, and with only a hint of a foreshadowing of age about her, a certain dignity and resignation at times in her manner.

It was a young medical student called Edwards who had the best chance of observing her behaviour. A cousin of Reymond's, he came to stay for a couple of months because he had some reading to do for an examination, and wanted quiet. It was certainly quiet enough down there, and he soon fell into a regular routine, which was only broken by occasional dances and week-ends in Dunnsport. After breakfast he used to go straight down to the beach with his books. He always went barefoot, first down the steps to the railway, all warm in the morning sun; then over the prickly cinders of the line; and then along the short, tunnel-like path through the bush to the sea. It was shady and sandy and uncannily silent in there, and one came suddenly out again to the sun and the sound of the waves. He used to work all the morning, then swim, then return to the house for lunch on the veranda, sleep awhile out of doors, and then go fishing (he never caught much) or walk along the line. If the weather was especially warm he had a second swim, usually worked again before supper, and spent the evening talking, or singing (rather badly) to Mrs. Reymond's accompaniment, while her husband sat on the veranda smoking his pipe. Almost the only variants to this programme were visits to or from their neighbours, none of whom lived very near. And once Reymond took Edwards out shooting, but they came back very hungry and almost empty-handed, and Mrs. Reymond laughed at them, with just a suggestion of bitterness in her gaiety.

It was winter time, and the weather was nearly perfect, only sometimes a little windy. There was a sort of drowsiness in the air which was very peaceful and pleasant, and only marred by Mrs. Reymond's slight uneasiness and by those trifling odds and ends of everyday troubles which tend, in isolated places, to become magnified into things of importance.

'I hope you'll still be here,' Reymond said to his guest once or twice, 'when the sardines come.'

The coming of the sardines, it seemed, was expected to take place at about the same time every year. It was the great annual event. Immense shoals (so Edwards was told) would pass slowly up the coast, close inshore, and pursued by innumerable seabirds and large predatory fish. At that time everybody stopped work and turned angler.

Edwards was still at Reymonds' when the sardines came. It was one day towards the end of June, a perfect day. Like most perfect things, it didn't last long, but a great deal happened in the time. There were no clouds and no waves. There was no wind. It was perfectly warm and still, and the sea undulated so lazily that the tides seemed to have lapsed, and the water was scarcely troubled at its edge. The sky above the horizon was a darker blue than the sea. At lunch-time the kitchen boy brought the rumour of the sardines' approach. An extraordinary atmosphere of tension and excitement was at once created, as often happens before some natural event, and all three seemed to have lost their appetites. Afterwards they noticed that the wind had got up a little, and the sea was no longer quite so calm, but this was usually the case in the afternoon.

At about two o'clock some dark stains were visible on the sea, rising and falling with the waves, the water round them disturbed, and birds wheeling overhead. A little later they heard voices from the beach and went down all armed with rods and nets and baskets. The servants had preceded them.

The sands, nearly always deserted, were now crowded with all kinds of people, men, women and children of all colours and ages. To the right and left, hundreds of fishing-rods rose into the air. Everyone was looking out to sea, and not very far out, for the dark patches, which were enormous shoals of sardines, had spread and spread, and coming nearer had become much larger. One could see distinctly the flashing of huge triangular fins and curving tails as the larger fish swam madly round their prey. One could also distinguish that most of the birds were gulls and gannets. Snow-white in the afternoon sun, the gannets fell like bombs, rising a moment or two later brown and wet from the waves, fish in beak. The tide, the current, the pursuers, and the inscrutable alliance of fate and nature, gradually drove the myriads of victims towards the beach, where excitement almost gave way to ecstasy. And when a wave at last drove the first edge of a shoal right up on the shore, so that in retreating it left a few silvery flounderers on the wet sand, a sudden movement ran right through the crowd, and an old Indian woman in a magenta skirt darted into the water with a basket. A moment later, and the sardines had really arrived. There was a certain poetic justice in the fact that nobody bothered about them — they had enemies enough already. No, the old hunter in the heart of man was after bigger game, and it was the pursuing fish that everybody wanted to catch.

The pitch of excitement was intense. It was the one mad day in the year. Not only were the sardines maddened with fear (or whatever in them corresponds to that feeling) of their pursuers, but the second fear now possessed them of being driven clean out of their element. As for the great fish-of-prey, the lust of the chase had driven them into such a frenzy that, with an utter disregard of consequences, many found themselves driven up by their own energy and the impetus of the waves right on to the beach, where their great metallic fins and steely tails grooved into the soft wet sand like the keels of ships that run aground in a fog. Until that moment their natural aversion to man had been in abeyance, and had they been able to consider him at all, they would no doubt have seen him simply as a rival. The air was thick with the wings and cries of birds, but they held a little more aloof than the fish.

Most remarkable of all was the behaviour of the crowd, which was very mixed. There were Indians and Mauritians from the sugar-mill a couple of miles away; Zulus from kraal and kitchen; poor whites and *bywoners*; people who rather fancied themselves, like the Scotch engineer from the mill, with his trousers now rolled up over the knees; one or two people of rather the same sort as the Reymonds; and a selection of the oddities who used to live in those parts, hidden away here and there in little houses in the bush along the coast. There was a gaunt woman, who was a vegetarian, lived by herself and did water-colours; an old Norwegian sailor who lived between the sun and the sea, wearing only a pair of khaki shorts, his torso burnt to the colour of rosewood and covered with fine gold hairs; and a family of Russian refugees — an old father who never left the house, a daughter who worked in Dunnsport, and a young son. Mrs. Reymond and Edwards used to make jokes about these last, especially the son, a tall, fair young man with wild, elemental eyes. Indeed, they had given him the nickname of 'the bush-baby', calling him after the large-eyed galago, that strange creature of the woods. And the 'bush-baby', like almost everybody else round about, whom they knew either by sight or by repute, was of course on the beach on this day when the sardines came.

The excitement of the hour had already worked an extraordinary, an almost magical effect upon the minds of all these people — an effect as violent and as magical as upon the fish. Divided at all times by a thousand barriers, of race, of money, of caste, of class, of language, of pride and fear, but especially by various kinds of colour-bar — the Indians and natives living in mutual contempt, the 'coloured' people looking down on their darker neighbours, the whites and near-whites looking down on everybody else, and being, in consequence, for the most part mistrusted in their turn — divided like this at all times, they were now, quite surprisingly, all brought to a level. Just as enemies will unite in a common fear of a common danger, so they will sometimes be united by something which makes an appeal to any emotion as primitive as fear — by a promise, for example, of something for nothing. In this case, one rather heavy touch of nature had made the whole world kin.

Mingled with the sounds of splashing and dashing, the cries of birds and children, could be heard the hiss of lines being thrown, and the whirr of unwinding reels. Here and there a great fish was hooked, and rods could be seen bent nearly double, as if they might snap at any second, jerking spasmodically without a pause, as if they had a motor bicycle on the hook instead of a fish. Except in the case of the old Norwegian sailor, it was mostly out of the question for one person to manage one fish; to every engaged rod there were at least two fishermen; and it was even possible to see an Indian, a Zulu, a white and a half-caste all united in a single effort — a rare sight indeed in United South Africa.

It was not long before Mrs. Reymond said to Edwards:

'Oh, look, Charles, there's the Russian bush-baby! And he's hooked a fish!'

There he was, a blond boy of less than twenty, in shorts and an open shirt, rather slender, with the large eyes of one who has learnt too young the meaning of hunger, and who has looked at death too near and too soon. He was staggering about in the sand, and looked almost as if he were doing some savage dance, straining every muscle to prevent himself being dragged into the sea, and to stop the rod, which was bent in the shape of a C and kicking like a sapling in a cyclone, from being jerked out of his hands or snapped in two. The servant who had come with him was holding him back by the waist, and two or three boys ran up to give a hand if needed. The whole effect was that instead of playing the fish they were being played by it.

Mrs. Reymond was fascinated. She had eyes for nothing else. Her husband was busy some distance away, and had apparently not caught anything yet. As for Edwards, he had already landed a fair-sized fish, and had handed his rod over to the kitchen-boy. Mrs. Reymond took no notice of either of them. Not even when a giant rock-salmon was caught by the naked hands of a group of children and dragged floundering out of the water, was her attention diverted. The Russian boy, or rather the Russian boy's fish, was gradually moving away to the left, away from the main scene of action, and Mrs. Reymond moved too. Edwards couldn't make out what was interesting her so much. It seemed to him that a dozen tussles quite as remarkable were going on at the same time.

Important things in life often happen so suddenly and unexpectedly that they simply take one's breath away; if they happen in other people's lives, and one is only a spectator, it is often a little difficult to grasp, let alone convey, the exact reason for them, their details and consequences. All Edwards knew was that at that moment he felt quite certain that something important was going to happen and that it wasn't going to happen to him. On the left of the beach was a group of jagged rocks, to which the Russian was gradually getting nearer, and his supporters were excitedly warning him to try and avoid them. But the fish was wild and perhaps wise as well, and plunged determinedly on in the same direction. Occasionally it reared itself out of the water, and in the late light it looked, to the heightened imagination of the spectators, as big as a dolphin. A moment later the Russian boy sprang up on to a high rock, and with a very precarious foothold seemed in danger of falling. But still he held on. Edwards expected Mrs. Reymond to say, 'Oh, isn't he plucky!' but she was far too intent to speak. He glanced back to see how far they had come from the crowd, when he heard her utter a sudden little cry, a most moving sound that seemed to come straight from her heart, and turning quickly round, he saw that the Russian boy had disappeared. She ran forward, her high heels sinking into the sand, and Edwards followed.

When they arrived at the rock the Russian boy was being lifted out of the water. His wet hair had fallen over his face, and he was bleeding horribly from the leg. By a miracle, the rod was neither broken nor lost, and a wiry Indian, up to his waist in eddying water, was holding it upright with all his strength, the butt end pressed against his hip. The Russian boy, the 'bush-baby', fainted from loss of blood. Fortunately both Edwards and Mrs. Reymond (who had done some nursing during the war) knew what to do. When the flow of blood had been checked by a rude tourniquet, the boy was carried up to the house and laid, by Mrs. Reymond's orders, on her bed. She looked round once for her husband, but he had been a good way off at the time of the accident, and not knowing what had happened was not yet back.

'Will you fetch the doctor, Charles?' she said, turning to Edwards. 'I'd rather you went than one of the servants.'

Edwards went. To reach the doctor meant a long ride through the reserve, and he did not return with him until ten. (All that is changed down there now — they have a telephone and a car and so on.) It appeared that the wound had been caused by a sharp bait-knife, worn casually sheathless in the belt, but there was also a slight fracture in the foot, caused by the fall. The consequence was, it was decided that the patient should remain where he was, and he did. It should be remarked that the fish was landed by the Indian; it was a 'springer', rather over five feet long, the shape and colour of a torpedo. Before it was cut up, the patient, the Indian and the splendid carcass of the victim were photographed together by Edwards. Mrs. Reymond was overjoyed.

'It was really you who caught it,' she said to her protégé.

Meanwhile Edwards went on with his work as usual, and Reymond went every day to see the patient's old father and report progress. Like all Russians, the old man was a great talker; like all Russian refugees, he let it appear that he had had something to do with the Court; anyway, quite a friendship sprang up between him and Reymond, whose visits to this new acquaintance grew longer every day. So Mrs. Reymond was left even more in touch with her patient than she otherwise would have been.

The change that came over her during the following days was most remarkable. All her restlessness seemed to have vanished, and she looked ten years younger. She was sometimes silent for several minutes, which was unlike her. And when she talked, it was about Boris — the progress of his cure, what he had told her about his early life, what he had said about this, that or the other. At times she was like a mother boasting of her child's cleverness, and it is no exaggeration to say that at other times she was like a young girl shyly praising a lover. When Boris was able to get up and hobble about with crutches she was so pleased that it would not have been surprising to hear her exclaim, 'See, he can walk!' Her continual pleasure was very evident, but she was inclined to be brusque with her husband, and even (so Edwards thought) to neglect him. And Edwards watched Reymond closely to see what effect this was having on him, but that mild-tempered man seemed to remain exactly as usual. Then one day, walking bare-foot along the veranda, Edwards happened to glance in at a window and saw Boris kissing Mrs. Reymond. When he had got over his surprise (which was not altogether a surprise) he wondered, being rather young and foolish, if he ought to draw Reymond's attention to what was going on. But fortunately he had enough sense to keep his mouth shut.

Boris soon gave up his crutches, and carried a walking-stick instead. He and Mrs. Reymond used to go for short walks together — very short walks, for they often walked just down the garden, crossed the railway line, followed the path through the bush, and seeking out some group of rocks on the beach, sat in the shelter of them for hours at a time. When Boris was almost well again, it became known that instead of going back to his father's cottage on the coast he was going to take up a job in Dunnsport. Two days before he went, Edwards happened to be passing through that silent tunnel of foliage between the railway and the beach, and trudging through the deep, dry sand, couldn't help overhearing voices coming towards him.

'So you see,' said Boris, speaking in his attractive foreign accent, 'that wouldn't really be possible . . .'

'But I shall *never* forget —' Mrs. Reymond answered, and her voice was quite transfigured with emotion.

Edwards coughed, and as he came face to face with them made some bright remark about the weather. As far as his own observation went, that was about the end of the whole affair.

Boris duly left, and for a week or two it was plain that Mrs. Reymond missed him grievously. Indeed, as if to hide the fact, she mentioned it casually more than once, and even pretended to joke about it. It would not be true to say that she was soon her usual self again. When she was resigned as far as she could be to the absence of Boris she seemed to have lost her former restlessness, and by contrast with her recent fervours, appeared definitely middle-aged. It was as if in the course of a few weeks she had made up the difference between her own age and her husband's, and a new peacefulness seemed to have asserted itself in their relationship, a mutual confidence. And then one day, during a walk along the beach, Reymond turned to Edwards and seemed about to speak. But it was plainly hard for him to do so, for he was not much of a talker at any time, and was quite unused to expressing his more intimate feelings.

'Oh, Charles,' he said, 'I want to explain to you something you mayn't quite understand.'

'Yes?'

'About my wife,' said Reymond, looking out to sea, 'and Boris.'

'Yes.'

'Why do you say "yes" like that? I suppose you have your own ideas . . . I suppose you wonder why I didn't do anything about it. That's just what I'm going to explain. Well, you know how things are with us, we have no children, and we don't see many people down here. Of course I don't mind that, but for my wife — for a woman, you know — it's not so nice. I could see for some time that she's been feeling it a bit. Of course she's not so used to a country life as I am . . . Well, I saw how it was after — well, after the sardines came. That boy just became everything to her. He was like a son and a friend and a sweetheart all rolled into one. Well, I'm not a terribly jealous man, but I can't say I altogether liked the look of things. But you see, if there's one thing I can't stand, it's when I feel that my wife's not happy. I thought it was better to let things run their course. I felt sure my wife would come down to earth again all right, and she did . . . Now I know nothing like that'll ever be likely to happen to us again. I dare say it's not so nice for a woman to feel that she'll soon be face to face with old age . . . And then you see, women are funny. She'd have been annoyed if she'd thought I wasn't jealous, and yet knowing that I *was* jealous somehow irritated her . . . Ah well, I'm sure it's all over now. . . . I don't know why I've told you all this, except that I didn't want you to get wrong ideas into your head. And I must say it wouldn't have been any easier if you hadn't been here — triangles are apt to have sharp corners. . . . And anyway, if you hadn't been here you'd have missed the sardines!'

'Which I wouldn't have missed for anything,' said Edwards. He longed to know how Mrs. Reymond had justified her behaviour after Boris's departure — had she repented with tears? had everything been taken for granted? or what? — but he didn't like to say anything. Besides, he wanted to appear understanding, a man of the world, and tried to look the part in silence. In any case, they had almost reached the house, and Mrs. Reymond was waving to them from the tea-table, which had been set on the veranda.

When Edwards left the South Coast his mind was quickly filled with his own affairs, but whenever he thought of the Reymonds he was haunted by that woman's voice saying 'I shall *never* forget . . .' and again he seemed to see her trying to hurry forward, her high heels sinking into the sand at every step, towards the last passion of her life.

# STORIES OF JAPAN

# A PIECE OF GOOD LUCK

## § 1

THE village of Omura, in the prefecture of F——, consists of one street of grey wooden houses. In front there is nothing but rice-fields. At the back there is an abrupt mountain, too steep for cultivation, and partly covered with pine trees. The view exemplifies the truth that in the Japanese landscape there is no middle distance. No traveller, glancing out of a train window, could expect to see a more typical country village: indeed, Omura is just visible from the railway, though it is doubtful if any passenger ever regards it. And although there is a station not very far away and bearing the name of the next village but one, it is seldom that any of the inhabitants of Omura go in a train. Why should they? Except petty officials and an occasional merchant they have very little reason to move. They live together something like a large family and in more harmony than villagers in most other countries, because there are so notably few differences or causes for differences among them. They are all so much alike, and everybody else's business is such common property as one's own that there is hardly any room for gossip. And there is very little news.

The seasons pass. Here a bare tree is suddenly in flower. On that fence of split bamboos the frail cups of morning glories carry drops of dew in their silken throats. A persimmon tree is hung with fruit long after the leaves have fallen. The last cosmos flowers are shaken by the autumn wind, and the feathers are ruffled back on the back of a bird. In January the *nanten* bushes at cottage doors are bowed down, with all their bunches of scarlet berries, under a weight of snow. Whenever the new moon appears, all the old thoughts are renewed.

The pines endure. The routine of work in the rice-fields is only varied by the slight variations in the weather. Even quite an intelligent European, were anything so unlikely to happen as that such a person should come here, might be overwhelmed or taken in by this surpassing pastoral peace. A Japanese of a literary turn might, on some summer's afternoon when the street is so placid that one can hear the feet of chickens scuffling in the dust, when one can hear the drops from a water-pipe falling one by one into a runnel at the roadside, when one can hear a drowsy cicada half-way up the mountain — such a man might be put in mind of an old short poem which seems to carry years, even centuries, of experience —

> The dragon-flies are flitting
> Above the village
> Where nothing ever happens.

Somebody yawns. The shadows slowly lengthen. A cat with no tail crosses the road, settles down to sleep in the sun, shuts its eyes, half opens them, shuts them again. . . .

Yet it would not be quite true to say that nothing ever happens. That is, it depends what you mean by nothing. For instance, children are born and people die. Further, the number of children who are born exceeds the number of people who die. So occasionally a new house goes up, a new collateral family is founded. This has been going on for some time, the process is slow, the change is all but imperceptible. Then again at times a rumour fills the air, a rumour which, though slight, is powerful enough to take hold of the whole body and threaten it with death, just as a man may take an insect between his fingers and (whether you call it caprice, fate or God's will) may let it fly away or else pinch out its entrails. Even at Omura the vibration of earthquakes is sometimes felt. Our imaginary European might feel it as a little link in a chain which includes fatal catastrophes of the forgotten past, dread disasters of the unknown future;

nervousness would be excusable, so would fear of God. Within living memory, however, nothing worse of the kind has happened than the dislodging of three tiles from the roof of the barber's shop.

Of course it is obvious that Omura (like Tokyo, or that city of the clouds, New York) is liable to change and accident. And we must take into account other things than changing seasons and acts of God. This is not a village where nothing ever happens, for there is a small cottage at the southern end where life has been in a way more eventful than in any other house. And when anything happens in life, somebody has to suffer for it. To the inhabitants of that house things have happened.

The reader might prefer to know about the 'average' life of the village, he might like to be lulled by some smiling chronicle of domestic bliss, some rural idyll, some cottar's Saturday night. If so, Omura is full of these things, and we are now at the wrong house. But if, on the contrary, the sight of an oldish woman and a young girl, neither in any way remarkable to look at, but living alone together, should provoke in us any curiosity at all, then we may rather disregard all those other lives.

These two are mother and daughter. Their name is Hara. The older woman is a widow, and she has survived two of her children. Even as a child, she had seen her own parents mauled by misfortune, but you would never guess all this from her face, manner and appearance — at least, not for some time. She is always cheerful, smiling and even laughing, but after some time one realizes that it is all put on. It is a mask. She conceives it to be her duty to present to the world a gentle smile, and nobody commends her for it. She is not really a very old woman, but she is old for her age, and is now practically bedridden. Her face shows marks of woe to a careful eye. As for her own eyes, they are kindly, but the rims are red, and in the winter when the wind is cold they water easily, and she looks exactly as if she is weeping, although she is really smiling all the time.

I will not harass the reader by describing her feelings at the death of her husband by violence; of one of her children, at a promising age, of a disgusting disease; and of another by a pure accident, which of course afterwards appeared to have been easily preventable. The village explained all this by the fact that the late Hara, stout-hearted, headstrong and boyish, had married her in defiance of the indications of the zodiac. In fact, by over-ruling his parents and defying the stars, he had been asking for trouble. To this theory the widow had always paid lip-service, perhaps to save trouble, to take the line of least resistance, but naturally the yearning of a woman's heart, especially when combined with that of a man's, is stronger than the frown of an astrologer: the astrologer may reserve the right to say, 'I told you so.' So the difference between the fortunes of the Hara family and those of the rest of the villagers may at once, if you like, be ascribed to the fact that the Haras began wrong. If you take the wrong turning at first, you are likely to reach the wrong destination at last; and nobody in Omura had ever before been known to marry against the indications of the heavens. Not that anybody was harsh or callous. They were spontaneously and constantly kind and most of them were somehow related to or connected with the family, whose two survivors could hardly have existed without some kind of support.

The daughter, Chiyé, was just seventeen, an ordinary country wench, a small, plain, healthy virgin, awkwardly bashful, with cheeks as round and hard and red as apples, no nose to speak of, and black wispy hair of the texture of horsehair. Not clever, but not an idiot. And perhaps, like all young women, a problem. The mother could easily find a home, and people would take in the daughter too. Before long Chiyé might be married off. But her mother secretly cherished another plan. Her late husband had a married sister in Tokyo whom she had only once seen since her marriage. They had been familiar in childhood, and still sometimes wrote to each other.

This sister was still living. Her husband, an official, was said to be rather well-to-do. If only Chiyé could go to them! The smiling widow brooded, lying awake in the night and listening to the girl's heavy regular breathing, and at last decided to write and make a suggestion to her sister-in-law. But before she could write, a letter came from Tokyo which happened to be a direct invitation for the girl to come.

People who have suffered a great deal sometimes suspect a sudden happiness: they think there is a catch in it somewhere. The widow, torn by a lifetime, mistrusted her own elation. She told the girl who, at the thought of Tokyo, was too scared to speak.

'It is a piece of good luck,' said the mother. 'And we must make the most of it.'

It was a piece of good luck, an extraordinary chance for the girl. It is not every day that a female bumpkin of Omura is offered a safe niche in the capital. But nearly everybody was dead against it. They said, in their cottage-wisdom, that it was madness for such a young girl to go to Tokyo alone.

'But she won't be alone,' said the widow, 'she'll be with her aunt.'

'Everybody knows the dangers of such a great city. Even her aunt can't protect her. They say that there are foreigners in Tokyo who just go about spoiling virgins. Why, only the other day in the newspaper — and not only foreigners —'

'I'm sure she'll be safe with her aunt and uncle.'

The widow was hopeful, and with the suffrage of a minority, wrote back her thanks and said the girl was coming. One or two people thought that this was as bad as the old story of Hara and the zodiac; and one or two said so, but not to the widow.

The village where nothing ever happens? Hara Chiyé was going to Tokyo! One early autumn morning a crowd of villagers could have been seen standing on the platform of the station at the next village but one. The girl herself, to be chaper-

oned by the guard, who was an acquaintance of a distant connexion, leaned out of the window, full of smiles, blushes and
confusion. Her sensations since the receipt of her aunt's letter
had been powerful, and corresponding to their outward manifestations. She was young and low-bred and showed what she
felt. From one moment to another she had hardly known
whether to feel joy at the excitement of the prospect and at the
envy of her friends, or embarrassment and shame at this launch-
ing out, or dread at leaving the village, or sorrow at leaving her
sick mother, from whom she had never been separated for a
single day. The two predominant sensations in this upheaval
were a mixture of bashfulness, sadness, and homesickness, and
also a vague anticipatory joy. She was by no means a pudding-
head.

Now, at some chance remark, she hid the lower part of her
face in her red cotton scarf, blushed to match it, blinked her
bright black eyes, and with a small fat hand in a pink cotton glove
put back a wayward wisp of horsehair from her forehead. Her
mother had not been able to come and see her off, and as Chiyé
stared at all the friendly valedictory faces in the station they
suddenly seemed almost strange or hostile. She thought of her
poor old mother and wondered when she should see her again,
gave a loud sniff, and another, and very nearly burst into tears.
She was saved by a piercing whistle, ten voices all speaking at
once, ten rustic bodies all bowing like grass in a storm, hands,
smiles, faces, farewells.

The train moved out of the station, and with a burning face
and beating heart she sank on to the seat, feeling that all eyes in
the long carriage were on her (as, indeed, most of them were),
and not daring, for several minutes, to glance up at the rack over
her head, where a small basket, containing all her worldly possessions, and a string bag of fat persimmons were trembling a little
with the vibration of the train.

## § 2

She had been unable to form any definite ideas about her aunt and uncle, so that she was at first neither overjoyed nor disappointed. Everything was so new and strange. Her aunt was very kind, even effusive, and smiled and chattered a great deal. It was not at all like her mother's smile, and in spite of all this cheerfulness Chiyé liked her uncle much better, quite an ordinary, elderly man, who was seldom at home and hardly took any notice of her except to speak to her as if she was a servant. Perhaps that was why she liked him. Or perhaps she realized intuitively his ordinary heart about the same time (it was very soon) that she saw through her aunt's cheerfulness to an inner core of hardness, selfishness, cupidity, and cunning. The fact that her uncle spoke to her as master to servant was not surprising, for it was practically as a servant that she worked, though of course she drew no wages, for the prosperity of her uncle was only an Omura legend, and even had he had money his wife would still have watched *sen* as carefully as she watched *yen*. Her aunt, who already had two children, expected to give birth before very long to another. For this reason, she explained, she was particularly glad to have Chiyé with her. So Chiyé, whatever she might have looked forward to, became a drudge. The house was in a poor part of Tokyo, cold in winter, hot in summer, dark, dusty, dirty, and obscure. Few visitors came. Her aunt went often to the public bath-house and gossiped for hours at a time. Chiyé looked after the house, the children, the clothes and the shopping. Her aunt then took to sleeping in the daytime.

'I'm sorry you have so much work to do,' she remarked once, with a radiant smile, 'but, you see, my coming confinement —'

She talked a great deal about her coming confinement, until the expected event took on an excessive importance in Chiyé's imagination, and when at last the child was born, the girl was so obsessed with the significance of its arrival that, although her work immediately increased, she devoted all her spare thoughts and time to playing with it, looking at it, kneeling by it, talking to it. Chiyé was not unhappy, but her aunt was, for, like so many people, she wanted money and did not know how to get it: her husband had lost some money unexpectedly and she herself also needed more, to say nothing of the children, now three in number.

Chiyé's mother now wrote much oftener to her sister-in-law as well as to her daughter. The widow said she hadn't been very well in the winter, but had picked up in the spring. She asked many questions and always expressed her hopes of seeing Chiyé again before long, though she must have known that such hopes were unlikely to be fulfilled. And Chiyé, when she had a moment to think, experienced pangs of longing to go back to Omura. But meanwhile her aunt thought of a plan. Chiyé had been just a year in Tokyo when her protector came to her one day and said:

'A friend of one of my friends knows a lady who keeps an important high-class hotel, and this lady asked my friend's friend to ask her to ask me if I knew of any young girl who wants a situation, as a vacancy has just occurred on her staff which must be immediately filled. Of course I at once thought of you. It's a wonderful chance, and I've accepted it for you, and you're to go as soon as possible.'

She paused significantly, as if waiting for gratitude, but Chiyé, whose heart was beating hurriedly, only stared at her with wide-open eyes.

'I'm sorry you have to leave us, but I think this is a real opening for you. And you can earn some money, which you'll be able to send to your mother —'

The girl thought that her aunt was rather over-eager, rather too ready with all this information. She felt a slight resentment that she had not sooner been told or consulted about it.

'But —' she said timidly, 'but, Aunt, do you think it is all right — I mean is it quite safe — for me to —'

'Chiyé, I have already paid for you a premium.'

'A premium?'

'Yes. There are so many girls who wish to get that place that at first we must pay some money for them to go in, then they work on trial for a month or two, then they get paid proper wages.'

'But —'

'So it is an excellent situation.'

'And you have paid —'

'It is not mine, but your uncle's generosity. Don't thank him, because you know it annoys him to be spoken to by a servant — well, by any girl, even about ordinary household things.'

'And I must go soon?'

'Yes, it will be better. The sooner the better.'

'But you do want me to go, Aunt?'

'No, no, of course not, but I'm thinking of your poor mother. It is time for you to try and send her something. You came to Tokyo to help to support her, you know, not to help me.'

Chiyé hid her face in her sleeve. She sobbed once or twice. When she looked up, her aunt had gone out of the room. But one of the children had come in, and was standing in the doorway with the baby tied on to its back. Chiyé got up and ran to the baby, loosened it, lifted it up and embraced it. Whenever she just glanced at its eyes a thrill ran right down her spine.

'Where's your mother?' she asked the eldest child.

'She's gone to the bath-house.'

Indeed, at this moment, a street away, her aunt was squatting in exceedingly hot water with three other ladies; the gold teeth of her smile gleamed radiantly through the cloudy steam, and the sound of her voice, flowing on continually in a stream of small-talk and home chat, mingled with the sound of the scalding hot water chortling out of a tap a yard from her nose, and helped to preserve for her the good name of a sociable and animated busybody.

Chiyé, although she was holding the baby in her arms, felt a faint but sickening sense of nameless apprehension, loneliness, helplessness. She was now to go among strangers! Not as a relation, but a servant. On trial. A premium. A real opening. Don't thank your uncle. The recent words of her aunt kept recurring in her mind, where every one of them had stuck. She was still full of hopes, but neither now nor later was she capable of telling herself the real truth. She was not conscious enough. The real truth was that she did not want to leave the baby, the true centre, had she only known it, of her life at her aunt's.

Less than a week later she set out, accompanied by that aunt, and carrying a basket and bundle, for the hotel where she was to work. They rode in a tram, and the older woman, smiling affably, talked all the way.

The Kaméfuku, or Lucky Tortoise, Hotel is hard to find, for it is at the end of a blind alley within a maze of narrow streets which all look much alike and none of which leads anywhere in particular. This part of Hongo-ku is dingy and dirty. It has never been anything else, but in the years after the great earthquake it was at its worst. To reach the hotel, in fact, one has to go through slums. The final approach is narrow, dark and smelly; as cold as the grave from October to April, and for the rest of the year sultry but sunless. The front of the hotel, such as it is, faces north, and is screened by a number of tuberculous trees and by the blank wooden walls of some cramped houses opposite. The prevailing colour may be called an unclean slate or battleship-grey. The alley-way, the houses, the trees are grey, the hotel is dead grey, and the lightless air is grey. The stinking water which runs, or fails to run, in the open drains at the side is dirty grey, the faces of the older inhabitants of this region are doughy grey, the past, present and future are muddy grey. And as Chiyé and her aunt entered the alley-way — the woman walking with some speed, assurance and determination, the girl lagging because of her load, her uncertainty and her short legs — a cold, dank, dead air touched her, like the grey lick of a gigantic tongue, and she shivered.

It is characteristic of the Kaméfuku Hotel that its dark portal does not face the alley-way. Like so many things in Japan, it is round the corner. But let not the reader for one moment assume that because of the prevailing neutral tints these surroundings are therefore destitute of that colour to which he has a right. Ah, no. Is this not the land of cherry blossoms, nay, of the Rising Sun?

It might be by now reasonably supposed that the Kaméfuku Hotel is only a resort of the indigent and obscure, of the mentally and physically grey, but this is not the case. It cannot be judged by its appearance. Chiyé and her aunt have only just reached the *genkan*. Let us at least wait until they get inside. There is another thing to take into account if one is trying to arrive at the true status of the house.

Although it is so unfortunate in its immediate surroundings, it is necessary to remember that this part of Tokyo is quite convenient and central. For instance, it is near the University, and some important schools, within easy reach of Kanda and Uéno, and served by various means of communication. The hotel is only two minutes from the trams. Yet in spite of all these facilities, it also has the advantage of being comparatively quiet. Most of the people who stay there do not do so simply because it is quiet and central, but also partly because of the other people who stay, or have stayed there. The hotel attracts, generally speaking, certain types of men. Chiyé will find them out for herself. She is already bowing at the entrance, blushing, palpitating, and by slipping out of her light wooden clogs on to the polished floor she stands also on the threshold of a new phase of her life.

§ 3

She bows and blushes before the proprietress herself, Mrs. Kikuchi, a big woman for a Japanese, a masterful and calculating widow, whose portly stocky front, always covered with an apron that was clean the day before yesterday, serves as a pedestal (the contours of the back view being apparently much like those of the front, only apronless) for a hard, square, puffy face. There is no reason to suppose that a Japanese landlady need be so very different from one in corresponding circumstances elsewhere. The Kaméfuku Hotel being in a slum conceals no tea-house tea-roses. Look at this heavy, costive face with the lustreless, dusty, drab hair drawn up and back on every side and screwed into a top-knot in the middle of the plateau above. Look at the shifty eyes; furtive, adaptable and quite unenthusiastic smile; and large, calculating, avaricious hands. This is Chiyé's mistress, and Chiyé accordingly touches the floor with her forehead.

The three women seat themselves round the firebox on the matted floor of a room just off the entrance, a room that may be called the office, for it contains a telephone and a broken gramophone, a calendar hangs on the wall, and in the corner a young man is seated doing accounts at a low desk littered with papers. He takes no notice at all of the women, except to glance with cold indifference at Chiyé. He is the younger son of the proprietress. His elder brother is out. His elder brother is nearly always out.

In spite of her aunt's cheerfulness, and the apparently maternal benevolence of Mrs. Kikuchi, Chiyé feels uneasy, helpless, victimized, and wants to weep. She is handed a cup of tea, and again blushes, muttering her thanks. But she is not so confused that she fails to notice underneath the formal mutual politeness of the two elder women some degree of intimacy and understanding. This surprises her, for she had supposed that they were not even acquainted, but she is far too innocent to suspect anything.

Before saying goodbye to Mrs Kikuchi, her aunt extracts a promise that Chiyé shall be allowed to come and see her from time to time, and then grinning and nodding, and bowing low four, five, six times, opens her oiled-paper umbrella, gathers her skirts closely with her bony left hand and steps out on her high clogs into the street. It has begun to rain.

The first few months that the girl spent in these new surroundings could not be called sensational, but nevertheless they were of singular importance to her, for she was now more cut off than she had ever been before from her relations and friends. If she had had much time to think and brood, no doubt Omura and her mother and the old and happy days (ah, they never seemed so happy at the time, but only when the traveller in the desert looks back to the leafy mountains does he understand what he has left) would have seemed very far away, far and near like a lover in a dream. But luckily she had to work hard, and work, though it may not be a cure, is at times a useful drug. Then it must also be remembered that she was not, strictly speaking, a thoughtful or brooding person by nature, but ready enough to be at home where she found herself and to accept happiness without seeking it. Her thoughts, like everybody else's, came to her from her feelings. Her reason was the slave of her passions; the belly, as the Chinese long ago discovered, being the home of the soul.

Even when she was tired there were usually a few minutes before she slept, and she sometimes lay awake at three or four in the morning — it was at those times that she felt herself, all unwitting, in the grip of nameless powers, and the longings and cravings that stirred her then were long afterwards to translate themselves in the brain of that bright and active daylight virgin into regrets, hopes and desires. And then she might sigh or smile, for nobody had taught her that it is useless to dwell on the past except to profit by it, and that it is useless to expect anything of the future.

She slept in a room with four other maids, and all five of them snored. It was the duty of each to look after a particular section of the untidy, rambling, scrambling building; all made, or nearly all, of wood and glass and paper; full of twists and turns and ups and downs; which sometimes broke out, as in the façade, into a 'foreign' aspect, and from whose windows one always caught sight of other windows or sunny corners of the roof. The girls also had to help with washing, washing-up and other activities. They were maids-of-all-work, and they all had to work unceasingly, though they occasionally had time off, when they could attend to their own clothes: but somehow if they ever settled down to talk or to read or write letters the telephone was sure to ring. The telephone in that room was apt to ring at any time, and the receiver and bell, hanging there black and shining, were like a perpetual warning, always on the verge of breaking silence.

'*Moshimoshi*! Hullo!'

And at the other end the voice of the younger son of Mrs. Kikuchi (for the elder one was nearly always out) could be heard, hard, insolent and peremptory. The young man never smiled. In the daytime he sat in the office and bullied the maids; at night he sat in the office listening to the wireless, talking to his mother or his friends, and occasionally bullying the maids over the telephone. He was one of those men who seem to derive sexual satisfaction from insulting female dependents. Until he married, six years later, this vocal sadism was almost his sole occupation.

Chiyé soon became friendly with a maid called Tsuya, a country girl who had been in Tokyo about six months longer than herself, but the others, for one reason and another, she did not like so much. One was rather old, one was rather cattish, one was rather dull, but still she got on with them, for they all had their good moments, and she herself was ready enough to get on with anybody at all times. In spite of her awkwardness she was gentle and unselfish. The vague feeling (most of her feelings were vague) of loneliness and nostalgia was not quickly got rid of. She did not only think of old village days and miss her mother.

Now she also missed the house and children she had just left, the family and surroundings of her aunt, and even that gossiping, scheming woman herself. Most of all she missed the baby she had looked after.

She had been less than a month in the place when she asked leave to go and see her aunt. Mrs. Kikuchi, with maternal condescension, readily agreed. Chiyé put her old red scarf round her neck, found her aunt all smiles, and spent a lot of time playing with the baby. The second time she went her aunt was out. And when she wanted to go a third time, Mrs. Kikuchi refused without giving any reason. Chiyé said nothing, but believing that during the next few days she noticed less benevolence in the manner of her mistress, she decided to discuss, or rather suddenly began to discuss the matter with her friend Tsuya in the servant's bedroom. It was a room in which the characters and idiosyncrasies of all the inmates, visitors and connexions of the hotel were sooner or later thoroughly and repeatedly discussed and compared. It was a temple of gossip, hearsay and invention, in which curiosity — an escape from dullness — was more conspicuous than malice — an escape from suffering.

The two girls chanced to be alone. Tsuya began by asking under exactly what circumstances Chiyé had come to work here. Tsuya looked so simple, but behind her sad, mild eyes was a quick brain, and by asking this question she had at once gone to the heart of the matter. Chiyé told the story of the 'opening' and the 'premium', and Tsuya kept on answering shortly, quite non-committal:

'Is that so? So?'

And then the telephone rang. It may easily be imagined who was at the other end. The conversation stopped.

Four days later they were on their way to the bath-house in the next street, when Tsuya came out with a piece of information. Quite by chance she had overheard that morning, in her wing of the house, part of a conversation between Mrs. Kikuchi and an elderly woman who was visiting somebody in the hotel. They had at first been talking about Chiyé's aunt, and it was this which had caught her attention. Then had come a reference to Chiyé herself. Somebody had said: 'And that was what you paid?' The answer was not clear. Then:

'The girl knows?'

'Not yet,' in Mrs. Kikuchi's voice. 'I shall explain to her when it is necessary.'

From these and other somewhat scrappy data Tsuya, who already knew something of Chiyé's aunt, had constructed a theory.

Chiyé began to tremble.

'I believe,' said Tsuya, 'that your aunt sold you to this hotel.'

'What?'

'Mrs. Kikuchi has certainly paid some money to your aunt. That means she has bought you. You can't escape. You're bound, just like a girl in a licensed house.'

'It's impossible,' said Chiyé, in the teeth of the facts. 'My aunt said —'

'And you believed her! Why should she pay a premium for you? Is she so rich? Does she love you so much?'

'She is my father's sister.'

'And she has taken advantage of that to enrich herself. It's well known that she's fond of money.'

'Oh, but I can't believe it —'

§ 4

Gradually, however, she forced herself to believe it. Her work seemed to increase, she hardly dared to look at her mistress, she could think of nothing else. . . . But surely she would get wages? She would be able to send something to her mother? Should she write to her mother and try and confirm the truth? No, she would be sure first. Without consulting Tsuya, she decided to ask permission once more to go and see her aunt. After hesitating for a day or two, she timidly approached Mrs. Kikuchi, feeling sure that the older woman could read her thoughts plainly.

'Why do you want to go?' said Mrs. Kikuchi. Chiyé thought she had an odd, shrewd expression.

'Only — only for a visit,' she faltered.

'Ah, so?' This was said in a strange way. 'Then you may go. But you must be back at six.'

She found her aunt at home, very kind and cheerful. She couldn't believe — and yet she must ask. After a time she became confused and agitated.

'What's the matter, dear? Aren't you feeling well?'

'I'm quite well, thank you,' she said slowly.

She realized that she simply could not bring herself to ask. She blushed, wondered if it was time to go back yet, and tried to forget herself by holding the baby. When she went away, her aunt, beaming and smirking, gave her some clothes for a present. Chiyé was so surprised at this unexpected and unusual generosity that she thanked her aunt profusely — and found herself already on the way back. She told the whole story to Tsuya.

'And so you didn't ask her after all?'

'Oh, I *couldn't*.'

'Well, it's certainly true.'

Her aunt wrote to her occasionally, but Chiyé always felt disagreeable now when she read these postcards. She tried to forget that she was a prisoner. She tried to forget her aunt, and though she longed sometimes to go and see her again, she did not ask for leave.

Now what was, in fact, the actual truth of her coming here? Her aunt, in exchange for the 'loan' of a considerable sum of money, had undertaken to surrender Chiyé, body and soul, to the hotel, on condition that the pledge could at any time be redeemed for an equal payment. It is hardly necessary to add that should the aunt ever by some extraordinary stroke of fortune come into any money she would, as a good mother, use it for the education of her children or some other worthy purpose. Mrs. Kikuchi was quite satisfied with her bargain — such a convenient form of contract. And Chiyé began slowly and painfully to learn by her own experience the universal truth that slavery always and everywhere survives its abolition.

What a life! And yet the girl had been brought up to nothing much easier. If she suffered now, it was not because she had come down in the world. On the contrary, she had arrived in Tokyo; and here she was. Chiyé may at times have longed to be else-where: who doesn't? But if she now no longer enjoyed the peace of Omura, if she was now separated from her mother and the scenes and friends of her childhood, she lived at any rate in Tokyo, a circumstance for which she knew many of those same friends envied her, and she was philosophical enough to console herself with this thought. Often, hurrying alone down an empty corridor to answer the telephone call of a new arrival, she would feel a pleasurable qualm of delightful anticipation. Her life contained elements of surprise which prevented it from being dull. A scrap of gossip in the maid's room would set her ears a-tingle and furnish her for days with food for speculation. Rumours, thoughts and dreams; occasional familiarities from one of the lodgers; the whole stress of character and circumstance made for variety.

She toiled, but she was not bored. Tsuya was her constant confidante. She became slightly thinner and paler but remained perfectly healthy. Such physical changes were for the better. She had never been ugly, and was now, she hoped — peeping in somebody else's mirror while she paused in dusting a room — she told herself that she was now less plain than she had been.

She began to take an interest in the newspapers, of which her somewhat elementary education allowed her to read a great part. Curiosity was born in her, and brought with it the usual results, especially ambition. She was able to formulate in her mind a definite wish to marry and bear a child. She wanted a home, a husband, a lover, an intrigue, a romance, a double suicide, a concrete hope to live for — anything she could get.

She read in the newspapers about the careers of exceptional girls, and saw no reason why she should not also be an exceptional girl. She might become a waitress in a café or restaurant; or an actress or film actress — she was not quite clear about the difference, if any, between these. She might learn some musical instrument, flower arrangement or needle-work, and earn money by giving lessons. Two girls from a high school were reported to have lately joined a ship for America as stewardesses — unheard-of originality! but she might do the same. She might become a woman painter or novelist. One of the other maids, indeed, had this last ambition, and had already written from memory a fragment of her experiences at a primary school. Fame and fortune await successful women writers. . . .

Perhaps this cultural trend in her dreams (rather than thoughts) was partly caused by some of the persons she had to wait on. The Kaméfuku Hotel has long been a resort of some of the lesser men of letters, and usually houses some sort of a novelist, a brace of poets and other intelligentsia not usually of the most popular or successful, nor perhaps of the most refined. Hidden away round so many corners, it is a convenient periodical retreat from wives and families, friends, creditors or the daily task. Even a best-seller may appear there for a week-end, not necessarily unaccompanied.

When such a person turned up, the house was at once in a flutter. The proprietress and her younger son were excessively obsequious, the bath steamed hotter, the cook worked harder, the maids pattered up and down the smooth bare floors of the passages. Once a well-known film actor, tall, strong and florid, arrived at dusk on a motor-bicycle and ordered everybody about, which they all enjoyed, fairly tumbling over one another to oblige him. The same thing occurred with a retired wrestler. And just at present the debauched son of an enormously rich factory-owner in the country was staying on the first floor, a lout who came to Tokyo at least twice a year, and always had the same room. He was so free of promiscuous tips and caresses, and was considered such an important visitor, besides being flushed with lust and coarse of speech, that the maids were always in and out of his room, especially in. The stories Chiyé heard of this rake naturally excited her imagination, and she wished in vain, half repelled and half fascinated, to get a chance of attending him, but her work lay elsewhere.

Tsuya related anecdotes of a lady with two husbands, a divorcee; of an eccentric young foreigner in a bleak back room who was visited by a young woman in dark clothes who always covered her mouth with her sleeve and looked melancholy, but had a silvery laugh when with him; and of an Indian, a gentle and handsome man who had had to leave the country because he was blackmailed. So Chiyé's mind was prepared by the fragments of many local dramas for anything to happen.

§ 5

Her peculiar care was a corridor with three rooms on one side and five on the other. Of these eight rooms, one, small and cold and facing north, was empty. The inhabitants of the other seven were not, with two or three exceptions, of surpassing interest to her. One was an old man, an odd recluse, who lived frugally, but was said to be very rich. He has no special part in this story, but that Chiyé rather liked him and attended him many times daily. He never rose before noon, only ate one light meal during the day, read meticulously three newspapers, went out every evening, and dressed in very good dark brown silk kimonos. He smoked vile stinking cigarettes, but nobody noticed that they were vile and stinking. His chief peculiarity was a completely bald head, quite round and smooth. He was sufficiently proud of this dome to wash it daily with care, and Chiyé had the duty of carrying to him at the bath a saucerful of white-of-egg, with which the old gentleman polished his glossy cranium for three or four minutes until it shone like red lacquer.

In the next room to him lived a young man with long hair who worked in an office. The long hair showed that he was musical, but the only sounds that ever came from his room were those of expectoration. However, he went out sometimes in the evening, looking very serious, and carrying with great care an *empty* violin-case. It was Chiyé who found this out, and she accordingly held him in some contempt. Later on, she saw a large volume of translations from Karl Marx lying on his table: its pages long remained uncut.

'Why do you buy such a book,' she asked, 'if you don't mean to read it?'

He answered with a surprising frankness, so that afterwards she found it easy to forgive him for being an intellectual snob.

'Some of my friends asked me if I was a Marx-boy,[1] and of course I had to answer yes. One must be in the fashion, one can't be thought an ignoramus, so, as everybody is reading Marx now, I bought this book.'

Next door to this youth lived a married couple, who were quite contented, and therefore of no distinction whatsoever. Beyond them, in a smaller room, were two university students in whom Chiyé took a special interest. They teased her in a friendly, off-hand way, and she became quite attached to them. Most of their time was spent in playing baseball or talking or reading about it, but when the time for examinations was getting near they sat up all night with wet towels on their heads, back to back, over law text-books. Neither of them ever passed an examination. Sometimes when they were out Chiyé would pause in her sweeping and finger their clothes and other belong-

[1] *Marukusu-boi.*

ings. It gave her an inexplicable thrill just to touch their baseball gloves and bats.

The only thing she regretted was that they never attempted to make love to her. They even teased her about her appearance.

Tsuya, although better-looking, seemed little luckier. She told Chiyé about a young man on the third floor who was the son of a general and quite rich, but never played baseball. He was always reading or writing, but he went out a great deal, for he gave lectures nearly every day in a high school and a university. He was lively and good looking, but he never had letters from women, and never took much notice of Tsuya, though he was quite polite to her. It was evident that she admired him very much, and took pains to please him. At one time she had never stopped talking to Chiyé about Minami — for that was his name — but lately she said little about him. No doubt she was disappointed because he practically ignored her.

Chiyé herself had once been sent up to his room on some errand, and had found him sitting on the matted floor before his low desk, which was littered with books and papers and illuminated by a standard lamp with a red shade. His sleeves were turned up, and he was busily writing. She had approached him timidly, for she knew that he was translating from a foreign language the history of the world: advertisements of the first and second parts had already appeared in the newspapers. When he looked up and spoke to her she did not think he was so handsome as one of her baseball students, but she could not help liking the manly charm and vivacity of his open face. His eyes were bright and intelligent, his colour good and his voice clear, but it was impossible not to notice that his mouth was a little drawn, that it could not escape, even when he smiled, a stigma of sadness. It was as if, in his face, there was a war between the forces of heart and head: the upper part of the face, even the bright smile, seemed to show the power and alertness of intellect and will, but the resigned mouth, and even sometimes the eyes, showed the fatally unconquerable power of emotion. Of all this, though, she only got a vague impression.

She would catch a glimpse of Minami in the corridors or at the door of the bathroom, or run into him just as he was going out, and she studied him from afar. Hearing by chance that his nickname among his students was Vitamin, she could see that the name suited him well, for he was restlessly eager in all his doings. Had she only known, he was in the throes of reason against romance, will against wish, that battle in which we are all engaged for life. Chiyé almost envied her she-friend the privilege of waiting on this serious and lively young man, but whenever she tried to talk about Minami, Tsuya made little response, so she gave it up.

An occasional letter from her mother, who seemed comfortably settled, would for several days send her thoughts back to Omura. Her mother told her to keep any money she might earn, a noble sacrifice on the part of that weak old woman in a country where children are bound to make noble sacrifices for their parents without expecting any gratitude. However, except for a little pocket-money, Chiyé had as yet had nothing from Mrs. Kikuchi, nor was she likely to get much out of that lady, who might fairly accurately be called her purchaser.

It has been said that in the care of Chiyé there was a small empty room facing north, but although it faced north it afforded only a very small glimpse of the northern sky. Chiyé sometimes slipped in there at the quietest part of the afternoon, and would stand a minute or two gazing up above the cold dark roofs into that serene and sunny immensity against which was printed a slender column of iron, banded with scarlet and black, the chimney of a bath-house, out of the top of which poured unceasingly a creamy and sulphurous plume of smoke, whose direction silently altered with the wind. But her attention would usually be attracted by giggling and singing quite near at hand, and she could look down at a row of windows only a few yards away, in deep shadow, and partly screened, whence the sound proceeded. That gloomy wooden barrack opposite was the dormitory of a girls' school, and this side of it so nearly touched one end of the Kaméfuku Hotel that it seemed that between them no ray of the sun ever shone. At night, though, an oblique segment of a moonray, cut by the angles of roofs, might travel into the canyon between the two buildings, and that dazzling light might reveal the motionless head and shoulders of a virgin, looking up at the purity of the night, and dreaming, just as if she were asleep.

Passing down her corridor one afternoon Chiyé noticed that the door of this room was open, and hearing voices, looked in. Her two baseball students were at the window, one shaking with laughter, and the other leaning out and calling to somebody. She hurried to another room where she could look out and see what was going on. They were talking familiarly to two schoolgirls at the opposite window. The girls were in paroxysms of giggling: one had her hair down and her hand over her mouth: the other, a beauty, was tying something to a long bamboo pole — such as is used for hanging out washing — the other end of which was held by one of the students. It was a letter.

'*Oi*,' cried one of the students, 'be careful!'

And the girls both doubled themselves up with excitement, blushing and shaking with laughter, their faces half covered by their silken sleeves.

So that was why the students ignored her! They were in touch with that lovely creature over the way. It was not jealousy that Chiyé felt, but rather disappointment, a sudden sickening sense of the futility of hope. She remembered how they always teased her — but she did not want to be teased, she wanted to be loved. She told the story to Tsuya, who showed great interest in it, but could only offer by way of consolation the news that the students were due to leave soon (for they had just failed again in their last examination), and then, she suggested, perhaps somebody more promising would take their place. She counselled hope, and Chiyé sighed, feeling lonely. Somehow she could not be on quite such intimate terms with Tsuya at present: it was just as if something had come between them, though of course, she assured herself, there was nothing that could possibly have done so.

§ 6

As it was a long time since she had been to see her aunt and her baby cousin, Chiyé asked leave to go. Mrs. Kikuchi, as usual, smiled slyly on her large drab face. It was impossible for Chiyé to gauge at all what the proprietress was thinking or how much she was hiding, for that inscrutable expression might conceal everything or nothing. Mrs. Kikuchi was a cunning woman, and like all cunning people she could not hide her tricks permanently from anybody really watchful: Chiyé, however, was sufficiently pure in heart to be gullible. Mrs. Kikuchi now gave her gracious assent, as if she had nothing at all up her sleeve.

An hour later Chiyé might have been seen walking quickly on her clogs down a narrow street in that dingy and overcrowded quarter with which she was so familiar, but she suddenly paused a moment, as if in surprise, for she had noticed that the shutters on the street side of her aunt's house had been drawn across the windows. This was odd. Chiyé hurried to the entrance. It was locked. She went round to the back. The kitchen door was also locked, and all the windows were shuttered. It was obvious that the family were away. Impossible! In a dustbin at the kitchen door there were some orange skins that looked quite fresh. Hoping against hope, and glancing up sideways, Chiyé rattled the door. There was no answer. For a moment she could hardly breathe, as if she had been suddenly immersed in cold water.

Then she remembered a friend of her aunt's was living next door who would tell her why the family were absent; but her call was now answered by somebody she did not know. She asked for the former neighbour by name.

'No, I'm sorry, she doesn't live here now, but went away some months ago.'

'Then, I beg your pardon, but can you tell me where my aunt is at present?'

'Your aunt?'

Chiyé explained. The neighbour frowned.

'The house is to let,' she said majestically, 'for the family have gone into the country for good. They left yesterday, and most of the furniture went last week.'

'Into the country!'

'I don't know the address, I'm sorry.'

As Chiyé came out, she saw a man in a fur cap and a long overcoat with a frayed velvet collar standing in front of the old house. He had taken a large piece of paper out of an imitation leather dispatch-case, and was pasting it obliquely on to the outside wall. It bore the words *To Let*.

She plucked up courage to ask him for her aunt's address. He looked at her with a broad smile, for he was a cheerful man. He was rather proud of his fur cap. When he spoke, the words simply poured out of his mouth. Chiyé smiled politely, and at last gathered definitely that her aunt had left Tokyo and was not coming back. He did not know the address, but no doubt she could get it from the landlord, who was away at present, having gone to visit his native place in the prefecture of N——, as his wife's nephew was about to marry, etc.

Chiyé thanked him, bowed and started back for the hotel. On the way she sat very upright in the tram, with a flushed face, and staring at her knees.

Mrs. Kikuchi affected surprise at the result of this expedition, and promised to make inquiries. And late in the evening, after her work was done, Chiyé sat down and wrote to her mother for information — she, at any rate, must have been told, and would explain. Then at last she confided it all to Tsuya, who was very sympathetic, but could not help reflecting on the cunning of the aunt and the proprietress, whom she felt convinced were in league; Tsuya told Chiyé yet once more that she had been sold by one to the other. Chiyé wept.

During the next few days she suffered from headaches. It was the end of the summer, and the change in the season, together with thoughts of what she could not help regarding now as her unfortunate situation, tended to produce in her a disturbed state of mind. September is the May of autumn, says an old poet; and it is true that in the fall of the year we may be liable to feel a restlessness akin to that we felt in the spring. Just as a person in the autumn of life makes a sudden final spurt, so we may feel in us again, when the heat goes and the sky becomes serene and clear, other clouds of heat, a precious madness and creative longing. And the less we know about it the more we are at its mercy, yet even the very wise have to obey it, just as they are forced always to do things which they fondly suppose they themselves have originated, planned or approved.

Chiyé, with her hand to her forehead, decided to go to a fortune-teller. She made this decision without consulting anybody: it was unusual for her to be so independent, but adversity instils desperation, and desperate people are apt to act for themselves. Besides, she who was now going to consult the zodiac no doubt had in her something of her father's wilfulness, the man who had defied the zodiac. Having, as a child, heard often enough of her head-strong father's misfortunes, she had every excuse for being superstitious. And so the generations vary: the children run away from the mistakes of the parents, but they run on pretty much the same sort of legs.

Mrs. Kikuchi felt she could safely let Chiyé out on a long tether now and then — if all the windows and doors are locked, the canary may certainly be let out of its cage for half an hour and given the freedom of the room — by analogy, one conquers by yielding — so with her craftiest smile she gave the girl an afternoon off for 'shopping,' and asked no questions. Chiyé had not the slightest intention of shopping — which she would have liked very much — for she had only just enough money to pay for bare necessities.

## § 7

She went first to Uéno, and then, feeling extraordinarily venturesome and reckless, got into the new underground railway just opened between that place and Asakusa. It was a wonderful experience, for while she was thinking what she would say to Tsuya when she got back, she found the train had already got to the other end.

She made straight for the fortune-teller's booths near the great temple of Kwannon (goddess of Mercy, Pity, Peace), for she had made a mental note of them on a visit to Asakusa (how long ago it seemed!) with her aunt and the children. She had not dared to ask or suggest anything at the time — and now here she was! First she climbed up the temple steps, where before that gigantic and cavernous portal she stood a moment in a group of worshippers. Under that overhanging cliff of carved scarlet wood she clapped her palms together softly, twice, to draw the attention of heaven; bowed her head; and asked for nothing but help. On her way down the steps she noticed a crowd of people gathered in an attentive ring about fifty yards away on the right, within the great compound, under a vast gingko tree whose leaves would soon turn pure yellow, and as she had plenty of time determined to go and see what they were so interested in. Flocks of fat doves rose and fell, flapped, strutted and cooed. Some were on the ground just before her feet. So tame! She held out her hand and made a small sympathetic noise, but the doves, sleek and iridescent, turned their backs to her because she had nothing to give them. But she was luckier when she reached the crowd, for she arrived just as some others, exclaiming with valedictory astonishment, were disembroiling themselves, so, slipping in, she got their good place.

In a round space three Chinese jugglers were performing, with the assistance of a Korean who spent all his time packing and unpacking, and seemed oblivious of everything else. The eldest Chinese was stout, middle-aged and wheezy, and his buffooneries were done with such an air of boredom that they were quite funny. Another was a boy. But the chief actor was a man of about thirty-five, who, like the others, was dressed entirely in black silk brocade, fitting tightly above the waist and ending in a loose divided skirt. He never kept still for a moment, and so held closely the attention of the spectators. At present he was blowing clouds of fire very rapidly out of his mouth and darting backwards and forwards to keep the air rushing in and out, while his associates kept up a continual patter in excellent Japanese. A moment later he was standing still, with his delicate hands on his hips, and the older man was pulling yards and yards of parti-coloured paper ribbons out of the now fireless mouth, with which, it seemed, all his tricks were done.

Chiyé looked at him carefully. His skin was redder than that of a Japanese, his hair was cut short and he looked animated and perfectly healthy. The eyes were small and rather flat, lidless, bluish underneath and with a metallic sparkle that seemed not quite natural. The cheeks were flushed, but perhaps that was their usual state. The nose had no bridge, and would have been effeminate had it not ended in a pair of widely-gaping nostrils. But it was the mouth that made his living, and it was the mouth that was remarkable, for in repose it was shapely, but showed itself capable of expansion and distortion. The lips were thick and red, and about them, even when fixed in some grotesque position, lingered a smile in which there was neither cruelty, nor contempt, nor humanity, but some other quality which had hints of these and yet seemed not to possess them.

Their owner now, for a change, occupied himself with some sleight of hand, while the boy and the Korean took out a basket from the bag on the ground. Then he went over to them and the other side, where he could not be seen so easily, and Chiyé turned her head to look at some girls among the spectators near her. Suddenly a loud murmur began to travel round the crowd, the girls gave a little scream and Chiyé could see the same actor coming round the ring. He seemed to be holding his hands before his face — now he paused right in front of her —

In his hands he was holding firmly the fore part of a shining black snake, whose little winking head curved alertly on its neck. Its tiny, slender body passed into his mouth, and was loosely held between his moist, caressing lips about which, as in his eyes, there was now some trace of contempt at the fascinated, gaping horror of the crowd. The long, smooth, tapering tail of the snake protruded several inches from his left nostril, where it flickered and twitched lithely and obscenely.

Somebody exclaimed aloud. Chiyé, panic-stricken, forced her way out of the crowd, tore her sleeve in doing it, ran in and out among the people until she could no longer hear those gasps of incredulity, could no longer see — She shut her eyes, but the sight that had so powerfully caught her imagination was already burnt into her memory. She tried for days to escape it, to forget it, to hide herself from it, but always that face, that mouth, would pursue — an image of pure evil.

She now made her way over to the fortune-tellers' booths, but she was trembling, and had to stand outside for several minutes. She felt hysterical: the excitement of what she had just seen, the prospective excitement of whatever she was just going to hear, were too much for her.

The fortune-teller before whom she at last found herself was an old man with a keen eye, which he never removed from her face except to watch some abracadabra he was arranging all the time with his hands. He condescended to receive from her in advance the sum of two *yen* and fifty *sen*, in return for which he told her a lot of astrological claptrap which she could not understand at all, but said clearly enough that if she worked hard her life would not be a failure, that she was not destined to return to her native place this year, that she must beware of a man with a scar on his right forearm, that her character prevented her from seeing the bad intentions of others because she lacked intuition, and finally that if she followed his advice she might live long. . . . But he had said nothing about marriage. She did not dare to ask him, but blushed vermilion, for his eye was fixed on her, and she was afraid he could read her thoughts.

'. . . and about marriage,' he said, and paused.

She waited, expectant, red, breathless.

He pronounced a long astrological sentence.

'But — but I don't understand,' she said anxiously.

'You will when the time comes,' he said cryptically.

How she longed to put another two *yen* and fifty *sen* into his hand! But her money was nearly finished. Suddenly she had an idea, and blurted out:

'And shall I have a baby?'

The seer narrowed his eyes.

'I see no reason why you shouldn't,' he said emphatically, and looking her up and down.

How delighted she was at this last piece of honourable condensation! What a marvellous prophet! When she left him she bowed as to a prince of philosophers, a celestial sage; and then, as it was late, the servant hurried home to the hotel.

§ 8

Two days later she received a letter. It was her mother's answer to the inquiry about the whereabouts of her aunt. Yes, her mother knew, but at first could not understand why Chiyé had not been told that her aunt's husband had been transferred permanently to Nagoya, and that the whole family were to be there for good. However, word had since come from her aunt that the removal had been so unexpected and hurried that there had been no chance to say good-bye to Chiyé, who was now fortunately safe in the care of her kind friend Mrs. Kikuchi, working well and quite happy, and who would no doubt later be able to pay a visit to Nagoya, etc. Chiyé's mother exhorted her to work hard and be a good girl and then one day she would be able to come back to Omura and see her loving parent. Her dear mother!

Chiyé showed this letter to Tsuya, who was praising the mother and once more abusing the aunt, who had no excuse for going away, she said, without saying good-bye to her ward — when the telephone bell rang, and Chiyé was ordered to present herself immediately at the office. She hurried downstairs, and when she got there, the second son of Mrs. Kikuchi (the eldest was out) kept her waiting a few minutes and then threw her a telegram, saying insolently that it had come the day before, and that she was a fool for not having yet removed it. A telegram? Chiyé rushed upstairs again to share it with Tsuya, who was just hurrying down.

'A telegram?' said Tsuya. 'All right, I'll be back before long, but Mr. Minami has just rung his bell, and I may be delayed —'

Chiyé carried the telegram to the light and opened it. It was from Omura. She read it through slowly three times and then stared at it. Her mother was dead.

The telephone began ringing again and again.

The effects of this news on her mind are better imagined than described, for she was stupefied by it. Whether she was stunned by the blow, whether she was one hardened or insensible to adversity, or whether she was able to put a stoic face on her troubles, it is certain that no ordinary observer could have judged from her appearance. She stood in the middle of the room with the telegram in her hand, and looked out of the window at a sunny patch of roof where on a wooden platform some blue and white clothes were waving in the wind: they had been freshly washed, and there was hardly a cloud in the sky.

All this time the telephone was ringing wildly, and Mrs. Kikuchi, who happened then to be on the same floor, came in to answer it. What was her amazement to see one of the servants actually in the room and ignoring the call! The stout old woman was not quick in her movements, but she was not slow in her understanding, and by the time she had taken the telegram from Chiyé and read it, the bell had stopped ringing. She said nothing and went out.

She would certainly have been on the verge of feeling sorry for the girl had not a doubt at once attacked her as to whether her own proprietary rights were not now perhaps in danger. Possibly some relation of the girl might wish her to return to her native village. Mrs. Kikuchi was a woman of business; she had two sons and a hotel, and she made up her mind to write to Chiyé's aunt and find out how the land lay.

Chiyé's grief was real, and her mind was much occupied, as people's minds often are at such times, in recalling and reconstructing early memories and precious hours and episodes. As her mind got into this habit of retracing forgotten paths it would often come, at odd and unexpected moments, upon some vivid situation whose very existence it seemed to have forgotten, and she was able to escape, to lose herself, to drug herself out of the present into a dream picture whose revival was more poignant than novelty.

These mental conditions were followed, as they often are, by a vague, a very vague craving to express them, and Chiyé, whom a kind of natural modesty never left, so that her tongue was not always willing to utter aloud the thoughts that arose in her — even supposing it could express them — now half wished to write with ink her heart's tears for her kindest and dearest friend and protector, her dead mother. It was a half-wish, and she was less than half-educated, and her character was only half-developed. It went the way of all half-wishes, and nothing was done.

To her friend and fellow-servant she told something of her feelings, and honest Tsuya was as usual a real prop. Tsuya could only console her with hazy hopes, but she meant well, and her sympathy was precious as far as it went — as far as it went, because the sympathies of Tsuya were now deeply involved with Minami, translator of the history of the world. What was more, Minami returned them.

The situation thus produced was piquant, to say the least, and the confidences Tsuya chose to make were the first influences that began to stir Chiyé out of her trance of memory, which nothing in her daily round had been able to do, although quite a time had elapsed since the receipt of the wire. Tsuya did not say much, but what she did say was pointed, and it was quite clear that between her and Minami a feeling of a true and noble intensity had come to exist. But how could it exist? Tsuya was a housemaid and Minami the son of an officer of high rank in the army. They were far too serious for there to be any question of a temporary liaison, and it seemed that things had already gone so far as a tacit admission that marriage alone would be satisfactory. Up to this Chiyé felt sure of her ground, and beyond it she feared to tread. The face of her friend was radiant and resigned, like that of one who endures in the knowledge of a glorious and speedy relief.

Meanwhile Chiyé was a little distracted by various changes in the house. Her baseball-playing students suddenly left, and a gentleman was due to come, who was said to have some connexion with the stage. The flutter below stairs was quite noticeable. It was variously asserted that he was a producer of films, a playwright, an actor, rich, poor, old, young and many other things. One would have hoped him to be, at the very least, youngish, dashing and prosperous. Was he married? Well, either a widower or divorced, it was not quite clear which.

He arrived late one afternoon in February, got out of a taxi, and was shown straight to his room by the proprietress herself, who seemed not only to have been expecting him but also to be acquainted with him. They went upstairs, he laughing shortly and abruptly and she wheezing with unctuous politeness.

Chiyé had the duty of helping him to change his clothes, of showing him to the bath, of bringing his supper and making his bed. She was as dry as she could be in her manner, for Jin (that was his name) spoke to her from the first with a careless and contemptuous familiarity she distrusted. Whenever she looked at him she could see that she feared him, and this gave him a pleasurable thrill of anticipation.

Jin was a man of thirty-nine, lean and sinewy, with hairy hands, a swarthy face, mauve lips and white teeth which always seemed to be grinning. His eyes were untrustworthy. He did not appear to work for a living, but always had money. He wore sometimes Japanese and sometimes foreign clothes, undoubtedly had some connexion both with theatre and cinema, and was reported by Mrs. Kikuchi to be well known as a tennis-player. He went out a great deal, but in spite of this Chiyé soon got to know and like him better. He was fond of a joke, and would scold her about some trifle until she apologized, and then laugh at her. This made her blush, and he enjoyed making her blush. Once or twice he pinched her arm, and once he asked her if she had ever been kissed.

'Chiyé,' said Mrs. Kikuchi, 'please be very polite and obedient to that gentleman, for he is related to me.'

She somehow could not feel angry with him, but did not want his attentions, even though they might only be playful. She talked about him to Tsuya, saying that she must have misjudged him at first. Tsuya answered rather absently, saying that he seemed quite a sincere gentleman.

And then an unexpected thing happened: Minami left the hotel.

'What'll you do now?' said Chiyé.

'I don't know,' said Tsuya. 'But I'm also going away for a time.'

'What! With him?'

'No, no, of course not. My father is ill, and I have to go home for a few days.'

Two days later she went, and until she came back Chiyé had a lot of extra work. Until she came back? She never came back.

## § 9

The story all came out a week later. All the newspapers were full of it, the hotel was buzzing with it and waves of excitement washed through every heart. It was briefly this:

Minami had become infatuated with Tsuya, and had decided to marry her. He accordingly went to his father, General Minami, to get permission, which was sharply and finally refused. He was told that he must be out of his senses to imagine that he could marry a housemaid, and was ordered to leave the Kaméfuku Hotel. The young man had submitted with a good grace to his father's anger, and asked for a few days' delay, which was granted. The father then repented of his anger and spoke kindly, but Minami had already made up his mind to ask Tsuya to elope with him. Tsuya was not the girl to say no. Minami then addressed to his father a letter which he asked a friend to deliver after another week: he said nothing of its contents.

Next he met Tsuya by appointment. She was dressed in her best clothes, and they went to the station and took tickets to one of the smaller lakes near the bottom of Mount Fuji. The train was over-heated, as the season was hardly yet early spring, and the outside air was bitterly cold. They had nothing with them but the clothes they stood up in. Minami, however, carried some money. Late at night they arrived by motor at a small hotel near Lake Kawaguchi. Their appearance excited the curiosity, if not the suspicion of the proprietor. In the first place it was an odd time for visitors. There was a lot of snow on the ground, the hotel was empty and there was absolutely nothing to do. Then this couple had brought no luggage. Madame Minami? She hardly seemed his social equal, though certainly a modest and not inelegant young woman. They spent the night there, and in the morning Minami must have guessed that he and his companion were regarded rather doubtfully, for he decided on their moving to another hotel, farther round the lake shore, where they arrived in time for lunch. In the afternoon they played ping-pong with the family of the proprietor.

The next morning Minami bought a lot of caramels and some soda-water, and announced that they were going out for a walk. His usual manner was consistently eager, and his voice high, so it would have been difficult to detect any additional excitement, had that been present in his manner. It was a cruel, dark morning and looked as if it might snow. However, the young couple went out. They walked a long way, and stopped at last in a lonely thicket of cryptomerias near the edge of the water. At about three in the afternoon Minami went alone to a hamlet about a quarter of a mile from the hotel, a hamlet through which they had passed in the morning. Here, at a little shop, the translator of the history of the world bought some more caramels, with which he returned over the snow under a black sky to his love.

Meanwhile, the letter he had written in Tokyo had been delivered to his father. It contained a polite and respectfully filial intimation that as he was not allowed to marry the girl of whom he had spoken, he proposed not only to leave Tokyo with her, but to leave this life itself. The distracted father at once raised the alarm, and two days later General Minami, the friend who had delivered the letter (everything should be arranged by a go-between), a police-officer and a manservant set out from the little hotel where the pair had spent the second night.

About midday these searchers found the thicket. A large hole had been scooped in the snowy ground and there, half in and half out, lay the naked body of Tsuya. She was dead partly from exposure and partly from poison. Her young skin had hardly lost its freshness, and the perfect contours of her body still suggested softness rather than stiffness, life supple rather than stark lifelessness. Near her lay the empty soda-water bottles and some little folded squares of paper from the caramels. There were traces of a fire, and it seemed that the girl's clothes had been used as fuel: the cold must have been extreme.

While these things were being examined, four dapper young men arrived on the scene, two press photographers and two reporters. The body of Minami was not found till the next day. He had hanged himself on a tree.

The newspapers were full of the story, and especially made much of the fact that the girl was still a virgin. They saw fit to use the word 'platonic'. The public curiosity was thoroughly aroused — for two days. A monthly magazine printed the story in its own way. Two schoolgirls lay in front of a train to show their sympathy. General Minami, the unfortunate father, remembered particularly the filial submission of the younger man to his will, and asserted repeatedly, too late, that if he had known it would lead to this he would never have refused his consent to the union.

Many people were able to realize the strength and sincerity of this double suicide. Some said young Minami had always been impulsive and excitable, and this was his final folly. One of his teaching colleagues thought his death foolish, and said so. Many older people sympathized with the father, and were inclined to condemn the son. The general did not say one word against the dead, and communicated very finely with Tsuya's family. Few of the younger generation were unstirred at the time of hearing, reading and discussing the story: very few remembered it long — a day seldom passes without a tale of suicide, a week seldom without one or two more or less sensational double ones.

Chiyé was thrilled to the marrow. Entranced, enraptured, intoxicated, her sympathy with the dead lovers was so great that she felt a kind of hopeful triumph, a kind of congratulatory enthusiasm. She could not feel grief at the death of her friend, and though she certainly missed her, the sense of loss was itself lost in thankful pride and joy that the love of those two had been consummated: she regarded death as a conclusion quite as complete as bodily union, or as bodily union followed by death. She laid hands on every possible newspaper, cut out every word relating to her friend, and read and re-read these cuttings until she practically knew them by heart. Then by a lucky chance she happened to be at the main door when an intimate friend of Minami's called for information: in the end he told her more than she could tell him. From him, and from other sources, she was able to add quite a lot of detail to what she already knew.

She learnt how the general had already vaguely proposed a certain bride for his son; and of the character of the general, who came from Kagoshima and was rigidly conservative and feudally strict with his family — all the money the son had earned by his lectures, had been paid in, as a matter of course, to the father, and the young man had lived (and died) entirely on the proceeds of his translations. Chiyé was also able to see a brother of the dead girl, from whom she heard indirectly that Tsuya had expressed frankly in letters home the nature of her affection for Minami. Those warm phrases glowed in Chiyé's breast for the remainder of her life. Indeed, the whole affair left her with a lasting emotion, whose untarnished freshness would recur to her years later, purely as a memory, or as a consolation in her own disconsolate hours, or more mysteriously, as a kind of nameless hope.

But it cannot be said that she now entered on a period whose chief reality was memory, either idealized or applied, for present events of the first importance were about to take possession of her life, a rudderless boat driven about, continually and with varying violence, by the intentions — good, bad or indifferent — of other people. In this she took after her mother, who, even before being tamed by misfortune, had always submitted naturally to the control of those who wished to control her. Buddha, that aristocrat, teacheth not the servile to rebel.

§ 10

'Oo! Mr. Jin did give my arm a twist this morning,' Chiyé exclaimed in the servants' bedroom, rubbing that member, and wrinkling her nose with an expression indicative neither of pain nor disgust.

Jin had done more than that, were it only known. He had given a twist to her life-story. He had also made plans to give a party, not for her, but for two intimates. The amiable twisting of her arm had gone with the information that she would have to wait on his guests, a duty she now looked forward to with positive pleasure.

Whatever her first impression of Jin might have been, she had quickly got to like him. He was always cheerful. He paid attention to her. He was familiar with her as no other man had ever been. But she did not let herself go. She did not for one moment try to convince herself that there was going to be anything like a repetition of the feelings Tsuya may have had for Minami. She now liked Jin's attentions, and though she hardly thought it within the bounds of possibility that he would suggest such a thing, she would have no objection to marrying him. She was now in a state of mind and body when marriage would do her good. She kept her head, but she by no means kept Jin at arm's length. On the other hand, she was not going to let him take liberties. She continued to play the fish very prettily. He was certainly hooked, and if she could help it he was neither going to get away nor be landed just yet.

'The two gentlemen I am expecting,' said he, 'are my intimate friends, and I want to give them a good supper. I was going to call in geishas, just to make things cheerful, but on second thoughts I won't. For one thing it's expensive, and for another there's no need. It's only to be a friendly little gathering. So you'd better dress yourself up as well as you can, and be as bright as possible. It's a pity you're such an ugly little thing—'

He flipped her ear.

'Oh, but yesterday you said I was a pretty little thing.'

'I was only joking, fool. Don't forget to have the *saké* properly warmed. I've already told Mrs. Kikuchi about the dinner.'

He speaks to me, she thought, going downstairs, just as if I was his wife. Mrs. Kikuchi also spoke to her about the coming evening, and advised her to smarten herself up and do her best: it was a good chance for her to show how clever she could be at waiting on the gentlemen, and pleasing them.

'Try to be bright,' said the old dame, 'and understand what the gentlemen say. Even if you don't, you must make them think you do, so mind you laugh at all their jokes. Nothing spoils a dinner so much as a dull waitress. Try to anticipate their wishes, and when they ask for anything get it as quickly as you can. Never ask them to repeat their orders, and don't keep them waiting. If they get a little tipsy, that won't hurt you, so don't worry. Of course they will expect you to drink with them, but you must just pretend — a sip here and a sip there — you understand? And don't forget to show plainly that you admire them. Men are very easily made fools of. Flatter them a bit, you see?'

The mistress actually nudged the servant, and smiled ponderously instead of winking. Chiyé had never really been able to dislike her, and now this kind and confidential manner made the girl's heart go out to her. This advice was so motherly and yet so sisterly in tone. At that instant they were as closely leagued as a pair of suffragettes. People are often as united by a common sex as by a common enemy.

Chiyé, feeling somehow that this was a critical evening, took great pains with her appearance. The result was good. Her hands were red, coarse and pudgy, and her wrists somewhat thick and strong, but her body was now at its best. She was not ungraceful in her movements, especially since the death of Tsuya. Her feet were small; she walked with small, simpering steps, the toes too much turned in; and occasionally, as she knelt or rose, an inch of pink skin appeared above her snow-white *tabi*. Her clothes were of fine flowered silk of several thicknesses, and the sleeves, as they swayed, showed the tantalizing edge of a bright red lining. Her neck, thickly daubed with liquid powder, supported a head which had greatly improved since the arrival of the awkward bumpkin girl from Omura, and which was crowned with a glossy black, perfumed coiffure decorated with gaudy pins. When she looked in the glass her black eyes sparkled in her pretty face with the quickness of a bird on a blossoming bough. Her eyebrows, by nature a little too heavy, had been shaved into a pair of thin blue-black curves like two quick strokes of a fine squirrel's-hair brush. Her mouth was ready to smile moistly. Excited by pleasure, a warmth rose to her cheeks. Her appearance caused surprise even among her everyday associates. There are such moments of transfiguration in every woman's life.

Jin was greatly struck when she first came into the room bringing trays with another maid, but as he was in the midst of conversation with his guests he made no comment, and affected not to notice her. When she came back alone the second time to wait, he spoke banteringly to her, and his guests began to take notice.

One of them, no longer young, tried, by the cultivation of a boisterous manner, to give an impression of his still having a young heart. The other had lately returned from China, and patriotic delight at his homecoming made him thirsty and talkative. In his cups he became garrulous, but nobody at first took much notice of him. Chiyé was kneeling between the other two.

When the old man tried to make her drink she showed a coy confusion of nature and art, and had to answer all sorts of pleasantries, not all of the most refined. The gentlemen were so free with her that she found no difficulty in finding repartees to match their sallies.

All at once there came up from the street the sound of the night-watchman's drum and his chanted warning of fire:

'*Shinanomachi, Shiocho!*'

The returned exile from China had now got on to his reminiscences, while the others steadily gorged and sipped their warm rice-wine. He was no lover of the Chinese, he declared, a cruel, dishonest and dirty race who ought to be the servants of the Japanese.

Suddenly, through and above the drunken laughter, the watchman's drum sounded much nearer, and his voice cried sadly and loudly, as if in the room:

'*Shinanomachi, Shiocho!*'

'I tell you,' shouted the speaker, red in the face, 'the Chinese don't understand the value of civilization!'

'If the cursed Americans were not so sentimental,' cried the old man, 'we could punish all the Chinese, and make slaves of them, and shoot every one of them down, the dogs!'

Chiyé half-consciously waited for the watchman's drum and drone again. It came, already less loud, and long-drawn-out, dying away in the distance, more like a voice of hope forsaken than of present danger:

'*Shinanomachi, Shiocho!*'

'A fire somewhere,' said Jin absently.

'Cruelty?' exclaimed the man from China. 'You! you don't know what cruelty means. They'd tear the skin off your face. I've seen two soldiers spend an hour pulling a young girl in half, and enjoy doing it.'

And he proceeded to tell them a story he could not have told sober. Only that morning, as a matter of fact, he had, in a crowded room, been heatedly defending the Chinese against every accusation, including this one and others much more trifling: truth by no means always lies in wine.

Chiyé alone was now sober, and into her mind there rushed the memory of that Chinaman she had seen at Asakusa, the one with the snake in his mouth, and she turned her head and hid her face in her sleeve. Her skin was creeping with horror.

'What! what's the matter?' cried Jin. 'Here, let's make her drink —'

And he caught her round the middle, pinioned her arms, twisted her backwards and called to the others to make her drink. One picked up a cup, but the old man grabbed a porcelain *saké*-flask and forced its mouth into hers. The china gritted against her teeth. She struggled and vainly shook her head as the warm liquid kept on jetting into her throat and up her nose, until she sputtered and choked.

At this moment one of the paper doors was slid back, and anybody noticing that could also have made out dimly in the dark passage the large kneeling bulk of a woman in a greyish-white apron. However, nobody in the room saw Mrs. Kikuchi, who had just looked in to see how things were going, and who now leaned forward with a slow cow-like movement, so that her head and massive bust were in the room. On her face she wore (she could afford to wear it) an almost good-humoured, an urbane expression of easy tolerance, and what practically came to a satis-fied smile, and then withdrew, sliding-to once more the sibilant screen.

Chiyé was released to fetch more *saké*, and the gentleman from China, red in the face, began to snooze. The old man talked heartily, and Jin felt very cheerful; but under his gaiety there was all the time a vague lurking anticipation, which found some satis-faction in an increasing wish to get rid of his guests. Perhaps this early spring night helped to cause the restlessness in his veins. When Chiyé came back he asked her the time.

'What, is it so late?' exclaimed the older man. '*Oi!*' And he began to try and wake his companion.

'Drink,' said Jin.

They drank, getting more and more noisy. Jin suddenly turned to Chiyé and said rapidly in a low voice:

'Go and order a taxi.'

She did not come back till the taxi had arrived, and then announced that it was at the door.

'Well, I don't want you to go,' said Jin, 'but your car's waiting at the entrance.'

'What? I never ordered a car,' said the old man.

'Of course you did,' said Jin. 'Are you so far gone that you've forgotten?' He turned to Chiyé for confirmation: 'Didn't you hear him?'

'Oh, yes, that was why I went to order it,' said she.

'Then tell it to go away, you wench,' said the old man angrily.

'You'll have to pay a lot if you keep it waiting,' said Jin. And so, bickering and protesting, the two guests were at last piloted downstairs and bundled into the taxi. It was about two o'clock in the morning.

Jin came back to his room and stretched himself on the floor. When Chiyé appeared he ordered her to take away the things and lay out the bed.

'But leave the *saké*,' he said, refilling his cup. 'And bring another bottle.'

She cleared away, and then opened the cupboard and drew out the mattress. He let her make the bed, and just as she was finishing, stepped behind her, threw his arm round her neck and tripped her up. They both fell on the mats. She gave a cry of surprise, but made no resistance.

'Drink some more,' he said, 'come on.'

He made her finish the last flaskful with him, cup for cup. She hardly knew what she was doing. Her windpipe was on fire, and her eyes watering.

'Now I must go,' she said, trying to stand up.

'No, no,' he said several times, with extraordinary and unnecessary emphasis. 'No, no. There is no need to go. Absolutely no need.'

They rolled over together on the floor. Suddenly she was afraid, and struggled to get up. He thrust his hand into her coiffure, which fell half apart, and one long coil of hair broke loose and unrolled almost to her knees. Against the smooth silk it looked like a rapturous black cascade in a drunken dream.

'Help me to bed,' he said, 'before you go.'

She helped him out of his clothes, standing behind him, and putting his scanty night kimono over his shoulders. She always remembered afterwards his long straight back, wide at the shoulders, narrow at the waist, muscular and golden. He tied his girdle and then turned, his face purplish white, and fondled her ear. Suddenly he threw her down, kicking, on the bed, and before she could get up had switched off the light.

'No, no, no,' she said, trying to get away, but he at once caught her again, and somehow she could not, she did not want to, she did not attempt to resist.

§ 11

She lay with him again the next night. She became his mistress. And there were no regrets. Looking back, she saw Minami and Tsuya, their young arms interlaced for a pillow. Looking forward, she considered the possibility of a home and a child. She liked Jin. She was happy.

He, however, had not the slightest intention of continuing to live with her for more than a short time. She clung to him with such faithfulness that he was in two minds what to let her think. But in truth she neither ventured to trust nor to doubt him. She was contented with the present, not absolutely content, but happier than she seemed to have been before, and happy in a new way which seemed somehow old and familiar. Jin could not make up his mind whether to promise a liaison he did not intend to continue or whether simply to let things drift and leave her guessing. He took the latter course, but she never attempted to guess, leaving everything to him, less from confidence than from force of circumstances. And suddenly he blurted out one day as if he were joking:

'Of course you've never imagined that I should continue to live with you?'

And laughed.

She looked at him without answering. There was no reproach in her gaze, no surprise. It was impossible for him to know what she really felt. And he did not greatly care.

Indeed, she felt neither surprised nor reproachful, worked as usual, but with a deep inward calm, a physical balance, that she had never known before. She continued to serve Jin, and he gave her presents, not valuable ones. Everybody knew that she lived with him and nobody made a fuss. When he was out or when she was alone or not working she sometimes picked up a newspaper. It gave her a unique pleasure, with its unexpectedness and sensational appeals to her imagination. She happened one day to see a loose sheet of the morning paper lying in the kitchen where the cook had put it down, and as she was just going up to her room picked it up and took it with her. There was at the bottom of the page, just above some advertisements, a short paragraph which cut her to the heart so that she never forgot it. It left, one might say, a scar on her memory. Yet the journalists could not have thought it important, or they would not have put it down there. Perhaps they wanted too much space that day for the arrival in Japan of the executive committee of the Pan-Pacific Peaceful Penetration Push from America.

In a poor suburb of Tokyo, said the paper, a child of three had been murdered. The circumstances were these. Two married women lived next door to each other. One was the mother of the child; the other, older, was barren. The barren one had become obsessed with her misfortune; unbalanced; until, maddened by that mother-and-child happiness always under her eyes, she had, in a paroxysm of suffering, put an end to it. She had confessed everything quite openly. That was all.

Into Chiyé's mind the effect of this story, though powerful, worked its way slowly. Eventually, it diverted her attention from the union with Jin, which still went on, to the hopes of becoming a mother; and with these hopes she was now entirely taken up. It was not that the two states of feeling were different things — there was only one flood of emotion: it had now set all in one direction. The first rare freshness and activity of her body, followed by some more disturbing sensations, made her pretty sure that what she most desired would happen, and she passed busy days in expectant peace. The time of waiting was then broken by two important events.

Late on a dark, steamy, rainy midsummer afternoon she returned from an errand and had hardly folded her umbrella when one of the maids said to her:

'You didn't tell me that Mr. Jin was leaving this afternoon: I went to his room to prepare tea, and found that he had already left —'

'No, I didn't, I'm sorry,' said Chiyé in an expressionless voice. Already left! She was taken completely unawares by this news. Somehow the fact that he had gone (she had half supposed he would go soon) did not matter to her so much as the fact that he had gone without saying good-bye to her. People glanced sideways at her to see how she liked being deserted, but there was no sign as to how she took it. A few days later she heard from Jin, and it was a nice letter. He kindly enclosed some money, but as she was now drawing a small regular wage from Mrs. Kikuchi, this tribute, or quittance-money, was not absolutely needed.

The shock of his going away she only felt in its entirety long afterwards. This was so often the way with her — things happened to her quickly, and not always unexpectedly, and she could not take them all in at once. Slowly the significance of facts, whose meaning she ought to have realized at the time of their occurrence, would bear gradually in on her; as a bank of clouds, at first ranged apparently immovably on the horizon, will soon, slowly toppling, advance, forced forward by some large wind too high up for humanity to feel, and, preceded by a few scarfy and dissolving forerunners, will spread, and darken, and over-spread the whole mild sky. The sky may be hidden for weeks, but the clouds do not last, continually changing their forms. Afterwards the sky is serener than ever.

She was not only slow to realize, but, once having realized, quick to forget or overlook (not necessarily to forgive) where most people would bear active remembrance or malice. Her anger, if it could be called that, did not last. And just at the moment when she had more or less forgotten things they had a way of forcing themselves back on her. It was a long time, for instance, since she had thought much about her aunt, but now who should walk into the Kaméfuku Hotel but that very woman! — the same as ever, only a little more so than usual.

In the same room, the office, where they had once sat together before, the three women, all bowing and smiling and getting politer and politer every minute, were once more assembled. In the background sat the younger son of Mrs. Kikuchi at his tele-phone and ledger: her elder son was not there, for he was nearly always out. This meeting was by no means merely formal. The aunt and niece were genuinely glad to see each other. Chiyé couldn't help sniffing and blubbering in her sleeve. Crocodile tears? Why should they be? She was not a person to feign emotion. That her aunt had sold her into her present life did not now sway her mind: the far-eastern character, with its elaborate traditional machinery of revenge, seems, whether from fatalism or inertia, often to know better how to forgive than the Christian character, whose business is supposed to be the turning of the other cheek. But Chiyé was soon filled with curiosity to know what her aunt had come for. Mrs. Kikuchi on this occasion was positively motherly, and looked at Chiyé almost with pride. As for the aunt, her affability was quite remarkable. After a barrage of platitudinous compliments had been created, she came down to business.

Now it had happened that a distant relation, some kind of cousin, had come to her from Omura with an offer to adopt Chiyé and eventually to arrange for her marriage and safeguard her future, at the same time asking the aunt her opinion, and suggesting that she should go to Tokyo and put the matter to Chiyé. The aunt had replied that Chiyé was in service, and could hardly be released without a considerable payment. This upset the cousin a little, but he did not yet withdraw his offer. Wishing to hear more details, he urged the aunt to go to Tokyo, which she agreed to do.

Her scheme was to see Mrs. Kikuchi and the girl together and to tell Chiyé at once of the cousin's offer: naturally thinking that the girl would be eager to go back to her native village, and that Mrs. Kikuchi, in order to avoid losing a good servant, might privately advance something to prevent it. This ingenious plan did not work out in practice exactly as she had foreseen. In the first place, Chiyé now surprised her very much by expressing very little wish to return to Omura! Mrs. Kikuchi had a twinkle in her eye. Her second son, with his mouth open, stared vacantly at the group. The puzzled aunt began to persuade. Chiyé wriggled her shoulders awkwardly. Mrs. Kikuchi said that the girl was very happy where she was, but that she should not attempt to try and force her to stay if she really wanted to go; — conquer by yielding! — however, as the girl was used to her work and now able to earn wages, no doubt she would be more prudent to stay where she was. The aunt, exasperated, smiled more winningly than ever; she positively beamed with rage. As she was again expecting an addition to her family, a small financial contribution to the home would have been welcome, especially as she had had the expense of coming to Tokyo. She did not know what to do. If she could see the girl alone, possibly she could persuade her, but obviously Mrs. Kikuchi would prevent that.

While she was hesitating she was lost, for the voice of one of the maids was repeatedly calling down the passage for Chiyé, who at once rose, bowing, and went out of the room. The subsequent conversation between the other two convinced the aunt that her attempt was hopeless, and that the only possible courses left to her were either to write to Chiyé and persuade her, or else to get the cousin to come to Tokyo, which might perhaps induce Mrs. Kikuchi to seek her as an ally in making the girl stay. By the time Chiyé returned to the room, her aunt had decided to leave, and after a lot of ceremonious leave-taking the visitor was bowed out. Mrs. Kikuchi, after this, could hardly have been more maternal in her manner.

The root of the matter was Chiyé's indifference. This requires little analysis, for she was now a person of one idea only, beyond which she cared for nothing. And it was not the idea that she was going to have a child.

§ 12

The idea which now possessed her was a terrible one. It was, that perhaps after all she was not going to have a child. To most people, no doubt, in such a position as hers, this would be cause for thankfulness, a matter of profound relief. But she was not most people. She was Hara Chiyé. She wanted one thing in the world, and have it she must. As for Omura — her aunt — Jin — the future — they were shadows in a dream.

She was alone, and she could not stand it any longer. If Jin had married her, she would not have been much less alone, for her loneliness was a matter of the deepest feelings in her whole

173

existence. She was utterly alone: only one comforter could come to her out of the world, and that comforter must come out of herself. She had not yet by any means given up her present hope. She only had the suspicion that she might be deceiving herself. She counted on her fingers the months since Jin had left her.

Once or twice a week she was allowed to go out for a bath. The bath-house was in the next street but one, and she usually got there when it was rather crowded. This afternoon, however, about a fortnight after her aunt's visit, the season being late summer, she got out much earlier than usual, and found only two people in the bath, married women of middle age, deep in conversation, a conversation that had begun somewhat obstetrically. They seemed to have plenty of leisure, for after twenty minutes they showed no sign of departure, while one or two other people came and went. One of the pair sat on the edge and dandled her stubby legs in the water, where they appeared curiously fore-shortened. The other sat on the bottom with only her head sticking out of the water, her hair screwed up in a top-knot, and never stopped talking for an instant. Chiyé far outstayed her usual time to listen to them.

'Where do you say it is?' asked one.

'At the Temmonji temple in Koïshikawa,' said the other, 'just over there — you know? The stone in question is on the right as you go in at the south gate, the main gate. Behind some trees, a cherry tree, I think, and some dark bushes.'

'Ah, so.'

'Quite a tall stone, six or seven feet high. They say it has been successful in a great number of cases.'

'Yes, I've heard that. They say one can see somebody there almost every day.'

'Oh, yes. One should go in the evening. That's the best time, they say.'

'And the wife of —'

'Yes, I was going to tell you. The wife of Mr. Hoshiai had

174

been to doctors, priests, fortune-tellers and all such people. She
was quite in despair, for she had already been married six years.
Then she prayed at this stone only three or four times — just
came in the evening, you know, and prayed — and now she has
a fine boy more than three months old.'

'Wonderful!'

'A very old stone. It is said to date from the time of Genroku,
but I hardly believe it can be as old as that.'

The speaker, dripping, clambered out of the water; so that
Chiyé suddenly realized how long she herself had been sitting
there, and hurriedly got out and dressed. As she came out in the
street her head felt quite fuddled with steam, but her heart beat
quickly as she at once began to think of a plan to visit the temple
of Temmonji in Koïshikawa.

How peaceful the streets were as she went back! Children
were playing, old men sat smoking and chatting at the open shop
fronts, and young women with babies on their backs could be
seen moving in the lighted interiors of the houses. At the corner
the policeman sat in his little kiosk with a red lamp, doing nothing. Arm-in-arm, some idle students in thin *yukata* clattered
along on high clogs. There was a smell of cooking, intermingled
with stray whiffs of scent and sewage. At a fishmonger's, the
electric shone wetly on the various glistening corpses of the fish,
all of whose noses were pointing in the same direction, and over
them a loud-speaker coughed from its black vulcanite throat a
lecture on English grammar. The boy from the macaroni shop
hurried past on his bicycle, pedalling frenziedly with his fat legs
in white tights, and balancing on one hand a lacquered tray laden
with bowls of hot, savoury food. A blind masseur tapped his
way along slowly, blowing now and then a plaintive whistle,
over against which could be heard the tinny whining of a mouthorgan.

An active young woman with a towel in her hand, clothes like
a servant's, and a slightly dishevelled appearance, turned down a

narrow and smelly by-street towards the Kaméfuku Hotel. She was not walking quickly, but there was an intent expression on her face, because above and between her eyes her smooth girlish forehead had a tiny pucker: it could hardly be called a frown. It was not dark yet, for the sky was perfectly clear, with a reflected glow as if turquoise-colour should become transparent. In luminous air floated a far and pinkish new moon, and almost immediately, no doubt, it would become possible to notice here and there the sparkle of a star. At the sky, however, that playground of everlasting change, Chiyé did not happen to look up. As she passed the kitchen window of the hotel she could hear the sizzling sound of frying.

She very soon contrived a chance to pay an evening visit to the Temmonji. She walked there in less than half an hour, entered the gate, and found everything as the woman had said. An old scarred stone, mossy, and roughly cylindrical in shape, with a round top, stood behind a small shrubbery. In the dusky shadows it had an ancient, awful secrecy, an almost godlike presence. Chiyé looked hastily round. There was nobody much about, though she could hear some footsteps on a flagged path, and distant motors and trams.

Before the monolith were one or two stone tablets with inscriptions, a few cheap sacred pictures damaged by the weather, a bamboo vase with a fresh spray of leaves, a small stone trough in which were the remains of fine powdery ash, a pile of small stones and a money box. Chiyé opened her left hand, and from its sweaty palm picked, with the forefinger and thumb of her right, two coins, which she dropped into this box; and then, groping with her right hand inside the flap of her left sleeve, drew forth a small pebble, which she added to the pile before her. Her only regret was that she had no incense to burn. She bowed her head, clapped her hands together inaudibly and prayed for a baby.

She prayed earnestly for some time, her eyes tight shut, and occasionally softly clapped, palm to palm again, her hot house-maid hands. At last she opened her eyes and bowed to that dark image. Turning to go, she saw that the overhanging boughs of a cherry tree near by were all tagged and knotted with paper prayers. And a great peace came on her, as if some responsibility, some load, some fear, had been taken from her. She may not have had the faith of certain conviction, but she was wonderfully soothed. Lying in bed that night, she snuggled down into the clothes and hugged her knees against her plump country breasts in a transport of nameless and unreasonable ecstasy.

This feeling of exaltation did not soon wear off. It was as if she shared some delightful secret with that wise and ancient pillar, whose inanimate silence was so full of divine wisdom. And when a letter came from her aunt, urging her to leave Tokyo, she only read it once and then thrust it away somewhere and forgot all about it. A month produced none of the desired symptoms, so she went to worship again.

This time she stopped in the twilight at a stall near the entrance of Temmonji to buy the devotional burning sticks she forgot before. As she came through the trees towards the shadowy corner of the temple compound, the figure of a young woman, elegantly dressed, and hiding her face in a lacy wrap, came from the direction of the stone and hurried past her, leaving in the air a trail of scent. Chiyé turned curiously to watch her; the figure went towards the great entrance gate, passed through and went down the steps. Chiyé moved across to the left and looked over the wall just in time to see the elusive and expensive visitor getting into a very large motor at the kerb. A servant in uniform closed the door, bowed and got in beside the driver. The headlights were suddenly switched on, the long car turned and glided away like a shadow after its swiftly travelling projection of white light.

Chiyé wonderingly approached her god. Before him was a spark at the tip of a still-burning joss-stick, from which a single thread of blue sweet smoke streamed waveringly upwards in the tranquil evening air. Still burning? So the rich also came to this place, the young wives of millionaires! It was quite enough to confirm her faith in the value of her prayers.

But to those prayers the stone returned a stony answer. She had confided to it her most intensely real, her most human feelings. She had prayed to it, and yet she never knew that it was simply a phallus. If she had known, she could have prayed to it no more fervently. When the extreme limit of the possible period of gestation was passed, she gave up hope, but still not absolutely.

§ 13

A second letter came from her aunt, blaming her for not answering the first, and repeating the same urgent advice. Chiyé wrote back a short and polite note saying she did not want to leave Tokyo; but she never made the slightest proper attempt to analyse her feelings until long after the letter had been posted. And then, when the idea of going back to Omura did suggest itself to her, somehow she always pushed it into the back of her mind, with the result that there the idea of her native place gradually underwent, after long preparation, a curious sublimation.

For example, once when she was very young, she happened, playing at noon in early summer with others of her own age, to come unexpectedly, behind a little farm surrounded with camphor trees, upon a whole field full of salmon-pink peonies. They had been planted by the owner simply for his pleasure, but going back another year to look at them she found he had had to convert the land into a paddy-field, for he was short of money, and Japan was short of Japanese rice. He never planted peonies again, but in her mind the field of quivering, globular, full-orbed strong, delicate, flesh-coloured flowers glowed on always in the rays of an ever-bright meridian sun. The shiny petals, seemingly

178

of the texture of strong silk, could be easily crushed with the fingers or slit with the nails, but the petals in her memory were indestructible.

In the Omura of her mind there was a field of peonies; in the Omura to which her body was asked to return there was only a muddy rice-field. This contrast did not only appear in vegetable affairs, it came in everywhere, all along the line. The distance between the two Omuras was always increasing, the one gleaming in a tender haze; the other bare as bones. In one her mother still lived; in one her mother was dead. One was the scene of old wholehearted hopes whose vagueness made them dearer, the Omura of her childhood; the other exhaled a faint whiff of disillusion, this Omura she could not go back to. Her mind had kept much of its childish quality, so let it not be supposed that she carefully reasoned out and balanced things for herself. As for saying to herself that if she went back her prospects would be better than if she stayed — she would never have dared to say such a thing, even had she been capable of saying it. There was nothing and nobody to push or drag her away, and so she stayed.

She had completely forgotten how her mother had said it was 'a piece of good luck' for her to go to Tokyo. Had she remembered, she would have agreed whole-heartedly. She would have said yes, she considered she was lucky to be in Tokyo still, she was lucky to be something more than a mere country girl. She regretted nothing, was neither particularly elated nor depressed, and hoped for she knew not what. How many people are in the same boat! She became friendlier with the other servants, and a busy gossip, though not a malicious one. She knew all that was to be known of the ins and outs of the affairs of everybody in the hotel and many people outside it. Every newspaper she set eyes on she set hands on, and gradually formed a bulky collection of cuttings (some of the earlier ones, including the well-worn accounts of the double death of Minami and Tsuya, were already yellowing with age) which she kept in a large cardboard box covered with red satin. In the same box there was a small doll.

She was given much of the marketing to do, and soon got familiar with the numerous tradesmen at the back door, the cheeky ones, the servile ones and the domineering ones. She proved herself a bargainer with the makings of a good housewife. Sometimes at her work, washing a floor, for instance, or hanging out blue-and-white clothes to dry on the breezy platform on the roof, or late at night just before undressing, she would indulge herself in a little pleasant melancholy: she would even think of going back to Omura. Then she could be heard crooning some sentimental folksong, like the *Sadobushi* which she had picked up somewhere:

> Towards Sado Island, towards Sado Island,
> Inclined trees and grasses;
> There's a dreamy and a happy land.

It is a kind of *Swanee River*, and she sang it in a tiny, far-away voice, not melodious at all, but so thin and shrill that it was almost like an insect's.

Sometimes when she was not aware of it the great body of Mrs. Kikuchi would pause at the top of the stairs, or at a door or window to watch her or listen to her for a moment at her work. Then both women, one unconscious of the other's presence, might be smiling secretly to themselves.

Hara Chiyé is still working at the Kaméfuku Hotel. She now fancies herself in love with the butcher's young man who comes twice a day to the back door. They are, indeed, likely to marry soon. If they do, Chiyé will of course hope for a child. Why not? Don't you remember? — That fortune-teller she went to said there was no reason why she should not have a child.

# THE PORTRAIT OF AN EMPEROR

ONE summer's day in the first quarter of the present century Yoshida Shojiro was appointed principal of a country school in the prefecture of F——. He was nearly forty, though he felt much younger, especially on that day. He regarded this appointment as an important step in his career. But still it was merely a step, for he was not without ambition. His father, a silk merchant, had left a flourishing business and three sons, two of whom had continued to trade with considerable success. Yoshida was often a little galled by the knowledge that his two brothers secretly despised him for his profession if not for his comparative poverty, and also by being aware that it was generally said of him that he ought to have been a business man. The fact is, he looked like and seemed to have the character of a business man, and knew it. He hoped to become in time a conspicuous official with a post in the Mombusho, or the director of a high school, or even an assistant professor in a university: once, but only once, in a dream, he saw himself actually as Minister of Education, with a telephone at his elbow: he unhooked the receiver and was just telling some secretary that, yes, if it could be fitted in, he would consent to lay the foundation stone on Thursday week — when the alarm clock woke him up. He earnestly believed that about an official of rank there is something more sacred, a more radiant aura, than there is about even a millionaire. This belief kept him going. It pulled him over those rare occasional moments of ennui, of doubt, of sick headache which are apt to occur even in the best-regulated officials. And so, when he was telling somebody about some clever thing he had done, he could afford, as an official, to say jokingly, 'You see, I am

quite clever at business. I ought to have been a business man.'
And having said this he would laugh or titter nervously.

This laugh was quite characteristic out of school hours, and
prevailed in all kinds of conversations, even serious ones. When
he laughed his eyes almost closed, and behind the projecting
teeth and shaking smile his quick calculating brain could do its
work. For he certainly had a quick, shrewd brain. It would be
quite unfair to say he deliberately used his cheerfulness as a mask.
It was simply a nervous laugh, which he naturally did nothing
to suppress, because he knew that to succeed one must be popular,
to be popular one must be polite, to be polite one must be cheerful. Of course, on official occasions he preserved the becoming
dignity. Also, he never smiled to his wife. She was a model
Japanese wife, silent, hard-working, obedient, trusting and trust-
worthy, a good mother and housekeeper, with some natural and
some acquired tact and good sense; in fact, a good, simple woman
altogether, and quite pleasant looking.

Another peculiar occasion for the smile to fade was when anybody happened to say something which might possibly, con-
ceivably, be interpreted in a sense at all adverse. For example, if
one said, 'Perhaps your little son is tired after his long walk?' or
'Don't you think it's rather cold weather for this time of year?'
he would immediately appear as though he thought one were
trying to 'get at' him—almost as if the fatigue of the infant
might be construed as a reproach to the virility of the parent,
or as if a caprice of the weather involved some personal responsibility. The answer to such polite conventional fatuities would
always be a shock and a contradictory 'No, no, no, not at all,' in
which there was no smile, but a quick touch of righteous indignation. In sum, one couldn't help feeling sorry for the nervous
weakness of the man. The sight of a man unable to find strength
in himself and trying to arm himself with authority is far too
common to provoke surprise.

Yoshida's management of the school is best hinted at by

quoting his retort to a subordinate, who had said, 'As a teacher, I thought it was right for me to —'

'You must always remember,' Yoshida impressed on him, 'that your first duty is not to be a good teacher, but a good official.'

The recipient of this reproof was a meek and spectacled young man who sometimes wrote poemlets about autumn dew and the shadows of dragon-flies' voices: he afterwards went away and of course never came to any good.

For the first year or two everything went smoothly enough. The principal was not popular, but he was not unpopular: he was accepted. His nickname was Mezamashi, which means alarm-clock. He made up for his strictness in school by resolute geniality outside it, and was more pleasing to his superiors than to those below him. Almost his only anxieties during those first years were the visits of inspectors and the occasional weakness of examination candidates, but these feelings were modified by a casual hint that intimated a possibility that he might after a year or two be recommended for promotion.

His family life was perfectly satisfactory. His wife was obedient and well-behaved, and without any obtrusiveness took a real interest in his career and in such details of the everyday routine as he chose to confide to her. She was proud of his ambition, and showed her pride by means of respectful sympathy. They had two dear little children, and everything in the garden was lovely.

Yoshida received a letter to say that on a certain day in about three months' time he might expect a special official messenger carrying a copy of that photograph of the Emperor which was just being issued to every school, college and university in the country, and advising him to prepare suitable ceremonies for its reception: the letter concluded by asking whether he had a proper place ready to house the photograph permanently.

From the moment when Yoshida read this letter a change began in him. Probably his wife was the first to notice it, though of course she said nothing to anybody and very little to herself. But she couldn't help wondering why he was getting so fussy about the reception of the Imperial photograph. Not that she failed to recognize its importance. In pure, unquestioning loyalty she was an example. One might have seen her, for instance, on public holidays, hanging out the national flag, a red spot on a white ground, and the reverence of her fingers and the radiance of her face had something almost hypnotic about them. But her gentle, cow-like placidity simply could not understand fussiness. As she had been educated to put up with everything, she said nothing.

The first thing Yoshida decided was to build a special little kiosk or shrine of reinforced *konkurito* to hold the precious gift. The tiny building should have no windows, and one double folding door to be opened only on occasions of national importance. But it must be very strong, rainproof, fireproof, burglarproof, foolproof and earthquakeproof. The school was in funds, so the work was at once sanctioned by authority. This was the only school in that part of the country which was to have the privilege of providing such exceptional security for the Imperial gift. Such photographs had usually been kept in a safe part of the main building.

There is no doubt that the authorities were favourably impressed, and there is no doubt that if Yoshida made the plan partly to impress them, he also did it from motives of genuine duty, loyalty and enthusiasm. He arranged a ceremony for the laying of the foundation according to Shinto rites and he himself was present in a frock-coat, striped trousers, a very high collar and black satin tie. As it was very hot, the month being June, he perspired freely, particularly after making his speech. But fortunately in the photographs which he had caused to be taken nothing like that was really obvious: in them his face seemed to shine with nothing but dutiful satisfaction. Naturally the whole school was present at this function.

While the building of the kiosk, or shrine, was going on, the principal came every day, and usually twice daily, to watch. He not only watched, he made inquiries, assertions, suggestions and positive contradictions, so that the workmen, patient, cheerful, stolid country fellows, became piqued. They said nothing to him. Perhaps it was just as well he did not know what they were saying to one another. One of them became so nettled that he ventured to oppose some trifling, but, as it seemed to him, unpractical order of Yoshida's with a polite and reasonable refusal. Yoshida lost his head, said he regarded this as an act of open rebellion against authority, dismissed the workman and communicated his name to the police, suggesting that an eye ought to be kept on him, as he was quite likely to stop at nothing short of lese-majesty. The police filed his name and kept an eye on him. Yoshida gave an account of everything to his wife as usual, and she, as usual, had not the slightest doubt that he had done perfectly right, and told him so.

Just before the concrete shrine was finished, an inspector arrived and officially inspected it. He congratulated the principal, who thereupon told him the whole history of the little structure, its virtues, and what it had cost and how long it had taken and how he himself had supervised its daily progress, and how, why and when the workman had been dismissed, etc. The inspector at first listened carefully and assented affably, but later he became a trifle bewildered by the principal's enthusiasm, and half mesmerized by the principal's vivacious unceasing laugh. Yoshida was confident that everything he had said to the inspector would be retold at headquarters. He repeated every word to his wife. She had no doubt that he was perfectly right, and her eager attention never waned, but at the end she did venture to hazard that he ought not to worry so much, as he was looking quite thin since the end of the summer. He gave her such a look for her presumption that she never again dared to offer him a word of advice. After all, she told herself, he was always right, and there could be no doubt that his zeal would eventually be rewarded with promotion — it was time for her to wash the baby.

Some time elapsed between the completion of the building and the arrival of the photograph, and others besides his wife began to notice the principal's excessive preoccupations. He was thirsty for congratulations, easily agitated about trifles, and the smallest school children had begun to feel nervous of him. It was found necessary to combine the two ceremonies of reception and installation, and this was a great disappointment to him.

When the great day came he got out of bed long before dawn to look at the sky. It was the first day since his marriage that he had got up before his wife. It turned out splendid autumn weather, and everything went off wonderfully well. Of course it was a whole holiday, there were flags and a band, local personages arrived in Ford cars, there were photographers, speeches, reporters — only a country affair, but very satisfying. All the teachers, children and spectators filed before the open shrine and bowed profoundly to the photograph dimly seen inside.

His wife shared his pride and pleasure. At midday, however, when the very bright hot sunshine made his black frock-coat look as grey as ashes, she had noticed that he was beginning to go bald. She said nothing, having no doubt that he was doing the right thing in losing his hair, for he had turned forty. Now that all this concern about the photograph had been duly arranged, she hoped he would settle back again into the usual routine. But in this she was somewhat disappointed, for although in a way he had certainly become calmer, a fundamental change seemed to have come into him lately. She could not understand his fussiness and increasing nervousness, and would have liked him to see a doctor. She said nothing, but showed this much of her thoughts in a letter to her sister in Osaka — 'He seems to worry about trifles,' she wrote, 'but perhaps will become calmer.'

He had now formed the habit of going every morning, fussily, on his way to school, to inspect the little shrine. In the town people commented on his devotion to duty, though it is doubtful if anybody actually used the word 'officious.' This habit was bad enough, but worse was to come. Time passes vaguely and impalpably in these country places. A rumour arose that a lesser Prince of the Blood might visit the town on his way to manoeuvres, and in the uncertainty of its truth Yoshida brought himself down to something like nervous prostration, but the rumour was never confirmed and the prince never came. Spring again gave way to summer; summer to autumn; and Yoshida began to go twice daily to inspect the shrine.

'If anything went wrong,' he told his wife, 'I should never forgive myself.'

She wanted to reply that nothing perhaps was likely to go wrong, but instead she murmured a soothing assent. He did not play with the children now so much as he used to. Perhaps he thought that as they were growing older he ought not to take too much notice of them, to spoil them. No doubt he was right. She heard indirectly that he was unpopular, but she put this down to jealousy, and as nothing came of it she did not worry.

The winter was uneventful, except that Yoshida refused to take a proper holiday, returning abruptly from a hot-spring resort after only four days. The time for promotion, he said, was getting near, and as he had lately read in the newspapers of a terrible case in which a school photograph had been lost in a fire, he was doubly anxious that nothing should go wrong. His behaviour was by now well known in the countryside, and though some people thought him to be the victim of a mania nobody said so, for one does not comment at all on anything even so remotely connected with the Imperial House. It is true that the Japanese sometimes understand the art of silent conversation, but it is also true that the swords of policemen have been known to transfix unspoken words. Yoshida, continued to do what he regarded as his duty, and nobody interfered with him. He was sometimes stared at.

One morning, late in February, he was awakened by the sound of water dripping from the eaves. He went to the window just after the sun had risen. The snow was melting rapidly and the thatched roofs of cottages smoked in the sun-thaw. After breakfast he went out cheerfully, wearing gum boots, a short black overcoat and a brown felt hat. His wife was delighted to hear him humming an old tune as he closed the gate behind him. The dazzling sunlight reflected from the thawing snow always put him in a good mood, and he felt almost as light-hearted as a schoolboy. But when he came in sight of the playground he saw that at school something was wrong. His heart throbbed painfully, and he walked quicker, splashing through the slippery mud and slush, but as he came nearer a sick terror took hold of the pit of his stomach. A crowd of children and some peasants were standing there, staring and pointing at — what? *What?* Yoshida almost ran. The spectators made way for him, saluted him, but when he said in his agitation, 'What's wrong? What's up?' they didn't answer. They pointed and stared. He then saw what was wrong. The door of the shrine was open, and the photograph had disappeared. A ray of the sun lit up the bare wall.

Everybody expected him to fall into a frenzy. But he was by no means the madman he was taken for. Not at all. He was a loyal and dutiful official, a servant of his Imperial lord and master. He behaved with exemplary calmness, quietly fastened the door of the shrine, ordered the lessons to continue as usual, summoned an emergency meeting of the teachers, told them what had happened, asked them to leave everything to him, telephoned for the police and explained what he had found, and then, on the stroke of the bell, entered his classroom as usual. He was invariably punctual, infallibly so, since he had learned by chance that his nickname was Alarm-clock.

At lunch-time he telephoned to the police again, who had as yet no news, returned to his classroom, and finally went home as usual — except that this afternoon he omitted to go near the shrine, only glancing over the heads of the school children at the broken lock on the door. When he came in, his wife saw at once that something had upset him, but she said nothing, and began to clean the mud off his gumboots. He had gone straight to his study and was very silent, so she peeped in to ask if she should bring tea. He was writing a letter. He started at her voice, and drew a sheet of blotting-paper over his writing.

'No, not yet. In half an hour,' he said.

She came back at the proper time with the tea, and he handed her the letter, already sealed up, and told her to take it at once to the post, which she did. She could not help noticing that it was addressed to a very exalted personage, and wondered why, half feeling all the time that something was wrong. She never suspected that it contained her husband's resignation from his position. In the street one or two people seemed to be staring at her curiously. At the post office a friend came up and exchanged several bows and after the usual compliments begged to offer her sincere condolences on the misfortune which had overtaken her respected husband. The poor woman was at once engulfed in a wave of nameless fear.

'What — what misfortune?' she asked.

The friend was utterly astonished and confused, and smiled politely.

'Is it possible that you don't know? Ah, how sorry I am that I should be the one to carry you such bad news. The Imperial photograph has been stolen from the school —'

'Is that so?'

'Some peasant took it, they say, whom your husband once dismissed. The rascally fellow wanted his revenge. Pray accept my condolences in this unspeakable affliction —'

The principal's wife had only one thought, to give and to give with all her might streams of pure warm sympathy as a cow gives milk. She ran back home with the small steps of habit, propriety and the dignity of a schoolmaster's wife. She ran through the wet streets as fast as she could for the narrow kimono, but when she got home Yoshida was already dead. He had eaten rat-poison. His face and body were horribly distorted and his children were staring at the corpse.

Only two other suicides were reported in the newspaper as having occurred on the same day. A young private in the Imperial army had done away with himself, overwhelmed at having mislaid a pair of slippers issued to him by his regiment. And further, a clerk in the Imperial bureau of communications, suspected of the theft of two yen from a colleague, had seen fit to throw himself from the roof-garden of a department store in the Ginza. But neither of these cases had such a large paragraph as Yoshida's.

The feelings of the widow were not what those of a European woman would be in circumstances at all parallel. She was deeply aware of the honourable behaviour of her late husband, a credit to his country, a starry flower in the annals of his family, a proud memory to his wife and children. Her love for him as a husband, her respect for him as a man of judgment, were rather strengthened than shaken. There was not the slightest doubt that he had, for the last time, done the right thing. As for her, she took the children and went to live with her sister in Osaka.

Her brother-in-law was no longer young, but he was very well off. His house was large and comfortable, and contained a miscellaneous collection of rich and poor relations, stray guests and visitors, dependents and retainers. He was, in fact, a *narikin*, a profiteer of the boom of 1920, quite simple and kind-hearted in spite of his wealth, and often showed special kindness to his sister-in-law's children. Yoshida's widow settled down to a quiet, regular, respectable life. Her health was good, like that of her children, she had everything she wanted, and a real affection for her sister. Although life in Osaka was an interesting change from former years, she had plenty of time to think about the past: but she never became morose, and rather pleased everybody with her cheerful staidness.

Among the more permanent occupants of the house were several students, and though she saw little of them, she sometimes heard pieces of gossip about them and even felt a vague motherly interest in their activities. She could not help noticing one of them, a young man called Wada, a sort of cousin of the family. He had long hair, and a pale face which indicated a mixture of devilry and sadness that attracted her very much. She had never had more than a few words, but wished she could have a long talk with him. She would have liked to ask him about his career, his ambition, and so on. While she was in this state of mind she chanced one day to overhear part of a conversation between two older members of the household. One voice sounded like that of her brother-in-law. They were talking about young Wada.

'He takes no interest in his work at the university.'

'So?'

'Refuses to compete in the examinations.'

'What! Really?'

'Speaks disrespectfully, associates with bad companions and clearly intends to go to the bad.'

'Ah, I'm very sorry to hear it. Women, I suppose? Some geisha or other?'

(The listener's heart beat a very little faster.)

'No, no. I only wish it were. It's worse than that. Much worse. The fact is, I'll tell you, he calls himself a radical —'

(The listener did not know exactly what a radical is, but she guessed instinctively that it was something bad.)

' — a radical. And he's actually on the black list of the police. It is more than a disappointment to me. It's a disgrace.'

'But perhaps he'll grow out of it. These young men —'

'Well, I hope so, but I fear — Do you know what he actually had the effrontery to say to me the other day? I told him he was disloyal to the Emperor. "I have got nothing against the Emperor," he said, "but after all he's only a man." "If you ever say or think such a thing again," I said, "I'll disown you." He didn't answer.'

'Ha!'

'And I may have to disown him —'

At this point Yoshida's widow lost the thread of the talk. For one brief second the remark of Wada had seemed like a flash of truth, for one instant she was on the verge of doubting, and then she was absolutely flooded with a proper revulsion of feeling. The blood mounted to her cheeks. For the first time in her life she felt something like anger. To think that that boy, that student, that lazy long-haired good-for-nothing, that *radical*, should mock at the Most Sacred Majesty for which her husband had died! To think that he should dare to *doubt*! She saw again the face of Yoshida on the floor of his room, the projecting teeth horribly exposed and slavered with yellowish foam, the familiar features fixed in the last grim purpose, the children watching. . . . All her pride, all her love, all her life, summoned up in her at this moment a magnificent renewal of the faith she had never lost.

She no longer wished even to think of Wada, and meeting him by chance the same evening she felt that she froze him with a smiling politeness that cut like a knife. Wada himself only thought her manners were rather stiff.

'I suppose,' he remarked to somebody, 'it is because she has lived nearly all her life in the country. A *petite bourgeoise*.'

Yoshida's widow's mind, which had never really wavered, was now for ever made up. As the years went by, she became formal and even prim, devoted to her children and to household affairs. But the words 'only a man' haunted her till her dying day.

1927

# THE SLEEPING HUSBAND

I FEEL a few lines are needed to explain how this fragment came into my possession. When I was living in one of the better quarters of Tokyo I happened to be acquainted with a certain officer in the army, my neighbour, and his family. Owing to circumstances which will appear below, this family had occasion to take refuge in my house for several days, and Madame S., the officer's wife, occupied much of that time in writing. When she left the house she was in a great hurry, and left her manuscript behind. I am not a scholar of the Japanese language, but as soon as I learnt that she had been writing personal memoranda, I wrote to her in Oita prefecture and asked her permission to have them translated and to allow me to print them abroad, without her name. This request surprised her so much that she at first refused, saying that she had never dreamed of writing those pages for any eyes but her own, and expressing shame and confusion at her carelessness in leaving the papers behind when she had to quit my house at a moment's notice. As she did not specifically ask for them to be returned to her, I pressed for her consent to a translation, urging her with the obvious remark that the fact she had written for the love of the thing and for her own satisfaction showed her to have something of the character of an artist: and I quoted an anecdote of a famous Chinese painter of old times, who said that he worked from the same necessity and inner law as the silkworm spinning her cocoon, that is to say, according to nature. I did not feel that this was an exaggeration, for if there was one thing that I particularly remarked about Madame S. in the short time that I knew her, it was her natural grace. At last she obligingly yielded to an importunate foreigner, and here is the result. The too literal translation I have simply recast, without adding or leaving out anything.

§ 1

[This first part was written in her own house, and carried to mine when she came. The first page seems to be lost.]

'. . . morning, and as I sit here I recall that it must have stopped snowing quite early last night. When I looked out this morning the sky was gem-like. I don't know what the time is now, but the sun has risen quite high in the sky, it makes the snow warm and the white layers on the roofs are rapidly melting. Glittering drops are falling from the eaves as heavily as if it were raining, and when the paper screens are shut and I see on them the shadows of the falling drops, I can almost imagine a sunny shower outside. I open them again, and the first thing I see is a young maple tree in the garden, which has been bent down under a mass of snow — now unexpectedly dislodged! so the young tree springs back to its former position. What a sugary, swishing sound that was! I remember how frightened I was as a child when I heard for the first time a bamboo cracking under a weight of snow in the middle of the night with a loud report.

'And now under the eaves there is quite a little runnel, and flakes of foam and bubbles float away, whirl away on it like boats on the rapids of Hozu. A light steam is rising from the ground. I wish I could continue for ever to look at the beauties of nature.

'In this room, on the mats just behind me, my husband is sleeping with his mouth open. His head is only a few feet from my knees, but it seems much farther away. Toki, the servant, is out, and has taken the children, so the house is unusually quiet. There are two sounds, the ceaseless drip-dropping of the melting snow and the snoring of my husband. I am in just such a position where a woman ought to be happy — between her sleeping husband and a quiet garden; and yet, although my children are healthy and I am devoted to them, although I am not starving, I am miserable. I don't complain aloud (how unthinkable!), so I'll just put down on paper as well as I can a few of my feelings. If I can get them out of me and see what they look like, then afterwards I'll destroy it all. One thing I'll remember is that my life is not as bad as poor Toki's has been. I'll try and say more about her than about myself, for she has told me so much, and as for writing about my own life I don't know how or where on earth to begin — not because so much has happened to me, but because — well, I don't know.

'What really surprises me is that even when I married I was so ready to expect the best from men. I didn't think they were angels, but then nor did I think they were devils : I don't think that now, but I know some of them come near it. Ah, this life is a dream. Before I married I must have been blind or deaf. I certainly couldn't have been ignorant, for there were plenty of signs and hints, even plainer things to guide me. Was I so innocent, or simply a fool? Was I more foolish than other girls? I wonder.

'I remember how we used to call all our men-teachers at the high school by the names of flowers, nicknaming them violet, peach-blossom, tiger lily, *kikyo*,[1] and so on. How absurd! Yet I believe I'd do the same again, I could do it now, for I am not disillusioned or cynical, I am simply unhappily married.

'To take, for instance, young Kishi, who has quite unwittingly caused most of this last unreasonable trouble, I know my love for him is a true thing, and there would be to me nothing ridiculous in calling him by a flower name. Which one would suit him? I can't think exactly now. Perhaps *yamabuki* — the single one, which I, unlike most people, have always preferred to the double. . . .

[1] The Chinese bell-flower.

196

'How angry my husband would be if he by chance read these words! Is there *anything* in this house which doesn't make him angry, at any time whatsoever? But I'm not afraid. I don't love secrets so much. I have already admitted to him that I still feel, and shall always feel, a sincere but innocent affection for Kishi. I love him with a pure, true love. Is it likely that I should have committed adultery with that mere boy, as I am accused of doing? No, no, I am quite the faithful wife. Oh, quite. But the only answer I got to my honest assertions, for my frankness, was a blow in the face with my husband's knuckles. It was not the first. But I'm going too fast. I'm not going to try and write my life (as if I could!), but I must go back a bit. . . .

§ 2

[This section was written in my house.]

'It is strange I should have stopped just there. The last words I wrote were "go back a bit". But where have I gone? Now I'm not even writing in my own house, but actually in a foreigner's. He's kind to the children and to me — rather over-polite to me, which is ridiculous. It's unnatural to be always saying "thank you" and "I beg your pardon" to a woman, but I can't help admitting that I like it. If I'm going to explain how I come to find myself here, in a foreigner's house, with the two children and Toki, I must stop this way of writing, it's too fluent and colloquial, like talking. And I began in such a high-flown way — well, I can't keep up such a formal style. I must be as brief as possible.

'Well, then, my esteemed parents are well-to-do as they have always been, but their reasons for marrying me to this man will always seem to me inscrutable. I have learnt to be dutifully filial to my father and mother, but I told them I didn't want to marry a soldier, and that I could never love this particular soldier. I never liked the look of him, and I was able to see him three times before my marriage. I have twice asked my parents to arrange a divorce, but of course it was useless to ask. How could I expect them to agree? Once, also, when my husband had spent everything and even borrowed money on account of one of his affairs with women, he forced me to go and ask them for money. This they also refused; so now I don't see much of them, though I write regularly. Nobody can call me undutiful, either as daughter or wife. I have long since got used to the indifference of my parents and the behaviour of my husband. He has been much worse during the last year. I have got used to his drunkenness and dirty talk to the children, but once he actually came in with his friend Captain H. and two geishas. It wouldn't be true to say that all were completely drunk, though the two men certainly were. The girls had been drinking. Not only did I have to endure this orgy in my house, I had to assist at it. I had to receive those women, and serve them with smiles. Why do I speak of it as if it were some extraordinary episode of the distant past? It may happen again. I have never complained, nor have I told anybody but Toki. She said she was sorry for me.

'Our house is too big for us, my husband said from the beginning, so one room has always been let, and the rest of us have crowded into two others. The lodger is a student, and I've got to know him and some of his friends quite well: one of them, called Kishi, happened to get ill. I was sorry for him, and liked him, and as he was poor and living in bad lodgings I asked him to come to our house and we would look after him till he got well again. My husband was away for the autumn manoeuvres, and then for another fortnight on some other duty. By the time he came back Kishi, after being with us about a month, had gone away quite fit to his rooms again. At his rooms, it seems, there is a young girl, the daughter of his landlady, who has long loved him in vain; and in the house next door is a private in my husband's regiment who loves that girl. She never looks at the soldier, and thinks only of Kishi, who never looks at her! It is easy to imagine the despair of the soldier, but I think he acted very foolishly. He wrote an anonymous letter to my husband saying that Kishi had slept with me for a month. What did he expect to gain? Did he think to make Kishi appear disreputable to the girl? Did he owe me some unknown grudge? Did he hope to win the favour of my husband, his superior? Whatever he hoped, the results were unfortunate. Perhaps I had been indiscreet to let Kishi sleep in the same room as me, but Toki and the children were there too.

'My husband came back suddenly, two days earlier than he was expected, drunk of course, seized me by the hair, and started blurting out the whole story with a lot of disgusting remarks which I have no wish to record. Our student lodger slipped out of the house and went and told Kishi to escape, as my husband was threatening to kill him; and then came back and tried to protect me. He kindly knocked my husband down, and we had no more trouble that night, only words.

'The next evening I went out to buy something, and when I came back my husband had drawn his sword and was ordering the children to kneel down, because he intended to behead them. They were too terrified to cry, and had already started to obey him. Their little eyes seemed much larger than usual. He was really wild, so our student lodger went for the police: but they refused to come, saying they had no right to rebuke a man in his own house unless some crime had actually been committed. When the lodger returned, my husband was kneeling on me and trying to pull out my hair: Toki had managed to hide the children. At last, leaving my husband and our lodger in argument, I went out with Toki and the children, and we spent the night safely in a police shelter. The two policemen on duty were awfully kind, and bought some goody-goodies for the children; one of them obligingly told me the story of his life.

'My husband has already got his revenge for my supposed

union with Kishi. He has arranged to be transferred to Oita prefecture, so well known for its roughness and remoteness, and I am ordered there with the children. My husband is taking several days to "celebrate" his departure from Tokyo, and our lodger forbids me to go to my own house at all. How we shall finish packing I don't know. Meanwhile I am taking refuge in this foreigner's house, and while we have been here Toki has told me all her history, so that I am ashamed now to have spoken of my own troubles. She knows better than I the meaning of lonely sorrow, yet how cheerful she is! She has worked for us for months, and there is always a smile on her face, which is almost a baby face, though she must be nearly twenty. I believe it is impossible for her to feel anger, but I know she can feel fear and other things deeply enough. I have never seen her appear either sad or annoyed at anything, and even in telling me her story she smiled all the time.

§ 3

'Toki had never told me anything of her experiences until quite lately, when she saw that I was just beginning to suffer. She said she was afraid I would get rid of her if I knew her story. Most people would refuse to keep such a servant, she said, and it's true. Certainly from her baby face I could never have dreamt what she has been through; and yet, now and again, I have almost suspected that there was something under the surface — she has a strange way of narrowing her eyes, especially in moments of doubt or apprehension, as when she is asked some unusual question. . . .

'Before I begin, I must put it down that I don't reproach anybody. If my parents choose to abandon me to such a husband, is it not because they believe that I belong now entirely to him and his family? Doesn't it require some sacrifice, some unselfishness on their part, to give me up? I can't help feeling that they love me dearly. If anybody read these pages they might think I was blaming my husband. I am not blaming him: I am unhappy with him, and I am sorry for my children. Nor would I blame anybody for Toki's life, for there's something wrong, something evil, that makes people bad. They are not naturally bad. Her father must love her as his daughter, and yet she says she can't see his love. I can see it, I can realize that he persecutes and bullies her because he loves her. I believe I can understand some of her feelings, though she told me her story without much comment, without saying very particularly whether people were good or bad, so I'll try and do the same. She doesn't seem to judge people by what they are, but by what they do — that is, if she judges them at all!

'Her father, she told me, is quite well off, but loves his money so much that he refused to let her go to a high school, which he could easily have afforded. Her home is in Chiba prefecture, and she has several brothers and sisters. She didn't speak much of her youngest days, but there are two incidents she particularly remembers, which she told me at the end, so I'll keep them to the end. It is quite plain that even as a child she was unhappy at home, and so as soon as she was old enough she ran away.

'Although she had never been there she ran straight to Tokyo, and went to a servants' exchange or employment bureau, where she was told to wait in an anteroom, but was almost at once shown into the manager's room. The manager was talking to an oldish man, who seemed to Toki to have a fine character. He sat a little aside while she answered all the manager's questions, but when she was asked what kind of work she wanted to do she didn't quite know what to answer. It was at this point that the older man leant forward, touched her on the knee and told her in a confidential tone that he was the head of a private detective agency. His firm, he said, were at present looking for some clever young women detectives — how would she like to try that? She had no money and she was hungry, so she said she'd like it very much.

' "Then," said the gentleman, "let's go along at once. It's all right, we'll take good care of you."

'And she went with him. It was already evening, so they didn't go to his office, but to a private house in the suburbs. Here she prepared supper, and they both sat down to eat it. The gentleman was very kind, and brought her some soda-water to drink. Very soon after this she either fell asleep or became unconscious, for the soda-water was doped. She says that she has no clear knowledge of what went on in the night, but she awoke late in the morning in a very confused state of mind and body, and the first thing she saw was a letter from her host which said that he didn't like to wake her up as she seemed so tired, that he had had to go out to business and that he hoped to return in the evening. Her first thought was to escape. But where could she go? She knew nobody in Tokyo. She was alone in the house. It would be better to wait and see what turned up. Anything would be better than going back home, back to the father and elder brother she particularly hated. . . .

'And in the evening the nice gentleman returned, bringing with him her father and that same elder brother. He had left early in the morning for Chiba prefecture, and, representing himself as a private detective, had informed the girl's father that by a lucky chance and his own adroitness he had already managed to trace the girl. If a considerable sum of money were immediately advanced to him, he thought he could lay hands on her. She might, he said, be in the town, but if she was found in the suburbs it would be necessary to pay a bit extra. On the way back he affected to inquire at an office, and then came straight to the house where he had left Toki. When she saw her father and brother she dashed out of the room, snatched a pair of scissors off a low table and locked herself up in the W.C. There, overwhelmed, maddened with rage and shame, fear and disappointment, she ran the scissors quickly over her head, and hacked off roughly but speedily the whole of her long and beautiful black hair. At the moment when the three men were about to force the door she walked out with an extraordinary jagged head, and dangling in her hand thick and lustrous hanks of hair. At first her relations were too surprised even to speak, but they soon hurried her out of the house and took her home. When they got back they were so ashamed of her escapade and of her appearance that they kept her shut up in one room. She says she was forbidden to leave it even for a bath, half-starved, and treated with cruelty. After three weeks of this frightful confinement she escaped to Tokyo again.

## § 4

'This time she went to quite a different employment agency, and as soon as she came there realized how much better it was than the former one. It was kept by a middle-aged man and his wife, simple folk, who asked her to spend the night in their house which was tacked on to the back of the office, and this she cautiously but willingly consented to do. The wife of the manager was really kind and motherly in her manner, and suggested that Toki would do well to become a hospital nurse.

'"Nursing," she said, "is a very special profession. There is something noble about such a calling. It is indeed a holy mission. And although one must work hard, it is an honour to belong to such a profession." Toki felt that this was quite true, and at once undertook to work in a hospital.

'It was not a very large hospital, so there were not many patients, and between them and the staff, which was also small, there was unusual intimacy. Toki's hair was of course still very short, and everybody thought that she had made it so for coquettish reasons, so she was at once nicknamed *Moga*.[1] This nick-

[1] A truncated Japanese form of *modan garu*, i.e. 'modern girl'.

name was used even to her ever-smiling face, and very soon familiar remarks were added, for the usual discipline of a hospital was not in evidence here at all. The familiar remarks gave way to solicitations.

'It hadn't taken her long to discover that all the patients were there to be cured of venereal diseases. Without having any idea as to what might become of her, she repeatedly urged the superintendent, or doctor in charge, to let her go; but it seemed that she had previously signed some sort of contract, though she was not aware of having done so. They told her that if she ran away she would be brought back, but that they would allow her to go after six months. She stayed there for six months, during which one of her patients died of general paralysis of the insane.

'About a week before she was due to go, she happened one evening when off duty to be walking in a park, not far away, when she luckily met a man she knew and liked, a distant and friendly connexion of her family. To him she described her situation, begging him to find for her another more tolerable, or at least to put her in the way of finding one. The face of her cousin (as she called him) was gloomy, but not unkind. His forehead was full of wrinkles, for he was a journalist by profession, and no stranger to domestic anxieties. His wife was consumptive, he said, and they were now living at Hiratsuka, and kept one servant. He suggested to Toki that she should come and look after his wife, be a companion to her and cheer her up a bit. His manner was agreeable, and his offer was made in kindness and sincerity, and although he warned her that she could expect neither money nor joy, she accepted the place with eagerness, and at once went there on leaving the hospital.

'Her cousin the journalist was nearly always away on business, so his wife, except for the servant, was much alone, for she had neither friends nor relations. The grass mats in the house were in places discoloured by blood, especially in one room, where the lady, whose malady was in an advanced stage, spent much of her time. Her wasted frame and haggard face, a ruin of loveliness, at once aroused the sympathies of Toki, who became a devoted attendant, an attendant to whom the unfortunate woman, knowing she must soon die, confided nearly all her thoughts. Those were not happy days; and the woman and the girl, as time went on, were nearly always alone, for the servant was apparently unpaid, and came in much less often now that Toki undertook so much of the work of the house.

'The slowly dying woman would sit talking, always in the same strain, smiling wanly as if to excuse the absolute hopelessness and nihilism of her words; in the middle of her smiling desolation she would frown, her whole face would contract in an agonized expression, and vainly clapping to her mouth a thin white hand she would be shaken, shaken, wrenched almost to death, with a protracted and harrowing spasm, that Toki was powerless to alleviate. The invalid had a habit of sitting in the dark, as electric light, she said, hurt her; and another habit of caressing a cat with mottled fur that seemed dear to her. Toki had an instinctive and superstitious dread of cats, but in any case the whole situation would be enough to affect anybody's nerves.

'Directly a moment came when the sun or moon was shining, when there was no wind or special cause for anxiety, when there was an air of gaiety or a silence with flowers, with the chirp of a bird or summery vibrations of insects; or if they were watching a globe with various goldfish; directly a moment came of bright peace, it was false, pain burst out, and all was spattered and stained. The end came soon.

'One breezy spring afternoon, about the time when the cherry trees are covered with flowers, Toki in the garden heard her name faintly cried. She ran in and found the poor woman in agony in the bathroom. She did what she could, and then hurried to fetch the doctor, who was away. She ran back. In the evening the woman died, choked by her own breath. It was already getting late when Toki found herself alone with the dead body. She hunted for her purse, and at once went to the post office to send a telegram to the absent husband. Unfortunately she couldn't remember exactly which newspaper he was working on. She knew it was one of two, and sent the telegram to the wrong one, after which she was burdened with the suspicion that she might have done so. The husband was not destined to return that night.

'By the time the girl got back to the house it was pretty dark and the wind was rising. A *mokuren*[1] tree at the gate, now still leafless, but full of winged white flowers, looked, she said, as if a whole flock of birds had waveringly settled on it, and were about to fly away again. Just then she remembered that she hadn't seen the cat all day. Where was it? She dreaded to open the door and go in. But of course she was still half expecting that the journalist would return. It never occurred to her to try and get somebody else to help her — besides, whom did she know that would do so? She went in and shut the door, her ears full of the wailing wind and her mind (more than her mind — her whole being) full of thoughts of the cat and the corpse. Everybody knows it is unlucky for these two things to be found together. She didn't know which to fear most. Was the cat inside the house or out? She had a firm idea that it must be inside, and although she dreaded now to open the sliding paper doors of the room where the dead woman lay, she forced herself to look and see if the cat was there. It wasn't; so she closed the room again carefully.

'Toki herself couldn't tell me at all what she really felt that night, but she must have been near to madness. She's a funny girl at the best of times. Which was more terrible, she considered, to have a light in her room or to have none? At all events, she had to put her head tight under the bedclothes, though nothing could drown the fitful screaming of the wind outside. She kept on thinking that she heard the husband at the door — the dead woman moving — the cat stealthily prowling. And she couldn't help thinking of that tree (which had been so gay and scented in

[1] The lily-flowered magnolia.

the morning sun, *that* morning, as far away as a dream) so near to her in the dark, a whole flock of ghostly birds, spirits of the dead, glimmering, fluttering, trying to fly away all together, but somehow failing, and still clinging all together on the bare and waving windy twigs.

'And then she heard a voice. Distinctly. A high voice. A cat's? A woman's? A ghost's? It was outside the house. It was inside the house? It was continually wailing. It didn't want to be let in. A sound she had never heard before, nor could ever hear again. It knew the woman was dead. Toki was afraid to listen to it, afraid to get up and let it in, afraid to be alive. But she couldn't stand the sound. She got up, prepared to pass through two dark rooms to the door to let it in. When she got up the sound ceased. Still she went bravely forward. She was afraid to go back. When she came to the entrance she saw the cat's eyes shining in the dark. It had been inside the house all the time.

'She shrieked and shrieked, but there was nobody to hear her. . . .

§ 5

'These peasants are too superstitious! In the morning she was afraid to get up, and didn't move until she heard a loud daylight knocking. It was the grocer's boy who had come as usual to the back door for orders. Trembling, she sent him to fetch the servant, who had been away for days. Then the husband appeared or was sent for and the house filled with people and light and air. The wind, the cat, the tree and the corpse are all present in her heart to this day.

'The husband had thought himself fully prepared for the woman's death, but now it affected him more profoundly than an unexpected shock could have done. Only three people went with him to the funeral — a friend of his, Toki and the servant. It was a warm sunny day, and Toki's mind was full of the misery of that broken woman, who had seared her heart with the confession of her loneliness, her meaningless existence, her lack of parents, brothers, sisters, friends, her utter resentful hopelessness. And the feeling which now took possession of Toki was one of limitless inescapable futility, the inanity of living, the dullness of dying. She no longer cared for anything. She missed nothing, wanted nothing, feared nothing, hated nothing. Until at last there rushed into this vacuum the desire to die. She prepared to leave the house, and the journalist was too self-absorbed even to ask her where she was going. She got into a train for Odawara. Why Odawara? Because she had once been there as a child, on some school excursion. She knew what it was like.

'On the evening of the same day as the funeral she was walking on the beach at Odawara. The weather of the morning was fulfilling its promise, and a tranquil moon lit a cloudless sky and a calm sea, the sound of whose ripples came occasionally to the ear like sighs of contentment. She sat down. An elderly woman approached her.

' "I beg your pardon, but I wonder what you're doing here?"

' "I came here to-day," Toki was prepared to lie without any hesitation, "to visit my relations, but their house has been moved — they've gone away."

' "Where are you going to stay, then, to-night?"

' "I'm not sure. Can you — can you tell me of a suitable hotel?"

' "I can't; for I think there's no hotel would admit a young girl like you alone."

' "Oh."

' "But if you like I'll be pleased to find you a room. I know a nice house near here that belongs to my friend, who will, I'm sure, give you a secure lodging for to-night. Won't you come with me now? It's getting late. How bright the moon is!"

'Toki went with her, and occupied a room as suggested at a very respectable house near the shore. The family went to bed early, and at about eleven Toki slipped out of the house and went on to the beach. A perfect spring night: but how fatal is spring to the young!

'The moon was now in quite a different part of the sky, but the sea was as calm as before. She looked carefully round her. There was no movement at all, except that in a distant house a light disappeared. After it had been put out she thought how yellow it had been. She turned to the sea, easily undulating, dusky, hazy, lazy, indifferent, peaceful, powerful. It was much warmer than she expected, and she waded out. When the water was up to her shoulders she paused, thinking she heard something, and then, satisfied, groped forward in the waiting ocean. She wanted to sink; the more she wanted to sink, the more she found herself swimming. She couldn't help swimming. She tried to swallow some water and spat it out again. But her clothes began to be heavy and dragging. She had now no will either to strike out or to sink. She rolled over on her side. The water closed over her head, but she came up again. This happened twice. Then she was fighting like a wild beast. Her body felt as if it would burst in two, her brain was full of cold and fiery salt, a hot and universal roaring filled her ears; but into that roaring came a quieter tune, and dreamily she seemed to be going, going down, down to nameless oblivion, to perfect peace. . . .

'She is not clear whether it was a watchman or a fisherman who saved her, for when she became at all conscious again she was lying in a hospital. Faces were staring at her. For a long time they meant nothing. And then she realised that they must be the faces of drowned men at the bottom of the sea. But could that be right? Surely they were not resolving themselves into a look of expectancy. Under the sea? They were like words, whose meaning was a series of questions, in an unknown language.

'No one had yet identified her, but a doctor in a white overall, and a policeman with a sword at his hip and white cotton gloves on his hands, were now doing their best to find out who she was.

At first, feeling in her very bowels the growing rebirth of fear, she pretended not to understand; and when the men pressed her for an answer, tightly shut her lips; and when they hung over her, persistent and threatening, she sobbed without weeping. But the policeman knew his duty, and as soon as she could stand she was marched off to the nearest police-box, where she stood, her heart wildly palpitating from fear and exhaustion, and her head sunk on her breast. She has described to me at length the combined efforts of three policemen cajoling, persuading, threatening, to force from her the name and address of her parents. I am surprised, for I have always found policemen so kind. Perhaps they really thought she was the escaped concubine of an eminent official (judging from the questions they asked her), or perhaps it was simply that they had nothing else to do: when men are idle they get so awfully cruel. Toki held out as long as she could, but at last there was no hope for it; and so she thought of a stratagem.

' "If," she said, "you'll promise on your words of honour not to communicate it to anybody at all on any pretext, then I'll tell you where my home is."

'They all promised.

' "I don't believe you," she said, "you're deceiving me."

'They protested their good faith, but she laughed. At this they solemnly undertook to convince her that they wouldn't under any circumstances betray her, but that in accordance with their duty they were bound to find out where she lived, and asserted that it they failed in this they would be severely punished.

'She told them.

'One of them laughed.

'She stared, as if bewildered.

'They at once sent a telegram to her family.

'This time her mother and brother fetched her home, after many bows, smiles, thanks and apologies to the policemen, begging them to excuse the behaviour of an insane girl. On the journey, she says, they treated her as a lunatic, but at home she was treated as a criminal.

'She managed to escape for the third time; and with the aid of her relation, the journalist, now of course a widower, she got a place with me, and I have done my best to treat her kindly. Before I end this writing I ought to mention two trifling episodes of her childhood, which, she says, have impressed her more than anything that has since happened in her life. They must have influenced her character. I wonder, by the way, what she thinks of people generally? She swore to me that she would never marry. Stupid thing!

'The first anecdote is this. When she was at the primary school in her native place she was in the same class as a certain little girl who was the daughter of one of the richest and most influential men in the neighbourhood. This child was accordingly a great favourite with the teachers, but Toki asserts that her character was not estimable. For some unknown reason the child hated Toki and was always trying to score off her. Now it happened that this little girl possessed a certain gaudy pencil-box, the gift of her father and the envy of her school-fellows. This object she put secretly into Toki's school bag, or satchel, with the eventual result that Toki was unjustly held up to the local world as a thief.

'It is unlucky to tell stories about fortune-tellers, but the other story shows how even when a child she had begun to be ridiculously superstitious. One day, returning from school, she stopped to listen to some quack fortune-teller in the street. This personage was impressively warning his audience that if in any of their houses the W.C. was built at the south-western corner, it was a positive indication that one of the inhabitants of such a house would certainly become a raving lunatic. Toki knew at once that her own home was built like that: perhaps she may again try to do away with herself, for, she says, she is still afraid of becoming . . .'

§ 6

[There the manuscript abruptly ends, and when I asked its author to continue it she said she was unwilling to do so, nor did she tell me how she had originally proposed to end it. The reader may have noticed that Captain S., the lady's husband, removed, as a result of his drunken jealousy and impulsive and brutal stupidity, his whole family to a distant part of the country, Oita in Kyushu. Toki wouldn't go with them, saying she preferred to stay in Tokyo. Perhaps she felt that in the capital there would always be more security, more chance to hide or escape when necessary. Madame S. managed to find her a place with a young-ish couple, who happened to be among my best Japanese friends, and in their house I occasionally saw her. After some time they lent me rooms, into which I gladly moved, and it was while there that a small incident occurred, which I may as well record briefly here, by way of an end-piece. When I had been in the house a couple of months my friends happened to go away for a week, so that I was alone in the house with Toki. She was a good servant, quiet and fairly thorough, though inclined to be forget-ful, and, out of pure thoughtlessness, a bit of a mischief maker. It was in the early summer and I was just getting over a slight attack of 'flu. Although the morning was bright and warm, I decided to stay in bed, for I still had a touch of fever. My bed, being a Japanese one, was on the floor, and the house and weather being both delightfully Japanese, I had opened the whole end of the room to the sunny air which filled the garden outside. I had been lying on my stomach and reading, but I put the book down and gazed up at the perfect sky, and listened dreamily to the faint fresh humming of new-born insects, when I suddenly became aware of a man standing just in front of me. My pillow was only six feet from the garden where he stood. He must have come in at the little garden gate, which was unusual, but I sup-posed he was some old pedlar who had come in that way by-mistake-on-purpose to avoid the servant, and perhaps to get round the master. Yet he was a bit too neatly dressed for a pedlar. He was not a very attractive old man. He stood with his hat in his hand, and I saw that his round head, bald in places, was covered with short white bristly down, and looked like the swollen breast of some unpleasant bird. His head he carried rather forward, for he had a slight stoop, and on his neck the skin was dry and mottled. His face was small, not an open face, and with no prominent feature. Eyebrows he lacked, but the place where they ought to have been was raised enquiringly, and the gaze of his pale eyes was fixed on me above a pair of old-fashioned spectacles, which had permanently slipped down, for like most Japanese he had no bridge to his nose. His mouth was curiously small, half open, looked as if it had never smiled, and disclosed regular rodent teeth.

This inglorious picture was not, I venture to assert, the figment of an invalid fancy. It definitely was a small, dry old man who was not pleasant. I was just going to tell him that there was nothing to-day, thank you, when he opened a little covered Red Riding Hood basket and took out a slip of paper, which he handed to me with the sort of hand you'd expect a man like that to have — a close fisted man. Poor beggar, I thought, being an experienced pauper myself. I don't blame him for *that*: money's certainly scarce enough. I can't read much of the Japanese script, but I was able to make out on this bit of paper the name of my absent host.

'Yes,' I said, 'he lives here. Did you want to see him? He's away now.'

I thought the old man was dunning for some forgotten bill to be paid. He then asked me what seemed an unnecessary question, scrutinizing me closely:

'Does anybody else live here?'

I was just going to say 'Yes, I do,' when I changed my mind and thought I'd call the servant to come and get rid of him, for I didn't feel well enough to go on being civil to this tedious old creature: I listened for Toki, thinking she was in the next room or in the kitchen beyond. In a paper house sound travels, but nothing could I hear just then. No doubt she had gone out shopping — it was no use calling. I turned to the old man again, wondering how to get rid of him, and thought of a good plan.

'I'm sorry,' I said, smiling politely, 'I don't understand.'

He then asked several more questions which, instead of answering, I met with as blank a look as I could command, and the old man, bowing and muttering, put down his basket and hat and went next door, where I heard him asking his questions again. Old devil, I thought.

Just then the sliding paper door of my room opened, and there stood Toki.

'My father!' she whispered, and dived into the large wall-cupboard behind me (in which the beds are usually kept) just as the old man returned with the woman from next door.

A nice position for me! At my head a furious parent, and at my feet — if he only knew it — his trembling child. I was at a disadvantage. I was a foreigner. I had to be polite. I had to act my part. My temperature was 38·8°. The two submitted me at once to a volley of leading questions, both leaning forward and trying to read my thoughts by outstaring me.

'I don't understand,' I protested with a smile and a shrug.

'Where is the servant who works here?' they demanded.

'Ah! the servant!' I said brightly. 'She's away just now.'

'Where is she?'

'I don't know.'

'When will she be back?'

'I don't know.'

They exchanged significant looks. 'How can you cook your meals without a servant?' they asked.

'I don't understand,' I said. But they wouldn't leave the question. They repeated it in all possible forms, with various antics, until only a moron could have failed to understand.

'Ah, so?' I said sweetly. 'Well, I look after myself when there's nobody to look after me.'

It was obvious that they didn't believe a word I said.

And now, while the old man went on with his cross-questioning, the woman left him, and I could hear her going round outside, peeping and poking into every room. If I made the slightest protest they would at once be positive of what they now strongly suspected — that I was hiding the girl. As the woman came back she stumbled over something, and plucked the old man's sleeve.

'Look!' she muttered, and they both looked down. 'Her clogs.'

Toki had left her clogs just outside! The most damning evidence.

'If you come back next Wednesday,' I said, 'somebody may be here.'

That would give me time to get her out of the way. . . . They both smiled scornfully, looking over my shoulder, to the right, to the left —

'This gentleman,' the woman explained, 'would like to wait here a little longer, in case the girl *returns*.'

'Certainly,' I said, 'please do.'

She left him, and he made himself somewhat at home, but instead of sitting down before me, he craftily moved, with an affectation of courtesy, along to the other end of the garden front of the house, and there sliding back a door, sat down with his feet in the garden and his head in the house, and in such a position that he had a commanding view of the four main rooms, including my own, and could hear the footfall of a mouse in any one of them.

The sun was now high in the sky, the dew on the leaves was all gone and a drowsy silence ensued: but silence was the last thing I wanted, for the girl might think the coast was clear and burst out at any moment! I coughed meaningly, but my cough might have meant 'Come out,' so I didn't do it again. Leaning far forward, I was in time to see the old man leaning far back and twisting his neck to peer into an inner room where a lot of Toki's sewing and odds and ends were scattered on the floor. He must have known that she was in the house. What I really feared was that he would come in and start looking in the cupboards. And if I tried to stop him, he would feel certain that I had something to hide. And in this most awkward of silences the girl might so easily emerge. . . . At last I could stand it no longer.

'I'm sorry,' I said, 'but I have to go out very soon. Won't you come back on Wednesday?'

I got up giddily, pulled on some clothes and started sliding the various doors together and closing everything.

'The servant here,' he said meaningly, grasping his wicker basket, 'is my daughter.'

'What!' I exclaimed. 'Is she really? Fancy! What a pity she isn't here to-day! Well, good-bye — I'm sorry your visit was useless — good-bye.'

I bowed him out and closed all the doors. When he had gone, I let the girl out. She thanked me, and then stood for quite a minute, her hands hanging limply at her side, her head down, not moving, and one of the most shocking expressions on her baby face that I think I have ever seen on the face of a human being. She seemed like an animal which, after struggling endless hours in a trap, after giving up all hope and being paralysed with raw terror, after being slowly frozen into madness, is suddenly set free — and has no feeling except an organic certainty that its liberty is somehow worse than its captivity.

Just for one moment she looked like that, and then lifted her head — with the smile restored to the baby face. It was very moving. She submitted to these events without any comment, for she was submissive; and soon started talking again quickly and gaily. She said she would rather die than speak to her father. And yet I must say that some time later the old man wrote, hoping for a reconciliation: was the father in him restored, or had he some scheme? She of course refused unconditionally. What can they have done to her at home? How mysterious and terrible are the relations between parents and children, and how little we know about them! And yet whenever she spoke about her home she used to smile. It was only then that I fully understood the words of Madame S. when she wrote: 'Toki can feel fear very deeply, but it is impossible for a nature like hers to be angry.']

'ARE you afraid of death?' old Kurodaké asked me suddenly, not fixing me with a hypnotic stare or anything like that. Indeed his eyes were cast down on the bowl of rice he was holding in his left hand, while his right, poised in mid-air, lightly held a pair of antique ivory chopsticks which he used to wash carefully and put away in an old lacquer case after every meal: he carried it about in his sleeve, as one might carry a spectacle-case. My eyes rested for a moment on his hands, which were of an extraordinary delicacy and agility, and young-looking; then I looked at his face as if to meet his question. He was still looking down, and there was a ghost of a smile on his lips, not a cynical smile, but tranquil, like the smile on the face of a carved *bodhisattva*. The other members of the family were looking at me expectantly, and Mrs. Shiroi, the old man's niece, tittered nervously and hid the lower half of her face in her sleeve as if she was a schoolgirl instead of a grandmother.

'What a strange question to be asked at breakfast-time,' I remarked defensively, and smiled politely. As if I had made a joke, Mrs. Shiroi lowered her sleeve and tittered quite openly; her husband showed even more front teeth than usual; and her son Hajimé laughed, I think out of sheer good nature. The old man, quickly manipulating his chopsticks as if they were part of him, took a couple of mouthfuls of rice and a small pickled plum, which he picked up as deftly as a watchmaker might pick up a jewel, and then raised his eyes, over which the lids drooped a little, and looked at me as if still awaiting an answer. As I was rather afraid of him, for his brain was as delicate and agile as his hands, I wanted to avoid giving a banal answer, which would have disappointed him, or a dishonest one, which he would at once have seen through.

'I think of death quite often,' I said. 'Sometimes I'm afraid of it, but not always. Sometimes, when I'm enjoying life and looking forward to things I want to do, I resent the necessity of dying and wish I could live for ever. Sometimes, when gloomy or disillusioned, I think I should welcome death. So I suppose it's a matter of mood.'

He nodded, with an air of appreciation, but said nothing: I dare say he found my reply too commonplace. Outside in the street, the clatter of daily life was increasing, but it was a hot morning, and it was going to be a very hot day, and somehow the tempo of life seemed already a little slowed down by the heat. One can be scorched in the summer in Hiroshima.

The old man was not the sort of person to whom one easily says, 'It's going to be awfully hot to-day, don't you think? Hajimé and I are thinking of going for a swim.' With the approach of age, Hajimé had explained to me, his great-uncle was withdrawing his mind from earthly things and in the autumn would retire, in the traditional way, to a lonely hide-out in the mountains, where he would sit at night listening to a distant waterfall and watching the moon rise above a grove of bamboos. So I said instead, 'But what made you ask me that question, sir, this morning?'

'I have seen some foreigners, of course,' said Kurodaké, 'but this is the first time I have had the chance of talking with one. It is very interesting for me.'

I bowed slightly, as if to signify that I would do my best not to be a bore, and looked out over his shoulder into the garden, to which the side of the room was open. It was a small, formal, flowerless garden, very clean, with evergreens, a fantastically-shaped rock, a stone lantern, a pool of water: everything was conventional and symbolical and orderly. Violent, emotional, deeply pessimistic, the Japanese soul (if one could speak in such a general way) evidently needed, I reflected for the thousandth time, a rigid scheme of everyday life to contain and direct its energies, to bound its fears and circumscribe its joys. After the slight first shock of surprise that the great-uncle had never before spoken to a foreigner, I remembered that he had hardly been out of Hiroshima in his life, and that Hiroshima was just a provincial town, through which foreigners might pass by train to Kobé or Shimonoseki, but in which there was seldom any reason for them to linger: he had succeeded, I had gathered from Hajimé, to a comfortable old-fashioned firm of *saké*-brewers, and had enjoyed ample leisure, which he had devoted to editing the works on occultism and esoteric Buddhism of a seventeenth-century writer, whose name I never could remember. The great-uncle, the garden, the noises in the street (among which the itinerant fish-pedlar's horn sounded forlorn and ancient), the stillness in the room where we were sitting, produced an overwhelming sense of continuity and inevitability.

Hajimé's father, a mild and modest gentleman of moderate means, who had never done a stroke of work or hurt a fly in his life, had unclosed a small black silk fan and was fanning himself without haste and without rest. His face was now composed, with no expression except of benevolence: he seemed to be waiting quietly for an interesting dialogue about death between his uncle-in-law and his foreign guest, and waiting quietly, too, for death itself: one could imagine him folding his fan, and leaning back with a sigh at last. Mrs. Shiroi, as a woman, knew that speculations about death boil no rice; on her knees beside the low black lacquer table, she was clearing away the breakfast things and no doubt thinking already about the preparation of luncheon, since even philosophers must eat. Hajimé said nothing. He was sitting cross-legged on a flat silk cushion and smoking a cigarette; his springy hair, which he wore long and parted in the middle, had fallen forward and was hanging over his eyes. I wondered what he was thinking.

'I suppose,' said the old man, who had put away his chopsticks, and was now playing with a chaplet of big amber beads as if he were telling them, 'that you think of death as the beginning of personal immortality?'

'Christians do,' I said; 'and I think many people feel that they live on in a way after death, not so much in the memories of those who have known them, as in the repercussions of their good and bad actions, however great or small, among those who have known them.'

'Ha!' said old Kurodaké, as if the right nail had now been hit on the head. ' But supposing there were no repercussions of that kind?'

'But there surely must be repercussions,' I said. 'Everything one says or does all one's life, or even refrains from doing, has consequences that cannot be measured. "Nor knowest thou what argument Thy life to thy neighbour's creed hath lent."'

Hajimé helped me to explain the meaning of this quotation.

'Yes,' said Kurodaké, 'I understand; I agree. But supposing that when you died your body was destroyed without trace, and your house, and all your possessions, and all your relations, friends and even acquaintances, and every personal relic or reminder of yourself?'

'You mean in an earthquake?' I said, for in Japan one is never long unconscious that one is menaced by the very earth one walks on.

'I mean more thoroughly than in an earthquake,' he said.

'Fire?'

'I mean more thoroughly than by fire,' he said.

'I can hardly imagine that.' I felt the conversation was getting a little dotty.

'I can imagine it,' said Kurodaké, and his eyelids drooped so low over his eyes that his expression suggested omniscience. It was uncomfortable, and I looked away.

'Have you in mind,' I asked, 'human destructiveness or an act of God?'

'Human destructiveness,' he said.

I glanced appealingly at Hajimé, but failed to catch his eye. A klaxon sounded suddenly in the street like an alarum, and made me jump. I had been warned that the summer was fierce in Hiroshima, and although the sweat was running down my face I had forgotten for the moment all about the projected swim. I told myself that the old man was dotty and must be humoured, but when I looked at his immobile eyes and his restless fingers playing with his beads I reminded myself that a madman lives by truths of his own, and that the sane must seem to him not only his persecutors, but his ignorant persecutors.

'In that case, you see,' Kurodaké went on, 'repercussions of personal acts would be of no importance. Everything would depend on the actions of the spirit after death.'

'It might feel revengeful,' I said.

Kurodaké laughed abruptly, but made no comment.

'I advise you to leave Hiroshima,' he said.

This was rather blunt.

'Oh!' I exclaimed, 'I hope I haven't offended you?'

'No, no, no!' He smiled almost broadly. 'I speak as a friend.' He instantly became grave again. 'What I have in mind is that you should die in the customary way — with repercussions — and avoid the new kind of death, which will impose a great burden of responsibility, and work, on the spirit. I desire your spirit to be at rest.'

I bowed again, and said: 'And the same to you.'

'You are not made,' he remarked, 'for a life of action. You should lead the life of a scholar or hermit.'

I thanked him for the advice, and he rose to his feet, springily and effortlessly, like a young man, and bowed himself out of the room. Mr. Shiroi had also gone, though I had not noticed his going.

Along with Hajimé, I asked a good many questions about his great-uncle. Kurodaké's wife, it appeared, was dead. He had one son, an officer in the navy, with whom he had quarrelled and whom he now never saw or mentioned. Hajimé did not know the nature of the quarrel, but in the family it was supposed that Kurodaké had wanted his son to be a quietist like himself, whereas the son had been determined to live an active life: the father had allowed the son to have his own way, but after, in due course, finding him a bride, he had refused to have anything more to do with him. And what sort of reputation, I asked, had Kurodaké? Among the business men of Hiroshima, said Hajimé, his great-uncle was regarded as slothful and unenterprising; among scholars he was held in respect; among servants and common people he was spoken of as a sorcerer — he had undoubtedly discovered missing persons and objects, of whose whereabouts he could not have had conscious knowledge, and he was said to have foretold future events of a private nature.

'And tell me, Hajimé, what do your father and mother think of him?'

'They respect him. He is continually urging my father to sell our house and go and live in the country, where he owns some land, near Ozu in Shikoku. My father has always lived in this house, which was built by his grandfather, and does not wish to leave it, but I think in the end he will agree.'

'Why? Because of this new kind of destructiveness which Kurodaké San prophesies, and which I must say I find rather fanciful? Is there some chemical industry in Hiroshima, where they do research into new explosives or something? But I had better not ask questions like that, or you'll think I'm a spy — although you know how little interested I really am in such matters.'

We did not go swimming that day, but lolled about with books and cold drinks and a gramophone. I felt uneasy all day, and all day it grew hotter and hotter. In the evening we were to go out in a boat to see the great annual religious festival, when, with much ceremony, a sacred object is rowed across to the sacred island of Miyajima. When I heard that Kurodaké would be with us, my feelings were mixed: I thought that with his alleged powers of divination he perhaps already knew more about me than I knew myself. . . .

After dark we were out on the water: so, it seemed, was half Hiroshima. There was no wind and no thunder, but the sky was overcast and the air more than sultry. Although we were only wearing thin cotton *yukata*, Hajimé and I were still very hot. Mr. Shiroi had taken off his panama hat and was still using his fan; his wife, whose hair had been newly dressed, looked demure in a matronly way — ladylike is perhaps the word; and Kurodaké, who sat with us in the stern of the motor launch, handed me a pair of field-glasses which he had thoughtfully brought for my use. He seemed in a less vatic mood, made jokes and laughed at other people's jokes and looked and behaved (though with dignity) more like a young man than an old one. At the same time his black *haori* coat, ornamented in the middle of the back and on the sleeves with a feudal crest in white (I can see it now — inside a circle, three wavy lines to represent running water), gave him a slightly hieratic air.

Battleships from Kuré, anchored along the line of the procession, were playing with their searchlights, turning them now on the countless boatloads of spectators, now on the sky, now towards the invisible horizon. There were lights everywhere, lanterns, torches; staccato music from a *samisen* came sharply amplified over the water; and in due course the holy boat arrived, propelled by naked oarsmen, standing and absolutely uniform and rhythmical in their movements, which were timed exactly with the thudding of drums struck by musicians in sacred vestments — those drums which are held against the left shoulder and struck with the flat right hand, and which are somehow much more dramatic than the drums of Europe. At the same time a very ancient chant arose from a party of seated singers — though singers seems hardly the word for the utterers of those deep, stylized cries, so eloquent of pain and of resignation to pain. In the middle of the boat, guarded by standing priests, a sacred ark glittered with gilding and lacquer and brocade.

Caught by a searchlight, this gliding coloured vision became instantly bleached and ghostly; excited by the heat and by *saké* and by the drums, and by the whole occasion, I thought again of death and destruction and of Kurodaké's phrase about 'the actions of the spirit after death'.

Near and far, fireworks were being let off: emeralds and rubies flowed in galaxies, hung suspended, drifted, vanished; bunches of luminosity, like magic laburnum or wistaria, suddenly hung over the sides of boats and seemed to produce magically in the water swarms of mauve or golden bees; there was a hissing and sputtering, and from our own boat a fountain of little globes, blood-red and incandescent white, played high out in a curve over the water. Looking back towards Hiroshima, one could see a huge *feu de joie*, no doubt in some open space like the parade-ground at the barracks or perhaps just outside the town; looking towards Miyajima, one could trace the progress of the holy boat and hear the ever fainter reverberations of the ritual chanters and the drummers. Seeing me looking in that direction, and knowing that Hajimé and I were going there the next day, Kurodaké told me several useful or interesting things about the sacred island. Then he said in quite a matter-of-fact tone of voice:

'It may interest you to know that on that island nobody may be born and nobody may be buried.' (I made a polite expression of interest, as if I was hearing this for the first time.) 'It is not generally known,' he went on, 'that in Hiroshima many people have been born who will never be buried.'

'Ah, is that so?' I said gravely, feeling that he ought to be humoured about his obsession. It was so hot that I felt disinclined to question him, and thought to myself that there had been previous instances of prophets dwelling on the future doom of the cities to which they belonged.

As we headed for home, two searchlights met above the distant bonfire and showed that in the windless air the smoke had risen like a tall column and had flattened out at the top: it appeared motionless.

'What a peculiar shape that smoke is,' I said, inspecting it through the field-glasses. 'It looks just like a poisonous toadstool.'

As soon as I had said this I thought it sounded rather precious. Why hadn't I said simply 'like a mushroom'? But the smoke was livid and discoloured; it *did* look rather like a poisonous toadstool. Mr. Shiroi nodded assent, displaying, in the pinkish light of a lantern hanging just over his head, an affable keyboard of teeth. Kurodaké said nothing. His eyelids were heavy, as if with sleep, but his eyes were open and were looking towards the smoke. When I looked again in the same direction the searchlights had vanished, the smoke was no longer visible, and the bonfire had died down. I wondered if I had imagined the thing, especially when I asked Hajimé if he had seen it and he said he had not.

I never saw Kurodaké after that night. He did not appear at breakfast the next morning, and Hajimé and I left before lunch for Miyajima, where we spent some happy days.

Some weeks later, when I was back in Tokyo, I had a letter from Hajimé in which he said that his great-uncle was no longer under his father's roof. One sunny day, walking in the street with Mrs. Shiroi, Kurodaké had exclaimed that *some* of the passers-by had no shadows. He had grown very excited, and had begun pointing wildly at one person after another, attracting much attention and creating something of a disturbance, which held up the traffic. Just as a policeman was approaching, Kurodaké fell to the ground in a fit. He had been removed to a mental hospital and some anxiety was felt about his condition.

Hajimé said his mother had been greatly distressed by the whole affair. Her embarrassment in the street had been extreme, but fortunately her great-uncle had mostly singled out young people, especially young girls, when he was airing his extraordinary delusion. He had only denounced two elderly persons as shadowless; one of them was Mrs. Tanaka, the bank manager's wife, who had been very much offended.

I still have Hajimé's letter: it is dated September, 1927.

1946.

# STORIES OF GREECE

# NAUSICAA

THE island of Corfu, so the guide books say, was the island of the Phaeacians. It was here that Ulysses swam ashore and was received by Nausicaa, and even to-day there are children to be found who bear that name. The first part of Greece to become a colony of Rome, Corfu was ruled later by the Byzantines, the Venetians, the despots of Epirus and the kings of Naples. Then after four centuries of Venetian domination it was occupied for a while by the French, until at the beginning of the last century it became a republic under Russian and Turkish protection. For fifty succeeding years it was controlled by the English, and at last in 1863 became part of the kingdom, now the republic, of Greece. What changes! Strange and various are the traces they have left. Old stones remain from the heroic age. The Byzantine Church of St. Jason and St. Sosipater, the procession in which the mortal remains of St. Spiridion (now vested in a company which pays handsome dividends) are carried in a silver coffin, the lousy monks at Palaiokastrizza, many a ruined convent and ikons in every house tell of the Christian era and tell of its decay. In the side of a forgotten rampart a fig tree has split in halves a stone lion of St. Mark. And on the esplanade a statue of the Venetian marshal Von der Schulenburg, brother of 'Maypole' Schulenburg, who was mistress of George I of England, crumbles slowly, a perfect specimen of the mock-heroic, and a reminder that the Christian era was also one of politics and war.

What else do the guide-books say? They direct you to the palace of the English governors, built in the elegant style which prevailed at the beginning of the last century. At a proper distance stands a piece of shoddy Italianate vulgarity typical of the end of the same century — the villa 'Achilleion' which formerly

belonged to the Kaiser. In the town library (though the guide-
books make no mention of this) there are first editions of Petrarch
and Erasmus Darwin, and in many a house may be found Venetian mirrors and Victorian lamps, Empire chairs and Turkish
silver. There is even a Chinese museum. Wherever you touch
the place you come upon this same extraordinary richness, an
accumulation of racial tendencies and historical survivals, an epi-
tome of Europe ever so faintly flavoured with Asia. And when
you leave the town, with its tall old pink Venetian houses, its
ghetto, its mouldering forts and decaying hatchments, you find
all round you a natural grandeur, beauty and fertility of a kind
that can be found nowhere else, a landscape alternately Homeric
and West Indian. Heather and sweet potatoes grow in the same
ground as the fir and the palm, while the olive trees so flourish
that whole groves attain a height of fifty or sixty feet.

But in spite of all these glories, there is certainly a curse on the
island. It becomes evident on certain days when the climate,
which is sub-tropical and capricious, becomes suddenly violent or
sultry, and brings with it low fevers and megrims; it is plain in
the decay to be found on all sides; it can be felt instinctively by
those whose instincts are sharp enough; and it can be learnt from
the fate of many of the distinguished people who have been
connected with the island. Capo d'Istria, regent of Greece, died
by the hand of an assassin; so did the Empress Elizabeth of Austria, who built the Achilleion; Kaiser Wilhelm II, her successor in
the property, lost his throne; while Count Constantinos Theo-
toki, that noble Corfiote character, lost his fortune, died a death
of lingering agony, and was attended to the grave, in spite of his
public spirit, by a mere handful of people. Nothing, however, is
more sinister than the atmosphere in which the inhabitants of the
island actually live, the aura, as it were, which emanates from
them. One expects them to be decadent, but one is not prepared
for such a degree of degeneration as that in which they live and
move. It is not simply that they are poor and live for the most

part in squalor, it is not simply that they share the generally low standards of living and physique common to most Greeks to-day, nor is it that, like the poor everywhere, they breed more children than they can feed. Nor can the climate be held solely to account, though it is certainly relaxing and demoralizing and must have hastened the decay of the common people as well as that of the formerly pretentious Corfiote aristocracy. No, the truth is that the blood is stagnant, and that ever since the long lazy centuries of Venetian domination, though some of the people have emigrated to Athens, to India, Turkey, Egypt or America, very little new blood has flowed in. Inbreeding has done and is still doing its work thoroughly. Cripples, half-wits, hunchbacks, are common enough; faces are pale, tissues flabby, blood and skin diseases very prevalent; and the unborn are often condemned to face this harsh world with as many handicaps as heredity and environment can well lay upon them. And if anybody feels any discontent, any enterprise, any energy, he goes to other lands to make his fortune, and is not over-anxious to return. If it is true, as it seems true, that some kind of spell hangs over the island, it is open to doubt whether the matter can just be explained scientifically, for if any place is haunted, Corfu is haunted; and if it is possible for a place to be singled out for bad luck, for a curse, then Corfu is such a place. In contrast to the fertility of nature, the orchards bowed down under many kinds of fruit, and the wild cyclamen which perfumes the mountain breeze, in contrast to the complexity of their history and the splendours of their past, the inhabitants have the appearance of victims. Whether nemesis is to be explained in terms of science or not, it is certain that nemesis has overtaken them.

Visitors to the island are not numerous, although it lies on the direct route between Brindisi and Athens, and this is perhaps because nothing is done to attract them. Consequently when tourists arrive, they seldom stay more than a few days. They drive to the Achilleion, they take a boat to Pontikonisi — especially if they are Germans, for this is Böcklin's 'Island of the Dead' — they climb to the top of the old fortress to enjoy what their Baedeker calls 'a superb ★ ★ View', they take a few photographs and a disapproving stroll through the town, after which there is nothing, they complain, to do. And it is true, that for many modern travellers, there is little to do. The hotels are few and bad, and their standards are those of the boarding house, the only amusements they provide being a tuneless piano, a copy or two of last week's *Continental Daily Mail*, and some furniture and Tauchnitz novels of the late 'nineties. Many people cannot bear scenery unless they can take it in small doses while they are rushing along in a motor, nor can they feel at all at ease in a place where life is frugal, lazy and corrupt. Cocktails, wireless programmes, and golf are not to be had for love or money; and when there is no taxi available, one must drive in a battered victoria, so that Americans sometimes go away uttering a wish that somebody would 'clean up' Corfu — and this in spite of the fact that the English have left a legacy of roads, water, sanitation, cricket and ginger beer. It is true that before the war some efforts were made to galvanize the place into some sort of flashiness. A casino, for example, was planned and built, but to-day its gardens are all overgrown with gigantic flowering yuccas, and the building itself, like every other available building in the place, has been used for the housing of refugee children from Asia Minor. The plaster is coming off the walls, and every afternoon a little girl with elephantiasis drags herself past on her way back from school.

In view of the general atmosphere of the place, which is provincial and nostalgic where it is not actually mournful and unhealthy, it is a little surprising that among the Greeks themselves Corfu is considered to be well worth visiting, not simply on account of its historical associations and natural beauties, but for a much stronger reason. It would be too much to say that the town has a reputation for gaiety, but one hears it said in Athens

that the Corfiotes have a certain licence of morals which is entertaining to the stranger. Nobody would assert that the Corfiotes,
or any other Greeks, are remarkable for a strict moral rectitude,
but what is the good of licence without enterprise? What is the
use of wickedness, at least as an attraction for tourists, if it is
accompanied only by anæmia, apathy and impotence, to say
nothing of poverty and squalor? In Corfu the flesh may be willing but the spirit is weak. Yet there is the fact, and there is no
getting away from it, that every year there are Greeks who come
to Corfu expecting to be amused. Just such a person might have
been seen, one evening at the end of last summer, strolling about
on the esplanade.

Napoleon Emmanuelides was wondering how to conclude the
day, which happened to be his forty-first birthday, and not finding any solution to the problem, he glanced at his watch. It was
exactly ten o'clock. He looked casually at the people sitting in
the cafés and at the passers-by, but they did not interest him
nearly as much as he interested them. They knew him for a
stranger, and some already knew him by sight, for he had been
here a week, and everybody noticed that he was always well-
dressed. The Greeks seem to attach an undue importance to
clothes. They will often look at a man's clothes before they look
at his face, while a slight shabbiness or incorrectness in their own
attire will cause them a discomfort which amounts to pain. Indeed, there are few countries where men dress so well and women
so badly. A Greek with the most precarious means will contrive
to look smarter than he is rich, while a Greek of any standing
will often appear more stylish than a man of similar standing
elsewhere. Emmanuelides was not exceptional in his tastes, and
as he strolled about was agreeably conscious of his appearance.
The night was warm for September, and he was wearing an
elegant fawn-coloured suit that fitted him perfectly, while everything else, shirt, socks, and so on, had been chosen to harmonize

with it. As he had grown older he had become more particular even than when young. His hair and teeth were scrupulously brushed, his moustache was fastidiously trimmed, and his nails had been so carefully manicured that they shone like polished pebbles, but he was very careful that his manners and appearance should not lead people to say that he was effeminate. 'Well-groomed' was how he would have liked to hear himself described, and he was proud of his extraordinary resemblance to one of the only European monarchs of our day with any pretensions to looks and style. Like that monarch (now an ex-monarch) Emmanuelides had his clothes made in England. To a casual acquaintance at the hotel he had remarked airily that he had only brought eleven suits with him to Corfu, and the acquaintance, who was not Greek, at once concluded that Emmanuelides was, besides being well-dressed, well-to-do. But in fact Emmanuelides was not by any means a rich man; his private income was small and his salary an ordinary one — he was employed by an international commission in Egypt in matters of local government. If his salary was moderate, his vanity, as has perhaps been made plain, was greater, or at least more patent, than is usual. Yet one could not very well dislike him on that account, for it was only the usual vanity of the Greek male, which is so frank and spontaneous and often goes with such good nature and vivacity, that it cannot be regarded as anything more than amusingly innocent — unless, of course, one is somehow made to suffer by it. If people are vain and unhappy and malicious they can be very unpleasant, but Emmanuelides, coxcomb as he was, had pretty much what he wanted in life, and though shallow, was not unkind. He was flattered by his friends, who were of various nationalities and as shallow and cheerful as himself; he was particularly flattered to be liked by English people, preferably those with titles or rank; he was flattered every now and again by being saluted in mistake for that king he so much resembled; women flattered him; and altogether he was quite gratified to find himself in a world which thought so highly of him and treated him so well.

But Corfu! This was another story! Never in his life had he been so disappointed by a place. Why, there was absolutely nowhere to go and dance of an evening; the theatre was closed; the women were dowdy and stuffy; the men provincial to a degree. After a week's stay he felt he had exhausted every pleasure the island had to offer. The hotel was as dreary as its inmates, German professors and American spinsters, and even the food was wretched. Fortunately he had brought an introduction to a man who had had to do with both the imperial owners of the Achilleion, and the anecdotes of royalty he heard from this man gave him some pleasure, but as he had come to Corfu thinking to find a little gaiety and international smartness, perhaps even a little illicit gaiety, he naturally felt frustrated. He had been to all the show places and had been more or less bored by them, had tried swimming and had caught a cold, had scratched the surface of local society and found it wanting, for he had not the wit to see how even its decay was enthralling and not unseldom comic. He was definitely disappointed.

Take to-day, for example. He had woken at nine, taken a bath, made his usual elaborate toilet, rung several times more than anybody else to call the servants, and after a final survey of himself in the mirror had sauntered out, well dressed and slightly scented, into the garden, where he consumed a light and leisurely breakfast. After this, while he was enjoying an English cigarette, he fell into conversation with a young American couple who were staying at the hotel. The man was a classical scholar who was just completing his first visit to Greece, and who, strangely enough, was more interested in the people than in the broken columns and the debris which fills the museums. He had a theory that the Greeks of to-day, in spite of the Byzantine tradition and in spite of their changed blood, are not entirely unlike the Greeks

of antiquity, especially in their vices. He had seen something of
the Greek colonists in America and had detected in them (he
thought) a certain matter-of-factness characteristic of their ancestors, the same love of money, the same obsession with politics,
the same jealousy of anyone among them who gave evidence of
possessing a few brains or a little power. In Greece itself he had
learnt to feel affection for a race he could never help admiring
in spite of its faults, and had been overjoyed to discover once or
twice in Athens types of men and women who seemed to him to
correspond physically to the beautiful creatures of early Attic art.
About them, as about the majority, he had no illusions, and now,
here in Corfu, he had come to regard Emmanuelides, whom he
saw at meals, and with whom he and his wife exchanged a few
words every day, as the very archetype of the modern Greek, not
the antithesis, but the late offspring of archaic glories. He saw
him plainly as one of those frivolous beings who abound in the
modern world, who are incapable of thought, who take nothing
seriously, who never seem to be without money though they
appear to do little or no work for it, who like wearing parti-
coloured shoes and silk shirts at expensive international resorts,
who are often not without a little culture and a little charm,
whose aim is pleasure and whose ambition is bound up with the
gossip-column and a little display; and he could not help seeing
him as simply one of those Greeks who, in their decadence, long
before Christ, had scattered abroad, to Rome, to Alexandria,
to Babylon, ready to act (so Juvenal noticed) as tame poets,
domestic philosophers, social parasites, speculators, quack
doctors, cheap-jacks, music-masters, rhetoricians, masseurs, or
mountebanks. He could not dislike him, though he saw
through all his shallowness and charlatanry; and as for his
wife, she really liked him, feeling rather pleased to be asked
if she knew why the Prince of Wales didn't marry, and if
she didn't think the tango had come to stay. One could not,
however, spend the whole morning, in this beautiful weather,

discussing such matters, so he pressed his wife's arm and said to Emmanuelides:

'Well, if you'll excuse us, I'm afraid we must leave you. They've brought a couple of bicycles around for us, and we want to get to Canone and back before lunch.'

And so Emmanuelides was left alone again, glancing at his shoes once more to see whether they had been properly cleaned. He stood at the entrance to the hotel, sniffing slightly, for he was not quite sure whether he had altogether lost the cold he had caught while bathing, and looked up and down in the sun-glare of the street, wondering how he should occupy the time until luncheon. He had already written postcards to all his friends, and felt disinclined to repeat the process again so soon. He yawned, with a slow, pleasurable, feline yawn, and then glanced at his nails, an occupation from which he was distracted by the arrival of a taxi. As soon as he saw it he decided at once to go for a drive, but he did not allow the chauffeur to guess his intention at once. The American couple had called the weather 'beautiful', but the month was September, in some ways the worst month of the year in Corfu, so he had been told, for it is then that the heat tells most, not because it is at its greatest but because of the unhealthy dampness with which it is overcharged; the air seems to have lost some essential ingredient, and becomes stale and listless, bringing no ozone from the sea; it is breathed with difficulty, like the atmosphere surrounding some other and crueller planet than this; the sea itself is silent, without ever a wave, and seems stagnant; at its edges whole banks of seaweed decay with a frightful and noxious stench; and at sunset the rock pools begin to coruscate with the transient gleams given off by tiny phosphorescent vermin; the very fish which are drawn from these waters seem, in September at least, to be either tasteless or touched with some almost imperceptible taint. Yes, decidedly the only thing to do on a morning like this was to move through the air in the hope of refreshing oneself. One might drive through the village of

Potamo, for instance — not because one was interested in picturesque poverty but because it was one of the places that people went to, and would form a topic of conversation with the American couple. The taxi-driver approached Emmanuelides and suggested a drive, but he shook his head. They exchanged a few words, and the taxi-driver became importunate, whereupon a thoroughly Greek conversation ensued. Emmanuelides called him a thief and a liar, they both invoked heaven, and their four hands went through a long series of eurhythmics and spasmodics which ended in the chauffeur's reluctantly agreeing to do the drive for half the price he had at first asked. Emmanuelides then put on a white hat and dark spectacles and got into the car. The chauffeur drove rather fast, hoping to get another fare on his return to the town, and it was noticeable that whenever there was a downward slope he switched off the engine for economy's sake. The car ran between hedges of prickly-pear, past thickets of bamboo and pink-and-white chapels, a cemetery with cypresses, a villa with palms, past fields of cabbages and egg-plants, but Emmanuelides was not much interested in what he saw, and began to ask the chauffeur some facetious personal questions. At one point, where it was necessary to slow down, a boy with wasted limbs and eczema ran begging by the side of the car, and Emmanuelides without any hesitation threw him a drachma, which at that time was worth about three farthings. The chauffeur was sulky, and as for the village of Potamo, well, why did people come and see it? Certainly the church was large, but all the houses were rotting or in ruin, there were pigs in the main street and the discoloured plaster was everywhere coming away from the walls. Certainly some of the peasant women were wearing their celebrated costume, but although their hands and feet were small they were not exactly beauties . . . And before he knew where he was, Emmanuelides was back again at the hotel. The dining-room was chilly, in spite of the heat of the day; the food was as poor as usual; and there was no liveliness among the visitors. Afterwards, following his customary routine, Emmanuelides took a long siesta, sleeping for more than two hours.

When he rose, he dressed carefully in a different suit to the one he had worn in the morning, and went out for a stroll in the town, where he had a little shopping to do. But directly he found himself in the narrow principal street, called after Our Lady of Victories, his progress was impeded by a crowd, he heard the slow strains of an approaching band, and was obliged to stand by for a funeral to pass. And what a funeral! After the band, which was playing a dirge stridently and slightly out of tune, came four popes and a number of young men holding candles. The bright westering sun, shafted between two rows of houses, shone full upon them, made the candle-flames almost invisible, and lit up the faces in such a way as to make them all livid or lurid, especially those already pale from sickness or debauchery. There were no women at all in the procession, but it did not produce any idea of restrained and manly grief or of the nobility of death. On the contrary, the sun was so merciless that it not only shone like a searchlight upon the funeral itself, but seemed to draw out grimly every suggestion of mortality in each living face and hand, showed up the greenish tinge of clothes once black, and made death seem but a matter of corruption, misery and degradation. The climax came with the arrival of the hearse, all varnished black angels, gilded knobs and twisted pillars, and drawn by two gaunt horses entirely caparisoned, except for the eyes and hooves, with a material which had once been purple velvet, but which the ruthless sun showed to have faded almost to grey and puce, revealing the tarnished braid of the borders and even small rents and darns in the side. Two of the mourners had faces quite disfigured with grief, several more had affected the same emotion, and all the rest were set in various expressions of dutifulness, habit, sympathy and indifference. The last slow feet followed the fading notes of the band, and the spectators felt no doubt of the reality of either the sting of death or the victory of the grave. Even the unserious Emmanuelides had been made to feel momentarily gloomy and uneasy, to remind himself that this was his birthday, and to wonder how long he was likely to be allowed to live. The atmosphere had become steamy again, and he wiped the sweat away from his forehead.

By the time he had done what he had set out to do, had sat in a café to watch the people and read the newspaper, had spent half an hour in conversation with a returned Greek-American who professed himself disgusted with the lack of comfort in his native island, and had finally returned to the hotel, it was nearly time to dress for dinner.

And now it was ten o'clock, and there were three hours to be whiled away somehow, for Emmanuelides never dreamt of going to bed before one in the morning. He was standing irresolutely under a tree in the esplanade when somebody stepped out of the shadows and touched him on the arm. It was a young man who was wearing a large cap which had been manufactured to look like tiger-skin. He had a pale face and neat black moustache, and it was clear from his roguish expression and insinuating manner that he was a pimp. Every instinct that was most frivolous in Emmanuelides immediately awoke, and he promptly began to ask the man a number of bantering questions, although he had not the least intention of being persuaded by him. Coquettish and chaffing, his behaviour was never more characteristic of the type of man to which he belonged, and the pimp soon saw that there was no business to be done and turned away to seek honester game, so that Emmanuelides found himself exactly where he had been ten minutes before.

Just at this moment the moon rose. An orange moon, not quite full, it suddenly looked out dramatically from a cloud-wreath above the mountains of northern Epirus on the other side of the strait, scattered its light on the sea, and with level rays cast a pale radiance upon the old fortress, the trees in the esplanade, the façade of the English palace, and the mouldy statues that stood here and there — an English governor in streaky bronze; Guilford, the eccentric philhellene, in marble; and especially the fantastic Schulenburg, in chipped periwig and sandstone toga, pot-bellied above his panelled trophies. Moonstruck, the whole scene had a touch of magic. Long shadows, and contrasts of light and shade, seemed to distort the proportions of things, and the esplanade became a stage set for any improbable happening; while by way of overture a blind fiddler had struck up in a café with an eerie Heptanese folk-tune. But although the appearance of the moon had given the hour and the place a sudden glamour, Emmanuelides saw little chance of anything happening to distract him, and on turning over in his mind the possible amusements — a primitive open-air cinema, a game of cards or billiards, a dull walk or conversation — he rejected each in turn. It was then, however, that an idea occurred to him. It is perhaps no exaggeration to say that the only ideas which ever occurred to him were those connected with his own pleasure, and this was accordingly one of them. Why, he reflected, should he not take a boat for an hour or two? He at once made his way to a landing-place he knew of, where there were always boats to be had, and sure enough there were several to choose from. But he did not choose a boat so much as a boatman, for what would be the good of spending time with a dreary companion? One of the boatmen was much younger than the others, and Emmanuelides at once got into his boat, at which the older men were rather annoyed.

As soon as he had pushed off, the young boatman looked narrowly at his passenger, feeling for him, as it happened, an aversion as instinctive as the attraction he had exerted over Emmanuelides. He could only think of him as a fool with money to spend, and felt towards him the usual Greek envy of anybody a little richer or happier than oneself, and that bitterness which can only be felt towards people of one's own kind. Emmanuelides could see the boy's black eyes sparkling in his handsome face, but he did not consider how far these good looks were due to poverty and hunger, and sought to please him by making amiable remarks. He was only answered shortly. The boat was not far from shore when some voices became audible, singing the words of a tango which had been the fashion in Greece for several months past, and the tune of which tended to haunt the least musical ear. It was a tune based on an indigenous Argentine melody, but had been written by a Polish-Australian Jew in Paris, and popularized by a negro comedienne with what the Greeks call a pancosmic reputation. With Emmanuelides it was a special favourite, and as the singers ashore left it off he took it up, humming it in a rather highly-pitched voice, grinning, and beating time with his foot on the bottom of the boat.

'Ah, how often I have danced to this tune,' he exclaimed.

The boatman, whose name was Spiros, made no comment, bending to the oar.

'Do you like dancing?' said Emmanuelides, without waiting for an answer. 'I love it myself. I usually dance every evening at the same cabaret, and forget all about the work I've done during the day. It's pleasure and exercise combined. But in Corfu there doesn't seem to be any dancing. What a dull place it is!'

'Where do you live?' said Spiros.

'Well,' said Emmanuelides, 'I live in Athens.' He was very cautious and reticent, or in other words he was telling a lie.

'Are you in business there?'

'Yes, in business,' he lied, and there was a silence broken only for a time by the creaking of the oars. 'And you?' said Emmanuelides in a soft voice. 'Tell me something about yourself.'

The boy laughed rather contemptuously, and said nothing. 'Dancing', in the sense that Emmanuelides used the word, to Spiros represented all that he felt he himself could never attain to, a world of ease and pleasure and money, and his envy of the older man became intensified at every word.

'Well?' said Emmanuelides expectantly.

'What do you want to know?' said Spiros, avoiding his glance.

'First of all,' said Emmanuelides, 'please stop rowing. We've gone quite far enough, and it'll do you good to have a rest.'

Spiros obediently put up the oars, and still said nothing. Emmanuelides, leaning forward, offered him a cigarette, which he took, and lighted. When the match lit up his face, Emmanuelides was quite struck with his good looks, so struck that he forgot to be discreet, and said suddenly:

'Do you know, I was lying to you just now.'

'Were you?' said Spiros. 'What about?'

'I told you I was in business at Athens, but I'm not in business and I don't live in Athens. I live in Egypt and I'm an official.'

'Ah,' said Spiros, 'not in Alexandria?'

'Yes, Alexandria. Why do you ask?'

'I only wondered . . . But why did you lie to me at first?'

'Well,' said Emmanuelides, 'at first I didn't quite trust you, because I didn't know you. But now I see that I can trust you, I see that you're a good boy.'

'But is there any secret about where you live?'

'Oh, you never know. I'm a stranger here, and an official. People sometimes talk —'

There was a pause. The moon had risen higher, and the Othonian islands could be distinctly seen, bathed in a golden mist.

'As you are an official,' said Spiros, not without hesitation, 'perhaps you can help me.'

'I'll do anything I can for you,' said Emmanuelides with an unexpected eagerness, leaning forward again. 'Let me be your friend.'

Spiros was a little suspicious of this generosity but he resolved to turn it to good account. It seemed to him an enjoyable sort of revenge, to take thorough advantage of the kindness of a person one despised. So he began talking a little of himself, making his story seem as pathetic as possible. He stressed his poverty, which was genuine; explained that his parents were both dead, which was true; said that he lived with his uncle, that his life was dull, that he helped the fishermen in the intervals of managing his boat, that he had no money and no future — all of which was equally true. Seeing how effectively he was playing on Emmanuelides' feelings, he was careful not to overdo his performance, but with silence, and an occasional catch in the voice, he worked wonders. It became clear that Emmanuelides was excited and interested, perhaps by the story, or by his moonlight excursion, by this variation from his recent boredom, or by Spiros himself.

'Have you any brothers or sisters?' he said, not because he wanted to know, but because he wanted to watch Spiros, to hear him talk, and to make it appear as if he took a very special interest in him. At this question the boy's manner and expression immediately changed. It was possible, even in the moonlight, to see his dark eyes dilate, to see that he had somehow been touched to the quick. And Emmanuelides, with an almost feminine alertness, missed nothing. Where Spiros had previously been speaking for effect, he now spoke with passion. The words hurried to keep pace with his thoughts.

'I have one sister,' he said, 'and it is with regard to her that I want to ask your help. Her name is Nausicaa. Three years ago she was married to a man who came from Egypt. We knew nothing of him, he was not a Corfiote, but my uncle said that she ought to marry him, and she did. When she went away, it was the worst day of my life. And although she promised to write, and although I have made inquiries, we have never heard a word from that day to this. I am longing to see her again, at least to have news of her, but I have a great fear. From things I have heard indirectly, I believe it is possible that she has been forced to become a prostitute in Alexandria.'

Emmanuelides was careful to utter a horrified exclamation.

'And this is where I ask you to help me. Can you inquire for me if she can be found? I can give you all particulars, and the name of the man she went away with . . .'

Emmanuelides felt a glow of satisfaction, felt that he had conquered this at first contemptuous boy, felt that by promising help he could complete that conquest. Laying his hand on the boy's knee, he said, in very gentle and emotional voice:

'But of course I will help you, *pallikaraki*. I'll make detailed inquiries directly I get back, and let you know the result. I'm sure she can be traced.'

And Spiros believed him, forgot his envy, felt that he really had found a friend, so that his whole attitude to Emmanuelides changed, and his reserve melted away.

They stayed out so long on the calm water that warm night that, by the time they returned, the moon was in quite a different part of the sky. After Emmanuelides had given the boy some money, he made his way back to the hotel, feeling very pleased with himself.

Shortly afterwards, he made a second excursion, spending the whole afternoon on the water with Spiros, renewing his promise and assurances in regard to Nausicaa, and making himself as amiable as possible. But in his own mind he had already decided to leave Corfu, and when, on their return in the evening, a little rain began to fall, he felt himself in danger of being bored again, for his curiosity about Spiros was now satisfied.

'I shall have to leave in a few days,' he said on landing. 'If I don't see you before then, be sure to come and see me before I go.'

And although Spiros regretted in some ways the prospective departure of Emmanuelides, his heart beat quicker at the thought of the possibility of his sister's being found, so he said good night to him with mixed feelings.

Before Emmanuelides reached the hotel the rain was falling

quite heavily. It continued to fall, on and off, for a week. Also, the weather was very cold, and because it was early in the season, the hotel was inadequately heated. The visitors were miserable, but none was more bored than Emmanuelides, who did not know what to do with himself, and attached himself rather too closely to the American couple. Their views on the charm of the Greeks became a little modified. Besides, not having been long married they were quite contented to be alone together, whatever the weather was like. One day, when it cleared a little, they went out bicycling again, largely with the idea of escaping for a time from Emmanuelides, but the bad luck which is characteristic of the island came upon them, and the woman fell off her machine and was slightly injured.

It was the morning of Emmanuelides' departure. He rose much earlier than usual, put on his slippers of soft red leather, and a dressing-gown of brocaded silk, and went over to the window. Not only had the rain stopped, but there was not a cloud in the sky. The room faced westwards, looking inland over a wide and varied panorama, which now appeared, with the sun's bright beams shining through the unsullied air as if through a crystal, clearer than he had ever seen it before. The sea was all diamonds, while between the rocky heights of San Salvatore on the right and those of Hagia Deka on the left, towers and trees and gardens were as finely coloured as those in a medieval illumination or oriental miniature, and just as the Middle Ages and the East are to be thought of as largely squalid and filthy, full of the corruption of earth and humanity, so were the houses of Corfu; but if those paintings are glorious projections of mortality, so too this aspect of the island seemed such a projection, with the white cliff cluster of the village of Pelleka over there (so poor and dirty really) looking now like a colony of love in Paradise itself, as if nature wished to show that she does not disdain the function of art, which can paint a heaven with earthy colours. The morning sky, the sunny white houses among green trees, the cries of children and the twinkling leaves below his window, were not unappreciated by the spectator, for he was tired of days of rain. But he was also tired of Corfu, not with the frantic ennui of the nervous and high-strung, but with the weak satiety of a dilettante. He was bored, and glad to go, and looked at the landscape without regrets. Indeed, it made him unwontedly reflective, for he felt it to be slightly sinister, and he remembered his birthday, the funeral he had seen, and the mad moon rising over the esplanade. Yes, he even became imaginative enough to think of the dirt and disease he had seen, which festered even now behind those white walls of near mansions and distant cottages; he remembered how he had been told only yesterday that Corfu had had the first lunatic asylum in Greece, and he saw madness brooding in innocent hamlets; he thought of the two madwomen he knew so well by sight as familiar characters in the town — one, young and dressy, who hurried off daily to stand motionless for hours under a tree in the square, muttering empty litanies; the other older and lousy, with a shock of curls, who strolled about scavenging and sometimes wept so vehemently as to cause laughter, hers seemingly the shrill grief of a buffoon. Already the magic of the light was slightly coarsened, soldiers were marching, a motor-lorry was passing, day was terrestrial, and Emmanuelides had finished his cigarette. He threw it away, and turned to shave and pack, glad to go, but feeling a slight irritation at the thought of a possible visit from Spiros.

As often, and perhaps usually happens, two human beings had each other in mind at the same moment, and Spiros was just dressing with a view to saying good-bye to Emmanuelides. He was dressing in borrowed clothes, while Emmanuelides was explaining to the valet-de-chambre that his tenth suit must not be crushed in the packing. From his childhood up Spiros had been familiar with the façade of the hotel. GRAND HOTEL BRISTOL AND ITHAKA was written in Greek and Roman letters above the door, and he seldom went past without exchanging a nod with the hall-porter, a distant connexion of his by marriage. But the idea of entering had never occurred to him. Even on the occasions when he had brought back a scarf or camera which somebody had left in his boat, there had always been a servant at the entrance to receive it. Not that the hotel was awe-inspiring; it simply housed a floating population of persons who were mostly foreign and therefore rich, or if not rich, able, under pressure, to pay. Yet this morning, so brilliant after the rain, Spiros went up the steps a little awkwardly and uneasily, proud and yet somehow ashamed of his blue serge suit and borrowed white collar that pressed a trifle tightly on his brown, muscular neck. The clear voices of two young women from 'Europe', from one of those pulsating cities that form the nerve centres of the world, rang with quick laughter and repartee, and he caught sight of their figures through the revolving glass door. They were tall and slender, dressed very simply and smartly, with a touch of care-lessness and scarcely any jewellery or paint, standing and moving in ways that were neither slack nor stiff, but easy with the ease and elegance of people who have never known for generations what it is to be without money or food, and who regard any momentary lack of one or the other as a joke. They both glanced at Spiros as he passed, with the quick, calculating glance of their species, and his gaze rested on each of them in turn, deliberately, independently, with that mixture of shyness and hostility that can be seen in the faces of peasants, children, animals and persons very highly organized. A moment later they had gathered up their things and gone out into the sunshine, while he went slowly upstairs. On the first floor there was some confusion but he found his way to Emmanuelides' room.

'Ah, there you are,' said Emmanuelides airily. 'You're very smart this morning.'

'These clothes do not fit me,' said the boy, looking at the luggage piled up in the middle of the room.

'You haven't yet tied on the labels!' Emmanuelides exclaimed to the servant. 'Please do it quickly.'

'You won't forget . . .' began Spiros.

'Now where are my keys? Ah, here they are! I thought for a moment I had lost them!' Emmanuelides smiled broadly.

'I came to say good-bye,' said Spiros, 'and to ask you not to forget . . .'

'To inquire, you mean? But of course I shall not forget . . .' He glanced at his watch. 'Ah, look at the time! I must hurry. An American lady who is staying here has had a bicycle accident, and her husband says she is determined to see me before I go. One must consider the ladies . . . And the ship sails in three-quarters of an hour!'

He moved out of the room, and Spiros followed, saying again: 'You won't forget?'

Emmanuelides looked back over his shoulder at the servant, who was still busy with the labels, and seeing that he was unobserved, for he had a horror of scandal, pinched Spiros' cheek.

'Good-bye,' he said facetiously, 'and be good.'

He began to walk away, smiling as usual, on his way to the room occupied by the two Americans, glanced down at his breast pocket to see that the corner of his handkerchief was properly displayed, and then turned round and said to Spiros:

'I'll make inquiries, but they may not come to anything. People move about, you know — it is not always possible to trace them . . .'

Twenty minutes later he appeared at the front door. Spiros saw him go, and then after a few minutes' conversation with the porter, stepped across the street in the splendid sunshine, walking aimlessly in the direction of his home. The air was wonderfully fresh after the rain. Two or three children were playing with a cat in an alleyway, and a stout woman came out of a doorway, gave them a quick glance, and then, looking in the opposite direction, called out in a sonorous voice, 'Nausicaa! Come back when I call you!' Spiros started, and involuntarily glanced round, just in time to see a tiny child appear at the top of some steps in response to its mother's call. When he reached the corner of the next street his ear caught the distant sound of a siren from the direction of the port. Familiar enough, that prolonged, vibrant wail had never meant so much to him. But the boat was leaving, and its cry was not one of expectation but of farewell. Its effect on him was that of a warning to abandon hope, the last cry of the ghost of an illusion, and it seemed as though that departing ship were leaving him utterly alone on a desert island. He no longer cared whether Emmanuelides made inquiries or not, for he felt certain now that Nausicaa would never be found. 'People move about, you know, it is not always possible to trace them . . .' When he considered how much he hated the man who had uttered those words, how instinctively and whole-heartedly he detested him, Spiros could not understand how he could have allowed himself to behave so amiably towards Emmanuelides. And because he was unwilling even to catch a glimpse of the departing ship, he turned and took a road that led directly away from the sea.

# THE CRISIS

ZAPPAGLOU, a wholesale tobacco merchant, formerly of Stamboul, is a very fat patriarchal creature with somewhat old-fashioned tastes, and when he retired to Athens with a small fortune he did not go and build himself a pretentious villa at Kephissia, but acquired from some impoverished relations a real old Greek house, dating from the days of the Turkish occupation and standing right in the very shadow of the Acropolis itself. The house is on the steep north side of the Acropolis, in that old quarter now threatened not only by the usual encroachments of modern life but even by the zeal of archæologists from the western world who have got an idea into their heads that all sorts of antique treasures must be hidden under these charming streets so crowded together on the slope — though of course all they will find is an assortment of broken bits of bad late sculpture and the usual lumps and odds and ends.

Zappaglou's house can easily be distinguished from a distance, because it has two cypresses and a large fig-tree in the yard. It is approached by some steps turning off from a very narrow passage called Mykonos Street, and surrounded by a thick old wall which is partly whitewashed and has two Byzantine capitals embedded in it (one of them upside-down) as well as what seems to be a section of a slender fluted column of great age. In this wall there is a gate, or rather a door, which leads into the yard, and as soon as you get inside you find a palm tree as well as the other trees already mentioned. There are various outbuildings on two sides, and on a third there is the house itself, covered with stucco of a very light fawn colour. There is an iron balcony, the windows have shutters, and the roof is tiled, while above it rise three or four of those elegant Venetian chimneys which are shaped like an inverted cone. In the yard there are usually to be found a nondescript dog, some washing hanging out, and some rather dirty children, while on the balcony above one is certain in good weather, during the mornings or late afternoons, to see Zappaglou himself, sitting in a white alpaca jacket and a pair of white cotton trousers which are cut so that they almost reach his armpits, in order to enclose his enormous paunch. On his wrist there is a tiny gold watch which he wears not because he really cares what the time is but because it gives him a feeling of authority. Its face, misty with the steam that continually rises from such a gross organism, is almost hidden in a forest of black hairs.

Sitting up there on his balcony, talking politics or food and wheezing cheerfully over his own jokes with his crony, a retired shipowner, Zappaglou is pretty well content. Of course there is an 'economic crisis' on. There always is nowadays. But that is not peculiar to Greece. And in any case the very words 'economic crisis' are Greek and have been so for a very long time, so that if the words creep into the conversation now and then they bring with them no disturbing novelty.

Where he sits Zappaglou has the Acropolis and his own house and family at his back and the best part of Athens spreads out before him. There, on the left, is the Theseion; there, on the right, is the Constitution Square and the formerly royal garden; and there is the rocky hill of Lykabettos with the white church like a lighthouse on its summit, and over there is Mount Hymettos, ready to turn violet when the sun has set. But if it is agreeable to Zappaglou to sit in such a commanding position, which makes him feel properly related to the history and traditions of his race and family and to the town and its contemporary life, he has other causes for satisfaction. A newspaper at his elbow — a progressive conservative newspaper — is ready to share with him his own opinions, and being a newspaper it puts no great strain on the intellect. His wife within there is ready to be argued with or to advise him, as she has done with sound common sense for the last forty years, and she is no doubt giving an eye to the preparation of supper in that kitchen which is a favourite haunt of his, for cooking is his hobby, and to see Zappaglou squeezing a few drops out of a lemon into his favourite soup is one of the most comfortable and heartening sights imaginable — the only thing is that if he were a little less fat he would be able to get nearer to the stove and his activities there.

Sometimes he glances down into the yard and calls out an order to a child or a servant, and sometimes he looks across to the outbuildings and thinks of their inmates, and certainly they give him plenty of food for thought. First of all, there is a whole family ensconced in three rooms at the end. These are the cousins from whom he took over the whole place. Hopelessly improvident, they would have let everything go to rack and ruin if he had not stepped in just when he did. And he has been kind enough to let them stay on, provided they keep to the other side of the yard. He only charges them a very small rent, which they are always backward in paying, and this gives his wife grounds for saying, 'You ought never to have let them stay on here. I advised you against it, but you allowed family sentiment to get the better of you, and now you see what comes of it, and I hope you're satisfied.'

Next to the rooms occupied by the cousins is a servant's room, and then, up a flight of stone steps, comes a room used by Zappaglou's youngest son, the apple of his mother's eye and the chief bane (a much more real one than the 'crisis') of his father's existence. In the first place, although Costa is supposed to be in the tobacco business with his elder and married brother and is paid a salary for that, he seems to be always in need of money. Then he will insist on living in that room and sometimes will not come near the house itself for two or three days at a time. He shows every sign of becoming one of those amiable wasters whom nature is liable to provide as sons to successful business men. And besides, it is he who is responsible for the presence in the only remaining room in the yard of Nikos and Timos.

Nikos and Timos are beggars, and they live in that room for nothing. Of course, old Zappaglou is not so mean that he minds doing a little something for charity, but when the beggars came he was already charitable in other directions, and there is the crisis to think of. Besides, although he has no real objection to Nikos and Timos, and rather likes them and especially the respectful way in which they always speak to him, their presence is useful as an argument against Costa. And in Zappaglou's conversations with his wife about their youngest son such arguments are needed, for she will admit no fault in the boy.

'I don't know where he picked them up!' Zappaglou exclaims irritably.

'They don't do any harm!' his wife retorts.

'And they don't do any good either,' he grumbles.

'Ah, well, you must put up with them. What with the crisis . . .'

'The crisis!' he roars. 'If anybody wants to get anything out of me they always start talking about the crisis! If people do anything wrong nowadays, they don't blame their own wicked hearts or their own laziness — oh no, not a bit of it! What do they do? They blame the crisis! Don't they understand that for a serious man life is always a crisis? I've always found it so. I've always been in a state of crisis, trying to avoid bankruptcy or overwork or starvation or family troubles or bad cooking. And the only way to overcome one crisis after another is by hard work. And that's what's wrong with Costa — he's afraid of work! And not content with being a beggar himself he must go and add two more beggars to the household!'

'He's not a beggar!'

'He will be one day!'

These discussions are never conclusive, and nobody is less affected by them than the subjects themselves. The way Nikos and Timos were brought to live under the unwilling patronage of old Zappaglou was this. His son Costa, sitting once in a café of ill repute at the Piraeus, saw the two beggars come in, one playing an accordion and the other singing, and taking a fancy first to the music and then to the performers, he prevailed upon his mother to allow them to come and live in the room in the yard, at that time empty, and there they have been for more than a year. They don't seem ungrateful.

'Like everybody else,' they say, 'of course we feel the effects of the crisis, and are thankful to have a roof over our heads.'

But when Nikos and Timos speak it is never possible to tell for certain whether there is not perhaps a trace of irony in the tones of their voices, for they are both, in a sense, people who have been quite disillusioned but whose disillusionment has partly healed, and people of that sort are apt to be both independent and mysterious. And then that 'we' of theirs is rather formidable. Neither of them is ever heard to use the word 'I'. Never was there such a mating of two natures. Yet they remain very definitely two natures, and when one speaks for both, it is because he knows the other would approve of what he says though incapable of saying the same himself.

'And how are "we"?' old Zappaglou sometimes asks them when he is in a good temper.

'We are very well,' they reply gravely.

Separate natures, and yet neither can be said to play a more active part than the other, as is so often the case in partnerships between two human beings. Nikos, who is blind, is the more beautiful of the two. He is rather tall for a Greek and holds himself very erect, while his blindness causes him to tilt his head back more than he would ordinarily do, and this tendency is becoming to him and brings into relief the harmonious regularity of his features. Timos is shorter. He is not blind, but nearly so. He suffers from a severe ophthalmia. His eyelids are scarlet and inflamed and nothing seems to do them any good.

These two expect nothing of life but what it has already given them. They do not dread death, but would prefer not to be separated. Their outlook on life combines the most unutterable melancholy and a constant gaiety. As for their time, that is mostly spent in the streets, where they beg. Nikos plays his battered accordion, of which the notes are surprisingly pure and plaintive. He sings also, in the most melting voice, a few snatches of old folk songs or of popular tunes like *Valencia*; while Timos, who can at any rate distinguish people from houses, approaches the former with a battered tin tray which he holds out for alms. It is a good idea, that tray. If you give them too little, your meanness lies naked in the sun until Timos chooses to pocket it.

§ 2

Rather late one afternoon, when Nikos and Timos were out begging, and Costa was down at the sea with his friend the sailor, old Zappaglou was sitting on his veranda. He had risen from his siesta and was now sitting there with his hairy paws clasped over his huge belly. He was waiting for his wife to bring him a large slice of an excellent melon which his sister had sent him, and his mental faculties had temporarily abdicated in favour of his salivary glands. Before the melon arrived, however, his attention was caught by the passing of a pedestrian up the lane just below the house. A foreigner, thought Zappaglou, a tourist no doubt, he has a white suit and is eating something out of a bag. But beyond that he registered no further impression, for he did not know that he would ever see the passer-by again. Besides, the melon had just arrived, and seemed much more important.

The passer-by, who was wearing a Palm Beach suit and eating

Turkish Delight out of a paper bag, was none other than Fletcher
B. Raper, newly appointed chief local executive organizer for
Greece of Study Trips in Bible Lands, Inc. Mr. Raper was
delighted with Greece and with Mr. Raper. And he thought
Turkish Delight was the swellest candy imaginable. He had a
large glabrous face, like an omelette in texture and a boiled
shrimp in colour. The eyes were keen but unseeing, the nose
was small, the nostrils were pinched, the mouth was thin, the
ears were large, the cheeks were like buttocks, the chin was
determined — and the whole, supported on a high, starched
collar, would have done very well for the head of an American
president, the only trouble being that an American president
nowadays has to have two O's in his surname, and Raper — well,
Raper hasn't even one. 'Raper Runs for President,' though,
sounded quite plausible.

At the moment Mr. Raper was not 'running for president'
but climbing to the Acropolis, and although the afternoon was
well advanced he continued to feel the heat. He had felt the heat
all the morning, and had not perhaps been wise to schedule visits
to three museums in the hot sun in as many hours. And instead
of taking a proper siesta after lunch he had been busy with a type-
writer in a hotel bedroom facing the sun. He thought he was
going up to the Acropolis to get cool and to improve his knowledge of that ancient spot, but he was just getting hotter and
hotter. He told himself he was a fool for not taking a taxi, but
with the crisis back home he figured to try and save something
out of his salary as local executive of Study Trips.

Turning a corner into an even narrower lane than the one he
had left, he came face to face with Nikos and Timos. He saw
that they were beggars and he saw that they were dirty. Whatever faults Mr. Raper may have had he looked very clean, and the
lousiness of the two beggars quite upset him. Also, he saw that
he would have to give them something, and that rather irritated
him. Nikos was standing in the middle of the way, and singing

in a low voice as if he was the only person in the world. He looked very tall, and the absolutely resigned and self-contained expression on his face made Mr. Raper feel somehow awkward. Timos, seeing a white blur approaching, went up to it with his tin tray, and said something in Greek. It was Greek to Mr. Raper. He had so far been too busy doing what he called 'studying up' statistics to learn much of the language, though he had already arranged for lessons; Greek art, literature, and mythology had also eluded him hitherto. He now produced a ten-drachma note and placed it reluctantly on the tray, and then, catching sight of Timos's inflamed eyes, hurried off up the hill, wiping his fingers on his handkerchief in case he had picked up some germs. Somebody ought to clean up these slums, he thought, and popped the last piece of Turkish Delight into his mouth.

Five minutes later he was seated in the shade behind a broken column near the Erechtheion. He had had to sit down on account of a slight feeling of giddiness. There were rumblings in his interior and he wondered if he had been wise to eat so much Turkish Delight, but he believed that if you *think* there is something wrong with you there soon *will* be something wrong with you, so he took out his pocket book to look at a list he had made of things he hoped to do on the following day. Mr. Raper was ambitious. He was proud of his new appointment, and he meant to make a success of it. He knew that he was lucky to get it in a time of world-wide crisis, and he also knew that if or when the crisis passed, heavy bookings could be obtained in the Middle West for Study Trips in Bible Lands. All that would be wanted would be a large-scale publicity drive.

Mr. Raper fell into a day-dream, into a doze. He was a romantic person, and as he sat there, leaning back against that ancient marble fragment, he dipped into his future, and found it as succulent as Turkish Delight. He imagined himself being interviewed by a correspondent of some great newspaper back home. He worked out the headlines:

U.S. EXECUTIVE, CHIEF LOCAL ORGANIZER OF STUDY TRIPS IN BIBLE LANDS, INC., TELLS CHARMS OF HELLAS — GREECE IMPORTS MORE FROM AMERICA THAN ANY OTHER COUNTRY — FLETCHER B. RAPER ADVISES TOURISTS TO COME BEFORE MODERNIZATION IS COMPLETED.

'I found Executive Raper strolling on the Acropolis in Athens, Greece,' the interview would begin. ' "Scarcely a century ago," he said, "this tiny country had a total population of hardly 600,000 but she now embraces a large area and a population of 6,204,684. The influence of the United States may be in part attributed to the presence in the United States of 498,231 persons of Greek birth. At the present time Greece imports more goods from the United States than from any other country in the world, and the United States, on its side, is the chief purchaser of Greek staple commodities. The principal public works now being carried on in this country are being carried on by well-known American corporations, and include the new American sewage farm on the plain of Marathon. If we sewage farmers could only get together we could drain the world, and if all the dollar bills for draining all the countries in the Balkans alone were laid end to end and converted into gold they would weigh more than Paraguay's war debt to Japan did before the slump.

' "Travel in Greece at this time is fraught with material discomforts, but doubtless within a few years the system of projected automobile highways will have linked up the sacred sites whose names have come down to us in history, and also at that time the whole country will be dotted with tourist hotels. We take our Greece for granted, little comprehending the giant economic strides this little country has taken, so my advice to all and sundry is to come and see historic little Hellas before American money and American enterprise have cleaned it up, which it sorely needs. What Greece wants is better roads, better ruins, and better toilet-paper. What would St. Paul have said, what would Poet Byron have said, what would Excavator Schliemann have said? *You* can visit Greece too. Visit mosquito-free Missolonghi — Ice-water in every bedroom — Dancing in the winter-garden every afternoon — Attend the Eleusinian Mystery Ball on Thanksgiving Night — Balls all the year round — Conjure up the classic past in eight thousand restful bedrooms, each with bath.

' "And what has America done here in Athens? Here in Athens we have the American School of Classical Studies, the American Friends of Greece, Athens College at Psychiko, the American College for Girls at Phaleron, and the new Y.M.C.A. located on Euripides Street. Say, where would Greece be without America? Where would America be without Greece? And where would waffles be without syrup? And where would the Parthenon be without a bum executive walking all around it? In the British Museum probably.

' "Yes, sir, all in all, the friends of Greece can hope and expect that in the course of the coming years, when once we have got over the crisis, this country, always one of the most interesting in the world, will become as well one of the most prosperous, independent economically as well as politically. Say, where should we be — where should I be, we be, where would you be, they be, without the street-car, the elevator, the radio, and the telephone? Visit the classic shores of Hellas before it is too late. Tread where Socrates trod, Plato argued, and Helen of Troy launched all those ships. Why, this land is so impregnated with history that it cannot fail to touch a responsive chord in even the least idealist among us. See the Ilissus by moonlight, see where Homer nodded, see the quaint Republican Guards in their ballet skirts." '

At this point Mr. Raper's dream took such an eccentric turn that it can no longer be reproduced here. And then he suddenly woke up, shouting, 'Say, who called me a bum executive?'

It was ten minutes before sunset, closing-time on the Acropolis and an irritable official was doing his voluble best to rouse Mr. Raper from his stony couch. He succeeded, and Mr. Raper was the last to leave the Propylea, which he did with the sun shining full in his eyes. Oh, that sun! Mr. Raper was sick of it. Mr. Raper felt sick and a little shaky at the knees, and a fine, cold perspiration broke out on his forehead. He took off his hat to cool his head, and began to make his way downhill.

§ 3

Five minutes before sunset Zappaglou, in a black alpaca coat and a straw hat, left his house for a short stroll. At the corner of Mykonos Street he was surprised to see again the foreigner he had seen earlier in the afternoon. But this time he was not walking purposefully along and eating sweets out of a bag. No, he was leaning against an old wall, had gone very pale, and was rolling his eyes in a way which made him look rather like a cow that is just going to calve. He must be ill, thought Zappaglou, staring. And as he stared the foreigner gave way at the knees and fell down face foremost in the dust, in a dead faint.

The leviathan was galvanized into action. He bellowed to a woman in a doorway for water, and as he was a hearty man and had a hearty voice, and as it was the evening hour when people are awake and about, he attracted a lot of attention. Heads popped out of windows, willing helpers appeared from nowhere, and curious people came running from near and far, while a rumour spread rapidly that an English lord had committed suicide as his heart had been broken by an unfaithful wife. Amidst a babble of excitement Zappaglou had Mr. Raper carried up to his house till he should recover, and sent somebody for a doctor.

Two streets away Timos heard people running and caught a fragment of excited questioning.

'Why are people running?' said Nikos. 'Is there a fire?'

Timos screwed up his scarlet, mucous eyes and looked after the blurred and hurrying figures.

'You may as well stop playing,' he said, ''till the people come back. There must have been an accident, and it has drawn them all away.'

Nikos smiled, and said nothing. He was standing very straight against a white wall under an overhanging fig free. The last rays of the sun shone full upon him, upon his lean figure and his calm, handsome and filthy face, which had not been shaved for two days, with its expression of peculiarly Balkan hopelessness oddly mixed with a subtle and perhaps ever so slightly disdainful smile. He looked a young dandy in his rags, as he still touched a note or two from his accordion with his long fingers.

'Even if I could see again,' he remarked in a dreamy voice, 'I doubt if I should go and look at this accident of theirs. Even if we could see all right, Timos, I doubt if we should be able to see this crisis they're always talking about.'

Behind his eyes there is some real world of his own. His blindness, by sharpening all but one of his senses, has produced in him a kind of inversion; he knows that, being blind, he is exceptional as the world judges, but it seems to him that *he* can see and the *world* is blind. What were all these people running for? It is the world, not Nikos, that is stampeded by a whim, swayed by phantom and fetish, ruled by rumour and by fear. He feels a kind of security, thanks to Costa and old Zappaglou and his wife, and thanks to Timos, and thanks to the public which supports him, as a whirlpool supports a feather or a straw. Perhaps when people glance at his upturned face they sometimes suspect that he may be able to see more calmly and deeply into things than they can. And no doubt the fragments of tunes that escape from his accordion suggest mystery to them, produce in them pangs of longing for something they have lost or will never attain.

Detaching a hand from the instrument he scratches himself in

straw hat and carrying a melon, got up and the tram slowed down, that the stopping-place had been reached, and he and his friend got out. But the merchant went up a steep street between stucco houses, a steep rough street with no traffic, going directly towards the sun, his shadow climbing behind him, and light billows of golden dust hanging in the air at his heels. Those two turned to the sea.

The road and the tramline were at the top of a cliff and curved out of sight together a few hundred yards farther on, but there was a steep narrow path, once a goat-track, down the face of a cliff leading to the bathing place, of which the existence might never have been suspected. This path they took, when the sun was already far past its zenith, for although early in the afternoon it was late in the summer.

The path led down to some steps cut in the rock (they had been used for at least two thousand years) and the steps led to a terrace, where there was a wine-shop, painted pink, with an open front, and overshadowed by a large and leafy fig tree which filled the air with its perfume. Crossing the terrace, which had on it a few tables and chairs, and a balustrade at the side, one became aware of the sound and smell of the sea twenty feet below. The keeper of the place, a man little more than forty, lean and healthy in a thin and dirty white sweater, his face rather lined yet young-looking, exchanged a cheerful greeting with the sailor, whom he had known all his life, and with Costa, a more recent acquaintance, who paid for the right to bathe (no tickets were issued), drawing a crumpled note from his trousers pocket.

They went as usual down the wooden steps to the wooden bathing cubicles, built in the shape of an L, with a wooden veranda in front of them looking on to the narrow beach, half shingle and half sand, and the sea.

'It always seems to me strange that you can't see the island from here,' said Costa, 'but I suppose it must be behind that cliff. I must swim a good way out and see if I can see it.'

'No, you mustn't try and do that,' said the sailor, but he gave no reason and did not say that he did not like Costa to go far away from him or that he feared the sea or the cramp that may overtake swimmers. He had already thrown his towel on the seat in one of the dark cubicles and was unlacing his shoes. Looking back at the sea over his shoulder Costa followed him in and closed the door. Having no windows, the cubicles were dark, but not so dark that it was impossible to see all the signatures and dates pencilled on the walls, all the erotic poems and drawings which, while the sailor undressed, Costa looked at with some curiosity. From outside came the splash of somebody diving, and two wet bathers hurrying along the veranda shook the whole rickety structure of the bathing cubicles.

They were soon in the water, where the sailor was less enterprising than Costa, for he had been smoking too much lately and was short of wind. The water was warm, and while the sailor stood in it up to his waist, exchanging a remark with one of the other bathers (as there were fewer than a dozen of them that day, many of the cubicles were empty) Costa was already swimming straight out to sea as if he meant to have a sight of the island, for it seemed to him reasonable that if one could see it from the top of the cliff one should be able to see it also from sea level, provided one swam out far enough.

'Come back,' cried the sailor. 'Don't go out so far!'

'It's all right,' cried Costa from a distance, laughing, and waving a glistening arm before swimming out farther.

When the sailor saw that Costa was determined to swim out farther, when he saw him swimming straight out in a leisurely but steady way, he plunged in after him and swam with furious energy until, short of breath, he caught him up. When Costa saw this he stopped, treading water, and they began to argue.

'Why do you want to stop me?' he said. 'There's no danger. If you had only let me swim for another three minutes I believe I should have caught sight of the island and then I should have been satisfied and should have turned back.'

'But I tell you, you can't see the island from here! And why should you want to see it from here when you can see it so easily from the top of the cliff? It isn't an important island. Nobody lives on it, and there is nothing on it but the ruins of a temple and some plants.'

'I know,' said Costa, 'but . . .'

'Please come back when I ask you,' said the sailor gravely. 'Come, let's race back to the shore.'

And knowing for certain that Costa would not, indeed could not refuse flatly to do what he asked, he struck out vigorously on his return journey to the beach. But Costa followed him half reluctantly, swimming back in his leisurely way, so that he got back to the beach some moments after his friend. They did not go into the water again that afternoon, but sat against some rocks in the sun.

'Before we settle down,' said the sailor, 'I'll go and get a couple of cigarettes.'

'Not for me,' said Costa. 'I don't want one now.'

'You don't want one? Very well, I shall get one for myself.'

He was lying on his belly, and the sun shone upon his slender, rose-brown back and the few faint black hairs like the traces of a very fine paintbrush at the top of his spine. He got up then and walked away, with a slow, proud gait, holding himself very erect, his feet now in the water and now out, as the waves broke and receded. Presently the shadow which was advancing from the cliff seemed to drop a veil behind him as he stepped into it, and he disappeared into the cubicle. He came out a moment later with the cigarette between his lips and a curl of blue smoke trailing away from his head, and meeting an acquaintance remained in conversation with him for some minutes, though they were too far away for Costa, reclining now on a smooth hot rock in the sun, to hear what they were saying. This disturbed him. He was of a jealous nature. The curtain of shadow fell away from the sailor as he advanced again (the cigarette now half smoked), walking with easy grace and a black rag round his loins, glad of the sun falling warm on his golden shoulders again, for with the summer so far advanced the shade in mid-afternoon was not quite so warm as it had been a few weeks before. The history of his extraordinary race glittered in his dark eyes. He was humming to himself the following song:

Water springs out of the earth, and out of the olive, oil,
And out of a lovely mother springs a strong young man;
Drop by drop the water wears away the stone
And a girl with mincing airs destroys the strong young man.

His voice was deep and low, and the old Klephtic melody sounded sad between the rocks and the sea.

A light warm breeze blew among the sunny rocks, and the top of a tram could be seen and heard passing along the top of the cliff. Three boys were playing in the water, and fragments of a heated argument about politics drifted down from the terrace under the fig tree. The sailor lay on his back looking up at the cloudless sky. From just below the base of the neck to the navel there was a distinct groove in his body.

The man who kept the place came down to talk. He stayed with them for some time, bringing cigarettes and some fresh figs on a plate.

'You'll be sleeping in Athens to-night?' he said.

'No, we shall be sleeping in Phaleron. But we're going to have supper here, soon after sunset.'

'Before you go,' said the owner, addressing himself to Costa, 'remind me to show you the mosaics in my cellar, where in ancient times there was a bagnio.'

'We must go and dress now, the sun's getting low.'

They got up slowly, brushing off the sand that had stuck to their skins, sticky with salt from the sea.

'I'll get a bucket of fresh water,' said the sailor as they walked back to the cubicles, and went to fetch it. It was very warm in the cubicle, on which the sun had been shining all day long, and as they were by this time both warm and dry they were in no hurry to dress. The sun still glinted through the cracks in the wall at the back, which faced west, and made little strips of light on their bodies where they sat. They could hear boys splashing in the sea and there was a sense of approaching evening.

When they had washed and dressed they went up to the pink house, but had no sooner reached the top of the steps leading to the terrace than they heard a low moan behind them, and looking down, saw a bather at the bottom of the steps in pain, still wet from the sea, and supported by his companion: he had cut his foot badly on some broken glass on the beach, and was being helped up to ask for iodine and bandages.

Leaving Costa, the sailor became at once engaged in a furious argument in which the owner was taking part (his wife came out of the café in her apron but did not stay a second to argue, running back for bandages), and the injured man, and his companion especially, who was trying to fix the responsibility for the injury — whose fault was it that there was glass on the beach? and whose fault that a foot had been cut on it? and who would pay the doctor's bill and who would compensate the injured man for being unable to go about his work for at least a week? The injured man had meanwhile turned quite pale. In contrast to his black hair his face had gone a clear honey colour like some antique mask, the eyelids lowered from faintness. He was helped inside — carried, for he felt unlike hopping on one foot, by his companion and by the sailor, to a chair. When the sailor came back to Costa there was a little blood on his white trousers, just below the knee.

'It'll wash out,' he said.

And yet that little stain was never washed out of their memories. They afterwards remembered this afternoon.

It was quiet now, the sun was setting, and everybody had come out of the water. Two or three lights began to twinkle on the pale blue battleship anchored out in the bay, the *Byron*, that looked more like some fantastic cathedral planted on an islet than like the death-dealing machine that it was.

They sat at a table drinking glasses of *ouzo* and watching the moon rising like an enormous bubble from the sea. There was silence again, and the moon began to shine down on the darkened sea. The owner came out to find out what they wanted for supper and to ask if they wanted to see the mosaics, so they got up and followed him.

The café itself was lighted with oil-lamps, and a door at the back led into what in prehistoric times had been a large cave, in ancient times a bathing establishment, and was now used as a cellar. They descended by steps into a circular room with recesses in the wall now occupied by hogsheads of wine. A second door led into a larger room, now used for storing things, where the owner flashed an electric torch upon the mosaics. There were two. One, somewhat damaged, of Phœbus-Apollo driving the small-headed, prancing horses of the sun; the other, in good condition, of a woman helping a warrior to arm.

'If these could speak,' said the owner, laughing rather slyly. 'they would tell some strange stories!'

The sailor said nothing, looking sidelong at Costa to see if he was pleased with the mosaics.

'Aren't they good!' said the owner.

'They're wonderful,' said Costa.

'We hardly ever show them,' said the owner. 'But you're privileged because you're a friend of *his*.' Smiling, he nodded towards the sailor.

'Thank you very much,' said Costa.

When they came out again the moonlight was brilliant, and they went back to their table at the edge of the terrace. It had been covered with a white cloth, and they asked the owner to join them at supper, which he did. They had red mullet with bread and a salad, resinated wine, and afterwards some black currant-grapes and coffee. A beggar came round, the moonlight was playing on the sea, and when he had gone a band could be heard faintly playing on the battleship *Byron*, now all twinkling with lights, for there was a party on board that night. In the distance the moon was shining on Hymettos, and here and there all over Greece it was shining on marble columns, some of which were still standing while others had fallen.

'I'm sleepy after bathing,' said the sailor. 'Let's be going soon.'

'Very well.'

'Oh, did I tell you that I'm going to be transferred to a submarine?'

'To a submarine! You never told me!'

The sailor smiled sadly, and with his black eyes flashing began to sing in a low but languorous voice:

'Drop by drop the water wears away the stone. . . .'

The night seemed full of an immense yearning when he stopped singing, and it did not vanish at the changed tone of his voice as he said, when they were getting up to go:

'Costa, from the top of the cliff you'll be able to see the island quite safely!'

Calling out 'Good night!' to the owner they passed under the fig tree and up the steps, but when they got to the top of the cliff they forgot to look at the island. Walking in silence, with linked arms, they felt for the moment content.

# LOCAL COLOUR

UPON certain kinds of Nordics the effect of living in Mediterranean countries is the reverse of bracing. The freedom, warmth and glamour of their surroundings begin to sap their intellectual or artistic activity and ambition. They drift into idleness and weaken in will. While constantly talking about what they are going to do and accomplish, they do nothing and make nothing, and at last discover that in gaining liberty and sunshine they have lost purpose and vigour. It is a matter of taste and temperament. You can't have everything.

But when the Nordic, young, enterprising and healthy, first finds himself enjoying freedom, warmth and glamour, the effect upon him is indescribably delightful. He is without responsibilities, he has a susceptible body and an impressionable mind; the sun warms his skin and the blood sings in his veins. Life is full of promise, he is ready for anything, and if anybody asks him if he doesn't feel the heat he says, 'No, I love it.'

Two people in this happy condition were sitting in basket chairs on the veranda of the best hotel in Athens. They were English undergraduates who had come to spend the long vacation in Greece. They were not sitting there alone. They had a guest — nobody less than Madame Hélène Strouthokámelos.

'Don't you feel the heat?' she said, looking from one to the other.

'Not a bit,' said Grant.

'We love it,' said Spencer.

It *was* extremely hot, all the same. The glare was dazzling. It was just that hour when nothing seems likely ever to cast a shadow again, and the air itself buzzes like a cicada. The young men, neatly dressed in light summer clothing, sat in easy attitudes, but there was much more assurance in their voices than in their feelings. They had brought a letter of introduction to Madame Strouthokámelos and in delivering it had added an invitation to lunch. And here she was in the flesh, and they felt rather shy. Spencer, the English one, was uneasy because he was wearing rather too pretty a tie, which he had bought in Paris, and Madame Strouthokámelos kept glancing at it every now and again as if it offered a clue to his soul. Grant, the Scotch one, had begun looking at the toes of his shoes, and that was always a bad sign with him. Just then an important looking man in a straw hat came up the steps, and catching sight of Madame Strouthoká-melos made her an obsequious bow, to which she replied with a cool nod. *Cool*, that was it. It was her coolness that was so disconcerting.

She was neither young nor middle-aged. She had dignity without stiffness, she was handsome, healthy, powerful. There was no powder on her face, she wore no jewellery, and her clothes were simple. She had taken off her little soft hat, just as a girl might have done, with a single gesture and laid it on the table at her side, and now she sat there with her head, most appropriately, against a white marble background. Spencer was facing her, Grant saw her in profile, and if they had been in the presence of Juno herself they could scarcely have been more impressed.

Before meeting her they had tried to imagine what she would be like, and they had invented a perspiring Levantine matron in black which the sun had faded, with a bluish moustache, bad teeth, and voluble French. And here was Juno at forty, or the Venus of Milo come to life, a woman of noble proportions, with naturally wavy hair, black, becomingly streaked with grey, and drawn back from a smooth forehead, from a face with regular features supported grandly on a firm neck like a cylinder of honey-coloured marble. Her skin was clear and honey-coloured too, and it made the white of her eyes and her fine teeth seem to be ever so slightly tinged with very pale blue. Her strong arms were bare, and her cool dress hung loosely over her firm breasts and clung against her hips and thighs. So much for her appearance. She had a manner to match it.

She had once had a baby — but rather a small one. It often happens with amazonian, mammoth, or merely muscular women that their offspring comes into the world as an embodied protest against size and strength — in fact, the little Strouthokámelos weighed at birth no more than four pounds. It was, however, her husband rather than her child who had mainly disappointed her. Had he been dutiful, she would no doubt have worn him out, but he was casual, and she lost him. Strouthokámelos had been a little too Greek in his nature for her taste — she had been 'finished' in Paris and Vienna, but they hadn't prepared her for what happened. And when it *did* happen she took pains to inform herself about aspects of life, of Greek life, to which she had hitherto paid little attention. And having been informed, she was resentful. What she could no longer ignore she blamed, frowned upon, or affected not to notice, according to circumstances. And whenever any reflection happened to be cast by foreigners upon the Greeks in general she hastened to proclaim her countrymen's conformity with Christian morality, with the finishing-school view of human nature, failing altogether to remind herself that they are scarcely a European people.

Madame Strouthokámelos was not a fool. She was very much the reverse. Like so many citizens of the lesser European countries she was an excellent linguist, equally at home in English, French, German and Italian. She had read a great deal and was still reading. She was a capable housewife, a born organizer and to some extent a woman of the world. She could stride through thistles in Thessaly, hold her own at the bridge table, make a speech or sack a maid, was a personal friend of the prime minister, and of course was fully equal to the present occasion. She glanced in the direction of the dining-room, and then said:

'Do you specially want us to have lunch here?'

'No,' said Spencer.

'Not if you know of anywhere better,' said Grant.

'Ah, I see you're the practical one,' she said, displaying her classical, milk-blue teeth. 'I don't know about *better*, but hotels are all the same everywhere. I think while you are in Greece you ought to do as the Greeks do. I know a little place down by the sea, towards Vouliagméni, where we could get a nice *Greek* lunch. Do you think you would like that?'

'We should love it,' said Spencer.

'I'm all for local colour,' said Grant.

'Ah, that's just it,' she said. 'If we go there, it will be *Greek*, whereas *this* . . .' She shrugged her shoulders, but there was a delicious smell of food wafted from the dining-room. 'Then we may as well go at once?' she said, rising to her feet.

Her hosts got up obediently. She was used to obedience.

'You've left your book behind,' she said to Spencer. 'What is it? May I see? Ah, Proust.'

'Do you like Proust?' said Spencer.

'He's very clever, of course, but I don't much care for the atmosphere.'

Spencer popped *Sodome et Gomorrhe* into his pocket.

'And now,' she said, leading the way, 'we'd better get into a taxi.'

The taxis, open touring cars, were lined up under some pepper trees on the opposite side of the road. Madame Strouthokámelos waved away the svelte hotel porter as if he was an insect, led the way, chose a taxi, instructed the driver brusquely, and climbed in. Spencer and Grant exchanged glances and followed. She made them sit one on each side of her, and the taxi drove off, rushing down the Amalia Boulevard towards the sea.

'She doesn't like men,' thought Spencer.

'She despises us,' thought Grant.

'It isn't many miles,' said Madame Strouthokámelos, and began asking them the usual questions about how long they were going to stay, where they were going, and so on.

'I'm afraid we Greeks are rather misunderstood or misrepresented,' she said. 'But there is a wonderful new spirit in the people. The refugees from Asia Minor have increased the population enormously, and have helped to consolidate the national feeling. The younger generation, the Greeks of your age, are manly and patriotic. I think there is great hope for the future.'

'*Manly*,' thought Spencer. 'She's thinking of my tie.'

'What is she getting at?' Grant wondered. 'Is this propaganda?'

It was propaganda.

'So I hope,' she went on, 'that although you'll be here such a short time you'll really be able to get in touch with the people a little and get an idea of what they're really like. That's one reason why I'm taking you to this place for lunch. I don't suppose any foreigner's ever been there before.'

'That's much more interesting than the hotel,' said Grant.

'Much,' said Spencer a little half-heartedly, remembering the smell of the hotel lunch.

'Hotels are *so* much the same everywhere,' she repeated.

They had passed Phaleron, and the conversation turned to Byron. They sped towards Glyphada, along what was then one of the only two decent roads in Greece, and the asphalt was like burnished steel. There was almost no traffic at this time of day. The sea was like a fiery glass and Byron had given place to the Greek language. The road was about to be very bad, when Madame Strouthokámelos, employing that language with great determination, brought the car to a standstill. They all got out, and she waited for her hosts to pay the fare. Then she led the way across a piece of waste land to a little white house by the sea.

There was no path. The way was through loose, burning sand which filled one's shoes. There were some prickly bushes about. They passed a pine tree, sighing to itself. The rays of the sun seemed to be vertical. Presently there was a crazy notice-board decorated with broken fairy-lamps and the inscription PANTHEON.

'Here we are,' said Madame Strouthokámelos as if she owned the place.

And immediately a man came out to welcome them. He treated his visitor with deference — she was known to have in-fluence in important circles; her bearing would have demanded respect in any case; and she had brought two young foreigners with her. Well, three lunches meant three profits. He led the trio round to the seaward side of the Pantheon.

'Now, surely this is better than the hotel!' cried Madame Strouthokámelos.

And indeed it was.

A veranda thatched with myrtle branches, and floored with the earth itself, on which stood three round tables covered with coarse but clean tablecloths, and chairs; and only a few yards away, the Aegean sparkling like a million diamonds. There was even a suggestion of a breeze.

The table at the far end was occupied. Four men, workmen or peasants apparently, were seated there, eating a cheerful meal. Beyond them were some rocks and bushes. At the corner of the house a single plant of maize had grown to a great height. It looked very green and was in flower. Beneath it some fowls were enjoying a dust-bath, and tied to one of the veranda-posts was a goat, recumbent in the shade. With clear yellow eyes which looked as though they missed nothing and saw through everything it watched what was going on. It looked so inde-pendent that one could not tell whether it was enjoying what it saw, enjoying a cynical attitude to what it saw, or simply indulging in sheer observation for its own sake.

The proprietor approached Madame Strouthokámelos for orders. She took off her little soft hat again, with the characteristic sweeping gesture, and then, with a clean, capable hand on which the nails were cut short like a man's, she patted her hair, though its wiry waves had not lost their shape.

'There's not much to choose from,' she remarked. 'Of course they weren't expecting us.'

'We leave the choosing to you,' said Grant.

She ordered red mullets, black olives, white bread, a tomato salad, with yaghourt and coffee to follow.

'It sounds marvellous,' said Spencer.

'You'd better taste it first,' she said. 'At least everything here will be fresh.'

The fact that she never wore gloves aided the general impression that she was 'classical' in appearance.

'And what are we going to drink?' she said.

Spencer stole a glance at the other table.

'What are *they* drinking?' he said.

'*Retsina*, probably,' said Madame Strouthokámelos. 'Do you know what that is? White wine with resin in it. It's very nice. Would you like to try some?'

Spencer and Grant said they would, though somebody had told them that it was perfectly revolting.

'I adore the goat,' said Spencer.

'Isn't *adore* rather a strong word?' said Madame Strouthoká-melos. 'It seems to me it stinks slightly.' She laughed.

'Exactly what are those people?' said Grant, looking at the other table.

'Oh, just country boys. It's a pity you can't talk to them. Very cheerful, aren't they? And they're really typical.'

They were, indeed, very cheerful, and had just ordered some more wine.

'Would you like to offer them some cigarettes?' said Madame Strouthokámelos. 'They would be very pleased.'

'Would they?' said Grant, and crossed rather shyly to the other table with an open cigarette-case. The 'country boys', even more shyly, helped themselves. And Madame Strouthokámelos, leaning forward graciously, addressed them in Greek.

'These are two young Englishmen,' she said, 'visiting Greece for the first time.'

The country boys expressed interest.

'So I've brought them down here to lunch, so that they can see a bit of the *real* Greece.'

The country boys registered approval and pleasure.

'I see you've got a guitar there,' said Madame Strouthokámelos. 'Won't you sing for these foreigners?'

The country boys laughed and looked at one another and then addressed themselves to one of their number who wore a lilac shirt, urging him to play. He took up the guitar just as the food arrived for the foreigners.

In spite of the heat Spencer and Grant were hungry, and the pleasant atmosphere and the pretty song that was now being sung to the guitar combined to whet their appetites.

'What a delicious lunch,' said Spencer.

'Perfect,' said Grant.

'I'm so glad you're enjoying it,' said Madame Strouthokámelos, and then, turning to the country boys, she suggested another tune for them to play. Her manner was gracious and patronizing and did not go down with them very well. However, the tune she suggested happened to be a favourite with Lilac Shirt, so he soon struck up with it. Drink had made him confident, and vanity made him self-conscious, so he became rather noisy, laughed, and now and then flashed a glance at Spencer and Grant. Madame Strouthokámelos wore an indulgent smile and nodded a gracious acknowledgment.

Conversation turned to the *retsina*. Grant thought it even more disgusting than he had anticipated — it tasted to him like pure turpentine, and he did his best not to make a wry face as he swallowed it. Spencer, who was rather romantic, pretended to himself and to the others that he liked it.

'It has such a nice *piny* sort of taste,' he said. 'But I don't think I could put away quite as much as *they* do — not in the middle of the day, at any rate.'

As he spoke he indicated the country boys, who had opened a fresh lot of wine and were getting very merry.

'Is that what they do every day?' said Grant.

'No, I think they must be celebrating rather a special occasion.'

The proprietor appeared in the doorway, looking genial above his apron. Somebody else had taken the guitar now and was playing a rapid syncopated tune. Lilac Shirt was looking rather flushed. His shirt had come unbuttoned, revealing a lean brown chest, very hairy. He was supporting the head of one of his companions in his lap, and making remarks which surely *must* be ribald. Spencer stole a glance at Madame Strouthokámelos. Yes, sure enough, she was looking at her plate, and a faint frown now marred her rather too regular features. Then Spencer looked at Grant, and Grant looked at Spencer and kicked him under the table, then they both looked at the other table, on which somebody was beating with a spoon just to add to the noise of the guitar and the laughing and the singing.

'They *are* getting gay,' said Spencer, in an affectedly innocent tone of voice.

'They have been drinking a little too much,' said Madame Strouthokámelos with an expression of something like distaste. 'Have you had enough to eat, or shall I order some cheese?'

'Aha,' thought Grant, 'she's trying to hurry us away just when it's beginning to get interesting.' And he said, 'Yes, please. I should like to try the cheese. I expect it's very good here.'

With obvious reluctance Madame Strouthokámelos ordered cheese. The proprietor made a laughing comment on his other visitors, but she did not reply.

At this moment one of the country boys rose to his feet. He was very slender, with lank black hair and rather sleepy-looking eyes. He was going to dance. The others clapped and uttered cries of delight, encouragement and facetiousness. The dancer raised his arms and spread out his hands and began to dance to the guitar. He was skilful and kept excellent time and for a moment it seemed as if Madame Strouthokámelos' slightly disdainful expression might vanish.

'The cheese is excellent,' said Grant.

Spencer lighted a cigarette.

Just then Lilac Shirt rose to his feet, approached the other dancer and clasping one hand round his partner's waist and the other round his loins he called for a tune. Shouts of laughter, and one of the remaining two began again on the guitar. Madame Strouthokámelos frowned once more. The frown was deeper this time.

The tune was a tango. Lilac Shirt proceeded to sway his partner into a caricature of a tango. With absurdly languorous movements they danced, still keeping excellent time with the music. Lilac Shirt's white trousers were, however, a little too tight for really free movement.

'How well they dance,' said Spencer, smiling. 'I think we ought to join in.'

He got another kick under the table.

He then saw that Lilac Shirt's way of holding his partner was perhaps a little too daring, a little too intimate, for the open air, at midday, in public. As the dance continued the goat rose to its feet — as if to get a better view. It stared with its pale amber eyes at the dancers, then turned to look at Madame Strouthokámelos — it was a look that spoke volumes, but banned volumes — and then again fastened its keen, glassy, unblinking stare on the dancers.

The guitar-player paused. Lilac Shirt, leaning against his partner who was leaning against one of the veranda posts, embraced him and kissed him on the mouth. This brought loud cheers from the other two. All four of them had forgotten the two foreigners and Madame Strouthokámelos — a fact which made her next words rather wide of the mark.

'They have forgotten themselves,' she said in a tone of disgust. 'They have drunk too much.'

Lilac Shirt's kiss was so prolonged that she averted her eyes and rose abruptly to her feet.

'We had better go,' she said in a quiet and furious voice, and picking up her hat she went round to the landward side of the Pantheon to demand the bill. Spencer and Grant followed to pay it. Glancing back, they saw Lilac Shirt and his partner disappear behind some rocks a few yards away.

As for the goat, it had settled down again, and was quietly chewing the cud. Its yellow eyes were shut for the siesta.

# STORIES OF ENGLAND

# NO GHOSTS

Mrs. de Paul-Pincus's visit to Quarenden Hall was short, but has not been forgotten. At the corner of a lane leading to Quarenden, a large maroon-coloured car slowed down, one afternoon last summer, in order to leave the main road. As it did so, the occupant glanced at the fingerpost and then told the chauffeur to go slowly as she wanted to have a good look at the country. A healthy, middle-aged woman, both fussy and determined, she was rather over-dressed in white with touches of black, and equipped with an Edwardian bust and one of those tiny little modern hats, pinched in at the top, so that she had at once an air of old-fashioned prosperity and of trying to keep up with the times. A bright young person in 1907 — her memoirs and her earlier novels equally make it plain — Zélie de Paul-Pincus, far less exotic than her name, has gradually ripened into a fairly successful woman of the world without losing her youthful archness. Indeed, that archness has contributed to her success. Her face, carefully made up, is enlivened by a pair of quick but not penetrating eyes, now slightly discoloured. She looked that afternoon as if she might have been on her way to a garden-party, with the pearls rising and falling on the powdered triangle of pink skin at the base of her neck, and her expensive clothes and full contours suggesting the opulence of summer only slightly shadowed by the approach of autumn. She looked a little out of place, gliding in her shiny, dark-red limousine between the brambly hedges of a country lane. Sitting comfortably there in her comfortable car, she vibrated a little, like a jelly decorated with cream, as she glanced from side to side with a shallow, practised eye, looking for local colour.

The road was narrow, the landscape typically English, with its sumptuous elms, its green grass, its fields of corn more delicately green, its savour of hay and meadow-sweet, and the continuous trilling of larks overhead. The car went slowly up a long incline, between hedges so tall that they shut out the view, and Mrs. Pincus looked absently at the back of her chauffeur's head. She had a sudden feeling that he was almost a stranger to her. She treated her servants with what she conceived to be dignity, and this prevented her from learning much about them. Her sudden qualm was followed by no resolve to learn more.

Towards the top of the hill, the hedges sank and revealed an untidier landscape. From the top, there lay open to the view a broad, wooded valley with a stream winding through it on its way to join the distant Gloucestershire Ouse, and in the middle, held together like a bouquet by the ribbony stream, the trees and towers of Quarenden itself. Mrs. Pincus made her chauffeur stop for a moment, and as she gazed at the view, her eye was not dreamy like the scene before her, but glinted like that of a hungry sparrow-hawk which catches an old but tender rabbit asleep and means to gobble it up at once.

Quarenden is an old and beautiful but not a very large house. Its chief interest is an increasingly rare one — it has been in the occupation of the same family since the early Middle Ages. 'There have been Potts at Quarenden since time out of mind,' Mrs. Pincus said to herself, resolving that when she came to 'use' the 'material' before her, she would substitute a more high-sounding name for that of Pott. She did not know the present Mr. Pott, and her visit to him was made possible by a paragraph in a local newspaper to the effect that Mr. Edmund Pott, following the example of other landowners, had kindly consented to allow certain portions of the grounds and Hall at Quarenden to be seen by the public on alternate Thursday afternoons throughout the summer for a fee of not less than a shilling per head, the proceeds to be given to the new county hospital. 'The Hall, certainly entitled to rank as one of the less known of England's stately homes, has never before been opened to the public, and Mr. Pott is to be congratulated on his public-spirited decision, which will afford a welcome opportunity in these hectic days of visiting this venerable relic of Merrie England. Once an abbey, founded by Odo, Bishop of Bayeux, the Hall passed through some stirring scenes of historic pageantry in mediæval times. Queen Elizabeth is said to have passed a night under its roof. . . .'

Mrs. Pincus, in her car, began to glide down into the valley, and then to be jolted a little, for the surface of the lane was rough. On either side the hedges had grown tall and ragged, and fat blackbirds flapped noisily off when they saw the car approaching — they whistled shrilly, and left the bunches of elder-flowers shaking in the still, warm air. And then the car came to a stop, in a warm, country silence, smelling slightly and wholesomely of cow-dung, with bees buzzing about among the dead-nettles and cow-parsley.

'I suppose this must be the way, ma'am,' said the chauffeur, looking rather doubtfully at an old five-barred gate which stood half-open under the hedge.

'I suppose it must be, Horsfall, though it seems incredible that this should be the only way to the Hall, this awful lane. Are you sure you came the right way?'

'Yes, I came the way they told me,' said Horsfall, 'but we can't go no farther with the car.'

'Well, I'm afraid I must walk. Will you open the gate? There must be some mistake.'

Unfolding a white sunshade, she began to make her way along a rough footpath across a meadow to the house, leaving Horsfall to drowse over a cigarette and a newspaper. She glanced anxiously at a distant and somnolent cow, and then began to compose a remark to make, if she got the chance, to Mr. Pott: 'I'm looking for material for a historical story I'm thinking of writing — but of course it's a secret!' She could see ahead of her a low stone bridge over the shadowy stream: it led, seemingly, straight to some neat lawns and the house itself. She felt uneasy. Surely this couldn't be the right way? Her assurance had not deserted her, but the summery silence seemed oppressive. She had expected to see a car-park and a throng of dressy visitors, and surely if one invited the public one didn't expect it to struggle over a meadow to the front door? A little puzzled, she paused to wipe one of her shoes on a tussock of grass, for it had got sullied in the meadow. She could almost have cried — everything seemed to be going wrong.

She had hardly taken two steps on to the bridge when she was startled by the loud quacking of innumerable ducks. There they were, flotillas of them on the stream, regarding her with bright suspicious eyes and quacking with surprise, tinged, it almost seemed, with resentment and even malice. To right and left the quacking spread; it was taken up by more and more ducks, which could be seen in the sunbeams under the willows and hawthorns, and away in the distance to right and left the panic spread, and a faint chorus of quack-quacking filled every pause in the louder protests near at hand. Had a fox appeared on the bridge the birds could hardly have made more fuss; had they been mastiffs and watchdogs they could scarcely have startled her more. But with an air of determination she passed over into the garden.

There were the grey walls of Quarenden, seemingly all staring windows; and here was a wide lawn with beds full of flowers; but not a soul was in sight. Had nobody, then, in the whole countryside come to see the house and help the hospital? She wondered if she should go straight up to the front door or if she should first approach the shabby grey-flannel backside of a stooping gardener which could be seen over there, just beyond the flower-beds. Yes, she would speak to him first. Getting nearer, she saw that a farther expanse of lawn was almost entirely covered with duck-pens made of wire-netting, and that he was busying himself with the construction of yet another.

'Good afternoon,' she said in the tone of voice she used when addressing servants.

The man, whose trousers were really extraordinarily shabby, jumped a little, for he had not heard her approaching across the grass. Then he straightened himself slowly, as a man does who is not as young as he has been, and confronted the stranger, holding out his arms at an angle from his body, for his hands were very dirty. He looked at her rather blankly for an instant, an oldish man with a white moustache and shrewd country wrinkles round a keen pair of eyes, and before he had time to reply to her greeting (for he had a country deliberateness) she said:

'Do you know if I can see the Hall?'

'Well, there it is,' said the man, nodding his head towards the house and smiling an odd smile which was at once benevolent, cynical and defensive. He waited for her to speak again, and she was a little taken aback. Was he really a gardener?

'I read in the paper that one could see over the house,' she explained, not without condescension.

'So one can, on certain days,' said the man, smiling, 'but this doesn't happen to be one of them, I'm afraid. I only show the house on every other Thursday, and this is one of the other Thursdays.'

The truth being now clear to her, Mrs. Pincus, cursing inwardly, thawed with appropriate haste.

'Oh, I *am* sorry!' she said. 'How silly of me to make a mistake about the day!'

'Well, as you're here,' he said, twinkling, 'I'll put a good face on it and show you the house. I expect you've come a long way. Only I warn you, I shall fine you a bit extra for the hospital as a punishment for coming on the wrong day. How do you like my ducks? In those boxes over there, eggs are being hatched out, here we have the youngest ducklings with their mothers, those are a fortnight old, those a month, and so on, until they're quite emancipated.'

'Dear little things!' Mrs. Pincus said gushingly.

'Paying little things,' said Mr. Edmund Pott. 'I shall have to go and wash my hands. Would you mind waiting for me in the hall? You'll find the front door open, I think.'

And he made off round a corner, while Mrs. Pincus, bridling with pleasure at the thought of a personally-conducted tour, of her luck at getting Mr. Pott to herself, sailed off into the shadow of the house. Her taste in interior decoration was merely fashionable, and when she found herself in the hall she was a little shocked. A high, plain room with a stone floor and windows far above one's head, it was crammed with an accumulation of centuries — especially of the last century. She felt that the antimacassars, the large bad Chinese vases stuffed with bulrushes and the photographs in elaborately carved Indian frames did not go very well with the old portraits and escutcheons.

'We sit in this room in the summer but not in the winter,' said Mr. Pott, reappearing with clean hands. 'This is the oldest part of the house —'

Unlike most guides to ancient monuments, he had developed two forms of monologue. When showing round large parties of visitors he stuck to facts and dates and two or three anecdotes; when showing round a small party or a single visitor he made the process more human and was more conversational, and derived amusement from the way they took his sallies and the remarks they made themselves. But Mrs. Pincus somehow failed to call out his natural amiability. He took a dislike to her, and was in any case annoyed at being interrupted in his work.

'I think I must have come by the wrong road,' she began.

'Oh, that doesn't matter! You came across the field, I expect. There is another way, but it's not much better, except that there's no field. We don't bother much about the road — after all, there are so many good roads nowadays, it doesn't matter if you strike a bad one now and then. They say that in the eighteenth century a man who lived here was making his way over a very muddy road when he saw a hat lying on the surface. He kicked it, and found it had a head inside. When they dug out the possessor of the head, they found he was on horseback. So really *we* can't grumble. . . . This is called the South Gallery.'

On the right, pictures; on the left, some pieces of sculpture after, but a long way after, Canova, mixed with cases of stuffed owls, and surmounted by trophies of arms from outlandish places.

'The young man in the blue coat is by Gainsborough.'

Mrs. Pincus had little knowledge of painting, but Gainsborough, she knew, was Gainsborough, and confronting the homely-faced Pott in the pale bue coat, she murmured:

'Charming!'

'He's usually thought very plain.'

'As a painting, though —'

'Oh, it's all right as a painting,' said Mr. Pott, walking rapidly into a large room with an ornate ceiling, a room that was very dusty and devoid of furniture, except for one table on which was the mouldy top of a christening-cake under a glass case.

'We don't use this room,' he said, 'but people look at the ceiling.'

Mrs. Pincus looked at the ceiling.

'I never look at ceilings myself,' said Mr. Pott. 'They give me a stiff neck. Can't see the point of painted ceilings.'

'I was going to say —'

'Please mind the step. This room was used to keep armour in when I was a boy. Armour — who wants armour? There's not much in it now but tennis rackets and old boots, as you see. . . . Now we go this way.'

'What a beautiful house you have,' said Mrs. Pincus. 'I'm thinking of —'

'Beautiful? Well, it may be, but I'm used to it. Ramshackle, I call it. It's all right now, but it's the winter that tells. I'm not as young as I was.'

'Of course, it's the *continuity* that's so wonderful!' she exclaimed, wishing he would talk about his family.

'Look out of the window and you'll see the stream,' he said. 'It was once the moat. This used to be a bathroom. I used to fish out of the window. There aren't many men in England can say that they've caught fish from their bathroom window.'

He was slipping into the public form of his monologue.

'No, indeed,' she said, thinking that living away in this hole might have made him a bit touchy, and that he must be humoured.

'I must confess,' she said, taking advantage of a pause, 'that I have at the back of my mind — but of course it's a secret! — an idea about writing an historical novel, and when I came here to-day I was quite shamelessly keeping a weather-eye open for local colour. Do you think you'd mind your house being described, as I imagine it to have been in Elizabethan times, in a novel?'

'Good God! In a novel? Afraid I never read 'em myself. Well, *I* can't stop you, can I? Afraid I shall never read it, so I shan't know what it's all about, shall I? Put me in, too, if you like. Old country fossil making a duck-run. *I* shall never know, shall I?'

He led the way up some stairs.

'Now we're going on to the roof so that you can see the view.'

They came out on to the roof. Part of it was flat. There were stone chimneys, and against one of them a garden seat, painted green. Leaning on a balustrade, they looked down on the lawns and flowers, they could see the glasshouses in the kitchen garden, and a sunlit bend of the stream all dotted with ducks, and there was a view of the only park-land remaining to Quarenden.

'What a heavenly afternoon!' said Mrs. Pincus. 'What an enchanting view! How lovely to live in such a peaceful place in these difficult times!'

A faint chorus of quacks came up from the distant ducks, as if in assent.

'Well, the times are just as difficult in peaceful places as they are anywhere else,' said Mr. Pott. 'A brother of one of the Regicides was drowned just at that bend in the stream. The Cromwellian troops were camped at the top of the slope. The siege lasted nearly two months. And there had already been a battle up there in the time of the Heptarchy. Fortunately, we aren't troubled by any ghosts.'

'What, no ghosts!' said Mrs. Pincus. 'Oh, but you must have!'

'Oh, but we haven't!'

'Oh, fancy there being no ghosts!' she said, with a disappointment half real and half feigned, and sat down on the seat.

'Lord, I should have warned you!' cried Mr. Pott.

'Warned me?' She smiled coyly up at him.

'The paint's wet.'

She stood up as abruptly as if she had been stung.

'Your beautiful dress must be ruined. Turn round. Yes, if I may say so, I'm afraid we've given you rather more local colour than you bargained for. Oh dear, I *am* sorry.'

The white seat of the dress was now barred with blotchy green stripes.

Mrs. Pincus's one consolation was that he had said, 'your *beautiful* dress'. She seized the chance of showing that she knew how to be gracious, and smiled, delighted that he should have put himself in the wrong.

'And I'm afraid there's nothing in the house that'll take it off,' he was saying.

'I shan't pretend I'm pleased,' she said, as they made their way downstairs, 'but it was really my fault, wasn't it? For being lazy. I was so entranced with your view and its associations that I felt I *had* to sit down and enjoy it for a few moments more.'

'I'm exceedingly sorry,' he said. 'Will you come and write your name in the visitors' book?'

She wrote her name, but he didn't even look at it. She had hoped he would say, although he didn't read novels, 'Ah, Mrs. de Paul-Pincus! Of course, I know your name very well.' Then she noticed a collecting-box for the county hospital.

'I wasn't going to ask you for anything,' he said, 'after ruining your clothes like this.'

'Oh, but you *must* take this,' she said, opening her handbag and producing a ten-shilling note.

'We could almost endow a bed with that,' he said. 'We only get a bob as a rule.'

'And I *did* come on the wrong day,' she said, gathering up her gloves.

He showed her to the door but no farther. As she crossed the bridge, a mocking, valedictory chorus arose from those hateful ducks. Horsfall saw her approaching rapidly across the meadow, and guessed that she must be out of temper. She asked him abruptly for his *Daily Express*, and told him to spread it out on the seat. He could not guess why until he opened the door for her to get in.

'Home, Horsfall,' she said crossly, but as he took his place at the wheel he could not help smiling.

'That was how she looked,' he afterwards told the cook, 'like a green blooming zebra.'

1934

# EVER SUCH A NICE BOY

You want to know how I first met Freddy? Oh, it's quite a long story. No, we don't come from the same place at all. You see, my home's near Gloucester. I was in service there with Major and Mrs. Trumbull-Dykes. Mrs. Dykes was ever such a nice lady, she was just like a mother to me and writes to me every Christmas, not that I haven't got a real mother, because of course I have, and she's always been good to me too, I couldn't wish for a better. Well, the Major used to suffer from rheumatism something terrible, he was always carrying on and saying the house was damp, though it was as dry as a biscuit. He wouldn't rest but they must move to Devonshire, nagging away all the time.

Well of course Mrs. Dykes wanted me to go with them, but I didn't like the idea seeing that I hadn't never been more than a few miles away from home. It was Mum that persuaded me. 'You've got a good home with them,' she said, 'you'd better go with them.' Of course, most of the things was sent off by train, and we was to follow by car, but there was a lot of luggage all the same, just like gipsies we were, all packed in with a kettle and I don't know what else. Of course, I hadn't never driven so far before and the Major drove ever so fast and it quite turned me up, what with the bumps in the road. 'Stop, Gilbert,' said Mrs. Dykes, 'Edith wants to be sick.' 'I don't *want* to be,' I said. 'I've *got* to be.' Oh, I *was* ashamed. 'Never mind, Edith,' said Mrs. Dykes, 'you'll feel better now.' 'You'll never make a sailor, Edith,' said the Major. Oh, if I was on the sea I think I'd die.

Of course, it was ever such a nice house that they had, just outside Paignton, everything easy to keep clean and the kitchen all white. The reason I didn't want to go away was I was afraid I would be homesick. It's funny, isn't it, when you get homesick?

You see, I was only a kid and me never having been away from home before I just cried and cried. 'Why, Edith,' said Mrs. Dykes, 'whatever's the matter? You're not homesick, are you? Aren't you happy with us?' And, of course, when she spoke to me so gentle that just made me cry all the more. 'If you're so unhappy,' she said, 'maybe it would be better for you to go home at the end of the month.'

Mind you, the Major was always a worry to her, you never knew what he'd be getting up to. I don't believe there was nothing between them and hadn't been for a long time, though I dare say the Major wished there was, so of course they always had separate bedrooms. Well, one afternoon about tea-time, yes, it must have been about tea-time because I was making the toast, the Major must always have his hot buttered toast for tea, there I was making the toast and the Major come into the kitchen. Of course, I didn't take no notice until he come up and caught hold of me. I asked him to let go and stop his games, but he wouldn't, so I hit at his hands with the toasting-fork to make him leave go of me. He had ever such big veins in his hands, they stood right out. 'Oh, you little vixen! You little spitfire!' he said. 'Well, you had no call to lay hands on me,' I said, 'whatever would Mrs. Dykes say?' And as he wouldn't stop his tricks I said 'Give over, will you!' and hit him again over the knuckles with the toasting-fork. 'Damn it, damn it,' he said, and then he run out. Just as I was getting tea ready to take into the drawing-room Mrs. Dykes come in, she'd been out shopping, and 'Oh, Edith,' she said, 'I'll just take the Major's tea up to him. He's ever so upset,' she said, 'he's hurt his hands something dreadful, he's resting in his room. He caught them in the mowing machine and they're all swollen up.' Of course I didn't say anything, but you should have seen the state his hands were in. Of course, I didn't mean to hurt him like that, but it was his own fault in a way, wasn't it?

My homesickness didn't get any better. I seemed to be always moping, so Mrs Dykes said I'd better go home at the end of the month. Well, only a couple of days before the end of the month I was cleaning the windows. It was a lovely morning, and when I was doing the window of the spare room I couldn't help noticing that there was a boy painting the roof of a shed in the garden next door, and when I was looking at him he looked up and saw me and he grinned and waved his hand. That's ever such a nice boy, I thought. Of course it was Freddy, though I didn't know at the time. I was ever so pleased. I didn't like to be too forward, but I waved back at him. Then I run downstairs to Mrs. Dykes and I asked her if I could stay with her instead of going home at the end of the month. 'Why, Edith, of course we should be very pleased,' she said, 'but whatever's made you change your mind so sudden?' Well, I knew I could tell her everything, so I said, 'I've just seen ever such a nice boy painting the roof of the shed next door, and he waved to me while I was doing the spare room window.' With that she run upstairs with me and looked out and when Freddy saw two of us he didn't know what to think. 'Yes, Edith,' said Mrs. Dykes, 'you're quite right, he *is* a nice boy.' So I didn't go away at the end of the month, and I just waited, hoping I'd see him again. I'd forgotten all about being homesick.

Next thing a note come to the house, addressed to 'Miss Edith.' Just like that, 'Miss Edith'. Of course it was from Freddy, asking me if I'd meet him at the corner on my evening out so we could go to the pictures. Oh, I *was* excited. I run and showed it to Mrs. Dykes and 'Of course, Edith,' she said, 'you'll have to go, but I wish we knew something about him. Isn't there anybody we could ask?' Well, next time the butcher's boy come round I said, 'Do you know anything about a fellow round here called Fred Carter?' 'Fred Carter?' he said. 'No, I can't say I do. What sort of work does he do?' 'I believe he's something in the building line,' I said. 'The only Fred I can think of,' he said, 'that's in the building line is Fred Baines, him that was painting that shed next door.' 'And what sort of a fellow is he?' I said. 'Oh, he's all right,' he said, 'but what do *you* want to know for? Has he been round here after you?' 'Don't be so nosey,' I said, but what I couldn't make out was if his name was Baines why did he call himself Carter, but it turned out that his stepfather's name was Baines so everybody used to call him Baines's boy though his name was really Carter.

So off I went to meet him, and 'Do be careful, Edith,' said Mrs. Dykes, 'don't let him take no liberties,' she said, 'until you're sure of him.' Oh, and do you know, he was *late*. Oh, I was that worried I could have cried, I thought he was just making game of me. Oh, I *was* upset, I thought I'd have done better to go back home after all. But just then he come up, all smiles, and we went off to the pictures, and we did have a lovely time. Of course after that everything was all right, but Mrs. Dykes said he must come to the house so she could see him for herself, and of course everybody liked him, you know how it is, people always do seem to take to Freddy, and after that he was always coming round, every night he used to come round, Mrs. Dykes was ever so kind, and the Major liked him too.

Then one evening, late it was, Mrs. Dykes come running down to the kitchen, screaming blue murder, 'Edith! Edith! Freddy!! Freddy!! Come quick, there's a man in my room!' Well of course we run upstairs and Freddy grabbed the poker and when we got up to her room there was nobody there but the Major. Do you know he'd got in through the window, thinking to surprise her, she wouldn't let him set foot in her room at all in the ordinary way. 'What on earth's all this?' he said when he see us. 'Why, Gilbert, it's only *you*!' said Mrs. Dykes. 'What do you mean by giving us all such a fright, creeping in at my window like that? Why, I thought it was a *man*!' At that Freddy and me couldn't help giving a laugh. Soon after that I left to get married, and I was sorry to leave in some ways; Mrs. Dykes cried when I went away, ever so good she was. Poor soul, I can't help thinking of her sometimes, with that Major of hers.

# THE NIGHT BEFORE THE WAR

Or perhaps it wasn't. It may have been a few nights before war was openly declared. It was one of those hot summer nights when 'Hitler' and 'Poland' had become the commonest words in the English language, when the Maginot Line had still to be proved a fond delusion, and when young men with neatly rolled umbrellas were beginning to look a little out of place and were expecting the fall of something heavier than rain. Not that Henry's habit of carrying an umbrella could be held against him. He was small, shy and conventional, and without his apparatus of umbrella, gloves, cigarette-case and so on he could hardly have faced the world; but one could easily guess that if he survived the coming war he would come out of it with a good record, for it would give him his first great chance of asserting himself.

At this time he was a civil servant with a small circle of conventional and unimaginative friends, and was living with a married cousin and her husband in a flat near Baker Street. At present they were away, and on this particular evening he had been dining out in Chelsea. When he returned, rather late, to the silent flat he found a telegram waiting for him. It was characteristic of him to open it not with his finger but with a paper knife. The telegram was to say that Violet had been taken ill and would he come at once. He rushed out of the house, not only without an umbrella but without a hat — such was his agitation — then got into a taxi and directed the driver to a rectory in Camberwell. Violet was the rector's daughter and she and Henry were virtually engaged, but he did not expect to be able to marry her until his sick old rich uncle was dead: the uncle had a really promising phlebitis, and in his heart Henry had been hoping that the phlebitis would work faster than Hitler.

Violet was indeed ill, but not dangerously, and Henry was allowed to sit and hold her hand for an hour or so. Then she fell asleep, so he tiptoed out of the room and after a short conversation with her mother, who insisted upon his drinking a glass of barley-water, he left the house. Although it was very late, it had occurred to neither of them that he might have spent the rest of the night there, and it did not occur to him until he was out of the house that the chance of finding a taxi thereabouts at such a time was very slight, that the tubes had stopped running, and that if there were still any buses they would be going in strange directions to remote termini.

Henry walked vaguely in the direction of Vauxhall in the hope of picking up a taxi. With typical prudence — a symptom perhaps of the activity of deep-seated and undiscovered coral-insects busy beneath the surface of his mind with the building of tiny galleries of anxiety and guilt — he felt in his pockets. He found that all the money he had on him was threepence-half-penny. He also found that he had come out without his key. A cold sweat came out on his forehead, for without it there was no means of getting into the flat before breakfast-time. He thought for a moment of going back to the rectory, but felt too shy: he did not wish to risk disturbing Violet, and he was too considerate to trouble her mother. Where, then, was he to spend the night? He thought of friends who might put him up, but one was out of town, another was recently married, others he was reluctant to disturb. An uneasy feeling in his intestines caused him to remember with distaste that the rectory barley-water had been luke-warm: Violet's father's stipend perhaps precluded an ice-box.

To Henry, whose life had been so sheltered and orderly, and as regular in its material comfort as that of a prosperous old lady, and to whom eccentricity and excess and even disorder had always been repulsive, there was something slightly scandalous and almost alarming about being at large at this time of night. He thought vaguely that he would go on walking. Perhaps he would walk about all night. He was afraid that if he stood still or sat down on a doorstep he would be arrested for loitering. How was he to know that before long he would be a seasoned veteran of mechanized warfare in the deserts of Africa?

His feelings were wonderfully mixed. The thought that Violet was not in danger filled him with relief and made him almost light-hearted: before the menace of coming events she was in any case doubly precious to him. Then there was the deep dread of the unknown and inevitable that lay against his heart in those days like an ulcer. Then there was an extraordinary sense of something like adventurous gaiety at finding himself at large in London at night, and unprotected by money, a key, a hat, gloves and an umbrella. For perhaps the first time in his life he was unsheltered; he had come face to face with that uncertainty which is the very beginning of the forming of a character; it was as if a mild ordeal to mark his attainment of manhood had been devised for him by some power unknown.

He was walking up the Vauxhall Bridge Road with a springy step, but the night was hot and he was sweating a good deal. There were very few people about. Approaching Victoria, he felt thirsty and turned into a squalid little snack-bar which was open all night. There was nobody in it except an old man behind the counter, who was bleary and greasy with heat and fatigue. Henry exchanged twopence for a cup of tea and asked the old man if he could put him up for the night. The old man said he couldn't, but a friend of his in Tachbrook Street might. Henry said he had only three-halfpence on him: would the friend take his watch as security for payment for his lodging? The old man said there was no harm in trying.

Pimlico was deserted. Had Henry known something of the strange ramifications of the life of that quarter, he would have felt even more adventurous. In his world the very word Pimlico, seldom used, could hardly be uttered without a note of superiority and even sarcasm; it suggested nothing but seedy squalor, it was a symbol of those vast, submerged areas of unsheltered life that were better ignored; non-intervention was the great weakness of Henry's world. Down an empty, brightly-lighted street he preceded the sound of his own footsteps while behind the hushed façades hearts were beating and rank dreams were acted. Henry knocked firmly at the house to which he had been sent. His hand had hardly left the knocker when a woman's voice shrieked inside the house, 'Do that again, you swine, and I'll scream the place down!' Henry started back in alarm, but evidently the remark was just part of an argument, for a man's voice replied, 'Oh, come off it! Why don't you put a kettle on, you silly —— ? I could do with a cup of tea.' Feeling *de trop*, Henry retraced his steps towards Victoria.

Whether as a result of the heat, or the rectory barley-water, or the tea he had drunk, or all the emotion he had felt earlier in the night, or the immense apprehension of the war quickening his metabolism, there now came upon him a pressing natural need. At Victoria it could not be satisfied, for everything was closed for the night. The last porter, like the last of the Barons or the last of the Mohicans, was leaving for home. Henry asked his advice, but the porter could not help him. For the first time in years Henry understood the resentment of the poor against the rich: for the price of a hotel room he could have had a bed and also what he far more urgently needed.

'It seems,' he remarked to the porter with a bitterness born of frustration, 'that in the capital of the British Empire after midnight a dog may, but a man mayn't — even if he has a penny. There aren't even any dark corners. If we're going to have a war, let's fight for the right to do what I want to do, when we want to do it.'

The porter grunted sympathetically, for one call of nature makes the whole world kin; and bade him a kindly good night.

By now in some discomfort, Henry directed his steps towards Hyde Park Corner. In Grosvenor Gardens a belated bird of paradise, who looked about forty-five, intercepted him and asked him if he wanted a naughty little girl — by which, so little are we able to see ourselves as others see us, she meant herself. He said he was sorry, not to-night; and it did just cross his mind that a bed was becoming a more expensive thing as the night wore on.

As he was passing St. George's Hospital he was hailed, from the direction of the Artillery Memorial, by an old lady seated at the base of that construction. More out of civility than curiosity, Henry crossed over to her: she might be mad or drunk, on the other hand she might be in need of help. He was a stranger to that moth-like population of fly-by-nights, conspirators, derelicts and eccentric loiterers that was loosed nightly upon the capital at about his usual bed-time.

'How dare they say it's round!' She said scornfully, in the sort of voice one might have expected to hear in a residential 'guest house' in Bournemouth. 'It's disgraceful, a regular plot! What was good enough for Our Redeemer is good enough for me. *He* never said it was round. Nowhere in Holy Writ is it called round.'

She looked fiercely up at him, evidently waiting for an answer.

'But *I* never said it was round,' he replied in self-defence, wondering what it was.

'Then you are a most unusual young man. An open mind, keep an open mind, and above all, don't jump to conclusions. Fear God and keep your bowels open.'

'I only wish I could,' said Henry irritably, for his pangs had not lessened.

'And what's to stop you, pray? You should eat bran. But I bless you for not saying that it's round.'

'But what is it?'

'Why, it's flat. I have proof.'

'But *what* is flat?'

'The earth, of course! What have we been talking about?'

'Of course,' said Henry, 'how stupid of me! But I'm afraid I must be on my way. Good night. Pleasant dreams.'

And he left the old fundamentalist sitting on her fundament and muttering to herself at the feet of a bronze image, complete with bronze overcoat, of one of those who died to make the world safe for heresy.

The Park was of course closed, and Henry, whose journey had by now become an endurance test, plodded up Park Lane. Opposite the Dorchester he came face to face with an upstanding young navvy, who asked him the way to Epping.

'But surely,' said Henry, momentarily half gulled, 'you're not going to Epping to-night! Besides, you're not going the right way.'

'How far would it be?' the young man asked innocently, looking at Henry with a disquieting directness. It was a faked air of innocence. Like Henry, he was looking for a night's kip. He hoped to be offered a bed or a shilling. No doubt he used the same technique every night, inquiring late, of kindly-looking and often slightly mellow middle-class strangers, the way to remote places.

'I'm sorry I can't help you,' said Henry, suddenly haunted by vague recollections of stories of blackmail. 'As a matter of fact I'm looking for a bed myself, and I've only got three-halfpence in my pocket.'

'Have it your own way,' said the man, and Henry left him with a falsely cordial good-night, to which he made no reply.

At the Marble Arch, Henry decided to make in the direction of Paddington. The night seemed hotter than ever. Upon locked iron gates he read the word *Gentlemen*. Keeping a stiff upper lip and grinding his teeth, he passed this outrage on civil liberty and entered the Edgware Road, a hopeless vista.

By now he had begun to feel that he was living in a nightmare. A white cat dashed past him so quickly that he was not sure whether he had seen it at all. Men in strange hats and boots with a seventeenth-century look were flooding the streets with hoses, and when he looked back, the Marble Arch appeared to be floating on a black lake. Farther on, two men were fighting in Titchborne Street. Locked together, they were still on their feet, and appeared to be performing a difficult and exhausting dance. Nobody was watching them and they might just as well have been trying to kill each other. Perhaps they were trying to kill each other.

Near Cambridge Terrace an open-fronted snack bar was still serving customers of nocturnal habit, and there was a cheerful clatter and chatter.

'Hullo,' said a young woman standing at the door. 'How are you getting on?'

'Well, I don't know, really,' said Henry, thinking to himself that she did not look at all like a tart. 'How are *you*?'

'Can't grumble. Long time since I've seen you.'

'Well, I've never seen you before in my life.'

'Flattering, aren't you!' said the young woman, smiling. 'You don't remember *me*!' And she thrust her face forward, as if she were showing a passport. It was the sort of face one might have seen somewhere, and Henry felt as one feels when a strange place suddenly seems familiar — have I been her before? When? How?

'I don't think I do,' he said.

'Of course you do!' she said, giving him a little slap on the lapel of his coat. 'And that long talk we had!'

'Where?' said Henry.

'Fancy asking me where!'

He felt that he was losing his grip on reality, and turned away.

'I'll be seeing you!' the young woman called after him.

Do I, he asked himself, naturally attract lunatics and impostors, or are all the nocturnal inhabitants of London streets, the people whom as a rule I never see, lunatics or impostors anyway?

At the corner of Praed Street he paused. Was he going to walk about all night, or what? Catching sight of a policeman, he remembered having heard that one could sleep, in case of necessity, at a police station. So he went up to the policeman, explained that he had accidentally locked himself out of his flat without any money, and asked what he had better do about a bed. Policemen, nurtured on suspicion, tend to take a low view of human nature, to look instinctively for ulterior motives and doubtful credentials, and to believe a man guilty, especially at night, unless he can prove himself innocent. This was not an agreeable policeman, and he looked at Henry with sour scepticism, which hardened, during Henry's further explanations, delivered with a falsely jaunty air, into hostile disapproval. Perhaps it was the tense expression that Henry wore — and small wonder — that caused the policeman to look him up and down so insolently. Henry did not lack spirit, and for fear of losing his temper he turned on his heel and made off, with what was meant to be an air of dignity, towards Paddington.

Delightful accidents do happen, and suddenly Henry saw, on a rapidly moving bicycle, a face he knew. It belonged to the nephew of the daily woman at his cousin's flat. This young man was by day an artists' model and by night a partner in a coffee stall, from which he was now returning to his home beyond Paddington Green with part of the night's takings. When he heard of Henry's troubles, he lent him some money, and crouching low over the handlebars, curved like the horns of a luck-bearing antelope, sped smilingly away.

Never did four half-crowns look so attractive. Henry made for the nearest hotel, but the night porter was hostile and suspicious, and seeing that Henry had no luggage and no hat he said the hotel was full. Farther on, where Bayswater begins, the wanderer was luckier. A more sympathetic porter showed him into a nice clean bedroom, in which, for six-and-six, he could sleep for a few hours: it would soon be daylight.

'Before you go,' he said, 'you might just show me where the —'

'Yes, sir, that little door just at the end there. Good night, sir.'

'Ah, little door, little door,' thought Henry, making for it as unerringly as William Tell's arrow made for the apple, 'if you don't lead to Paradise, you lead to something very like it. No pilgrim ever arrived more thankfully at a long-sought shrine than I at this little door. This gleam of white tiles and frosted glass is more precious to me than ivory and diamonds ...'

Once he was in bed, he was so tired that he felt wide awake. Ideas, images and phrases rushed through his head like a garbled film. The Marble Arch floated on a black lake. 'How far,' said a voice, 'is it to Epping?' 'They say it's round,' said a bronze soldier, stepping off his pedestal, and at the end of a vast, deserted street, brilliant with electric light, Henry saw himself knocking at a door that would never open. He thought of the war that might begin at any moment, of things that he had to do in the morning, of Violet, and how extraordinary it was that in the greatest city in the world it should be so difficult, so nearly impossible, for a man to relieve himself.

He decided not to wait for his uncle's money, but to urge Violet to marry him at once. He reflected that if he had been married, he would have been highly unlikely to have found himself locked out and wandering in the streets of London. Yes, yes, he thought, society protects itself against the pauper and the outcast. If you won't sleep respectably in a conjugal bed, says society, then you shan't have a bed at all; you shall wander the streets, and, what's more, I won't even allow you to answer a call of nature, for to commit a nuisance is to incur a penalty.

He saw suddenly that this night marked a stage of his growth, a turning-point in his life. He felt as if he had been liberated, as if he had passed a difficult test. Without an umbrella, without a key, without money, he had come nearer than ever before to being himself. Love and death were staring him in the face, and he could stare back at them without flinching, for with the aid of one he could master the other. He was filled with an extraordinary sense of confidence, power and well-being.

The blind had not been drawn and an elaborate floral pattern on the lace curtain was visible in the light thrown up from a lamp in the street. He had a sense that he had never known before of identification with London; he understood, in the hallucination of fatigue, the differing humanity of all those whom he had by chance encountered during these last hours; his heart warmed to them because he knew for the first time that we are all wanderers on the face of the earth; he had become a man, with the strength of a man. Closing his eyes, he imagined himself alone with Hitler, fighting to kill and absolutely confident of being the winner. Then the memory of the feel of Violet's hand as he had held it became intensely real to him, beyond words heartening, life-giving and soothing; and so he fell asleep.

# A WEDDING GUEST

'THE day after to-morrow,' said Madam Cardoon, 'I'm goin' to a weddin'.'

'Something special?' said her late husband's nephew, who knew she had some classy friends.

Her only reply was a twisted, mocking smile, and she turned to draw back the black-out curtains in order to inspect the weather. It was a morning in January, 1945, and the nephew-by-marriage, on belated Christmas leave, was spending a couple of days with his aunt. The relation between them was simple. She was a lonely old woman and liked to mother him, a process to which he had no objection. Besides, she fascinated him, for she was unlike anybody he had ever known: she seemed to live almost entirely in the past, a fantastic past that was reflected in her manner and appearance, her style and setting.

Juliet Cardoon lived in an 'upper part', consisting of two floors over a junk-shop in a byway of Bayswater: she was much impoverished. The narrow, plain-fronted, brick house had not originally had a shop on the ground floor; it had been built in the eighteenth century, probably by some successful small tradesman who wished to live out in the country but within easy reach of London. No doubt it stood then in an acre or two of its own, but now it was all hemmed in with heavy, decayed Victorian houses and small shops, except at the back, where a noisy garage had been reduced to silence and ashes by incendiary bombs. Some of Madam Cardoon's windows had been blasted, and from time to time pieces of plaster fell from the ceiling into her hair or her soup.

The rooms were not large, but they were neatly proportioned and lined with their original panelling, from which their occupant had long ago had layers of wallpaper stripped in order that the old wood might be seen and touched. It was characteristic of her to have found these rooms and to be living in them. Although she had some good pieces of furniture and some rare and even beautiful stuffs, glass and china, this constricted abode had to contain the accumulated surviving belongings of an acquisitive woman who had formerly been used to much more space and many more possessions, a woman who could never bear to throw anything away, believing that everything may 'come in useful' some time, and who was governed by a sort of fetishism in regard to material objects. In short, the rooms were overcrowded and had evidently been like this for a long time. There were too many draperies, too many photographs, and too many oddments, especially on the mantelpiece — a jade cup to hold spills, two precious fans, a brass cow studded with turquoises, a row of *netsuké*, a Persian bowl filled with pot-pourri, and a cloisonné incense-burner now used as a receptacle for buttons. Each of these objects, if touched by a visitor, was apt to start its owner off on a long train of reminiscences, and each seemed to contribute something to the peculiar faded odour of this boudoir-like den, an indefinable, faintly disturbing, but not disagreeable odour, as of some stale sweetish fungus. And about Aunt Juliet herself there was wafted also a cognate aroma, as of an old sachet in a box of subfuse clothes, long unopened. One never saw a moth or even a fly in this establishment.

It seemed fitting that Aunt Juliet herself should tinkle as she moved, with amulets on a bangle, and a pendant knocking against a brooch, and that she should tend to wear collars of old lace or panels of old brocade which had nothing to do with fashion, but which certainly had a style of their own, or rather her own; and all these things went with her straight back; her fluffed-out, indestructible-looking grey hair; her eyes, into the faded blue irises of which, with oncoming age, a milky fluid seemed to have seeped; her evidently tight stays; the long, pointed toes of her shoes, dark bronze in colour and ornamented with paste buckles; her somewhat stately deportment; and her antique habit of saying 'comin'' and 'goin''.

Juliet Cardoon was not in the least self-critical or introspective, so she had no compunction about her attachment to the past. The past had interested her, excited her, made her, and she did not choose to part with it nor feel any compulsion to try and adapt herself to the present. The war-time silence of the streets was a positive joy to her: it would have been a greater joy if broken occasionally by the clop-clop of horses' hooves. Bombs and all that sort of thing had merely acted as a fixative; she had been frightened, certainly, but it had never occurred to her to take shelter or to mind being alone in the house. 'If I'm goin' to be blown up,' she used to say, 'I'd rather be blown up comfortably in me bed.' She was the kind of woman who, if burnt at the stake, would have found time to remark that she had always thought there was nothin' to beat a real cracklin' log-fire.

Although her nephew was not a very articulate young man and had only the vaguest sense of period, he could appreciate to some extent the glamour of his aunt's past. He understood that it had been linked with high life in the days when high life really was high, that is to say, expensive, not open to all the world, and still marked by the remains of feudal grandeur. Her own origins were provincial and commonplace, but the comfortable evangelical home in which she grew up had seemed to her, from quite an early age, chiefly a place to escape from — not because she was unhappy, but because she was expansive. She was a clever, energetic child, with a flair for persons and things that were lively, fashionable and what in those days was called 'fast' — things and persons more or less under a ban, at home, of disapproval. She was ambitious, and had ideas about making a career: she once horrified her father by saying she wished she could go on the stage. Opportunity did not knock at her door, but threw it open and snatched her out into the great world for

313

which she longed, for when still very young she married a young London lawyer of great promise and useful connexions. Her sister Jenny, an almost equally vivacious being, married soon after a young but successful gynæcologist already in practice in Harley Street.

All four of them were social climbers, not in the narrow and purely snobbish sense, but because they all wanted to get on and be well off and to enjoy themselves and to be in what they would have called 'the swim'. They were well equipped for both the climb and the swim. Both men were able, personable and shrewd, and apart from their professional successes, their social talents and ambitions were adroitly reinforced and even surpassed by those of their wives. The society in which they climbed was chiefly that of the clients, rather than the professional associates, of the two husbands.

Now Juliet felt, quite early in her married life, that it would not be enough for her to give charming little dinners (a good cook, her husband used to insist, was the very foundation of all things), to dress smartly, to be playfully 'clever', to know a little of everything that was going on in public and something of what was going on in private. No, she must launch out in some new direction, so that her name, and her husband's name, might be associated with some interesting activity, something up-to-date, modish, sought after. The way was clear, for she was childless, and she had a particular talent which she now resolved to turn to account. Juliet had always had an extreme interest in the chairs people sat on, the carpets their chairs stood on, the fireplaces by which they warmed themselves, the lamps that lighted them, the curtains that framed the weather they looked out upon: even as a child she had been in the habit of planning the decoration of imaginary rooms and houses.

And so it happened that, at the turn of the century, she had succeeded in setting herself up as an interior decorator. She called herself Madam Cardoon, opened a combined office and showroom (which she called her *atelier*) in Davies Street, filled it with an assortment of choice old objects and startling new ones (some of them imported from Paris, Munich and Vienna), obtained the services of a capable young sissy of good family as manager, left the management of her own house to a housekeeper, and then set to work. An interview which she gave to a fashion journal and in which she spoke with more confidence than she actually felt (though that was not small) was seen by Mrs. X, at that time a 'great friend' of the Prince of Wales. Mrs. X, reading the interview, remembered having lately met Mrs. Cardoon at a garden party, remembered also a useful service performed for her by Mrs. Cardoon's husband when she wished to arrange a legal separation from Mr. X, and decided to get Mrs. Cardoon — or 'Madam Cardoon, Adviser on Decoration', as she now called herself — to do up the house she had taken in Great Cumberland Place, and to do it up so effectively that women who saw it would be envious and men would be bewitched into seeing it as part of Mrs. X's personality, like her clothes, her jewels, her scent, and her voice.

Juliet let herself go, and the drawing-room in Cumberland Place became a nine weeks' wonder. She painted the ceiling black, which was unheard of, and the floor white (so was that), and covered it with plain mauve rugs (their plainness, even more than their mauveness, was a startling novelty), and planted upon them a sofa so commodious that if Madame Récamier had been the Dionne Quintuplets she would have been quite at ease upon it, and so comfortably upholstered that sharp tongues speculated on the uses to which it was likely to be put. Little more need be said about that room except that above a dull gold dado the walls were covered with a satin paper in which broad black stripes alternated with mauve stripes, both being sown with little white and gold hearts, and that a prodigious electrolier hung from the ceiling in a wealth of sinuosities representing nymphs apparently caught in a cataract of melting toffee that had congealed for ever:

in the palm of each hand of each nymph was a socket, and in each socket was an electric light bulb. The rest of the house, as decorated by Madam Cardoon, is described in the pages of *Milady at Home* for the year in question; it is enough to say that the bathroom was the first in London to be entirely lined with looking-glass for it to be understood that Madam Cardoon was, as they say nowadays, on the up-and-up. Emulation is the sincerest form of envy, and the 'atelier' in Davies Street and the young man with the very tall collar and very narrow trousers soon had as much work as they could cope with. In brief, Madam Cardoon had made her name.

'You ought to write the story of your life,' the nephew-by-marriage had more than once said, after his aunt had been in a reminiscent mood. He was quite right; particularly as in the course of her career as a decorator Juliet Cardoon had sometimes found herself called in not merely to 'advise' socially eminent women about their new chintzes and wallpapers, but to listen to their confidences. They saw that she was young but they regarded her as already a woman of the world, and the fact that she was not, or rather had not been originally, a woman of precisely *their* world made them in a way more ready to confide in her: besides, she had charm, she listened with every appearance of sympathy, she had good sense, was discreet, never gossiped unkindly (it was noticed) about her other clients, and had (what was more) a shoulder positively formed for weeping on — it had been saturated, quite early on, by a lonely celebrity who thought she had been wronged and was glad to seize a chance of relaxing the tiresomely 'brave' smile with which she faced the world.

The transition from Edwardian splendours to the Bayswater hide-out was neither abrupt nor recent. First came the sudden death of Cardoon from heart-failure, then the revelation that he had made such ample provision for his two children by a mistress whose existence Juliet had not even suspected, that very little was left for Juliet herself. Juliet could have gone on with her 'atelier' and made a very good thing of it, but she had lost heart, so she sold out, took up Christian Science, put it down, and went to live with her sister Jenny for a time; then, after the first world war, she lapsed into Bayswater and a reclusive life.

'No,' she told her nephew, 'I shan't be writin' any memoirs. If I put in only the pleasant things the book wouldn't be true, and if I put in the truth it wouldn't be pleasant. I'm not grumblin', I've had a good life in some ways, better than most as far as I can see, and I've got me friends, and very old friends, some of 'em — otherwise I shouldn't be goin' to this weddin'.'

And all the trinkets at her wrist rattled and tinkled as she made a vague, slightly helpless gesture — as if she were accepting the truth of some proverb — that it's a long lane that has no turning, perhaps, but no —

'Things aren't always what they seem,' she said, with such a strange emphasis that this trite remark had an almost startling effect. 'I'll tell you a story,' she said, 'but you mustn't breathe a word of it to a soul. You promise? . . . Once upon a time, in the days when I took an interest in other people's houses, I went to stay at a small country place belongin' to Lord and Lady Crotchester. It was full of dreadful Victorian stuff (though I'm told people are collectin' it nowadays) and they wanted it freshenin' up a bit. I could see that Connie Crotchester had somethin' on her mind, but I couldn't imagine what. She and her husband seemed to have all the luck — looks, health, money, position. But no, they wanted a child, and they couldn't bring it off, and she was haunted by a fear that her husband would get to hate her if she failed to present him with an heir. I asked her if she thought it was her fault or her husband's. She said she was sure it was hers, as there had been no want of tryin' on his part. I can see her now, wringin' her hands and turnin' her beautiful head away as she spoke. "Oh, nonsense," I said. But I asked her all the same why she didn't see a good doctor. She hadn't apparently thought of that. So I told her about me sister Jenny's husband. I said he was a gynæcologist, but that all sorts of people went to see him about their private troubles, men as well as women. So she said she'd think about it, so I said it was no good thinkin' about it, she'd better *do* somethin' about it. Well, she went to see him, and within a year she was the mother of a beautiful boy. . . . Now don't look so cynical, you wicked boy! Me brother-in-law wasn't that sort of man. In any case, he wouldn't have been such a fool as to jeopardize his professional standin', and he had his own children to think of. . . . I need hardly tell you that Connie Crotchester spoke very highly of him.

'A year or two later another couple, whom I didn't know, Sir Portland and Lady Place, were also troubled at bein' childless. In this case, I believe, there was no doubt that the fault (or shall we say disability? — it seems unkind to call it a fault) lay with the husband. Well, Sir Portland went to see me brother-in-law, and again a child was born — only one, a daughter, but still that was better than nothin' . . .

'Well, Jenny's dead, and her husband's dead, and as you've promised to keep this all to yourself, I'm goin' to tell you a con-sultin'-room secret. When Jenny was a widow, I asked her, for I was dyin' of curiosity, how these two miracles were done. The explanation was quite simple, but a bit startlin'. It was Raikes.'

Again the gesture, the tinkling bangle.

'Rakes?' said the bewildered nephew, curious but faintly embarrassed. 'What are they?'

'Raikes was a big, handsome young man with a heart of gold. He was their butler in Harley Street . . .'

'Gosh!' said the nephew.

'Now the funny thing is that the weddin' I'm goin' to next week is the weddin' of the young Lord Crotchester and Miss Place. Of course *they* don't know, and Raikes himself doesn't know now — he was killed by a bomb, poor fellow, in '41.'

Again the twisted smile; and perhaps because there was something entirely shameless in it, the nephew, in an access of boyish *pudeur* or shyness, hid his face for a moment in his hands; and as he did so he felt almost suffocated by that sweetish, unchanging, pervasive odour, in which his aunt's outrageous memories were preserved as if in some embalming fluid suddenly become transparent.

# PRINCE EUGENE

## AND HIS TIMES

An Historical Novel

BY

### L. MÜHLBACH

AUTHOR OF FREDERICK THE GREAT AND HIS COURT, THE MERCHANT OF BERLIN,
BERLIN AND SANS-SOUCI, JOSEPH II. AND HIS COURT, ETC.

TRANSLATED FROM THE GERMAN

By ADELAIDE DeV. CHAUDRON

NEW YORK
A. L. FOWLE, Publisher
1907

23232

# CONTENTS.

## BOOK I.

## BOOK II.

## BOOK III.

## BOOK VII.

## BOOK VIII.

# PRINCE EUGENE AND HIS TIMES.

## BOOK I.

### *PRINCE EUGENE, THE LITTLE ABBÉ.*

### CHAPTER I.

#### THE COUNTESS OF SOISSONS.

"Is that your last word, madame?" said Louvois, in a tone so emphatic as to be almost threatening.

"My last word," replied the countess, haughtily. "My daughter is too young to marry, and were she older, I would not impose a husband upon her who was not the man of her choice. She shall bestow her hand and heart together."

"Do you mean that it is impossible for your daughter to love my son?" asked Louvois, hastily.

The countess raised her shoulders and smiled superciliously, while from her large black eyes there darted forth a glance that spoke volumes to the mind of the irritated minister.

"It would appear," said she, "that there can be no sympathy between the Mancinis and the Louvois, and that their antipathies are to be perpetuated from generation to generation."

"You would remind me of the similarity which the fate of my son as a wooer bears to that of his father?" asked Louvois. "I do not deny it; the repulse which twenty-one years ago I received from Olympia Mancini, she repeats to-day in the person of her daughter. But it may be that on some other occasion the Mancinis shall be repulsed by the Louvois."

"A threat?" said the countess, angrily.

Now it was the shoulders of the minister that were raised. "I have sowed love and reaped hate," said he, quietly.

The countess laughed. "Ah," said she, "I see that you have remodelled your speech according to the pious formulary of Madame de Maintenon, and that you seek for your troubadours among the prophets."

"Yes—the Scriptural prophets satisfy *my* cravings for knowledge," replied Louvois, smiling. "Pity that everybody else is not as orthodox as I!"

"What do you mean?" asked the countess, uneasily.

"I mean that it would be better for the Countess de Soissons if she imitated the discretion of Madame de Maintenon, and eschewed association with those unholy prophets who draw their inspiration from the stars."

"Do you think so? And yet the book of the stars is inspired and contains truth, for therein it stands written that our two families will never be united by the bonds of love. What is the use of striving against destiny? Fate has willed our enmity, and we must submit with resignation," said the countess, with an affected drawl. "You see," added she, pathetically, "how beautifully I fall into your new-fashioned dialect, and how harmoniously my dulcet notes mingle with those of the court chorus."

"I remember the dulcet notes of a poem written years ago, which were wont to edify the court with a strain that would sound inharmonious there to-day. What would De Montespan and De Maintenon say to such discordant lines as these?" And Louvois began to hum the following:

> "La belle Olympe n'a point de seconde,
> Et l'Amour a bien réuni
> Dedans l'infante Mancini
> Par un avantage suprême
> Tout ce qui force à dire : J'aime !
> Et qui l'a fait dire à nos dieux !" *

"What they would say?" replied the countess; "why, they would listen approvingly to a rhapsody which time has falsified, and imagine that I wince to hear it sung. But they would be in error. I thank you for recalling to my mind the golden vision of the past, wherein a king knelt at my feet, and

* "Les Nièces de Mazarion," par Renée, p. 177.

Louvois lived upon my smiles. She who can look back upon conquests such as these, can afford to despise the contrarieties of the present, while she plumes her victorious wings for future flight, wherein she shall attain indemnification for the trifling vexations of to-day."

"I wish you may realize your joyous anticipations," replied Louvois, with a sneer. "But if you will allow me to draw your horoscope, you will confess that I am a wiser seer than your dear friend La Voisin."

For one moment the features of the countess contracted painfully, but she mastered her emotion and was able to reply with a tranquil smile,—"Do so, your excellency, I am all attention."

"I read in the stars that snares encompass you, Countess de Soissons. You have enemies, numerous, powerful, and crafty. At their head stands the queen, who can never forgive you for having opened one of her letters, and having stolen thence a note addressed to the king, which accused her of secret machinations with Spain. Then there is poor Louise de la Vallière, who for your cruel sarcasms shed such oceans of tears—"

"She is in a convent."

"True, but the scars of your persecutions are upon her heart; and although she may be a Christian, think you that she has ceased to be a woman? Third—among the number of those who hate you is the Marquise de Montespan, to whom the brilliant assemblages at the Hôtel de Soissons are a source of mortification, for she can never forget that, on more than one occasion, the king has forgotten his rendezvous with her, to linger at the side of his fascinating hostess. And we must not overlook the pious De Maintenon, who lives in constant terror lest some day or other your presence should recall to the king that golden vision of his youth, whereof Olympia Mancini was the enshrined divinity. For this reason you are more obnoxious to the ex-governess than De Montespan herself. The star of the latter favorite is already on the wane, whereas yours may rise again at the bidding of Memory. These four women have long meditated your destruction, and many are the thorns with which they have strewed your path in life. But, to compass your ruin, there was wanting *one* strong arm that could concentrate their scattered missiles, and hurl them in *one* great bomb at your head. Countess de Soissons, that arm is mine—I, Louvois, the trusted minister of the king, the friend of De Maintenon, the mightiest subject in France—I am the man whose arm shall strike on behalf of your enemies, of whom in me behold the chief ! You have thrown me your gauntlet, and I raise it. I proclaim myself your foe, and since there must be war between our races, we shall see whether for the future the Mancinis may not be made to suffer through the Louvois ! This is my horoscope, and now mark well my last words: La Voisin the soothsayer was arrested last night."

All the self-control which she could gather to meet this sinister disclosure, could not smother the groan which was upheaved from Olympia's sinking heart.

Louvois affected not to hear it. He bowed low and prepared to take his leave. The countess made no effort to detain him; she was too frightened for circumspection, and she followed his retreating figure with eyes that were all aflame with hate. Nor did their fiery glow abate when, having reached the door, Louvois turned and confronted her.

He surveyed her calmly, but his eye returned hate for hate, and so for a moment they stared at each other, while there passed between the two a silent challenge, which both felt was to be fought out to the death.

After a pause Louvois spoke. His mouth dilated with a cruel smile, which, when its mocking light was seen, betokened peril to those who offended him.

"Madame," said he, "not only has La Voisin been arrested, but her private papers have been seized." So saying, he bowed again and disappeared behind the portière.

## CHAPTER II.

### THE LABORATORY.

THE countess listened to his echoing footsteps until they were no longer audible, nor did she move until she heard the roll of the carriage which bore him away.

Gradually the sound of the receding vehicle melted into distance, and a deep silence ensued. This silence first roused the countess from her lethargy. A tremor convulsed her limbs ; her dilated orbs which had been fixed upon the door relaxed, and wandered from the silken hangings of the walls to the gilded furniture around her; from the tables of Florentine marble to the rainbow-tinted chandeliers, whose pendants swayed to and fro in the sunshine. And now they rested dreamily upon a picture which, conspicuous for size and beauty, hung immediately opposite to the sofa whereon she was reclining. It was the full length portrait of a handsome youth. He was not tall, but he was gracefully proportioned. His shoulders were broad; and, rising from the midst of a slender throat, adorned with a fall of lace, appeared his stately head crowned with a wealth of long, brown curls. His face was of a beautiful oval, his complexion clear, his mouth wreathed with happy smiles. The brow was high and arched, and the fine gray eyes beamed with hope and energy. In one hand he held a rose, which he extended to a person not represented in the picture; the other hand, half-veiled by its overhanging fall of gossamer lace, rested carelessly on the table, while close by lay two rose-buds, which seemed just to have been dropped from the half-open fingers. Over an arm-chair in the background was thrown a mantle of royal ermine, which partially concealed the kingly crown that surmounted its high carved back.

The eyes of the countess were fixed upon this picture with an expression of tender sadness, and slowly, as if yielding to an influence altogether objective, she rose from her seat and advanced toward the portrait, where she remained gazing until her sight was dimmed by tears, while the youth smiled ever, and ever held out the rose.

What golden tribute had his homage brought to her ambition! What ecstasy had it poured into her heart! How truly had she loved that princely boy, who, careless, happy, and fickle, was bestowing upon other women the roses which for her had withered years ago, leaving upon their blighted stems the sharp and cruel thorns of his inconstancy!

Since then, twenty-three years had gone by; she had become a wife and the mother of seven children, but the wound still festered; the old sorrow still sang its mournful dirge within a heart which to-day beat as wildly as ever, and felt a pang as keen as when it first grew jealous, and learned that not she, but Marie, had become the divinity whom Louis worshipped.

Marie, too, had been forsaken, and had stifled the cries of her despairing heart by marriage with another. The fate of both sisters had been the same—a short dream of gratified ambition, followed by long years of humiliation. It seemed that the prosperity and happiness of Cardinal Mazarin's nieces had been coexistent with his life, for when the eyes of their uncle closed in death, the light of their fortunes grew dim and expired.

The portrait of Louis XIV., which was calling up the spectres of so many buried joys, had been painted expressly for Olympia Mancini. It represented his first declaration of love to her, and had been sent as a souvenir of "the brightest hour of his life." He had barely reached his thirty-seventh year, and yet this winsome youth had been transformed into a demure devotee, who, despising the vanities of the world, had turned his heart toward heaven, and spent his life doing penance for the sins of his early manhood!

And this transformation was the work of a woman who had neither beauty, youth, nor birth to recommend her to the favor of a monarch—a woman who had been the paid governess of the king's bastards, and was not even gifted with intellect enough to cover her other deficiencies!

These last thoughts brought a smile to the face of the countess. Turning suddenly away from the portrait she crossed the room with rapid steps, and placed herself directly in front of a large Venetian mirror which occupied the space between two windows. It gave back the reflection of an exquisite figure, whose outlines contributed much to the grace with which the folds of a blue satin dress fell in rich profusion around it. The white shoulders were scarcely concealed by a shawl of superb lace, and the arms, still round, were set off by costly bracelets. The raven hair, with not a trace of time's finger to discolor its glossy blackness, fell around her face in curls as delicate as the tendrils of a grape. Her brow was smooth and polished, her eyes aglow with passionate longing, and, as her lips curved into a complacent smile, they disclosed two rows of pearly teeth, compact and without a fleck.

Yes, she was not deceived. Olympia de Soissons was a handsome woman, and with so much comeliness, such ready wit, and such unrivalled powers of conversation, she might gird up her loins to do battle with her rivals. Was not Madame de Maintenon her elder by three years? And as for De Montespan, was she not wasting away into an old woman? If they had found it possible to win the heart of this sensual Louis, why not she? This heart had once been all her own, and why should not she, who combined the beauty of one mistress with the shrewdness of the other, dispossess them both, and re-enter into possession of her old domains?

She smiled again, and saw how well her smiles became her. "Yes," said she to herself, "yes, I will recall this truant merlin, and he shall return to perch upon the hand he used to love! I will be mistress of his heart and mistress of his realms. She foretold it all, and gave me the charm wherewith to work the spell."

But as she gave utterance to these last words, her lips began to quiver, and her fine features were distorted by some sudden pain. She had just called to mind the fearful intelligence of La Voisin's arrest.

"Great God! If my letters should have been found among her papers! What, oh what would be *my* fate?"

She shuddered—and in place of the triumphant vision of a heart recaptured, a monarch at her feet, there arose the fearful spectacle of an execution which, four years before, she had witnessed at the bloody Place de Grève. Once more she saw

2

the square, black with a mass of human beings, who, jeering, shouting, and cursing, moved hither and thither like the waves of a turbulent ocean; at every window that looked out upon the place, she saw gayly-dressed ladies who peered anxiously out to catch a glimpse of one gloomy object that loomed darkly up from its centre. She saw the crowd give way and part, as, keeping pace with the dull sound of a muffled drum, a sad procession entered upon the scene. At its head marched a battalion of soldiers, and behind them, seated in the felon's cart, came a pale, beautiful woman, who ever and anon pressed to her quivering lips the crucifix held out to her by a priest —that last link of sympathy between the convict and his fellow-creatures. At the criminal's side, in symbolic robes of sanguinary red, was the executioner that was to sever this slender tie, and wrench the spirit from the body to whose guardianship God had committed it on earth. Silently the hideous cortége moved on, while the crowd fell back to let it pass, until the scaffold came to view. How joyously the sun's rays seemed to play around the glittering axe that was to end a career of secret crime ! How eagerly the high-born dames bend forward to catch sight of the criminal, as, leaning on the arm of the priest, she tottered to her doom! Olympia remembered only too well the moment when the drum ceased its "discordant sound," and when the silence was so oppressive that the low voice of the condemned was heard uttering her last prayer. She knelt beside the block—a circle of light was described upon the air—and the head fell upon the blood-besprinkled sand.

The Countess de Soissons sickened as she remembered that the woman whom she had seen executed was one of high position, no less a personage than the beautiful and fascinating Marquise de Brinvilliers. Neither her rank, her charms, nor the strenuous efforts of her powerful friends, had been adequate to save her from the headsman's axe. She had been convicted of poisoning, and had shared the fate of other malefactors of less repute. Her confidante La Voisin had been arrested at the time, but as nothing proved her to have been an accomplice of her former mistress she had escaped conviction.

Something new with regard to the fortune-teller must have

transpired, for Louvois had considered her arrest as an ill-omen for the Countess de Soissons. Not only for Olympia, however, was the arrest of Catherine a calamity, for she was the trusty counsellor of many a noble lady who, before suspicion had sullied her name, had been the dear and intimate associate of the Marquise de Brinvilliers.

The countess had turned away from the contemplation of her mellow charms, and was on her way to her boudoir. She bolted the door within, and, crossing the room, mounted a chair that stood by the side of a tall mirror set in a thick gilt frame. She touched a spring, when the mirror glided noiselessly aside, revealing a dark recess within the wall.

Olympia slipped through the opening, which closed behind her, darted up a narrow staircase, and, hastily drawing a key from a pocket concealed within the folds of her dress, she unlocked the door of a room whose aspect was anything but appropriate to the pursuits of a lady of quality.

It was to all appearances a kitchen, for one entire side of it was occupied by a hearth full of recesses, each one of which contained a furnace fitted up with iron utensils for cooking. On the mantel, which corresponded to this immense hearth, were ranged pipkins and other vessels of different sizes, interspersed with rows of phials and flasks containing liquids of every imaginable color. On a massive oaken table, in the centre of the apartment, were placed a number of bowls and dishes, and near them lay a disorderly pile of papers, books, and pamphlets.

Olympia approached the hearth, stooped over one of the furnaces, and from a fagot lying near gathered a few small sticks. Over these sticks she poured a fluid from one of her flasks, and then rubbing them briskly together, they began to emit sparks. She placed them under the furnace, added a little more fuel, and in a few moments had a good fire.

She now sprang to her feet, and hastily pushing aside a row of pipkins, opened a small door which had been concealed behind them, above the mantel. From a recess within the wall she took a brass-bound casket, which she placed upon the table.

The casket contained some books, papers, and several diminutive phials. One of these phials she held up to the light, contemplating its contents with manifest satisfaction.

"Herein lies the spell that is to lure my faithless monarch back again. La Voisin may rot in prison, but her mantle of science has fallen upon me, and her secrets are mine. Her last, best gift shall restore me to my throne. Not only did she leave me the means of success, but she foretold the certainty of that success besides. It must be so: La Voisin never erred in her predictions, and I shall triumph!"

Pressing the phial to her lips, Olympia hid it beneath the folds of her lace tucker, murmuring the while, "I shall sip of this nectar anon; for the present, I must provide for discovery."

She took the papers that lay in the casket, and weighing them in her hand said musingly:

"How light they are, and yet how heavy was the gold with which I purchased them! 'Tis a pity they should be destroyed: what if I should forget? But no! oblivion of their treasured secrets were impossible to me; so away with you! You might turn traitors, and I had best anticipate treachery by destruction."

Then followed the books and the contents of the phials remaining in the casket. The blue flames leaped high as these last were added to the cremation, and the room became oppressive with their unwholesome vapor.

"The window must be opened," said Olympia. "This odor might betray me. People might suspect me of having cooked arsenic in my kitchen instead of onions."

With these words she opened the casement, and the noxious cloud passed slowly out into the air.

"Now all is safe. Louvois can send as many bailiffs as he lists, and should they poke their inquisitive noses into my sanctum, they will find nothing for their pains but an innocent laboratory wherein the Countess de Soissons prepares her cosmetics, and makes experiments in the chemistry of the toilet."

She replaced her casket, searched the mantel carefully, and then glanced sharply around the room to assure herself that she was alone and undiscovered.

Yes! Alone, the witnesses of her guilt consumed, and their ashes etherealized throughout space.

The countess smiled, and, as she locked the door of her laboratory, her spirits revived and her thoughts once more reverted to the ambitious dreams of the morning. When she had reached her boudoir again, and the complaisant mirror had resumed its place, she drew the flask from her bosom, removed the glass stopper, inhaled for a moment its perfume, and then, raising it to her lips, drained the contents to their last drop.

"And this philter is to make me mistress of your heart, King Louis! How I long to begin my reign!"

A slight rustling was heard outside, and the guilty woman trembled anew. She concealed the phial, and listened breathlessly, while her straining eyes were fixed upon the door as though they had hoped to see through its panels of oak whether friend or foe stood without.

A slight knock was heard, and now, in spite of herself, the Countess de Soissons grew pale and shivered. What if the myrmidons of Louvois had come with a *lettre de cachet!* What if—No! not even *he* would go so far in his enmity to the niece of the great cardinal, the relative of the reigning Duke of Savoy, and the daughter-in-law of the Princess Carignan.

So she summoned resolution enough to cross the room, draw back the bolt, and to say in a loud, imperious tone: "Come in."

The door opened, and admitted a young man. The countess no sooner recognized him than she smiled, and, with a slight elevation of her shoulders, said, "Nobody but you."

"Nobody but me," replied the youth, sadly. "I come to ask of my gracious mother an interview."

## CHAPTER III.

### PRINCE EUGENE.

THE countess inclined her head in token of assent ; but, as she did so, her eyes rested on the diminutive form of her son with an expression that savored of disdain. The look was un-motherly, and seemed to say, " How can a man of such insig-nificant appearance be the son of the stately Countess de Sois-sons ? "

And indeed to a careless observer the words were not inap-propriate to his dwarfish proportions. His head, which, be-tween his excessively wide shoulders, was perched upon the top of a very long neck, was too large, much too large for his body. His face was narrow, his complexion swarthy, his sal-low cheeks high and sunken. A nose slightly turned up, gave an expression of boldness to his countenance, increased by the shortness of his upper lip, which exposed to view two large front teeth that were almost ferocious in their size. On either side of his high, narrow forehead, his hair, instead of being worn according to the prevailing fashion, was suffered to fall in long elf-locks about his ears. Notwithstanding all these dis-advantages, his eyes were so superlatively beautiful that they almost persuaded you into the belief that he was handsome. From their lustrous depths there streamed a meteoric splendor, which, more than words, revealed the genius, the enthusiasm, and the noble soul to which Nature had assigned such un-worthy corporality.

Those speaking eyes were fixed upon the countess in tender sadness, while, in a respectful attitude near the door, he awaited her permission to approach.

She languidly extended her hand, and, Eugene coming for-ward, bent over and imprinted upon it a heartfelt kiss.

" My dear mother then consents ? " said he, humbly.

"I know of no reason why I should refuse," replied the countess, carelessly. " Neither am I able to divine wherefore you make your request in a tone of such unusual solemnity. One would suppose that the little abbé has come to invite his mother to a confession of her sins, so portentous is his demeanor."

"Would I could receive that confession," exclaimed he, earnestly ; "would I could look into my mother's heart and read the secrets there!"

"Indeed! and have you come hither to catechise your mother. then ?" said the countess, with a frown.

"No, dear mother, no," cried Eugene, eagerly ; "I have come to ask of you whether I may walk with head erect before the world, or whether I must die because of our dishonor ?"

"An extraordinary alternative to present for my decision, certainly ; and I confess that I am very curious to learn how it happens that I can assist you in your dilemma. Speak, then, and I will listen."

With these words the countess threw herself indolently into an arm-chair, and motioned Eugene to a seat. But he only advanced a step or two, and gazed wistfully upon her handsome, hardened face.

"Mother," said he, in a low, husky voice, "the soothsayer La Voisin has been arrested."

"Ah! what else ?" asked the countess, with perfect composure.

"Her house is guarded, every corner has been searched, and her papers have all been seized."

"And what else ?" repeated the countess.

Her son looked up, and a ray of hope shot athwart his pale and anxious face. "Nothing is talked of in Paris," continued he, "but the strange revelations connected with her arrest. It is said that she not only drew the horoscope of those who were accustomed to visit her, and gave them philters, but—but—"

"But," echoed the countess as her son paused.

"But that she prepared secret poisons, one of which, called 'La poudre de succession,' was specially designed for the use of those who wished to remove an inconvenient relative."

This time the countess was silent ; her brow contracted, and she shivered perceptibly.

An involuntary cry burst from the lips of her son, which recalled her to a sense of her imprudence.

"What ails you?" asked she, abruptly. "Have you seen a ghost, that you cry out in a voice so unearthly?"

"Yes, mother, I have seen a ghost—the ghost of my father!" And while the countess grew pale, and her eyes dilated with fear, her unhappy son sank upon his knees before her, and clasped his hands with agony of apprehension.

"Mother, have mercy on me, and forgive me if, in the anguish of my writhing soul, I ask you whether you are innocent of my father's death?"

"Has any one dared to accuse me?" asked she, with a scowl.

"Ay! And so publicly, that men spoke of it together as I passed them in the streets to-day. Need I say that I was ready to die of grief as I heard the epithet of murderess applied to the mother who to me has been the ideal of beauty, goodness, and excellence, which my heart has worshipped to the exclusion of all other loves! My brain was on fire as I dashed through the scornful crowd, and made my way to you, mother, here to look upon your dear face, and read in your eyes your innocence of the hideous crime. We are alone with God: in mercy tell me, are you innocent or guilty?"

As he raised his face to hers, the countess saw there such powerful love struggling with his anguish, that her heart was touched, and the angry words she had meditated died upon her lips.

"These are cruel doubts wherewith to assail your mother, Eugene," said she, after a pause. "Follow me, and in the presence of your forefathers you shall be answered."

With a lofty bend of the head, she left the room, followed by her stricken child. They crossed a spacious hall, and traversed one after another the apartments of state which were thrown open to guests on occasions of great ceremony, and led to the grand hall of reception. At the farther end of this hall, under a canopy of purple velvet, surmounted by a ducal crown, were the two thrones which, on the days of these state receptions, the Count and Countess de Soissons were privileged to occupy in presence of their guests, provided his majesty were not of the number. This right they held by virtue of their connection with the royal house of France, and their close relationship to the Duke of Savoy. At the time of the marriage of his niece with the Count de Soissons, Cardinal Mazarin had obtained from Louis XIV. an acknowledgment of her husband as a prince of the blood, and, by virtue of this acknowledgment, his right to attend without invitation all court festivities, to appear at the public and private levees of the king, and in his own palace to sit upon a throne.

On either side of the throne-room of the Hôtel de Soissons were ranged the portraits of their ancestors, in armor, in ducal or episcopal robes, in doublet and hose, or in flowing wigs. Silently the mother and son walked by the stately effigies of princes and princesses, until they had reached the farthest portrait there.

With outstretched arms the countess pointed to the likeness of a handsome man, clad in a rich court-suit, which well became his aristocratic figure. As he gazed upon the pleasant smile that illumined a face expressive of exceeding goodness, the eyes of young Eugene filled with tears.

His mother surveyed him with a curl of her lip.

"Tears!" said she. "And yet you stand before the portrait of your father, whom you accuse me of having murdered!"

"No, no," cried her son, eagerly, "I did not accuse, I—I—"

"You inquired," interrupted the countess, disdainfully. "And by your inquiry you insinuate that such a crime by the hand of your mother was not only possible, but probable."

"Unhappily, I have more than once seen La Voisin in your boudoir, mother."

The countess affected not to hear. "Then a son considers himself justifiable in asking of his mother whether or not she poisoned his father; he should do so with the sword of justice in his hand, not with an eyelid that trembles with cowardly tears."

"Mother, have pity on me," sobbed Eugene, throwing himself at her feet. "Do not answer my cruel question, for I read your innocence in the noble scorn that flashes from your eye, and beams from every feature of your dear, truthful face. Pardon me, beloved mother; pardon your repentant child."

"No, I shall not pardon the poltroon who, believing that his mother has disgraced his escutcheon, weeps like a woman

over wrongs which he should avenge like a man. But I fo
got. The little abbé of Savoy is not accustomed to wear a
sword; *his* weapon is the missal. Go, then, to your prayers,
and when you pray for your father's soul, ask forgiveness of
God for your heartless and ungrateful conduct to his widow."

"Dear, dear mother, have pity!" sobbed Eugene, still kneeling at her feet.

"Was there any pity in your heart for me when you asked
that shameful question?"

"I was demented," cried he; "maddened by the sneers
that were flung at me in the streets to-day."

"And, to console yourself, you joined in the popular cry.
' *Vox populi vox Dei*,' I suppose, is your pious motto."

"Mother!" cried Eugene, springing to his feet, "crush me,
if you will, under the weight of your anger, but do not stretch
me upon the rack of your scorn. I am no devotee; and, if the
king, my family, and yourself, are forcing me into a career
which is repugnant to every instinct of my manhood, pity me,
if you will, but do not insult me."

"Pity you!" sneered the countess. "I am a woman; but
he who would venture to pity *me*, would receive my glove in
his face for his insolence. Go, faint heart! You are fit for
nothing but a whining priest, for there is not a spark of manhood within your sluggish breast. No generous blood of the
princes of Savoy mantles in your sallow cheek; 'tis the ichor-
ous fluid of the churchman Mazarin that—"

"Mother!" thundered Eugene, with a force that gave the
lie to her derisive words—"mother, you shall go no further in
your disdain of me, for the blood of Savoy is seething within
my veins, and I may, perchance, forget that she who so affronts my father's son, is my mother!"

"You have already forgotten," replied the countess, coldly.
"My answer to your infamous charge shall be made not to
you, but to your ancestors."

So saying, she bent her steps toward the ducal throne, and
seating herself thereon, addressed her son:

"Eugene of Savoy, Prince of Carignan, Bourbon, and
Piedmont, bend your knee before the mother that bore you,
and hearken to her words."

The prince obeyed, and knelt at the foot of the throne.

The countess raised her arm, and pointed to the portraits that hung around. "You have been witnesses," said she, addressing them all, "to the outrage which has been put upon me to-day by him who inherits your name, but not your worth. If I am the guilty wretch which he has pronounced me to be, strike me to the earth for my crimes, and justify his parricidal words. But you know that I am innocent, and that, with bitter tears, I lamented the death of my murdered husband!"

"Murdered!" exclaimed Eugene. "It is, then, true that he was murdered?"

"Yes," replied the countess, "he was murdered, but not by bowl or dagger."

With these words, she rose, and, slowly descending from her throne, she returned to the spot which she had left, and gazed mournfully upon her husband's portrait. "He was a noble, brave, and gallant prince," said she, softly. "He loved me unspeakably, and wherefore should I have taken the life of him whose whole pleasure lay in ministering to my happiness? What could I gain by the death of the dearest friend I ever had? Ah, never would he have mistrusted his Olympia! Had the envious rabble of Paris defamed me while he lived to defend my honor, it is not your father, Prince Eugene, that would have joined my traducers and outraged my womanhood, as you have done to-day!"

"Forgive me," murmured the prince.

"Yes, my beloved," continued she, addressing the picture, "they accuse me of murdering thee, because they seek my ruin as they compassed thine."

"Who, dear mother, who?" cried Eugene, passionately. "Who are the fiends that murdered my father and calumniate my mother?"

"They are Louis XIV.," exclaimed the countess, "his minister Louvois, and his two mistresses, De Montespan and De Maintenon."

"The king!" echoed Eugene, in a voice of such fury, that his mother turned her eyes from the portrait, and stared at him with amazement.

"You hate the king?" said she, hurriedly.

"Yes," said Eugene, his eyes flashing fire; "yes, I hate him."

"And why ? "

"Do not ask me, mother; I dare not say wherefore I hate the king."

"Then I will tell you why. You hate him because you believe the scandalous reports which my enemies have spread throughout Europe as regards my relations, in years gone by, with Louis. You believe that your mother was once the king's mistress, and that, to hide her shame, she borrowed the name of the Count de Soissons."

Eugene made no reply.

"Ah, why have I no son to shelter me from these infamous suspicions ! Why must I live and die under such false and disgraceful imputations ? "

"Then, it is not true ? " cried Eugene, joyfully. "You did not love the king, mother ? "

"Yes, I did love him," said she, calmly, "and loved him as an Italian alone can love."

Eugene groaned, and covered his face with his hands.

"I do not deny the love," continued the countess, " for it was all the work of Cardinal Mazarin. He brought me from Italy, and bade me win the king's heart and become a queen; and when he did so he added a recommendation to me to be a good, dutiful niece, and never to forget who it was had helped me to a crown. I saw the youth whom the cardinal desired me to love : the handsomest, wittiest, and most accomplished cavalier in France. I obeyed but too willingly, and Louis became the idol of my life."

"Then it is true that my mother was beloved by the king ? " said Eugene, sternly.

"Beloved by him, but never his mistress ! " returned the countess, proudly. "Yes, he loved me as I did him, with the trust, the strength, the passion, that are characteristic of a first love. I was ambitious for him as well as for myself, and would have had him a monarch in deed as well as in name. I led him away from the frivolous regions of indolent enjoyment to the starry realms of poetry, art, and science ; and, had Louis ever risen to the fame of Numa, I should have merited that of Egeria. But this conflicted with the ambition of the cardinal. He had no sooner comprehended the nature of the influence I exerted over his royal tool, than he poisoned his ear by insinuating that ambition, not love, was the spring of all my efforts to elevate him to the level of his magnificent destiny. Poor, weak Louis ! He was anything that Cardinal Mazarin chose to make him ; so at the word of command he ceased to love, and went to make an offering of his accommodating affections to Marie. She made him take an oath never to look at me again."

"Did he respect the oath ? "

"Just so long as he loved Marie. I need not tell you that I suffered from his inconstancy. I was inexpressibly grieved; but pride upheld me, and Louis never received a word or look of reproach for his faithlessness. Meanwhile your father offered his hand, and before I accepted it he was made acquainted with the history of my heart. I concealed nothing from him, so that he was at once the confidant of my past sorrows, and their comforter."

"Thank you, dear, dear mother," said Eugene, tenderly. "In the name of all your children, let me thank you for your noble candor."

"I married the Prince de Soissons, and here, in presence of his assembled ancestors, I swear that I have kept unstained the faith I pledged him at the marriage-altar. Let the world belie me as it will, Olympia Mancini has ever been a spotless wife. So true is this, that Louis, when he had abandoned Marie, and had tired of his queen, returned to me with vows of a love which he swore had been the only genuine passion of his life ; and when, as my husband's loyal wife, I repulsed the advances of his sovereign, that sovereign became my bitterest enemy. Not even after he had consoled himself with the insipid charms of that poor, flimsy creature, La Vallière, did Louis relent ; his animosity, because of some witticism of mine on the subject of his hysterical mistress, has pursued me throughout life ; not only me, but every member of my family. For a mere epigram I was banished from Paris, and your father stripped of a lucrative and honorable office. We managed after a time to return to court, but my enemies were more

powerful than I.   Through the jealousy of the Marquise de
Montespan I was a second time banished ; but before we left,
your father fought two duels with noblemen who had circu-
lated the calumnies which the marquise had originated concerning me.   The Duke de Noailles was wounded, and the Chevalier de Grand Mercy killed.   Although the challenges had
been honorably sent and accepted, the Count de Soissons was
summoned before the king and publicly rebuked.   Oh, let me
speak no longer of the contumely we endured during those
bitter days !   My husband died, blessing me, and cursing the
selfish monarch who had ruined us both."

Eugene clinched his hand.   "I shall remember the curse,"
cried he, "and it shall be verified if God give me strength,
mother!"

"Yes, avenge us if you can, Eugene, but, until the day of
reckoning come, we must be politic and wary.   Be silent and
discreet as I was, when, on being allowed to return to Paris, I
humbled myself for my dear children's sake, and not only
swore to write no more epigrams, but went in person to sue to
Madame de Montespan for pardon and protection!"

"Mother, is it possible !   Far better had it been for us to
die obscurely in some provincial village, than purchase our
admission to court at the price of such humiliation as that !"

"No, no—I had sworn to be revenged upon my persecutors,
and no plan of *vendetta* could I carry out in a provincial village.   Do you remember what I told my sons on the day of our
return to the Hôtel de Soissons ?"

"Ay, mother, that do I.   You said : 'Bow your heads in
ostensible humility, but never forget that the Bourbons have
robbed you of your inheritance.   Never forget that if you are
poor, it is because on some idle pretext of a conspiracy that
never could be proved, Louis XIV. sequestered the estates of
the Counts de Soissons.'   These were your words, and you see
that I have not forgotten them.   They are the steel on which
I have sharpened the hate I feel for the King of France.   And
now that its edge is keen, why may I not lift it against the
man who belied my mother, and murdered my father ?   Oh
mother, mother, why will you force me to become a priest ?"

"What else could you become ?" asked Olympia.   "The

king is your guardian, and he it is that from your childhood
has destined you for the church."

"I hate this garb," exclaimed Eugene, touching his cassock.
"My vocation is not for the priesthood, and, if I am called
upon to utter compulsory vows, I feel that I shall disgrace my
cloth. Dear mother, loosen the detested bonds that bind me
to a listless and contemplative life ! Gird me with a sword,
and let me go out to battle with the world like a man!"

The countess looked disdainfully at the diminutive figure
of her son, and raised her shoulders with contempt. "You a
soldier !"

"Yes !" exclaimed Eugene, passionately. "Yes ! My soul
abhors the cloister, and yearns for the battle-field. While
you have fancied that I was studying theology, I have been
poring over the lives of great commanders; and, instead of
preparing my soul for heaven, I have trained my body for
earthly strife. Look not so compassionately upon my stature,
mother. This body is slender, but 'tis the coat of mail that
covers an intrepid soul, and I have hardened it until it can bid
defiance to wind or weather. With this arm I curb the
wildest horse, nor will its sinews yield to the blow of the
most practised swordsman in France. I have studied the
science of warfare in books ; my life has been one long preparation for its practice, and I cannot, will not relinquish
my day-dreams of glory."

"There is no help for it, I tell you. All princes of the
blood are wards of the king ; your royal guardian has chosen
your profession, and you must either submit or bear the consequences of his wrath."

"What care I for his wrath ? Let him give me my freedom, and I will promise never to seek my fortune at his
hands."

"At all events, wait for some favorable opportunity to rebel, Eugene. We are poor and dependent now, and your
brother's scandalous marriage has forever marred our hopes
of seeing him heir to the duchy of Savoy. To think of a
Prince de Carignan uniting himself to the daughter of the
equerry of the Prince de Condé ! What a disgrace !"

"My brother consulted his heart and not his escutcheon,"

replied Eugene, with a smile. "He followed the example of his father, and may God bless him with a wife as beautiful and as virtuous as his mother!"

The countess, who had begun to frown at Eugene's apology for his brother, could not resist this filial flattery. She gave him her hand, which he kissed devoutly.

"You no longer believe me guilty, my son?" said she. Eugene knelt and murmured: "Pardon, dear, dear mother! My life will be all too short to expiate my unworthy doubts, and to avenge your wrongs."

"Avenge them, but do not exasperate the king. Imitate Richelieu and Mazarin, and the priest's gown will no longer be distasteful to you. They were great in the field and in the cabinet, and both possessed more than regal power, for both were the rulers of kings."

Eugene was about to reply, but Olympia raised her hand in remonstrance, and continued:

"I exact of you, for a time at least, *apparent* submission and perfect silence. When the hour is ripe for retaliation, you shall strike, and repay me for all that I have endured at the hands of the king. But, for the present, breathe not the name of Louis above a whisper. I have a deadlier foe than he to encounter now. Louvois, Louvois, I dread above all other men; and if you have the strength of a man in your arm, Eugene, let the force of its vengeance fall upon the head of him, whose animosity is more potent than that of all my other enemies united."

"It shall crush him and all who seek to injure you, mother. Revenge!—yes, revenge for your wrongs, for my father's death, and for *my* bondage!"

"Ay, revenge, Eugene! A man may wear the garb of an ecclesiastic with the heart of a hero, and to your brave heart these Princes of Carignan commit my cause! Come, let us leave our ancestors to their grim repose. May they lend their ghostly aid to the arm that wields the carnal weapons of our righteous vengeance!"

As she turned to leave the gallery, the train of her blue satin dress became entangled in the claws of the lion which supported the throne. Eugene stooped hastily to release it, and, instead ot dropping it again, he smiled affectionately upon his mother and placed himself in the attitude of a page.

The countess looked pleased at the attention, and said, "Have you learned, among your other accomplishments, to be a trainbearer?"

"Yes, mother, I have learned to be *your* trainbearer, but to no other mortal would I condescend to do such service."

But Olympia was not listening. She was day-dreaming again, and the substance of her dreams was as follows:

"How soon, perchance, the court of France may bear my train along, while I, victorious and exultant, crush the head of my enemies beneath my heel! I feel the glow of the philter as it courses through my veins, warming the blood that shall mantle in my cheeks, kindling the fire that shall flash from my eyes! The hour is nigh when I am to make my last supreme effort for mastery over the heart of Louis: if I fail—I have an avenger in Eugene, who—"

At this moment an outcry was heard in the streets, and as Olympia opened the door of her cabinet, she was confronted by her steward, who, unannounced, stood pale as death before his astonished mistress.

---

## CHAPTER IV.

### THE RIOT.

"WHAT, in the name of Heaven, is the matter?" exclaimed she. "Whence these discordant yells without, and how comes it that you enter my private apartments without a summons?"

"I trust your highness will pardon my boldness; the case is too urgent to admit of formalities, and I come to receive your instructions as to—"

Here the voice of the steward was overpowered by the yells of the populace without, and for several moments the countess and her son stood in speechless amazement, waiting an explanation. "What can it mean?" asked she at last.

3

"Your highness," replied the trembling steward, "the court is filled with an infuriated mob, who rushed in before we had time to close the gates."

Eugene, with an exclamation of dismay, would have darted to the window, but the steward raised his hand imploringly.

"Do not let them see you, prince," cried he. "They have torn up the pavement, and with the stones have shattered the windows of the lower story."

"Then it is a riot," said the countess, "and the *canaille* of Paris have rebelled against the aristocracy."

"Unhappily, your highness, their anger is directed exclusively against the Hôtel Soissons, and, if I judged by the number of our assailants, I should say that all Paris has joined in the attack. Not only the *canaille* are here, but, as I was hurrying to the *corps de garde* to ask for protection, I saw more than one well-dressed personage descend from his carriage and come thither to increase the number of our enemies."

"I understand," said the countess, setting her teeth, "the anger of the mob is directed against *me.*"

"Mother," whispered Eugene, "they must be the same men whom I met in the streets, and whose jeers drove me thither to add to your misery the stab of my unfilial doubts."

"Did you say that you had sent off for guards?" asked she of Latour.

"Yes, your highness. I went at once to the headquarters of the *corps de garde*, and the officer of the day promised immediate succor."

"It will not be sent," returned Olympia. "But hark! What tumult is this?"

"They are battering the palace-doors," said Eugene, who, in spite of the steward's entreaties, had approached the window and was looking down upon the mob. The palace de Soissons fronted the Rue Deux Écus, from which it was separated by a tall iron railing. The enclosure was filled with a throng so dense that there was scarcely room for them to move a limb; and yet, in their regular assaults upon the palace-doors, they seemed to be obeying the commands of some unseen chief.

Eugene surveyed the scene with something of that calm but powerful interest which possesses the soul of a commander about to engage the enemy.

"The multitude increase," said he. "If they continue to press in much longer, the court will be so thronged that no more missiles can be thrown."

At that very moment the windows were assailed by a hailstorm of stones, one of which fell at Olympia's feet. She touched it with the point of her satin slipper, remarking as she did so, "This is a greeting from Louvois."

"For God's sake, your highness, be not so rash!" exclaimed Latour, as a second stone flew over the head of the prince, and shattered part of a cornice close by.

Eugene had not moved. He heeded neither steward nor stone, but stood with folded arms, looking upon the terrible concourse of his mother's accusers. His face was very pale and resolute; it expressed nothing beyond stern endurance; but the eye was threatening, and the dwarfish figure had expanded until the abbé was forgotten, and in his place stood the implacable foe of Louis XIV.

"Yes," said he, "I was right. The crowd is so dense that they now threaten one another, and, unless they force the entrance to the palace, they will be crushed by their own numbers."

"They will never force the entrance," said Latour. "The door is barred and bolted, and they may bombard it for a day before they ever make an impression upon the stout plates of iron with which it is lined."

"Ay," replied Eugene, with a smile. "Catharine de Medicis knew how to build a stronghold. She knew from experience what it is to face an insurrection, and took her precautions accordingly. We owe her a debt of gratitude for our security—Good heavens!" cried he, interrupting himself, "they have found means to send us another salvo."

A shower of stones came rattling toward the very window where he stood, one of which struck the countess on the shoulder and caused her to wince.

Once more Latour besought her to take refuge in another apartment.

"You have said that they cannot force the entrance; what do you fear?" said she.

"I fear the stones, your highness."

"Then I will prove to the rabble that I, no more than Cardinal Mazarin, am to be terrified by stones," returned Olympia, approaching the window and placing herself at the side of her son.

The multitude, as they recognized her, broke forth into a wild shout of abhorrence.

"Look! there is the woman who murdered her husband, and would have murdered her children too!" "There is the wretch who would have poisoned the king!" "There stands the accomplice of La Voisin!" "And while her tool languishes in prison, she has no right to breathe the free air of heaven!" "Away with her to the Bastile!" "To the Bastile, to the Bastile!" "No! let her be burned for her crimes!"

"Louvois! Louvois!" murmured Olympia, her brow reddening with humiliation.

Another yell from the besiegers was silenced by a loud voice, whose words of command rose clear above the tumult.

"I knew it," said Eugene, "they have a leader. There is a method in these manifestations which shows that they are not the disconnected efforts of a many-headed monster."

"Great God! And the guards are not even to be seen!" cried Latour, who stood with folded hands, murmuring snatches of prayer for help.

"Nor will they be seen," added Olympia, in a low voice.

Eugene was glancing now at his mother, now at her persecutors. As his eye wandered from one to another of the uplifted and angry faces below, he saw two men somewhat elevated above the rest, who with their outstretched arms were giving the signal for a fresh onslaught. No demonstration, however, followed the command, for the people had gravitated into one solid body, of which no portion was capable of independent action.

"Now," thought the prince, "now would be the opportunity for retaliation. If I had but the means!—Latour," continued he, aloud, "do the iron gates of entrance open within or without?"

"Without, your highness."

"So that if we could get access to the street, we might cage up these base-born villains, might we not?"

"Yes, your highness; but he who shuts the gates must undo the chains by which they are fastened back."

"Who has the keys?"

"I, your highness. I have them now upon my person."

"There are outlets by which you could gain access to the gates without facing the people?"

"Certainly, your highness," began Latour; but his words were drowned in another outburst of howlings from the maddened mob, and another discharge of stones whizzed through the air, crushing the mullions of the windows to splinters, and dashing their fragments of shivering glass into the very faces of the unfortunate besieged.

"If the guards would but come!" said Latour, reiterating for the twentieth time his doleful refrain.

"Since it appears that they have no intention of coming," replied the prince, "we must e'en take this matter of defence in our own hands. Hasten, Latour, to the street—undo the fastenings, and quick as thought lock the gates!"

"But, your highness, do you suppose that I shall be suffered by that infuriated crowd to lock or unlock the gates at pleasure?"

"Never fear; their faces are all turned toward the palace. You will have accomplished the thing before they know that you have undertaken it. Take two other men with you, who, as soon as you release the chains, must fling the gates together, while you relock them. Now be dexterous, and you will have performed no unimportant feat of strategy."

"I will do my best, your highness."

"Before you go, summon the household to my presence. How many men are there at home to-day?"

"Twelve, your highness."

"Enough to settle with two thousand such wretches."

Latour darted away on his double mission, and the prince turned to his mother, who, undaunted and defiant, still stood

before the window contemplating her assailants, giving back
look for look of scorn and abhorrence.

"May I beg of my dear mother permission to absent myself
for a while?" said Eugene.

The countess looked round with inquiring eyes. "Whither
would you go, my son?" asked she.

"I wish to give some orders to the domestics, to arm them,
and assign to each man his post."

"Where will you find weapons, my son?"

"I have among my effects a small collection of fire-arms.
They are all in good order, and all loaded. I have nothing to
do but distribute them, and place my men."

The countess smiled. "In good sooth, I begin to believe
that you are fitter for a soldier than for a churchman.
But you are not in earnest when you speak of using fire-
arms?"

"Why not? We are attacked, and, obeying the laws of
necessity, we defend ourselves. Unfortunately, we are forced
to remain on the defensive; I only wish I had an opportunity
to attack."

"But what means that new outbreak of fury?" asked the
countess, returning to the window.

"It means," cried Eugene, joyfully, "that Latour has been
successful, and the gates are locked. The ruffians have discovered the snare, and they howl accordingly. Now to my
garrison; I must station it with judgment, for it is not numerous."

"I will accompany you, my son," said the countess. "I
would not miss the sight of the first exploit of my future cardinal, him who promises to unite in his own person the wisdom
of Mazarin with the prowess of Richelieu!"

The servants were assembled in the hall, whither they had
taken refuge from the stones and splintering glass, that were
flying in the palace windows. They were not a very valiant-
looking body of troops, but their commander made no comment upon their dismayed faces. He merely counted them
and spoke to his valet.

"Darmont, conduct these men to the armory, and provide
each one with a musket. Let them handle the guns carefully,

for they are heavily loaded. Bring me my pistols also. And now, away! and return quickly."

Silently, and, to all appearances, not much edified by these recommendations, the domestics followed Darmont, while Eugene returned to his station at the window.

"Not only have they a leader," said he, "but I believe that they were instigated to make this attack, mother."

"No doubt of it," replied Olympia; "and since Louvois has dared so much, we may infer that he has the sanction of the king for his brutality."

"Look!" cried Eugene, catching her arm, "there is the leader!—that tall man in the brown suit, with bright buttons, who stands upon the stone seat, near the gates."

"I see him," returned the countess. "He is speaking with two men who are directly in front of him. This person looks familiar to me: I have surely seen that tall figure and those wide shoulders before. If his hat were not drawn so far over his brows, and we could but see his face, our doubts as to the source of this outrage would speedily be solved."

"He has been giving instructions, for the two men are addressing the crowd. I fear we must look out for another bombardment."

And so it seemed; for the mob, having recovered from their momentary fright, were evidently preparing for action. Hundreds of brawny arms, each one of which grasped a stone, were raised into the air; while as many stooping forms were seen, crouching close to the ground, that they might leave room for the slingers to hurl their missiles without impediment.

"That is a good manœuvre," said Eugene. "Their leader understands strategic warfare. They are ready, and await the word of command. It comes! Stand back, mother!"

A crash was heard, but not a stone had been aimed at the windows. "Ah, I understand," cried Eugene. "They are trying to force the door, and so obtain their release. Thank Heaven! Here comes the garrison, a handful of braves who, I hope, are destined to change the fortunes of the day.—Now," continued he, advancing to meet them, "listen to me. There are twelve of you, and the hall has seven openings. Leave the central window free, and station yourselves two at each one of the other six. Throw open the casements, cock your guns, and be ready for the word of command. Darmont, give me my pistols."

With one of these in either hand, Eugene stationed himself at the window in the centre, while his mother stood by his side.

"They are about to favor us with another volley," said the prince. "Neither they nor their leader have as yet remarked the changed aspect of the palace-windows."

"The hat of the leader is purposely drawn down, and, while he succeeds in concealing his features, he loses sight of the danger which threatens from above. So much the better for us; but I do long to have a sight of his face," returned the countess.

"You shall have your wish," replied Eugene, with a smile. "I will knock off his hat, and your curiosity shall be gratified."

"How will you manage to do that?"

"You shall see," said he, raising the pistol that he held in his right hand.

He fired, and when the smoke had cleared away, the face of the leader was exposed to view. The ball had struck the hat, which had fallen, and now a pair of dark, sinister eyes were glaring at the spot whence the insult had been sent.

"Have a care," said the prince, leaning forward and addressing the crowd. "If you send another missile against these walls, I will have twelve of your lives!"

The men, who were just about to fling their stones, paused and stared at one another in dumb perplexity.

Their leader, pale with rage, gave the word of command.

Eugene heard it, and called out in clear, defiant tones: "If the leader of this riot attempt a repetition of his order, I will break his right arm."

"Another volley, men!" shouted the chief.

A second report from the window was heard, which was answered by a yell from below. Eugene's ball had pierced the elbow of the leader, and the dismayed crowd had made a hasty movement toward the gates.

"Do you not see that there is no egress for you except through the palace ? Look at the murderess there, instigating her whelp to new crimes! She exults over your weakness, and laughs at your panic. On! on! Batter down the doors!"

"On!" echoed the mob; and their stones were flung with such frenzy against the palace-doors, that its very walls trembled.

"Fire!" called out the sonorous voice of Eugene, and in another moment might be seen the sinking forms of twelve of the rioters, while, among the others, some were pale with fright, and a few cried out that they would be revenged.

"Revenge is for those whom you have insulted and attacked," replied the prince, deliberately. "You have made a cowardly assault upon a noble lady, and not one of you shall leave this place alive!—Make ready! Take aim!" continued he to his men.

The click of the locks was distinctly heard, and in the crowd each man fancied that one of those carbines was aimed at his own head. The mob was losing heart; not even their leader was to be seen or heard. He had taken refuge in a sheltered corner of the court, where his wounds were being bound up by his lieutenants. Inconspicuous as he was, however, the sharp eyes of Olympia had followed him to his retreat. Not for one moment did she lose sight of him; she was determined to solve the enigma of his identity. As the last bellicose words of Prince Eugene rang through the ears of his dismayed followers, the wounded ringleader flung back his head with such sudden haste, that its masses of dark, tangled hair were entirely thrown aside, and the face that was revealed by their removal, caused the countess to start and utter an exclamation of surprise. As Eugene was about to give the command to fire, his mother caught his arm, and whispered in his ear:

"My son, I now think that I can tell you the name of yonder caitiff there, and, if I have guessed rightly, it were better for us to cease hostile demonstrations, and capitulate."

"Capitulate!" cried the prince, indignantly. "Capitulate with the rabble! Who can be this man that has so suddenly cowered the heart of my noble mother?"

"I think that he is the son of Louvois," whispered she.

"Ah, the presuming Barbesieur, who would have given his name to a Princess de Carignan?"

"Yes—the same. His beard is dyed, and he wears false locks, but, spite of his disguise, I feel sure that it is Barbesieur. And I warn you, Eugene! harm not a hair on his head, for he is the favorite son of the mightiest man in France —mighty and vindictive. Kill as many of the rabble as you will; but give positive orders to your men not to touch Barbesieur Louvois."

"I ought to command them to fire on no other man, for he is responsible for the acts of every rioter here."

"That would be to cast your entire family into the very jaws of destruction. These men who call me murderess, could not be made to believe that I have the tenderness of a mother for my children; but you, Eugene, who know how dearly I love you all, you can understand that no revenge would be sweet that was purchased at the expense of my children's welfare. Spare, then, I implore you, the man who holds your destinies in his unfriendly hand."

"So be it," sighed Eugene, and he went from man to man, saying in a low voice, "Direct your fire toward the left." He then took his station at the central window, and, raising his arm, called out a second time: "Make ready! Take aim!"

The multitude heard, and their exceeding consternation found utterance in one prolonged shriek of horror.

"Do not fire!" screamed a hundred voices. "Do not fire! We are defenceless!"

The order was countermanded, and the self-possessed defender of the beleaguered palace advanced his head and contemplated the ignoble faces of his enemies.

"You acknowledge yourself baffled, then? You are willing to retreat?"

"Ay!" was the ready response of every rioter there.

"You swear to desist now and forever from your infamous attack upon this palace? You swear never more to make use of vituperative epithets toward the family of the deceased Count de Soissons?"

"We swear, we swear! Open the gates! Let us out! Let us out!" was now the universal cry.

"Not so fast. Before you have my permission to retire, I must have unequivocal, outspoken evidence of your repentance and conversion. You have presumed to asperse the good name of the Countess de Soissons. Take back your injurious words, and cheer her now, right lustily. Cry out three times, 'Long live the noble Countess de Soissons!' and, if your acclamations are to my mind, I will open the gates."

The reply to these conditions was a greeting so enthusiastic and so unanimous, that you would have sworn the mob had assembled before the hôtel to tender to its inmates a popular ovation.

"Miserable *canaille!*" muttered their chief; "they are base enough to hurl their stones at *me*, if that beardless manikin up there should require it of them, as a peace-offering to his immaculate mother!"

"I told your excellency that you could not trust them," replied the companion on whose arm he was leaning. "It is a dangerous thing to be identified with any action of theirs."

"You were right, François. Give me your arm, and let us try to reach the gates, so as to be the first to escape from this accursed man-trap."

"You have cheered the countess but once," cried Eugene to the multitude. "Do you wish me to renew our strife?"

"Long live the noble Countess de Soissons!" was the prompt reply. And, without waiting for a third suggestion, they shouted again and again, "Long live the Countess de Soissons!"

Olympia's flashing eyes rested proudly on her son. "I thank you, Eugene: you have avenged me effectually. All Paris will be filled with lampoons on the ridiculous repulse of the valiant Barbesieur and his followers."

Eugene made no reply. His eyes were fixed upon the personage whom they supposed to be the son of Louvois, and the prince knew perfectly well wherefore he seemed in such nervous haste to reach the gates.

"He hopes to escape without recognition," muttered Eugene, "but I must have a word with him before we part."

"Open the gates!" clamored the populace anew; then suddenly there was a cry of alarm which was echoed from man to man, from group to group, until it shaped itself into these words: "The guards! The guards!"

---

## CHAPTER V.

### BARBESIEUR LOUVOIS.

THUNDERING down the street came a troop of horsemen, who halted directly in front of the palace-gates.

"Louvois' spies have been reporting the failure of his son's warlike expedition," remarked Olympia, and the guards whom *we* had vainly called to our help, have come in hot haste to protect our assailants."

By this time the officer in command was at the gates making vain efforts to open them.

"What does this signify?" asked he. "And what is this multitude about in the court of the Hôtel de Soissons?"

"Look at the palace-windows and the palace-doors, and you will read your answer there," replied Eugene. "I closed the gates against a furious and misguided mob; but we have come to terms, and I am about to liberate them. I crave your indulgence for these poor fellows: they have been deceived, and knew not what they did, and I hope that you will make good the forgiveness I have extended to their fault, by allowing them to go hence without molestation."

"If so," replied the officer, "I shall be happy to confirm you highness's clemency by carrying out your order for their release."

"Is it possible," asked the countess of her son, "that you are in earnest? You intend to suffer those wretches to go away unharmed! Because I asked your forbearance for one man, shall this vile horde be snatched from the hands of justice!"

"Do you suppose that justice has any intention of overtaking them?" asked Eugene, with a significant smile. "Believe me, dear mother, I do but anticipate the object for which the guards were sent, and spare myself and you the humiliation of publishing to the world that neither law nor justice takes cognizance of the wrongs of the Countess de Soissons. These men have come hither to succor our enemies, not us."

"Ah, my son, I begin to appreciate you. You have inherited the sagacity of your great uncle," returned Olympia.

"Open the gates! open the gates!" cried the rioters.

"Will your highness be pleased to send some one to release your prisoners?" asked the captain of the guardsmen.

"I shall be there myself, in a moment," was the reply.

"You!" exclaimed the countess. "Would you expose yourself to the vengeance of the populace, Eugene?"

"They will not molest me. Barbesieur Louvois has reached the gates, and I must greet him ere he goes.—Come, Latour and Darmont, and show me the way by the private staircase. The rest of you keep your posts and be watchful, for the struggle may be renewed, and it is just possible that I may have to order you to fire.—And now shall I conduct my mother to her boudoir?"

"No, my son, I remain here to observe what passes below, nor will I retire until I shall have seen the ending of this curious spectacle."

Eugene bowed and withdrew. "Go before, Latour," said he. "I am unacquainted with the private inlets and outlets of the palace."

Latour obeyed, saying to himself: "They may well make a priest of this virtuous youth, who knows nothing of the secret windings of his own hotel. His father and his brother were wiser than he; and many a night have they gone in and out on visits of gallantry, when they were young enough to be as squeamish as he, or old enough to have reformed their ways."

"Give me the keys," said Eugene, as they emerged from the side-entrance. "I will unlock the gates, and when I cry 'Halt!' do you seize upon a man whom I shall point out to you as he attempts to force the passage in advance of his confederates."

"Let us alone for holding him fast, your highness."

Eugene went a few steps farther; then, turning round, he said: "Yes—grasp him well, but be careful not to take him by the right arm, for I believe that it is wounded."

As he spoke these merciful words, Eugene blushed, for he saw a derisive smile on Latour's face.

"I was in error," thought the steward. "Such a soft heart ought to have been lodged in the body of a woman."

They had now reached the palace-front, where, in return for the obsequious salutation of the captain of the guard, Eugene slightly inclined his head.

"You came late to the rescue," said the prince. "Had you answered the requisition of my steward, you would have spared me the painful necessity of wounding a dozen of those poor devils."

"Was there bloodshed?" returned the officer.

"Of course there was. You can hardly imagine that I quieted these turbulent rioters with a lullaby. Yes, there has been bloodshed, and I have had satisfaction for the affront offered to my house to-day. I hope you hold me justified in my method of procedure."

"Perfectly justified, your highness."

"Then the matter rests here, and peace is proclaimed. From my amnesty, however, I except one man, him who is responsible for all the evil that has been done by his followers."

"Your highness has only to point him out, and I will have him arrested forthwith."

"You give me your word of honor that he shall not escape punishment?"

"My word of honor, your highness."

"Latour and Darmont, station yourselves one on either side of me, while I unlock the gates."

They took their positions, and Eugene slowly drew out his ponderous keys. They were heard to click in the locks, and at the welcome sound, there was a shout of joy from the imprisoned rioters. They pressed eagerly forward—the gates parted—and the crowd began to pour out into the streets. Eugene soon perceived the tall form of the ringleader, although he had borrowed the hat of his companion, and wore it slouched far down over his face.

As he approached the entrance, Eugene gave the signal agreed upon, and he was seized by Latour and Darmont. But they had forgotten the precaution given them as regarded his wounded arm, for as they touched him he had been unable to suppress a cry of pain.

"Hold him, Latour," said the prince, "and you, Darmont, close the gates so that only one man may pass at a time. Some of those guards might be of service to us. Have I your permission to employ them, captain ?"

Eight men were ordered to dismount and to station themselves at the gates, which, spite of the tremendous pressure from within, they managed to secure, so that each man as he passed could be scanned by him, who, notwithstanding his delicate build and diminutive stature, was unquestionably the hero of the day.

"Now that the court is empty, you can see what devastation has been committed," said he to the captain of the guard.

"Yes, indeed," replied the latter, raising himself in his stirrups to overlook the railing, "they have uprooted the whole pavement."

"And have seriously damaged the windows," added Eugene. "For all this destruction we have to thank yonder churl," continued he, pointing to a man of almost gigantic stature, who was struggling to free himself from the hands of Latour and Darmont. "Not content with the laurels he has won as the ringleader of a mob, he has aspired to achieve renown by defaming women. He has incited the populace to asperse the good name of my honored mother, and by Heaven, he shall suffer for every opprobrious word that has fallen from the tongue of every base-born villain that followed him hither!"

"Your highness shall yourself dictate his punishment," replied the officer, courteously.

"Then order your men to capture the twelve last rioters that leave the enclosure, and let their leader, who is a thousand times more guilty than they, oversee the restoration of the pavement, and himself remove yonder Druid's temple, that lies before the central window there."

"Never!" exclaimed the giant, redoubling his efforts to

escape, and writhing so vigorously that Latour and Darmont
had to strain every sinew to retain their hold of his huge
body.

Eugene eyed his prisoner with withering scorn. "You
hear him, captain! He says 'Never!' as though it were for
*him* to decide whether or not my judgment is a righteous
one. And yet I think it most moderate amends to make for
such immeasurable wrong."

"Indeed, your highness, it is most disproportionate to the
enormity of the offence. It is only too merciful!—Here! Eight
men to carry out the orders of the noble Prince of Savoy!"
shouted he, peremptorily.

The crowd, meanwhile, by this time convinced that submission was their only alternative, were passing slowly and silently through the gates. They were so completely subdued,
that not one ventured a remonstrance. They were intent each
man upon his own retreat, and nobody was troubled about the
fate of the chief.

"There are just twelve men within the enclosure," said the
officer. "Instead of capturing them singly, close the gates,
and secure them all at once."

"But first let us admit my distinguished prisoner.—Thrust
him in, Latour, and conduct him to his task. He must expiate
his offence against the Countess de Soissons, by removing
that heap of stones, which were cast by his command
against my palace-doors. If he prove intractable, bring him
to his senses by administering a blow or two with a stout
cudgel."

The chief, who for a few moments had been hoping by
affected submission to withdraw the attention of Eugene from
himself to his followers, gave a howl of rage, and looked
around for his companion. The latter, instead of passing out
with the crowd, had remained voluntarily in the enclosure
with the twelve who were to suffer for all.

They whispered together, after which the subordinate, approaching the captain of the guard, said: "Captain, I come to
offer myself in the place of my poor brother, who, having been
wounded in the arm, is helpless, and incapable of removing
the smallest of those stones."

"What says your highness?" asked the officer of the prince.

"I grant the petition, for it is reasonable. Let him confine himself, then, to the superintendence of the work."

"Captain, I crave permission to conduct my brother to a surgeon, where his wound may be dressed. It is impossible that any man can be so brutal as to require him to stay here with a bullet in his arm," said the subordinate.

"The bullet was no impediment while outrage was to be committed on the property of the Countess de Soissons," thundered Eugene, "and I exact that he remain."

"Your highness's commands shall be obeyed," replied the officer.

"Captain," said the ringleader, dragging himself forward, while in his tremendous strength he forced his captors along with him, "captain, I must have a word in private with you. I have something of importance to communicate, and you must come nearer that I may whisper in your ear."

So imperious was the sound of his voice that the captain involuntarily obeyed, and bent down his ear to listen. Although the latter was on horseback and the former on foot, his tall figure was almost on a level with the officer's head.

He spoke a few low words, the captain started, and, quickly raising his head, he surveyed the gigantic chief from head to foot. He then conferred with him a few moments, after which he addressed himself in a very embarrassed manner to Eugene.

"Your highness, this poor man complains so piteously of the agony he endures, that it would be cruel to detain him any longer. If you have no objection, I will send him to the surgeon, accompanied by four of my men, who, when his wound shall have been dressed, can reconduct him hither."

"He will not return," replied Eugene, with a shrug. "He will find means to escape the vigilance of the police. So be it. Let his wounds be dressed, and let him depart whither he lists. But I have a few words of adieu to speak ere he goes."

So saying, he approached his tall adversary, and so commanding was his presence, so fiery his eye, and so proud his de-

4

meanor, that Eugene of Savoy looked mightier than the wide-shouldered giant before him.

"I wish merely to say to this fellow that he is a knave," said the prince. "Yes, captain, a knave, although you start to hear me call him thus. I neither know his name, nor wish to know it; but I shall recognize him among a thousand, and, if ever I meet him again, I will give him a knave's portion—a sound horsewhipping. And now away with him! His presence is intolerable!"

"I go," replied the other, pale and trembling with rage. "But beware, little priestling, how you cross *my* path! If ever you dare intrude yourself upon my sight, I will crush your diminutive carcass as an elephant does a crawling worm!" He went, followed by him who had claimed him as a brother, and accompanied by four guardsmen, who rode at some distance behind their prisoners.

"And now, captain," said Eugene, "since your sympathizing heart has made it impossible for you to allow justice its way, you will, I presume, see fit to appoint another man to supervise the repairing of my court-yard."

"I myself will attend to it, your highness," said the officer, bowing to his saddle-bow. "Not only that; I will send workmen to replace the broken panes and restore the window-frames, so that by to-morrow no trace of the damage done shall remain."

Eugene laughed. "You are certainly most accommodating! As much so as if the city guard had participated in the riot! Adieu, sir! And may this be our last meeting of the sort!"

Accompanied by his two domestics, he re-entered the palace. His twelve men were at their posts, and the countess was still standing at the window whence she had witnessed the scene below.

Eugene dismissed his household, gave orders to have his weapons carefully replaced in his armory, and then, with a deep inclination to his mother, he asked if he might now conduct her to her boudoir.

She gave a smiling assent, took his proffered arm, and returned to her cabinet. Once there, she turned toward her son, and, contemplating him for the first time in her life with pride and admiration, she thanked him warmly for what he had done.

"My dear son," said she, "I must congratulate you upon your strength of character. Believe me, you looked mightier far than Louvois' overgrown Titan. If he surpassed you in stature, your great soul towered far above his lofty person. I could not hear what you were saying to those two men, Eugene, but I read in the glance of your fearless eye that your words were such as would have rejoiced my heart to overhear. In that moment my soul went far out into the future, and there I saw you great, glorious, renowned. You know, Eugene, that I have sometimes strange revelations of things hidden from ordinary mortals: I have visions that are prophetic, and I tell you that you are destined to earn imperishable fame. Go, my son, and fulfil your destiny!"

Eugene, his features illumined by enthusiasm and radiant with hope, covered his mother's hand with kisses, and again besought her forgiveness for his unfilial behavior in the gallery. "Dear mother," said he, tearfully. "are you indeed reconciled to your unworthy child?"

"Yes, Eugene, yes. When you compelled that unwilling multitude to do me homage, I forgave you from my heart. I have always loved you as my child, but from this day forward I honor you as my deliverer. Come to my arms and take the mother's kiss that shall consecrate you to glory."

Eugene, intoxicated with happiness, threw himself upon her bosom, and was clasped to her heart. "With this kiss I greet the hero whose exploits shall shed new lustre upon his princely house. God bless thee, my son! Sweeter lips may meet thine in the glow of a love more passionate, but never will they kiss thee with a tenderness more true than does thy proud mother this day!"

"And never will I love woman more tenderly than I do my precious mother. You were my ideal of womanly perfection as a child, and your adored image will be my soul's divinity to the latest hour of my life! Never again will I doubt you; were the whole world to scorn you, I at least will believe in you, and honor you with a faith as implicit as that which leads man to martyrdom for his Re-deemer's sake."

"Believe in me, and trust me," returned the countess, again impressing a kiss on her son's forehead. "And when you are great and powerful, think of this hour, my child. 'Tis one of the brightest of my life; one of the few wherein I have unveiled my heart to mortal man. Think of it, then, Eugene, when you wear the hat of a cardinal, and—"

"What, mother! You would devote me to the priesthood, after all that has passed between us to-day!"

"'Tis your only path to renown; 'tis the only ladder by which ambition can climb to power. With Louis' favor, you may become a cardinal and a statesman; without it you will never become a field-marshal. We must take fate as we find it, Eugene; not whine because we may not fashion it to our own liking."

"Then be it so: I submit. But I tell you, for the last time, that under my priestly gown there will be heard the wild and unseemly throbbings of a heart that not only pants for glory, but yearns for love."

"Cardinals may hope for both," returned Olympia, with a strange, unpleasant smile. "Ask the widowed Queen Anne, whether Richelieu knew how to love. And ask her whether Mazarin was not as fond as he was sagacious. But enough of day-dreams: we must return to the affairs of real life. There has been a demonstration of serious import against me to-day. I must oppose it by another. Louvois and his minions must learn that I am not to be intimidated by their menaces, nor to be browbeaten by their contumely."

Near her hand, on a porphyry table, lay a golden bell—a marvel of Benvenuto Cellini's workmanship. The countess took it up and rang.

The steward answered the summons, and begged to know what her highness was pleased to command.

"Let the palace-doors be thrown open, that the people may know how little I fear their dislike. Send all the lackeys out, and let them announce to the court that to-day I hold a special levee, and that my rooms will be opened to visitors at nine this evening. Let the equerry be informed that in half an hour I shall take a drive in my open calèche, with six horses and two outriders, all in livery of state."

The steward bowed and left the room. When he had gone, the countess again addressed her son: "In half an hour the court will be assembled at the Pré aux Clercs; no doubt it would gratify more than one of those envious Parisians were I absent to-day. But they shall not enjoy any such satisfaction. They shall greet me as usual, and I—I—I intend to approach the king!"

"And I, dearest mother," said Eugene, "beg to be allowed to accompany you in your ride."

"You shall do so, son of my heart," exclaimed Olympia, giving him her hand. "I see that you are not only the child of my love, but bone of my bone and flesh of my flesh. Yes, Eugene, you shall be my knight, and no loving maiden was ever prouder of her cavalier than I shall be of mine!"

## CHAPTER VI.

### THE STATE RECEPTION.

THE commands of the countess were promptly obeyed. All Paris (that is, the Paris of the aristocracy) were informed that a special reception would be held at the Hôtel de Soissons, and messengers were dispatched with official announcement of the same to the royal household. The ponderous gates were flung wide open to admit the carriage of state. Eugene's superb gelding was led out by his jockey; while near the open portière stood the equerry whose office it was to hand the countess to her carriage.

Her turnout was magnificent. The frame of the carriage was of dead gilt, while above the burnished wheels rose its body, in shape and color like the wonderful lily of the Amazon. Its exterior of snowy whiteness was relieved by the rich coloring of the arms of Carignan and Soissons emblazoned on the panels; the interior was cushioned with purple velvet embroidered in gold. To this sumptuous vehicle were harnessed six white horses, whose head-gear of velvet was adorned with ostrich-plumes so delicate, that, as the air breathed upon them, they looked like wreaths of snowy vapor. Perched high above the hammer-cloth, which in color and material corresponded with the inner decorations of the carriage, sat the chubfaced coachman, his head buried in the vast expanse of a flowing wig, and surmounted by a gold-and-purple cocked hat. The handle of his coach-whip was of steel inlaid with gold, and he flourished it with as much ostentation as if it had been the baton of a field-marshal. Behind this princely equipage were two footmen in state livery ; on either side were two out-riders.

The countess emerged from her palace-doors, clad in mantle of sky-blue velvet bordered with gold. She was followed by the prince, who, as the equerry advanced to assist his mistress, gently waved him away, and took his place. Olympia smiled fondly upon her son, and with graceful negligence sank back among her luxurious cushions.

The equerry approached for orders. "Let the coachman drive leisurely through the streets, and still more slowly when we enter the Pré aux Clercs."

Eugene mounted his impatient gelding, and his mother, inclining her head to the equerry, gave the signal for their departure.

Slowly went the cortége, through the Rue des Deux Écus and along the Quartier St. Honoré, while from every house, as they passed, the windows were cautiously opened, and sneering faces looked down upon the vain pomp with which Olympia de Soissons would have sustained the falling ruins of her good name.

But things grew worse, when the outriders would have opened a passage for the carriage through the crowded streets. As soon as the people recognized the liveries, all the conventional homage with which they were accustomed to greet such splendor, was transformed into scorn.

"The poisoner! the poisoner!" they cried. "She braves us in the open streets! Away with her! Away with the accomplice of La Voisin!"

The object of all this contumely preserved an appearance

of consummate indifference to it all; but her son! her unhappy son blushed with shame and anger. He turned his sympathizing eyes upon her, whom he believed to be an impersonation of every feminine virtue, and she replied to his glance by an unconscious smile.

At last they reached the Pré aux Clercs, the fashionable promenade of the day. Here the aristocracy were accustomed to drive, the king and queen invariably appearing there to receive, sometimes, in the case of the former, to pay homage. How often had he leaned upon the carriage of Olympia, while princes and princesses of the blood had been obliged to wait behind, until the Countess de Soissons was ready to move on, and allow them to proceed! And how they had flattered and praised, and curried favor with the divinity of the hour!

"It must all be enacted anew," thought the ex-favorite, as she slightly raised her head to see if the king was in sight. "The philter will work: from the moment I catch his eye, he is mine! This was La Voisin's promise."

Yes—the royal equipages were there, at the other end of the shaded avenue, and, following in their wake, were those of the court. Olympia cast aside her nonchalance, and raised her head that she might be seen. The crisis had come! She was now to quaff the intoxicating drink of success, or drain the poisoned chalice of defeat!

She could see the very smile on his face as he whispered flattering words in the ear of some beauty who was in advance, and whom Olympia could not recognize. One moment more, and *her* equipage would pass! He would meet her eye, and the passion of his youth would be rekindled in his heart, never more to die out!

But what commotion was this among the lords and ladies that surrounded the king? His majesty spoke with his chief equerry; the equerry sprang forward, and presently the royal equipages came rushing by, close, close to the calèche of the countess, who vainly sought to meet the eye of Louis, for he was conversing with the queen, and his head was turned away.

Scarcely had the royal carriages been put in motion, before the entire cortége followed at the same rapid pace. Princes

and princesses of the blood,—dukes, counts, and marquises,—
duchesses and marchionesses, rushed by so swiftly that not
one of her court friends had time to give so much as a passing nod to her who nevertheless was allied by marriage to the
reigning Duke of Savoy.

The last equipage had just gone by. "Is it the will of your
highness that we follow?" asked the equerry.

The countess inclined her head, and the equerry passed the
word to the coachman: "Follow the cortége." But the horses
stirred not a foot.

Eugene repeated the order, when the coachman slowly
shook his head. "Impossible, gracious prince, impossible!—
The countess would never forgive me, and I should be despised
by every coachman of distinction, were I so far to forget my
duty as to suffer that an equipage bearing the ducal arms of
Savoy should follow the carriage of a nobleman so insignificant as the Vicomte de Charlieu. Why, he goes back but ten
generations!"

Eugene smiled and delivered the portentous message to his
mother.

"He is right," replied she; "and were he wrong, it would
avail me nothing to contend with him on a point of etiquette.
The coachmen of people of quality are more tenacious of their
rights than the noble families they serve. Not long ago, the
Duchesses of Chartres and of Luynes waited four hours in the
rain, because, having met in a very narrow street, neither one
of their coachmen would back out, to give the other an opportunity of passing. I must imitate their patience, and wait for
the return of the cortége, to take my proper place."

The decision of the countess being transmitted to the
coachman, he nodded approvingly. "I thought her highness
would understand," replied he. "Our place is after the Duchess de Bourbon, the sixth carriage from that of his majesty.
The coachman of the Duke de Cheneuse knows it as well as I
do, and he will yield us precedence as soon as he sees me ready
to fall in."

They waited—the countess in perfect composure, her large
black eyes cast upward in complete forgetfulness of the actual
state of things around her; Eugene, with visible annoyance

on his face, darting anxious and uneasy glances down the avenue through which the king was expected to return. And so passed an hour, at the end of which the avenue was still and empty as a desert. It now became apparent that his majesty had selected some other route by which to reach the Louvre, and Olympia, awaking from her golden day-dreams, began to realize the exceeding awkwardness of her position. For the first time her heart faltered, and a cloud passed over her face.

Eugene rode up to the portière, and addressing the countess in Italian: " Mother," said he, " if we remain here any longer, I shall choke with rage."

" Home," said Olympia to the equerry. " Home! Quick! Urge your horses to their fullest speed!"

On the evening of that eventful day, every reception-room in the Hôtel Soissons was thrown open, and the palace front was one blaze of light. But the steward had been obliged to close the gates, and station four armed men within them, to protect the entrance from the rabble who had again begun to assemble, again begun to threaten.

The countess was either ignorant of this unpleasant circumstance, or she considered it beneath her notice. From her carriage she had passed to her cabinet, whence she had never emerged until compelled to make her toilet for the evening. Her temporary discouragement overcome, she entered the throne-room magnificently attired, sparkling with jewels, and radiant with feverish expectation. She was still upheld by the confidence she reposed in La Voisin's predictions, and the firm faith with which she clung to the virtues of her philter.

She could not, however, repress the scowl that darkened her brow, as, glancing around her vast suite of empty rooms, she beheld not one visitor!—no living being besides her own three daughters, the young Princesses de Carignan, who came forward to kiss her hand, and pay her their tribute of affectionate admiration.

She paid very little attention to their sweet flattery; her restless eyes wandered from door to door, where not a form was seen but those of the four lackeys, who were in waiting to announce the distinguished guests as they arrived,

The mocking echo of her tread, as she traversed the void which should have been filled with a courtly throng, sounded ominous in her ear, and the haughty woman began to quail. She had heard it said that when a ship was doomed to destruction, no rats were ever known to leave port in its hold. Was she a sinking ship? Was her doom sealed? Once more her longing eyes sought the lofty, open doors, through which so often the court had passed to do her homage on her throne, and she shivered almost perceptibly. But she forced a smile, and observed to her eldest daughter: "Our guests are unusually late to-night. Even the Duchess de Bouillon, generally so punctual, has not yet made her appearance."

"Even your adorer, Marshal de Luxemburg, mamma, is not yet here," returned the princess, with a smile.

The countess looked sharply at her daughter. Why had she mentioned the name of De Luxemburg? Why named him in conjunction with the Duchess de Bouillon? Did Johanna know that these two were her confidants, and that they were accustomed to visit La Voisin together? That only five days before, they had met in the den of the soothsayer, to have their horoscope drawn for the last time? Did Johanna know that through De Luxemburg's efforts Louis's valet had been bribed to rob him of a lock of his hair, without which the precious philter could never have been distilled? Oh, no! She was silly—nervous—the events of the day had disheartened her, and she was growing to be a craven. How should Johanna know her secrets? The allusion to the marshal was accidental.

The wax-lights were growing fearfully short, and still the invited guests tarried. Never in her life before had Olympia condescended to rest her gaze upon the faces of those who served her; to-night she could not resist an inclination to glance for one moment at their countenances. As she looked athwart those features, erst so submissive and so reverent, she saw significant smirks, and an expression of disdain for which she could have felled them to the earth.

Meanwhile the three princesses, their lips distorted with forced smiles, stood around their mother, sometimes raising their anxious eyes to her stormy face, sometimes exchanging uneasy glances one with another; but not one of them daring to break the oppressive silence by a single word.

At last the painful lull was broken by a slight rustling. The door of the anteroom was opened, and a solitary figure was seen traversing the long suite of apartments.

"Eugene," exclaimed Johanna. "Our little abbé!" And, delighted to put an end to their embarrassment, the sisters went forward with outstretched hands to meet him.

But Eugene could not respond to their greeting. His eyes were fixed upon the chandelier, under whose blaze he beheld a pale, sinister face, and a tall, haughty figure; his mother, attired with regal splendor, looking every inch a queen; but ah ! a dethroned queen, for her subjects had deserted her. and among them "there was none so poor to do her reverence."

He approached her, and, as she silently extended her icy hand, he covered it with loving kisses. "I had hardly expected to find my dear mother here before me," said he, with a smile.

"Why so, Eugene ?" asked Olympia.

"Because the hour for your reception was fixed for nine o'clock, and it has not yet struck nine."

"The countess glanced quickly at the clock on the sculptured mantel-piece. "It is almost ten," said she.

"Your clock is nearly an hour too fast," said Eugene, who had followed the direction of his mother's eyes. And he drew out his own watch.

She looked at it a moment. "True—your watch is slow, Eugene. You knew, then, before you came hither, that no one had yet arrived ?"

"Dear mother," responded Eugene, "you think—"

"I think that you are a tender, loving son," said she, interrupting him. "But it is not necessary to deceive me, dear boy. I know that it is almost an hour past the time I had appointed; but that signifies nothing. It was not known until late that I would receive to-night, and this is the reception-day of the Duchess de Luynes. My guests will naturally have gone thither first, and they will come later to us."

"You are quite right," replied Eugene. "But would it not

be better for you to retire to your cabinet and rest until the
company arrive ? I will call you as soon as the rooms begin
to fill."

She shook her head slowly. "No—I remain here. It
would be cowardly to retire now. Let us calmly await our
distinguished guests. They will be coming very soon."

Eugene bowed his head in obedience·to her commands, and
stationed himself by the side of his sisters. There was another
long silence, interrupted by the slow, inflexible strokes of the
clock, which announced the hour of "ten."

Great drops of anguish stood out upon the pale, high forehead of the prince, and his sisters could no longer restrain
their tears. The countess alone looked resolute: her features
betrayed no emotion whatever; but about her mouth there
hovered a vindictive smile, and in her eyes there was a light
like that which glitters in the serpent's head that looks out
from the deadly jungles of India.

"Would that I could breathe poison into the veins of yonder staring menials at the door !" said she to herself.
"Would that I could blind their staring eyes with lightning !
But for them I might leave this fiery furnace of shame, and
hide my face within the privacy of my own room !"

A sound was heard without, and the Princess Joanna unconsciously clasped her hands with delight, exclaiming,
"There comes a carriage !"

The countess turned around, and glanced fiercely at her
unsophisticated daughter. "Is there anything remarkable in
the sound of a carriage, that it should occasion so much joy,
mademoiselle ? Are carriages so rare within the gates of the
Hôtel Soissons ?"

The door opened, and the gentleman-usher, with his gilded
staff, appeared on the threshold.

"Madame la Marquise Dupont de Lanin," cried he, and the
lady followed the announcement at once.

Often had the poor old marquise attended the levees of the
Countess de Soissons, but never before had she been accorded
so distinguished a reception. She was tolerated in the *salons*
of Paris on account of her high birth and connections ; added
to which she had a tongue in her mouth like a two-edged

sword, which flew hither and thither about the reputations of those who slighted or forgot her claims to courtesy.

To-night she was most graciously, most cordially welcomed. Like the dove which brought the olive-branch to Noah, the marquise was a messenger from dry land. The waters had subsided—the deluge of their troubles was over.

With wreathed smiles and flattering words, Olympia came forward to greet her first guest. The old marquise received the unprecedented attention paid her without the least manifestation of surprise. With her sharp old eyes, she traversed the empty vastness of the gilded halls that were wont to swarm with the *crême de la crême* of Paris, and understood the matter at once. She had scarcely had time to reciprocate the politeness of her hostess before two other carriages rolled into the court-yard and two more distinguished names were announced by the usher.

This time an old duchess and an equally venerable viscount entered the room of state. Their social *status* was similar to that of the marquise: they belonged to the species whom the world is compelled to invite, but whom it detests, because they never have been known to decline an invitation. But they, too, were heartily welcomed, and, by one not initiated in the mysteries of the hour, they would have been set down as the countess's dearest friends.

Eugene took no part in the conversation which ensued. He had again resumed his taciturn and unsocial demeanor, and now, with folded arms, he stood in the deep recess of a curtained window, sometimes looking gloomily out into the night, anon glancing at the little knot of adventurers, and personages of doubtful reputation, who occasionally added another to the meagre group that were around his mother. Olympia strove to converse gayly with her assemblage of insupportables, but she was chafing like an infuriated lioness.

"If Marianna and De Luxemburg would but come ! I might, at least, learn how I stand at court, and find out why the king returned to the Louvre by an unusual route. Heavens ! how long will I be able to smile upon these hateful bores ? How long sustain the burden of this insufferable lie ?"

The evening waned, and neither Marianna, De Luxemburg,

nor any other member of the court circle appeared, to silence
the apprehensions or soothe the wounded pride of the haughty
Countess de Soissons.   But late—very late—when she had relinquished all hopes of another arrival, the doors were flung
open, and the usher, in a loud voice, announced : "His highness the Duke de Bouillon !"

## CHAPTER VII.

### HELP IN TIME OF NEED.

OLYMPIA, who, with three or four wrinkled old fops, and
as many withered dames, had just taken her seat at a card-
table, kissed her hand, and received her brother-in-law, with a
profusion of smiles such as never before had greeted his entrance into the *salons* of the Hôtel Soissons.

He seemed to be totally unconscious of her blandishments,
as, with a slight inclination to the company, he came very
close to the hostess, and, regardless of etiquette, whispered
something in her ear.

His communication must have been of a nature to excite
mirth, for she threw back her head, and, laughing rather more
boisterously than was her wont, rose quickly from her seat.

"Of course, my dear duke," said she, so as to be heard by
all who were around ; " of course you shall have the drops
for my sister.   I regret to hear that she needs them.   Come
with me to my cabinet, and you shall receive them from my
hand.   I will even taste them in your presence, that they may
not be suspected of containing poison.   Follow me, if my kind
friends will excuse us for a few moments."

With a graceful bend of her head, the countess crossed the
room, and disappeared with her brother-in-law.   From the
window to which he had retired, Eugene had seen and heard
what was passing, and in the stern expression of the Duke de
Bouillon's face he had read something of more significance
than a whispered request for headache-drops.   No sooner had
his mother left the room than he followed her, and as she was

about to enter her cabinet, he laid his hand upon her shoulder :

"Pardon, dear mother," said he, in fond and deprecating tones. "I merely wish to say, that during your interview with my uncle, I will remain in the little room adjoining. You may want me, perchance, to execute some commission— it may be to bear an apology to our guests."

"It will be better for Prince Eugene to take part in our conference," said the duke, with his usual moroseness. He is the only son you have in Paris, and, as the representative of the family, it is proper for him to hear what I am about to communicate."

"I consent," replied Olympia, calmly. "I have no secrets from my son, and your highness may speak without reserve what you have come hither at this unusual hour to say."

With these words she entered her cabinet, the others following silently behind. The duke closed the door and looked around, to see that there were no other occupants of the room. He peered curiously at the heavy folds of the satin curtains which concealed the windows, and, having satisfied himself that no listeners lurked behind, he spoke.

"You are quite sure that we cannot be overheard?" said he, addressing the countess.

"Perfectly sure," replied she. "Of these walls it may be said, that, unlike walls of ordinary construction, they have no ears. Speak without apprehension. But above all things let us be seated."

"No, madame, let us remain as we are, and hearken to my words. You know that La Voisin was arrested last night."

"I know it. Monsieur Louvois brought me the news this morning, and it was corroborated by the rabble that attacked us not long after his departure from the palace. It is said that La Voisin is a toxicologist, and that she has been in the habit of selling poison to her patrons. Was this what you came to say?"

"With this I intended to open my communication, madame. That La Voisin has trafficked in poisons is proved, and she will assuredly mount the scaffold for her crimes. But

the next point is to inquire to whom her *poudre de succession* has been sold."

"Has the question been put to La Voisin ?" asked the
countess, carelessly. "They have only to inquire of her;
doubtless she will reveal the names of her friends."

The duke came nearer, and looked sternly in her face.
"The question has been asked, and it has been answered,
madame."

The countess shuddered, but recovered herself instantaneously. Momentary as it was, however, Eugene had seen the
motion, and now his large dark eyes were fixed upon his uncle
with a look of steady defiance.

"The confessions of La Voisin can be of no significance to
the Countess de Soissins," said he, haughtily. "She cannot
have made any declaration that would compromise a noble
lady ! "

"Nevertheless she has compromised one of the noblest
names in France," returned the duke. "She was forced to
reveal the names of her confederates."

" Yes! they have been as cruel as they were to poor Brinvilliers; they have taken her to the *chambre ardente !*" cried
the countess, in a trembling voice.

"Yes, madame, she was taken to the *chambre ardente*,
stretched upon the rack, and then she confessed."

"Confessed what ?" gasped Olympia.

"She confessed to have sold her *poudre de succession;* to
have foretold the future, and to have prepared love-philters."

" I do not know that there is treason in drawing horoscopes
and brewing love-philters," returned the countess, with a
forced laugh.

" It is treason to brew love-philters, when they are designed
to take effect upon the King of France," replied the duke. "It
is also treason to steal a lock of his hair wherewith to prepare
the philter."

"Did she say this ?" screamed the countess, with the fe-
rocity of a tigress at bay.

"She did. The lock of hair was obtained by Marshal Luxemburg, who bribed the valet of his majesty; the philter was
prepared for the Countess de Soissons."

"Her tortures must then have unsettled her reason," cried Olympia. "To end her agony, the poor delirious wretch has confessed any thing that her executioners may have suggested."

"You are mistaken. When she had fully recovered her senses, she repeated her declaration word for word. She signalized three persons as her trustiest confidants. Two of the three were her accomplices; the third is merely accused of having made use of La Voisin to raise the devil. The two who are accused of murder are Monsieur de Luxemburg and Madame de Soissons."

"The third?" said Olympia, hoarsely.

"My own wife," returned the duke, mournfully. "Not having been accused of crime, she has not been sent to the Bastile; his majesty has graciously permitted her to be imprisoned in her own hotel."

"Not sent to the Bastile!" echoed the countess, with a shudder. "Has—any one been—sent there?"

"Yes. Two hours ago Monsieur de Luxemburg was arrested, and he is now there in a criminal's cell."

The countess uttered a cry of anguish, and tottered to a seat, for her trembling limbs refused to support her. She put her hand to her head, and looked wildly around.

"And I?—am I to be arrested?"

"Yes, madame. The *lettre de cachet* has been sent by Louvois to the king, and—"

"And the king!" said Olympia, almost inaudibly.

"His majesty has signed it."

The countess pressed her hands upon her heart, and then, suddenly springing to her feet, she burst into a loud, frenzied laugh. "He has signed! He has signed!—And you—you—" muttered she, with a scowl at the duke, "did you offer to act as bailiff for the king?"

As though he would have confronted a world to shield her from harm, Eugene threw his arm around his mother's waist, and stood between the two.

"If such be your errand, Duke de Bouillon, you must first be the assassin of her son. No blow shall reach her, until it shall have pierced the heart of her only protector!"

"Not so grandiloquent, my little abbé," replied De Bouillon, superciliously. "Methinks, were I so disposed, I might snap the feeble thread of your existence, without any extraordinary display of valor, but I have no desire to deprive the countess of so valiant a knight. I come, not to arrest, but to deliver her. I come to save herself from the headsman, her family from the foul blot of her public execution."

"Avenging God!" murmured the miserable woman.

"You must fly, Olympia," continued the duke, compassionating her fearful condition, "you must fly, and without delay."

"Fly!" exclaimed Eugene, furiously. "Because a degraded wretch like that La Voisin, in her delirium of agony, has spoken the name of the Countess de Soissons, she shall become a fugitive from justice? No, mother, no! Remain to confound your calumniators, and, with the good sword of Right, and Truth, pierce the vile falsehood to its heart's core!"

The duke shook his head. "Let not ill-advised heroism tempt you to defy your legions of accusers. Be you innocent or guilty, you are prejudged, and will be condemned. Believe me, the danger is urgent, and it were sheer imbecility to confront it."

"You say the king has signed?" replied she, with a vacant stare. Then clasping her hands, she burst into a flood of tears, repeating o'er and o'er the piteous words, "Oh no! No! No! It cannot be! It cannot be!"

"Nevertheless, he has done it; done it at the instigation of Louvois and De Montespan. But mark me well, and you too, abbé—listen to what I am about to say. The king himself it was who sent me hither to warn you; it is he who urges you to flight. That you may have time to escape, the *lettre de cachet* is not to go into effect until to-morrow morning. But the morrow is close at hand: hark!—the clock strikes eleven, and you have but one hour. If after midnight you are found within the gates of Paris, your doom is certain. The spies of Louvois are close at hand; they watch before your palace-gates, and await the twelfth stroke of the iron tongue that speaks from the towers of Notre Dame, to force their way into the very room wherein we stand. If they pass the threshold of the palace you are irretrievably lost!"

The countess spoke not a word in reply. They scarcely knew whether she had understood the terrible import of the duke's appeal. She had remained motionless, almost breathless; her face white as death, her large orbs distended to their utmost, gazing, not upon the tangible objects that were before them, but upon some fearful pageant that was passing within the shadowy precincts of her soul.

Her lips began to move, and she muttered incoherent words. "Ah! is it so?" said she, almost inaudibly. "The end of that bright dream! The philter! What!" cried she with sudden energy, "he warns me? He grants me—one—one hour!" And then, overpowered by the reality of her supreme desolation, she opened her arms, and looked defiantly above, as if invoking the wrath of that Heaven which had forsaken her.

"Olympia," said the duke, touching her arm, "you have but three-quarters of an hour to quit Paris."

"Dear mother," implored Eugene, "decide quickly whether you go or remain."

She shuddered, and, with a deep sigh, suffered her arms to fall listlessly at her side.

"I must drink of this chalice of humiliation," said she, mournfully. "I must fly."

A groan of anguish broke from the depths of Eugene's suffering heart, while a strange look shot athwart the countenance of the duke. The groan was that of faith that faltered ; the glance was that of doubt made certainty.

"I must make my escape," iterated Olympia in a tone more resolute. "If Louvois has effected the arrest of a woman allied to the royal family, it is because he is secure of her conviction. Rather than become his victim, I will endure the shame of flight. Time enough remains to me for justification."*

"Justification shall come through me !" cried Eugene, raising his right hand as though taking an oath.

* The countess's own words.—See Amadée Renée, "The Nieces of Mazarin," p. 207.

"Countess, countess," urged De Bouillon, "you have but half an hour."

"You are right," returned Olympia, summoning all her resolution to her aid. "Time is flying, and I must be diligent."

"I promised his majesty not to leave you until you were on your way, Olympia," was the duke's reply, "and I shall remain to fulfil my promise."

"And I, mother," added Eugene, "will never leave you until you are in perfect safety."

"Then let us prepare," was Olympia's rejoinder. "You, duke, be so kind as to collect my papers and money. They are in that ebony secretary at your elbow. Here are the keys. You will find a casket therein, where all that you find may be deposited for the present. I myself will gather up my jewels and such clothing as cannot be dispensed with. Eugene, my son, go at once to the stables : order my travelling-chariot, and see that eight of my swiftest horses are attached to it. In Brussels I shall find a friend in the Spanish viceroy. Send forward relays to Rheims and Namur ; and let the men be clad in liveries of dark gray. Hasten, my son ; before half an hour, I must be hence ! "

When Eugene returned, he found his mother waiting. The duke hastily threw over her shoulders a travelling-cloak bordered with fur, and Olympia, drawing the hood closely around her face, prepared to quit the room.

"Shall I not call my sisters to bid you adieu ? " asked her son.

"No," said she, calmly. "Their absence would be remarked, and nothing must arouse the suspicion of my guests. I leave to you, Monsieur de Bouillon, the task of communicating my flight to my daughters. May I request you to bear a message to the king also ? Tell him that whenever he will pass his royal word that I may return without danger of incarceration, I shall be ready to appear before my accusers, and defend my calumniated reputation.* Give me your arm,—and yours, Eugene : we are late."

Silently, and without a single expression of regret, she went

---

* Her own words.—See the " Letters of Madame de Sévigné," vol. iii.

through the lofty corridors of the hôtel, until she reached the private staircase by which Eugene had passed to the street that morning. The servants had assembled to bid her adieu, and, as they tendered their good wishes, she bent her lofty head with the condescension of a queen. Before descending, she addressed a few words to the steward :

"I am forced to leave Paris for a time, Latour. My enemies refuse me the poor privilege of remaining here to refute the absurd charges preferred against me by the senseless rabble that are in their pay. During my absence, I leave you in full command of my household. You shall receive your wages until you decide to seek employment elsewhere. Farewell all!"

The chariot with eight superb horses was at the postern, and around it stood the lackeys in their liveries of sombre gray. The countess took her seat in the carriage, and, bending forward to kiss her son, said, "Bear my greetings to your sisters, Eugene."

"Will my gracious uncle accept this commission?" asked he, turning to the duke.

"Why not you?" asked Olympia.

"Because my place is with you, dearest mother," was the simple reply of her devoted child, while he took his seat at her side.

"It is right," remarked the duke, "and I begin to feel considerable respect for our little abbé!"

"I shall compel respect from more than the Duke de Bouillon," thought his nephew.

"Farewell!" said Olympia, with as much self-possession as if she had been starting for a tour of pleasure. "Tell the king that I forget to pity my own impotence in compassionating his."

The carriage rolled away, first under the illuminated windows of the rooms of state, where the unconscious Princesses de Carignan were doing their best to entertain the motley assemblage, that had been so suddenly deserted by their mother; then along the dimly-lighted streets where Eugene's heart beat with painful apprehension lest the crowd should recognize the fugitive ; then they entered the avenue where the court had turned its back upon Olympia and her extravagant hopes, and at last—they reached the gates.

Meanwhile the Duke de Bouillon had returned to the *salons,* where he announced the departure of the countess to her guests ; the servants had dispersed, and returned to their usual employments, all except one, who crept stealthily out, and, turning the corner, advanced a few paces into a dark and narrow alley. Two horsemen were waiting his appearance there.

" Has she gone ? " asked one.

" Yes," replied the man ; " and relays have been ordered to hasten her escape."

" What route did she take ? "

" She goes to Brussels, by the way of Rheims, Rocroy, and Namur."

" Here are your four louis d'ors."

With these words, the two horsemen galloped away, turning their horses' heads toward the palace of the minister of war. In the porte-cochère stood Louvois himself, who, motioning them not to dismount, spoke a few low words, and then handed to each one a package of letters and a purse of gold.

" Fly with all speed," said he, in his parting injunctions. " Kill as many horses as you list—I pay for their carcasses ; but see that at every station you arrive a full hour before the countess."

He then entered his carriage, and drove to the Louvre to inform the king that his royal commands had been obeyed, and that the Countess de Soissons had been suffered to escape.

As the chariot that was bearing away the disgraced Olympia drove through the barrier and entered upon the high-road, the two horsemen galloped past, and so completely did they distance the unhappy travellers, that in a few moments the echo of their horses' feet had died away into silence.

## CHAPTER VIII.

### THE FLIGHT.

IT was a glorious night—a night of sapphire skies, radiant with stellar diamonds—one of those nights whose beauty intensifies pleasure, and whose gentle influence soothes pain ; which, to the joyous heart seem to prefigure heaven ; to the sorrowing are like the healing touch of the Almighty hand, which, in exceeding love, has stricken it with a passing pain.

But not a ray of hope or consolation refreshed the dreary wastes of the heart of Olympia de Soissons. She had withdrawn herself from the embrace of her son, and leaned far back into the corner of the carriage. But for the glare of her large, black eyes, as they reflected the light of the lamps on either side, she might have been asleep, so motionless she lay ; but, whenever Eugene turned a timid glance upon her rigid features, he saw that she seemed ever and ever to be looking away from him, and far out upon the black and shapeless masses of the woods through which they journeyed all that night.

He had tried to divert her by conversation; but to his remarks she had made such curt and random replies, that he desisted,and left her to the bleak solitude of her own reveries.

And thus they passed the night. With fresh relays of eight spirited horses, they travelled so swiftly, that when morning dawned, the lofty towers of the Cathedral of Rheims were seen looming through the mist, and the coachman drew up before the gates.

But, although a courier had been sent in advance to order it, no relay was there. The coachman turned to Eugene for instructions.

"This is most unfortunate," replied he, "for it compels us to enter the city and change horses at the royal post-house. While arrangements are being made there, will it please my dear mother to leave her carriage and partake of some refreshment ?"

The countess replied with a silent bend of the head, and

Eugene sent forward a courier, with orders to have breakfast prepared. The carriage passed the old Roman gate, and entered the city, made famous by the coronation of so many kings of France. The rattle of the wheels over the rough stone pavement made the countess start with apprehension of she knew not what, and she withdrew cautiously from sight.

"It is well that the roll of this clamorous carriage cannot awaken our foes," said she, as they stopped before the post-house.

Her rejoicings were premature ; for the master of the post-horses came leisurely forward, his face expressing a mixture of rude curiosity with careless contempt.

"You want post-horses ?" asked he, with a familiar nod.

Eugene's large eyes flashed fire. "It would appear," said he, "that you do not know to whom you have the honor of speaking, or else you would remove your hat."

"Oh, yes, I know who you are," answered he, insolently. "That is the Countess de Soissons, and you are the little abbé, her son. But I keep on my hat, for it is cool this morning, and it suits me *not* to remove it."

"It suits you, then, to be a boor, a barefaced—"

"Peace, Eugene !" interrupted Olympia, in Italian ; "peace, or you will cause me some detention that may imperil my life. See ; in spite of the undue hour, how many men are around our carriage. They are not here by accident. Their presence only proves that Louvois' couriers have anticipated us ; and if ever we hope to pass the frontiers of France, we must be discreet."

"And I may not, therefore, chastise this varlet ! I must sit tamely by while he insults my mother !"

"He is but a tool, Eugene. Spare the instrument, and strike the hand that directs it against me."

"By the Eternal God, I will smite that hand !" said Eugene, while the master of the post-horses stood staring at Olympia with an expression of familiarity that would have cost him his life, had she been free to take it. But sweet as the honey of Hybla, were the words she spoke.

"Good sir, would you be so obliging as to furnish us with eight horses ?" said she, almost imploringly.

"Eight horses! for that light vehicle ? It looks much as if you were trying to make your escape, and were sore pressed to move on."

"I am, indeed, sorely pressed," said she, in tones of distress; "hasten, I implore of you, hasten!"

"You cannot have them before half an hour," said he, turning on his heel, and re-entering the house.

The countess now called to one of her footmen : "Go, see if we can have a room and some breakfast."

The man obeyed, but returned almost immediately, with a most embarrassed expression.

"They have no vacant room, and say that your highness need not trouble yourself to leave the carriage, in search of lodgings, were it even for five minutes."

"Then go and bring us each a cup of chocolate," replied the countess, with a sigh.

The footman renewed his petition, and this time returned, accompanied by a woman, who, in angry haste, approached the unhappy fugitives :

"You are the Countess de Soissons ?" asked she, with a bold stare.

"Yes, madame, I am; and I hope you will do me the favor to serve us a cup of chocolate."

"You do—do you ? Well, I have come out here to tell you that I shall do no such thing. How do I know that your breath may not poison my cup and—"

"Woman!" cried Eugene, springing up from his seat.

His mother put him firmly back. "I command you to keep silence," said she, imperiously. Then, resuming her colloquy with the woman who stood by, with arms akimbo : "I will tell you how you can oblige me without any risk to yourself."

"How, pray ?"

"Sell me, not only the chocolate, but the cups that contain it. I will give you a louis d'or for each one."

The woman's eyes glistened with greed of gold. "Two louis d'ors for two cups of chocolate !" said she to herself, "that is a brave trade for me. You shall have them," added she aloud, "I will fetch them in a moment."

And off she pattered with her slipshod shoes into the house. The countess then addressed her son, who, leaning back in a corner of the carriage, sat with his head buried in his hands.

"Eugene," said she, emphatically, "if you are to accompany me any farther, it must be as a peace-loving abbé not as an irascible soldier. If you incense these people against us, your indiscreet zeal will cause me to be captured. I have no longing for death ; I desire to live until my son, the mighty cardinal, has trampled under foot the least as well as the greatest of my enemies."

"Oh, mother, I have not only *your* injuries to avenge, but mine ! I have the burning shame of yesterday to wipe out, although the wound of my humiliation can never be healed."

"Time—Nature's sweet balm—heals every wound, and in our days of adversity let this be our consolation. To the sharp lash of Destiny the wise man will bow in silence ; but if the blow be from the hand of man, it is from the crucible of the suffering it imposes that must come the strength wherewith we retaliate ; from the depths of our wounded hearts that must spring the geysers of our seething revenge. It would gratify me to have you the companion of my flight, but, if in the impotence of your wrath you seek to defend me, it will be better for us to part.—Ah, here comes the chocolate ! I confess that I rejoice to scent its fragrant aroma. Let us drink, and afterward you will decide whether you subscribe to my exactions, or return to Paris."

The cups were cracked, without handles, and of coarse pottery—the thrifty housewife having taken care to select the worst of her wares to barter away. The countess smilingly accepted hers, and, as Eugene was putting his impatiently away, she took it herself from the servant's hands.

"Drink," said she, "and hearken to a saying of our uncle, Cardinal Mazarin: 'When a man is troubled in spirit, he must strengthen himself in body. The world is a great campaign against contrarieties with which we must daily anticipate a skirmish. And above all, on the eve of a great battle, the soul, which is the chief, must see to it that his soldier, which is the body, is in a condition to do him service.' These were the words of a wise man, and they are worthy of being remembered. Drink your chocolate, my son, for you well know that we are about to go into action."

He took the cup from his mother's hand, and, without another word, emptied it of its contents. The woman, meanwhile, had been watching her cups, lamenting their approaching destruction, which, spite of the tremendous price at which they had been purchased, she looked upon as a sacrifice greatly to be deplored. Seeing that the catastrophe was approaching, she stepped forward to receive her pay. In her hand she held a large pan of water, which she raised to a level with the portière of the carriage.

"Now, madame," said she, "you have had your chocolate, give me my louis d'ors."

From her jewelled purse Olympia drew out two gold-pieces, which she offered to the woman. But, instead of receiving them, she cried out in a shrill voice:

"Drop them in the water. After a few hours I may venture to touch the gold that has passed through your hands!"

The crowd, whom curiosity had drawn around the carriage, now burst out into a shout of applause.

"Right, right, Dame Margot! You are a prudent woman! Nobody knows what might come of handling her louis d'ors."

Olympia smiled. "Yes," said she, "you are a wise woman, and, as a token of my admiration for your prudence, here are three louis d'ors instead of the two I had promised."

So saying, she dropped three gold-pieces in the basin. The woman blushed, and looked ashamed. The crowd were astonished, and here and there were heard a few murmured words of sympathy. "That was very kind, was it not? After all, she may not be as bad as they say. It may all be a lie about her poisoning her children!"

Olympia heard it, and a proud smile flitted over her beautiful face. The woman still lingered at the carriage-door. "And the cups?" asked she, wistfully. "I suppose you will break them, will you not?"

"No," replied the countess, speaking so that she might be heard by the people. "No, my good woman, I will not break them : they shall lie in the basin, so that, like the gold, they may be purified until you find them worthy of being used again!"

And again her jewelled hand was extended, and from her slender fingers the cups were carefully dropped into the basin.

"Your highness," exclaimed the woman, abashed, "I thank you a thousand times for your generosity, and I hope you will forgive my rudeness. I would not have been so forgetful of the respect I owe to a lady of your rank, if I had not been put up to it by other people. From my heart I beg your pardon, madame."

"You are sincerely forgiven," replied Olympia, gently. "I am accustomed to contumely, and when unjustly persecuted I follow the example of my Saviour—I forgive those that hate and revile me."

"Did you hear that?" whispered the multitude one to another. "And do you mark what a beautiful countenance she has? Instead of being a murderess, she may be a pious saint. Who knows?"

"No," cried the vender of chocolate, bravely diving her hand into the basin and withdrawing her louis d'ors, "no, she is no murderess, she is a benevolent, Christian lady."

"She is a benevolent Christian lady," shouted the people, and in less than five minutes the countess was as popular as a prince who has just ascended the throne.

A third time the magic purse was drawn forth, and two more louis d'ors glittered in the hand of Dame Margot!

"May I ask of you the favor to give this to those good people, that they may drink my health?" said Olympia.

"You are an angel," cried Margot, while her eyes grew moist with sympathizing tears.

"Yes, an angel!" echoed the crowd. "So beautiful! So good! So bountiful!"

They were still in the height of their enthusiasm when the half hour had expired, and the post-horses were brought out and harnessed. The postilion sounded his horn, and the coach man cracked his whip.

"Long live the noble Countess de Soissons!" cried Dame Margot, and "Long live her highness!" echoed the converts.

while the carriage thundered through the streets, and the countess threw herself back and laughed.

"Miserable rabble!" said she, "whose love and hate are bought with gold, and whom philanthropists regard as the exponents of the Divine will! '*Vox populi vox Dei*,' forsooth!" —Then, turning to Eugene, who, during the whole performance, had remained sullenly silent, she continued: "Have you decided whether to leave or accompany me? If the latter, it must be in the character of a diplomatist, whose weapons are sweet words and shining gold."

"I go on with you, mother, as your loving and obedient son," said Eugene, kissing her hand—even the one which still clasped the wonder-working purse. "I have no right to despise this tiny necromancer, for, by its beneficent power, you have been rescued from dangers which I, a man, and not a coward, was impotent to avert. I submit, dear mother, to your dictates—no longer your champion, look upon me henceforth as your subject."

The voice was very mournful in which Eugene made this profession of vassalage, and at its conclusion his eyes were veiled by tears of burning humiliation. His mother affected not to perceive his emotion, as she replied in her blandest tones:

"I thank you, my son. Your decision is a most filial and meritorious one. The two days that have just passed over your head have proved to me that, whatever may be your career, you are destined to render it illustrious either by statesmanship or prowess. Whether as an ecclesiastic, a politician, or a soldier, you will certainly attain distinction."

"Mother, as a soldier, I *may* attain distinction; as a churchman, never. For the present I accept my fate; but blessed will be the day on which I go into the world free to feel the power of my manhood, and to shape my fortunes with my own hand. Let women rise to dignity through royal favor and family influence; man's only ally should be his own strong arm. Far nobler to me is the lieutenant who wins his epaulets upon the battle-field, than the prince who is born to the command of an army."

"Have a care how you speak such high-treason at the court

of Louis XIV.," replied his mother. "It would be repeated to his majesty, and never would be forgiven."

"I hope to do many things in my life that will be repeated to his majesty of France—perchance some of which may never obtain his forgiveness," replied Eugene, quietly. "But let us speak of the present, and of you, beloved mother."

Olympia threw herself back against the soft upholstery that lined the back of the carriage. "Rather let us speak of nothing, my child. Neither of us had any rest last night : I would gladly sleep awhile."

She closed her eyes, and finally Nature asserted her long-frustrated claims. In a few moments, the humiliations, the fears, and the sufferings of the unhappy Olympia, were drowned in the drowsy waters of profound sleep.

She was not long permitted to remain in oblivion of her woes. Her repose was broken by the hoots and hisses of another vulgar crowd, that swarmed like hornets about the carriage-windows. They had arrived at another station, where, in place of finding post-horses, they were met by another mob as vituperative as the one they had encountered before.

Eugene thrust open the portière, and, leaping into the very midst of the rioters, he drew out his pistols. "The first one of you," cried he, "that proffers another injurious word, I will shoot as I would a vicious dog ! "

"Hear that sickly manikin ! He is trying to browbeat us ! " cried some one in the crowd.

"Yes, yes, trying to browbeat us ! " echoed the chorus.

"Yes—by the eternal heavens above us ! " exclaimed the prince, "The first that moves a foot toward us, dies ! "

His eyes flashed so boldly, and his attitude was so commanding, that the people, ever cowed by true courage, faltered and fell back.

Just then Olympia opened the door on her own side of the chariot, and, without the slightest manifestation of fear or anger, stepped to the ground, and, with one of her bewitching smiles, made her way to the very center of her foes. Her voice was soft and low, but, to a practised ear, it would have seemed like that of a lioness, who, forced to temporize, was longing to devour.

"Good people," said the leonine siren, "pardon the iras-cibility of this young man. He is my son, and, when he heard his mother's name aspersed, his anger got the better of his dis-cretion. Is it not true," continued she, turning to a woman who had been most vociferous in her maledictions, " is it not true, dear friend, that a son is excusable who grows indignant when he hears his mother accused of deeds the very thought of which would fill her with horror ? Perhaps you, too, have a son that loves you, and who, knowing you to be a good and pious woman, would never suffer any man to attack your good name."

"Yes," replied the woman, entirely propitiated, "yes, ma-dame, I have a son who certainly would defend my good name against any man that attacked it."

"Then you will make allowances for mine, and speak a kind word for him to your friends here, for we mothers understand one another, do we not ? And any one of us is ready to shelter the good son of some other woman ? Are we not ?"

"That we are," returned the woman, enthusiastically. "I will protect your son, never fear." And, with her arms up-raised, she dashed through the crowd, and addressed those who were nearest to Eugene, and who, partially over their panic, were just about to remember that they were many against their one opponent.

"Let him alone !" cried she. "He is her son ! You see that we have been deceived by those who told us that she had poisoned her children. How should this one love her, if she were so wicked ?"

"Dear friends," cried Olympia, so as to be heard by all around, "you have been shamefully imposed upon, if you were told that I poisoned my dear children. I have given birth to seven, who are all alive to testify that their poor mother is innocent."

"All seven alive! Seven children, and not one dead!" exclaimed the "dear friend" whom Olympia had specially ad-dressed. "Just think of that ! Why, of course she is inno-cent."

And here and there the shrill voices of the women were

heard repeating the words, "She is innocent, of course she is innocent!"

"You perceive, then," continued the countess, pursuing her advantage, "that I have powerful enemies, since they precede me on my journey with slanderous falsehoods, and try to turn the honest hearts of the villagers of France against me and my son. I see that they have been here, and have bribed you to insult me."

"That is true," cried a chorus of rough voices. "We were paid to insult you and to refuse you post-horses."

"Well, then," returned Olympia, with one of her most enchanting smiles, "I, too, will give you money, but it shall not be to bribe you to resent my injuries. It will be to dispose of as your kind hearts deem best."

She threw out a handful of silver, for which some began to stoop and scramble, while others, emboldened by the sight of such a largesse, crowded around, stretching out their hands for a "souvenir."

"Whoever, at the expiration of fifteen minutes, furnishes me eight fresh horses, shall receive eight louis d'ors as a token of my gratitude," said the sagacious Olympia.

No sooner were the words spoken, than every man there flew to earn the token. In less than a minute the ground was cleared, and naught was to be seen but a few women and children, still bent upon searching for the silver.

The countess returned to her carriage, where she found Eugene, looking embarrassed and ashamed. He immediately apologized for his involuntary disregard of her injunctions.

"Dear mother, forgive me ; in this last dilemma I have conducted myself like a madman, while you have shown that you possess true heroism. I see how very much wiser you are than I ; and I solemnly promise to attempt no more violence, where personal violence is not offered to us. But to say that I could exchange my weapons for yours, I cannot. I never shall learn to dissimulate and flatter."

His mother slightly raised her shoulders. "You will learn it in time, when you will have learned to despise your fellows as I do.—But see! Heaven be praised, here come the horses."

In a few moments, eight brown hands were outstretched to receive the gold, and, amid the huzzas of the multitude, the Countess de Soissons pursued her journey.

---

## CHAPTER IX.

### THE PARTING.

EUGENE looked gloomily out of the carriage-window, and heard a succession of deep sighs.

"Shall I tell you why you are so sad?" said Olympia to her son.

"I am sad because I feel my miserable impotence," replied he, moodily. "I am sad because I must at last acknowledge that Mazarin was right when he said that gold was the only divinity devoutly worshipped on earth."

"Speak not slightingly of gold," cried Olympia, laughing; "it has probably saved my life to-day. Unluckily we are far from the end of our journey, and I may not have enough of this precious gold wherewith to purchase forbearance as we go."

"We are not far from the frontier, and once in Flanders, you are safe."

"Not so. There are no bounds to the realms of this yellow divinity. Its worshippers are everywhere, and Louvois will seek them in France and out of it. But I think I have a device whereby we may outwit our mighty oppressor, and avoid further contumely."

"What is it, mother?"

"I will take another and a less public road. You shall go with me as far as the boundaries. We can pass the night at Rocroy, and part on the morrow: you to retrace your steps, I to continue my flight in a plain carriage, with two horses and no attendants."

"I have promised to submit, and will obey you implicitly," returned Eugene, respectfully. "Since you command me to go, we will part at Rocroy."

6

"Ah!" sighed the countess, "I would we were there, for indeed I am exhausted, and yearn for rest."

Many hours, however, went by, before they reached Rocroy, and, wherever their need compelled them to stop, they met with the same insults; the same efforts were to be gone through, to propitiate the rabble; and Eugene was forced to endure it all, while his martyred heart was wrung with anguish that no words are adequate to picture.

At last, to the relief of the prince, and the great joy of his mother, who was almost fainting with fatigue, the fortress was reached, the foaming horses were drawn up, and the officer in command was seen coming through a postern, followed by six of his men.

It was the custom in France to search every vehicle that left the frontier; and, in compliance with this custom, the officer advanced promptly to meet the travellers. The countess had so often submitted to this formality, that when her name and destination were asked, she avowed them both without the least hesitation.

"I hope," added she, "that the declaration of my name and rank will exempt me from the detention usual in these cases, for I am in great haste, and you will oblige me by ordering the gates to be opened at once."

"I am sorry to disoblige your highness," replied the officer, with a supercilious smile, "but that very declaration compels me to refuse you egress through the gates of Rocroy."

"What in Heaven's name do you mean, sir?" exclaimed Olympia, alarmed.

"I mean that Monsieur Louvois's orders are express that the Countess de Soissons shall not be suffered to pass the fortress, and his orders here are paramount."

With these words the officer turned his back, made a sign to his men, and in less than a minute the party had disappeared, and the inexorable gates had closed.

The countess sighed wearily. "Let us go farther," said she. "In the next village we will at least find lodgings, and rest for the night."

The horses' heads were turned, and the tired animals urged on, until a neighboring town had been reached, whose stately inn, with its brightly-illuminated entrance, gave promise of comfortable entertainment for man and beast.

Three well-dressed individuals stood in the lofty door-way, and as the carriage drove up they came forward to meet it. Eugene, shielding his mother from sight, asked if they could alight to sup and lodge there for the night.

"That depends upon circumstances," replied one of them. "You must first have the goodness to give us your name."

"My name is nothing to the purpose," cried Eugene, impatiently. "I ask merely whether strangers can be accommodated with supper and beds in this house."

"The name is every thing, sir, and, before I answer your inquiry, I must know it—unless, indeed, you are anxious to conceal it."

"A Prince de Carignan has never yet had reason to conceal his name," said Eugene, haughtily.

"Ah! your highness, then, is the Prince de Carignan! And may this lady in the corner there be your mother, the Countess de Soissons?"

"Yes—the Countess de Soissons; and now that you are made acquainted with our names—"

"I regret that I cannot receive you," interrupted the host. "Were you alone, my house and every thing within my doors would be at the service of the Prince de Carignan, but for his mother we have no accommodation. We are afraid of noble ladies that use poison."

The words were scarcely out of his mouth, before he sprang up the steps, and closed the doors of the inn in their faces.

"Ah!" muttered Olympia, between her teeth, "such cruelty as this is enough to drive any one to the use of poison! And if I live I will be revenged on yonder churl that has sent me out into the darkness, denying me food and rest!"

"Whither will your highness go now?" asked the footman; and, by the tone of the inquiry, Olympia felt that her menials were rapidly losing all respect for a "highness" that could no longer command entrance into a public inn.

"Take a by-way to the next village, and stop at the first peasant's hut on the road."

The coachman was growing surly, and the poor, worn-out

horses were so stiff that they could barely travel any longer.
The village, however, was only a few miles off, so that they
were not more than an hour in reaching a miserable hovel, at
the door of which was a man in the superlative degree of astonishment. He, at least, had never heard of Louvois and
Louvois's orders, so that, for the promise of a gold-piece, he
was easily induced to receive the desponding party. But his
only bed was of straw, and he feared their excellencies would
not be satisfied with his fare.

"My friend," said Olympia, "to an exhausted traveller a
litter of straw is as welcome as a bed of down;" and, with a
sigh of relief, she took the arm of her son, and entered the hut.

"Are you married?" asked she, taking her seat on a wooden
stool, near the chimney.

"Yes; and here is my wife," said he, as a young woman,
blushing and courtesying, came forward to welcome her distinguished visitors.

"Have you a wagon and horses?" continued the countess.

"A wagon, your excellency, but no horses: we have two
sturdy oxen, instead."

"Would you like to earn enough money to-night to buy
yourself a handsome team?"

"Yes, indeed, we would," cried husband and wife simultaneously.

"Then," said Olympia to the latter, "sell me your Sunday-
gown, let me have something to eat, and throw down some
clean straw in the corner, where I may sleep for a few hours.
When I awake," added she to the man, "harness your oxen,
and take me in your wagon beyond the frontier, to Flanders.
If you will do this, you shall have fifty louis d'ors for your
trouble."

The peasant grinned responsive. "That will I," cried he,
slapping his thigh; "and, if you say so, I'll take you as far as
Chimay, which is a good way beyond the frontier."

"Right," said the countess, joyfully. "To Chimay we go.
Now, my good girl, bring me your best holiday-suit."

The young woman ran, breathless with joy, to fetch her attire, while the man went out to feed his oxen. Olympia then
addressed herself to Eugene:

"Now, my son, we are alone, and I claim the fulfilment of your promise. You have seen me to a place of safety, and you must return to Paris. Listen now to my commands, perhaps the last I may ever give you."

"Command, dear mother, and I will obey. But do not ask me to abandon you to the danger which still threatens you."

"You exaggerate my danger, Eugene; and, by remaining with me, you increase it. You are too impulsive to be a discreet companion, and I exact of you to leave me. Disguised as a peasant-woman, and travelling in an ox-cart, my foes will never discover me, and I have every hope of reaching my destination in safety."

"It is impossible," persisted Eugene, his eyes filling with tears.

"My child, must I then force you to do my bidding?"

"No force can compel me to do what I know to be craven and dishonorable," cried the prince. "Mother, I must not—cannot obey."

"For one short moment, the eyes of the countess flashed fire, but as suddenly they softened, and she smilingly extended her hand:

"Well—let us contend no longer, dear boy ; I see that, for once, I must succumb to your strong will. Here comes the woman with my disguise. Go out a while, and let me change my dress. Send the footman with a little casket you will find in the carriage-box. Here is the key. And, Eugene, do beg the man to send in our supper, that it may be ready for us when I shall have metamorphosed myself into a peasant-woman."

About fifteen minutes later, the countess called her son. "How do you like me?" she said. "Am I sufficiently disguised to pass for that fellow's wife? What a strange picture we will make—you and I, seated on a sack of wool, and drawn by a pair of creeping oxen ! 'Tis well for you that you are an abbé ; were you any thing else, you could not venture to travel by the side of a woman of low degree. But—come, let us enjoy our supper ; I, for one, am both hungry and sleepy."

She drew a stool up to the table, which was spread with a clean cloth, and covered with platters of bread, butter, and cheese. Between two wooden bowls stood a large pitcher of milk. These bowls the countess filled to the brim, and handed one to her son.

": Pledge me a bumper, and wish me a prosperous journey," said she, playfully, while she put the cup to her lips, all the while narrowly watching Eugene.

He followed her example, and drained his bowl to its last drop. Then, striving to fall in with her mood, he said:

"You see how obedient I am, and yet you know that I am not one of those that would be content to live in a land flowing with milk and honey."

"Thank you," replied his mother, "for this one act of obedience. I could wish you were as submissive in other things. But—what is the matter, boy? You are pale."

"I do not know," stammered Eugene, his tongue seeming paralyzed. "I am sick—I want—fresh air! Some air, mother!"

He attempted to rise, but fell back into his seat.

"Mother," murmured he, while his features were becoming distorted by pain, "have you drugged—"

He could articulate no longer, but gazed upon his mother with fast-glazing eyes, until slowly his dull orbs closed, and his head dropped heavily upon the table.

"Three minutes," said the countess, quietly. "Only three minutes, and he sleeps soundly. La Voisin was a wonderful creature! What a high privilege it is to reign over the will of another human being with a might as mysterious as it is irresistible? And greater yet the privilege of dispensing life or death! Why did I not exercise that power over the proud man that follows me with such unrelenting hate? Ah, Louvois, had I been braver, I had not endured your contumely! Poor, weak fool that I was, not to wrestle with fate and master it! But—it is useless to repine. Let me see. Eugene will sleep four hours, and, ere he wakes, I must be beyond the frontiers of hostile France."

She left the little room and joined the peasant's wife.

"I have prevailed upon my son to return to Paris," said she, in that caressing tone which she had practised so successfully through the day. "His health is delicate, and the hard·

ships of our hurried journey have so exhausted him that he has fallen into a profound sleep. Do not disturb him. I entreat of you, dear friend, and, when he awakes, give him this note."

She drew from her pocket-book a paper, and, giving it to the woman, repeated her request that her dear boy should not be disturbed.

"I will take my seat at the door, madame, and await the wakening of Monsieur l'Abbé, to deliver your highness's note. But will you too not rest awhile, before you go on? I think you look as if you needed sleep quite as much as your son."

"No, no, thank you, I must reach Flanders before sunrise," replied Olympia, "and do beg your husband to use dispatch, for I am impatient to start. Will you also be so obliging as to call my servants? I must say a few words to them before we part."

When the men came in, their mistress, in spite of her costume, wore a demeanor so lofty, that they were afraid to betray their cognition of her disguise, and were awed back into their usual stolid and obsequious deportment.

"You have witnessed," said the countess, "the persecutions that have been heaped upon me since yesterday, and of course you are not surprised to find that I have adopted a disguise by which I may hope to escape further outrage. You have both been among the trustiest of my servants, and to you, rather than to my son, I confide my parting instructions. He is now asleep, and I will not even waken him to take leave; for he would wish to accompany me, and so compromise both his safety and mine. I therefore journey in secret and alone. As for you, be in readiness to return to Paris by daylight, and do all that you can for the comfort of my son on the way."

"I served his father," replied the coachman, "and will do my duty by his son, your highness. Rely upon me."

"And I," added the footman, "will do my best to deserve the praise your highness has so kindly vouchsafed to us, by serving my lord and prince as faithfully as I know how."

"Right, my good friends. You will always find him, in return, a gracious and generous master. You will have no difficulty in procuring relays or lodging on your return to

Paris : oblige me, then, by travelling with all speed, for it is important that my son arrive quickly. And now farewell, and accept this as a remembrance."

Dropping several gold-pieces into the hands of each one, their proud mistress inclined her head, and passed out of the hut.

"If your highness is ready," said the peasant's wife, meeting her on the threshold, "my husband is in his wagon waiting."

"In one moment," replied Olympia; "I must return to take a last kiss from my son."

She hastened back to the little room, and, stepping lightly, advanced to the table, where Eugene, his head supported by his arms, lay precisely in the position wherein she had left him. She lifted the masses of his shaggy, black hair, and gazed wistfully upon his pale face. "And if the stars are not false," whispered she, tenderly, "this feeble body enshrines a mind that shall win renown for the house of Savoy. God bless thee, my fragile, but great-hearted Eugene! As I gaze upon thy pallid brow, my whole being is inundated by the gushing waters of a love which to-night seems more than maternal! So should angels love the sons of men! Take from my lips the baptismal kisses that consecrate thee to glory! May God bless and prosper thee, my boy!"

She bent over the sleeping youth and kissed his forehead o'er and o'er. When she raised her head, among the raven masses of Eugene's hair there trembled here and there a tear, perhaps the purest that ever flowed from the turbid spring of Olympia de Soisson's corrupt heart.

One more kiss she pressed upon his clasped hands, and then she hurried away. The cart was before the door; she took her seat, and slowly the creeping oxen went out into the darkness, bearing away with them a secret which, to the wondering peasant-woman, was like Jove's descent to the daughter of Acrisius.*

Four hours passed away, and the power of the drugged cup

---

* Louvois's hate pursued the Countess de Soissons to Brussels, where the beggars were bribed to insult her as she passed them in the streets. She was so persecuted by the rabble that, on one occasion, when she was purchasing lace at the convent of the Béguines, they assembled in such multitudes at the

was at an end. Day was breaking, and, although by the uncertain light of the gray dawn, no object in that poor place was clearly defined, still everything was visible. Eugene raised his head and looked, bewildered, around the room. He saw at once that his mother was not there, and with a gesture of wild alarm he sprang to his feet.

"Mother, my mother!" exclaimed he.

The door opened, and the smiling peasant with a deep courtesy came forward to wish his highness good-morning.

"Your mother, excellency, has been gone these four hours," said she.

"Gone! Gracious Heaven! whither, and with whom?"

"She went to Flanders, excellency, with my husband. Do not feel unhappy, sir, I beg of you; my husband is a good, prudent fellow, and he will take her safely to Chimay. Here is a paper she left for you, and she bade me say that, as soon as I had given you an early breakfast, you would return with your servants to Paris."

Eugene clutched at the note, and returned to the table to read it. Its contents were as follows:

"My dear child, you would not obey me, and yet I could no longer brook the danger of your attendance. Although I am no adept in the art of poisoning, yet I have learned from La Voisin to prepare harmless anodynes, one of which I mingled with the cup of milk you took from my hand to-night. You sleep, dear Eugene, and I must go forth to meet my fate alone. Your knightly repugnance to what you looked upon as a desertion of your mother, has forced me to the use of means which, though perfectly innocent, I would rather not have employed. I knew no other device by which to escape your too loving vigilance.

entrance, that the nuns, to save her from being torn to pieces, were compelled to permit her to remain with them all night. Finally the governor of Netherlands was driven to take her under his own personal protection, by which it became unlawful to molest her further. After the governor became her champion, the prejudices of the people wore gradually away, until at last Olympia held her levees as she had done in her palmy days at the Hôtel de Soissons.—See Abbé de Choisy: Mémoires, p. 224. Renée: "Les Nièces de Mazarin," p. 212.

"Go back to Paris, my Eugene, and go with all speed, for there you can protect, there alone you can defend me. There are my enemies; and, although I dedicate you to the church, I would not have you put in practice that precept of the Scriptures which enjoins upon you to forgive your traducers, and bless those who despitefully use you. No, no! From my son's hand I await the blow that is to avenge my wounded honor and my blasted existence. Farewell! The spirit of Mazarin guide you to wisdom and success! Olympia."

"I will avenge you, my own, my precious mother," said Eugene, his teeth firmly set with bitter resolve. "The world has thrown its gauntlet to us, and, by Heaven I will wear it on my front! I have swept the dark circle of every imaginable sorrow, and my soul is athirst for strife. 'Tis a priestly office to vindicate a mother's good name, and I shall be the hierophant of an altar whereon the blood of her enemies shall be sacrificed. And now, dear maligned one," continued he, kissing the words her hand had traced, "farewell! Thou wert my first passionate love, and in my faithful heart nothing ever shall transcend thee!"

Half an hour later he was on the road to Paris; but, desirous to escape notice, Eugene travelled without footmen or outriders, and confined himself to a span of horses for his carriage. The simple equipage attracted no attention, and no one attempted to peer at its silent occupant, so that on the morning of the next day he had arrived in Paris.

It was a clear, bright morning, and perchance this might be a reason why the streets were unusually crowded; but as the prince was remarking what a multitude were astir to enjoy the beauty of a sky that was vaulted with pale-blue and silver, he observed at the same time that all were going in one direction. The throng grew denser as the carriage advanced, until it reached the Rue des Deux Écus, when it came to a dead stop. And after that it advanced but a few feet at a time, for the whole world seemed to be going, with Eugene, to the Hôtel de Soissons.

At last they reached the gates, and the prince was about to alight, when, directly in front of the palace, and within the court, he saw the sight which had attracted the multitude thither.

Before the principal entrance of the palace were six horsemen, two of whom in their right hands held long trumpets decked with flowing ribbons. Behind these, bestriding four immense hosses of Norman breed, were four beadles in their long black gowns, and broad-brimmed hats, looped up with cockades. Behind these four were two mounted soldiers, dressed like those in front, in the municipal colors of the city of Paris, and in place of trumpets they carried halberds.

As he saw this extraordinary group, who had apparently selected the court of the Hôtel Soissons wherein to enact some ridiculous pageant, Eugene could scarcely believe his dazzled eyes. He looked again, and saw the horsemen raise their trumpets to their lips, while the air resounded with a *fanfare* that made the very windows of the palace tremble in their frames.

The multitude, that up to this moment had been struggling and contending together for place and passage, suddenly grew breathless with expectation, when a second *fanfare* rang out upon the air; and, when its clang had died away, one of the black-robed beadles cried out in a loud voice:

"We, the appointed magistrate of the venerable city of Paris, hereby do summon the Countess Olympia de Soissons, Princess of Carignan, widow of the most high the Count de Soissons, Prince Royal of Bourbon, and Prince of Carignan, to appear within three days before our tribunal, at the town-hall of our good city of Paris."

The trumpet sounded a third time, and another beadle continued the summons:

"And we, the appointed magistrate of the venerable city of Paris, do hereby accuse said Countess Olympia de Soissons and Princess de Carignan of sorcery and murder by poison. If she hold herself innocent of these charges, she will appear within the three days by law granted her wherein to answer our summons. If she do not appear within three days, she shall he held guilty by contumacy, and condemned."

Scarcely had these last words been pronounced, when the people broke out into jubilant shouts over the fearless rectitude of the honorable city fathers, who were not afraid to lift the avenging arm of justice against criminals in high places.

Amid the din that followed, Eugene escaped from his carriage to the private entrance, through which twice before he had passed in such indescribable anguish of heart.

Not a soul was there to greet the heir of this princely house, or bid him welcome home. The servant, who, after his repeated knockings, appeared to open the door, gazed at his young lord with a countenance wherein terror and sympathy were strangely mingled.

" Are the princesses at home? " asked Eugene.

" No, your highness, they took refuge with their grandmother, the Princess de Carignan."

" Took refuge! " echoed Eugene, staring at the man in dumb dismay.

" Yes, my lord, they were afraid of the people, who have gathered here by thousands every day since the countess left. This is the third summons that has been made for her highness, and at each one the people of Paris have flocked to the hôtel with such jeers and curses, that the poor young ladies were too terrified to remain."

"They acted prudently," replied Eugene, recovering his self-possession. "But where is the steward? And where are the other servants?"

"Latour accompanied the princesses, your highness, and has not returned. The remainder of the household have taken service elsewhere."

" What! my valet, Dupont?"

" He thought your highness had left Paris for a long time, and looked for another master."

"Then how comes it that you are here, Conrad?"

" I, my lord? Oh, that is quite another thing. I belong to a family that have served the Princes de Carignan for three generations. I myself have served them from my boyhood, and if your highness does not discharge me, I shall not do so, were the hôtel to be attacked by every churl in Paris."

As Conrad spoke these words, Eugene turned and looked affectionately at his faithful servant. "Thank you, Conrad, for your loyalty and courage; I can never grow unmindful of such devotion. From this day you become my valet, and if you never quit my service until I discharge you, we will roam the world together as long as we both live!"

Tears of gratitude glistened in Conrad's honest eyes. "Then to the day of my death I remain with my dear lord," replied he, kneeling, and devoutly kissing the hand which Eugene had extended. "And I swear to your highness love and fealty, while God gives me life wherewith to serve you."

"I believe you, Conrad," replied Eugene, kindly, "and I thank you for the solitary welcome you have given me on my return to this unhappy house. Your loving words have drowned the clang of yonder trumpets without.—And now let us part for a while: I feel inclined to sleep."

The prince turned into a hall that led to his apartments, and entered his bed-chamber. He had scarcely taken a seat, and leaned his weary head upon his hand, before the trumpet pealed another blast, and the beadle again summoned the Countess de Soissons to answer before the tribunal of justice for her crimes!

The people shouted as though they would have rent the canopy of heaven; and Eugene, overcome by such excess of degradation, burst into a flood of tears.

# BOOK II.

## CHAPTER I.

### MARIANNA MANCINI.

For a day Eugene remained in his room, while Conrad kept vigil in the antechamber without. The unhappy prince had longed so intensely for the privilege of grieving without witnesses, that he felt as if no boon on earth was comparable to solitude. Not only his affections, but his honor, had been mortally wounded: what medicine could ever restore it to life?

And through the long night Conrad had listened to his slow, measured step, as forth and back he had paced his room in the vain hope of wooing sleep to

> "steep his senses in forgetfulness."

Finally day dawned, and Conrad then ventured to knock and inquire whether his lord would not breakfast. The door was not opened, but Eugene thanked him, and refused. The poor fellow then threw himself down on the carpet and slept for several hours. He was awakened by his father, the only servant besides himself that had remained to share the humiliations of the family, and who now came as bearer of a letter from the Duke de Bouillon, which was to be delivered to the prince without delay.

Delighted to have a pretext that might gain him admittance to the presence of his master, Conrad sprang up and knocked. The door was just sufficiently opened to give passage to the latter, was hastily closed, and the bolt was heard to slide. But two hours later Eugene appeared, and greeted his two faithful attendants with a gracious inclination of the head.

"Now, Conrad," said he, "I am ready to oblige you by taking my breakfast. Immediately after, I shall go out, and, as

I go on an affair of importance, order the state-coach, two footmen, and two outriders. What makes you look so blank? Does it seem singular that I ride in state through the streets of Paris?"

"God forbid, your highness!" exclaimed Conrad, "but—"

"But—"

"But we have no footmen—no outriders, your highness."

"True," said Eugene, "I had forgotten. But I suppose that the rascals may be found and re-engaged. Go after them, Conrad, and—stay—where is the steward?"

"He went with the princesses to the Hôtel Carignan, your highness."

"True—true—you told me so yesterday. Go to him, Conrad; bid him return and resume his duties, for the Hôtel de Soissons must be open, and I must have a household befitting my rank. Be as diligent as you can, my good fellow, and let the carriage be before the entrance in one hour."

"But first, your highness must breakfast."

"And how can I breakfast if all the servants have deserted? Or has the cook been more loyal than his companions?"

"No, your highness; he went with the rest, but he is in the neighborhood, and will be glad to return."

"I am rejoiced to hear it. Fetch him, then, and let him provide breakfast. But, above all things, find me footmen and outriders. I would rather go out hungry than without attendants."

"Your highness shall have all you desire," returned Conrad, with alacrity ; and he kept his word. An hour later, the state-coach stood before the portal of the palace, and the outriders and footmen were each man in his proper place. The prince had partaken of an excellent breakfast, and was advancing to his carriage.

When he saw old Philip, the coachman, he gave him a look of grateful recognition, and inquired whether he had recovered from the fatigues of their uncomfortable journey.

"I endured no fatigue, your highness," was the old man's reply. "I was on duty, and had no right to be fatigued."

"Bravely answered," returned Eugene. "I see that you,

at least, are unchanged, and I may rely upon your loyalty. And the rest of you," continued he, looking searchingly around at the captured deserters, "you have returned, I perceive."

"Your highness," replied one of them, eagerly, "I had the honor of accompanying you to Flanders."

"Oh, I do not allude to you, Louis. I know that I can count upon you."

"We, too, are loyal, your highness," replied the others, "and are ready to serve you from the bottom of our hearts. The hôtel was empty, and we had supposed ourselves to be without places. But we are only too happy to return."

"Very well, I shall have occasion to test your fidelity this very day. Conrad, get in the coach with me. I desire to converse with you in private."

Conrad dared not disobey, although to sit opposite to his master in a carriage, seemed to him the acme of presumption. He took his seat with a look of most comic embarrassment, and stared at the prince as though he suspected him of being suddenly attacked with insanity.

"To the Hôtel Bouillon!" was the order given, and the coach went thundering through the gates toward the Quai Malaquais. It was stared at, precisely as before, when Eugene and his mother had attempted to join the royal cortége at the Pré aux Clercs. The people sneered at the equipage and escutcheon of a countess, who, for three days in succession, had been publicly summoned before the tribunal of justice; but of the young prince, who was the solitary occupant of the coach, they took no notice whatever. He was not guilty, therefore he provoked no curiosity; he was not handsome, therefore he attracted no attention. As lonely and heart sick his head reclined amid the velvet cushions, whose silken threads seemed each a pricking thorn to give him pain, Eugene's resolves of vengeance deepened into vows, and he swore an oath of enmity against his mother's enemies, which long years after he redeemed.

Conrad was perplexed, and ashamed of the honor conferred upon him ; but when after a long pause Eugene began to speak in low, earnest tones, the embarrassed expression of the valet's countenance gave place to a look of interest, and finally he ventured a smile.

"Indeed, your highness," replied he, "it shall be accomplished to your entire satisfaction, and old Philip will be delighted to be of the party. He is already burning to revenge himself upon the Louvois family for taking precedence of carriages that have the right to go before them; and he has more than once approached the coachmen of the nobles thus insulted, for their cowardice in suffering it."

"Well—you will both have an opportunity of exhibiting your powers to-day in the Pré aux Clercs, and I only hope that the court will be there to witness it."

"Philip will not fail, your highness, nor I either."

"Thank you. There may be an affray, and perchance a blow or two in store for you; but I will reward you handsomely. But what is this? The carriage has stopped, and we have not yet reached the Hôtel de Bouillon."

Conrad sprang out to ascertain the cause of their detention.

"Your highness," said he, returning, "we cannot proceed any farther. The street is blocked up with carriages that extend all the way to the entrance of the hôtel. Some of them are equipages of the princes of the blood."

"Then I must go on foot, and you and Philip can profit by your leisure to discuss the manner of your attack. But by all means let it be in the Pré aux Clercs, where all these carriages will be filled with occupants."

So saying, Eugene alighted, and hurried to the hôtel. Its large portals were flung wide open, and streams of elegantly-dressed courtiers and ladies were entering the palace. In such a crowd, where the men were in glittering uniforms, and the women, resplendent with diamonds, wore long trains of velvet or satin, borne by gayly-attired pages, nobody had eyes for a little abbé, clad in russet gown, with buttons of brass ; so that Eugene was more than once forced back before he made his way to the state apartments. Step by step he advanced, until at last he reached the centre of the room, where the family were assembled to receive their distinguished guests.

The duke, in the uniform of a general, stood in the midst

7

of the group. At his side was the duchess, the celebrated
Marianna Mancini, the rival of Olympia de Soissons, not only
in the affections of Cardinal Mazarin, but also in those of the
king. When the heart of Louis had wearied of the elder
sister, its capricious longings fluttered toward the younger, for
whose sake he deserted La Vallière, and to whom, for a season,
he swore every imaginable vow of love and eternal constancy.

Marianna had gained wisdom from the experience of her
sister. Quite convinced of the transitory nature of a king's
favor, she formed the bold design of capturing the hand as
well as the heart of his majesty of France. Perhaps Louis
fathomed her intentions, and resolved to punish her ambition,
for he suddenly manifested a willingness to marry the Spanish
princess, whom Mazarin had vainly endeavored to force upon
him as a wife ; and Marianna, like her sister, sought consolation in marriage with another, and became Duchess de
Bouillon.*

Years had gone by, but Marianna was still a court beauty,
and she still possessed a certain influence over the heart of her
royal admirer. She alone refused to do homage to De Montespan, and she alone ventured to interrupt the pious conversations of the king with his new favorite De Maintenon.
When the obsequious courtiers were vying with each other as
to who should minister most successfully to the vanity of the
monarch that considered himself as the state ; when princes
and princesses listened breathlessly to the oracles that fell
from his inspired lips, the Duchess de Bouillon was not afraid
to break their reverential silence, by conversing at her ease
in a tone of voice quite as audible as that of his majesty.

She stood in the midst of that brilliant throng, accepting
their homage as though she had been born to a throne, and
dispensing gracious words with the proud consciousness that
every smile of hers was received as a condescension. And
yet, in that very hour, the Duchess de Bouillon was under impeachment for crime. Her summons had been sent " in the
name of the king ; " but everybody knew that it was the work
of Louvois, and everybody knew equally well that the com-

* This is a mistake. The one whom Louis loved was Marie Mancini,
Princess of Colonna.—TRANS.

pliment paid to the duchess that day, was especially gratifying
to the king, who himself had suggested it as a means of vex-
ing his arrogant minister.

That morning, his majesty had held a grand levee, which
was punctually attended by all who had the inestimable privilege of appearing there. Louis received his courtiers with
that gay and smiling affability which was the result of his
temperament, and had procured for him from one of his ador-
ers the surname of Phœbus. But, all of a sudden, a cloud
was seen to obscure the face of the sun, and the dismayed
sycophants were in a flutter to know what was passing behind
it. The firmament had darkened at the approach of the Duke
de Vendôme and the Cardinal d'Albret.

"My lords," said the king, curtly, "I am surprised to see
you here. Methinks the proper place for you both this morning would be at the side of your relative, the Duchess de Bouillon."

"Sire," replied the young duke, "I came to see if the sun
had risen. I behold it now; and since the day has dawned
on which my aunt is to appear before her accusers, I hasten
whither duty calls, to take my place among her adherents."

"And you, cardinal?" said Louis, to the handsome brother
of the Duke de Bouillon.

"I, my sovereign, am accustomed to say my orisons before
turning my thoughts to the affairs of this world. Now that I
have worshipped at the shrine of my earthly divinity, I am
ready to admit the claims of my noble sister-in-law."

The king received all this adulation as a matter of course,
and, without vouchsafing any reply, turned to his confessor.
Père la Chaise looked displeased; he had no relish for court
nonsense at any time; but what availed his exhortations to
humility, if his royal penitent was to have his ears poisoned
with such abominable stuff as this!

Louis guessed somewhat the nature of his confessor's vexation, for he blushed, and spoke in a mild, conciliatory tone:

"Pardon me, father, if this morning I have ventured to
permit the things of this world to take precedence of things
spiritual. But a king should be ready at all hours to do justice
unto all men; and as this is the day fixed for the trial of a

noble lady of France, for crimes of which I hope and believe that she will be found *innocent*, I have deemed it proper to show my impartiality by upholding those who have the courage to avow themselves champions or defenders of the Duchess de Bouillon. Come, father, let us hasten to the chapel."

He rose from his couch, and, with head bowed down, traversed his apartments, until he reached a side-door which communicated with the rooms of the Marquise de Maintenon. On either side were long rows of obsequious courtiers, imitating as far as they could the devotional demeanor of the king; and, following the latter, came Père la Chaise—the only man in all the crowd who walked with head erect. His large, dark eyes wandered from one courtier to another, and their glances were as significant as words. They asserted his supremacy over king and court; they proclaimed him the ambassador of the King of kings.

At the threshold Louis turned, and, letting fall the mantle of his humility, addressed his courtiers.

" My lords," said he, imperiously, " we dispense with your attendance in chapel this morning, and you are all free to go whithersoever you deem best."

With a slight bend of the head, he passed through the portière and disappeared. The courtiers had comprehended the motive of their dismissal : it was a command from his majesty to repair to the Hôtel de Bouillon. They hastened to avail themselves of the royal permission, and one and all were shortly after in presence of the duchess, offering sympathy, countenance, and homage.

---

## CHAPTER II.

### THE TRIAL.

WHILE she received her numerous visitors with cordiality, Marianna Mancini tempered her affability with just enough of stateliness to make it appear that their presence there was a matter of course, and not of significance. She had arrayed herself with great splendor for this extraordinary occasion of mingled humiliation and triumph. She wore a dress of rose-colored satin, whose folds, as she moved, changed from the rich hues of the carnation to the delicate tinge of the peach-blossom. Her neck and arms were resplendent with diamonds, and her whole person seemed invested with more than its usual majesty and grace.

She saw Eugene, who was making vain endeavors to approach her. With mock-heroic air, she raised her white arm, and motioned away those who were immediately around her person.

"Let me request the mourners," said she, "to give place to the priest, who advances to hear the last confession of the criminal. Poor little abbé! How will he manage to sustain the weight of the iniquities I shall pour into his ears?"

A merry laugh followed this sally, and all eyes were turned upon Eugene, who, blushing like a maiden, kissed his aunt's outstretched hand, but was too much embarrassed to reply to her greeting.

"Prince," said a tall personage coming forward, "will you allow me to act as your substitute? My shoulders are broad, and will gladly bear the burden of all the sins that have ever been committed by your charming penitent."

"I dare say, Monsieur la Fontaine," replied Eugene, recovering himself, "and they will incommode you no longer than the time it will occupy you to weave them into a tissue of pleasant fables."

"Thanks, gallant abbé!" cried Marianna, pleased. "You look upon my crimes, then, as fiction?"

"Yes, dearest aunt," said Eugene, resolutely; "they are, I heartily believe, as fictitious as those attributed to my dear and honored mother."

As he spoke, Eugene's large eyes looked courageously around, to read the countenances of the men that were listening. Whatever they might think of the mother, the chivalry of her son was indisputable, and no one was disposed to wound his filial piety by so much as a supercilious glance.

The silence that ensued was broken by La Fontaine. "Did

you know," said he, "that Madame de Coulanges had been summoned to trial yesterday?"

"Yes," replied the duchess, "but I have not heard the result. Can you tell it to us, my dear La Fontaine?"

"I can. The judges paid her a compliment which I am sure she has not received from anybody else, since the days of her childhood."

"What was it?"

"They gave in a verdict of——innocent."

A hearty laugh followed this satire of La Fontaine's, and the duchess indulged in so much mirth thereat, that her eyes sparkled like the brilliants on her person, and her cheeks flushed until they rivalled the deepest hues of her pink dress.

"Ah!" cried La Fontaine, bending the knee before her, "La mère des amours, et la reine des grâces, c'est Bouillon, et Venus lui cède ses emplois." *

"Go on, go on, fabulist!" cried Marianna, laughing.

La Fontaine continued:

> "Ah, que Marianne a de beautés, de graces, et de charmes;
> Elle sait enchanter et l'esprit et les yeux;
> Mortels, aimez-la tous! mais ce n'est qu'à des dieux,
> Qu'est reservé l'honneur de lui rendre les armes!" †

"Do you, then, desert and go over to my enemies?" asked the duchess, reproachfully.

"I!" exclaimed La Fontaine, rising to his feet. "Who could so calumniate me?"

"Why, did not you say 'elle sait enchanter'? And is not that the very crime of which I am accused?"

La Fontaine was about to make some witty reply to this sportive reproach, when the Duke de Bouillon announced to the duchess that she must prepare herself to appear before her judges.

"I am ready," was the response, and Marianna passed her arm within that of her husband.

"My friends," said she, addressing all present, "I invite

* La Fontaine's "Letters to the Duchess de Bouillon," p. 49.
† See Works of La Fontaine.

you to accompany me on my excursion to the Arsenal. Come, Eugene, give me your other arm. It is fit that the criminal should go before her accusers between her confessor and her victim."

"Madame," returned Eugene, frowning, "I am no confessor. A confessor should be an anointed of the Lord, which I am not."

"Not anointed!" exclaimed the duchess. "I have an excellent receipt for unguent given me by La Voisin; and, if you promise that I shall not be made to mount the scaffold for my obliging act, I will anoint you myself, whenever you like."

"Mount the scaffold!" cried La Fontaine. "For such as you, duchess, we erect altars, not scaffolds. True, you have bewitched our hearts, but we forgive you, and hope to witness, not your disgrace, but your triumph."

And, indeed, the exit of the Duchess de Bouillon had the appearance of an ovation. The streets were lined with people, who greeted her with acclamations, as though they were longing to indemnify one sister for the obloquy they had heaped upon the other. The aristocracy, too, felt impelled to avenge the insult offered to their order by the impeachment of the Countess de Soissons. In the cortége of the Duchess de Bouillon were all the flower of the French nobility; and such as had not joined her train were at their windows, waving their handkerchiefs and kissing their hands to Marianna, who, in a state-carriage drawn by eight horses, returned their greetings with as much unconcern as if she had been on her way to her own coronation.

Next to her equipage was that of the Countess de Soissons; and bitter were the feelings with which Eugene gazed upon the multitude, who, but a few days before, had driven his mother into exile. He was absorbed in his own sorrowful musings, when the carriage stopped, and it became his duty to alight and hand out his aunt.

She received him with unruffled smiles, and they entered the corridors of the Arsenal. Behind them came a gay concourse of nobles, drawn out in one long glittering line, which, like a gilded serpent, glided through the darksome windings of that gloomy palace of justice.

The usher that was stationed at the entrance of the council-chamber was transfixed with amazement at the sight. He rubbed his eyes, and wondered whether he had fallen asleep and was dreaming of the fairy tales that years ago had delighted his childhood. And when he saw the duchess smile, and heard her ringing laugh, he was so bewitched with its music that, instead of challenging her train of followers, he suffered them every one to pass into the chamber without a protest.

At the upper end of the hall of council, seated around a table covered with a heavy black cloth, were the judges in their funeral gowns and long wigs, which floated like ominous clouds around their sinister faces. Close by, at a smaller table similarly draped, sat the six lateral judges of the criminal court, and the scribes, who were prepared to take notes of all that was said during the trial.

When Marianna came in, with her cortége stretching out behind her like the tail of a comet, the pens dropped from their hands and the solemn judges themselves looked around in undisguised astonishment.

The duchess, affecting complete unconsciousness of the sensation she was creating, came in smiling, graceful, and self-possessed. While the frowning faces of the judiciary scanned the gay host of intruders, who were desecrating the solemnity of the council-chamber with their levity, the duchess advanced until she stood directly in front of their table, and there she smiled again and inclined her head.

The judges were still more astounded—so much so, that they were at a loss how to express their indignation. It took the form of exceeding respect, and their great black wigs were all simultaneously bent down in acknowledgment of the lady's greeting.

The only one among them who allowed expression to his displeasure was the presiding judge, Laraynie, who, with a view to remind the criminal that her blandishments were out of place, stiffened himself considerably.

"The Duchess de Bouillon has been summoned before this august tribunal to answer for the crimes with which she has been charged," said he, severely. "Are you the accused ?"

"My dear president," returned Marianna, flippantly, "how can you be so absurd? If you have forgotten *me*, I perfectly remember *you*. You were formerly amanuensis to my uncle, Cardinal Mazarin, who promoted you to the office, because of your dexterity in mending pens. Yes, I am the Duchess de Bouillon, and nobody has a better right to know it than you, who wrote out my marriage contract, and were handsomely paid for your trouble."

"Our business is not with the past, but the present," replied Laraynie, haughtily. "The question is not whether you are or are not the niece of the deceased Cardinal Mazarin, but whether you are or are not guilty of the crimes for which you have been summoned hither?—"

"Which summons, you perceive, I have obeyed," interrupted the duchess. "But I pray you to understand that I acknowledge no right of yours to cite a duchess before your tribunal, sir. If I come at your call, it is because it has been made in the name of the king, my sovereign and yours!"*

"You have obeyed the citation, because it was your duty to obey it," returned Laraynie. "But I see here a multitude who have come neither by indictment nor invitation. It is natural enough that the Duke de Bouillon should accompany his spouse on an occasion of such solemn import to her safety; but who are all these people that have obtruded themselves upon our presence?"

"Did you not comply with my husband's request that I might be accompanied to the Arsenal by a few of my friends?"

"Yes—his petition was granted."

"Well, then," replied Marianna, turning toward the brilliant assembly that had grouped themselves around the room in a circle, "these are a few of my most particular friends. You see on my right the Dukes de Vendôme and d'Albret, and the Prince of Savoy; on my left, the Prince de Chatillon, and others with whose names and persons you were familiar in the days of your secretaryship under Cardinal Mazarin."

* The duchess's own words.—See Renée, "The Nieces of Mazarin," p. 395.

"To our business!" cried Laraynie, angrily. "We will begin the examination."

"First let me have a seat," replied the duchess, looking around, as though she had expected an accommodation of the kind. There was not even a stool to be seen in the council-chamber. But at the table of the judges stood a vacant arm-chair, the property of some absent member ; and in the twinkling of an eye Eugene had perceived and rolled it forward. He placed it respectfully behind his aunt, and resumed his position on her left.

This bold act was received by the judiciary with a frown, by the other spectators with a murmur of applause, and by the beautiful daughter of the house of Mancini with one of those bewitching smiles which have been celebrated in the sonnets of Benserade, Corneille, Molière, St. Evremont, and La Fontaine.

She sank into the luxurious depths of the arm-chair, and her "particular friends" drew nearer, and stationed themselves around it.

"Now, gentlemen," said she, in the tone of a queen about to hold a levee, "now I am ready. What is it that you are curious to know as regards my manner of life ? "

"First, your name, title, rank, position, age, and—"

"Oh, gentlemen ! " cried Marianna, interrupting the president in his nomenclature, " is it possible that you can be so uncivil as to ask a lady her age ? I warn you, if you persist in your indiscreet curiosity, that you will compel me to resort to falsehood, for I positively will not tell you how old I am. As regards the rest of your questions, you are all acquainted with my name, title, rank, and position. Let us come to the point."

"So be it," replied the president, who was gradually changing his tone, and assuming a demeanor less haughty toward the duchess. " You are accused of an attempt on the life of the Duke de Bouillon."

"Who are my accusers ? " asked Marianna.

"You shall hear," replied Laraynie, trying to resume his official severity. " Are you acquainted with La Voisin ? "

"Yes, I know her," said Marianna, without any embarrassment whatever.

"Why did you desire to rid yourself of your husband?" was the second interrogatory.

"To rid myself of my husband!" cried the duchess, with a merry laugh. Then turning to the duke, "Ask him whether *he* believes that I ever meditated harm toward him."

"No!" exclaimed the duke. "No! She has ever been to me a true and loving wife, and we have lived too happily together for her ever to have harbored ill-will toward me. Of evil deeds, my honored wife is incapable!"

"You hear him, judges; you hear him!" exclaimed Marianna, her face beaming with exultation. "What more have you to ask of me now?"

"Why were you in the habit of visiting La Voisin?"

"Because she was shrewd and entertaining, and because she promised me an interview with spirits."

"Did you not show her a purse of gold, and promised it to her in case these spirits made their appearance?"

"No!" said Marianna, emphatically, "and that for the best of reasons. I never was possessed of any but an empty purse —a melancholy truth, to which my husband here can bear witness. That I may have promised gold to La Voisin is just possible, but that she ever saw any in my possession is impossible."

Marianna glanced at her friends, who returned her look with approving nods and smiles.

"You deny, then," continued the judge, not exactly knowing what to say next, "you deny that you ever made an attempt to poison your husband?"

"I do, and I am sure that La Voisin never originated a calumny so base. But I confess that I was dying to see the spirits. Unhappily, although La Voisin called them, they never came."

"You confess, then, that you *did* instigate La Voisin to cite spirits?"

"I certainly did, but it was all to no purpose. The spirits were excessively disobliging, and refused to appear."

Another murmur of approbation was heard among the friends of the duchess, some of whom applauded audibly.

"You are accused not only of raising spirits, but of citing the devil," pursued Laraynie, in tones of marked reproof. "Have you ever seen the devil?"

"Oh, yes! He is before me now. He is old, ugly, and wears the disguise of a presiding judge."

This time the applause rang through the council-chamber. It was accompanied by shouts of laughter, and no more attempt was made by the amused spectators to preserve the least semblance of decorum. The president, pale with rage, rose from his seat, and darting fiery glances at the irreverent crowd, whom the duchess had named as her particular friends, he cried out :

"The trial is over, and I hereby dismiss the court."

"What—already ? " said the duchess, rising languidly from her seat. "Have you nothing more to say to me, my dear President Laraynie?"

Her "dear president" vouchsafed not a word in reply; he motioned to his compeers to rise, and they all betook themselves to their hall of conference. When the door had closed behind them, Marianna addressed her friends.

"My lords," said she, "I must apologize for the exceeding dulness of the scene you have just witnessed. But who would ever have imagined that such wise men could ask such a tissue of silly questions? I had hoped to experience a sensation by having a distant glimpse of the headsman's axe, and lo! I am cheated into an exhibition of President Laraynie's long ears!" *

"Come, Marianna," said her husband, passing her arm within his. "It is time for our drive to the Prè aux Clercs; the king and court are doubtless there already."

"And I shall annoy Madame de Maintenon by entertaining his majesty with an account of the absurd comedy that has just been performed in the council-chamber of the Arsenal."

So saying, Marianna led the way, and, followed by her adherents, left the tribunal of justice, and drove off in triumph to the Pré aux Clercs.

---

* The duchess's own words. This account of the trial is historical.—See Rénée, " The Nieces of Mazarin," p. 395.

# CHAPTER III.

## A SKIRMISH.

INSTEAD of accompanying his aunt from the council-chamber to her carriage, Eugene fell back, and joined two young men, who were walking arm in arm just behind the duke and duchess.

They greeted him with marked cordiality, and congratulated him upon the presence of mind with which he had captured the judicial arm-chair, and pressed it into the service of his aunt.

" My cousins of Conti are pleased to jest," replied Eugene. "Such praise befits not him who removes a chair, but him who unsettles a throne."

" Have you any such ambitious designs? " asked Prince Louis de Conti, sportively.

" Why not? " returned his brother, Prince de la Roche. " It would not be the first time that such a feat had been performed by an ecclesiastic. Cardinal Mazarin removed the throne of France from the Louvre to his bedchamber, and what Giulio Mazarini once accomplished, may perchance be repeated by his kinsman, the abbé."

" Who tells you that I am a priest? " said Eugene.

" First—your garb; second, the will of your family; and third, the command of the king."

" You forget the will of the individual most interested. But of that anon—I have a request to make of you both."

" It is granted in advance," exclaimed the brothers with one voice.

" Thank you, gracious kinsmen. Will you, then, accept a seat in my carriage, and drive with me to the Pré aux Clercs ? "

" With pleasure. Is that all? "

" Almost all," replied Eugene, laughing. " What else remains to be done, must be performed by myself."

" Ah! There is something then in the wind? May we ask what it is? "

"You will witness it, and that is all I require of you. But here is my carriage. Be so kind as to step in."

Conrad stood at the portière, and, while the young Princes de Conti were .entering the coach, he drew from under his cloak a slender parcel, which he presented to his lord.

Eugene received it with a smiling acknowledgment. "Is all prepared?" he asked.

"Yes, your highness. Old Philip is in ecstasies, and the other lackeys are like a pack of hounds on the eve of a fox-chase."

"They shall hear the fanfare presently," returned Eugene, following his cousins, and taking his seat opposite to them.

"What is that?" asked the Prince de Conti pointing to the long, thin roll of white paper which Eugene held in his hand.

"I suspect that it is a crucifix, and Eugene is going to en-trap us into a confession," returned De la Roche, who loved to banter his cousin.

"We shall see," replied Eugene, opening the paper, and exhibiting its contents.

"A whip!" exclaimed De Conti.

"Yes, a stout, hunting-whip!" echoed De la Roche. "Are we to go on a fox-hunt, dear little abbé?"

"We are, dear, tall prince, and we shall shortly set out."

"Things begin to look serious," observed De Conti, with a searching glance at the pale, resolute face of his young rela-tive. "You do not really intend to chase your fox in presence of the king?"

"Yes, I do. I intend to prove to his majesty that I am not altogether unskilled in worldly craft, and, as regards my fox, I intend that all Paris shall witness his punishment."

"You mean that you have been insulted, and are resolved to disgrace the man that has insulted you?" asked De la Roche.

"You have guessed," said Eugene, deliberately, as he un-wound the long lash of the whip, and tried its strength.

"But Eugene," said De Conti, earnestly, "remember that such degradation is only to be wiped out with blood, and that your cloth will not protect you from the consequences of so unpriestly an act."

Eugene's eyes flashed fire. "Hear me," said he. "If my

miserable garb could prevent me from vindicating my honor as a man, I would rend it into fragments, and cast it away as the livery of a coward. A man's dress is not a symbol of his soul; and so help me, God! this brown cassock shall some day be transformed into the panoply of a soldier. But see! The carriage stops, and we are about to taste the joys ineffable of seeing the King of France drive by."

Two outriders in the royal livery were now seen to gallop down the *allée*, as a signal for all vehicles whatsoever to drive aside until the royal equipages had passed by.

In this manner Louis was accustomed to exhibit himself to the admiring gaze of his subjects, and to bestow upon them the unspeakable privilege of a stray beam from the "son of France." Never had he shed his rays upon a more numerous or more magnificent concourse than the one assembled in the Pré aux Clercs; for the Duchess de Bouillon had just entered with her cortége, and the allée was lined on either side with splendid equipages and their outriders—pages, equestrians, and foot-passengers.

His majesty was gazing around, bowing affably to the crowd, when he perceived the Duchess de Bouillon, and caught her eye. Louis waved his hand, and smiled; and this royal congratulation filled up the measure of Marianna's content. At that moment his face was illumined by an expression of genuine feeling, perhaps a reflection of the light of a love which had shone upon it in the golden morning of his youth.

The king's coach had gone by; following came the equipages of the royal family, and the princes of the blood: then—

"My dear cousin," said Eugene, "be on your guard, and if the glasses of our carriage-windows begin to splinter, close your eyes, for—"

At this moment the coach darted suddenly forward, and took its place behind the royal cortége. There was a tremendous concussion of wheels and shafts, a crash of broken panes, a stamping and struggling of horses; and, above all this din, the frantic oaths of the coachmen that had suffered from the collision.

"What do you mean, you ill-mannered churl! What do

you mean by driving in front of my horses?" cried a loud and angry voice.

"What do you mean yourself, clown!" was the furious reply of the Jehu addressed. "My horses were merely advancing to take the position which belongs to them of right, and how dare you stop the way!"

"Do you hear?" asked Eugene, with composure. "The drama begins, and I and my whip will shortly appear on the stage. It was my trusty old Philip who began the fray, and— it has already gone from words to blows, for it seems to me I heard something like a box on the ear—"

"You did indeed!" exclaimed the Prince de Conti; "but what on earth can it mean?"

"You will find out presently," replied Eugene. "But wait a moment, I must listen for my cue—"

"Your cue will have to be a thunder-clap, if you are to hear it above all this racket," said De la Roche, slightly lowering one of the windows, and looking cautiously out. "Devil take me! but it is a veritable pitched battle. These knights of the hammer-cloth are dexterous in the use of their fists, and every one of your servants, Eugene, are engaged in the fight!"

The prince's last words were lost to his listeners, for a tremendous crash drowned his voice, and something fell heavily to the ground.

"This is my cue," cried Eugene. "Come—I am about to make my début." And before he had time to rise from his seat, the portière flew open, and Conrad hastily took down the carriage-steps.

"Is his coach overturned?" asked the prince.

"Yes, your highness, and he is inside. His footmen tried to get him out; but with the help of some of our friends we fell upon them, and so gave them plenty of occupation, until your highness was ready to appear."

"Well—let him out, Conrad. I am ready for him! Come," added he, turning to his cousins. "Come, and let us survey the field."

In truth, the Pré aux Clercs, at this moment, resembled a battle-ground. Although the royal cortége had long gone by, the promenaders were too curious to follow; they all remained to see the end of this turbulent opening. Every one had witnessed old Philip's manœuvre, and everybody knew that the point of attack was the carriage of Barbesieur Louvois, for the footmen of the Countess de Soissons had been seen to seize the horses' reins, and force them out of the way.

And now the coaches were all emptied of their occupants, who crowded around the spot which Eugene, with his two cousins, was seen approaching. They began to comprehend that this was no uproar among lackeys, but a serious misunderstanding between their masters. The Dukes de Bouillon, de Larochejaquelein, and de Luynes, the Princes de Belmont and Condé, and many other nobles of distinction, came forward and followed Prince Eugene to the field of action. The coachman and lackeys of Barbesieur Louvois were trying to force the footmen of the Countess de Soissons to right their overturned coach. Old Philip cried out that the Princes de Carignan took precedence of all manner of Louvois of whatever generation, and that he would not stir. His companions had applauded his spirit, and both parties having found allies among the other retainers of the nobles on the ground, the battle had become general, and the number of fists engaged was formidable.

The tumult was at its height when the clear, commanding tones of Eugene's voice were heard.

" Churl and villain ! " exclaimed he, " are you at last in my power ? "

In a moment every eye was turned upon the speaker, who, just as Barbesieur was emerging from the coach-window, seized and held him prisoner. The belligerent lackeys were so astounded, that on both sides the upraised fists were suspended, while old Philip, taking advantage of the momentary lull, cried out in stentorian tones:

" Armistice for the servants ! Their lords are here to decide the difficulty ! "

Down went the fists, and all parties gazed in breathless silence at the pale, young David, who confronted his Goliath with as firm reliance on the justice of his cause as did the shepherd-warrior of ancient Israel. Eugene was pale and collected, but his nostrils were distended, and his eyes were aflame

8

Barbesieur's great chest heaved with fury, as he felt himself in the grasp of his puny antagonist, and turning met the glance of the son of Olympia de Soissons.

For a few moments no word was spoken. The two enemies exchanged glances; while princes, dukes, counts, and their followers, looked on with breathless interest and expectation.

Barbesieur now made one supreme effort to escape, but all in vain. With one thrust of his muscular arm, Eugene forced him back into the coach, his nether limbs within, his great trunk without the window.

"Miserable coward," said the prince, "who to escape from the dangers of a fray among lackeys, have taken refuge in the carriage of a nobleman! Monsieur Louvois will assuredly have you punished for your presumption; but before he hears of your insolence toward him, you shall be chastised for the injuries you have inflicted upon me."

"Dare harm one hair of my head," muttered Barbesieur, between his teeth, "and your life shall be the forfeit. My father will avenge me."

"So be it; but first, let me avenge my mother," cried Eugene, raising his whip on high.

"Eugene, Eugene," exclaimed the Duke de Bouillon, trying to reach his kinsman in time to prevent the descending stroke, "you are mistaken. This gentleman is no intruder in the coach of the Louvois; it is Barbesieur de Louvois himself!"

"It is you that are in error," returned Eugene, holding fast to his prisoner, who looked like some great monster in a trap. "This is not Monsieur Louvois; this is a leader of mobs, an instigator of riots. He is the knave that incited the people of Paris to malign my mother, and to stone her palace.—Here! Philip! Conrad! Men of my household, do you not recognize this man?"

"Ay, ay!" was the prompt response, "he is the very man that led on the rabble."

"He is. The captain of the guard allowed him to escape, but before he left I promised him a horsewhipping, and I never break my word.—You are a villain, for you have defamed a noble lady.—Take this! You are a liar, for you have accused her of crime.—Take this! You are a poltroon, for while you were inciting others to violent deeds, you hid your face, and denied your name.—Take this!"

At each opprobrious epithet, the lash fell heavily upon the shoulders of Barbesieur, and every blow was answered by a cry of mingled pain and rage. The multitude looked on in silence, almost in terror; for who could calculate the consequence of such an indignity offered to such a family!

"And now," said Eugene, throwing the whip as far as he could send it, "now you are free! My mother's defamer has been lashed like a hound, and her son's heart is relieved of its load."

So saying, he turned his back, and joined the group, among whom his cousins were awaiting his return.

"Which of you, my lords," said he, "cried out that I was mistaken in the identity of yonder knave?"

"It was I, Eugene," replied the Duke de Bouillon.

"But you see your error now, do you not, uncle? since not only I, but my whole household proclaim him to be the ringleader of that riot, which forced my mother into exile."

"And yet he is assuredly Barbesieur Louvois," laughed the Prince de Conti.

"Well—we shall see," was the reply. "He has disengaged himself from his coach-window, and if he is a gentleman he will know what he has to do."

And Eugene returned to the place where Barbesieur was now standing, calling out to his friends to follow him.

"Are you quite sure, my lords, that this individual is Monsieur Louvois?"

They answered with one voice, "We are!" while all eyes were fixed upon the tall figure which, now relaxed and bent with shame, resembled the stricken frame of an old man; while his eyes were sedulously cast down, that they might not meet the glance of the meanest man who had witnessed his disgrace.

"I am still incredulous," said the prince. "But I reaffirm that this is the brutal ringleader of the mob that attacked my mother's home, and since I am ready to swear upon my honor that it is he, have not I performed my duty by chastising him ?"

"Yes, Prince of Savoy, if you are sure that it is he," was the unanimous reply.

"I can prove that it is he. When, in spite of my warning, he uplifted his right arm to urge the rabble to a new attack on the palace, I aimed a bullet at his elbow, and it reached its mark. Now, if this man be Monsieur Louvois, and not the knave I hold him to be, let him raise his right arm, and so brand me as a liar."

As he heard this challenge, Barbesieur trembled, and his face paled to a deadly whiteness. His right hand was buried in the breast of his coat, and well he knew that every eye was riveted upon that spot. He made one superlative effort to straighten his arm, but no sooner had he moved it than he uttered a stifled cry of pain, and the wounded limb fell helpless to his side.

"My lords," said Eugene, inclining his head, "you see that I am no calumniator. This is the churl who maligned my mother's name."

"And I am Barbesieur Louvois!" cried the *churl*, gnashing his teeth with rage. "I am Barbesieur Louvois, and you shall learn it to your sorrow, for my father will avenge the insult you have offered to his son."

"Your father!" echoed the Prince de Conti. "But yourself! What will *you* do to mend your bruised honor ? A nobleman knows but one means of repairing that."

Barbesieur blushed, and then grew very pale. "You see that I am incapable of resorting to this means," replied he, in much confusion.

"Then you will not challenge the Prince de Carignan ?"

"It is not in my power to send a challenge. My right arm is useless to me."

"Sir," said De Conti, haughtily, "there are blots on a man's honor, which can only be wiped out with blood ; and when the right hand is powerless, a nobleman learns to use his left."

"I claim the privilege of waiting until I shall have regained the use of my right hand," returned Barbesieur with a sinister glance at De Conti. "I cannot be sure of my aim with an unpractised left hand ; and when I meet this miserable mani-kin, I wish to kill him.—Eugene of Savoy, you have offered me a deadly affront ; and as soon as my wound is healed, you shall hear from me."

"Don't give yourself the trouble of sending me a challenge," returned Eugene coolly, "for I will not accept it."

"Not accept it ! " echoed Barbesieur, unable to suppress the gleam of satisfaction that *would* shoot across his countenance. "Your valor then, which is equal to put opprobrium upon a defenceless man, will not bear you out to face him in a duel ? What say these gentlemen here present, to such behavior on the part of a prince of the ducal house of Savoy ?"

"When I shall have spoken a few more words to you, they can decide. You have so outraged my mother, the Countess de Soissons, that the falsehood with which you have befouled her honored name can never be recalled! Not content with forcing her, by your persecutions, into exile, your emissaries preceded her to every point whereat she sought shelter, and incited the populace to refuse her the merest necessaries of life ! For wrongs such as these, nothing could repay me but the infliction of a degradation both public and complete. I have disgraced you ; the marks of my lash are upon your back, and think you that I shall bestow upon you one drop of my blood wherewith to heal your stripes ? No ! I fight with no man whom I have chastised as I would a serf ; but if you have a friend that will represent you, here is my gauntlet : let him raise it.—Gentlemen, which of you will be the proxy that shall cleanse the sullied honor of Barbesieur Louvois with his blood ?"

"Not I," said the two Princes de Conti, simultaneously.

"Nor I," "Nor I, "Nor I ! " echoed the others.

"Nor I," cried the Duke de la Roche Guyon, stepping for-ward so as to be conspicuous and generally heard. "I am the son-in-law of Monsieur Louvois, and unhappily this man is the brother of my dear and honored wife. But he is no kins-man of mine ; and if I raise this glove, it is to return it to the Prince of Savoy, for among us all he has not an enemy. He stands in the midst of his friends, and they uphold and will sustain him, let the consequences of this day be what they may."

With a deep inclination of the head, the duke returned his glove to Eugene, who, greatly affected, could scarcely murmur his thanks.

With glaring eyes and scowl of hatred, Barbesieur had listened, while his brother-in-law's repudiation of the tie that bound them to one another had deepened and widened the gashes of his disgrace. With muttered words of revenge, he mounted the horse of one of his grooms, and galloped swiftly out of sight of the detested Pré aux Clercs.

" Gentlemen," resumed the Duke de la Roche Guyon, " I am about to seek an audience with Monsieur Louvois, to relate to him the events that have just transpired ; and to exact of him as a man of honor that he will seek no revenge for the affront offered to his son. Which of you, then, will accompany me as witness ? "

" All, all," cried the cavaliers, with enthusiasm. " We sustain the Prince of Savoy, and if Minister Louvois injures a hair of his head, he shall be answerable for the deed to every nobleman in France."

" And you, dear Eugene, whither are you going ? " asked De Conti, putting his hand on his cousin's shoulder, and contemplating him with looks of affectionate admiration.

" I ? " said Eugene, softly. " I shall return home to the hall of my ancestors, there to hang this gauntlet below my mother's portrait. Would that kneeling I could lay it at her feet ! "

He was about to turn away, when De Conti remarked, " I wonder whether Barbesieur will have the assurance to attend the court-ball to-night ? "

" We shall see," replied Eugene, with a smile.

" We ! Why, you surely will not present yourself before the king, until you find out in what way his majesty intends to view your attack upon the favorite son of his favorite minister ? "

" I shall go to the ball to ascertain the sentiments of his majesty. You know how I abhor society, and how awkward I am in the presence of the beau monde ; but not to attend this ball would be an act of cowardice. I must overcome my disinclination to such assemblies, and learn my fate to-night."

## CHAPTER IV.

### LOUVOIS' DAUGHTER.

"ARE you really in earnest, *ma toute belle* ?" said Elizabeth-Charlotte of Orleans. "Are you serious when you relinquish your golden hours of untrammelled existence, to become my maid of honor ? "

The young girl, who was seated on a tabouret close by, lifted her great black eyes, and for a moment contemplated the large, good-natured features of the duchess ; then, smiling as if in satisfaction at the survey, she replied :

"Certainly, if your highness accords me your gracious permission to attach myself to your person."

"And does your father approve ? Has the powerful minister of his majesty no objection to have his daughter enter my service ? "

"I told him that if he refused I would take the veil," returned the young girl, with quiet decision.

The duchess leaned forward, and contemplated her with interest. "Take the veil!" exclaimed she. "What should such a pretty creature do in a convent ? You are not—you cannot be in earnest. Let those transform themselves into nuns who have sins upon their consciences, or sorrow within their hearts : you can have had no greater loss to mourn than the flight of a canary, or the death of a greyhound."

The maiden's eyes glistened with tears. "Your highness, I have lost a mother."

"Oh, how unfeeling of me to have forgotten it ! " exclaimed the duchess. "But, in good sooth, this heartless court-life corrupts us all ; we are so unaccustomed to genuine feeling, that we forget its existence on earth. Dear child, forgive me ; I am thoughtless, but not cruel. Give me your hand and let us be friends."

The girl pressed a fervent kiss upon the hand that was out-stretched to meet hers. "Oh!" cried she, feelingly, "my grandmother was right when she told me that you were the best and noblest lady that ever graced the court of France."

"Did your grandmother say that, love?" asked the duchess. "I remember her as one of the most delightful persons I ever met. She was a spirited, intelligent, and pure-minded woman; and many are the pleasant hours we have passed together. I was really grieved when the Marquise de Bonaletta disappeared from court, and went into retirement."

"She left the court for love of my mother, whose marriage was a most unhappy one; and who, although she had much strength of mind, had not enough to cope with the malignity of the enemies that were of her own household."

"Your father was twice married, was he not?"

"Yes, your highness; and, by his first marriage, had a son and a daughter. With the latter, the present Duchess de la Roche Guyon, my mother lived in perfect harmony, but her step-son, Barbesieur, hated her, and finally caused her to quit her husband's house, and take refuge with her mother, the Marchioness de Bonaletta."

"I remember," returned the duchess. "Both ladies left Paris at the same time, and nothing was ever heard of them afterward. They retired to the country, did they not?"

"Yes, your highness. My grandmother had inherited a handsome estate from her husband; and thither they took refuge from the persecution of Barbesieur—my brother, and yet the enemy who, before I had attained my sixth year, had driven me to a state of orphanage, by alienating from me my father's affection. Well—I scarcely missed his protection, for dear mother's love filled up the measure of my heart's cravings for sympathy, and her care supplied every requirement of my mind. But my happiness was short-lived as a dream; my mother's health had been sorely shattered by her many trials, and I was not yet fourteen when it pleased God to take her to Himself."

The duchess listened with tender sympathy. "I see, dear child," said she, "that you are a loving daughter, for two years have gone by since your misfortune, and yet your eyes are dim with tears."

"Ah, your highness, time has increased, not lessened, my sorrow. The longer the separation, the harder it is to bear, and I know not from what source consolation is to flow. For a time, however, I had the sympathy of my grandmother to soothe my grief. We visited her grave, we spoke of her together. For love of her who was so eager for my improvement, I applied myself heartily to my studies. Hoping, believing that she looked down from heaven upon her child, I strove to prove my love by cultivating to their utmost the powers which God had bestowed upon me."

"And no doubt you have become such a learned little lady, that you will be quite formidable to such triflers as we," said the duchess, with a smile.

"No, indeed, dear lady. I am slightly proficient in music and painting—these are my only accomplishments."

"Ah, you love music? How it delights me to know this, for I, too, am passionately fond of it! When I was a maiden in Heidelberg, I used to roam about the woods, singing in concert with the larks and nightingales ; and my deceased father, the Elector Palatine, finally declared that I was no German princess, but a metamorphosed lark, whom he constantly expected to see spread out her wings, and depart for Bird-land. Sometimes, when my reveries are mournful, I could almost wish myself a lark, hovering over the fields that lie at the foot of our dear castle at Heidelberg, or nestling among its towers, wherein I have passed so many joyous hours. Now, if I were a Hindoo, I would look forward with pleasure to the day of my transmigration ; for as a lark, I would fly to my dear native home, and sing the old air of which my father was so fond :

' The sky that bends over the Neckar is fair,
   And its waters are kissed by the soft summer air '—"

As the duchess attempted to hum this familiar strain, her voice grew faint, and her eyes filled with tears. She dashed them hastily away.

"My dear child," said she, after a pause, "I know not why

your sweet companionship should have brought to mind visions of home and happiness that are long since buried in the grave of the past. I seldom indulge in retrospection, Laura ; it unfits me for endurance of the heartless life we lead in Paris. But sometimes, when we are alone, you will let me live over these sunny hours, and—"

Again her voice faltered, and she buried her face in her hands, while Laura looked on with sympathetic tears.

There was a silence of several moments, at the end of which the duchess gave a short sigh, and looked up. Her face was quite composed, and, smiling affectionately upon her young companion, she resumed their conversation.

"And now, dear child, go on with what you were relating to me. My little episode of weakness is ended, and I listen to your artless narration with genuine pleasure. You lived with your grandmother on her estate, and you were tenderly attached to each other ? "

"Yes, indeed, I loved my grandmother to adoration. My lonely heart had concentrated all its love upon her who loved *me* not only for my own, but for my mother's sake; and we were beginning to find happiness in our mutual affection, when death again snatched from me my last stay, my only friend. My dear grandmother would have gone joyfully, but for the sake of the poor child she was leaving behind. When she felt her end approaching, she sent for my father, who obeyed the summons at once. He arrived in time to receive her last injunctions. They had a long private interview, at the end of which I was called in, and formally delivered over to the guardianship of my father, who promised me his love and protection. But my grandmother added these words, which I have carefully treasured in my memory :

"'If you should ever need advice or countenance from a woman, go to the Duchess of Orleans. She is a virtuous and benevolent princess, and will befriend you. With her for a protectress, you will be as safe from harm as in the sheltering arms of your own mother.'"

The duchess extended her hand. "I thank your grandmother, dear child, for her confidence in my benevolence: if I have never deserved it before, I will earn it now; and be assured that in me you will find a loving protectress. But why should you need any influence of mine ? Your father is the most powerful subject at court, and the whole world will be at your feet. Young, handsome, and rich, every nobleman in France will be your suitor."

"But I can never marry without love," replied Laura, enthusiastically. "Love alone could reconcile me to the exigencies of married life, and *I* must choose the man that is to rule over my destiny. Let me be frank, and confess to your highness why I desire to place myself under your protection. My father is trying to force me into a marriage with the Marquis de Strozzi, the Venetian envoy. He is young, handsome, rich, and may perhaps become Doge of Venice. He is all this—but what are his recommendations to me? I do not love him! More than that, he is the friend of Barbesieur, and therefore I dislike him. The match, too, is of Barbesieur's making : he it was that influenced my father to consent to it. I have already declared that, sooner than marry the marquis, I will take the veil. But my vocation is not for the cloister, and therefore I implore your highness's protection. I beseech you, give me the place made vacant by the marriage of your maid of honor, and save me from a life of misery. In my father's house I am solitary and unloved: but even loneliness of heart I could endure, if I were permitted to endure it in peace ! But a compulsory marriage is worse to me than death! Save me, dear lady, and I will be the humblest and most obedient of your subjects !"

The duchess smilingly shook her head. "I am afraid," said she, "that the daughter of Louvois will not be permitted to accept the office you ask, my child. Do you know that my maids of honor are paid for their services ?"

"Yes, your highness ; but I crave permission to serve you without salary. I am rich, and, as regards fortune, independent of my father. On condition that I assume her name, my grandmother left me the whole of her vast estates. I have wealth, then, more than enough to gratify my wildest caprices; —but no mother—no friend. Oh, take pity on me, and befriend a poor orphan !"

"A poor orphan !" laughed the duchess. " A rich heiress,

you mean—a marchioness of fifteen years, who is possessed of sufficient character to dispute the mandates of the powerful minister of the King of France ! But your resolute bearing pleases me. You are not the puppet of circumstances, nor is your heart hardened by ambition. It follows whither youthful enthusiasm beckons, and scorns the rein of worldly restraint. I like your spirit, Laura, and I love *you.* You may count upon me, therefore, as far as it lies in my power to serve you. But understand that I am not a favorite at court. The king honors me occasionally with his notice ; but the two great magnates, the 'powers that be,' De Montespan, and her rival De Maintenon, both dislike me. They have reason to do so, for I do not love them. I am at heart an honest German woman, and have no taste for gilded corruption. I honor and love my brother-in-law, whom God preserve and bless ! But if the Lord would take these two marchionesses to Himself, or send them below, to regions more congenial to their tastes than heaven, I assure you that I would not die of grief at their loss. De Montespan is merely a dissolute woman, who abandoned her husband and children to become the mistress of a king. But that De Maintenon ! Her hypocrisy is enough to turn one's stomach. She not only supplants her benefactress in the affections of her lover, but dresses up her sins in the garments of a virtue, and affects piety ! She teaches his majesty to sin and pray, and pray and sin, hoping to compound with Heaven for adultery, by sanctimony: perchance expecting, as brokerage for her king's regenerated soul, an earthly reward in the shape of a mantle edged with ermine ! When I think of that Iscariot in petticoats, I am ready to burst with indignation !"

The duchess grew so excited that she had to wipe her face with her embroidered handkerchief. After cooling herself for a few moments, she resumed :

"Yes ! and to think that the princes of the blood and the queen herself, are obsequious to these two lemans of a king ! May I freeze in the cold blast of royal disfavor, before I degrade my rank and womanhood by such servility ! And mark this well, little marchioness, if you take service with me. Who goes to court with me, pays no homage to the mistresses of the king.—But why do you kneel, my child? What means this humility?"

"How otherwise could I give expression to my reverence, my admiration, my love?" exclaimed Laura, her countenance beaming with beautiful enthusiasm. "And how otherwise could I thank my God that so noble, so brave, so incomparable a woman is my protectress! Let me kiss this honored hand that has never been contaminated by the touch of corruption!"

"You are a sweet enthusiast," said Elizabeth-Charlotte, bending down and kissing Laura's brow. "In your eye there beams a light that reveals to me a kindred spirit. Beautiful, young, hopeful though you be (and I am none of these), there is a congeniality of soul between us that leaps over all disparity, and proclaims us to be friends. Come, dear child, to my heart."

With a cry of joy, Laura threw herself into the arms of the duchess, who held her fast, and kissed her o'er and o'er.

"Sweet child," exclaimed she, "your spontaneous love is like a flower springing from the hideous gaps of a grave. I greet it as a gift of God, and it shall reanimate within me happiness and hope. You are but fifteen, Laura, and I am a mature woman of thirty; but my heart is as strong to love as yours; for many years it has pined under clouds of neglect, but the sun of your sympathy has shone upon it, and, warmed by its kindly beams, it will revive and bloom."

"And oh how I shall love you in return!" cried the happy girl. "As a mother whom I trust and revere—as a sister to whom I may confide my girlish secrets—as a guardian angel whose blessing I shall implore. But in the world, and when I bear your train, I will forget that I am aught but the lowliest handmaiden of her royal highness, Elizabeth-Charlotte, Duchess of Orleans."

"And when we are alone and without witnesses, we will speak of those we have loved; and I, alas! of some whom I have not loved; for, Laura, *my* marriage was a compulsory one. The altar on which I pledged my faith was one of sacrifice; and I, the bride, the lamb that was immolated for my country's good. Ah! many tears have I shed since I was Duchess of Orleans ; but your tender hand shall wipe them away, and in your sweet society I shall grow joyous again. We will sing the ditties of my fatherland ; and, provided no one is within hearing, I will teach you our German dances, which, because of the corruption that dwells within their hearts. these French people stigmatize as voluptuous. With such a birdling as you to carol around me, the lark that once dwelt in my heart, will find its voice again, and awake to sing a hymn of thankfulness to God, who has enriched me with the blessing of your love."

"And I, dear lady, will try to deserve the happiness He has vouchsafed to me, by loving all His creatures—even Barbesieur himself."

"Ah! Barbesieur!" echoed the duchess, thoughtfully. "I doubt whether he or your father will consent to give you to me, Laura. Nobody knows better than Monsieur Louvois, how unimportant a personage at court is the Duchess of Orleans."

"He must give me to you or to the cloister," exclaimed Laura, quickly. "And not only relinquish me, which would be no great loss, but my worldly good s, which are an important item in his estimation. I am ab olute mistress of my fortune, and nobody but the Chevalier Lankey has a word to say in the matter. As for him—dear old fellow! he is the tenderest guardian that ever pretended to have authority over an heiress ; and he loves me so sincerely, that if I were to come and say that, to save me from misfortune, he must stab me to the heart, he would do my bidding, and forthwith die of grief for the act."

"I can almost believe you, absurd child ; for you are an enchantress, and therefore irresistible."

"Yes—I am irresistible," replied Laura, throwing her arms around the duchess's neck, "and I vow and declare that it is my good pleasure to live forever in the sunshine of your highness's presence ; so I consider myself as accepted and installed."

"With all my heart, if your family be propitious ! And with a view to reconciling them, I must create an office for you of more dignity than that of a mere maid of honor. You shall be lady of the bedchamber ; and I will announce your appointment with all due formality to the king, the court, and my own household. You retain the title of maid of honor, because that gives you the right to remain constantly attached to my person; but, except on days of extraordinary ceremony, you shall be dispensed with the duty of following me as train-bearer."

"I shall be dispensed with no such thing!" cried Laura, playfully ; "I do not intend to delegate my duties to anybody; above all, a duty which to me will be a privilege."

"We shall see, you self-willed girl," was the reply, "for I shall forbid you in presence of my household, and, for decorum's sake, you will be forced to obey. Neither shall you inhabit the third story of the main palace, in common with the other maids of honor ; you shall occupy the pretty pavilion in the garden, and have an independent household as befits your rank and fortune. Now, as regards your table. You know that, by the laws of French etiquette, nobody is permitted to sit at table with the princes or princesses of the blood ; and my lord, the duke, is so stringent in his observance of these laws, that he would faint were he to witness a breach of them. When his royal highness, then, dines with me, you will be served in the pavilion, and are at liberty to invite whom you please to share your repasts ; but happily, I am honored with his presence but twice a week ; and on all other days, we shall breakfast and dine together. The duke spends two days out hunting, and the other three with his mistress, Madame de Rulhières. You look surprised to hear me mention this so coolly. Time was, when I felt humiliated to know that mine were not the only children who kissed my husband, and called him father. The caresses he bestowed upon his mistress, I never grudged. She robbed me of nothing when she accepted them. As the wife of a man whom I did not love, I could aspire to none of the joys of wedded life ; I have contented myself with fulfilling its duties, and so conducting myself that I need never be ashamed to look my dear children in the face. But enough of this : let us return to you. You will keep your own carriage, use your own liveries, and be sole mistress of your house and home, into which the Duchess

of Orleans shall not enter unannounced. You will find it
larger than it looks to be. It contains a parlor, sitting and
dining rooms, a library opening on the garden ; a bed-room,
three chambers for servants, and two anterooms, large enough
to accommodate your worshippers while they await admission
to your presence. This is all I have to offer my lady of the
bedchamber. May I hope that it is agreeable ? "

"Agreeable ! " exclaimed Laura, affectionately. "It will
place me on a pinnacle of happiness. And now that I have
heard of all the favors, the privileges, and the honors that are
to accrue to me from my residence in the pavilion, will my
gracious mistress deign to instruct me as to the duties I am to
perform, in return for her bounty ? "

"Wilful creature, have I not already told you ? On occasions of state you are to be one of my trainbearers ; and when
his majesty comes to visit me, you station yourself at my side.
Then you are to drive out with me daily, and as you alone
will be with me in the carriage, we can have many a pleasant
chat, while the maids of honor come behind. And we must
be discreet, or they may inform monsieur of the preference
which madame has for her lady of the bedchamber ; and then,
Heaven knows what the duke might do to us ! Let us hope
that he would not poison you, as he did my poor little Italian
greyhound, a few weeks ago. He hated the dog because I
loved it, and because it was a present to me from my dear
brother Carl. So be wary and prudent, Laura : these maids
of honor have sharp ears, and it is not safe to talk when they
are waiting in the anteroom, for some are in the pay of De
Maintenon, and you will not have been here many days before
one of them is sold to your father. I can scarcely believe in
the reality of my new acquisition, for much as I regret to tell
you so, Laura, you cannot enter my service until Monsieur
Louvois comes hither to make the request himself. Otherwise,
monsieur and Madame de Maintenon would spread it about,
that I had forcibly abducted the Marchioness de Bonaletta, and
torn her from her loving father's arms."

"My father will be here to-day to comply with all the
formalities that must precede my installation," replied
Laura. "And, if your highness will admit him, I shall

have the happiness of being in your train at the court-ball to-night."

"Of course I must admit him, since you will it, my queen of hearts. By what magic is it that you have won my love so completely to-day, Laura?"

"By the magic touch of my own heart that loves you so well, dear lady—so well, that I ask no other boon of Heaven but that of deserving and returning your affection."

"Until some lover comes between us, and robs me of my treasure," said the duchess, with a smile. "Have you seen the brigand yet? Do you know him?"

Laura laughed. "He is a myth—I have no faith in his existence," said she.

"He exists, nevertheless, my child, and will make his appearance before long; for you are destined to have many suitors."

"But none that approaches my ideal of manhood. Where shall I find this hero of my dreams?—not at the court of France, your highness. But—should he ever come out of the clouds, brave, noble, wise, as I have pictured him, then, oh then! I should follow the destiny of woman; leaving all other beings, even my gracious mistress herself, to cleave unto him, and merge my soul in his! Were I to love, the world itself would recede from view, leaving all space filled with the image of the man I loved! Better he should never come down from the moon—for, if he comes, I am lost!"

---

## CHAPTER V.

### THE COURT-BALL.

THE magnificent halls of the Louvre were open to receive the guests of his majesty Louis XIV. Balls were "few and far between" at the French court, and the festivities of the evening were significant, as betokening triumph to De Montespan and mortification to De Maintenon.

For Louis, like Mohammed's coffin, was suspended between

9

the heaven of De Maintenon's pious attractions, and the earth of De Montespan's carnal fascinations. Neither the exhortations of Père la Chaise, nor the affectionate zeal of De Maintenon, had as yet overthrown the power of De Montespan ; and more than once, when wearied with the solemn dulness of the former, had he sought refuge from drowsiness in the rollicking companionship of the latter, who, if she *was* a sinner, wore the livery of her master, and sinned honestly and above-board. De Montespan always profited by these little intervals of tenderness, to obtain some signal favor from Louis, which had the effect of perplexing the court, and rendering it a doubtful matter to those who would fain have gone over to the victorious party, which of his two mistresses was truly sovereign of the king's unstable affections.

Such a concession was this ball, wrung from Louis, first by coaxing, and finally by pouting and tears. De Montespan was elated, for it was a double triumph; it was given at her request, and was to take place on her birthday.

And De Maintenon, of course, was proportionally crestfallen. But, after shedding just as many tears as she deemed appropriate, Scarron's widow was clever enough to understand that wisdom lay in acquiescence. She wiped her eyes, and suffered herself to be caressed into a good-humor ; was more amiable, more sprightly, more fascinating than ever, with not a trace of disappointment in her looks, save that which lay in the unusual paleness of her face.

Louis was so touched by her magnanimity, that he absolutely begged her pardon ; and she was so overcome by the condescension of his majesty, that she asked permission to be present at the ball.

"He was only too happy!" that is to say, he did his best to conceal his consternation at the unheard-of proposition. Sainte Maintenon at a ball! What would she do in so unrighteous a place ? And worse—still worse : what would his other charmer say when she heard of it ? What outbreak of indignation might not be expected, when De Montespan was told that her ex-governess was to be present at a ball given in her own honor ? Between his saint and his sinner, Louis was sorely perplexed. But he might have spared himself all uneasiness. De Montespan was not in the least ruffled at the tidings ; she rather enjoyed the idea of setting off her own splendor against the shabbiness of her rival.

But the court was in a state of anxious excitement on the subject. Everybody was dying of curiosity to see the meeting of the rivals, and the effect that was to be produced by their presence on the poor deserted queen.

To which of the favorites will the king throw his handkerchief ? With which of the two will he converse most ? Will he feel at ease as he treads the minuet under the eyes of the devotee ? Or will he venture to recognize *her* in presence of the courtesan ?

Such were the questions that were continually asked, but never answered by the elegant crowd which thronged the halls of the palace that evening. The rencontre of Eugene and Barbesieur was for the moment forgotten. It was not likely that either one of the disputants would venture to appear at court, until the king had decided to which party belonged the blame of the affray; but, as regarded the brush that was imminent between the king's mistresses, that was a matter which concerned everybody, and everybody was in a flutter to know the result.

The lord chamberlain having announced that the court was about to make its entrance, the throng pressed forward to the Gallery of Apollo. Four immense chandeliers lit up the gorgeous frescoes on the ceiling, and poured a flood of radiance upon the line of stately courtiers and elegant women who were the guests of the king's leman that night. The ladies coquetted with their large fans, whispered with the cavaliers close by, and dispensed smiles and bewitching glances upon those who were too far for speech until the master of ceremonies flung open the doors, and announced " his majesty the king."

There was at once profound silence ; and in a moment every head was bent, and every eye sought the floor. The men bowed low, the women courtesied lower, and nothing was to be seen but a chaos of jewels, velvet, brocade, and llama, surmounted by feathered, flowered, or ringleted heads, and long, flowing wigs.

The one personage who had the right to hold himself erect in the presence of this reverential multitude—the king—appeared, followed by a glittering train of marshals, chamberlains, officers of the royal household, and pages. His majesty traversed the gallery and approached the throne, which, for this festive occasion, was hung with white velvet, studded with golden lilies. Not far from the royal arm-chair stood a lady, whose sad eyes looked wearily upon the pageant, and whose pallid lips had long since forgotten how to smile. It was Maria Theresa, the queen. She had made her entry before the king, but it had scarcely been remarked. She was a deserted wife, and, being without influence at court, had no favors to bestow. She was, therefore, altogether *sans conséquence.*

Nevertheless, she was the queen-consort, and Louis, extending his hand, and inclining his royal head, assisted her to mount the throne. As soon as the kingly pair were seated, his majesty's voice was heard—

" My guests are welcome."

As if by enchantment, feathers, flowers, curls, and wigs, all rose up out of chaos, and every eye was turned upon the handsome person of the sovereign.

While all this had been going on Eugene of Savoy stood erect, nor once cast down his flashing eyes before the lightning of the royal presence. He had entered quietly, had retired to the recess of a window, and, as the crowd had simultaneously become a heap of garments, he had curled his lip in contempt. Suddenly his eye grew soft, and his mouth relaxed into a smile. Not far from the throne he had seen one head— one beautiful head, and had met the glance of a pair of glorious eyes, which were quietly surveying the scene, and, as Eugene thought, enjoying it with an expression of suppressed amusement.

Who could she be, that, while every other person there had lost his individuality and merged it into one monstrous concretion of obsequiousness, had preserved her balance, and stood undazzled by the rays of the sun of France ? As young as she was lovely, whence came the mingled self-possession and unconsciousness which made her an observer instead of a worshipper ? Eugene had never seen this beautiful creature before ; but from the depths of her starry eyes there streamed a light that went straight to his heart, making strange revelation of some half-forgotten bliss which, in an anterior state of being, might once have been his own.

But how came she hither ? What had her fair, unclouded brow, her innocent face, her maidenly bearing in common with the vain, voluptuous, and corrupt women around, who were so lost to shame as not only to do homage to the king's mistresses, but to envy them the infamous distinction of his preference ?

Their eyes met ; and in her glance of astonishment Eugene fancied that he saw mirrored his own surprise at her extraordinary defiance of courtly servility. She too seemed to ask, " How is it that you stand so proudly erect, when every other head is bent in reverence before our sovereign ? Who are you, that presume to—"

But the king and his suite passed between them, and the beautiful face was lost to sight. In its place, Eugene beheld the haughty monarch who had caused such bitter tears to flow from the eyes of his dear, exiled mother ; and the thought of that beloved mother led to remembrance of his father's death, and to the tyranny which would make of his father's son an unwilling priest.

Meanwhile the king had seated himself on the throne, and the princes and princesses of the blood had approached to pay their homage. Not a sound was heard in that splendid gallery, save the subdued tones of Louis, who was conversing with the Duke of Orleans ; for, until the former rose to make his *grande tournée*, etiquette required of his adoring subjects to be dumb.

A slight hum, however, began to be heard at the lower end of the hall, and all eyes were turned toward the door which opened to admit the woman whom the king delighted to honor.

Her tall figure was set off to great advantage by a dress of purple velvet, embroidered with silver. From her voluptuous shoulders drooped a mantle, edged with richest ermine ; and her swelling bust was scarcely concealed by a drapery of sil-

vered gauze. On her bosom she wore a fleur de lis composed
of emeralds, pearls, and diamonds, and on her magnificent
brow glittered a diadem of brilliants worthy the acceptance of
an empress.

So haughty was her bearing, and so obsequious were the
salutations which greeted her entrance, that but for the pale
statue that occupied a seat next the king, Madame de Montespan might have been mistaken for the queen.

Eugene's eyes had sought and found the young girl, whose
sweet vision had been displaced by the king, but who now, in
full view of the company, stood immediately behind the chair
of the Duchess of Orleans. Would *she* bow her incomparable
head before that exalted harlot? Would *she* outrage her
maidenhood by acknowledgment of De Montespan's title to
consideration? No! Thank God, she was true to her pure,
womanly instincts. Her face crimsoned, her delicate brows
were slightly drawn together, and her head was unconsciously
raised, as if in protest against the public scandal of this woman's intrusion.

When Eugene saw this, his heart leaped with joy, and he
yearned to throw himself at her feet.

"In Heaven's name who can she be, that fairy-queen, who
fears not mortal man?" thought he. "Who—"

But suddenly his eye shot fire, and the expression of his
face was transformed. He had met the glance of Barbesieur
Louvois, who, under shelter of De Montespan's favor with
Louis, and the protection of his father, had intruded himself
into the company of the proudest nobles in France. How was
it possible that the master of ceremonies had allowed to a disgraced man the privilege of appearing before the king and
queen?

"Gracious Heaven!" thought Eugene, "are honor and
shame but empty words? Is this, indeed, the Marchioness de
Montespan, whose entrance is greeted like that of a sovereign,
while the Countess de Soissons wanders in foreign lands, a
fugitive from justice? Justice?—No! A fugitive from oppression, and the kinsman who should have protected her—her
oppressor! And is yonder swaggering cavalier the caitiff
whose back is smarting with the lash of my hunting-whip?

And those smiling courtiers there, who take him by the hand —are they the noblemen that upheld me in the act? By Heaven, they greet him as though, like me, his veins were blue with the blood of kings! But no!—not all! The Princes of Conti have refused to recognize him: they bow to the minister of war, but pass without a word to his son. For that act I shall hold them ' in my heart of hearts,' nor forget their manliness while I live to honor worth and scorn servility!' "

Eugene looked affectionately at his cousins, until his eyes filled with tears of gratitude; but they were unconscious of the comfort they had ministered to his wounded heart, for they were not aware of his presence in the ballroom.

The king had not yet ended his long conversation with the Duke of Orleans. The company stood still and expectant, and the Marchioness de Montespan began to exhibit signs of impatience. She had hoped that the ceremonial of compliments to and from the royal family would have been over before her entrance; and now that she had been there fully ten minutes, the king seemed as unconscious of her presence as ever.

But—thank Heaven! the colloquy was at an end; the king has risen, and has signified to the queen that the princesses of the blood may rise also. He descends from his throne, and De Montespan's heart is wild with joy. The moment of her triumph approaches; Louis is about to lead her out for the minuet, and so proclaim her queen of the festival. She smiles ineffably; in her eagerness, she almost rises from her tabouret to meet him, but—what can he intend to do? Has he not seen her?—He turns away, and—now he extends his hand to another!

De Montespan was perfectly overwhelmed, and, all etiquette forgetting, she actually rose from her seat and took a step forward, that she might see who was the person that had been so singularly honored by the king.

Who was it? Why, nobody but Sainte Maintenon, who, without pomp or parade, had entered the room, and had taken her tabouret with as much simplicity as she would have seated herself in church.

Her toilet, as well as her demeanor, presented a singular contrast with that of her sparkling rival. Her dress was of dark velvet, buttoned up to the throat. Her wealth of beautiful black hair was fastened up with a barbe of gossamer lace, and the only ornament she wore around her neck was a delicate gold chain, to which was attached a miniature of Louis set in superb brilliants.

And upon this wearisome, insipid, old-fashioned puppet, the King of France had bestowed his attentions. De Montespan would have given her diadem to have been permitted to vent her humiliation in tears ; but pride restrained her, while she looked on, and saw how the king led De Maintenon to the queen, an honor hitherto reserved for princesses of the blood. And with what feline humility she knelt and pressed her majesty's hands to her unholy lips ! Oh ! De Montespan could have taken her life when she saw this!

And she—she for whom this gay assemblage were called together, sat unnoticed and alone; her expected triumph, defeat —every hope she had cherished of love reciprocated, and ambition gratified, transformed into despair, by one little act. The king had given his hand to her rival!

---

## CHAPTER VI.

### THE LADY OF THE BEDCHAMBER.

THE conversation between the king, the queen, and Madame de Maintenon, was long and interesting. When she saw the former rise and incline his head, De Montespan's heart fluttered with expectation; but his majesty stopped before the Duchess of Orleans, and there he lingered so long that everybody wondered what could be the attraction there. Presently Elizabeth-Charlotte turned to the young girl who stood beside her, and presented her to the king. How beautiful she was ! How enchanting her smile, how charming her blushes !

She was evidently a stranger, and De Montespan set her down as an enemy, for she had not complied with the customs of the court, by which every lady introduced there was expected to leave a card for the mistress of the king. An enemy, then, she must be—perchance, a rival! But who was she?

"Yes, who is she?" thought Prince Eugene, as, transfixed with admiration, he gazed upon her lovely face.. "I *must* know," exclaimed he aloud, while he pressed forward to make the inquiry.

There was no one near to whom he could address himself, for he now for the first time remarked that he stood quite alone. He began to be aware that his friends were shy and kept aloof; but Eugene had come to this ball to prove that the son of the Countess de Soissons was not to be browbeaten by king or courtier; and he went on and on until he stood so near to Louis that he could look him full in the eye.

The *grand monarque* knit his brows, and presumed that the Prince of Savoy would understand the hint, and withdraw; but Eugene paid no attention to the Olympic frown, or affected not to see it.

Louis, who had been chatting with the little Duke of Maine, strode angrily forward and addressed the prince:

"I judge from your eyes, little abbé, that you have come hither to ask some favor of us to-night?"

"Then my eyes belie my purpose, your majesty," replied Eugene, quietly. "I have no favor to ask of any one."

"I understand," said the king, slightly raising his shoulders. "You have come for an answer to your last petition?"

"Pardon me, sire, I have presented no petition whatever to your majesty."

"If you have not, your mother, the Countess de Soissons, has presented one for you. She begged me, not long ago, to appoint you prebendary of a cathedral: as she has thought proper to abscond from my dominions, I have had no opportunity of answering her request. When you write to her, you can tell her that it is refused. Prince Eugene of Savoy leads too worldly a life to deserve promotion in the church. Bullies are not apt to distinguish themselves as ecclesiastics."

"Sire, I thank your majesty; for the sentiments to which you have just given utterance release me from further obligation to enter upon a career for which I have neither inclination nor calling."

To these bold words Louis vouchsafed no answer. He annihilated the offender with a glance, and passed on. Then turning to the Duke of Orleans, he said in a voice that was intended to be generally heard, " I cannot imagine what that little abbé of Savoy wants here to-night. His face brings me bad luck." *

This was enough to damn Eugene forever at the French court. It was the *anathema maranatha* of his sovereign, and cast him out from association with all loyal subjects. Nobody in those vast halls would have been seen in his vicinity; his best friends would not now have ventured one look of sympathy or kindness toward a nobleman so publicly and pointedly insulted by royalty. He was henceforth a proscribed man.

The Princes de Conti were sorely grieved, but they dared, no more than their compeers, risk the displeasure of the king by upholding their outraged kinsman. The eldest one, however, managed to whisper a word or two in passing.

" Dear Eugene," said he, " do be reasonable, and put an end to this abominable scene by going home. Our hearts are all with you, but we dare not affront the king by the smallest demonstration on your behalf; he is looking out for it, and would revenge himself effectually. We went this morning with De la Roche Guyon to Louvois, and obtained his sacred promise to ignore your difficulty with his son, and allow it to be settled between yourselves. But he has evidently not kept his word; for the affair has been misrepresented to the king, and the insult you have received is a proof of it. Go away for a few weeks until it blows over, and all will have been forgotten."

" I have no desire to have my affairs forgotten; I trust that they may be remembered," replied Eugene. " But hark! the music.—We are to have the, ineffable privilege of seeing the king dance. Doubtless you have already secured a partner, and I will not detain you."

The music was heard, and his majesty went through the usual form of requesting the queen to open the ball. She answered, as she was expected to do, that her health was too

* The king's own words.—See " Memoirs of the Duke de St. Simon," vol, x

feeble for her to enjoy dancing, and she hoped his majesty would excuse her, and find another partner.

This was always a time of suspense and excitement at court-balls; for the lady who was then selected by the king was, *de facto*, the queen of the festival. The minuet's enticing measure was calling upon its votaries to commence; but, until the king had made his choice, no one could stir.

Madame de Montespan's heart began to throb anew with hope. This time she was sure of being chosen, for De Maintenon did not dance ; and, after all, what signified a few words with the queen, compared with the glory of being led out to the dance by the king ?

Her eyes sparkled with animation, her mouth began to ripple with happy smiles, and oh! triumph and joy! the king was seen coming in that direction.

But again he stopped to speak with the Duchess of Orleans. What could he want of her ? If De Montespan had been within hearing, she need not have wondered, for Louis merely requested the pleasure of her hand for the dance.

Elizabeth-Charlotte looked up in astonishment.

"I hope I have not fallen into disfavor," said Louis, answering the look. "You are not about to refuse me ?"

"Oh, sire," replied his sister-in-law, laughing, "I am merely overcome with your condescension. But your majesty knows," continued she, seriously, "that since my father's death I have never danced. I was enjoying myself in this very hall while he was expiring at home ; and from that unhappy day I have never desired to dance again. Moreover, I am a miserable partner, and you would be ashamed of me."

"How ashamed ?" asked Louis, amused at his sister-in-law's artlessness.

"I mean, sire, that strive as I will, I am always behind-hand in a dance. I am like the snail, who, being invited to a wedding, arrived there a year after, and found herself the first guest that had come to the christening. As she entered the garden she fell into a ha-ha, whereupon she said, 'More haste, worse speed.'"

Louis laughed heartily. "Then I am refused, dear sister," said he, "and I must acquiesce in your decision. But I must have satisfaction for the affront. You must find a substitute."

"A substitute!" exclaimed the duchess, reddening with anger, as she fancied she saw the king's eyes wander to the tabouret whereon De Montespan still waited and smiled. "Surely, your majesty would not ask of me—"

"Why not?" cried Louis, enjoying her perplexity. "Why may I not ask you to procure me a substitute of your own selection? It is not much for you to do—is it?"

As he spoke, the eyes of the king rested unequivocally upon an object which he perceived just behind the chair of the duchess. She understood, and hastened to repair her blunder.

"Sire," said she "may I ask of your majesty a favor? My new lady of the bedchamber has just arrived in Paris, where she is a perfect stranger. "Will you be so gracious as to give her this proof of your royal favor? She is not only my favorite attendant, but the daughter of your majesty's minister of war, and—"

"And she is, above all things, herself—the beautiful Marchioness de Bonaletta," interrupted the king, with somewhat of his youthful courtliness and grace. "You propose her as your substitute, do you not?"

"Yes, sire—if your majesty is so good."

"So good! I shall esteem myself most happy in the acquisition of so charming a partner. Does the Marchioness de Bonaletta consent?"

With these words, Louis offered his hand; and Laura, without embarrassment or presumption, accepted the honor conferred upon her, and was led out to the dance. A murmur of admiration followed her appearance, but she seemed quite unconscious of the impression she had made. Her lovely countenance was neither lit up by pride, nor suffused by bashfulness. Her cheeks were slightly flushed by natural modesty, and her sweet, unaffected bearing enhanced her incomparable beauty of person.

Even De Montespan herself could not withhold her tribute of admiration. At first she had darted glances of hatred toward an imaginary rival; but a calm survey of Laura's pure and angelic expression of face reassured her. This girl had no mind to entrap the king, and if Louis had not courage enough to dance with *her* (De Montespan), in presence of that canting hypocrite De Maintenon, perhaps it was quite as well that he had provided himself with a partner *sans coquetterie*, and therefore *sans conséquence*.

Madame de Maintenon, too, had remarked Laura, as, gracefully emerging from her concealment behind the seat of the duchess, she had unostentatiously accepted the king's invitation to dance.

" What a union of tact with tenderness of heart is apparent in all that his majesty does," said she to the Duke de Maine, who was standing beside her. " This young girl is the personification of innocence and purity, and his majesty's selection of her as his partner proves that he not only desires to pay homage to youth and beauty, but also to virtue and modesty."

" How beautiful she is !" murmured a young cavalier, who, with Barbesieur Louvois, was watching the dancers.

"Why do you sigh ?" replied Barbesieur. "You ought rather to be proud of your future bride."

"My future bride !" echoed he, dolefully. "I would she were, my dear friend. But although your father has so graciously given his consent, I am as far from obtaining her as ever."

"It you wait for that," whispered Barbesieur in return, "you may wait until the day of judgment. My sister is one of those incomprehensible beings that loves opposition for opposition's sake. If she is disdainful, it is precisely because she is quite as much enamored of you as you are of her. She is a sort of chaste Artemis who is ashamed of her preference for a man, and would die rather than confess it."

"She enchants me at one moment, and drives me to despair the next," sighed the marquis.

"No need for despair," was the reply. "My dear marquis," continued Barbesieur, coming close to the ear of the Italian, "what will you give me if I promise that you shall become her husband ?"

The eyes of the marquis glowed with desire, and his swarthy face was tinged with red. " What would I give ?" cried he, as he caught a glimpse of Laura on the dance. "The half of my fortune, the half of my life, if, with one half of either, I might call her mine ! "

"Nay," said Barbesieur, with a sinister laugh, "I am neither robber nor devil. I wish neither your fortune nor your soul in exchange for my wares. Laura is so headstrong, that she will have to be forced into happiness, and made to take what even now she is longing to snatch. So if I make you both happy, you will not then object to giving me a few of the crumbs that fall from your table ? "

"I will give you any thing you desire, and my eternal gratitude to boot, if you will help me to become possessor of that angel."

"I am passionately fond of hunting, and the Marchioness de Bonaletta has the most tempting bit of woods that ever made a hunter's heart ache to call it his. Now if you marry Laura, you become her guardian, and have absolute power over her property."

"I care nothing for her property," cried the marquis, passionately. "Her beauty, her sweetness, and her noble birth, are wealth enough for me. In the golden book of Venice the name of the richest noble there inscribed is the Strozzi."

"Everybody knows that, dear marquis, and therefore you will not refuse the reward I claim from my sister's own possessions. 'Tis but meet that she make a present to her brother on her wedding-day. So, then, we understand each other : immediately after the ceremony of your marriage, you make out a deed by which you relinquish to me the usufruct of the Bonaletta estates in Savoy for life. Who gets them after me, I care not."

"I consent ; and add thereunto a yearly pension of one thousand ducats. Does that content you ? "

"Your liberality is really touching. A thousand ducats to boot ! They will fall like a refreshing shower into a purse that is always as empty as the sieves of the Danaides. It is a bargain. You wed Laura Bonaletta, and I get her estates, and one thousand ducats a year."

"Here is my hand."

"And mine.   In one month you shall both be on your way to Venice ; you a happy bridegroom, and she—your bride."

## CHAPTER VII.

### THE LADY OF THE BEDCHAMBER.

THE dance was over, and the king reconducted Laura to her chaperone.   "My dear sister," said he, "the fascinations of the partner you selected for me are almost enough to reconcile one to a refusal from yourself.   I am convinced that I have been the envy of every cavalier present.   I withdraw, therefore, that I may not stand in the way of the fair Laura's admirers."

And gracefully saluting his partner, the royal flirt betook himself at last to poor De Montespan, who had tact enough to smother her chagrin, and give him a cordial reception.   It was better to be noticed late than never.

"Your highness," whispered Laura, bending over the back of the duchess's chair, "pray command me not to dance any more.   Do you see that swarthy, sinister face over there, close to Barbesieur ?   It is the Marquis de Strozzi staring at me already.   He is about to come hither, and if you do not assist me I shall have to dance with him."

"Never fear, darling," whispered the duchess in return. "They shall not rob me of you so soon.   Take your place, and, being on duty, no one can claim you, were it the wild hunter himself."

Laura hastened to resume her station, and, in doing so, glanced toward the window, where stood the pale young man whom she had noticed before.   Their eyes met again, and again she blushed.   Laura bent her head, and, feigning to arrange a displaced ringlet on the head of her mistress, she said, in low, earnest tones : "Pardon me, gracious mistress ; but will you tell me who is that young cavalier in the recess of the window opposite ?"

"Certainly, my dear," replied the duchess in the same tone

of voice. "He is one whom all the courtiers avoid to-night—miserable timeservers as they are—for he has fallen into disgrace with your father and the king. He is Prince Eugene of Savoy."

"Prince Eugene!" echoed Laura. "He who laid the weight of his whip over Barbesieur's shoulders this morning!"

"Yes, the same, and he has been publicly rebuked for it to-night. Your father has received full satisfaction, Laura; for, not only has his majesty offered a pointed slight to the man who disgraced Barbesieur, but he has paid him a signal compliment by opening the ball with his sister."

"If I had imagined that any thought of Barbesieur mingled with the compliment paid me by the king, I would have refused to dance with him."

The duchess looked up astounded. "Why, Laura, such an insult to his majesty would almost amount to treason. For Heaven's sake, never utter such sentiments at court, child!"

"What care I for the court?" cried Laura, her eyes filling with tears. "I am overwhelmed with the shame of having been made use of as a tool wherewith to humiliate the noble Prince de Carignan! But I shall repair the wrong I have done him, and that in presence of the court!"

"Thoughtless, impulsive child, what would you do?" said Elizabeth-Charlotte, anxiously. "I really believe you are ready to go up and give him a kiss, by way of proving that you are not a party to his humiliation to-night!"

"Perhaps I am!" exclaimed Laura, passionately. "The prince was right to punish Barbesieur for his cowardly attack upon a noble lady; and my brother-in-law, De la Roche Guyon, was one of those who justify him. I, too, applaud his spirit; for, in avenging his mother, he avenged mine. This morning, when no king was by to uphold the calumniator, all these nobles were the friends of the prince, and not one of them would lift the gauntlet which, with his brave hand, he flung to the world. And to-night they desert him!—They are not worthy to touch the hem of his garment!—But I will take his hand—the noble hand that had disgraced his mother's traducer beyond the power of royalty to undo!"

"You will do no such thing, you dear little madcap !" returned the duchess, glancing admiringly at the beaming countenance of the beautiful enthusiast. "You have a brave heart, dear child ; but you must not allow it to run away with your judgment. You must keep your place at my side, nor let magnanimity get the better of discretion. The latter is a cardinal virtue in woman. But—see how the Marquis de Strozzi devours us with his eyes ; he is waiting until I cease speaking to come forward and claim your hand. Be comforted—he shall not have it. Here he comes—let the chamberlain have a chance to present him."

So saying, she turned away from Laura, and began to fan herself vigorously, while the marquis and the chamberlain advanced.

"Your royal highness," said the latter, reverentially, "may I present the Marquis de Strozzi ? "

"I am acquainted with him," interrupted the duchess. "He needs no introduction.  How do you like Paris, marquis ? Why are you not dancing this evening ? "

"Your royal highness has anticipated my wishes," was the reply.  "I am anxious to dance, and crave your permission to offer my hand to the Marchioness de Bonaletta."

"I regret to disoblige you," answered the duchess, "but you see that she is on duty, and etiquette forbids her to leave her post, except for two dances.  His majesty has had the first, and for the second she is engaged."

"Then I shall follow her example, and decline to dance," returned De Strozzi, with his burning glances rivetted upon Laura's face.

She drew back haughtily.  "The Marquis de Strozzi will oblige me by following the example of some other person.  I have no desire to be remarked by him in any way."

The marquis's brow grew dark, and his eyes glowed like coals of fire.  But he made an attempt to smile as he replied, "However I might be inclined to obey your commands, I have it not in my power to comply with a request so unreasonable."

The duchess saw how the crimson blood was mantling in the cheeks of her "dear little madcap," and she thought it

10

prudent to put an end to the skirmish by rising from her seat.

"I will take a turn through the ballroom," said she. "Come, marchioness."

She came down from the platform reserved to the various members of the royal family, and mingled with the gay groups below, addressing here and there a greeting to her friends, or stopping to receive their heartfelt homage. Side by side came the duchess and her lady of the bedchamber ; the latter all unconscious of her beauty, enjoying the scene with the zest of youth, unmindful of the fact that at every step she took, her admirers increased, until the cortége was as long as the trail of a comet.

But one face she sees—the noble countenance of Prince Eugene—who, as she approaches the window near which he stands, looks as though the morning sun had shone upon his heart, driving away all darkness and all night. She sees that joyous look, and with a wild bound her heart leaps to meet his. Her brow crimsons with shame, and she presses close to the duchess, as if to seek protection from her own emotion.

Elizabeth-Charlotte misunderstood the movement, or she may have guessed the longing that was struggling with decorum in the heart of her young attendant. She advanced toward the prince, and signed for him to approach.

Eugene started forward and stood directly in front of them. "How is the Princess de Carignan?" asked the duchess, kindly, "and why is she not here to-night? I hope she is not indisposed !"

"Your highness," returned Eugene, with a smile, "she is ill with a malady that has attacked every member of our family."

"What malady, prince?"

"The malady of royal disfavor, your highness."

"That is indeed a fearful malady, prince, for it rarely attacks the innocent."

"Pardon me, your highness," returned Eugene, calmly, "since the death of Cardinal Mazarin 'tis a heritage in our family, and—"

"Madame," said a voice behind the duchess, "be so good as to take my arm. The queen desires your attendance."

Eugene looked up, and saw a small, effeminate personage, magnificently attired, and wearing the broad, blue band of the order of St. Louis. He recognized the king's brother, the Duke of Orleans.

The duchess, with a sigh, laid her arm within that of her husband; but, disregarding his frowns, she remained to say a parting word to the victim of kingly displeasure.

"Give my regards to the princess, your grandmother, and tell her that if her indisposition lasts, I will go in person to express my sympathy with you both."

"Madame," said the duke, angrily, while, with little regard to courtesy, he almost dragged her along with him, "you will do no such thing. I cannot understand your audacity; still less will I countenance it. The Prince of Savoy has been so pointedly slighted by his majesty, that no one dares be seen conversing with him; it seems to me that you set a shameful example to the court by noticing one whom your king has been pleased to reprove."

"It seems to me that my example would be worse, were I to ignore my acquaintances because they happen to be momentarily out of favor at court," replied Elizabeth-Charlotte. "Such miserable servility may beseem a courtier, but it ill becomes our princely station. And if the king speaks to me on the subject, I shall say as much to him, for his majesty has a noble heart and will approve my independence."

While their royal highnesses were thus interchanging opinions on the subject of court ethics, a scene was being enacted behind them, which, had he witnessed it, would have called forth the indignation of the duke.

The Marchioness Bonaletta, as a matter of course, had followed her mistress; but during his short colloquy with the latter, Eugene had received so sweet a smile from her attendant, that he followed at a distance; resolved, since he could do no more, to gaze at her until the ball was over. In spite of the throng which closed as fast as the ducal pair went by, Eugene saw that the marchioness had dropped her fan. It became entangled in the train of another lady, and finally was dragged to the floor.

Eugene rescued it from destruction, and hastened with it to its owner, who appeared just to have discovered her loss.

"You are looking for your fan?" said he, with a beaming smile.

"Yes, prince," replied she, giving him in return a look that almost maddened him with joy—it was so kind, so, gentle so sympathizing.

"I have been so fortunate as to find it," replied he, in a voice whose music thrilled the heart of her to whom he spoke. "And to be permitted to return it to you, confers upon me the first pleasurable sensation I have felt since I entered this unfriendly palace to-night."

"I am happy to have been the means," she began. But just then the Duke of Orleans turned around, and his indignation may be imagined when he saw the Prince of Savoy in conversation with a lady of the duchess's household!

"Call your lady of the bedchamber hither," said he, imperiously. "That little abbé has the assurance to follow us, as though to defy his majesty, and prove to the court that, if nobody else esteems him, he has friends in the household of the Duchess of Orleans. Send that young lady on some errand."

The duchess walked a few steps farther, then turning around she beckoned to Laura. "Come, Marchioness de Bonaletta, I must present you to the queen."

"Ah!" thought Eugene, as he took up his position in the window again, "if I may not follow her, at least I know her name! Marchioness Bonaletta—what a pretty name it is! I have never heard it before, nor have I ever seen any thing that reminded me of her lovely person. 'Tis plain that she is a stranger at this corrupt court. Those limpid eyes, that brow of innocence, those heavenly smiles—O my God! what sudden thrill of joy is this which pervades my being? What flood of ecstasy is this which drowns my soul in bliss! Oh, angel of beauty—"

But his raptures were suddenly brought to a close by the sight of Louvois, who with his son joined the party of the Duchess of Orleans. He did not like to see him so near his angel ; but his uneasiness increased to positive pain when he saw her extend her hand, and greet him with one of her sweetest smiles.

"So," thought Eugene, "she is like the rest ! Louvois is the favorite of the king, and of De Maintenon, and therefore she greets him as though he were a near and dear friend. But what is it to me ? I came here to show his majesty that I shall maintain my rights in the face of his displeasure, and here I shall remain, though she and every other woman here do homage to my foes. What is the Marchioness Bonaletta to me ?"

But, in spite of himself, his eyes would wander to the spot where she stood, and his heart seemed ready to burst when he beheld Barbesieur approach her. He spoke to her and she answered him ; but Eugene could see that she was displeased. Could he have heard the words she addressed to Barbesieur, he would have hated himself for his unworthy suspicions, and would have acknowledged that she was not like the rest.

"So my lovely sister has refused to dance with the Marquis de Strozzi ?" said Barbesieur.

"Yes," was the curt reply.

"And may one venture to inquire why ?"

She darted a glance of contempt at him. "Because he is your friend."

Barbesieur laughed. "I really believe that you are in earnest, my candid sister. It is enough for a man to be my friend to earn your enmity."

"You are right," said she, deliberately.

"But you will hardly go so far as to say that it suffices for a man to be my foe, to be your friend," said he with an ugly frown.

"What if it were so ?" said she.

"If it were so, I would advise my sister not to provoke me too far. I would advise her not to make any more demonstrations of regard to the little abbé of Savoy, and to remember that she *is* my sister."

"When I heard of all that took place this morning at the Pré aux Clercs," said Laura, "I remembered it to my shame and sorrow."

Barbesieur grew pale with rage and hissed into his sister's

ear—"Have a care, girl, how you rouse me to retaliation! I can crush you like a worm under my heel; and as for yonder princely beggar, be assured that I shall remember him to his cost."

"Which means that you will bring suit against him, and obtain damages," replied she, contemptuously; "for you know that the Prince of Savoy will not condescend to fight a duel with Barbesieur de Louvois."

"I would not make myself ridiculous by fighting with such an apology for a man; but I will crush him as I would any other reptile that attempts to injure me. There shall not be a day of his life that does not bring him some pang which he shall owe to the hate of Barbesieur de Louvois. And I counsel *you* not to imitate his audacity, for—"

"Why, you scarcely expect me to bestow a horsewhipping upon you?" laughed Laura. "But I am not afraid of you, Barbesieur; it is not in your power to injure me."

"If you are not afraid of me, so much the worse for you; I should have thought that you had learned from your mother, how Barbesieur de Louvois nurses his hate, and how it blossoms into misery for those on whom he bestows it."

Laura's eyes filled with tears, and her voice faltered. "I did learn it from her martyrdom; but she was not like me. She submitted where I would resist."

"Resistance will only increase the bitterness of your punishment, and once more I warn you not to make friends of my enemies, and not to offer slights to my friends. The Marquis de Strozzi wishes to marry you; your father is anxious for the match—*so am I*, and you shall marry the marquis, of that be assured. He has asked you to dance, to-night, and you shall dance with him, too. This plea of an engagement is a falsehood. Where is your partner?"

"I will remind him of our engagement, now that I am prepared to fulfil mine," answered Laura. And, yielding to an impulse of aversion to Barbesieur, resolved to give him then and there proof unquestionable of her contempt; impelled, too, by an enthusiastic longing to sympathize with one whom all had united to slight, and forgetful of the social restraints which it is always unwise for a woman to overleap, Laura pressed through the crowds that were assembling for the dance, and stepped so proudly by, that all wondered at the solemn earnestness of her mien, more resembling that of a priestess than of a young maiden at her first ball.

If all other eyes were gazing upon her, those of Eugene were riveted upon her advancing figure with mingled rapture and wonder. He had long since forgotten the rudeness of the king and the contumely of his courtiers. Laura's image filled his heart, and left no space therein for painful emotions. He had watched her countenance while Barbesieur had been speaking to her, and had guessed that their colloquy was anything but friendly. He had seen her turn suddenly away, and now she came nearer and nearer, until her dazzled worshipper lost all sense of time and place, and his enfranchised soul went out to meet hers.

But at last she came so near, that he wakened from his ecstasy, and remembered that he had nothing in common with that high-born girl ; for, shame had fallen upon his house, and royalty had turned its back upon him.

But he had scarcely time to pass from heaven to earth before she stood directly before him, her starry eyes uplifted to meet his, her sweet voice drowning his senses in melody.

" Prince," said she, in clear, self-possessed tones that attracted the attention of those immediately around, " it appears that you have forgotten the engagement you made to dance with me this evening. Pardon me if I recall it to you."

So saying, she extended her little hand to Eugene, who, bewildered with joy, was almost afraid to touch the delicate embroidered glove that lay so temptingly near his. He was afraid that he had gone mad. But Laura smiled, and came a step nearer ; whereupon he gave himself up to the intoxicating dream, and led her away to the dance.

They took their place among the others, but the dancers looked upon them with glances of uneasiness and displeasure. How were they to know that they might not be compromised by their vicinity to an ostracized man, and how did they know that the king was not observing them, to see how they would receive this bold intruder ?

They might have spared themselves all anxiety ; for, in the

first place, the king was in another room, at the card-table, and, in the second place, their sensitive loyalty was soon relieved from its perplexities.

As a matter of course, Laura's generous indiscretion had been witnessed by Barbesieur ; not only by him, however, but by her father and the Duchess of Orleans. Barbesieur, enraged, would have followed, and torn her violently away, but Louvois' hand was laid upon his shoulder, and Louvois' voice (imperious even in a whisper) bade him remain.

"No *éclat*, my son : we are the guests of his majesty."

"But I cannot brook her insolence," muttered Barbesieur, in return. "She is my sister, and before she shall dance with a man that has insulted me, I will fell him to the earth, were the king at my side to witness it."

"Be quiet, I command you, or you shall sleep to-night within the walls of the Bastile," was the reply. "God knows that you ought to avoid notoriety ; for, your affair with Prince Eugene has not covered you with glory. Retire, then, if you cannot control yourself, and I will find means to put an end to this foolish demonstration of your sister."

The means were at hand ; they were concentrated in the person of his royal highness the Duke of Orleans. He had been about to join the dance, when he, too, witnessed the terrible sight of Laura de Bonaletta standing at the side of the little abbé of Savoy !

With a hasty apology to his partner, the Duchess de Chevreuse, he strode away and joined madame. Elizabeth-Charlotte saw him coming and heaved a sigh.

"Now for a tempest in a teapot !" thought she. "To be sure, the anger of my lord is not much like that of a thundering Jove ; yet I don't know but what it is better to be struck dead by lightning, than to live forever within sound of the scolding tongue of a fishwife ! I must try, however, to be conciliatory in my tones, or poor Laura will get into trouble."

So she smiled as graciously as she could, but her affability was lost upon the duke. He was in a towering passion.

"Madame," said he, in a low, but snappish voice, "do you know that your lady of the bedchamber is dancing with the Prince of Savoy ?"

The duchess turned around, as if to see whether Laura were not at her post. "True enough," replied she, "she is not here. I was so absorbed in my conversation with the queen that I had not missed her. I suppose she thought I could spare her for a while, and so allowed herself to be persuaded to dance."

"But when I tell you that she is dancing with Prince Eugene!—with the son of the Countess de Soissons!" cried the duke, impatiently.

"I understand your highness. The prince is in disgrace, and has the plague. But you must pardon my little marchioness, for she is new to court customs, and does not know how contagious is her partner's malady. She will learn prudence, all in good time, and, perchance, become as obse—I mean as discreet—as the rest of us."

"You will be so good as to begin her education at once, by reproving her sharply for her indecorous behavior here to-night," said the duke, beginning to stammer.

"When he stammers," thought his wife, "he is in a rage. I had better try the effect of soft words. What would your highness have me say?" added she aloud.

"I would have you send a peremptory message to the marchioness to quit the dance immediately; and, if she does not obey, I would have you go yourself and—"

"My dear lord," whispered madame, laying the weight of her hand upon monsieur's arm, "do you forget that she is the daughter of Louvois, and that we dare not affront her lightly? And have you forgotten that her father has promised to obtain for you, from his majesty, the woods of St. Germain. In accordance with your desire and that of her father, who is powerful enough to command everybody at this court, I have taken this young girl into my service since this morning. Would you undo what I have done for your advantage?"

"But it is an outrage," murmured the duke, somewhat pacified. "It is an outrage against his majesty."

"I will put an end to the outrage then, but I will do so by gentle means.—My Lord Marquis de Valmy, I am suffering terribly with a *migraine*, and am compelled to retire. Will you bear my apology to the Marchioness de Bonaletta, and say that I regret to be obliged to interrupt her pleasures, but must request her attendance."

The marquis hastened away with his message, and just as Prince Eugene had so far recovered himself as to be able to address a few murmured words of thanks to his beautiful partner, just as she was looking bashfully into his face, and had seen that his large black eyes were moistened with tears, she heard a voice at her side :

"Madame is suddenly indisposed, and regrets to say that she requires the attendance of the Marchioness de Bonaletta. Her highness is sorry to be obliged to interrupt you, mademoiselle."

"I will have the honor of conducting mademoiselle to her highness," replied Eugene, regaining in a moment all his self-possession.

Laura had just laid her arm within his, when monsieur approached with most undignified haste.

"Give me your arm, mademoiselle," said he. "Her highness has requested me to accompany you to her seat."

And without a word or look significative of his knowledge that Eugene was nigh, the duke placed Laura's other arm within his own, and stalked away.

The prince left the dancers, and retired again to his window-seat. He was pale with the shock of his sudden disappointment, but was callous to the fresh insult offered him by the king's brother. Still less was he conscious of the titter that was going around at his expense, or of the scornful looks directed to him from the eyes of many who until that day had called themselves his friends. He had neither eyes, ears, nor understanding, for any creature but the one who had braved the ridicule of the court, and the displeasure of its sovereign, to show her sympathy with a man in adversity. He must—he *would* see her again ! He must thank her for her magnanimity, let the consequences be what they would !

He darted forward toward the door through which the Duke and Duchess of Orleans were passing, with their suite. On the stairway he caught a glimpse of Laura's white satin dress, and one look at her beautiful face. He made a desperate effort to follow, but before he could put his foot on the top step, the Duke of Orleans and his suite, returning to the ballroom, stopped the way.

"Too late! too late!" groaned Eugene. "But I will see her again, if it costs me my life!"

The carriage of madame, meanwhile, was rolling homeward. She and her attendant were seated opposite each other, both keeping a profound silence. At length Laura could bear it no longer. Gliding from her seat, and kneeling at the feet of the duchess, she took her hand and pressed it to her lips.

"Dear lady," sobbed she, passionately, "have I done wrong? If I have, reprove me; but speak. Your silence is harder to bear than rebuke."

The duchess, no longer able to keep up her affected displeasure, put her arms around the young girl, and kissed her forehead. "I certainly ought to reprove you," said she, "for your conduct has been almost unmaidenly, but I have not the heart to chide you for indiscretion that springs from the overflowing of a generous nature. You have violated every rule of etiquette and decorum; but what would you? I am the least conventional of beings myself; and, instead of condemning you, I positively admire your impropriety. You have raised a tempest about your ears, child: but I will do my best to defend you against the king, monsieur, and the censorious world. Against your father and your brother you can defend yourself."

"They may think of me whatever they please," cried Laura, joyfully. "I shall not defend myself against anybody, for *you* are not displeased, and *he!*—oh, I believe that I conferred upon him one moment of happiness!"

"He! Who? Of whom do you speak?"

"Of Prince Eugene," murmured Laura, blushing.

"Prince Eugene!" echoed the duchess.

"Yes," exclaimed she, passionately, "of him, the noble, brave knight, who, like another St. George, sets his foot upon the dragon of this world's wickedness, and towers above its miserable worshippers, like an archangel!"

"Great Heavens! what has possessed the girl?" exclaimed the duchess. "She speaks of that little abbé as if he were an impersonation of manly beauty!"

"And so he is ! His eyes are aflame with the light of a noble soul, and his face is as that of a demi-god !"

"A demi-god !" cried madame, clasping her hands. "I do believe she has fallen in love with him !"

Laura buried her face in the folds of the duchess's dress. "Pray for me, dear lady," sobbed she ; "pray for me. Never would my father consent to bestow my hand upon the son of the Countess de Soissons, and I !—oh, if I should love him, I would forsake the whole world for his sake. Alas ! alas ! I believe that he is lord and sovereign of my heart, for it bounds to meet his, as though it felt that he was master of its destiny !"

## CHAPTER VIII.

### FIRST LOVE.

FOUR days had elapsed since the ball, and its events, triumphs, and contrarieties were already forgotten. Nobody bestowed a thought upon Prince Eugene, who, concealed from view by the thick cloud of the king's dislike, had fallen into complete oblivion.

Nobody said a word about the ignominious punishment administered to Barbesieur de Louvois, for the king had treated him with consideration ; and his majesty's countenance had healed his stripes, and cured his wounded honor. So that Barbesieur de Louvois was greeted with the courtesy due to a noble knight, and Eugene of Savoy was spurned as a base-born churl.

Was it for this that he was so pale, so silent, and so shy ? Was it for this that he sat alone in his room for hours, murmuring words of passionate tenderness, and extending his arms to heaven, as if he expected some seraph to visit him in his desolate home ? Was it for this that by night he paced the length of a garden-wall, and stood with folded arms before its trellised gates ? Had sorrow and slight unsettled his reason ?

If they had, there was "method in his madness," for his

steps were ever directed toward the same place, the hôtel of the Duke of Orleans.

On this fourth day after the ball, at dusk, Eugene left the Hôtel de Soissons, and took the way, as usual, toward the Palais Royal. Its long façade was dimly lighted, and every thing within seemed hushed.

" I am fortunate," thought he ; " the duchess has dismissed her attendants, and *she* has retired to the pavilion."

He continued his way along the side-wing of the palace, until he arrived at the garden which occupied the space now contained between the Rue Vivienne and the Bourse. This magnificent garden was refreshed by plashing fountains, and decorated by noble trees and gay parterres ; but it was encompassed by a high stone wall, of which the summit was defended by short iron spikes whose uplifted points gave warning to all passers-by that intrusion into this paradise was attended with danger.

But what cares love for " stony limits," or when did danger ever intimidate a stout heart ?

Eugene was now at the extreme end of the garden. The deep, unbroken stillness of solitude reigned around. At times, and at a distance, was heard the faint rumbling of a coach ; but otherwise nothing interrupted the loneliness of the place and the hour. For, although nine o'clock had just sounded from the tower of St. Jacques, all Paris was at rest, save the few aristocrats who were on their way to balls and banquets, or the houseless wretches who, with their dark lanterns, were searching the gutters for a lost penny.

So that Eugene was unobserved, and had full opportunity to draw from his cloak a package which proved to be a rope-ladder of silk ; to unroll, and fling it over the garden wall. It caught in the prongs, and in a few moments he was within the enchanted walls of the palace where Laura de Bonaletta dwelt.

She was alone in her pavilion, in the room which led into the garden, and its glass doors now stood wide open. She had thrown aside her court-dress, and was now attired in a white peignior edged with delicate lace. Her feet were encased in slippers of blue satin embroidered with silver, and her hair, stripped of all ornament, was twisted into a coronal around her graceful head.

She had dismissed her attendants, and sat beside a table of white marble, holding in her hand a book which she seemed to read—yet not to read. She turned its pages, and her eyes were fixed upon them, but little saw Laura of their contents, she was looking into another book, the book of her own heart ; and mysterious were the pages thereof, half painful, half pleasant, to peruse.

Around her all was silent. From time to time the night wind sighed through the branches of the trees without, and a few sorrowing leaves fell rustling to the ground, while she, her book now laid aside, and her pretty hands folded in her lap, gazed and gazed at sky and earth, at moonlit paths, and darkly looming trees, but saw nothing of them all. Something broke the perfect stillness. It was neither summer breeze, nor rustling leaf ; 'twas the crackling gravel that was being displaced by approaching footsteps. The sound was all unheeded by Laura, who heard nothing but the voice of her heart as it sang its first anthem of love.

The moon emerged from a silver cloud, and Eugene's figure darkened the threshold. For one moment he contemplated the beautiful picture before him, then with noiseless steps he approached and knelt at her feet.

"Kill me for my presumption," whispered he, "for I deserve death. But I would rather die at your feet than live another hour out of your sight."

Laura spoke not a word in return, but neither did she cry out in terror or surprise. She merely gazed at Eugene with distended eyes, whose mysterious expressions he dreaded to interpret.

A feeling of anguish inexpressible pervaded his being. "I thought so," murmured he, bitterly. "I thought so ; and yet I could not have done otherwise. Had I known that I was to be racked for my temerity, I must have sought you, alone and unattended—sought you as I would my Maker, when no curious eye was upon me to see my tears, no mocking tongue to echo my sighs ; but when, unfettered by the bonds of a conventional world, I was free to pour out the oceans of love that are drowning me in their sweetness; and then!—to live or die, as you should determine. I love you! Do you hear? I love you! And with such strength of love, that if I am unworthy; if, poor, ill-favored, unfortunate, the Prince of Savoy may not aspire to your hand, then call your people, and drive me hence; for whether you welcome or whether you spurn, you still must hear me, while my yearning heart cries out for judgment. Speak, beloved! I await my sentence—is it life or death?"

He raised his pleading eyes to hers, and as they met, her beautiful head drooped lower and lower, until it almost touched his own. He felt the soft touch of her hands upon his shoulders, and heard the thrilling accents of her trembling voice, as, in tones so inaudible that none but a lover's ear could have guessed their sweet import, she whispered these words:

"I was waiting for thee."

With a wild cry of rapture, Eugene caught her to his heart, and imprinted one long, loving kiss upon her lips. Then he gazed upon her with an expression of passionate tenderness, which transfigured his homely features and lent them beauty.

"Say that thou lovest me," cried he, "oh, say it again—again—again."

"I love thee," repeated Laura, "I love thee, Eugene. When first our eyes met, I knew that my heart had found its sovereign. Oh, sweet vassalage, that never again will seek enfranchisement! Oh, happy bondage, than liberty more precious! Bondage that makes me thine, and thou mine forever!"

"Ay, forever!" echoed Eugene, while tears streamed from his eyes at sound of her delicious avowal. "We love each other! Oh, my Laura, what magic in those blessed words! We love each other! I could weary echo with repetition of the sound: WE! 'Tis the first time in my life that my name has ever been joined with that of a fellow-being. My brothers, who enjoyed the privileges of their birth and rank, looked down with contempt upon one who was condemned to the obscurity of the priesthood; my young sisters feared me, and I

was too shy to ask for their love ; in my proud and beautiful
mother's heart there was no room for the son, to whom fate
had allotted no share of her loveliness and grace. Alone in the
midst of a family circle, alone in society, alone in the world, I
thrust back into my sorrowing soul the hopes, the loves, the
aspirations of youth, and refused to listen to their pleadings.
But in the depths of the night, when no mortal was by, and
I stood alone in the presence of God, I called them up, and
bade them weep with me that life and light were denied them.
I mourned, and prayed for deliverance, but no friendly voice
ever bade me be comforted. And so I lived, shunned and despised by my fellows."

"No, no, my Eugene, not shunned and despised," exclaimed
Laura, while her gentle hands wiped away the tears that were
streaming down her lover's cheeks. "You belie yourself and
the world. It may not love you, but it has divined your worth."

Eugene answered with a faint smile. "My worth is small,
beloved ; but no human being has ever divined the secrets of
my ambitious heart. But ah ! how changed is life to me to-
night ! I went to that ball to throw down the gauntlet of my
hate before Louvois and his son. I was rebuked by the king,
slighted by his nobles ; but I had no eyes to see, no pride to
resent their insults. When I saw thee, the sun shone upon
my heart, and there was light and love within. But oh ! when
thou camest so near that I felt the perfume of thy breath upon
my cheek, and the touch of thy hand within my hand, then I
was born again to a life of hope and happiness. My soul's
better half was found, and nevermore shall it wander from
my side. I am here at thy feet to ask thee for my wife. I
have neither wealth nor repute to offer thee : I am a poor ap-
panagist, a prince without fortune or distinction. But, dearest, if thou wilt be mine, I swear by all the imprisoned aspirations which thy coming has liberated, that the wife of Eugene
of Savoy shall have pride in her husband ! Be mine, be mine,
and I will make thy name illustrious !"

"I am thine," said Laura, fervently, "for time and for
eternity. I care not whether thy name be obscure or thy fortunes adverse ; I love thee as thou art." And so saying, she
extended her hand.

He grasped it in his own and covered it with rapturous kisses. "From this blissful hour, then, thou art my betrothed ; and to-morrow I shall ask the consent of madame to our marriage. Or hast thou relatives whom I must know and propitiate ? "

At this innocent question, Laura's youth and animal spirits got the better of her sentiment. She laughed heartily. "What !" cried she, " you do not know who I am ? "

" No, sweetest ; I know not, I care not who thou art. What have I to do with thy surroundings ? I love thee—only thee. If thou hast father and mother, I will throw myself at their feet, and beg their blessing for us both."

Laura's hilarity had all vanished. As Eugene had spoken of her father and mother, her cheeks had blanched, and the smile had died from the rosy lips. " Alas !" cried she, clasping her hands, " he knows not who I am ! "

" I know thou art an angel, and that is enough to make me the happiest of men."

" True, true," murmured Laura. "When my grandmother retired from court, he was but a boy."

" And had I been a man, what to me are the comings and goings of the ladies of the court ? " said Eugene, simply. " But why art thou troubled, my beloved ? "

" Alas ! alas ! " murmured Laura, her eyes filling with tears. " May God grant that you spoke the truth, Eugene de Carignan, when you said that you cared not who was my father or my mother ! "

" So help me Heaven, I do not care ! " was the fervent response, while he gazed passionately upon his new-found treasure.

She bent her head, and lowered her voice to a whisper. "Eugene," said she, almost gasping for breath, "I bear my mother's name ; but I am the daughter of your bitterest enemy, Louvois."

Eugene started back in horror. "Louvois ! Louvois !" echoed he, mournfully. " And Barbesieur, her brother !"

" Not my own brother," cried Laura, terrified at the effect of her revelation. "Before I had seen you, I approved your act, and bade God bless the son that had avenged his mother's

wrongs upon her traducer. Ah, Eugene ! my affianced, say
that you do not hate me ! I knew that you were the son of
the Countess de Soissons, and yet I loved *you!*—perhaps the
more, that Barbesieur was your enemy."

"And I love *you*, my own one, despite your parentage. I
love you so far beyond all feelings of pride or enmity, that I
am ready to humble myself before my mother's enemy, and be
to him a son."

"He will never receive you as such," cried she, bitterly.
"Woe is me, if he should learn what has transpired to-night
between us ! He would part us by force."

"Part us he shall not !" exclaimed Eugene, passionately,
while he flung his arm around the maiden's slender waist, and
pressed her wildly to his heart. "Thou art Louvois' daughter,
but my betrothed."

"I am Barbesieur's sister, but thou art my affianced !"

"Neither daughter nor sister of any man, my Laura ; thou
art thyself—and being thyself—mine."

"Thine for life and death," was her reply, "and from this
hour I know no will of mine."

"Then, ere thy father suspects our love, it must be sancti-
fied before the altar of God. Our faith once plighted there, no
hand of mortal can wrest thee from my side. Art ready to
speak the irrevocable words that bind us together as man and
wife ?"

"I am ready," replied she, clasping her hands, and looking
solemnly up to heaven. "If, in my eager acquiescence, I seem
unmaidenly, forgive me ; but I dare not be coy, Eugene ; we
have no time for conventional reserve, and I must act as becomes a brave and trusting woman, for every moment is
fraught with danger. I am surrounded by spies, even of my
own household, and, until I hear the blessing of the priest, I
shall disbelieve my own happiness."

"Then hear me, dearest. I know how crafty are the spies
of Louvois, and I tremble lest the whispering breeze betray
our secret. Yes, we must be diligent, so diligent that Fate shall
stand between our love and all contingency. For two days
I shall part from thee—long days that will steep my soul in
darkness ! But day after to-morrow, at this same hour of the

evening, I shall be here with the chaplain of the Princess de Carignan, an old and dear friend, who will bless our bridal. As witnesses, I will be accompanied by my kinsmen, the Princes de Conti, two of the worthiest nobles of France. Be in readiness, my best beloved, that not a word need be spoken until we are married. Then away with me to the Hôtel de Soissons, where those who love, may seek thee in thy husband's home."

"So soon?" murmured Laura, blushing. "Shall I leave my dear mistress without a word? Is *she* not to share our secret?"

"Assuredly not; for it would burden her with a painful responsibility. It would be her duty to betray you, artless child."

"Oh, I will not speak!" exclaimed Laura, eagerly. "I will be silent; and when—when we are married, we will beg so humbly for forgiveness that she will have to grant it."

"You must leave a note declaring everything; for with our marriage ends all secrecy. I will neither see you nor write until the appointed time. Dismiss your household as early as possible, and, if all is propitious, place a light in yonder window. If I see it, I will enter with the priest, and, lest there should be interruption, he will begin the ceremony at once."

"Alas, Eugene!" said Laura, looking anxiously around, "some evil spirit is about. It whispers me that this shall never be! Speak to me—in mercy speak! Let me hear thy voice, for even now its sinister threatenings are freezing the blood in my veins!"

"Nay, sweet one, fear nothing! My love shall compass thee with a charm that shall keep away all evil spirits, and make thy life a waking dream of bliss."

"How can I ever prove to thee how much I love thee?"

"Thou wilt prove it to me when, day after to-morrow, thou forsakest father and brother, to cleave to me alone; for never will my mother's son take the hand of Barbesieur Louvois."

"Nor my mother's daughter," cried Laura, vehemently, "for she, too, has a debt of hatred to pay to the man who broke that mother's heart. And believe me, our marriage will avenge us both; for it will end his contemptible intrigues to sell my hand to whomsoever chinks most gold in his. And now, dear Eugene, good-night!"

"Must I be exiled so soon, Laura? What have I done to be thus driven from paradise?"

"Nothing—nothing," stammered she. "But my mother's name has made me fear that—that I am wrong to hold such long parley with you in secret and at night. Methinks I see that mother's pleading eyes before me, and oh, Eugene! whenever they rest upon me thus, 'tis because danger threatens! Go, beloved, and God be with you!"

"I go," sighed he. "I would not stay one moment to wound your sweet scruples, my madonna. One more kiss, and then—good-night!"

They walked side by side until they stood upon the threshold. Eugene put his arm around her waist, and kissed her fair brow.

"Look," said she, "at yonder star that is just emerging from a fleecy cloud. It soars joyously upward now, and shall be to us an omen of hope and happiness. Farewell."

"Farewell!" was the sad response, and Eugene went slowly down the dark avenue, until he was lost in the gloom of night. Laura lingered for a while, listening to his footsteps, then resumed her seat at the table.

A half hour went by, and Laura sought her chamber. To her surprise she found her waiting-woman stretched at full length on the carpet, in a deep sleep, so deep that her mistress had much trouble to waken her. When, at last, she had been made to rise, she seemed scarcely to know where she was, or to whom she was speaking.

"I beg your ladyship's pardon," said she drowsily, "I was dreaming. I thought I heard robbers in the house, and when your ladyship spoke, I was struggling."

"God be thanked, there are no robbers here!" returned Laura, kindly. "Perhaps you heard the sentry's step in the park, and you ought to know that the Palais Royal is strictly guarded. But why are you not in bed with the rest? I dismissed you all."

"I have no right to retire before my mistress," returned the girl, obsequiously. "Therefore, I sat in your ladyship's room to await you, but sleep overcame me, and I humbly crave your pardon. Shall I close the door that leads to the garden?"

"What! still afraid of robbers, Louise?" laughed Laura. "Well—close the door, if you will—good-night."

"Can I do nothing for your ladyship?"

"Thank you—yes. Open the door of Madame Dupont's room, and let me feel that I am within hearing of my dear old Cerberus. That is all."

The waiting-woman did as she was bidden, and then retired to her room, but not to sleep. She seated herself before a table, drew out her portfolio, and began to write. Now and then she paused and looked up, when the sinister light that shone in her eyes streamed through the room like the phosphorescent glow of the lichen that moulds in the churchyard.

She wrote the whole night long, and day dawned before she rose from her task.

"Ah," sighed she, "for such a service surely he will return to me! I have repeated their conversation, word for word, not a sigh or a kiss have I forgotten. Who but his poor Louise would have served him so faithfully! 'Tis a vile trade, that of a spy; nor would I have accepted such a mission for all the gold in the king's treasury; but, for love of Barbesieur Louvois, I would sell my own sister to infamy—why not his?"

While thus soliloquizing, she had left her own room and crossed the corridor that led to the men's apartments. She opened the door of one of the rooms without knocking, and going directly up to a bed she touched the sleeper, and having wakened him, whispered:

"George, awake—awake!—rouse up quickly! '

"What is it?" mumbled George, stretching himself.

"Hist!—It is I, Louise. Dress yourself as speedily as you can, and away with this packet to your master. Give it to no messenger, but place it in his own hands, and he will reward you magnificently, for you will have done him a great service."

She glided away and returned to her own room, leaving the door open. In less than fifteen minutes George stood before her, equipped for secret service. "Mademoiselle Louise," whispered he, "I shall be with Monsieur de Louvois in ten minutes ; for I have the key of the postern, and can slip out and back again without anybody being the wiser for my little excursion."

"So much the better. Away with you, and the sooner the better ! "

George went on his way, and Louise stood in her doorway until she heard him softly open and close the outer door below ; then she threw herself upon her bed to sleep. Her last words were these :

"Oh, faithless but loved—now can I dream that thine arms are around me once more ! "

---

## CHAPTER IX.

### THE BETRAYAL.

THE sun was high in the heavens when Laura awoke, and rang for her waiting-woman. Mademoiselle Louise. fresh, smiling, and officious, came at once from the anteroom, and began the toilet of her mistress. She seemed to take more pleasure than usual in gathering her magnificent dark coils into a net of gold and pearls, and to linger more admiringly than ever over the last little touches given to the lace that bordered Laura's négligé of spotless white mull.

She certainly was one of the loveliest of created beings, and so thought good Madame Dupont, as her ex-pupil came into the dining-room, and imprinted two hearty kisses on her withered old cheeks. They sat down together to breakfast, and George, looking as innocent as if he had just awaked from the sleep of the righteous, came in with their morning chocolate. All went on as usual, except with the young marchioness, who, instead of laughing and chatting of Italy, and Bonaletta, as she was accustomed to do with her "dear Dupont," sipped her chocolate in silent abstraction. Breakfast had long been over, and still she sat in her arm-chair, looking dreamily into the garden, her head leaning on her hand, her lips sometimes rippling with a smile, sometimes opening with a gentle sigh.

She had been plunged in her blissful reverie for almost an hour, when the door was opened, and George appeared before her.

"Your ladyship," said he, "a man without desires speech with you."

"Who is he, George?" asked Laura, reluctantly returning to the world and its exigencies.

"He will not say, my lady. He wears no livery, but says that your ladyship knows whence he comes and why. He has a bouquet which was forgotten yesterday evening."

Laura darted from her chair; then, blushing deeply, she stopped, and recalled her wandering senses.

"Admit him," said she, trying to speak carelessly. "I will inquire what this means."

"Oh, 'tis a greeting from him," thought she; but before she had time to surmise any further, the door reopened, and a young man entered the room, holding in his hand a superb bouquet of rare and exquisite flowers.

"Who sent you hither?" asked Laura, with wildly-beating heart.

"A cavalier whose name I do not know," replied the young man, looking timidly up at the dazzling vision of beauty that stood before him. "I am first clerk in the largest establishment of the *Marché aux Fleurs*, and the gentleman who bespoke the bouquet ordered the handsomest flowers in our collection. Your ladyship sees that we have filled the order with the greatest care; for this bouquet contains specimens of our rarest and most expensive flowers. To be sure, the gentleman paid an enormous price for it, saying that nothing we could furnish was too costly for the occasion."

Laura had listened with wonderful patience to all this idle babble. "Give me the flowers," she said. "They are indeed most beautiful, and I am grateful for them, both to you and the amiable unknown who sends them."

"He is very small; of sallow complexion, but with large black eyes," replied the clerk, while, with an awkward scrape and bow, he presented the bouquet to Laura. "He was so pleased with our selection, that he kissed one of the flowers,"

Before she had time to control her tongue, Laura had exclaimed, " Which one ? "

" The blue one, your ladyship, called *Comelina cœlestis*."

Laura looked down at the *Comelina cœlestis*, and fain would she have robbed it of its kiss, but she consoled herself with the thought that she would rifle it of its sweets as soon as the messenger left.

He came closer. " Your ladyship," said he, in a very low voice, " I bear a message, as well as a nosegay. Is there any one about, to overhear me ? "

" No one," replied Laura, breathless and eager.

" Search the bouquet, and under the *Comelina* your ladyship will find something."

Laura's rosy fingers were buried in the flowers, and she drew from its fragrant hiding-place a small slip of paper.

" Your ladyship is requested, if you consent, to return, as an answer, the four first words of the note."

Laura unrolled the paper, and read : " *Not to-morrow, but to-day*. Danger threatens, and we must anticipate.—E."

Her face flushed, and her eager eyes were fixed upon that little scroll which, to her and her lover, was of such great import. What could it mean ? She read it again and again, until the words danced before her reeling senses.

The clerk came closer yet. " Your ladyship," whispered he, " I must take back my answer. Somebody might come in."

" The answer ? " gasped she, scarcely knowing what he said. " True, true, there must be an answer." She stood for a moment irresolute, then a shudder thrilled through her frame, and she felt as if some evil spirit had again come nigh. She raised her eyes to the face of the messenger, as though she would have looked into the penetralia of his thoughts.

" I am to write four words ? " asked she, plaintively. " You know, then, where he lives ? "

The clerk replied without the least embarrassment : " Pardon me, I told your ladyship that I was unacquainted with the cavalier. He awaits my return in the flower-market, and lest I should be too long absent, he hired a *fiacre* to bring me forth and back."

"He awaits my answer," thought Laura. " Oh, it must be so ! He shall not be left in suspense ! "

She went hurriedly to a table, and wrote, " *Not to-morrow, but to-day.*"

"Here," said she, " is my answer, and before you go, I beg you to accept this for your trouble."

She was about to hand him a purse of gold, when he retreated, and raised his hand in token of refusal.

" I thank your ladyship, I have already been paid, and have no right to a reward from you. May I be permitted to take my leave ? "

"Yes ; hasten, I implore you," returned Laura, wondering at his disinterestedness.

Scarcely had the commissionnaire taken his leave, when the door of the antechamber was opened, and a lackey announced :

" Madame, her royal highness the Duchess of Orleans ! "

Laura hastily thrust the paper in her bosom, and, coming forward, kissed the hand of her friend. But as she did so, she felt the blood rush to her temples, and bent low her head to hide her confusion.

"I could not stay away any longer," began the unsuspecting duchess. " For three days monsieur has been confined to his room with some trifling ailment, for which peevishness seems to be his only palliative. He is one of those who, when he sneezes, imagines that the earth is shaken to her foundations ; and when he snuffles, that all the angels in heaven drop on their knees to pray for him. With some trouble, I prevailed upon him to give me one hour wherein to make some change in my dress. I have accomplished the change in fifteen minutes, and the remainder of the hour I come to spend with you."

"Thank you, dear friend," replied Laura, who had now recovered her self-possession, and was sincerely glad to see the duchess. Then leading her to a divan, the graceful young hostess dropped down on a cushion at the feet of her royal guest, and continued : "I have been wondering why I did not see my gracious mistress ; I thought she had forgotten me."

" How could you do her such injustice ? " replied Elizabeth-

Charlotte, affectionately. "I have been longing for the sound of your carolling voice, and the sight of your beaming face. Let me look at you," continued she, taking Laura's head between her two hands, and gazing upon her with fondest admiration.

Poor Laura could ill bear the test of such loving scrutiny. She blushed scarlet, and her long black eyelashes fell at once under the searching look of the duchess's round blue eyes.

"Laura!" exclaimed she, anxiously, "something ails you, my darling; what have you on your heart that you are hiding from me?"

"Dear, dear duchess," stammered Laura, "I have nothing to—"

"Nay, child, do not stoop to untruth—"

"I cannot—I will not," cried Laura, bursting into tears. "I have a—secret—but you shall know it—soon."

"Gracious Heaven!" cried the duchess, turning very pale, "what has happened? What evil tidings am I to hear?"

"No evil tidings, my dearest mistress, no evil tidings! Nothing but joy—joy unspeakable. Do you remember what I told you on that happy morning of the ball, that if I ever loved I would leave even your dear self to follow the man of my choice? Well!" cried she, her face breaking out into bright smiles, while glistening tears lay like dew-drops upon her rose-tinted cheeks, "he is here! He came down from the moon on yesternight, and brought two great stars in his head instead of eyes; stars that I had no sooner looked upon, than I fell madly in love. Oh! he was sen hither by the good God, and it is His will that I love him, and forsake all others, to follow whithersoever he leads!"

"Is she mad?" cried the duchess, in alarm. "Yesternight? —came from the moon?—Who came, Laura?"

"God and my mother know his name, and both have blessed us; but I dare not tell it yet—not even to you. Pray ask me no more—for I may not say another word."

"Not say another word?" said the duchess, shaking her head, and looking reproachfully at her favorite. "Then there is something wrong in this headlong love, and it is no message to your heart from above. Afraid to say more to your best friend—to her who replaces your mother?—When saw you this preterhuman being? Who?—Great God!" cried she, suddenly, putting her hands to her heart, "can it be! Yes —it must be Prince Eugene!"

Laura clapped her hands, and then threw herself in the duchess's arms. "Yes—you have guessed—it is he whom I shall love to-day, to-morrow, and forever. But not another word, my own dear mistress. To-morrow you shall know all, and be assured that there is no wrong either done or to be done—I can say but this to-day, that he certainly came down from the moon, and is the only luminary whose rays shall ever shine upon my heart!"

While Laura was pouring out her childish half-confidences, her disinterested friend, the commissionnaire, was similarly engaged in the anteroom with Master George.

This latter worthy, after a few whispered words from the former, excused himself to the lackeys of her royal highness, who were in waiting there, and retreated to the corridor with the clerk.

"Now, George," whispered he, "mark what I tell you. Your master says that the coachman must be ready with the travelling-carriage of the marchioness at ten o'clock to-night; that Mademoiselle Louise must secretly pack up some of her lady's effects and her own, and have them conveyed to the chariot throughout the day; and that all must be done so that her ladyship shall suspect nothing."

"It shall be done. And so her ladyship is to go on a journey at ten o'clock to-night? What an hour to set out!"

"Yes, at ten o'clock precisely, and the blessing of God go with her!"

# BOOK III.

## CHAPTER I.

### THE DISAPPOINTMENT.

ALL was bustle and confusion in the Hôtel de Soissons. A crowd of workmen filled its halls; some on ladders, regilding walls and ceilings; some on their knees waxing the inlaid floors; and others occupied in removing the coverings, and dusting the satin cushions of the rich furniture of the state apartments. The first upholsterers in Paris had been summoned to the work of preparation, and the general-in-chief of the gilders stood in their midst, giving orders to his staff, and sending off detachments for special service. He held in his hand a roll of paper resembling a marshal's baton, with which he assigned their posts to his men. Some of his subalterns approached, to ask in what style the walls of the reception-rooms were to be decorated.

"I must see the Prince of Savoy about that," said he, with a flourish. And he took his way for the prince's cabinet. "Announce me to his highness," said he, ᴜᴏ he entered the antechamber.

"His highness is at home to nobody to-day, sir," replied Conrad.

"He will be at home for me," said the decorator, complacently. "Say to the prince that I desire an interview on business of great moment, connected with the embellishment of the hôtel; and without a conference with himself we cannot proceed. I am Monsieur Louis, the master of the masters of decoration."

Conrad, quite awed by the stateliness of Monsieur Louis, went at once to announce him, and returned with a summons for him to enter the cabinet.

Eugene met him with a bright smile of welcome, and asked what he could do to assist Monsieur Louis.

"Your highness," replied monsieur, "my workmen have gilded, waxed, and dusted the apartments, and the important task of decorating them is about to commence. I am here to inquire of your highness what is to be the character of the decorations. Are they to have a significance that betokens Honor, Friendship, Art, or Love?"

Eugene could not repress a smile as he asked whether, for the expression of these various sentiments, there were different styles of decoration.

"Most assuredly," was the pompous reply. "It depends entirely upon the nature of the guest or guests to be entertained. If your highness is to receive a personage of distinction (a king, for example), your decorations must be emblematic of respect. They must consist of laurels, lilies, and banners. If a friend or one of your own noble kinsmen, the decorations have no special significance; we mingle flowers, festoons, and pictures that are not allegorical. If you invite a company of artists, poets, musicians, and the like, the principal decorations surmount the seat of the Mæcenas who entertains, and the rest of the apartment is left in simplicity."

"But you spoke of a fourth style," said Eugene, blushing.

"Indeed I did, your highness; and on that style we lavish our best efforts. If the guest is to be a bride, then our walls and ceilings must be ornamented with rich designs emblematic of love. We must have cupids, billing doves, and wreaths of roses, mingled with orange-flowers. Added to this, the decorations must begin in the vestibule, and be carried out in character, through the entire palace."

"Well," said Eugene, his large eyes glowing with delight, "let your decorations be appropriate to a bridal."

"Impossible, your highness! This style requires great originality of conception, and time to carry out the designs. It would require a hundred workmen, and then I doubt—"

"Employ more than a hundred," returned Eugene, "and it can be done in a day. Indeed it must be done, and—I ask of you as a favor not to mention to any one in what style you are decorating the Hôtel de Soissons."

"Your highness, I will answer for myself, but I cannot answer for the discretion of a hundred workmen, who, precisely because they are asked to be silent, would prefer to be communicative."

"Well—do your best, but remember that your work must be done to-day."

"It shall be done, your highness, and when you see it, you will confess that I am the first *décorateur* of the age."

So saying, Monsieur Louis made his bow and strutted off.

Eugene looked after him with a smile. "He is proud and happy," said the prince, "and yet he merely embellishes the palace wherein love's festival is to be held. But for me—oh, happiest of mortals! is the festival prepared. Laura, adored Laura, I must speak thy name to the walls, or my heart will burst with the fullness of its joy! How shall I kill the weary hours of this day of expectation? How cool the hot blood that rushes wildly through my veins, and threatens me with loss of reason from excess of bliss! I am no longer a solitary, slighted abbé; I am a hero, a giant, for *I am beloved!*"

At that moment the door was hastily opened, and Conrad made his appearance.

"Your highness," said he, "a messenger is here from her royal highness, madame, and begs for an audience."

Eugene started, and his brow clouded with anxiety. "A messenger from madame," murmured he. "What can—how should the duchess?——But—Conrad, admit him."

"Speak," cried Eugene, as soon as the messenger entered the room. "What are her royal highness's commands?"

"Her royal highness the Duchess of Orleans requests his highness Prince Eugene of Savoy to visit her immediately. And that no delay may occur, her royal highness's equipage is at the door, waiting for his excellency."

Eugene answered not a word. With an imperious wave of the hand, which was justly interpreted into a command to clear the passage, he strode on and on through the corridors of the Hôtel de Soissons, crushing with his foot Monsieur Louis's choicest garlands, that lay on the floor ready to wreathe the walls and mirrors of the rooms of state.

Monsieur Louis was shocked at such desecration ; but still more shocked was he to observe what a change had come over the face of the prince since their interview scarce half an hour ago. Reckless of the ruined garlands that followed his track, pale and silent, he went on and on, down the marble staircase, and through the vestibule, until he flung himself into the coach, and cried :

"On, for your life ! urge your horses to their topmost speed !"

The coachman obeyed, and went thundering down the streets, little heeding whether the equipage that bore the royal arms trod down half a dozen boors on its way or not.

It drew up with a sudden jerk before the Palais Royal ; and the messenger, who had followed on horseback, asked if his highness would follow him. He had madame's orders to introduce her visitor without further ceremony, by a private staircase, leading to her own apartments.

Doubtless the duchess had heard the carriage as it stopped, for, when Eugene entered the anteroom, she was standing in the door of her cabinet, visibly impatient for his arrival. She beckoned him to approach, and closed the door with her own hand.

She gave him no time for ceremonious greeting. "God be thanked, you are here !" exclaimed she. "Put down the por-tière, that no one may hear what I have to say." Eugene obeyed mechanically, and loosening its heavy tassels, the crimson satin curtain fell heavily to the floor.

"And now," cried the duchess, indignantly, "now, Prince Eugene of Savoy, I command you to tell me the truth, and the whole truth ! What have you done with her ? How could you be so unknightly as to take advantage of her innocent and affectionate nature, to wrong one of the purest and most perfect of God's creatures ! My heart is like to break with its weight of sorrow and disgrace ; and, had it not been for Laura's sake, I would have laid my complaint before his ma-jesty. But I must not expose her to the world's contumely, and therefore I endure your presence here. Tell me at once what have you done with my darling ?"

Eugene could scarcely reply to this passionate appeal. His

senses reeled—his heart seemed to freeze within him. He thought he comprehended ; and yet—

" Who ? Who is gone ? Oh, duchess, be merciful ; what mean these words of mystery ? "

The duchess eyed him scornfully. " Base seducer, dare you question me ? Do you strive to delude me into believing that you do not know of whom I speak ? I demand of you at once the person of the Marchioness de Bonaletta ! "

" Laura ! " cried Eugene, in a tone of deepest despair. " Laura gone ! And you say that I enticed her away ! "

" Tell me the truth, tell me the truth," cried madame.

" The truth ! " groaned Eugene, while the duchess started from her seat, and grasped both his hands in hers.

" Have mercy," stammered he, trembling as if an ague had suddenly seized him. " Is she no longer—here ? "

" She is no longer here," echoed the duchess, staring in astonishment at the writhing features of the unhappy prince.

" You know not where she is ? " gasped he, faintly.

" No," cried she, " no ! You look as though you were yourself astounded, Prince Eugene ; but you will no longer deny your guilt when I tell you that my poor innocent child has told me all."

" What—all ? " asked Eugene.

" She told me that you were lovers. And now, prevaricate no longer ; it is useless and renders you still more infamous."

" What more did she say ? " asked Eugene, unconscious that his tone was as imperative as that of an emperor.

" Nothing more. She merely told me that in two days I should learn all. Alas ! I have learned it to my cost, and to her ruin ! "

" And you accuse *me* of enticing her ! Great God ! if my heart were not breaking with anguish, it would break that such baseness could be attributed to me. Would that I could answer you, duchess, but God in heaven knows that I was ignorant of her departure, until I learned it from yourself ! "

" Was ever a man so bold in falsehood ! " cried the duchess, losing all command of her temper. " I have in your own handwriting the proof of your wickedness. Now mark me ! This morning, the second woman in waiting of the marchioness came frightened to my apartments to tell me that her mistress, her woman Louise, and George, had disappeared from the pavilion, no one could surmise when. I was so overcome with terror that I hurried to the pavilion, and alas! found that it was indeed so. Neither her own bed, nor that of the servant who accompanied her, had been occupied. I looked everywhere for some clew to the mystery, when, on the floor near her morning-dress, which hung on a chair, I found this scrap of paper, which, as it is signed with your initials, you will not deny, I presume."

With eyes that flashed fire, she almost dashed the paper in his face. Eugene took it, and, having given it one glance, he turned pale as death, and it fluttered from his palsied hands to the floor.

"Heavens, what can ail him!" cried the duchess, sympathizing, in spite of herself, with his sudden sorrow. He was ghastly as a spectre, and his whole frame shook like the leaf of an aspen.

"I did not write it," gasped he, but almost inaudibly; for his teeth chattered so that he could scarcely articulate a sound.

"What!" exclaimed the duchess, now thoroughly convinced of his innocence, and feeling her terror increase with the conviction, "what! you did not write these words?"

He shook his head, but no sound came from his blanched lips. He laid his hands upon his heart as if to stifle its anguish; then, raising them to his head, he pressed them to his temples, and so paced the room for a while. Then he came and stood before the duchess, whose compassionate eyes filled with tears as they met his look of anguish. Finally, he heaved a long sigh, and spoke.

"My name has been used to deceive her," said he. "She has never seen my writing, and thus she fell into the snare."

"But I cannot comprehend who it is that possessed such influence over her as to frighten her into silent acquiescence of the fraud. Laura is young, but she is prudent and resolute. These words had some meaning which could be referred to you, or she would not have understood them."

"Ay," returned Eugene, solemnly, "they were chosen with satanic shrewdness. They referred to our plans of to-day, and

12

signified that I had anticipated the time for our marriage.
Ah! well I know what happened; and well I know why
Laura made no resistance! At ten o'clock she extinguished
all the lights in her parlor save one; and as soon as this signal had been given, four men, whose faces were concealed, entered the house. One of them was a priest, two were witnesses,
and the fourth—O God! that fourth one! Who was he I
know not; but I shall learn—alas! too soon. Without a
word (for such had been our agreement) he took her hand, and
the priest read the marriage ceremony. When the names had
been signed, *he* raised my Laura in his arms, bore her through
the postern to a carriage, and, O God! O God! tore her from
me forever!"

"But how come you to know these particulars, who knew
not even of her flight?"

"Duchess, it *was* to have taken place to-night, and *I* was
to have been that bridegroom. We were overheard, and those
accursed words, 'not to-morrow, but to-night,' were sent in
my name. She thought to give me her dear hand, while I—
I—"

He could not proceed. He gave one loud sob, and burst
into tears. Those tears, bitter though they were, saved his
reason.

The duchess, too, wept profusely. "Poor prince!" said
she, "well may you mourn, for you have lost an angel of
goodness and—"

"No!" interrupted Eugene, fiercely. "Say not that she is
lost to me! I must find her, for she is mine,—and I must find
her ravisher. Great God of heaven!" cried he, raising his
clasped hands, "where shall I find the robber that has so
cruelly despoiled us both?"

"Stay!" cried the duchess. "I know of a man that was
her suitor, and whose suit was countenanced by her father and
her brother. She told me of it herself, and, to avoid their
persecutions, took refuge with me."

"His name, his name, I implore you, his name!"

"The Venetian ambassador, the Marquis de Strozzi."

"I thank your highness," replied Eugene, approaching the
door.

" Whither do you go ? "

" To seek the Venetian ambassador."

" And compromise Laura ? You do not know that things transpired as you imagine. She may merely have been removed by her father, to part her from yourself. And suppose the marquis was no party to her flight ? You would make her ridiculous—nay, more ; you would sully her name, so that every gossip in Paris would fall upon your Laura's reputation, and leave not a shred of it wherewith to protect her from the world's contempt."

Eugene wiped off the great drops of sweat that beaded his pallid brow. "You are right," said he. "She must not be compromised—no, not even if I died of grief for her loss : there are other means—I will go to her father."

Elizabeth nodded her head approvingly. "Yes—that you can do. You may confide her secret to her father. Take the same carriage that brought you hither, and, to make sure of obtaining speedy admission to Louvois' presence, announce yourself as my envoy."

"I thank your highness," replied Eugene, and, inclining his head, he moved toward the door. The duchess followed him, and, taking his hand affectionately, pressed it within her own.

" I see that you love my darling as she deserves to be loved, and you would have made her happy. Forgive my injustice and my hard words. I was so wretched that I knew not the import of my accusations."

" I do not remember them," returned Eugene, sadly. " But one thing fills my heart—the thought of my Laura's loss. Farewell, dear lady. Now, to question Louvois ! "

## CHAPTER II.

### THE FOES.

GREAT was the astonishment of the household of Louvois, when, hastening to do honor to the liveries of the royal house of Orleans, they saw emerging from the coach Prince Eugene of Savoy.

"Announce me to Monsieur Louvois," said he.

The message passed from vestibule to corridor, from corridor to staircase, and finally reached the antechamber of the minister's private cabinet. In a short while, the answer was forthcoming.

"His excellency begged to decline the visit of his highness the Prince of Savoy. He was particularly engaged."

"He is at home," replied the prince; "then I shall certainly alight, for I must and will see him."

So he entered the house, and traversed the vestibule. The lackeys made no effort to stop him, for he looked dangerous; but they were certainly astounded at his boldness, who forced himself into the presence of the minister, when *he* had declined the proffered visit.

Eugene, disregarding their amazed looks, asked the way to the cabinet, and no one ventured to refuse. So he was passed from lackey to lackey, until he reached the antechamber. "Here," said the servant that had accompanied him, "here your highness will find a person to announce you."

Eugene bowed his head, and entered. The "person" was certainly within; but in lieu of announcing the prince, he stared at him in speechless astonishment.

Eugene paid no attention to him, but moved toward the door leading to the prime minister's cabinet. When the valet saw this, he flew across the room to stop the intruder, and, placing himself directly in his way, he bowed and said, "Pardon me, your highness. You must have been misinformed. His excellency regrets that he cannot receive your highness's visit to-day. He is particularly engaged."

"I have no visit to make to his excellency," replied the

prince without embarrassment. " I am the envoy of her royal highness the Duchess of Orleans. Announce me as such."

The valet soon returned, and, holding up the portière so as to admit Eugene, he said, " His excellency will receive the envoy of her royal highness the Duchess of Orleans."

Louvois was standing near a writing-table, from which he appeared at that moment to have risen. His right hand rested on a book, and he stood stiff and erect, awaiting an inclination from Eugene, to bend his head in return. But the prince advanced so proudly that Louvois involuntarily made a step toward him, and then recollecting himself, stood still and frowned visibly.

" You came under false colors to claim an audience from me, prince," said he. " As you found (indeed, you should have known) that I would not receive you in your own name, you borrowed that of her royal highness ; taking advantage of the respect due madame, to force yourself into my presence. What is your business ?"

" In supposing that I have used her royal highness's name to force myself upon you, you are mistaken," replied Eugene, calmly. " If you will take the trouble to look out of yonder window, you will see that I came hither in her highness's own coach."

Louvois stepped to the window, looked out, and, affecting astonishment, exclaimed, " True enough ; there are the royal liveries, and you have told the truth. You really must excuse me."

" I do excuse you ; for I do not consider that one bearing the name of Louvois is in a position to affront me by doubting my word."

" Lucky for you," returned Louvois, with his sinister laugh ; " for there is not likely to be much harmony between the two families. And now to business. What message do you bear from madame ?"

" Her royal highness informs Monsieur de Louvois that on yesterday night, the Marchioness de Bonaletta disappeared from her pavilion in the Palais Royal. As Monsieur de Louvois is well posted in all that takes place in or about Paris, her royal highness is convinced that he is no stranger to this occurrence, and she requires that her lady of the bedchamber be returned to her, or she be directed where to find her."

" Is that all ? " asked Louvois, after a pause.

"That is all that I have to say *for the Duchess of Orleans.*"

" You are so very emphatic that I infer you have something else to say, after all. Am I right ? "

" You are."

" Well, you may speak. But first, allow me to ask how you happen to be her highness's messenger ? Was it by way of sympathizing with the Marchioness de Bonaletta, that you took service with her mistress ? "

" My lord prime minister," returned Eugene, proudly, " I serve myself and the requirements of my honor only."

" Ah, indeed ! And does this respectable lady pay you well ? "

" She bestows upon me wherewith to pay those who venture to attack *her* name."

" Ha ! ha ! Then you must have heavy payments to make, not for yourself only, but for your mother."

Eugene clinched his fist, and made a motion toward his cruel enemy, but Louvois calmly raised his hand.

" Peace, young man," said he ; " the hour for reckoning has not arrived. I respect, in you, the representative of madame, and you shall depart from my house uninjured, *to-day.* Take advantage, then, of your opportunity ; say all that you have to say, and spare yourself the trouble of sending me your petitions by writing."

" I have no petitions to make to you, oral or written. I came hither to claim for her royal mistress the Marchioness de Bonaletta, your daughter."

" And I repeat my question. How came *you* to be the chosen ambassador of her royal highness, on this strictly private affair between herself and me ? "

" I was chosen," replied Eugene, breathing hard and growing pale, " because I love the marchioness."

Louvois laughed aloud. " You love my daughter, do you ? I admire the sagacity which directs your love toward the daughter of the prime minister of France, and the richest heiress within its boundaries. I congratulate you upon your choice."

"Yes," repeated Eugene, "I love her, although she is your daughter. And so dearly do I love her that, for her dear sake, I submit to be affronted by my mother's traducer, because that traducer is the father of my Laura. As regards your absurd insinuations respecting her wealth, they pass by me as the 'idle wind which I respect not.' And now, that I have satisfied your curiosity, be so good as to answer me. The Duchess of Orleans wishes to know where is her lady of the bedchamber: Eugene of Savoy demands his bride."

"Demands his bride? This is too presuming! But I must be patient with the representative of madame. Know, then, ambitious manikin, that, with a father's right to save his misguided child from your artifices and from the ridicule of the world, I rescued her from ruin last night, and, to secure her honor, gave her in marriage to an *honorable* man."

Eugene was as overwhelmed with this intelligence as though he had not foreseen it from the first. His wail was so piteous that Louvois himself felt its terrible significance, and started.

"You forced—forced her to give her hand to another?" gasped he.

"Forced! I perceived no reluctance on my daughter's side, to her marriage. She spoke a willing and distinct assent to the priest's interrogatory. I ought to know, who myself was one of her witnesses."

"That merely proves that she was deceived by the lying note that you forged in my name. How, in the sight of God, can a father so betray his own child!"

"It was sent with my approbation, but written by Barbesieur, as a slight token of acknowledgment for your cowardly attack on him at the Pré aux Clercs. Your mother was right, it appears, when a few weeks ago she told me that no sympathy could exist between her race and mine; and that every attempt at love between us was sure to end in hate. Quite right she was, quite right. And now, Prince of Savoy, your mission is fulfilled. Tell the Duchess of Orleans that her lady of the bedchamber is secure, but cannot return to her service: she is under the protection of her husband,"

"I will tell her," replied Eugene. "I will tell her that all honor, all humanity, all justice, forgetting, a father has cruelly betrayed his own daughter, and has cursed her life forever. Your wicked action has broken the hearts of two of God's creatures, and has consigned them to a misery that can only end with death. I say not, 'May God forgive you.' No! may God avenge my Laura's wrongs, and may he choose Eugene of Savoy as the instrument of His wrath! for every pang that rends the heart of my beloved, and for every throe that racks my own, you shall answer to me, proud minister of France: and, as there lives a God in heaven, you shall regret one day that you rejected me for your son-in-law."

Without another word or look toward Louvois, he left the room, and returned to his carriage. When he re-entered the cabinet of madame, his ghastly face, the very incarnation of woe, told its own story.

"You bring me evil tidings," said she, mournfully. "My darling is lost to us both!"

"Alas, my prophetic heart! She is married!" was his cry of despair.

"Poor Laura! poor Eugene!" sobbed the duchess, unable to restrain her tears.

"If you weep, what shall *I* do?" asked Eugene. "Why do you take it so much to heart?"

"Why?" exclaimed she. "Because I am no longer young, and I have lost my last hope of happiness. You, at least, have life and the world before you."

"And I," said he, languidly—"I am young, and have a life-time wherein to suffer. The world is before me! Yes; but it is a waste, without tree or flower. With scorched eyes and blistered feet, I must tread its burning sands alone. Forgive me, dear lady, if I ask permission to go. If I stay much longer, my aching head will burst."

"You are wan as a spectre, my poor Eugene," returned the duchess, laying her hand upon his arm, and looking him compassionately in the face.

"And, in truth, I am but the corpse of the living man of yesterday," sighed he. "Let me go home, that I may bury myself and my dead hopes together."

The duchess rang for her gentleman in waiting, and requested him to accompany the prince to his carriage, and thence to the Hôtel de Soissons ; but Eugene gently refused the proffered escort, and begged to be allowed to depart alone. He turned away, and as the duchess watched his receding figure, she saw him reel from side to side, like a man intoxicated.

At last he was at home. He had strength left to alight, to ascend the long marble staircase, whose balustrade was now hidden by a thicket of climbing jessamines, and to enter the antechamber leading to the apartments of state.

Monsieur Louis, with the élite of his workmen, was decorating its walls with hangings of white satin, looped with garlands suspended from the bills of cooing doves. When he beheld the prince, he came triumphantly forward.

"See, your highness, this is but the vestibule of the temple ! When you will have seen its interior, you will confess that it is worthy the abode of the loveliest bride that ever graced its princely halls."

Eugene neither interrupted nor answered him. He raised his large, mournful eyes to the festooned roses, the gilded doves, the snowy, shimmering satin, and to his fading senses they seemed gradually to darken into cypress-wreaths and funereal palls. He pressed his hand upon his bursting heart, and fell insensible to the floor.

## CHAPTER III.

### THE REPULSE.

EIGHT weeks had passed away since the disappearance of the Marchioness de Bonaletta—eight weeks of suffering and delirium for Eugene of Savoy. A nervous fever had ensued, which, if it had well-nigh proved mortal, had proved, in one sense, beneficent ; for it had stricken him with unconsciousness of woe. Blissful dreams of love hovered about his couch, and lit up with feverish brilliancy his pallid countenance. At such times *she* seemed to sit beside him ; for he smiled, held out his hand, and addressed her in words of burning love and ecstasy. Perhaps these joyful phantasms gave him strength to recuperate from his terrible prostration, for he recovered ; and, after four weeks of struggle between life and death, was declared convalescent. His grandmother and his sisters had nursed him tenderly throughout, and they had the satisfaction of hearing from his physician, that to their loving care he owed his restoration to health. The poor sufferer himself could not find it in his heart to be grateful for the boon. With returning reason came awakening anguish, sharp as the first keen stroke that had laid low the beautiful fabric of his ephemeral happiness.

But he was resolved to face his sorrow—not to fly from it. "It shall kill me or make a man of me, whom no shaft of adversity can ever wound again," thought he. He confided his troubles to no one, little dreaming that his secret was known not only to his grandmother and his sisters, but to the Princes de Conti, who, throughout their long watches by his bedside, had heard the history of his love, its return by the beloved one, and its disastrous end. But each and all respected the secret, and tacitly agreed to cover it with a veil of profound silence.

So Eugene suffered and struggled alone, until the tempest of his grief had passed, and light once more dawned upon his soul. His dreamy eyes, in whose depths one visionary object had been mirrored, now rested upon things with quick and apprehensive intelligence ; his ears, that had been pained with one monotonous dirge of woe, now opened to the sounds of the outer world around ; and his thoughts, which hitherto had kept unceasing plaint for their buried love, now shook off repining, and hearkened to the trumpet-call of ambition.

One morning he called Conrad, who (accustomed of late to see his master reclining languidly on a sofa, seemingly interested in nothing) was quite surprised to find him in the arsenal, busily engaged in examining and cleaning his arms.

Conrad could not repress a smile, and a glance of mingled astonishment and delight. Eugene saw it, and replied at once.

" You see," said he, gently, " that I am better, Conrad. I

was very slow to recover from my severe illness, but I believe that I am quite sound again. I thank you for all your self-sacrificing devotion to me, during that season of suffering; and never while my heart beats will I forget it. Let me press your friendly hand within my own, for well I know that your highest reward is to be found in my esteem and affection."

Conrad grasped the hand that was so kindly proffered, and tears of joy fell upon its pale, attenuated fingers.

"My dear lord," sobbed he, "how you have suffered! and oh, how gladly I would have suffered for you!"

"I believe it, good, true heart; but let us try to forget the past, and make ready for the future. First—tell me whether the letter you took for me yesterday is likely to reach the cabinet of his majesty."

"Yes, your highness," replied Conrad, with a happy smile. "My cousin Lolo washes the plate at the Louvre, and is engaged to be married to the king's second valet. I gave it to her, and charged her, as she valued her salvation, to see that Leblond remitted it."

"So far, so well, then. Order my state-carriage, livery, and outriders; and then return to assist me in dressing. I must go to court in half an hour."

While Eugene was preparing to visit the king, his majesty with his prime minister was in his cabinet, writing; while, not too far to be out of reach of his majesty's admiring eyes, sat the demure De Maintenon, profoundly engaged in tapestry-work. The conference over, Louis signed to Louvois to gather up the papers to which the royal signature had been attached, and to take his leave. Louvois hastened to obey; put his portfolio under his arm, and was about to retire, when the king bade him remain.

"Apropos," said he, "I was about to forget a trifle that may as well be attended to. I have received a letter from Prince Eugene of Savoy. There is a vacancy in the dragoons, and the little prince asks for it. Methinks it can be granted."

Louvois smiled. "What, your majesty! Give a captaincy of dragoons to that poor little weakling? Why, he would not survive one single campaign." As he uttered these careless words, he glanced at the marquise, who understood him at once.

"In truth," observed she, in her soft, musical voice, whose melody was as bewitching as that of the sea-maids of Sicily "in truth, poor Prince Eugene seems as unsuited to the career of a soldier as to that of an ecclesiastic. The dissipated and debauched life which, in imitation of his mother, he has led since his boyhood, has exhausted his energies. He is prematurely old—older far than your majesty."

A complacent smile flitted over the features of the vain monarch. "He certainly looked more dead than alive the last time we saw him, and since then he has been very ill, has he not?"

"Yes," replied Louvois, carelessly, "and for a long time his recovery was considered doubtful."

"Madame told me of it," resumed the king. "She seems very much interested in the little prince."

"Madame is the impersonation of goodness," observed De Maintenon, "and by her very innocence is unfitted to judge of character. The old Princess de Carignan imposed upon her credulity with some story of an unhappy attachment, while veritably his illness is nothing more than the natural consequence of his excesses."

Louvois thanked his coadjutor with a second glance, and the marquise acknowledged the compliment by a slight inclination of her head, imperceptible to the king.

"Be all this as it may," replied the latter, "I cannot refuse so paltry a favor to the nephew of Cardinal Mazarin. If we do no more, we ought at least to throw him a bone to gnaw." *

"Sire," said Louvois, hastily, "you do not know Prince Eugene. He is a dangerous man, though a weakly one, for he is possessed of insatiable ambition. He desires renown at any price."

"At any price!" repeated Louis, with a shrug. "Such a poor devil as that covet renown at any price!"

"Sire!" exclaimed Louvois, earnestly, "he is an offshoot

---

* Louis' own words.—"Mémoires de Jeanne d'Albret de Luynes," vol. i., p. 85.

of the ambitious house of Savoy, and a stranger besides. Strangers always bring us ill-luck."

"You are right," interposed the marquise, with a sigh. "Strangers never bring us any but ill-luck."

Louis turned and fixed his eyes upon her. Their glances met, and there was such unequivocal love expressed in that of the pious marquise, that her royal disciple blushed with gratification. He went up to her and extended both his hands.

She took them passionately within her own, and covered them with kisses. Then raising her eyes pleadingly to his, she whispered, "Sire, he is the son of his mother ; and if your majesty show him favor, I shall think that you have not ceased to love the Countess de Soissons, and my heart will break."

Louis was so touched by the charming jealousy unconsciously betrayed by these words, that he whispered in return :

"I will prove, then, that I love nobody but yourself."

"Be so good," added he aloud to Louvois, "as to say to the usher that the Prince of Savoy will have an audience."

This being equivalent to a dismission, Louvois backed out of his master's presence, and retired. As he was passing through the antechamber, congratulating himself upon having effectually muzzled his adversary, the minister saw his pale, serious face at the door. Eugene was in the act of desiring the usher to announce him.

"His majesty awaits the Prince of Savoy," said Louvois, and he stepped aside to allow him entrance.

Eugene came in, and the door was closed. The two enemies were alone, face to face ; and they surveyed each other as two lions might do on the eve of a deathly contest.

"It has pleased you to make an attempt to beg a commission in the army, and to address yourself directly to the king," said Louvois, after a pause. "And you presumed to do so without the intervention of his majesty's minister of war."

"I have no business with the servants of his majesty," replied Eugene, tranquilly. "If I have a request to make, I address it to the king my kinsman, and require no influence of his subordinates."

"Sir !" exclaimed Louvois, angrily, "I counsel you—"

"I desire no counsel from a man whom I despise," interrupted Eugene.

"You shall give me satisfaction for this word," returned Louvois, laying his hand on his sword. "You are a nobleman, and therefore—"

"And therefore," interrupted Eugene again, "you shall have no satisfaction from me, for you are *not* a nobleman, and I shall not measure swords with you. Peace, monsieur," continued he, as Louvois was about to insult him, "we are in the antechamber of the king, and a servant may not resent his grievances within earshot of his master. Take care that you become not too obstreperous, lest I publish to the world the story of your crimes toward your unhappy daughter. And now let me pass : the king awaits me."

With these words Eugene crossed the antechamber, and stood near the door that led to the king's cabinet. There he stopped, and, addressing the indignant minister—

"Now, sir," said he, imperatively, "you can go out to the vestibule and send the usher to announce me to his majesty."

Louvois made a rush at the prince, and almost shrieked with rage. "Sir, this insolence—"

But at that moment the door of the king's cabinet opened, and the voice of Louis asked, "Who presumes to speak so loud ?" His angry glances were launched first at one and then at the other offender, and, as neither made any reply, his majesty resumed :

"Ah, you are there, little abbé ? You asked for an audience : it is granted."

He returned to his cabinet, Eugene following. The marquise was assiduously occupied with her tapestry, but her large eyes were raised for one glance ; then, as quickly casting them down, she appeared to be absorbed in her embroidery.

The king threw himself carelessly back in an arm-chair, and signed to Eugene to advance.

"You would like to command a company of dragoons ?" said Louis, shortly.

"Such is my desire, your majesty. I wish to become a soldier ; I hope—a brave one."

Louis surveyed him with scorn. "I cannot grant your

request," said he. "You are too sickly to enter my service."

He then rose from his chair and turned his back. This of course signified that the audience was at an end; but, to his unspeakable astonishment, he felt the touch of a hand upon his arm, and, turning round, beheld Eugene!

"Is that all your majesty has to say to me?" said the prince.

"That is all," cried Louis, imperiously. "The audience is at an end—begone!"

"Not yet," replied Eugene, "not yet."

Madame de Maintenon uttered a cry of horror, and her tapestry fell from her hands.

"Do you know that you are a traitor?" exclaimed the king.

"No, sire. I am but a man who, driven to despair, can no longer withhold the cry of a heart wrung by every species of contumely and injustice. Were I tamely to submit to all that you have done to wound me, I were a hound unfit to bear the name of nobleman. By the memory of Cardinal Mazarin, your benefactor, nay, more, the spouse of your mother, I claim the right to remonstrate with your majesty, and to ask you to reverse your decision."

"You have summoned to your aid a name which I have ever cherished and honored," replied Louis. "For his sake I grant you fifteen minutes' audience. Be quick, then, and say what you will at once."

"Then, sire, may I ask if you remember the solemn promise you made to the cardinal on his death-bed?"

"I do."

"To the man who, during your minority, transformed a distracted country into a powerful and peaceful empire, you promised friendship and protection for his kindred. But how has this promise been fulfilled? The family of Mazarin have, one and all, been given over to persecution and injustice, and that by a sovereign who—"

"Prince," cried Louis, "you forget that you address your king!"

"My king! when has your conduct ever been to me that

of a king, and therefore of a father ? I know that my uncle was once king of the King of France ; and by the God above us ! he was a gracious monarch, for he left to his successor a prosperous kingdom and an overflowing treasury ! "

" Which was not fuller than his own private purse," retorted Louis.

" The cardinal named you his heir, sire—why did you not accept the heritage ? "

" Because I would not enrich myself at the expense of his family," replied Louis, haughtily.

" Because you knew very well that what you affected to relinquish, that the world might admire your magnanimity, you intended to take back by piecemeal. And to do this, you have persecuted the unhappy family of your best friend with an ingenuity of malice that is beneath the dignity not only of your station, but of your manhood ! "

" Sire," cried Madame de Maintenon, hastening to the king, " I beseech you, drive from your presence this insolent madman."

" Let him speak," said Louis, in a voice of suppressed rage. " I wish to see how far he will carry his presumption."

" Sire, it reaches past your crown, as far as the judgment-seat of God, where it stands as your accuser. Sire, what have we done to merit your aversion ? My mother—that you allowed your minions to traduce and drive her into exile ? My father—who fought and bled for you, that you offered him public insult, and so wounded his proud spirit, that he died from the effects of your cruelty ? My sisters—that you have robbed them of their patrimony ! And I !—what have I done that you should hold me up to the mockery of your court, and deny me the paltry boon of a petty commission in your army ? I had forgiven your public affronts, so unworthy of a king and a gentleman ; and I had offered my hand and sword to your majesty as proofs of my loyalty and superiority to resentment. As a kinsman and your subject you have repulsed me : for the future, know me as an alien and enemy."

The king laughed scornfully. " Puny braggart, what care I for your enmity ? "

" Time will show, sire ; and, as truly as a lion once owed

his life to a mouse, your majesty will repent of your injustice to me."

"I never repent," returned the king, hastily.

"A day of repentance must come for all who have sinned, and it must dawn for you. Beware lest it come so late that the prayers of yonder sanctimonious marquise avail you nothing."

"By heavens!" cried the king, starting from his seat and clutching his bell, "my patience is exhausted. This arch-traitor shall—"

But Madame de Maintenon was at his side in a moment. "Sire," said she, beseechingly, "in the name of the love and loyalty I bear my sovereign, pardon this misguided youth. Remember that the highest prerogative of power is the exercise of mercy. I, for my part, forgive him freely, and I thank God that I am here to mediate between him and your majesty's just anger."

"You are an angel," cried Louis, clasping her hand in his own, and covering them with kisses. "You are an angel whom God has sent for my happiness in this world and the next." And turning to Eugene with a lofty gesture, he said: "Go, young man. Madame de Maintenon's magnanimity has earned your pardon. Go—that I may forget you and your existence."

"Sire," replied Eugene with emphasis, "I do not intend that you shall forget me. In your pride of power, you have likened yourself to a god, but, great as you are, you shall rue the day on which Eugene of Savoy turned his back upon your kingdom!"

"So you persist in believing yourself to be a man, do you?"

"Yes, sire; such is my conviction. I aim at renown, and, in spite of my enemies, of my poverty, and of my friendless condition, I have strength and energy to attain it. I am no longer a subject of France. I bid farewell to my country forever."

With a slight inclination of his head, and without waiting for permission, he turned his back, and left the room.

Louis gazed upon his receding figure, with an expression

so strange, that Madame de Maintenon in great alarm flew to his side. His eyes were fixed, and great drops of sweat stood out upon his forehead. The marquise wiped them away with her handkerchief, all the while whispering words of tender encouragement.

Louis shivered, and seemed like one awakening from a dream. His eyelids fell, the strained eyeballs moved, and he tried to smile.

"Dearest friend," said he, "I know not what has happened; but, as the Prince of Savoy disappeared from my sight, a voice seemed to speak to my soul, and say that his threats had been prophetic, and that I would dearly rue the day on which the nephew of Mazarin had left me in anger. Can such things be? or am I the sport of—"

"Sire, sovereign, beloved," cried the marquise, kneeling and clasping his knees in her arms, "give no heed to this mocking voice. 'Tis but a temptation of the Evil One. Let us pray together."

"Yes, let us pray. Send for Père la Chaise, and let us away to the chapel."

---

## CHAPTER IV.

### THE FAREWELL.

PRINCE EUGENE, meanwhile, was on his way to visit the Duchess of Orleans. She met him with unaffected cordiality, and gave him a hearty welcome.

"Indeed," said she, extending both her hands, "I am rejoiced to see you again. I made you many a visit of inquiry during your illness; and it pained me deeply to hear from your grandmother that no effort of those who love you had so far prevailed upon you to leave your room. I am glad to see that your heart is returning to us, for you know that I am foremost in the rank of your friends."

"I know it, gracious lady," said Eugene, feelingly, "and for that reason I am here."

"And although you are pale, you are looking well. You

have a brave spirit, Eugene, and have met your sorrow like a man."

"Yes. Suffering has made a man of me, and he that has received its chrism with courage has overcome grief. I have come to give your highness a proof of my fortitude. I "— but he paused, and his face grew of a deadly pallor, while a convulsive sigh was upheaved from his bosom.

"Speak, poor boy," said the duchess, compassionately.

"I wanted to ask if your highness has news from the Marchioness de Bonaletta?" resumed he, with an effort.

"Yes," replied the duchess, mournfully.

"Has she written to you?" was the hurried rejoinder.

The duchess shook her head. "She has not, and thereby I judge that she is closely watched. For, if my darling were free to do so, she would long ago have poured her sorrows into my heart. Sometimes I feel her soft arms twining about my neck, and hear her voice, as, in the simplicity of her trust, she said to me one day : 'Pray for me, that I may never love, for if I should, I would forsake every thing for the man of my choice—even yourself, my best friend.'"

"She spoke thus?" cried Eugene, brightening.

"She did ; and, not long after, she glided up to me, and, giving me a kiss, said : 'I have found him, I have found him —him whom I shall love throughout all eternity.' 'Gracious Heavens !' I exclaimed, 'it is not Prince Eugene !' whereupon she kissed me again, and said, 'But it *is* he ; and I shall love him forever !'"

"Ah ! I thought I had been stronger !" murmured Eugene, his eyes filling with tears. "I had armed myself against misfortune, but the memory of her love unmans me."

"Poor Eugene ! I have been thoughtlessly cruel : forgive me, for you are the first one to whom I have dared, as yet, to mention her name. Let me not probe your wounds further, but tell you at once what I know. I have heard from Laura through the medium of her father only. The day after her shameful immolation, he communicated his daughter's marriage to the king ; and, the evening after, gave a grand ball in honor of the event. He excused her absence, and the secrecy attending her wedding, by saying that her betrothed having

been suddenly summoned away, he had yielded to the solicitation of the lovers, and had consented to have them married
without formality."

"Liar and deceiver!" cried Eugene, gnashing his teeth.

"Ay, indeed, liar and deceiver!" echoed the duchess.
"And I had to sit there, and hear him congratulated; and listen to the flattering comments of his guests, every one of
whom knew that not a word of truth was being spoken on
either side. Of course I had no choice whether to absent myself or not ; I was ordered to appear, and to confirm the lie.
And once or twice, when my face unconsciously expressed my
indignation, my husband was at hand to remind me that my
lady of the bedchamber had married with my consent and
approbation! The day after, Louvois distributed largesses
among his household, and bestowed princely sums upon the
poor, all in honor of the happy event! For a whole week I
could neither eat nor sleep for grief and anger. I can never
recover from this blow. If *you* had robbed me of Laura, I
could have forgotten my own loss in her gain ; but to know
that she is chained to the galley of an unhappy marriage
almost breaks my heart!"

"She is not chained to that galley," said Eugene; "the oath
she took was not to the man whom the world calls her husband—it was pledged to me. But do not fear that I will lay
claim to her, duchess. Far be it from me to take one step that
could endanger her safety, or unsettle her convictions. If *she*
considers the oath binding which she took to one man, supposing him to be another, I will bear my fate with resignation;
but if she scorns the lie that calls her *his* wife, she will find
means to let me know it ; and, let her summons come when it
may, I shall be ready to obey it. Let her heart seek mine, and
I will take care that renown shall tell her where to find
me."

"I feared as much," said the duchess. "I knew that you
would not remain at this false, corrupt court. Whither do
you travel?"

"I shall follow my brother. Your highness knows that he
was banished for having married the girl whom he loved,
whose only fault was her obscure birth. He is in the service

of the Emperor of Austria ; and, if his imperial majesty will accept of me, I, too, will join the Austrian army."

"And you will live to replace the lost myrtles of your love with the laurels of fame."

"God grant that you may be a true prophetess ! And now, your highness, I have one more favor to ask. May I visit the room in which I saw her last ? "

"Come. We can take a turn in the park, and enter the pavilion as if by accident. Every thing is just as she left it."

Accompanied by two maids of honor, and followed at a distance by two lackeys, they descended to the gardens. For a time they confined their stroll to the principal walks ; but when they had reached the pathway that led to the pavilion, the duchess, turning to her maids of honor, requested them to await her at the intersection of the avenues, and continued her way with the prince. Not a word was spoken on either side until they had ascended the steps leading to the room where, in one short hour, Eugene had seen the birth and death of his ephemeral happiness.

He opened the door ; then, standing on the threshold, gazed mournfully around him. Not an object in the room was missing. There, in the embrasure of the window, stood her harp ; there, on the table, lay her books and drawings ; and there, alas ! hung the silver chandelier whose solitary light was to have guided him to his bridal. Every thing was there, as before, and yet nothing remained, for she, who had been the soul of the habitation, had left it forever !

And now, as his wandering gaze rested upon the arm-chair where, kneeling at her feet, he had received the intoxicating confession of her love, he started forward, and, burying his face in its cushions, wept aloud.

The duchess, meanwhile, had remained outside on the *perron*. She would not invade the sanctity of Eugene's grief by her presence, for she felt that, in a moment of such supreme agony, the soul would be alone with its Maker.

Presently she heard the door open and Eugene joined her on the balcony. For a while he looked at her in silence ; then his lips began to move, and she caught these words, uttered almost inaudibly :

"I am about to go.   Will you grant me one more request?"
"Yes—what is it?"

"You told me that, when she confided to you her love for me, she put her arms around your neck, and kissed you.   May I have that kiss from your lips, dear duchess?"

Instead of a reply, Elizabeth embraced the poor youth. "God bless you, Eugene!" said she, fondly.   "Go forth into the world to fight the battle of life, and win it."

---

## CHAPTER V.

### A PAGE FROM HISTORY.

THE year 1683 was full of significance for Austria.   It was a period of victory and defeat, of triumph and humiliation. Austria's wounds were many and dangerous, but her cure was rapid.   In the spring of this momentous year she was threatened simultaneously from the East and the West, and she had every reason to fear that she would be similarly assailed from her northern and southern frontiers.

Her troubles originated, as they had often done before, with Hungary—that land of haughty Magyars and enthusiastic patriots.   Leopold I. ascended the throne in 1658, and from that time forward every year of his reign had been marked by intestine wars.   Sometimes, by force of numbers, the rebellious Hungarians were, for a time, held in subjection ; but the fire of patriotism, though smothered, was never extinguished in their hearts.   Deep buried under the ashes of many a deluded hope, it lived on, until some friendly breath of encouragement fanned it to activity, and its flames leaped upward, and defied the emperor anew.

Hungary would not submit to be considered as a provincial dependency on Austria.   She claimed the constitutional rights guaranteed to her from time immemorial, and recorded in the golden bull of King Andreas.   In 1654 the Emperor Ferdinand had promised, both for himself and his successors, that this constitution should be held inviolate ; that all foreign troops should be withdrawn from Hungary, while no Hungarians should be called upon to fight elsewhere than on their native soil ; that the crown lands were to be inalienable ; all offices bestowed upon native-born Hungarians ; Protestants secured in the exercise of their religion ; and no war undertaken, nor treaty concluded, with any foreign power, without the consent of the Hungarian Diet.

The Emperor Leopold had promised to ratify the constitution. But, in 1664, Austria declared war against Turkey, and called for money and troops from Hungary. The Magyars, not having been consulted as to the expediency of the war, refused to have any thing to do with it. With the help of France, peace was made with the Porte ; and, as soon as his foreign difficulties were settled, Leopold bethought himself of his turbulent Hungarians at home. Austrian troops were marched into Hungary, and the Protestant Magyars, in the enjoyment of high offices, were superseded by Catholics.

The indignation of the Hungarians knew no bounds. They took up arms, and swore never to lay them down until they had freed their native land. The revolution broke out in 1670 ; and such was the fanaticism of the patriots, that their banners bore the cross as their emblem, and every soldier wore a cross upon his shoulder. By this sign they swore eternal enmity to the detested Austrian lancers ; and, however they might be outnumbered, they hoped in God, and rushed by thousands to fill up the ranks whence thousands had fallen. Undaunted by reverses, undismayed by danger, new armies of warriors seemed to spring from the blood of the slain. Nor were the brave Hungarians without sympathy in their struggle for freedom ; they had allies both powerful and efficient.

Two of their ablest generals, Zriny and Frangipany, had fallen into the hands of the Austrians, and had perished ignominiously on the scaffold ; and another hero, Count Tököly, had fallen at the siege of Arva. But his son survived, a boy who had been rescued from the enemy and conveyed to Transylvania. There he was taught to hate the oppressors of his country ; and no sooner was he of an age to serve, than he entered the army. He brought with him succor from Prince Apafy, of Transylvania, and the promise of aid from the Porte,

Fired by the enthusiasm of young Emerich Tököly, the Hungarians renewed the contest with Leopold, and fortune so favored their youthful leader, that he conquered Upper Hungary, marched to Presburg, drove out the Austrians, and called an imperial Diet to consult as to the propriety of deposing the Emperor Leopold from the throne of Hungary.

But Emerich did not tarry at Presburg to attend the Diet. He marched on to Buda to confer with Kara Mustapha, the grand-vizier of Mohammed IV., on the affairs of Hungary. The victories of the young hero had more effect upon Mustapha than any amount of pleading could have done ; he was therefore prepared to receive him favorably. Mustapha was ambitious, covetous, and vindictive ; he had latterly felt some uneasiness as to the security of his own influence with the Sultan, and he burned to reinstate himself by gaining a victory or two over the Austrians. Moreover, he thought of the booty which would follow each victory ; and, in the hope of retrieving his defeat at St. Gotthard's, he concluded a treaty with Count Emerich, which was specially directed against Austria. He promised, in the Sultan's name, arms, money, and men ; and, as an earnest of the friendship of his new ally, Emerich was declared King of Hungary.

Under the ruined walls of the fortress of Fulek, which Emerich had taken from the enemy, Mustapha handed him the diploma of royalty which had been drawn up in Constantinople ; at the same time bestowing upon him the rank of a Turkish general, and presenting him with a standard and a horsetail.

The newly-appointed king pledged himself, in return, to consider the Sultan as his lord-paramount, and to pay him a yearly tribute of forty thousand florins. He was so elated with his title, and so desirous of humiliating Austria, that, to free himself from the emperor, he consented to become a vassal of the Porte. He signed the treaty, whereupon Kara Mustapha rejected the proposals of alliance which Leopold was making, and began to dream of extending the dominion of the Crescent, and of founding a Moslem empire in the West, whose capital should be Vienna. He dismissed the Austrian ambassadors with cold indifference, and promised the Sultan that the green banner of the Prophet should carry terror and devastation into the very heart of Austria. This was the danger which threatened the emperor from the East. He had equally powerful enemies in the West. Hungary had sent ambassadors to the court of Louis XIV. These ambassadors had been received in Paris as the accredited envoys of an independent and recognized kingdom ; and King Louis, a son of the Catholic Church, had carried his hatred to Austria so far, that he entered into a secret alliance with the unbelieving Porte, and promised assistance to the Protestant rebels of Hungary. This assistance he sent at once in the form of money and arms. French officers were dispatched to Hungary, to join the insurgents and discipline their soldiers. And, while Louis was secretly upholding Turkey and Hungary, he was calling councils at home to establish claims to a portion of the imperial dominions of Austria.

These juridical councils were established at Metz and Brisach, and they had instructions from Louis to reannex to his crown all the domains which had ever been held in fief by any of his predecessors, however remote. They began by summoning the lords of the Trois-Evêchés to acknowledge their vassalage to France ; and they went on to cite before their tribunal the Elector Palatine, the King of Spain, and the King of Sweden ; all and each of whom were called upon to do homage to the king, or have their possessions sequestrated.

All Europe was aghast at these monstrous pretensions, but nobody ventured to put them down, for Louis had a standing army of one hundred and forty thousand men, while the German empire, still suffering from its losses in the Thirty Years' War, could scarcely put into the field one-third of this number.

So that, without the drawing of a sword, Louis was suffered to possess himself of the important city of Strasburg, and subsequently of all Alsatia. Finally he claimed the cloister of Wasserburg and the province of Germersheim, and pushed his greed and arrogance to such a height, that Germany at last awakened from her lethargy, and found resolution enough to protest against the aggressions of this royal robber. Louis, in return, proposed to call a universal council at Frankfort, and have his claims investigated. This was agreed to, and each sovereign sent his plenipotentiaries. Meanwhile the King of France kept possession of all the lands in dispute, and stationed his troops at Strasburg, and at every other town in Alsatia.

Here was danger enough for the Emperor Leopold, from the west ; while, north and south, his horizon darkened also. The ambitious Victor Amadeus, seeing that Austria was encompassed by enemies, now bethought himself of annexing Lombardy to his dominions, while there was every reason to fear that the bold and enterprising Peter the Great would extend his frontiers to the Baltic Sea, and, with quite as much right as Louis ever had to Strasburg, declare Dantzic to be a part of his Russian territories.

## CHAPTER VI.

### THE EMPEROR LEOPOLD I.

THE Emperor Leopold had just returned from early mass. Throughout the services, and during the excellent sermon of his celebrated court-preacher Father Abraham, the face of his imperial majesty had worn a troubled aspect ; it had not even brightened at the appearance of the Empress Eleonora. But when, in his cabinet, he saw his professor of music, Herr Kircher, Leopold smiled, and his brow cleared at once. The professor was occupied in putting a new string to the emperor's spinet, which the evening before had been broken by his majesty at a concert ; and, having his back turned to the door, was not aware of the emperor's entrance until the latter laid his hand upon Kircher's shoulder.

The musician would have risen, but Leopold gently forced him back into his seat, observing that it was unbecoming in a teacher to rise at the entrance of his pupil.

"Of his pupil, your majesty, to whom there remains nothing for a teacher to teach ; for in good sooth, if your majesty felt disposed, you are competent to fill the chair of a musical professorship, or to become the *maestro* of your own imperial chapel."

"I prefer my own position," replied Leopold, laughing, "although there are times when the berth of an emperor is not an easy one. But when as at present I am here with you, then I am truly happy, for your conversation and music awaken in me pleasant thoughts and noble aspirations. Let me enjoy the hour, for indeed, Kircher, I need recreation."

The emperor sighed, and sank slowly into an arm-chair, where, taking off his plumed hat, he threw it wearily down on a tabouret close by.

"Has your majesty any cause for vexation?" asked Kircher.

"Not for vexation, but much for sorrow," returned Leopold. "Let me forget it, and if you have no objection, take up that piece of music on the table, and give me your opinion of it."

Professor Kircher obeyed at once. "Your majesty has been composing, I perceive, and your composition is in strict accordance with the rules of counterpoint."

"I have translated my sorrows into music," returned Leopold. "I could not sleep last night, and there was running through my head the words of a sad and beautiful Latin poem. I rose from my bed, and treading softly so as not to disturb the empress, I came hither, and set the poem to music. It gave me indescribable pleasure, and I wish you would try it, that I may know whether my interpretation has meaning for others as well as for myself."

"My voice will not do it justice, your majesty; let me call Vittorio Carambini to sing it, while I accompany him."

"No," returned Leopold. "Carambini's voice would so beautify my composition, that I would not recognize it. I prefer to hear it from you. So sit you down, dear Kircher, and begin."

Kircher made no further opposition, and commenced the prelude. The emperor leaned back his head, and closed his eyes, as he was accustomed to do, when listening attentively. Reclining among the purple-velvet cushions of his luxurious arm-chair, Leopold presented a handsome picture of imperial comeliness. His fine figure was set off to advantage by his close-fitting Spanish doublet of black velvet ; his short Spanish cloak, looped up with large diamond solitaires, fell in graceful folds from his shoulders, gently stirring with its golden fringe the feathers of his hat that lay beside him. The pale, regular features of the emperor harmonized with the splendid costume which, from the days of Charles V., had been in fashion at the imperial court of Vienna. Leopold had made one modification, however, in his dress. In spite of his dislike to the King of France, and all things French, he wore the long curled wig which Louis XIV. had brought into vogue.

His whole attention was absorbed by Kircher, who, with a wig similar in fashion, but more modest in dimensions, sat playing and singing the "Schmerz-Lied." He sang with great feeling, and he, as well as the composer, felt the power and beauty of the music.

It died away in gentle sighs, and there was a pause. Then the emperor in a low voice said, "Thank you, Kircher ; you have given me great pleasure."

"Your majesty, it is I who should thank you. Your composition is a masterpiece ; and, instead of criticising my miserable performance, you praise it."

"Do you really like it, then ?"

"Like it ! It evinces genius, which is something more than a conformity to musical rules. It is a gift from Heaven, whence surely all musical inspiration descends. The man that could listen to your 'Schmerz-Lied' without emotion has no soul ; and, to him that could hear it with eyes undimmed, God has denied the gift of tears."

"Kircher," said the emperor, with a delighted smile, "I thank you a thousand times for your approbation. It emboldens me to confess that I felt tears in my eyes while you sang. To you, a musician, I may say as much ; for you know that, to write a song of sorrow, a man must have known sorrow himself. I fear that my 'Schmerz-Lied' will have to give place to *embateria*, and our spinet to the discordant drum."

"And will it come to open war with the Porte ?" asked Kircher, sadly.

"I fear as much," sighed the emperor. "Is it not singular

that I, a man of peace, and lover of art, should be forever
compelled to be at war with the world? And is it not hard
that a potentate should be continually forced into measures
which he abhors, and stand before his fellow-creatures in a
character that is not his own? History will depict me as a
heartless and bloodthirsty monarch, while no man has ever
more deprecated the shedding of blood than I. My only comfort is, that, if my poor subjects suffer, it is 'ad majorem Dei
gloriam.'"

And Leopold, who was not only a disciple but a lay member of the order of Jesuits, bent his head, and made the sign
of the cross.

"Your majesty alludes to the bloodshed in Hungary?"

"Yes," said Leopold, mournfully; "for I love those poor
Hungarians, though they be heretics and rebels, and I long
for the rising of the sun of peace upon their unhappy land.
O Kircher, if we could but be at peace abroad and at home,
how happily would our days glide by! My court should be
the paradise of poetry and love, the home of art, and the temple of all wisdom and science."

"Your majesty is already the patron of all the arts; and
artists are proud to hail you as their brother. Are you not
both a composer of music and a performer? Do you not rival
Hermann, Schildbach, and Hamilton, in painting? And did
you not astonish Fisher von Erlach with the suggestions you
offered him in the planning of the palace of Schönbrunn?
And in all your majesty's dominions, is there a bolder horse-
man, a more valiant sportsman, a more graceful dancer than
yourself?"

"To hear you, Kircher," said Leopold, laughing, "one
would suppose that you were describing the attributes of Phœbus-Apollo."

"And so I am," laughed Kircher; "for out of the letters of
your majesty's name, *Leopoldus A*, did not Sigismund von
Birken compose the anagram, 'Deus Apollo?'"

"It is very easy to make anagrams by misplacing a few letters, my dear Kircher; but to convert a poor terrene German
emperor into a Magnus-Apollo, would require the upheaval of
mountains by Titan hands, from now until the millennium.

I would be content to be myself, were I regarded as a beneficent and peace-loving monarch. *Consilio et Industria* is the motto of my choice—a motto, which, though inappropriate to a god, is pertinent as the device of a Leopold. I would wish to govern with judgment, and labor industriously for the welfare of my people, accepting with Christian resignation whatever it pleases my Maker to apportion. All I ask of Providence is some little leisure for the cultivation of my favorite art. From music I derive such indescribable enjoyment, that, if I could, I would die within hearing of its delicious melody. And, since I have said so much, Kircher, I will go on to request of you, that when my end draws near, you will attend to the fulfilment of my wish."

"A melancholy duty you assign to me, gracious sovereign," sighed Kircher. "But if I outlive you, it shall be lovingly performed. Let us hope, however, for Austria's sake, that you will survive me by many years."

"Life and death are in the hands of God," returned Leopold, reverently. "And now let us speak of matters less serious. Here is the score of a new opera, lately sent to me from Rome. It is called 'La Principessa Fidèle,' and is composed by Scarlatti, who, as you know, is winning a great reputation."

"Yes," growled Kircher, "he is winning reputation by tickling the ears with soft strains which convey no meaning to the heart."

"Well, well, maestro, let us hear, before we decide," replied Leopold, laughing.

Kircher placed the score upon the desk of the spinet, and began to play. The emperor threw himself back again into his arm-chair, and, closing his eyes, listened with an expression of great satisfaction.

But his pleasure was of short duration. Scarcely had Kircher finished the first grand aria, before the door opened, and the chamberlain of the day presented himself. Leopold frowned, and, raising his head, asked somewhat impatiently, "Well,—what is it?"

"The members of your imperial majesty's council of war are in the anteroom, and solicit an audience."

"Ask them to assemble in the small council-chamber, and I will join them in a moment." Then, turning to Kircher, the emperor shook his head. "Something unusual must have happened for the council to assemble at such an early hour. You see, Kircher, that in these troublous times an emperor can have no leisure hours ; and, however I may yearn to remain, I must leave you."

"Shall I return to-morrow morning ? " asked Kircher.

"Happy is the man who can dispose of the morrow," sighed Leopold. "It is more than an Emperor of Germany dare do. I must first ascertain what news my council bring me ; but, under any circumstances, come, Kircher ; for if I am not here, some distant strain of your music may reach my ear to lighten my cares of state."

Resuming his hat, the emperor left the cabinet, and joined his ministers in the council-chamber.

---

## CHAPTER VII.

### THE COUNCIL OF WAR.

THE president, vice-president, and three members of the council, awaited the entrance of the emperor. The president, the Margrave of Baden, stood in the embrasure of a window, engaged in a whispered conversation with the vice-president, General Count von Starhemberg. whose eyes were continually wandering to the spot where the Duke of Lorraine was profoundly engaged in the contemplation of a full-length portrait of Charles V. Beyond, in the recess of another window, stood the Counts von Kinsky and Portia, conversing in low but earnest tones ; both from time to time glancing at the Duke of Lorraine with an expression of aversion which neither attempted to disguise from the other.

"Do you think his majesty will bestow the chief command upon his brother-in-law ? " asked General Count Portia.

"Yes," replied Count Kinsky, with a shrug. "The emperor is so inordinately fond of the Duke of Lorraine that he fancies him endowed with military genius."

"General," whispered the Margrave of Baden to Count Starhemberg, "I wish to say something to you in private. Can I rely upon your discretion?"

"Your highness does me honor," was the reply, "and I promise absolute silence as regards any thing you may be pleased to communicate."

"Then I will go to the point at once. The Duke of Lorraine must not have the command of the Austrian army. Do you sustain me?"

"Ah! Your highness, too, hates him."

The margrave smiled. "My dear general, that little word 'too' proves that we are of one mind. Yes, I hate the Duke of Lorraine, not *per se*, nor for any evil quality that I know of. I hate him as one dangerous to the welfare of the state, and too influential with its ruler, the emperor. Though he has the reputation of being a great general, he longs for peace and retirement among his books and maps at home; and he would rather submit to be humbled by foreign powers than declare war against their aggressions, however insolent. In other words, he hates bloodshed, and, if he is a soldier, he is one that loves the pen far more than he does the sword."

"Your highness is right," returned Count Starhemberg; "the duke is no soldier, and his appointment to the chief command of her armies would be a misfortune for Austria. And, worse yet, he is so opiniated that he never will listen to advice."

"Therefore we must work together to avert his appointment. We need a young commander, brave, ambitious, and eager for renown."

"Like Prince Louis of Baden?" asked Von Starhemberg, smiling.

"Yes, like Prince Louis of Baden, said the margrave, emphatically. "He is quite as brave and skilful as the duke; but he is modest, is willing to listen to advice, and to be guided by the experience of good counsellors. Instead of ruling the war department, he will be ruled by it, and thus we will have unanimity both in field and council. It is to your interest, therefore, to defeat the Duke of Lorraine, and secure the appointment of my nephew."

"Your highness can count on me ; but I am not very sanguine of success."

"It may be easier of accomplishment than you think ; at all events let us make the attempt. We must represent war as inevitable ; and, having given an account of the formidable preparations making by the enemy, we must counterbalance it all by a glowing exposition of our own strength and resources. This will arouse the duke's spirit of opposition, and he will forthwith discourse on the horrors of war. I will take advantage of his disinclination to fight, to suggest that, with such sentiments, he had better not aspire to command our armies. In your quality of vice-president you come forward to sustain my— Chut ! Here comes the emperor."

All the members of the council bowed low, except the Duke of Lorraine, who, having his back to the door, had not perceived the entrance of the emperor. Leopold crossed the room, and the thickness of the carpet so muffled his footfall that he had his hand on his brother-in-law's shoulder before the latter had become aware of his presence.

"What are you thinking of ?" asked he, with an affable smile. "You appear to be absorbed in admiration of our great ancestor."

"Yes, your majesty," replied the duke. "I was admiring the beauty of his noble countenance, and thinking of the pride you must feel when you remember that you are his descendant, and that his blood flows in your veins."

Leopold bent his head in token of assent. "You are right ; I *am* proud of my descent. Such an ancestry as mine should inspire a man to noble deeds ; and if I encourage pride of birth in my subjects, it is because I believe it to be an incentive to virtue and honor. Remembering, then, with mingled gratulation and humility, that we are the posterity of Charles V., let us determine to-day to act in a manner worthy of our great progenitor ; for, by your haste to assemble here this morning, I judge that we have weighty matters to discuss. Be seated, and let us proceed to business."

So saying, the emperor glided into his arm-chair, which

14

stood behind a semicircular table, immediately under the portrait of Charles V., and his five counsellors occupied the tabourets around.

"And now, my lords," exclaimed Leopold, "let me hear what it is that brings you hither at an hour so unusual."

"Dispatches from General Count Caprara, your majesty," replied the Margrave Herman of Baden.

"And from France and Poland, likewise," added the Duke of Lorraine.

"Let us hear from General Caprara. We sent him to Turkey to make a last effort at pacification. Our propositions, through him, were such as must have proved to the Porte our earnest longing for peace. Why did the general not present his dispatches in person?"

"Your majesty, it is out of his power to do so," was the reply. "Your majesty's proposals were haughtily rejected, and, in their stead, conditions were made which the general could not accept. The grand-vizier was so incensed, that he arrested your envoy, and forced him to accompany the Turkish embassy back to Constantinople. He then marched his army to our frontiers, carrying along your majesty's legation as prisoners of war. At Belgrade one of the secretaries managed to make his escape, and to conceal on his person the letters and documents of the general, which he has ridden day and night to deliver into your majesty's hands."

"What is the purport of these documents?" said Leopold, who had listened with perfect calmness to this extraordinary recital.

"First, your majesty, they contain an account of the general's peace negotiations. They were all rejected, and the grand-vizier has refused to renew the truce which has just expired. He requires new conditions."

"Name them," said Leopold.

The margrave drew from his portfolio a document, and began to read.

"Austria shall pay yearly tribute to the Porte. She shall raze every fortress she has erected on the Turkish frontier. She shall recognize Count Tököly as King of Hungary. She shall deliver to him the island of Schutt, the fortress of Comorn, and all other strongholds in Hungary, and place him on an equal footing with the Prince of Transylvania."

"Which means neither more nor less than a declaration of war," cried the emperor ; "and General Caprara would have been a traitor had he listened to such insulting proposals. My patience with this arrogant Moslem is exhausted, and further forbearance would be a disgrace. We have no alternative : we must go to war, trusting in God to defend the right. Our cause is a holy one ; and perhaps, with the blessing of Heaven, it may be granted us to drive the infidel from Europe forever. Go on, margrave. What other news have you ? "

"Important information, your majesty, as to the strength of the enemy's forces. The Sultan, at Belgrade, reviewed an army of two hundred thousand men, all fully equipped, and anxious to retrieve their losses at St. Gotthard. They have carried their fanaticism to such an extent that they talk of planting the Crescent where the Cross now looms from the towers of St. Stephen's in Vienna. Kara Mustapha himself told General Caprara that, in a few weeks from now, a Sultan of the West would seat himself on the throne of the Emperors of Germany."

"God will punish his blasphemous boasting," returned Leopold. "God will not suffer the Christian to perish before the might of the Paynim. The die is cast for war, for war ! At least, such is my conviction ; but if any one here be of opposite mind, let him speak boldly. Freedom of speech in this chamber is not only his right, but his solemn duty."

"War ! war ! " echoed the councillors, four of them vociferously, the Duke of Lorraine deliberately, and so slowly, that his voice came as an echo of the words that were spoken by his colleagues.

The emperor was a little surprised. "Your highness is then of our opinion ? " asked he.

"I am, your majesty. War is inevitable, and we must risk our meagre forces against the two hundred thousand men of the Sultan."

"True, we are not so numerous as the enemy," observed the Margrave of Baden, "but our men are as well equipped and as enthusiastic as those of the Porte, and, under the leadership of such a hero as the Duke of Lorraine, we are certain of victory."

The duke shook his head. "The greatest general that ever led an army into battle cannot hope for victory, when, to forces immensely superior to his own, he opposes troops neither well armed nor well provided."

"Happily," replied the margrave, "this is not the case with our men. Without counting the auxiliaries that will be furnished by the princes of the empire, we shall oppose a hundred thousand men to the Turks. Moreover, we have been preparing for war, and for several months have taken measures to arm our troops and provision them for a campaign."

"Permit me to dispute your last assertion," replied the duke, whose mild countenance kindled, and whose soft eyes began to glow. "It is my duty to speak the truth to his majesty, and I shall do it fearlessly. No, my liege, we have *not* a hundred thousand men, and our soldiers are ill equipped and ill provided. As regards the auxiliaries of the princes of the German empire, your majesty knows that their deputies have been in Frankfort for months without having yet held one single council to deliberate on the expediency of sending or not sending re-enforcements to our army. I grieve to say so, but the truth must be spoken. We have an insignificant army, which, of itself, is inadequate to repel the Turkish hordes ; and, should they march to Vienna, our capital must fall, for I regret to say that no measures have been taken for its defence. There are but ten guns on the bastions ; the trenches are so dry that they can be crossed by foot-passengers, and the garrison consists of our ordinary city guard, and one thousand troops of the line. For Vienna to withstand a siege in this defenceless condition is impossible ; and, should the Turks be allowed to march hither, your majesty would have to surrender."

"Your majesty," interrupted Count Starhemberg, vehemently, "leave to me the defence of Vienna, and I swear that, sooner than deliver your capital to the Turks, I will perish under its ruins."

"And I," added the margrave, "solemnly adjure your majesty not to confide the chief command of your forces to the

Duke of Lorraine, for it is evident that he does not desire so perilous an appointment. His highness has no confidence in our ability to prosecute the war successfully ; and no general can lead his soldiers to victory who beforehand is convinced that they are destined to suffer defeat."

"No general can lead his soldiers to victory who refuses to contemplate the possibilities of defeat," exclaimed the Duke of Lorraine, whose handsome face began to show traces of anger. "To estimate his strength at its real value, he must at least learn something of the size and condition of his army. It is the duty of a commander-in-chief to see with his own eyes, and decide from his own observation ; for him, the men and stores that are exhibited to view on the green cloth of a table within the walls of a council-chamber have no significance whatever."

"Does your highness accuse me of an intention to deceive his majesty ?" cried the margrave, haughtily. "Do you—"

"Peace, gentlemen, peace !" interrupted the emperor. "We are here to war with the stranger, not with our own flesh and blood. Every man present shall speak his mind without censure from his colleagues ; and he who prevaricates is no true subject of mine. You are all free to discuss our difficulties ; it remains for me to decide in what manner they shall be met. I beg to recall this fact to Count Starhemberg, who unsolicited has offered to take upon himself the defence of Vienna. My heartfelt thanks are due to the Duke of Lorraine for his frank exposition of our disabilities ; he is now, as ever, the champion of truth and right. Has the Margrave of Baden any further dispatches to lay before us ?"

"No, your majesty," answered the margrave, pale with anger.

"Then let us have those of his highness of Lorraine," returned Leopold, with an affectionate glance at his brother-in-law.

"I have couriers, your majesty, from Count von Mansfeld and from Count von Waldstein."

"Let us hear the news from Paris first," replied Leopold, slightly frowning. "Let us hear from our hereditary foe, who, under pretence of coming to our rescue, pillages our property while the house is on fire. We know full well that this fair-spoken Louis is in secret league with our foes at home and abroad, and we confess that when he invited us to be sponsor to his grandson, we accepted the honor with an ill grace. By-the-by, has the young dauphin been baptized?"

"Yes, your majesty, and Count von Mansfeld was your imperial majesty's proxy. After the ceremony the king held a long and gracious conversation with your majesty's representative, in which he expressed his great sympathy with your majesty, and requested Count Mansfeld to say that he remembered you night and morning in his prayers."

"The King of France will deceive neither the Lord of heaven nor His servant the ruler of Austria, with his prayers," exclaimed Leopold, with some show of warmth. "He merely means to say that he intends to give us nothing more substantial. Would he but content himself with cold neutrality, we would be willing to accept his prayers instead of his works. But while he prays for us, he gives aid and comfort to our enemies, who are less our enemies than such a sanctimonious friend. But, enough of the King of France! To such an offensive message I have no answer to return."

"Count von Mansfeld left Paris at once, your majesty, and proceeded to Spain to urge the claims of his imperial highness, the Archduke Charles, to the Spanish succession."

"Now let us hear from Count von Waldstein and Warsaw."

"Count von Waldstein was received with distinguished consideration. The King of Poland, at least, is your imperial majesty's friend. You remember that his wife is a French woman?"

"Yes," replied Leopold, shaking his head, "and a woman whose birth is not illustrious enough for her station."

"She is, nevertheless, Queen of Poland, my liege, and is recognized as such by the Poles. When the grandson of the King of France was born, he purposely sent notification of the event to the King of Poland, ignoring in his dispatches the queen. This omission of a courtesy, customary among royal heads, offended the queen; and to her resentment we are to attribute the gracious reception given to our ambassador. My liege, our alliance with Poland is a fixed fact. A treaty has been concluded, by which John Sobiesky pledges himself to sustain Austria against Turkey, furnishing at once forty thousand men who are ready for action as soon as needed."

"To what are we pledged in return for this?" asked Leopold.

"Merely to furnish on our part sixty thousand men, and to consult with his majesty as to our operations."

"To consult with him!" repeated the emperor. "This looks as though he expected to take part in our plans for the prosecution of this war, instead of recognizing us as commander-in-chief."

"To exact such recognition from him would be unseemly," replied the duke. "The King of Poland is a great captain as well as a crowned head; and it would ill become us to dictate to a warrior, from whom we should all regard it as a privilege to receive advice. Moreover, as a crowned head, John Sobiesky is entitled to the first rank in the field as well as in the cabinet."

"He is nothing more than an elected ruler," observed Leopold, with a shrug. "For want of a better alliance, I must content myself with that of John Sobiesky; but I put the question to you—suppose he were to come to Vienna, how should I receive or entertain an elected king?"

"With open arms, if he come to deliver us from our foes,"* was the prompt reply. "Welcome are all who visit us as true friends, but doubly welcome those who come in time of need. The King of Poland has been the first prince to respond to our offers of alliance, the first to co-operate with us in our struggle with the infidel."

"But he will not be the last," interposed the Margrave of Baden. "I, too, have good news for you, my liege. The Elector of Bavaria, to whom I wrote for aid in your majesty's approaching troubles, has promised not only a considerable body of troops, but offers to command them in person. The Elector of Saxony, too, I think, will co-operate with us. The council of the states of the German empire also are in session at Frankfort, to consult as to the expediency of joining your majesty's standard."

* The duke's own words.—See Armath, " Prince Eugene of Savoy," vol. i.

"And before the electors equip their men, and the council make up their mind, the Turks will have marched to Vienna, unless we make a junction with the King of Poland and intercept them on their way. Each day of delay increases the peril, for they are already on this side of Belgrade. Unless we can oppose them now, we are lost, and all Bavaria, Saxony, and the states of the empire, cannot avert our doom."

"Then, in God's name, let us act at once," cried the emperor, rising from his seat. "President of the war department, let your troops be in readiness to march, and see that our men are equipped and provisioned."

"Your majesty's commands shall be obeyed."

"Duke of Lorraine," continued Leopold, "I appoint you to the chief command of my forces. Go forth, and, with the blessing of God, do battle for Christendom and Germany."

"I accept, your majesty," returned the duke, solemnly bending his head. "Victory is in the hands of Almighty God; but bravery, loyalty, and struggle unto death, I promise, on behalf of your majesty's army."

"Count Rudiger von Starhemberg," resumed the emperor, "your petition is granted. To you I commit the defence of my capital."

"Thanks, your majesty," exclaimed Von Starhemberg fervently. "I will defend it with the last drop of my blood; and if Vienna fall into the hands of the infidel, he shall find nothing left of her stateliness, save a heap of ruins and the lifeless bodies of her defenders."

"To you, Counts Portia and Kinsky, I commit the direction of the war department, in conjunction with your colleague, the Margrave of Baden. Let couriers be dispatched to all the European courts with information of our declaration of war against the Porte. Let it be announced to the world that, for the good of Christendom, Leopold has grasped the sword; and, in this new crusade, may he confound the unbelieving Turk, and glorify the standard of the Christian, in the name of the Father, of the Son, and of the Holy Ghost. And may the Blessed Virgin, the Mother of Christ, vouchsafe her protection and her prayers!"

# CHAPTER VIII.

### THE PLAINS OF KITSEE.

ON the first of May, 1683, the Emperor Leopold reviewed his troops on the plains of Kitsee, not far from Presburg. To this review, all who had promised to sustain Austria were invited. Her appeals had at last roused the German princes to action ; but they had been so dilatory in their councils, that not one of them was prepared for war.

The army assembled on the plains of Kitsee was not numerous. There were thirty-three thousand men in all, who, with their faded uniforms and defective weapons, made no great show.

The emperor, as he emerged from his tent, looked discouraged. Sternly he rode forth on his richly-caparisoned gray horse, and, when his men greeted him with enthusiastic shouts, he bowed his head in silence, and sighed heavily.

He turned to Charles of Lorraine, who rode a few paces behind him, and said :

"Come hither, Carl." The duke obeyed at once, and at one bound was at the emperor's side. "Tell me, Carl," said he, anxiously, "how many infantry are there here ? "

"Twenty-two thousand, your majesty."

"And cavalry ? "

"Twelve thousand mounted troops."

"About what may be the strength of the enemy ? "

"Your majesty, our scouts report that the combined forces of Turkey and Hungary amount to more than two hundred thousand."

Leopold raised his eyes to the calm, self-possessed face of his brother-in-law. "You say that, as quietly as if it were a pleasant piece of news ; and yet methinks we are in a critical position."

"Your majesty, I have known this for so long a time that I am accustomed to contemplate it with equanimity. Before our decision was made, I was timid and irresolute ; but since the die is cast, I am bold and self-reliant, for I know that I will either conquer or die."

"You think success then a possibility! With thirty-three thousand men, you hope to repulse two hundred thousand ?"

"The King of Poland adds forty thousand to our number, the Electors of Bavaria and Saxony are making preparations to re-enforce us, and the other princes of Germany will soon follow their example. The Moslem has put out all his strength for one decisive blow ; the longer we avoid an engagement the weaker he grows ; while time to us brings accession of numbers, and lessens his chance for reaching Vienna."

The emperor shook his head. "That you are a hero, Carl, I confess : this hour proves you one. But I cannot share your hopefulness. When I look around me at all these men, and think that they are death-doomed, my heart grows faint, and my eyes dim."

"Do not think so much of the number of your troops, sire; look at their countenances. See those stern, resolute faces, and those fiery eyes. Every man of them chafes to march against the infidel—"

"Hurrah for our emperor !" cried out a lusty voice, close by. "Hurrah for our general, Charles of Lorraine !"

"Ah, Christopher Ill, are you there ?" cried the duke, cordially.

"Yes, your highness," replied the cuirassier, while his horse stepped a few paces in front of the ranks. "Yes, your highness, I am here to fight the infidel with a will as good as I had at St. Gotthard's twenty years ago. That was a glorious day ; and I thank God that I am alive to see your highness win another victory as great over the insolent Turk."

"You think, then, that we will be victorious, Christopher ?"

"Ay, indeed, your highness, for God is with us."

"Bravely spoken," said the emperor, gazing with visible satisfaction at the wrinkled face and snow-white beard of the old cuirassier.

The Duke of Lorraine signed to him to advance. "Your majesty," said he to Leopold, "allow me to present one of your bravest soldiers, Christopher Ill. In all the army there is not a man as old as his youngest son, and I venture to say that he is the oldest man in Europe under arms."

"That is a broad assertion," replied Leopold. "How old may you be, Christopher Ill ?"

"Last Thursday I was a hundred and nine years old, please your imperial majesty," said Christopher, bowing to his saddle-bow.

"A hundred and nine years old !" cried Leopold, incredulously. "Nay—that is impossible. No man of that age could sit a horse or carry a sword as you do."

"Your majesty, it is said in Holy Writ, that, when our forefathers were five hundred years old, they were young and lusty ; and I can assure my emperor, that when once I am on my horse, with my sabre in hand, I will fight with the best lad of twenty years. I mount rather stiffly, because of a wound I received at Leipsic when we had the ill-luck to be defeated by Gustavus Adolphus."

"Why, man, do you mean to say that fifty-two years ago you were in the army ?"

"Yes, sire ; and there I received the wound from which I still suffer to-day. The battle of Leipsic was far from being my first : it may have been the twentieth, but I am not quite sure. When first I entered the service, I used to mark our battles with a red cross when we were victorious, and a black one when we were unfortunate ; but, after I had been in the army for twenty years, I stopped. There were too many fights to record."

"But you can remember your first battle, can you not ?"

"Certainly, sire. I began, as I am likely to end, by fighting the Porte ; and we defeated him then, as we assuredly intend to do now."

"When was it ?" asked Leopold, with interest.

"Eighty years ago, sire, when the Hungarians and Turks made war upon the Emperor Rudolph the Second. Yes, even then, the dogs were after Vienna, and those mutinous Hungarians were giving trouble to your majesty's forefathers. The Emperor Mathias, who succeeded his brother, made a treaty with them for twenty years, for we had as much on our hands as we could manage, with the rebels of Bohemia. They rose again and again under the three Ferdinands, but we brought them down at last. I have served under six emperors, and all have vanquished their enemies, even as my last gracious sovereign Leopold shall do. Long live our Leopold, the conqueror of the Turks!"

" Long live our Leopold!" shouted the cuirassiers, delighted with the condescension of the emperor to Christopher. The shout was taken up by the other troops, until it resounded like rolling thunder along the plains of Kitsee.

The emperor greeted his army with something like a reflection of their enthusiasm, and then returned to Christopher.

" Christopher," said he, " you have served under six emperors, and have done more than your duty toward Austria. I give you your discharge, for he who has worked faithfully all day has a right to rest when night sets in. I appoint you castellan of my palace at Innspruck ; and, in addition to your salary, bestow upon you a pension of four hundred florins."

" Thank your majesty, but indeed I cannot go," replied the old man, resolutely. " I hardly think the Turkish hounds will ever get as far as Innspruck, so I must e'en go forward with the army to fight them wherever they are to be met. My night has not yet set in, sire."

" What!" cried Leopold, laughing, " you refuse ?"

" Yes, your majesty. I crave neither pension nor sinecure. I intend to follow the army, and, if God calls me hence, then I shall be willing to rest ; but before I go I hope to mow down a few Turks' heads to take to St. Peter, for him to use as balls when he plays ninepins. But, if your imperial majesty will grant it, you might do me a favor."

" What is it, my brave cuirassier ? tell me."

" Your majesty, will you allow me to present my sons, grandsons, great-grandsons, and great-great-grandsons ? They are all in my regiment."

" The Eleventh Cuirassiers of Herberstein, your majesty," added the Duke of Lorraine.

" Ah," cried the emperor, in a voice intended to be heard by all the men, " that is an old and renowned regiment. Were you in it, Christopher, when it was commanded by the great Dampierre in 1619 ?"

"Yes, your majesty, I was the first man enrolled. I was there when the regiment rescued the Emperor Ferdinand from a body of insurgents, who had surrounded his imperial palace, and were trying to compel him to abdicate. Just as they were forcing the gates, the trumpets of Dampierre sounded an alarm, and the emperor was saved. The cuirassiers galloped into the midst of the insurgents, and dispersed them like so many cats."

"And to reward their loyalty and opportune aid," cried the emperor, "Ferdinand conferred upon the Eleventh Cuirassiers the privilege of riding through Vienna, trumpet sounding and colors flying, and of pitching their tents on the Burgplatz."*

"Hurrah ! Hurrah ! The emperor knows our history," shouted Christopher Ill.

"Hurrah ! Hurrah !" echoed the regiment, and once more through the plains of Kitsee rang the jubilant cry, "Long live Leopold ! Long live our emperor !"

"And now," said the emperor, when the shouts had died away, "now let me see your children, my brave veteran.— Baron Dupin," added Leopold, addressing himself to the colonel of the regiment, "will you permit them to step out of their ranks ?"

Baron Dupin bowed, and, riding to the front with drawn sword, he called out : "All the descendants of Christopher Ill—forward !"

There was a general movement among the cuirassiers, and fifty-four men rode up, and clustered around their common ancestor. There were bronzed faces with white beards— others with gray ; there were men in the prime of life, and others in the flower ; there were youths approaching manhood, and lads that had scarcely emerged from childhood ; but from peeping bud to fruit that was about to fall, they one and all resembled their parent stem ; every mother's son of them had Christopher Ill's aquiline nose, and large, sparkling eyes.

"Your majesty perceives," said the old man, looking proudly around him, "that if I have sabred many a Turk's

---

* This is historical, and in 1819, on the two hundredth anniversary of the rescue, the privilege was extended to the present time.—See Austrian Plutarch.

head, I have replaced each one by that of a Christian ; so that I owe nothing to humanity for the damage my sword has done.—Now, boys, cry out, ' Long live the emperor ! ' "

So the boys, young and old, echoed the shout ; the regiment took it up, and for the third time Leopold's heart was cheered by the enthusiastic affection of the army.

" Well, Christopher," said he, gayly, " although you reject my pension for yourself, you will not, I hope, reject it for your sons. Let it be divided between them, and long may you live to see them enjoy it ! "

With these words, the emperor raised his hat, and waving it in token of adieu, he returned to his tent, far happier than he had left it some hours before.

" Carl," said he to the Duke of Lorraine, " I thank you for presenting Christopher Ill to my notice. That old man's spirit is catching, and I feel the pleasant infection. I recognize the might of bravery, and it seems as if my small army had doubled its numbers. This veteran, who in his person unites the history of six of my predecessors, has taught me that individuals are nothing in the sight of God. Six emperors have succumbed to the immutable laws of Nature, but the house of Hapsburg is still erect. What, then, if I meet with reverses ? The Lord has given me a son, who, if I should be unfortunate, will prop up our dynasty, and avenge his father's misfortunes."

" We will try to leave him none to avenge, sire. Your men are full of loyalty, and God will preserve your majesty's life until your son is fit to be your successor."

" His holy will be done ! " said Leopold, crossing himself ; then, having given orders for an advance upon the fortress of Neuhäusel, he changed his dress preparatory to starting for Vienna.

He had just been equipped in his black travelling-suit when Prince Louis of Baden entered the tent, followed by a young man whose simple costume presented a striking contrast to the magnificence of the uniforms around. He wore a brown coat buttoned up to the throat, leaving visible merely the ends of his cravat of costly Venetian lace. Ruffles of the same encircled his white hands, which, it was easy to see, had never been hardened by work, or browned by the sun. His face, though youthful, bore traces of thought and suffering ; and his bearing was self-possessed, although every eye was upon him.

"Whom bring you hither ? " inquired Leopold, with a smile.

"Your majesty, I bring nothing but a young Savoyard : nevertheless I predict that, one of these days, he will be one of the great generals of the world."*

"I am not so presumptuous as to expect that I will ever rival Prince Louis of Baden or Charles of Lorraine," said Eugene. " All I have to ask of your majesty is the favor of being allowed to serve under them."

There was a pause. Everybody looked in amazement at the bold being who, all court etiquette disregarding, had ventured to address the emperor without being spoken to by his majesty ; but *he* was perfectly unconscious of his blunder. He looked so frank, so modest, and yet so unembarrassed, that the emperor was disarmed, and a smile flickered over his pleasant face.

"I see that he is a stranger," was Leopold's deprecatory remark. " Present him, your highness, that I may welcome him to Austria."

The prince, taking the young man by the hand, led him up to the emperor.

"Sire, I have the honor to present you my kinsman, Prince Eugene of Savoy. He has come to Austria to join his brother, and, like him, to serve under the Austrian flag."

"Prince Eugene of Savoy, you are welcome to Austria," said Leopold, graciously.

Eugene answered the salutation by a low bow, and then calmly raised his head. But Prince Louis of Baden whispered in his ear, " The Spanish genuflection—quick ! bend the knee ! "

Eugene looked surprised, for he had not understood the warning. But the emperor had overheard, and came once more to the rescue.

* The Margrave of Baden's own words.—See Armath, " Prince Eugene," vol. i., p. 23.

"Never mind the Spanish genuflection," interposed he, with a good-natured laugh. "The prince is not my subject; he has been educated in France, where people know little or nothing of the customs and usages of our court."

But scarcely were the words out of Leopold's mouth before Eugene had approached his arm-chair, and had fallen on one knee.

"Sire," said he, in his soft, melodious voice, whose tones went straight to the emperor's heart, "allow me to consider myself as your subject, and to render you homage according to the usages of your majesty's court. It is my misfortune to have been educated in France, and thereby to have lost twenty years of my life."

"Why lost?" inquired Leopold. "What was wanting in France to make you happy?"

"Every thing, sire!" cried Eugene, warmly. "And the only thing I did not want was thrust upon me."

"What was that?"

"The tonsure, sire. I begged the King of France for an insignificant commission in his army; I was scornfully repulsed. And now that I have shaken the dust of his dominions from my feet, I never wish to return thither unless—"

"Well," said the emperor, as Eugene paused. "Finish your sentence. 'Unless'—"

Eugene raised his magnificent eyes until they met those of the emperor. Then, in a calm voice, he continued:

"Unless I could do so as his majesty's victorious enemy." *

"Your majesty sees that he is the stuff of which heroes are made," observed Louis of Baden.

"You do not love France?" said Leopold.

"Sire, my family and I have suffered persecution at the hands of the French monarch, and I yearn for satisfaction. Your majesty sees how unfit I am to be a priest, for I cannot love my enemies, nor do good to those who despitefully use me."

"Let us hope that you will learn this lesson later. Meanwhile you seem more fitted for the career of a soldier than the vocation of a churchman. Your appearance here reminds me

* Eugene's own words.—See René, "Mazarin's Nieces."

of my own youth. I, too, was destined for the priesthood, and wore the garb of an abbé. I was a younger son, and nothing but an appendage to royalty. But it pleased God of His servant to make a sovereign, and to send as His messenger, death. My brother Ferdinand, the hope of Austria, died, and I stepped forth from my insignificance to become the heir to a mighty empire. Your brother Louis has frequently mentioned you to me, and from him I learned that at the French court you were known as 'the little abbé!' If of me, who was once a novice, Almighty God has made an emperor—of you, little abbé, He may make a great warrior!"

"Sire, my fate is in His hands ; but all that lies in my own, I will do to serve your majesty as your loyal subject, hoping to follow from afar in the footsteps of the distinguished models before me." At the same time, Eugene bowed low to the Duke of Lorraine.

"Will you take him as your pupil?" asked Leopold of his brother-in-law. "No one in Austria can teach him better how to win laurels."

"With your majesty's permission, I accept the task," replied the duke. "But he must expect to find me a hard master, and, as my pupil in war, to have little leisure for aught else."

"You see," said Leopold, gayly, "what a miserable lot you have chosen for yourself. You have fallen from Scylla into Charybdis, my poor youth."

"I have my Ulysses, your majesty, in his highness of Lorraine. I give myself up to his sage guidance."

"If Prince Eugene is as ready with his sword as with his tongue, my enemies will have to look out, methinks," cried Leopold. "So take him along, Duke of Lorraine, and of the little abbé of the King of France make a great captain for the Emperor of Austria."

"With your majesty's permission, I will confer upon him the rank of colonel, and the first vacancy that occurs. Until then, prince, you can accompany me as a volunteer."

"As a volunteer for life, your highness," replied Eugene ; "and, although I have already to thank his majesty for much gracious encouragement, I feel more grateful to him for plac-

15

ing me under your highness's orders, than for any other of the favors he has so kindly bestowed upon me to-day."

"I am glad to know it," returned the emperor. "Follow your leader, then, my young friend ; and see that, although you have relinquished the priesthood, you hold fast to Christianity. We part for a time, but we shall meet again before long. Let us hope that it may be to give thanks to God for victory and peace."

The emperor then rose, and, followed by his officers, left the tent. His carriage stood without, and in a few moments, amid the respectful greetings of his staff, and the hurrahs of the army, he disappeared from the plains of Kitsee.

The Duke of Lorraine signed to Eugene to follow him. Laying his hand gently upon the prince's shoulder, he said : "Young man, you have requested me to be your instructor, and I have accepted the office, for you please me, and my heart inclines toward you. Let me then begin at once. I wish to give you some advice."

"I am all attention, your highness."

"Weigh well your words, before you give them utterance. You will find enemies in the Austrian ranks, as well as in those of the Turkish army. You have already gained a few ; and by-and-by, if you are not careful, you will have as many as myself."

"What can I have done, your highness, during the half hour I have spent in his majesty's tent, to provoke enmity from the strangers around me ? That you should have enemies, I comprehend ; for distinction always calls forth envy. But I, an unknown youth ! who could envy me ? "

"Those who saw how graciously you were welcomed by the Emperor of Austria. But that is not all. You have offended your kinsman, Louis of Baden. It was he who presented you to the king. He is a brave and distinguished officer, and deserved all the compliments you bestowed upon me. Believe me, if you know your own interest, you will select him for your model and master in the art of war. He will be flattered at your preference, and will serve you efficiently. His friendship is worth having."

"I love Louis of Baden from my heart," said Eugene ; "and,

*after* your highness, he has the first place in my consideration
and esteem."

"*After* me, say you? Give him the first place, and he will
procure you rapid advancement. For myself, I am unpopular, and if you love or respect me, do so in secret. You will
not long have been an Austrian officer before you make the
discovery that it is not politic to praise Charles of Lorraine."

## CHAPTER IX.

### THE BAPTISM OF BLOOD.

WAR had begun. Kara Mustapha advanced into Austria,
looking neither to the right nor the left, marching onward,
onward to Vienna. Such obstacles as he encountered on his
way he removed by the might and strength of his forces, as
an elephant lifts his ponderous foot to crush a pigmy lying in
his path. His march was through burning villages and devastated fields ; the glare of his torch illumined the sky, the blood
of his victims reddened the earth. Austria's desponding hopes
were concentrated upon the Duke of Lorraine ; for the King
of Poland had not arrived, and the Elector of Bavaria was yet
undecided.

The army of the allied enemies increased daily, while that
of the Austrians was decimated partly by contagious diseases,
partly by a division of their forces, for the defence of the
only fortress which was in a condition to arrest the advance of
the Turks.

The duke's army, which now numbered twenty-three thousand men, was encamped in front of the fortress of Raab ; for
here the Turks would make their first attack, and to possess
Raab was to hold the key of Upper Hungary and Central Austria. The army had halted there in the course of the afternoon, but, as night approached, the hum of action gradually
ceased, and gloomy silence reigned throughout. No groups
of merry soldiers gathered round the camp-fires with laugh, or
jest, or mirthful song. Some slept from exhaustion and dis-

couragement, others sat mournfully gazing toward the east, which, unlike the dark horizon around, was lit up with a fiery glow, that marked the advance of the ferocious invaders. In one tent pitched on a hillock that overlooked the camp-ground, a faint light shone through the crevices of the curtain ; and this glimmering spark was the only sign of life that was to be seen. The rest of the camp was in utter darkness.

The tent whence beamed this solitary light was that of the commander-in-chief, to whom his scouts had just brought intelligence which necessitated prompt action. He had sent for General Caprara and Prince Louis of Baden ; and when his interview with them was at an end, he dispatched his adjutant for Prince Eugene of Savoy.

In a few moments Eugene raised the hangings of the tent and silently saluted his commander. The latter seemed not to have perceived his entrance. He stood before a table, leaning over a map on which he was tracing and retracing lines with his fingers. Eugene stepped closer, and followed the motions of the duke with his eyes. He seemed to understand them ; for his countenance expressed anxiety and astonishment.

A long pause ensued, after which the duke raised his head and spoke :

"You have been here for some time ? "

"Yes, your highness ; I came as soon as I received your orders."

"I saw the shadow of your head on the map. You were watching my fingers attentively. I was glad to see that you were interested. What did you infer from your inspection of the map ? "

"I will try to tell your highness as well as I can," was the modest reply. "You began by drawing a line from Stuhl-weissenburg with three fingers. This represented the Turkish army, composed of three columns. Your forefinger represented the left wing, your third the right wing, and your middle finger the main body of the army. The two wings were then detached, and made a circuitous march to capture the fortress of Wesgrim. They again joined the main army, and I saw, with astonishment, that the consolidated forces had flanked

Raab, Comorn, and Leopoldstadt, had passed by the shores of the Neusidler Sea, and were now encamped on the banks of the Leitha."

"You have guessed most accurately," cried the duke, who had listened in amazement to Eugene's reply.

"It was not difficult to do," remarked the latter. "Since I have had the honor of serving under your highness, I have studied this map daily. I know every thicket, every forest, every stream laid down upon it. The whole country which it comprises is as familiar to me as if I surveyed it all at a glance. It is not, then, surprising that I should understand the movements of your highness's fingers."

"*You* think it quite natural—I consider it extraordinary. But you have raised my curiosity to know whether you also were able to interpret what followed."

"After accompanying the enemy to the banks of the Leitha, your highness stopped, raised your hand, and laid your finger upon the fortress of Raab. This, of course, denotes the position of our own army, and the direction in which we are to move."

"Move ? We came here to defend this stronghold."

"We have been flanked, and have nothing to gain by a defence of Raab. With your finger, then, upon Raab, you were deliberating as to the route we are to take ; since it is evident that, if we are not prompt, we will be cut off from Vienna. You made two divisions of *your* army. One finger traced a line across the island of Schütt to Presburg, and thence to Vienna ; this, I presume, denotes the march of the infantry. The other finger, on the left bank of the Danube, drew a line from Wieselburg to Hainburg, and this route would be for our cavalry—it is too rough for foot-soldiers."

The duke listened with growing interest, and when Eugene ceased, he put his arm affectionately around the neck of the young officer, and exclaimed, "I congratulate you, Eugene. You will be a great captain. You will be a better general than I. Let us hope that you will also be a more fortunate one— that you will complete what I have begun—avenge Austria's wrongs on France, and restore her to her place as one of the four great powers. You have not only the instincts of a soldier, but the quickness and penetration which constitute military genius. My pupil, I think, will ere long become my master."

"Ah !" replied Eugene, "unless you keep me as a pupil, I shall never become a master."

"The little that I know you shall learn from me, Eugene. I have predicted for you a glorious career, and, as far as lies in my power, I will contribute to your success. But success is as much the fruit of policy as of genius. You must not proclaim your preference for me to the world ; it will impede your advancement. To obtain promotion you must be an ostensible adherent of my enemies ; and for this reason I shall give you some command near the persons of General Caprara and Louis of Baden."

"Your highness, Louis of Baden is not—"

"My enemy, you would say ? Believe me, I know human nature better than you do ; but I have no resentment against Louis on account of his animosity. He is young, ambitious, and capable ; it is therefore but natural that he should covet my position. He will obtain it, for all my enemies will give him their suffrages, and chief among them all is the Margrave Herman. I, on the contrary, have but one friend—the emperor."

"But the emperor is a host within himself," cried Eugene.

"If you think so, it is because you are unacquainted with the intrigues of the Austrian court. The privy council has more power than Leopold ; and the veritable ruler of Austria is the minister of war, who, from his green-covered table, plans our battles and commands our armies. What do you suppose are my instructions from the war department ? I must first, with my thirty-three thousand men, hold the entire Turkish army in check ; I must garrison Raab, Comorn, and Leopoldstadt ; I must defend fifty miles of frontier between the pass of Jublunkau and Pettau ; I must oppose the passage of the enemy to Vienna ; and having accomplished all these impossibilities, I must end by giving him battle wherever and whenever I meet him." *

"Impossible, indeed ! " cried Eugene, indignantly.

* Kausler, "Life of Eugene of Savoy."

" And, for that very reason, assigned to me as my duty.
For, as I shall certainly not accomplish it, there will be an outcry at my incapacity, and a pretext for my removal. I shall
fulfil my obligations nevertheless, as conscientiously to foes as
to friends. I have borne arms for the emperor against France,
Sweden, Hungary, and Turkey ; if it serve his interests or those
of Austria, I am ready to struggle with his enemies at home ;
but, if my championship is to be dangerous to my sovereign or
to my country, I shall resign without a protest. As for you,
my son, the path of glory is open to you ; perhaps before another sun has set, you may flesh your maiden sword in the blood
of the infidel. You have anticipated my intentions. We are
about to march to Vienna. Do you hear the signal ? The
men are being awakened ; and in one hour we must be on our
way. I sent for you to bid you farewell. So far, you have
been attached to my person, and I have learned to esteem and
love you. But the opportunity for you to distinguish yourself
is at hand, and I must no longer retain you by me. I assign
you to your brother's regiment of dragoons. It belongs to the
brigade of Prince Louis, and the division of General Caprara.
I part from you reluctantly, but I do it for your own good ;
and I hope soon to make honorable mention of my favorite
officer to the emperor."

" My dear lord," answered Eugene, in a voice that trembled
with emotion, " I will do all that I can to deserve your approval. I care for naught else in this world ; and if after a
battle you say that you are satisfied with me, I shall be richly
rewarded for any peril, any sacrifice."

At this moment the curtain of the tent was drawn aside,
and the duke's staff entered. He waved his hand in token of
adieu to Eugene, at the same time saying :

" And now, colonel, Prince of Savoy, you will join your
brother's regiment. It has received its orders, and is in readiness to depart."

Eugene bowed low and left the tent.

The Austrian camp was now alive and in motion, but the
men were spiritless and taciturn. Conscious of the immense
superiority of the enemy, they advanced to meet him with
more of resignation than of hope. Not only were they out-

numbered, but their foe was one whose every step was marked
by incendiarism and murder.    The zest, the incentive to gallantry, was gone ; and, believing that they were going forth to
death, they went like victims to an inevitable doom.    Far different were the feelings with which Eugene mounted his horse,
and crossed the field to join the division of General Caprara.
He found Prince Louis of Savoy already in the saddle, awaiting his arrival.    The brothers greeted each other with fondest
affection.

"Dear Eugene," said Louis, "my heart is joyous, since I
know that we are to go in company.    How sweet and home-
like it is to have you with me !    By-and-by, we shall see you
cutting off Turks' heads as if they were poppies."

"For each one that I send to his account, I mean to claim a
kiss from my beautiful sister-in-law."

"You are welcome if you can get them," laughed Louis.
"But Urania is not prodigal of her kisses, Eugene ; I never
was able to obtain a single one until she became my wife.
But let us not speak of her.    Love is any thing but an incentive to valor ; and just now I almost envy you who have
never loved.    If you intend to be a soldier, twine no myrtle
with your laurels until you shall have attained renown."

Eugene's brow darkened, and a gleam of anguish shot
athwart his countenance.    "I shall never," began he—

But just at that moment the trumpet's peal was heard, and
Prince Louis, galloping off, gave the word of command to
move on.

And now was heard the roll of the drum, the clang of arms,
the stamp of horses, and the measured tread of men.    The infantry took the left, the cavalry the right bank of the Danube.
When morning dawned, the camp lay far behind them, but
the road was long that led to Vienna.

The two Princes of Savoy rode together.    Little had been
said by either one, but whenever their eyes met, each read in
the glance of the other that he was dearly loved, and then they
smiled, and relapsed into silence.    After riding in this way for
several miles, Prince Louis spoke.

"I wish to ask you something, Eugene.    But promise not to
ridicule me."

"I promise, with all my heart."

"Then tell me—do you believe in dreams and presentiments?"

Eugene reflected for a while and then said, "Yes—you know that our family have every reason to believe in dreams. Mine have often been realized ; and often too, I must confess, that they have deceived me—but still I am a believer."

"Well, then," said his brother, "I shall meet my death to-day."

Eugene shuddered. "Meet your death!" exclaimed he. "This is a grim jest, dear Louis."

"No jest, brother ; a serious prediction. Last night I saw myself mortally wounded, and I heard the wailing of my wife and children, when the news of my death was brought to them. It was so vivid that it awakened me. Dear Eugene, if I fall, be a brother to my Urania, a father to my children."

"I will, I will, Louis, but God forbid that they should need protection from me ! Were you to die, I should lose my only friend, for whom have I to love in this world besides yourself, dear brother ?"

"Nay, Eugene," returned Louis, "I cannot be your only or your dearest friend, for you do not trust me. From our cousins, the Princes de Conti, I learned that you had endured some great sorrow at the hands of Louvois, the French minister of war. I have waited for you to confide your troubles to me, but— Great God ! What is the matter ?"

Eugene had reined in his horse with such force, that it seemed to be falling back upon its haunches. His face was deadly pale, and his hand raised imploringly.

"My head reels," murmured he, in return. "I dare not think of the past, much less speak of it. Dear, dear brother, do not exact it of me. Be content to know that, for three days of my life, I was happy beyond the power of man to express—but for three days only. What followed almost cost me my reason ; and the mere mention of my misfortune unsettles it to-day. Give me your hand, and let us drop this subject forever, Louis. I have *no* past ; futurity is everything to me."

"So be it," replied Louis, grasping his brother's hand with fervor. "From this day we are comrades for life !"

Their hands remained clasped for a few seconds : then, as by a simultaneous impulse, the brothers struck spurs into their horses' flanks, and galloped swiftly onward. The troops were allowed to halt but once during the day ; they went on and on until sunset, when they arrived within sight of the market-town of Petronelle. Between the city and the tired troopers was a wide plain, whose uniformity was broken here and there by the ruins of ancient Roman fortifications.

Suddenly there was a cry, a clash of swords, and a clang of trumpets uttering strange sounds ; and, as the regiment of the Princes of Savoy was defiling along a passage between the ruins, a troop of Tartars that had been in ambuscade behind, sprang out, uttering the most hideous yells.

"Forward !" cried Prince Louis, brandishing his sword.

"Forward !" echoed Eugene, joyfully, spurring his horse into their very midst. For a while the brothers fought side by side, Louis with calm intrepidity, Eugene with the instinct, the enthusiasm, the inspiration of genius. His sword mowed down the Tartars as the reaper's scythe sweeps away the grass ; but unhappily the attack had been so sudden, and the cries which had accompanied it so frightful, that the Austrians became panic-stricken, and their ranks disorderly.

In vain the elder Prince of Savoy tried to rally them ; in vain Eugene, followed by a few veterans, called upon them to charge ; his reckless gallantry availed him nothing. Finally his arm with its unsheathed sword, dropped discouraged at his side.

"Lost, lost !" cried he to his brother. "Lost and disgraced !"

"Yes, by Heaven, they are flying !" was the despairing reply. But as he spoke the words, he saw that he was in error. The galloping horses were coming nearer and nearer, and now they saw that re-enforcement was at hand. The Duke of Lorraine with his cavalry was flying to their rescue, and the fight was resumed. The dragoons, encouraged by the sight of their commander-in-chief, now charged the Tartars, and they in their turn began to fly.

Prince Louis was eager to pursue them, and, calling his men, the chase began. His horse outstripped the others, and unhappily was so conspicuous a mark, that the arrow of a Calmuck, hidden behind the ruins of a triumphal arch, pierced his breast. Maddened by pain, the animal leaped so high in the air that his rider was thrown to the ground ; and while the horse rushed on, his master was trodden down by his own dragoons, who, in the eagerness of pursuit, trampled their unfortunate commander to death.

The enemy had been repulsed, and the troops were in better spirits. Eugene rode from rank to rank, repeating the same words, " Where is my brother ? Where is the Prince of Savoy ? "

Not a man there could answer his questions, for not one had seen his leader fall. At length, it was remembered that a wounded horse had been seen madly rushing over the plain, but the excited troopers had given no heed to the circumstance ; it was an occurrence too common in an engagement, to arrest them for a moment from their pursuit of an enemy.

Eugene's heart was bounding with joy, and he had been seeking his brother to give and receive congratulations. His countenance, which had been glowing with pride, became suddenly disturbed ; his flashing eyes grew dull and leaden, and so for one moment he sat, stricken and motionless. But he started from his lethargy, and crying out to his men, " Follow me ! " they galloped away to the spot where the dying and the dead were heaped together near the ruined arch where the Tartars had been concealed.

In an instant the unfortunate youth saw the body of his brother. He flung himself from his horse, and knelt down by his side. Gracious Heaven ! was that bruised and shapeless mass all that remained of the comeliness and grace of Louis of Savoy !

Eugene bent down, and, lovingly as a mother lifts her newborn infant, he raised his brother's mangled head, and rested it upon his arm. The hot tears that fell upon that poor, bleeding face, awoke the small remnant of life that was pulsating in the dying prince's heart, and his filmy eyes unclosed. Their light was almost extinguished, but Eugene saw that he was recognized, for the feeble spark kindled, and the pale lips fluttered.

"My dream!" were the words he uttered, "my dream!"

"No, no!" cried Eugene, in piercing tones of anguish, while with his trembling hand he stroked his brother's hair and wiped the death-dew from his brow.

"Eugene," murmured Louis, "my wife—my chil—"

"Oh! they shall be mine—mine, beloved," was the passionate reply.

"Kiss me, brother, and—bear the kiss to my Urania."

Eugene stifled his sobs, and kissed the pale, cold lips. A shudder crossed the frame of the dying man, a torrent of blood gushed from his lips, and moving his head so that it rested close to his brother's heart, he expired.

With a groan, Eugene fell upon his lifeless body. How long he had lain there he knew not, when he felt a gentle touch upon his shoulder. He looked up, and beheld the Duke of Lorraine.

"Prince Eugene," said he, "war has claimed from you a terrible sacrifice. You have lost a brother whom you most tenderly loved. But a soldier must conquer grief; and who more than he should remember that death, however painful, cancels all human woes?"

Eugene rose slowly to his feet, and raised his hand all purple with his brother's gore. "See," said he, "my brother has given me the baptism of war, and now I dedicate myself to strife. This blood-besprinkled hand shall smite the Turk, shall ruin his fields, shall devastate his towns.—Ah, Louis! Ambition has hitherto been my incentive to glory, but revenge is stronger than ambition, and revenge shall lift me to greatness!"

The setting sun poured down a stream of light upon the speaker, who, small, delicate, and insignificant, seemed transfigured into the genius of war. The dragoons around looked upon him with awe; and, long years after, they were accustomed to relate the circumstance of Prince Louis's death, and Prince Eugene's vow.

# CHAPTER X.

## VIENNA.

"THE Turks, the Turks! The Tartars are coming! The Duke of Lorraine has been defeated! We are lost!"

Such were the cries in Vienna, on the morning of the 8th of July, 1683. A courier from the Duke of Lorraine had brought news of the unfortunate skirmish near Petronelle, and had warned the emperor of the approach of the enemy. Leopold had acted upon the information at once, and preparations were making by the royal family to evacuate Vienna.

This fact was no sooner known throughout the city, than thousands of its inhabitants prepared to follow. If the emperor deserted his capital, it was because he knew that it must fall; and those who loved their lives were determined to fly. From palace to hut there was but one common feeling—a frenzied desire to go elsewhere—anywhere rather than remain to be butchered by the infidel.

Whosoever possessed a carriage, a wagon, a cart, was an object of greater envy than he who counted his treasures by millions. Incredible prices were offered and received for the roughest of conveyances. Before every house stood vehicles of every kind, crowded with fugitives, upon whom the poorer classes gazed with longing eyes; many of them, by dint of tears and prayers, obtaining liberty to hang on the wagons as they drove away.

And now amid the throng arose a cry. "The emperor! the emperor!"

Yes—he sat in his imperial carriage, pale, mournful, silent. And at his side, sorrowful as he, was the Empress Eleanor. Behind them, in another carriage, came the aja, with the crown prince of Austria in her arms. Alas! not even for that innocent babe was there safety to be found in the doomed city.

The people, like madmen, rushed through the streets behind the imperial cortége. Whither their sovereign went, they determined to follow ; for with him, they fancied, they would find refuge from the terrible Turk.

The retinue of the emperor took the way toward the Danube, and the long train of carriages thundered over its wide bridge. At intervals the people shouted :

"Follow his imperial majesty ! Whither our sovereign travels, we must go for safety !" And for six hours the bridge was thronged with passengers ; some in vehicles, some clinging to vehicles ; ladies and lackeys together in rumbles, or together hanging to the carriage-doors. Never in his life had such a cortége followed the Emperor of Austria ; and certainly a procession more mournful had never accompanied a sovereign before. Leopold's destination was Linz ; but the way was tedious, the roads sandy, and the sun's rays scorching. Poor horses ! they were white with sweat ; but still the drivers urged them on, for relays there were none. Terror had almost depopulated the country. Toward nightfall the fugitives were compelled to halt, for their tired animals were too stiff to travel farther, and themselves were weary and hungry.

They had reached a small village, where Leopold gave orders to have beds and supper prepared for his pale and worn-out empress.

"Ah, yes !" sighed she, "I am hungry and sleepy."

But from some mismanagement, the wagons containing the beds and provisions of the imperial family had either stopped on the way, or had never left Vienna.

The poor empress folded her hands and began to pray. The emperor bowed his head. "My house is sorely in need," said he, sadly, "but we are all in the hands of Almighty God. Whithersoever it be His will to exile us, I am ready to go : and may His holy will be done !"

The imperial pair then left their carriage, and, a bed being made of the cloaks of the pages, they laid them down to sleep under the dark-blue vault of the spangled heavens. But, at the dawn of day, they resumed their journey. The horses had rested, and the gentlemen of the imperial household had procured some homely refreshments for the famished monarch and his family. It consisted of eggs, milk, and black bread ;

but hunger lent it savor, and their majesties ate with more relish, perhaps, than they had ever done before.

They set out again. Their way now lay over cornfields, where the farmers, with their maids and men, were gathering the wheat, and binding it into sheaves. They, too, were in terror of the Turks ; but, when they saw the imperial cortége slowly plodding its way through the sandy road, they stopped their work, and, coming up to the portières, intruded their coarse, brutal faces into the very carriages themselves. They stared at the empress and jeered at the emperor ; inquired how he liked his crown, and why he did not wear it on his head. They added that it was a fine thing to be on a throne, to be sure ; but emperors had a right to their share of trouble in this world, quite as much as other people ; perhaps they deserved a little more than others.

When the officers and pages around heard this insolent scoffing, they drew their swords, and would have made short work of the boors ; but Leopold forbade the use of violence. "Let them alone," said he, mildly. "They are quite right. It is easy to be a monarch while the sun shines, and the empire prospers ; let me hope to prove to my subjects that I can bear my reverses with humility and fortitude. Let these people alone ; for all trials come from above, and in His own good time God will help us, and end our tribulations."

The peasants, ashamed, slunk back into their fields, and the imperial retinue went on to Linz, while for those that had remained in Vienna there ensued a period of danger, hardships, and terrible endurance.

Count Rudiger von Starhemberg, who had been chosen to defend Vienna, entered upon his perilous responsibilities with enthusiasm and energy. Rich and poor, great and small, were called upon to contribute to the general welfare. Nobles of high degree worked on the defences ; ladies brought baskets of provisions to the laborers ; and the mayor of Vienna, by way of setting the example to his inferiors, carried sand all day in a wheelbarrow to the fortifications. But bravely as they worked, each day augmented their danger. The sentinels on St. Stephen's towers could see, by the reddened heavens, that the Turk was approaching. On the 12th of July the sum-

mit of the Kahlenberg was seen to be in flames ; and the besieged had no need to be told that a monastery had been destroyed, and its occupants perchance put to the sword.  Kara
Mustapha invested Vienna, and sent to demand the surrender
of the city.  It was refused, and the siege was begun.

The Turks pitched their tents at the distance of several
miles, and began to mine.  Meanwhile a terrible fire broke
out in Vienna which threatened destruction to its inhabitants.
Driven onward by a high wind, it consumed street after street,
and at length approached the arsenal, within whose precincts
were a shot-tower and the powder-magazine.  Thousands of citizens were at the engines, making despairing efforts to arrest
the conflagration ; but the licking flames came fast and faster
toward the shot-tower.  The wretched Viennese had given up
every hope of salvation, when Count Guido von Starhemberg,
the nephew of the commanding general, rescued Vienna at the
risk of his own life.  Accompanied by a few soldiers, he entered the tower, and deluged the powder-barrels with water.
Animated by the noble devotion of the young count, others
followed him with new supplies.  The windows of the powder-
magazine were then walled up, and the fire extinguished.

Scarcely had the Viennese recovered from this threatened
catastrophe before danger assailed them from another quarter.
The Turkish lines grew closer around the city, and the Duke
of Lorraine, who, in the interim, had arrived, and had encamped on an island in the Danube, was forced back to Mora-
via, there to await the long-promised succor of the King of
Poland, and the long-procrastinated re-enforcements of the
Elector of Bavaria.

Within the gates their foes were sickness, discouragement,
hunger, and mutiny.  With these intestine enemies Count von
Starhemberg battled manfully.  His own spirit and courage
were the weapons he used to keep down discontent.  Day and
night he was in the trenches ; and when, by skilful counter-
mining, his men had succeeded in taking the lives of a few
hundred Turks, Count von Starhemberg embraced the miners,
and took the earliest opportunity of rewarding them.

Undaunted by the Turkish bullets, he visited the ramparts
three times daily, until finally he was struck by one of the

balls that were constantly aimed at him, and severely wounded in the head. He was picked up insensible, and carried home ; but Rudiger von Starhemberg had no time to be sick : so three days after he rose from his bed, and, with his head bound up, mounted his horse, and returned to his post.

His short absence had been productive of much evil in Vienna. It had dispirited the timid and emboldened the insubordinate. But Count Rudiger had an iron will, and no sympathy for weakness that endangered the state. An officer having neglected his watch, and permitted the Turks to intrench themselves in front of a bastion whereof he had the guard, Count von Starhemberg gave him his choice between the gallows and a *sortie* wherein he should meet the death of a soldier. The officer chose the latter alternative, and died after performing prodigies of valor.

Two soldiers had resisted the commands of their captain. Both were arrested, and one of them accused the other of having instigated him to insubordination. In presence of their regiment they were made to throw for their lives, and he who threw the lowest number was taken out and shot.

From the fulfilment of their duty to the country, Count von Starhemberg would exempt neither age nor sex. Two boys of less than twelve years of age were accused of having secret understanging with the enemy, by which, for a rich reward, they were to open the gates at night, and deliver the city into Kara Mustapha's hands. Count von Starhemberg investigated the matter thoroughly, and, the fact having been proved upon the boys, they were executed.

But hunger and disease were fast decreasing the ranks of the besieged. The hospitals were so crowded with patients, that no more could obtain admittance ; and the commander, who seemed to have an expedient for every disaster, appealed to the women of Vienna to receive the sufferers in their houses. They responded, as woman does, to the claims of humanity, and, carrying their devotion further than was required, they visited the hospitals, and brought food to the men on the ramparts, to refresh and invigorate them as they worked.

But unhappily, the day came when substantial food was no longer to be gotten. The city was invested, and no supplies

16

could come from without. The Duke of Lorraine had promised re-enforcements toward the end of the month ; and yet the 30th day of August had dawned, and no help was vouchsafed.

But there was yet another night to pass before they would despair of his coming. Crowds of men assembled on the towers of St. Stephen's, that they might hear from the lips of the sentinels the first tidings of joy ; in the churches women and children were on their knees imploring Heaven to send them succor ; while without the Turks, who had just begun a fresh assault, were thinning the ranks of their defenders, and adding to the mournful numbers of the widows and orphans of Vienna.

By morning the Turks had mined a passage to the stronghold of Ravelin. Thither rushed the men with pikes, sabres, and clubs ; and behind them came their wives and daughters with boiling pitch and oil, with sacks of sand and ashes, to throw upon the invaders as they emerged from their subterranean passage. The expedient was successful ; the enemy was repulsed with loss, and the fall of Vienna averted for another day.

A messenger from the emperor had managed to pass the Turkish lines, promising help to the brave besieged, could they but hold out till the middle of September ; but, after ten weeks of struggle, patient waiting, and hope deferred, two weeks seemed an eternity. Nevertheless the indomitable Starhemberg reanimated their courage, not only by words, but by his noble and unselfish endurance of hardship, his fearless defiance of danger. They had resisted fifteen assaults of the enemy, and had made twenty-one sallies outside of the defences. He knew that, if they chose, their valiant souls would sustain them for two weeks longer, and his burning words prevailed.

Once more they rallied, and defended themselves with desperation. Though shells were bursting over their houses and at their feet, though sickness was raging in their hospitals, and hunger was wasting away their kindred, they swore to resist for two weeks longer. So they could but save Vienna, their fatherland, and their emperor, they were willing to endure their sufferings to the bitter end. The Turks pressed closer, but every foot of ground cost them thousands of men ;

and their advance was disputed by heroes whose bodies were weakened with fasting and sickness. Not a morsel of bread or of fresh meat was to be seen ; for a while a cat was esteemed a great delicacy ; and, finally, when the rats were exhausted, the poor, famished Viennese were glad to eat mice.

Meanwhile Kara Mustapha went about in his litter, calling upon his men to exterminate these obstinate starvelings, bestowing rewards upon those who had distinguished themselves, and beheading with his own cimeter such as displeased or offended him. After each one of these visits of the commander to his trenches, the Turks made a fresh assault on the city. Had they made a general attack, the besieged were lost ; for there were within the walls of Vienna but four thousand men capable of bearing arms, and these were so exhausted by hunger, that they might easily have been overpowered. No amount of heroism could supply the want of bodily strength ; and at last Count von Starhemberg himself was forced to acknowledge that they must ere long capitulate.

Every night from the towers of St. Stephen's signal-rockets proclaimed to heaven and earth the distress and despair of the people of Vienna ; while the burning eyes of the brave commander were strained to see a responsive light, and his ears intent to listen for the answering boom of the cannon that was to have announced approaching succor. One week of the two had painfully ebbed away ; in eight days more Vienna would be sacked, and the Crescent would replace the Cross !

## CHAPTER XI.

### THE RE-ENFORCEMENTS.

ON this same 8th of September—so fraught with discouragement to the suffering inhabitants of Vienna—the Duke of Lorraine held a council of war in his tent with his allies. The King of Poland was there, burning with ardor to rescue the capital of Austria ; the Elector of Bavaria had arrived with heavy re-enforcements, which, added to the troops furnished by Saxony, Swabia, and Franconia, swelled the army to eighty-four thousand men. Other volunteers from various parts of Germany had joined the standard of Austria, and all were eager to uphold the cause of Christendom against the unbelieving infidel.

For three days the Polish troops had been occupied building a pontoon bridge, upon which, on the 8th day of September, the allied forces began to cross the Danube.

The first to cross were the King of Poland and the Duke of Lorraine. No sooner had they gained the opposite bank than the army broke out into one universal shout of joy.

John Sobiesky's fine face was beaming with exultation. With a triumphant smile he turned to the duke, who, with his usual serious expression of countenance, was watching the troops while they came across.

"The Turks are lost!" said Sobiesky.

"They were lost from the moment your majesty came to our rescue," was the courteous reply. "From the moment that you assumed the chief command, I felt certain of success."

"My dear duke," said the king, warmly, "I am not so dazzled by your generous praise as not to know which of us is the greater general of the two. If I have accepted your highness's gracious relinquishment of the chief command to me, I shall take good care not to exercise it without advice from yourself. But I am in no trouble now as to the issue of our contest with the Turks. They are already beaten. A general who, at the head of two hundred thousand men, suffers us to construct this bridge within five leagues of his camp, is a man of no ability. He is as good as beaten."*

"Provided we reach Vienna before our poor hungry countrymen will have been forced to surrender."

The king's eyes flashed. "Ay, ay, indeed!" exclaimed he, eagerly; "every thing depends upon that. The main question is, to march to Vienna as quick as possible."

"There are two roads to Vienna," replied the duke.

The king nodded affirmatively. "Yes; the road lying

* John Sobiesky's own words.—See Kausler, "Prince Eugene of Savoy," vol. i., p. 22.

through the valley of the Danube is level ; the one that leads to Vienna by the Kahlenberg is steep and toilsome."

"But much shorter," added the duke.

"Let us then select the route over the Kahlenberg," answered the king. "Your highness understands giving sound advice under the garb of a passing observation."

Their conversation was just then interrupted by the appearance of two young horsemen, who bowed respectfully as they rode by. One wore the rich and becoming uniform of the Polish lancers—this was the crown prince of Poland ; the other, more simply attired, was Prince Eugene of Savoy—the youngest colonel in the Austrian service.

At a signal from the King of Poland, the youths reined in their horses.

"My son," said the king, touching the Polish prince on the shoulder, "let me congratulate you that you are about to engage the enemy under the command of one of the most distinguished generals of the age."

The duke shook his head, and smilingly addressed Eugene : "Prince of Savoy," said he, "you see before you a king whose least glory is his crown. Let him be your model, and when you confront the enemy let the thought of John Sobiesky's fame urge you to deeds of prowess."

"Your highness," replied Eugene, "not only when I confront the enemy, but every day and every hour of my life, will I look back with emotion to the time when I beheld the two most eminent commanders of the age contemplating each other's greatness without envy, and accepting each other's suggestions without cavil ; and I trust that, from the sight, I may receive inspiration as far as lies within my capacity, to emulate their moral as well as their military worth."

"You will ere long have the opportunity of showing us, how proximity to John Sobiesky inspires men to valor," replied the duke. "We are about to march to Vienna. Which road would you take, if you had to choose for the army ?"

Eugene's large black eyes wandered over the horizon until they rested on the summit of Kahlenberg. "If we gain those heights, we overlook not only our friends, but the entire camp of the enemy."

"Well answered," said John Sobiesky. "You are a military man by intuition, I see, and are destined to make a figure in the world. You are small in person, but would be great in council. Men of your size and build are more frequently gifted with military genius than those of lofty stature. I suppose," continued he, smiling, "that it is because the brain which reasons, and the heart that feels, lie close together, and so can help each other. But," said he, interrupting himself, "here comes the Elector Max Emmanuel. Allow me to bid him welcome."

The Duke of Lorraine followed him with his eyes, as, in company with the crown prince, the king rode forward to meet the handsome Prince of Bavaria.

"The Poles did well," said he to himself, "to prefer John Sobiesky to me ; and, if I had known him personally, never would I have been his competitor for a throne. He is better fitted to reign and govern than I."

"Has your highness any commands for me?" asked Eugene.

"Yes, my dear young friend," replied the duke, solemnly. "We draw near to Vienna. Avenge your brother's death, but prize and cherish your own life. Do not wantonly expose your person, nor seek for danger ; for he alone is a hero whose valor is restrained by prudence. I shall place you, nevertheless, where danger is imminent, and glory to be earned ; so that, when I recommend you for promotion to the emperor, the world may not say that you owe your advancement to favor."

"Your highness's advice shall be followed to the letter," replied Eugene, earnestly. "I will despise danger, that I may avenge my brother ; yet will I guard my life, that I may be the protector of his wife and children. But nothing will more inspire me to heroic deeds than the friendship which you so condescendingly evince for me. May God bless and reward you for your sympathy with my suffering heart!"

At the end of three days, the army gained the heights of the Kahlenberg. The men, tired and sleepy, dispersed, and threw themselves down to rest under the trees ; their commanders rode farther to the mountain's brow, and there, beneath the fiery rays of the setting sun, lay prisoned Vienna and her Turkish jailers. But above was a cloud of smoke and dust, through which ever and anon leaped columns of fire, while the air was heavy with reverberation of cannon. The Turks were storming the city.

The besieged, mindful of their promise, were defending themselves with desperation. With imperturbable calm, Count von Starhemberg headed every sortie, and his quick eye perceived every little advantage that could be taken; while his wise precautions saved many a life, and warded off many a peril. His redoubts were no sooner damaged than repaired; trench after trench was dug; street by street defended with palisades, improvised of rods and beams.

As night came on, the heavy firing of the Turks ceased, and a dead stillness followed the terrible boom of cannon. The streets were ploughed with balls, the ashes of many a consumed building were scattered about by the wind, while here and there a fitful blaze was seen issuing from a shapeless mass that once had been the stately home of some proud Austrian noble. Pale, ghastly figures wandered among the ruins, searching for food, which, alas! they rarely found. But, amid this "abomination of desolation," they still lifted their eyes to heaven for help, and still clung to hope of rescue.

Count Starhemberg, as usual, had ascended the tower of St. Stephen's; while in the city below every form was prostrate in prayer. With his own hand he fired the nightly rocket, and watched its myriads of stars as they shot heavenward, illumined the darkness, and then fell back into nothingness. His heart beat painfully, as the last scintillations went out, and left but the pall of night behind. But he gazed on in silence, and in anguish unutterable. Suddenly he unclasped his rigid hands, for oh! joy! joy! there was light on the summit of the Kahlenberg; the signal darts up into the sky, and from Herman's peak the cannon proclaims that help is nigh!

One cry of rapture burst from the lips of all who stood around the commander; the warder grasped his speaking-trumpet, and cried out to the crowd below, "The signal is answered!"

The sound was caught up by the eager multitude, the blessed tidings were borne from street to street, and the people with one accord knelt down and thanked God. Noble and simple, aged and young, all hastened to St. Stephen's. Men clasped hands ; and strangers that had never met before, embraced one another like friends and kinsmen. Hope had softened all hearts, joy's electric touch had made a thousand interests one : men were no longer segregate, their lives were blended into one great emotion.

Count von Starhemberg was so overcome, that for some moments his tongue refused him utterance. When he spoke, his voice, so accustomed to command, trembled and grew soft —soft and gentle as that of a young maiden.

" Will some one fetch me pen and paper ? " said he. And when a portfolio was brought for him to write upon, he could scarcely command his hand while it traced these few words :

" Lose no time ; in Heaven's name, be quick, or we are lost ! "

" Who will venture to swim across the Danube, and deliver this paper to the Duke of Lorraine ? " added he.

Three young men volunteered at once. Count von Starhemberg chose the one that seemed the strongest, and gave it to him.

" Promise me that you will deliver it or die ! "

" I promise," was the reply of the young man, who, without tarrying another moment, sprang down the steps and disappeared.

In a few hours, another rocket from the mountain-top announced the safe arrival of the messenger, and promised speedy relief.

Yes, deliverance was at hand. At gray dawn, the army were ready to march, and the King of Poland, the Duke of Lorraine, and Louis of Baden were in the saddle. When all were assembled, John Sobiesky dismounted, and kneeling before the altar of Leopold's chapel, addressed a prayer to Heaven for a blessing on the approaching struggle. In his priestly robes, within the chancel, stood Marcus Avianus, the inspired Capuchin whom the pope had sent to Germany to preach this new crusade. His burning words had done as much for the cause of Christianity as the stalwart arms of Austria's best warriors ; and now, as he raised his hands on high, and eighty thousand men knelt to receive his blessing, their hearts throbbed with joy, for they felt that the God of battles would be with them that day.

The rites done, John Sobiesky bestowed the honor of knighthood upon his son, "thereby commemorating the proudest day of their lives ;" and at the conclusion of the ceremony, he addressed the Polish army, exhorting them to fight as became a Christian host in a cause "where death was not only the path to glory, but the way to heaven."

"I have but one command to give my men," said he, in conclusion. "Let them follow their king, and wherever he is to be seen, there let them know that the battle rages fiercest."

A tumultuous shout was the answer to this exhortation. It gathered strength as it passed along the ranks, until it awoke a thousand echoes from the mountain-tops around ; while the rays of the sun, like a consecrating fire, glistened from the point of every bayonet, and flashed from the blade of every waving sword.

The cheers of the Christians were borne on the summer air, until the sound reached the very camp of the Turks. It sent consternation to the heart of Kara Mustapha, as he lay smoking his hookah under a tent of silk and velvet. For sixty days he had besieged Vienna with his hundreds of thousands. Against its obstinate defenders warfare had failed ; and now that hunger was about to do what he had vainly tried—to paralyze their valor, here came succor, to render his victory doubtful. For he well knew that the Christians were full of ardor, while his Turks were tired of fighting. That he might excite their thirst for blood, he assembled all his prisoners, men, women, and children, together, and, within view of his army, ordered them all to be massacred. The work of death began, and the expiring cries of his victims were the Paynim's answer to the shouts of the Christians, that were raising their hearts to God.

That fearful wail was heard, too, by the beleaguered men

of Vienna ; and the thought of their butchered kindred gave strength to their famished bodies. They hungered no longer for food ! they thirsted for blood.

And now the bells, which for sixty days had been silent, rang out their alarum, calling all to the last great struggle. The sick raised their heads, and felt the glow of health thrilling through their fevered veins ; the aged worked like youths —the youths like demi-gods. And full of hope, full of valor, the brave citizens of Vienna awaited the coming of their liberators.

The main body of the allied army was commanded by the Electors of Bavaria and of Saxony ; the right wing, by John Sobiesky ; the left, by the Duke of Lorraine and Louis of Baden. The plan of the attack had been made according to the suggestions of the King of Poland.

At the side of Louis of Baden rode Eugene of Savoy, his sorrows all forgotten in the excitement of the occasion. His countenance beamed with animation, his eyes darted fire. His black war-horse, too, partook of his enthusiasm : he pranced, leaped into the air, and neighed as if in defiance of the barbs that were to bear his enemies into battle that morning.

"My dear cousin," said Eugene to Louis, "I implore you let me go early into action. Give me something to do as soon as we are in sight of the enemy, and thereby prove me your love."

"You shall have your wish, Eugene. Your division is to open the engagement. As soon as you hear the discharge of the cannon from the heights of the Kahlenberg, you advance."

With a joyful wave of the hand, Eugene sprang forward, and placed himself at the head of his dragoons, where, rigid as a statue, he stood with his eyes raised to the summit of the Kahlenberg.

The first shot rolled like thunder through the valley gorges. The men grasped their muskets, the horses pawed the ground. The second, the third, followed, and every eye glistened, and every heart throbbed. The fourth—*the fifth!*

"*En avant!*" cried Eugene ; and the dragoons galloped

forward. They were to drive the enemy from the valley of the Nussberg, and force the pass of Heiligenstadt. But the Turks disputed every inch of the ground, making breastworks of every hillock, trenches of every hollow. They defended the way with such desperation that the Austrian cavalry began to waver.

An exclamation of fury was heard from the lips of Eugene. "Victory or death!" cried he; and with these words the intrepid youth struck spurs into his horse, and sprang through the pass; his sabre, flashing like lightning through the air, as right and left it dealt destruction to the Janizaries that disputed his passage.

Amazed at such prowess, the dragoons gave one simultaneous cheer, and leaped into the enemy's midst. From that moment they moved on like a granite wall; onward in the track of their gallant commander, all peril disregarding, they fought their way, until, inspired by his heroism, encouraged by the soul-stirring tones of his blithe young voice, they won the pass, and forced the enemy back.

Meanwhile the imperial and Saxon forces had advanced from the Kahlenberg, in one dense column, the sight of which had sorely shaken the confidence of Kara Mustapha in his power to resist them.

On swept the mighty mass, and in a few moments the deep thunder of the cannon reverberated along the mountain gorges; the clashing of swords and the rattling of musketry mingled with the cries of the wounded, and the groans of the dying; while all above was fire and smoke. The passes were reddened with blood, which drop by drop flowed down their declivities, until it met another life-destroying current on its way; and both glided onward to the Danube, empurpling its waters with the mingled gore of Christian and Paynim.

The battle raged, without any decisive advantage, until long after noon. At four o'clock, however, the Ulans of the King of Poland were about to be overpowered by superior numbers, when re-enforcement came in the form of a charge on the right wing of the Turks, by the troops under Charles of Lorraine. Those flying squadrons, beneath whose horses' hoofs the ground is trembling as if upheaved by an earthquake, are headed by Eugene—the indomitable Eugene. On his foam-flecked steed, with a sword in his hand that is gory to the hilt, comes the "little abbé," who was too much of a weakling to obtain a commission in the army of the King of France. If his mother could see him now, she would confess that he was no fit aspirant for a scarlet hat.

Side by side rode Eugene and Louis of Baden, both heading that bloody chase. Over heaps of corpses, over struggling horses, falling timbers, through smoke and fire, they dashed toward the gates of Vienna. Count Starhemberg was there with his handful of braves, making gallant resistance to the Janizaries. But for the mad charge of Eugene, the little garrison would soon have been cut to pieces. But the attack on their rear surprised the Janizaries; they fell back, only to be confronted by the Duke of Lorraine, and, believing resistance to be useless, they fled.

The King of Poland meanwhile was within the gates engaged in a hand-to-hand fight with the enemy in the streets. He was not left long to struggle without help. Once more Eugene and his cavalry came to the rescue; and now the Turkish legions are flying for their lives, while the Christians are shouting for joy and victory!

Kara Mustapha, who was to have made his seat of empire at Vienna, has suddenly become a panic-stricken adventurer. With that singular absence of fortitude which so often distinguishes tyrants in adversity, he fell to weeping like a child, and went whining for protection to the Khan of Tartary.

"Save me, save me!" was his cowardly cry.

The khan shook his head. "We know the King of Poland too well," said he. "Nobody can withstand him."

And from this moment nothing was thought of, in the Turkish camp, but flight. Kara Mustapha's war-horse, with its housings of purple velvet worked in pearls, was too heavy to bear him away from Vienna; he mounted a fleet-footed Arabian, and sped away without thought of the treasures he was leaving behind. His costly tent, his girdles of diamonds, his cimeters inlaid with rubies and sapphires, his six hundred sacks of piastres, all fell into the hands of John Sobiesky.

While joy and jubilee prevailed throughout the streets of

Vienna, Eugene of Savoy was on his way to the dwelling of his widowed sister : but, while he sorrowed with Urania and her orphans, his name was being borne upon the trumpet-blast of fame, as chief among the heroes that rescued Vienna from the infidel.

# BOOK IV.

## CHAPTER I.

### THE FALL OF BUDA.

As a signal that the conference was at an end, the Emperor
Leopold rose from his arm-chair. The president and vice-
president followed his example, and the other members of the
council bowed and retired. The Margrave of Baden and
Count von Starhemberg remained standing by the green table,
while the emperor, who had crossed the room, now stood vacantly staring out of a window, drumming with his fingers on
one of the panes.

His two counsellors were perfectly *au fait* to the import
of this drumming; it meant that the emperor's thoughts were
with his army, which was still in the field, although three
years had gone by since the siege of Vienna. During this
protracted struggle both parties had fought bravely, but neither
one had as yet prevailed against the other. In 1684 the Austrians had gained a brilliant victory over the allied enemy;
but, in the course of the same year, the Turks, by their obstinate valor, had forced the Duke of Lorraine to abandon the
siege of Buda, which, since then, had remained in their possession, and gave them entire control of Hungary.

The emperor's thoughts, then, were at Buda, while his fingers still drummed on the window-pane. At last he turned
around.

"Any news from the army?" asked he, hastily.

"None, your majesty," replied the margrave. "Since the
news of the junction of the Duke of Lorraine's forces with
those of Prince Louis of Baden and Max Emmanuel, nothing
further has been heard as to the progress of the siege."

"And that, of course, signifies that there is nothing good to be told," added Von Starhemberg. "If the Duke of Lorraine had met with any success, he would not have failed to send a courier with the tidings."

"Unhappily, since he has had command of the army, he has had many more reverses to communicate than victories," replied the margrave, with a sigh.

"You forget his brilliant victory at Gran last year," returned the emperor. "Away with your petty ill-will toward the duke! Forget your personal grievances in admiration of his heroism."

"Sire," replied the margrave, somewhat impetuously, "there are personal grievances which will not allow themselves to be forgotten. The Duke of Lorraine, in his dispatches, has not only accused me of neglect in the provisioning and arming of his troops, but has also declared me unqualified for my position, and has recommended another man as minister of war."

"And yet you retain your position," replied the emperor; "so that neither one of you has influence enough with me to injure the other. I have great confidence, nevertheless, in the judgment of my brother-in-law; and, if occasionally he is of opinion that battles are not to be planned on the green table of a council-chamber, but in the field by the man, who is to fight them—not in *theoriæ* but in *praxis*—I am inclined to think that he is right."

"One thing I hope that your majesty will do me the justice to remember," answered Von Starhemberg, in a tone of vexation. "It is this: the war department, at my suggestion, advised that Buda should not be assaulted, but that the passes lying behind the city should be seized, Stuhlweissemberg besieged, and Buda, by this means, cut off from all intercourse with Turkey. Thus it would have fallen without bloodshed: whereas we have nothing to expect, as the result of a second direct attack, but the news of a second repulse."

"Should the Duke of Lorraine be forced to raise the siege a second time, I hope that the war department will remember that it was I, and not my commander-in-chief, who rejected their advice. So that, if we should be unfortunate, mine be the blame of the disaster, for I ordered the attack."

At this moment the door of the council-chamber was opened with some precipitation, and the chamberlain of the day appeared on the threshold.

"What do you come to announce?" asked Leopold.

"Sire, a bearer of dispatches from his highness of Lorraine."

"Ah, *lupus in fabula*," said the emperor, with a smile. "Well—let in the *lupus*."

"Your majesty," interrupted the Margrave of Baden, "would it not be better for me to receive the dispatches, and communicate their contents to you? The news of another disaster will be a great blow: your mind should be prepared to receive it."

"I am prepared for whatever it may please God to assign," replied Leopold, reverently. "If the news be bad, it is my duty to confront it like a man; if good, let me taste it pure, as it comes from the lips of the messenger. Let him enter!"

The chamberlain stepped back, made a sign to the page in the anteroom, and both sides of the door were flung open.

"Our bearer is a person of distinction," said Leopold to himself. "Both doors are opened for a reigning prince, a grandee of Spain, or—"

Just then the bearer of dispatches appeared—a small, slight person, in a simple uniform, but his breast well covered with orders, both Austrian and Spanish.

"Prince Eugene of Savoy!" exclaimed Leopold, with evident pleasure. And he made several steps toward the prince.

"Prince Eugene of Savoy," muttered the margrave, with an ugly frown; for well he knew that such an envoy would never have been chosen to be the bearer of evil tidings.

Meanwhile Eugene rapidly crossed the room, and knelt before the emperor.

"You forget," said Leopold, raising him, "that a knight of the Golden Fleece is not obliged to conform to the court custom of kneeling. His order kneel before the Almighty alone. Moreover, as grandee of Spain, your highness has a right to appear with covered head."

"Sire, I came hither neither as a grandee nor a knight. I came as the squire of my noble lord, the Duke of Lorraine, and as the soldier and subject of my emperor. Let me, then, greet my sovereign as my heart dictates."

With these words Eugene knelt again.

"Now," said Leopold, "rise, loyal subject, and satisfy my impatience. Tell me, in one word, has Buda fallen?"

"Yes, sire," was the exulting reply.

The emperor raised his grateful eyes to heaven, while his two councillors exchanged glances of dissatisfaction. Leopold saw this, and addressed himself to both.

"Gentlemen," said he, "pray remember that you were opposed to the siege of Buda, and that it was undertaken at the request of the Duke of Lorraine."

"Your majesty told us that you had commanded it yourself," answered the margrave. "The duke, then, has merely carried out orders!"

"Orders given because of his request. He proved to me that Buda could be taken; and, when I commanded this second attempt to reduce it, I merely yielded to his better judgment. But let us change the subject.—You are most welcome," continued he, to Prince Eugene. "And now let us hear the details of your glad tidings."

"Sire, the siege of Buda is an epic, worthy of the pen of a Homer. None but a great poet can do justice to the deeds of valor of the Duke of Lorraine."

"Try you, nevertheless," replied Leopold. "But hold! It were selfish to enjoy your narrative alone. The empress and the court shall partake of our happiness to day. Count von Starhemberg, oblige me by opening the door, and recalling the chamberlain."

The count reluctantly obeyed, and the chamberlain reappeared.

"You will announce to the ladies and gentlemen in waiting, that I request the presence of the court. I myself will conduct the empress hither." Then, with a wave of his hand to Prince Eugene, he added, "Await our return."

Not long after, the empress, conducted by her imperial husband, entered the room and took her seat. The ladies and gentlemen in waiting stood behind, and the margrave and Count von Starhemberg were on either side of the emperor.

17

"And now, Prince Eugene of Savoy," cried Leopold, "let us hear the details of the fall of Buda."

All eyes were turned upon Eugene, who, without boldness or bashfulness, calmly surveyed the brilliant assembly before him. In his plain, dark uniform, his black hair worn naturally and without powder, he presented a striking contrast to the courtiers in their magnificently-embroidered Spanish doublets, and huge, powdered wigs.

He began his narrative, by alluding to the fact that for one hundred and twenty years, in spite of six different attempts on the part of Austria to retake it, the ancient capital of Hungary had been in the hands of the Turks. He quoted the well-known saying of John Sobiesky, "Buda has drunk such torrents of Christian blood, that every handful of earth around its walls is red and moist with gore." He made a few brief remarks on the subject of the last unsuccessful attack, two years before ; and then, with all the enthusiasm of a warrior-poet, he entered upon the narration of the seventh siege.

He spoke of the various stratagems, sallies, and skirmishes that preceded the final assault. On the 18th of June the city was invested, and by the end of July the allied army had effected an entrance, and captured so many streets that the besieged had been compelled to retire within the fortress. At the same time, combustibles were thrown into the magazine, which exploded with fearful destruction, and the Duke of Lorraine, compassionating the condition of the brave old commander, Pacha Abdurrahmen, sent a messenger, advising him to capitulate. Abdurrahmen, for all answer, informed the duke that Allah and the Prophet would shortly punish the audacity of the Christians, and, by way of anticipating Divine justice, he caused one hundred Saxons, who had been captured a few days before, to be hanged within view of the besiegers.

This vindictive act was the signal for a new assault, and the fortress was attacked on three sides. The assailants were several times repulsed, for the Turks fought like demons. Undismayed, they stood upon the walls, pouring fire and shot into the Christian ranks until the hair was singed from their heads, and their scorched clothes dropped from their bodies.

If the allies were heroic in their attack, the Turks were not less so in their defence. Finally the women, too, were seen, some carrying ammunition, some bringing refreshments to the gunners, while others, singing wild strains of Turkish embateria, hurled stones from the walls upon the invading army.

More than two thousand Austrians had fallen, but they had succeeded in establishing themselves within one of the bastions, and had thereby obtained possession of the prison-tower. The day following, however, Abdurrahmen sprung a mine, which killed one hundred of the imperial troops, and so terrified the others, that they retired in confusion, and the bastion remained in the hands of the Turks.

Once more the Duke of Lorraine offered terms to the besieged, which a second time were indignantly refused. For the grand-vizier had arrived with re-enforcements, and on a plain just behind the city of Buda his troops were drawn up in battle array. The besieged now commenced an attack upon the besiegers ; one of their bombs burst almost at the feet of the Duke of Lorraine, killing and wounding several of his staff ; another fell into a heap of hand-grenades, which produced a frightful conflagration.

On the first of September Abdurrahmen was again summoned to surrender. The white-haired hero presented two documents to the envoys, one of which was from the high-priest of the Prophet at Constantinople, the other from the Sultan. The first enjoined it upon the pacha, as a religious duty, to defend Buda as the key to the Ottoman empire ; the other contained these few emphatic words : " Either fall as a martyr before the sword of the invader, or die as a traitor by the blade of the headsman."

" You see," added Abdurrahmen, calmly, " that no discretion is allowed me. I must prevail against you, or fight until I fall."

This decided the question of capitulation forever ; and although the grand-vizier was there with his reserves, the Duke of Lorraine determined to storm the fortress anew. It was a desperate resolve ; but, like Abdurrahmen, he had made up his mind to conquer or die.

At this point of his narration, Eugene paused for breath.

The emperor, perceiving that he was fatigued, made a sign to one of the pages in attendance, who thereupon placed a chair for him—a compliment never before paid by a sovereign of Austria to any man below the rank of a reigning prince.

"Prince Eugene of Savoy," said Leopold, "as a grandee of Spain, and a knight of the Golden Fleece, you have a right to be seated in the presence of your sovereign. Make use of the privilege, then ; for if you stand much longer, I see that you will not have strength to finish your recital ; and I would not abridge it by a word. It sounds like martial music to my enraptured ear."

"Sire," replied Eugene, accepting the chair, "'tis no wonder if the boom of the cannon sound like music to the son of Charles V. ; above all, when it thunders to proclaim your majesty's success. On the 2d of September began the last assault upon the fortress of Buda. It was impossible not to admire the intrepidity of our enemies : to a man, they seemed to have sworn, like their commander, to defend the post or die amid its ruins. But your majesty's troops were as resolute as they. After a terrible conflict fought over the bodies of their slain comrades, they cut to pieces a detachment of Janizaries that had been sent to oppose their passage.

"'No quarter !' was the watchword of the Moslems. 'No quarter !' cried the Christians in return. 'No quarter !' shouted the Bavarians, as they mounted a breach in the fortress, and fought hand to hand with its frenzied defenders. The latter poured out in such numbers that the Bavarians wavered, and perhaps might have been repulsed, had not the gallant Louis of Baden mounted the breach himself, and called upon his men to follow. They obeyed ; the Bavarians rallied, and the prince ordered a fresh attack. Thanks to his valor and able generalship, the Turks were forced back, and fled in confusion ; some finding refuge within the walls, others, in their dismay, plunging into the moat. The Bavarians followed the fugitives, and now from every castle-window waved the white flag of surrender.

"To the hero of Buda, the brave Abdurrahmen, our commanders would gladly have granted an honorable retreat. But he refused mercy at the hands of his admiring antagonists. Alone he stood, sabre in hand, defending the breach against our advancing troops, until he fell, pierced by twenty balls, while the bodies of his slain foes lay like a monument of his heroism around him. With the death of Abdurrahmen the struggle ceased, and that night, as a last act of defiance, the Turks sprung a mine in the fortress, and reduced it to a heap of ruins.

"The next morning, the grand-vizier retreated, and the plan of attack, inspired by the genius of the Duke of Lorraine, had destroyed the prestige of the Sultan in Hungary. Scarcely inferior to this great commander was the ability displayed by Prince Louis of Baden, and Max Emmanuel. No man who beheld them can ever forget the sight of these two great heroes, handsome and brave as Hector and Patroclus.

"Sire, my tale is ended. Buda has fallen, and its conquerors have immortalized themselves."

"You say, your tale is at an end, Prince Eugene," replied the emperor, smiling. "But you have omitted something in your recital."

"What is it, your majesty?"

"You have not once mentioned the name of the Prince of Savoy; and yet he must have been there. You have exalted the genius of the Duke of Lorraine, and you have likened his two generals to the heroes of antiquity. It is said that the Prince of Savoy is the inseparable companion of Prince Louis and Max Emmanuel. Where, then, was he, while his friends were gaining immortality?"

"Sire, he was with them; but, as he did no more than his duty, I have nothing further to say."

"It is your duty, as bearer of dispatches from your commander-in-chief, to answer my inquiries, let them relate to whomsoever they will. Where were you, then, while your friends were astonishing you with their valor?"

"He was at their side, your majesty. Before the siege, the three friends had sworn never to surrender to the enemy. It was therefore natural that the Prince of Savoy should follow the example of his superior officers, and imitate their gallantry."

"But was he in no danger? Was he not wounded?"

"Sire, on such a day, no soldier could hope to escape from danger ; above all, the officers who led them into action. The Prince of Savoy's horse was shot under him, and he himself was slightly wounded in the hand by an arrow."

"Where was he stationed on that last day ?"

"He was ordered to skirmish with the enemy, and prevent them from making sorties on the besiegers."

"A hard task, for one so young."

"Yes, sire ; for it condemned him to inaction, while his comrades were gaining glory. But before the close of the day, fate befriended him. The grand-vizier having made no attempt to join the besieged, the Prince of Savoy was so fortunate as to come in with his dragoons, just as the Bavarians were about to be repulsed from the breach."

"Ah ! I thought so !" exclaimed Leopold ; "and doubtless his appearance had much to do with the successful storming of the castle. And how did the Duke of Lorraine reward his gallantry ?"

"Sire, he was rewarded far, far beyond his deserts. The Duke of Lorraine, in presence of the army, folded him in his embrace."

"That was well done. Come hither, Prince Eugene. I, too, would reward you as the Duke of Lorraine did."

Eugene hastened to the emperor, who folded him in his arms, and then led him to the empress.

"Your majesty," said he to his wife, "I present you a young hero, who for three years has been gaining renown in the service of Austria. I recommend him to your favor, and beg that you, too, will bestow some reward upon him."

The empress turned her soft blue eyes upon the prince, who bent his knee, and kissed the hand she extended to him. "I will pray for you," said she, "as long as I live ; and, as a testimonial of my regard, I beg you to accept my husband's portrait."

Unclasping from her neck a heavy gold chain, to which was attached a miniature set in brilliants, she threw it over Eugene's shoulder with these words :

"Let the emperor's likeness be to you a souvenir of your past heroism, and may it inspire you for the future to serve him with loyalty and love."

"Your majesty," replied Eugene, "of my own free will I chose the Emperor of Austria for my sovereign ; but from this day forth I am pledged to serve him as his native-born subject : and the chain so graciously bestowed by your majesty, I shall wear as emblematic of my fealty, for life."

The emperor signed to Eugene to rise, and addressed himself to all present. "Vienna, too, shall have her share in this day's joy. The crescent, which for more than a hundred years has proclaimed to the world that Austria's capital was once in the hands of the infidel, shall be taken down from the tower of St. Stephen's. We have won the right to displace the accursed emblem, and it shall once more give place to the symbol of Christianity !"

The crescent of which the emperor spoke, had been on the tower of St. Stephen's since the year 1529, when Vienna was besieged by the Sultan Soliman. His guns were being constantly directed against the tower ; and the Viennese having sent a deputation to request that the Turks would not demolish their beautiful cathedral, Soliman consented to spare it on one condition. This was, that the cross should be removed, and the crescent take its place. In their extremity, the promise was made ; and, from that day, the Christian church had borne the hated symbol of Mohammedanism.

At the fall of Buda, Leopold refused to be bound any longer by the promise extorted from his ancestors ; and, in commemoration of the capture of this important post, a cross was erected on the tower, with this inscription : "Luna deposuit, et crux exaltata. Anno quo Buda a Turcis capta, MDCLXXXVI."

## CHAPTER II.

### THE FRIENDS.

WITH the capture of Buda, the campaign of 1686 closed. The army went into winter quarters, and the officers all congregrated in Vienna, there to indemnify themselves for past hardships by a few months of recreation.

Eugene of Savoy participated very little in the gayety of court-life. While his companion-in-arms, Louis of Baden, plunged headlong into the vortex of pleasure, the shy young Frenchman led a most retired existence, in his little hôtel in the Herrengasse. He had purchased this residence for his brother's widow and children, intending to make it not only their home, but his own. The young widow, after spending two years with her brother-in-law, forsook the world and retired to a convent, there to lay her burden of grief at the feet of her Lord. Her children she committed to the care of their great-grandmother, the Princess de Carignan; and Eugene was left to the solitude of a bachelor home, without one friendly voice to bid him welcome to its cold hearth.

Even Conrad, his faithful Conrad, was absent. Eugene had sent him to Turin with messages to Victor Amadeus, which he had not thought it prudent to write. For Conrad was not only loyal and affectionate; he had proved himself a person of such uncommon ability, that he was now his lord's secretary, no longer his servant. He had the care of his money, the administration of his affairs, and was his trusty and confidential friend. Eugene missed him sorely; for Conrad had accompanied him "that night" to the Palais Royal, and although Laura's name had never passed his lips, still her lover found some solace in the companionship of the man who had tended him during that dreadful illness, and who, he knew full well, had learned from his unconscious lips the secret of his love and its blight.

Eugene was in his cabinet. He had been engaged in the study of mathematics, and the perusal of Julius Cæsar's campaigns; after which, by way of recreation, he sat down to his escritoire, and, unfolding a sheet of paper, began to make plans of palaces and gardens.

He was so absorbed in his drawing, that he neither heard nor saw the door open, and give entrance to a handsome young man in a rich Spanish costume. For one moment the visitor paused on the threshold, and smilingly surveyed Eugene; then, crossing the room on tiptoes, he laid his hand upon the prince's shoulder.

"I certainly thought I would surprise you inditing a poem

or a letter to the lady of your thoughts, and here I find you drawing plans!"

"Max Emmanuel!" exclaimed Eugene, rising joyfully, and embracing his friend.

"Yes, Max Emmanuel, who, having paid his devoirs to his imperial father-in-law, has come with all haste to ask how it fares with his friend. The servants told me you were in your cabinet, so I forbade them to announce me, and made my way hither all alone, that I might take you by surprise, and find out whether you loved me as much as I do you. Seeing you intent upon writing, I was quite confident that I was about to discover a great secret—when lo! I see nothing but a sheet of drawing-paper, covered with porches and pilasters. Tell me the truth, Eugene—why is it that, instead of worshipping Aphrodite, like other youths, you are doing homage to the household gods of domestic architecture?"

"Why, my dear Max, domestic architecture interests me, because I expect to build houses, and lay out grounds. I do not worship Aphrodite like other youths, because—because I know her not."

The elector looked searchingly into Eugene's solemn eyes. "Are you in earnest?" asked he. "Do you intend me to believe that you are unacquainted with the ecstasies and tribulations of love?"

"No," replied Eugene, sadly, "for I am too truly your friend to deceive you, Max. I have loved, but my love was unfortunate; and the wound it has made in my heart is too painful to be probed. Dear friend, let us speak of it nevermore!"

"On the contrary, let us speak of it together without reserve. A hero like Eugene, who has faced death, and so often wrested victory from his enemies, can surely contemplate such a wound as Cupid's dart inflicts upon a man! But tell me, what are unfortunate loves? mine have all been crowned with myrtle, and smothered in roses."

Eugene was silent for a time; then raising his large, melancholy eyes, till they rested affectionately upon the bright, laughing countenance of his friend, he spoke: "I can well believe that you know nothing of the pangs inflicted by unhappy love ; for you are handsome, distinguished, and gifted. I, who am none of these, can tell you what it is to love adversely. It is to love with passion ; to be parted from the object of your love ; and not to know whether she, like you, is constant to her vows, and suffers from your absence, as you do from hers. Pray Heaven that love may never come to you in such a shape as this."

"No danger of me contracting the malady," replied Max ; "I am constitutionally incapable of receiving it. I pluck the fruit or flower that grows nearest, never suffering my imagination to run away with my longings. But never mind me and my sybaritic interpretations of the tender passion. Are your woes irremediable ? Is the lady married ?"

"In the eyes of the world she is."

"But not in the eyes of God, you would say. Then her marriage must have been compulsory or fraudulent ?"

"It was fraudulent."

"Then hie we to the pope for justice ! His holiness will not refuse it to such a brave crusader as you, and I myself will be your advocate. Give me pen and paper. I will write at once, send your signature and mine to the petition, and dispatch it by a courier this very day ; and then the world will see whether we, who stormed Buda, may not storm adverse fortune also."

"Dear friend, neither the pope nor you can storm my adverse fortunes. I must hear from my beloved whether she is true to me before I take one step to possess myself of her. For three years I have waited in vain for her summons ; and yet my longing arms are outstretched to clasp her, and never while I live will they encircle the form of another !"

"Nay—these are the enthusiastic ravings of recent disappointment. For a few years longer you may sorrow for your first love ; but oblivion will come, all in good time, and you will end by loving some other woman as deserving as your absent mistress, and more attainable. After all, ambition, not love, is the business of life ; and Cytherea's groves grow not a flower that can compare with the laurels which fame places on the brow of the conqueror. It is well for me that I am ten years your senior, else I should have been obliged to come behind you, Eugene, and pick up your cast-off leaves."

"The Elector of Bavaria is not a man so easily set aside," was Eugene's reply.

"And yet efforts are continually being made to set him aside," cried the elector, hastily.

"Who could be so presuming as to lay his sacrilegious hand upon the well-earned laurels of a warrior so distinguished as your highness?"

"Who? You know quite as well as I, that it is the Duke of Lorraine."

"Ah!" exclaimed Eugene, with enthusiasm, "who can compete with him? He is the greatest man of the age. As learned as he is brave ; as prudent as he is resolute ; a wise statesman, an unrivalled general ; equally distinguished in the cabinet and the field. How fortunate I have been in having him for my master in the art of war!"

"You are modest," said the elector, derisively. "As for me, I have no ambition to follow any master in the art of war. I wish to carve out my own plans and schemes, and I am weary of being subject to the will of the Duke of Lorraine."

"He is commander-in-chief of the army," urged Eugene. "No army can be without a head, to which all its members must be subordinate."

"But why must that head be Charles of Lorraine, pray?"

"You surely would not dream of supplanting *him!*" cried Eugene.

"Yes, I would ; and I have determined to submit to his dictation no longer. If I cannot have a command independent of the Duke of Lorraine, I shall withdraw my troops, remain in Bavaria, and leave my father-in-law to fight his own battles with the Turks."

"You will do no such thing," said Eugene, laying his hand upon the prince's shoulder, and looking anxiously into his face. "You will not endanger the great cause for which we have fought together by the interference of petty personal jealousies. No, Max Emmanuel, you are too magnanimous to sacrifice the interests of Christendom to such considerations.

Moreover, you have gained too much renown as a general, to be overshadowed by the reputation of any man."

"I do not know *that*. I only know that the Duke of Lorraine is in my way, and that for the future he must stand aside, or I resign my commission in the imperial army. But these are matters of future discussion. We will postpone this altercation until the opening of our next campaign. Meanwhile—do you know what brought me hither this morning? I come to snatch you away from cold contemplation, and introduce you to society."

"I have no taste for society," replied Eugene, shrinking from the very thought. "I love solitude; and mine is peopled with delicious visions of the past, as well as glorious aspirations for the future."

"Of what nature are your aspirations? They point to military distinction, I hope. Do they not?"

"Yes; and I trust that I shall attain it honorably. Fate will assign me my place; the rest remains for me to do. I have too much to learn, to mingle with the world."

"Man learns not only through the study of books, but through that of human nature," exclaimed Max Emmanuel; "and you need never hope for greatness unless you gain knowledge of the world. I have come to entice you away, and I will not be refused."

"Whither would you entice me?" asked Eugene, smiling.

"To the paradise of pleasure and of lovely women—to Venice!"

Eugene started, and a glow overspread his pale face. "To Venice!" echoed he. "To Venice!"

"Ay, prince—to Venice," repeated Max Emmanuel. "To live over the 'Arabian Nights,' by joining the great carnival."

"I have heard that Venice is the seat of all elegance and refinement, and that no man who has not graduated in its school of gallantry is considered perfect in worldly accomplishments."

"Then you perceive that you, who are so ambitious, must go with me to Venice to receive your diploma as a gallant. My heart beats with joyful impatience as I think of the delights that await us. The carnival is to be unusually brilliant this year. The Prince of Hanover, the Margraves of Baireuth and of Baden, the brave commander-in-chief of the republican armies, Morosini, and Admirals Molino and Delphini, are all to be there. Morosini himself has written me an invitation to the carnival, and you must accompany me."

"No, your highness," replied Eugene, seriously. "I have not been invited; there is therefore no reason why I should go."

"But if I tell you that I will consider it as a proof of your friendship," persisted the elector, "then I hope you will no longer refuse me. Indeed, you would do me the greatest favor."

"How could it possibly be a favor?" asked Eugene.

"I will tell you how. *I* am impulsive and easily led away: *your* principles are firm as a rock. I have known you for three years, and have closely observed your character, Eugene. You are sensible, honorable, and independent; you are reserved, yet sincere—brave, yet discreet. You are more than all this—you are an honest man, rejoicing in the fame of others, and never blind to worth because of envy or longing for notoriety."

"My dear, dear friend," interrupted Eugene, "you overrate me beyond—"

"No, I do not overrate you," was the elector's reply. "I appreciate you—that is all; and I want you for a counsellor. You know how a reigning prince is surrounded by flatterers; how his follies are heralded to the world as virtues; and, above all, you know how many snares are spread for such a gilded butterfly by artful women, who long, not only for his heart, but for his gold; above all, when he calls himself a prince, and is the son-in-law of an emperor."

"You have a poor opinion of women," smiled Eugene.

"They have given me no reason to think well of them. I know the whole sex to be fickle, coquettish, and heartless; and yet I am forever being led astray by their siren voices. And when the wicked enchantresses smile and swear that they love me, I am ravished—albeit, I know that every word they utter is a lie."

"You mean when they smiled and swore, I presume," said Eugene ; "for such delusions must have ended with your marriage. The husband of the beautiful Archduchess Antonia need not fear the wiles of Phryne or Lais."

"Pardon me," replied the elector, with a woe-begone expression of countenance, "they have become doubly dangerous, since they are forbidden fruit. I never was intended to be a model of conjugal fidelity, and my heart beats fearfully when I think of the starry eyes, the raven hair, the pearly cheeks of the fair women of Venice! I have very little confidence in my own valor, if I have to meet them single-handed. Do, Eugene, come with me ; let us be companions-in-pleasure as we have been companions-in-arms. I depend upon you to fortify my virtue in the hour of need."

"Your true and loving friend I am and will be ever," replied Eugene ; "but do not ask me to go to Venice. I am too poor to go thither in such distinguished companionship."

"It is understood that you go as my guest ; there can then be no question of riches or poverty. I have engaged a palace for me and my suite ; my household are already there, and you have nothing to do but to make yourself at home. Every thing I possess is at my friend's disposal."

"Which means that your highness considers me as one of your suite, and perchance intends to supply me with pocket-money ?" said Eugene, proudly.

"Nay, Eugene," replied the elector, offering his hand, "I meant nothing that could offend my friend. I meant that he should share with me as a brother whatever I possess.

"There are two things, your highness, which no man can share with another. One is his mistress, the other his honor. I am poor, and therefore I cannot share with you your advantages of fortune ; I am obscure, and scorn to shine by the borrowed light of your highness's exalted station. Sooner would I dwell in a cottage than in a palace at another man's expense."

Max Emmanuel had at first regarded Eugene with unmixed astonishment ; then the expression of his handsome face had changed to one of admiration and tenderness. As the prince ceased, the elector rose from his chair, and took both his friend's hands.

"You are, indeed, one of Nature's noblemen," continued he, affectionately. "Your view of this matter is, as usual, exceptional ; but it is the highest view that can be taken of such an offer ; and, although I am the loser thereby, I honor you for the refusal. I must then renounce the pleasure I had promised myself of having your company to Venice," added the elector, with a sigh.

"Perhaps not," returned Eugene. "Any thing on earth I would do to prove you my friendship ; and I *may* go to Venice, not for the sake of its beautiful women, but for the pleasure of bearing you company."

"Thank you for that 'may,' Eugene. But let your decision be a speedy one, I implore you ; for I long to quit a court that bristles with so many tiresome Spanish formalities. I would be glad to start to-morrow, but I will wait for you. How long must I wait ?"

"Only until my secretary returns from Turin. I expect him to-day."

"So much the better. Let me hear from you as soon as possible."

"I will."

The elector rose and took his leave, while Eugene returned to his escritoire, and tried to resume his occupation. But his thoughts were straying to Venice, and his hand lay listless on the paper.

"To Venice !" murmured he. "To Venice—perchance to Laura !"

As he pronounced her name, he broke into one wild ejaculation of joy.

"See her ? Oh, yes !" cried he, passionately. "Gaze into my Laura's eyes, I must—should the sight cost me my life ! But—no !" faltered he, suddenly. "I must not see her. She has forgotten me ; and perhaps at this very hour, when my heart throbs to bursting at the thought of meeting her again, she jests with her husband at the silly episode of her foolish fancy for me ! Perhaps she rejoices at her escape from alliance with the disgraced family of the De Soissons, and blesses Heaven for—peace, doubting heart ! I *will* believe—I *will* hope—Laura, my Laura.—Ah, Conrad, are you here at last ?"

And Eugene, springing from his seat, clasped Conrad's hands within his own.

"Yes, your highness," replied Conrad, his face beaming with joy to see his dear lord. "I have just alighted, and must apologize for my dusty garb. I did not stop to change my dress."

"You were right—quite right, and it needs no apology. Tell me the result of your mission. Did you speak with the Duke of Savoy in person?"

"Yes, your highness, he was so kind as to grant me two audiences. I related to him the entire history of your embarrassments, and their cause. I told him of the sequestration of your estates by the covetous King of France, and of the debts which this act of injustice had compelled you to leave in Paris. He asked me what was your pay as colonel in the Austrian service. I told him that the pay was fluctuating as to amount, and uncertain as to receipt; but at its maximum it might reach the sum of ten thousand florins a year. Upon this, he said: 'Ten thousand florins a year to maintain a prince of the house of Savoy, and one of the most distinguished officers in the imperial service! Well may he be straitened in purse!' Then I took courage, and told his highness that you could not possibly live on less than fifteen thousand florins, and that you appealed to him to assist you in maintaining the dignity of the ducal house of Savoy, and saving its representatives from absolute penury."

"And what was the answer?"

"He requested me to return the next day, which I did. I was most kindly received, and his highness said that he hoped he had found a remedy for your embarrassments, my lord. Although forbidden by the laws of Savoy to pay a salary to any man not in the service of his own dukedom, he would be happy to assist your highness from his own privy purse, until he had arranged matters in a manner more satisfactory and more secure. Prince Antony of Savoy, who is in a dying condition, possesses the revenues of five abbeys, which his highness of Savoy hopes to have transferred to your highness, thus securing to you a fixed and certain income, not subject to the sequestrations of the King of France."

"Without waiting for permission
he turned his back and left the room."

" He wrote no letter ? "

" No, your highness. The duke gave me four rouleaux of three hundred ducats each for present need, and bade me take them as his answer to your highness's letter."

Eugene smiled. " Therein I recognize my prudent cousin, who dares not trust his promises to writing. But I thank him for his golden answer. How much did you say you brought, Conrad ? "

" Twelve hundred ducats, my lord, which will cover all expenses until the opening of the spring campaign, when your pay is due."

" But, my dear Conrad, you forget that we have debts to pay. And, by-the-by, what news do you bring from Paris ? "

" Your highness's creditors there were so astounded at the prospect of being paid, that I almost regretted to be obliged to disturb the tranquillity with which they had accepted their losses. They were so grateful that they bade me say they would be perfectly satisfied with yearly instalments of any amount your highness would be pleased to pay. So I made arrangements to close your whole indebtedness at the end of three years."

" A long time for those poor fellows to wait for their dues," said Eugene, shaking his head. " Conrad, if we obtain the transfer of those abbey revenues, the first sum we receive therefrom goes to my creditors in Paris. Remember that." *

" I shall be very sure to remember it, my lord ; for it will be an occasion of rejoicing to many an honest tradesman, each one of whom will bless your highness's magnanimity."

" Magnanimity ! I call it bare justice ! " said Eugene. " Give me the memoranda."

Conrad presented the package, which his lord opened, examining each account until he had seen all.

" I miss one account here which I would gladly pay," said he, with some embarrassment.

" The account of Monsieur Louis ? " was Conrad's prompt reply.

---

* The payment of Prince Eugene's debts was regarded as something ultra-honorable by the people of Paris, and the Duchess Elizabeth-Charlotte speaks of it in her letters as a noble action.—See " Letters of Elizabeth-Charlotte."

Eugene made a motion of assent, while Conrad continued :

"My lord," said he, averting his eyes from the prince, "I went to Monsieur Louis, as I did to your other creditors. He said that he could not accept payment for decorations which had never been completed. He would always hold sacred the remembrance of the day when your highness fell insensible upon a heap of garlands that were to have ornamented your reception-rooms, and *he* had been near to lift you in his arms. He told me this with tears in his eyes, my lord ; pardon me if I have awakened painful reminiscences by the recital ; but he begged me to convey his message, and I felt bound to comply."

For some moments Eugene kept silence. After a pause, during which Conrad dared not meet his eye, the prince replied :

"Conrad," said he, "if I should ever afford to have a princely retinue again, I will take Monsieur Louis into my service. At all events, if I ever build a house, he shall decorate it, and shall be well paid for his work.—And now to other things. Did you see her highness the Duchess of Orleans ?"

"Yes, my lord. Her highness was walking in the park when your letter was handed to her. She sent for me at once, and received me in the little pavilion."

"The pavilion ! The pavilion ! Go on."

"She inquired minutely as to your health, prospects, and condition. She asked if you were cheerful. I told her that you were always in high spirits on the day of a battle. Then she would have me relate to her the dangers you had incurred, spoke of her grief at hearing you had been wounded, and seemed never to tire of your praises. Then she sat down and begged me to wait until she wrote you a short letter. Here it is, my lord."

Eugene broke the seal ; then, as if ashamed of the emotion that was welling up from his agitated heart, he looked at Conrad, who understood the appeal, and withdrew.

As the letter was opened, a small bit of paper fell from its folds, and fluttered to the carpet. Eugene, without observing it, began to read his letter. It ran thus :

"I cannot refrain from sending you a greeting in my own hand. My dear prince, I hold you in affectionate remembrance ; let me hope that you have not forgotten me. Every thing remains here as when you left ; false, frivolous, and, to me, as antagonistic as of erst. I have never been happy since *she* was so cruelly forced away from my protection. I have had news of her. My daughter, who lives in Turin, made a visit to Venice lately. I had begged her, if possible, to give me tidings of ——, and to give her my hearty love. They met for a moment, when she pressed into my daughter's hand a little note for me. I opened it, but it contained only the slip of paper I enclose. Be assured of my sincere and constant friendship. Elizabeth-Charlotte."

"The paper ! the paper !" exclaimed Eugene, as, with trembling hands, he opened the sheet, and found nothing within. "Great God ! the duchess has forgotten to enclose it, and I must away to Paris, this night, this very—"

Just then his eyes rested on the carpet, and there at his feet lay the treasured paper. It contained these words :

"I am a prisoner—watched day and night. Have you, too, forgotten me ? I cannot believe it ; and, after three long years of silence and of suffering, I still await your coming."

As Eugene read these tender words, he sank on his knees, and pressed the paper to his lips. "Forgive me, my Laura," murmured he. "I was weak in faith, and unworthy of you. But I will love you all the more for my injustice. I come ! I come !"

He rose from his knees, calling for Conrad, who was in the antechamber, awaiting a summons to return. Great was his astonishment when he beheld Eugene advancing toward him, his lips parted with a happy smile, his eyes beaming with animation, his whole bearing transformed. What could it mean ?

"Conrad," cried he, and his very voice had a joyful peal, like the chime of marriage-bells—"Conrad, we must leave Vienna this evening. Let everything be in readiness. If we have not gold enough with our cousin's ducats, borrow more ; but be ready to go with me at once. Stay—I had almost forgotten. Go to the palace ; see the chamberlain of his highness the Elector of Bavaria, and tell him to announce to the prince that Prince Eugene of Savoy leaves this evening for Venice. That is all. Make haste, Conrad! Away with you, and fly back as soon as possible, for I tell you that we must be on our road before night!"

## CHAPTER III.

### THE MARQUIS STROZZI.

THE Marquis Strozzi was alone in his cabinet, pacing the room with clouded brow and compressed lips. Now and then he stopped before the window which opened on a balcony overlooking the Canale Grande; and the sight of the gayly-decked gondolas that shot hither and thither with their freight of youth and youthful glee, seemed to intensify his discontent, and rouse him to positive anger.

"They are shouting their stupid welcome to these foreign princes," muttered he, "and presently *she* will be attracted by the sound, and seek to know what it means. My God!" ejaculated he, striking his forehead, "this love is the curse of my life. It will drive me to madness, and yet—and yet I cannot overcome it. To work, then, to work! I must increase my number of spies."

In the centre of the room, on a table of Florentine mosaic, lay a little golden bell, fashioned by the master-hand of Benvenuto Cellini. The marquis rang it gently, and, before he had replaced it, a secret door in the wall slided back, giving entrance to a masked figure, enveloped in a long black cloak.

Strozzi surveyed him for a moment, then, throwing himself upon a divan, he was lost in contemplation of the frescoes by Paul Veronese, which decorated the ceiling of this luxurious apartment. Meanwhile the mask had carefully closed the door, and stood respectfully silent.

Finally Strozzi condescended to speak. "Take off your mask." The man obeyed, and Strozzi gazed upon a sinister face, disfigured by a long, purple scar, which reached from the left temple to the chin.

"Do you know," continued the marquis, "that if you were to appear unmasked in the market-place, every child in Venice would recognize you, Antonio?"

"Yes, excellenza," was the humble reply.

"How did you come by that scar?" sneered the patrician.

Antonio moved impatiently, and glanced imploringly at the marquis.

The latter merely repeated the question.

Antonio heaved a sigh, and his head dropped to his breast.

"It was inflicted by my father," murmured he, almost inaudibly.

"Speak louder," said Strozzi. "Why did he inflict it?"

The man's eyes shot fire, but he dared not remonstrate. His glance fell before the cold glitter of Strozzi's black orbs, as he muttered in reply, "I was trying to get at his money, when he rushed in upon me, and gashed my face with a dagger."

"Upon which *you* plunged your poniard into his throat, and made an end of your respectable parent on the spot."

"Excellenza," cried Antonio, in tones of deep emotion, "I had but raised it to ward off the blow, when my father rushed upon it, and so met his fate."

The marquis laughed. "Rushed upon it—did he? Of course you are an innocent lamb of a parricide, and the judgment passed upon your act was a most iniquitous one. It was doubtless a shame that you were publicly maimed, and then led back to prison to await your execution. Possibly you may remember the night that followed your punishment, when a priest entered your cell, and, on condition that you paid him implicit obedience for five years, offered you life and the release of your paramour—the woman for whose sake you murdered your father."

"Poor Caterina!" sighed Antonio. "To think that, for the life of a babe not a day old, she should be imprisoned for five years!"

"Why, then, did she murder it?" asked Strozzi.

"To save herself from the vengeance of her husband, excellenza. But I—I have kept my word, and have served you faithfully, have I not?"

"Yes—you are a tolerably submissive hound," said Strozzi, scornfully. " How long before your bondage ceases ? "

"Excellenza, it was in January, 1683, that you appeared to me in the dress of a priest, and saved me from the headsman. I owe you still one year, one month, and twenty-six days of service."

"You are accurate—very ; but mark me ! If you fail in the least point, the contract is null. I neither release your Caterina nor you."

" I am your slave, and have no will but yours."

" 'Tis well. What have you learned to-day ? "

"As regards the gracious marchioness, but little. She drew, played on her harp, and embroidered, as usual, and wrote a letter, which she committed to the hands of that demoiselle Victorine, who gives out that she was sent to her ladyship by her friend the Duchess of Orleans."

"I know—I know. Where is the letter ? "

" Here it is, excellenza."

The marquis examined the seal, to see that it had not been tampered with by his underlings. "Any thing further?" added he, raising his eyes to Antonio's woe-begone face.

"Very little, excellenza. The signora went twice to the balcony to look at the gondolas, Mademoiselle Victorine watching her from within. The second time she went, she clasped her hands all of a sudden, blushed, and leaned so far over the balustrade that mademoiselle made sure that there was something unusual on the canal. Pretending that she had some question to ask as to the signora's dress, she followed, but the signora was so absorbed in what she saw, that she did not remark her tire-woman."

" What was it ? " asked Strozzi, breathless with expectation.

"The Canale Grande was so crowded with splendid gondolas that it was hard to say what had attracted the marchioness's attention. But after a moment or two of waiting, Mademoiselle Victorine saw that one of the gondolas was stationary just opposite to the palace."

" Whose gondola ? Who was in it ? " cried Strozzi, imperiously.

"Besides the gondoliers, the gondola contained a young man, so simply dressed, that he could not have been anybody of distinction, for he wore a brown doublet with plain buttons. Mademoiselle concluded that the lying-to of the gondola was accidental ; he was too insignificant to have interested the signora."

"What do *you* think ?" asked Strozzi, eying him searchingly.

"I think it was premeditated, but I will soon find out."

"What steps have you taken to—? But no !—go on—go on. What took place afterward ?"

"Nothing, excellenza ; for after this gondola, came that of my lord the marquis, and the signora retreated hastily to her room."

"Ah !—Now tell me what you have done ?"

"I posted one of my men, with his gondola, under the balcony. He is to remain there, watching every gondola that passes both by day and by night. I have stationed men at every entrance of the palace, who are to give admittance to all who present themselves ; but who are to require the names and business of all who leave. Even those who are in your excellency's pay are to be searched—for example, Mademoiselle Victorine."

"You are a well-trained dog," laughed Strozzi. "I really believe that I will have to set you and your child-murderess free, some of these days. Go, now, and bring me word who was in that gondola."

Antonio resumed his mask, and disappeared through the door, which closed, and left no trace upon the wall.

At this moment, there was a knock at the door of the antechamber, and a woman's voice was heard, asking admission.

"Lucretia !" said Strozzi, rising and undoing the bolt.

A lady entered the room. She was enveloped from head to foot in a veil of costly Venetian guipure, fastened to the braids of her raven-black hair by two large brilliants. Her face had been concealed by the veil, but, as the door closed behind her, she threw it back, and exposed to view a countenance of remarkable beauty.

"Look at me, Ottario," said she. "Tell me candidly—am I handsome enough to bewitch our guests, those princely bears of Germany ? "

The marquis surveyed her critically, just as a painter might examine a fine picture. He looked at her pale, pearly skin, her scarlet lips, her delicately-chiselled nose, and her low, wide forehead, so like that of the Capitoline Venus. Then he gazed into her dark, flashing eyes, at once so languishing and so passionate, with the beautiful arched eyebrows that gave such finish to their splendor. The black hair, like a frame of ebony, surrounded the face, and brought out the graceful oval of her cheeks. Strozzi then followed the luxurious outline of her well-developed bust, prisoned in a bodice of blue velvet, which rested on her white shoulders like an azure cloud upon the bosom of a snowy mountain-peak. The skirt, also of blue velvet, was short in front, that it might not conceal a fairy foot encased in blue satin slippers ; but, behind, it fell in a long train, whose rich folds lay on the carpet, perfecting the grace and elegance of the beautiful living picture.

"You are certainly charming," said Strozzi, at last—"quite charming enough to bewitch a dozen German princes, supposing your husband to offer no impediment to the spell."

Here she drew out a fan of coral and gold, and, opening it with a snap, began to fan herself. "Caro amico," said she, "you speak as if you were ignorant of the character and virtues of Count Canossa, when you yourself are the very tradesman that sold me to him."

"You use very strong expressions, Lucretia."

"Do I ? Not stronger than are warranted by the transaction. You sold me to him to rid yourself of your mother's dying charge, and you did it, although you knew him to be a man so depraved that nothing on earth was sacred in his eyes —not even the virtue of his wife."

"Why, that," replied the marquis significantly, "is so much the better for you."

"You mean that otherwise he would not have married me ?" asked Lucretia.

"I mean that he would have examined more carefully into the truth of the rumor which accused the sister of the Strozzi of having a *liaison* with a gondolier ; of having fled with him to Padua, and of having been caught and brought back to Venice, while her patrician lover was sent to the galleys."

"I wish he had done so," was the reply, "and then you would have been compelled to save my honor by allowing me to marry Giuseppe. Do not laugh so heartlessly, Ottario. I loved him not only because of his manly beauty, but because he was honorable and worthy of a woman's purest love. His only fault was that of having loved me. You sent him to the galleys ; and I—I, too, have been condemned to the galleys, and chained to a felon for life. Well I know that he covered my indiscretions with his name for a stipulated sum, which my generous brother paid to save my reputation, and he gambled it away before the expiration of a year. Our palace resembles a ship that has been visited by corsairs. It contains nothing but a pile of lumber, for which not even a pawnbroker would give a bajocco. Were it not for your alms, the Countess Canossa would starve."

"Alms, call you my gifts ?" said Strozzi, casting his eyes over her rich toilet. "They dress you up handsomely, methinks."

"But there they end," objected the countess. "I have neither lackeys nor diamonds, neither gondola nor gondolier, and my saloons are so shabby that I can receive no company at home. You give me as little as decency permits."

"If I gave you diamonds, our dear Canossa would steal them ; and if I furnished your parlors, he would gamble away the furniture in a night."

"You know the worth of the husband you selected for your mother's child, and doubtless you had your own private reasons for sacrificing her to such a man. His worthlessness, too, furnishes an excuse for your niggardly allowance to me. The very dresses I wear are the price of dishonor. I often feel ashamed of the part I play toward your wife, Ottario, and I know not but some day I may throw myself at her feet and acknowledge my treachery."

"If you do, your acknowledgment will be forthwith conveyed to my ears, and the doors of the palace Strozzi will be closed to you forever."

"I know it," sighed the countess ; "and the fear of this expulsion binds me to your wicked will."

"Never mind what binds you, so you serve with fidelity ; and, above all things, I charge you to be watchful during the coming week. I will not be able to keep my wife much longer from participation in the social pleasures of Venice."

"Why not? You have spread a report of her insanity, and nobody will ever give a thought to her absence."

"But she may desire to witness the carnival herself."

"How so? when she has invariably refused to be presented to any one as your wife?"

"She might change her mind, and claim her right to be presented to the doge and dogessa. She may wish to take part in the carnival, because of a fancy for some foreign prince !— Great God ! when I think of such a possibility," cried Strozzi, interrupting himself, "I feel as though I were going mad for jealousy !"

"Poor fellow !" said Lucretia, "I pity you. You live with a perpetual dagger in your heart."

"And it will kill me unless you are loyal to your office, Lucretia. Promise me to watch this woman closely. Listen to me.—She may wish to go out, and if she does, it is quite natural that you, as well as I, should accompany her. Swear that wheresoever you may be together, you will not for one moment quit her side, or take your eyes off her person."

"For what do you take me, pray? Do you suppose that I attend the carnival to yawn at the side of your wife? or do you imagine that such eyes as mine were made for nothing better than to stare at a woman?"

"You will have as much opportunity as you can desire to use them to your own advantage, Lucretia, for Laura will not go out often."

"What will you give me in return for my self-denial?"

"If the carnival passes off without misadventure, I will buy you a splendid gondola, with two gondoliers dressed all in silk."

"Give them to me now, and if I neglect my duty, then take

them back. But do—do give them to me to use during the carnival."

"Very well, you shall have them to-morrow morning. And you swear that my wife shall neither give her hand nor speak to any man in Venice, and that you will report her very glances to me?"

"I swear to guard your golden apple like a good dragon. And to-morrow I shall join the great regatta," added she, clapping her hands like a petted child. "Now, Ottario, listen to *me*—I have just come from your wife's apartments with news for you."

"What is it?" gasped Strozzi, clutching at the arms of his chair.

"The beautiful Laura is no longer the cold vestal that came to Venice as your wife. Her eye is bright, her cheek is flushed, her lips are parted with womanly longing. I congratulate you upon the change. Your love has at last awakened a corresponding sentiment, and now is your time to woo and win. I came hither to tell you this and make you happy. Do not forget my gondola! Addio, caro amico, addio!"

She kissed the tips of her rosy fingers, and then, coquettishly drawing her veil around her shoulders, she bounded off like a gazelle, through the corridors of the palace.

"I wish I had your frivolity," murmured her brother, sinking back upon the cushions of his divan. "I would that love, for me, were but the episode of the hour!—But hark!—twelve o'clock—the hour for my visit to her who is at once the blessing and the curse of my life!"

He was about to quit the room, when he heard a rustling at the secret door. "Come in," said he, and the mask re-entered the room.

"You, Antonio! Already returned?" asked Strozzi, surprised.

"Yes, excellenza. I know the name of the young man in the gondola which stopped before the palace this morning."

Strozzi was too much agitated to speak. He signed to the man to go on.

"It was Prince Eugene of Savoy. He arrived in Venice

yesterday, and has taken the little Palazzo Capello, next to the Palazzo Manfredino, which since this morning is occupied by the Elector of Bavaria."

Strozzi was now as pale as a corpse ; his brow darkened, and his limbs trembled so that he was obliged to sit down. He mastered his agitation as well as he could, and resumed his questionings.

"You are quite sure, Antonio ? "

"Perfectly sure, excellenza."

"And yet the Prince of Savoy is not among the invited ? "

"He came alone. The Marquis de Villars had rented the Palazzo Capello for himself, but he has given it up to Prince Eugene, and has accepted the invitation of the elector to occupy a suite on the ground floor of the Palazzo Manfredino. The Prince of Savoy and the elector are intimate friends ; for no sooner had the former arrived, than he left his address at the Palazzo Manfredino ; and the latter had not been here an hour before he was at the hôtel of the White Lion, where Prince Eugene had taken lodgings. By noon, the elector had obtained the relinquishment of the Palazzo Capello for the prince, and the Marquis de Villars had taken up his quarters at the Palazzo Manfredino."

"From whom did you learn all these details ? "

"From one of the gondoliers that rowed Prince Eugene this morning, my half-brother Beppo. 'Whither shall I row you, excellenza ?' asked he. 'Anywhere,' said the prince, in excellent Italian, 'but take me to see your famous palaces.' 'The Foscari, for example ?' inquired Beppo. 'Yes, and the Strozzi, which, I am told, is one of the finest residences in Venice.' So they rowed to the Strozzi palace, and there the prince bade Beppo stop for ever so long a time. The prince will spend the entire carnival here. He has bought a gondola, and his secretary is on the lookout for gondoliers, an Italian valet, and a commissionnaire."

"You will offer yourself as his commissionnaire, then," said Strozzi, with a sinister scowl. "And be sure you get the place—do you hear ? "

Antonio bowed, and the marquis continued : "In fifteen minutes return to me, and meanwhile—begone ! "

Without a word of reply Antonio disappeared; Strozzi pressed down into the wall the spring by which the door was opened, and then, taking up his plumed hat, betook himself to the apartments of his wife.

---

## CHAPTER IV.

### LAURA.

SHE lay half buried in the yellow satin cushions of a soft ottoman. Her large, dreamy eyes were fixed upon the ceiling, whereon groups of flying Cupids were pelting one another with roses. Her lips were parted with a happy smile, her fair brow was serene and cloudless, and her cheeks were tinged with a faint flush like that of the rose that is kissed by the first beams of the rising sun. She was the same beautiful, spirited, hopeful being that had lived and loved in the pavilion of the Palais Royal.

She lay dreaming and smiling, smiling and dreaming, when the velvet portière that opened into her boudoir was drawn aside to give entrance to the Marquis de Strozzi. Yesterday his visit had been a martyrdom to Laura; to-day she was indifferent to it: she was far beyond its influence, nor did she acknowledge it by so much as a glance.

But when he stood directly before her, and would have stooped to kiss her hand, she withdrew it with a gesture of aversion, although her countenance yet beamed with happiness.

The marquis saw that she was excited, and he frowned. "You seem in good spirits to-day, Marchioness de Strozzi," said he, moodily.

"I am indeed in good spirits when I can endure your presence with tranquillity, nor start at the sound of a title which is not mine. I am not the Marchioness de Strozzi."

"I do not know how that can be, when you are indubitably my wedded wife."

"No, no, I am no wedded wife of yours, nor am I bound to

you by the lying vows that gave me into your keeping. For three years, I have endeavored to make you understand this, but you are singularly obtuse."

"I can never be made to understand that the woman who in presence of her father and brother, promised to be unto me a faithful wife, is not my true and lawful spouse."

"My vows were not for you; they were made to another."

"Nay—I can show your signature to the contract, and the pope himself cannot undo our marriage."

"Our marriage!" exclaimed she, haughtily. "There is no marriage between you and me, and be assured that there never will be. I would sooner die than become your wife. Hear me," continued she, passionately. "If I thought that I was indeed bound to you, I would—ay! I believe that I would commit the crime of suicide. Could you convince me that the hand which received your accursed ring was indeed yours, I would gather up all my strength of hate to strike it off, and dash it in your face."

"Great God! And I love you to madness!" cried he, throwing himself on his knees, and clasping her hands so convulsively that all her writhings could not release them. "I love you, I love you, and am doomed to love you, albeit your cruelty is driving me to madness!"

"'Tis the punishment of your crime toward me," answered Laura, coldly. "You have sinned against love, and God has punished you through love that shall be forever unrequited. Accept your fate, and be resigned."

"I cannot do it, Laura, I cannot do it! My love for you is like a deadly poison that sets my blood on fire. It must be requited, or I shall die a maniac. Oh, have pity! have pity!"

"Pity for *you!*" said she, contemptuously.

"Look at me," cried he, imploringly. "For once in your life, Laura, turn your eyes upon me without hate, and see how love has corroded my very life. Three years ago I was a happy man—to-day I am not yet thirty, and my hair is gray, and my face wrinkled. Life has no charms for me, and yet I am too cowardly to die, and leave you to another. Oh, Laura, look at me, and be merciful! Deliver me from the hell in which your hatred has plunged me!"

"Nay—your sufferings are the purgatorial fires whereby you may perchance be purified from the guilt of your treachery toward an innocent girl. Marquis de Strozzi, now look at *me*. Am I, too, changed since three years of misery unspeakable?"

"No," sighed he, "you are as beautiful and youthful as you were when first I saw you in Paris."

"You are right," replied she. "I am altered neither in appearance nor in heart. And do you know why? It is because Hope—bright-eyed Hope has sat day and night by my side, whispering sweet words of encouragement, bidding me be firm; imparting to me strength to endure the present, and to enjoy the future. I feel it in my soul that he will come sooner or later to liberate me from my bondage."

"If he ever comes, I will murder him!" hissed Strozzi.

"You will try, but you will not succeed. God protects him, and he wears the invisible armor of my love to shield him from your hate."

"Very well. Pray for him if you will; but, as sure as I live, I will find his vulnerable heel!"

As he said this, Laura turned pale, and Strozzi remarked her pallor with a malicious pleasure. "Ah! your faith is not strong! My poisoned arrows will find the flaw, and upon him shall be avenged every pang that you have inflicted upon my bleeding heart. You know that he is here—I see it by your altered demeanor."

"Yes, yes, I know it."

"Be not too overjoyed thereat; for the daggers of my bravoes are keen and sure, and the lagoons are deep, and give not up their dead."

"You would not sully your soul with secret murder!" exclaimed Laura, shuddering.

"That would I. He is my rival, and he shall be put out of my way—that is all."

"No—that is *not* all. You dare not murder a prince, a hero upon whom the eyes of all Europe are fixed in admiration. Such a man as he is not to be put out of the way with impunity. Were you to murder Eugene of Savoy, know that I myself would be your accuser; and your uncle, the doge himself, is not powerful enough to save your head from the executioner."

"What care I for the executioner's axe, who for three years have been stretched upon the rack of your aversion? So I make sure that he has gone before me—so I have the sweet revenge of sending him to Tartarus, what care I how soon I follow him thither?"

"You are a monster!" exclaimed Laura.

"I am the work of your hands," replied Strozzi. "If I am a monster, my perdition be upon your head. And now, mark me! I came hither to have one decisive interview with you. Prince Eugene is in Venice; you are aware of it, for you sent him a greeting from your balcony this morning, as his gondola lay in front of the palace."

"Your spies are vigilant," said she.

"Yes, they serve me well, and they are ubiquitous. They mark each smile and report every tear that tells of silent joy or grief upon your face. They are with you when you pray; they watch you while you sleep, so that your very dreams are not your own. Now you are my wife, howsoever you may protest against the name, and you shall not sully that name, be assured of it. If, by word or look, by movement or sign, you allow Prince Eugene to suppose that you recognize him, he shall expiate your disobedience to my will by death. I am afraid that you do not believe me; you think that I make a mere threat to terrify you into submission. Is it so?"

"Yes, marquis, it is so. You are treacherous and cruel; but, abhor you as I may for the misery you have inflicted upon me, I do believe you to be one degree above a bravo. You are not a coward—you would not consent to be an assassin."

"You flatter your keeper, that you may disarm him."

"No; I speak the truth. I hate, but do not despise you to such a degree as to believe your threats."

"So much the worse for you. I would enjoy the privilege of plunging a dagger into his heart with my own hands; but I must deny myself that satisfaction. It is safer to employ a bravo, and to pay him. You know how dearly I loved my mother, do you not?"

"Yes, I have heard of it from your sister."

"Well—that portrait hanging over your divan is my mother's. Doubtless, had you known it, you would have banished it from the walls of your boudoir for hatred of her son."

"I have all along known that it was your mother. But I loved my own too deeply ever to offer disrespect to yours. I have often raised my imploring eyes to that mild face, and have poured out to her spirit my plaint of her son's cruelty."

"Raise your eyes to it again, then, and inform her that it rests with you whether her son shall become an assassin or not. For, by my mother's soul, I swear that, if ever there comes to pass the most trifling interchange of thought between Prince Eugene and the Marchioness de Strozzi, he shall die—die, if I have to expiate the deed upon the scaffold! Do you believe me now?"

"I must believe you," returned Laura, sickening with disgust. "But while conviction despoils you of the last claim I supposed you to possess to the name of a man, it does not terrify me for the life you would destroy. God, who has protected him on the field of battle—God, who has created him ' to give the world assurance of a man '—God, who is the shield of the pure, the brave, the virtuous, will not suffer the Prince of Savoy to fall under the dagger of your hired bravi!"

" Nous verrons.—And now, signora, let us speak of other things. The carnival this year is to be of unusual splendor; a number of foreigners of distinction have visited Venice to witness it. Lucretia, without doubt, has apprised you of all this?"

"She has."

"So I presumed; for Lucretia is fond of gossip. She would gladly induce you to go into society, knowing that a woman of your beauty and extreme youth cannot appear in the world alone, and that she would naturally be the person to accompany you. Would you like to see the regatta?"

This proposal terrified Laura, for she comprehended that he was in earnest when he threatened Eugene's life. The marquis read her thoughts, and replied to them.

"I shall shun no occasion whatever that may justify me in keeping the oath you heard me take a while ago. And, therefore, you are welcome to appear at the regatta. The doge will

19

be there in the Bucentaur, attended by all the court. As you have refused to be presented as my wife, you cannot take your proper place among the ladies of rank. But it is not too late. If you wish, I can present you to-day."

" No—no," cried Laura, "I do not wish it."

"Then perhaps you would like to go *incognita*. It will be many years before another such regatta is seen in Venice."

"True, I would like to see the sight," said the poor young victim. And to herself she added : "I might perchance see *him*."

" Be it so, then, signora ; your wishes are my commands."

"But I would like to see without being seen," added she.

"Indeed !" exclaimed Strozzi, with a wicked sneer. "Then I will see that your gondola is closely curtained. Will you allow me the honor of accompanying you ? "

"As if I were free to refuse," said Laura, with quivering lip.

" One thing more," said the marquis. " It is the custom for all who join in the festivities of the carnival to appear in a costume of some foregone century. May I commission my sister to select yours ? "

" I would like to select for myself."

The marquis bowed his head. "As you please. The tradesmen of Venice will be delighted at last to have a look at the beautiful wife of the Strozzi."

Laura shrank visibly. " I will not go," said she. " Let the Countess Canossa select my costume. It matters little to me : but be so good as to see that the gondola is well curtained."

"I will not forget it," answered the marquis, as he bowed and left the room.

Laura's eyes followed him until he had crossed her whole suite, and had closed the door behind him. Then, yielding to the bliss of being left a few moments alone, she opened her arms, and, kneeling before her *prie-dieu*, poured out her heart in prayer to Heaven for Eugene's safety. Then, throwing herself again upon the divan, she began to dream. She saw her gondola approaching his ; she saw her lover—her spouse, and made one rapid movement of her hand. His gondola touched hers ; she flung aside the curtains and leaped into the boat with him.

But as she dreamed, there floated over the water the sound of song. This was no unusual sound on the Canale Grande, but the music was not Italian ; it was no languishing barcarolle, such as Venetian lovers were wont to sing to their mistresses ; the air was foreign—the words were French. She heard them distinctly ; they were the words of her own, dear, native language !

"It is he ! " cried she, springing out upon the balcony.

Yes, it was he ; he had called her with an old familiar air, and, while he looked up in rapture, the music went on, for the singers were in a gondola that followed.

Laura was so wild with joy that she forgot the marquis, his spies, and his threats. Snatching the first bouquet that presented itself, she made an attempt to throw it to her lover. But she had not calculated the distance, and it fell far short of its destination.

"An evil omen," murmured she, and then she remembered the horrible threat of the marquis. She gave one ejaculation of terror, and bounded back into her boudoir.

About fifteen minutes later, Strozzi entered the room. In his hand he held a bouquet of beautiful roses, which he presented with mock courtesy.

"Signora, you were so unfortunate as to drop your bouquet in the lagoon not long ago. The mermaids will be glad to receive so fair a gift from so fair a hand. Allow me to replace it."

"On the contrary, I must request you to take your roses away from my boudoir. I do not like the odor of flowers, and I threw mine into the water because their perfume oppressed me. I regret that you should have taken so much useless trouble."

"And I beg pardon for interrupting your reveries," said Strozzi, with a sarcastic smile, as he bowed and retired with his bouquet.

"Gracious Heaven, I was watched ! Am I, then, given over to enemies, and is there not one being here that I can trust ? "

At this moment a door opened, and a young girl entered the room. "Victorine !" exclaimed Laura, joyfully, "come hither.    God has sent you to me to shield me from despair."

The girl came smilingly forward, and, kneeling at her mistress's side, looked affectionately at her, saying in Laura's own tongue :

"What ails my dear mistress ? "

"Victorine," replied Laura, gazing earnestly into the maiden's eyes, "Victorine, do you love me ? "

Victorine covered her hand with kisses, while she protested that she loved her mistress with all her heart.    "Dear lady," said she, "did I not leave Paris for love of her whom her royal highness cherished as a daughter ?    Was I not sent to you by the Duchess of Orleans, that you might have one true friend among your troops of enemies ?    And now that I had hoped to have proved to my dear mistress my devotion, she asks if I love her ! "

"True, Victorine, I have no right to doubt your attachment. And certainly I have proved that I trust you, by committing to your care my letters to the duchess.    Ah, Victorine, when will you bring me an answer to those letters ? "

"The answers cannot have reached Venice as yet, dear mistress," said Victorine, soothingly.    "But I came to tell you something.    May I speak ? "

"Yes—speak—speak quickly ! "

Victorine went on tiptoe to the door, and, having convinced herself that no one was near, she came close to Laura, and whispered in her ear : "Madame, one of the foreign princes has been here to call on you."

"Who ?  who ? "

"Prince Eugene of Savoy," said Victorine, as though she was afraid the breeze might betray her.

Laura shivered, became deadly pale, and could scarcely gather courage to say, "He was refused entrance ? "

"Yes, the porter told him that the marchioness was in bad health, and received no visitors."

"That was well.    Go, Victorine, and tell the servants to convey neither message nor card of Prince Eugene of Savoy to me.    I will not receive him.    Go, go quickly, and then—"

"And then ? " said Victorine, coaxingly.

Laura was silent for a while ; then, putting her arms around Victorine's neck, she drew the young girl's head upon her bosom. "Try to find out where Prince Eugene is staying, and go to him. Say that you come from the Marchioness Bonaletta, and you will be admitted to his presence. Now tell him word for word what I shall say to you. 'To-morrow the Marchioness Bonaletta will attend the regatta. Her gondola will be closed, but whosoever wishes to recognize it can see her as she descends the stair and enters it. Let the gondola be closely followed, and when a hand holding a nosegay of roses is seen outside the curtain, let the gondoliers be instructed to come as close as possible to the hand, so that the two gondolas collide. Then—let the prince await me.' Do you hear, Victorine ? "

" Yes, dear mistress, I hear, and will report your words faithfully."

"Tell him that Venice is alive with spies and bravi, and oh ! bid him be careful how he exposes himself to danger. Now go ! and may Heaven bless you for your fidelity to a wretched and betrayed woman ! "

Victorine withdrew. But before leaving the palace, she betook herself to the cabinet of the marquis, where they had an interview of some length. No sooner was she dismissed, than she retreated to her own room, drew out a purse of gold from her bosom, chinked its contents, emptied them out on the table, and counted them with rapture.

" Ten ducats ! Ten ducats for each intercepted message," said she. " I shall soon be rich enough to leave this abominable marsh of a Venice, and return to my dear Paris ! "

Having locked up her gold, and tied the key of her chest around her neck, she directed her steps to the hôtel of Prince Eugene.

## CHAPTER V.

### THE REGATTA.

PRINCE EUGENE was watching the little French clock on the marble mantelpiece of his dressing-room, wondering, in his impatience, whether it ever would strike the hour of twelve, the hour at which he was to witness the departure of the Strozzis for the regatta.

Mademoiselle Victorine had delivered her mistress's message, and the heart of her lover was once more bounding with joy. His eyes flashed with a light which, except on a day of battle, had never been seen within their sad depths since the dreadful period of his parting with Laura. Forgotten was all the anguish of those three long years ; forgotten all doubts, forgotten all fears. She loved him ; she was true to her vows, and he would bear her away from her ravisher to the spouse that was hers before Heaven.

But how long—how unspeakably long—the hours that intervened between him and happiness ! He was wishing for some interruption that would break this monotonous waiting, when the door opened, and Conrad came forward.

"My lord, I have found a commissionnaire for you ; one who professes to know Venice and its golden book by heart."

"Introduce him at once: I wish to speak with him."

Conrad opened the door and signed to some one without, when the commissionnaire advanced and bowed.

"Why are you masked ?" asked the prince, who remembered the warning which Laura had sent him the day previous.

"Excellenza, every Venetian of good character has a right to wear a mask during the carnival."

"And every criminal can take advantage of the right," replied Eugene. "Behind a mask every man has a good character, for nobody knows who he is."

"I beg pardon, excellenza. The republican fathers, through their sbirri, know every man in Venice. If you will take the trouble to look around you in the market-place, you will see how now and then a masker is touched on the shoulder, when his mask drops at once, or he escapes among the crowd to avoid public exposure."

"Then, I suppose that a stranger has no hope of seeing the beautiful women here?" observed Eugene, smiling.

"Pardon me; to-day, at the regatta, no masks will be worn, and your excellency will see all the beauty of Venice, both patrician and plebeian."

"Why, then, do *you* wear a mask?"

"I wear it habitually, having a fancy to go about incognito."

"Nevertheless, you must remove it now, for I cannot take a man into my service incognito."

The man raised his left hand, withdrew the mask, and revealed to sight a face that was colorless save where it had been marked with a deep-red scar from temple to jaw.

"You are indeed conspicuous, and not to be mistaken by those who have seen you once. Whence came this scar?"

"I received it two years ago, excellenza, at the taking of Prevosa."

"You have been a soldier, then?" asked Eugene, his countenance at once expressing interest.

"I have, indeed; and but for the loss of my right hand by the sabre of an infernal Turk, I would be a soldier still."

"You have written the conquests of the republic upon your body, my friend," said Eugene, kindly. "But your mutilations are so many orders of valor; they are the ineffaceable laurels which victory places on a brave man's brow."

A slight flush overspread the sallow face of the ex-soldier, and his eyes sought the floor.

Eugene contemplated him for several moments with the sympathy—even the respect—which a military man feels for extraordinary bravery, as attested by such wounds as these.

"With what manner of weapon were you cut in the face?" said he. "Not with a sabre, for the scar is curved."

"It was not a sabre-cut, excellenza," replied the man, in a low, tremulous voice. "I was in the breech, fighting hand to hand with a Turk, whom I had just overthrown. While I was stooping over his prostrate body, he drew forth a yataghan and gashed my face as you see."

"I knew it was a dagger-thrust," replied Eugene. "Well, this scar shall be your best recommendation to me, for I, too, am a soldier."

"Excellenza, I thank you, but I have other and weighty recommendations from my employers. Moreover, here is my license as commissionnaire from the Signiory."

So saying, he would have handed the prince a document with a large seal appended to it, but Eugene waved it away.

"I prefer the license to serve that is written on your body, my friend. You have been a brave soldier, you will therefore be a faithful servant. You say that you are well acquainted with Venice?"

"Ay, indeed, signor; I know every palace and every den, every nobleman and every bravo, in Venice."

"You are, then, the very man I need. Make your terms with my secretary. But be loyal to me, and remember that the scar you had received in your country's service was the only recommendation I required when I took you into mine."

"Excellenza!" exclaimed the man, kneeling, and raising the prince's doublet to his lips, "I will bear it in mind, and serve you faithfully."

"I believe you, my brave! Rise and tell me your name."

"Antonio, signor."

"Antonio.—Well, Antonio, you accompany me to the regatta to-day."

"My lord," said Conrad, entering the room, "your gondola is below, and his highness the Elector of Bavaria is here."

A deep flush of joy overspread Eugene's countenance as he advanced to welcome his friend. Max Emmanuel had chosen the gorgeous costume of a Russian boyar. His dress was of dark-blue velvet, bordered with sables, and buttoned up to the throat with immense brilliants. On his head he wore a Russian cap, with a heron's plume fastened in front by a rosette of opals and diamonds.

Eugene surveyed him with undisguised admiration. "You are as gloriously handsome as a Grecian demi-god," cried he, enthusiastically. "I pity the lovely women of Venice to-day, when they come within sight of the hero of Buda."

"I absolve them all from tribute except one," returned Max.

"What! In love already!"

"My dear young friend, I saw yesterday on a balcony a black-haired beauty far beyond peri or houri of my imagination!—majestic as Juno, voluptuous as Venus, with eyes that maddened, and smile that ravished me. Unless I find this houri, I am a lost, broken-hearted man!"

"Then you have not yet begun your siege?"

"Impossible to begin it. The Duke of Modena was with me, and you know what an enterprising roué he is. To have pointed her out to him would have been to retreat with loss. So I was obliged to say nothing: but I will see her again if, to do so, I have to reduce Venice to a heap of ashes!"

"Peace, thou insatiable conqueror, or amorous ambition will intoxicate you. You are certainly just the very cavalier to storm and take the citadel of a woman's heart; but you are the Elector of Bavaria, a reigning prince, and son-in-law of the Emperor of Austria."

"My dear Eugene, no ugly moral reflections, as you love me! I am here to enjoy the glow of the warm blood that dances through my veins—to sip the ambrosia that pleasure holds to my lips—in short, I am, body and soul, a son of the short-lived carnival that begins to-day. Don't preach; but pray if you like, for my success, and help me in my need."

"Help you? I should like to know how I am to do that!" said Eugene, laughing. "But stay—I have a man in my service who professes to know everybody in Venice. So, if you should see your houri to-day, point her out, and doubtless Antonio will tell us her name. Ah! Twelve o'clock at last!— Come, come, let us go."

"You have not made your toilet, Eugene. What costume have you selected?"

"The very respectable one of a little abbé," was the reply.

"Respectable, if you will, but excessively unbecoming, and unworthy of the Prince of Savoy. I perceive that you, at least, have no wish to make conquests to-day."

"No—all my victories I hope to win by the help of my good sword."

"Do you go with me in my gondola, reverend sir?"

"I in your magnificent gondola, at the side of such a Phœbus-Apollo! I might well despair of making conquests in such company; and, for aught you know, I may be desirous of attracting the attention of some fair lady who is not taken by appearances."

The elector looked up in surprise. He had never heard an expression like this from Eugene's lips before; and now he saw clearly that his demeanor had changed, that his eye was restless and bright, his cheek flushed, his whole countenance beaming with some inward hope or realized joy.

"Eugene," said he, touching his friend's shoulder, "Venice holds the secret of your love; and you have tidings that have lightened your heart. I read them in your eyes, which are far from being as discreet as your lips."

"Perhaps so; but the secrets of love are sacred—sacred as those of the confessional. Nevertheless, I may confide in you sooner than you expect, for I may need your help as well as you mine."

The two young men went out arm in arm, followed by the suite of the elector, and, behind them, by Conrad and Antonio.

"Who is that mask?" asked Max, as he passed by.

"My new commissionnaire, Antonio—he that is to tell us the name of your belle."

They were by this time on the marble stairs that led to the water, where side by side lay the superb gilded gondola of the Elector of Bavaria and the inconspicuous one of the Prince of Savoy.

As the two princes were descending the stairs, a gayly-dressed nobleman sprang from the gondola of the elector, and advanced respectfully to meet them.

"Monsieur le Marquis de Villars," said Max, bowing, "I am happy to see that you have accepted a seat with me."

"It is an honor for which I am deeply grateful, your highness," replied the marquis; "and one which I accept in the name of my gracious sovereign, for whom alone such a compliment can be intended."

"You are mistaken, marquis; I invited you that I might enjoy the pleasure of your company to-day. Allow me, Prince of Savoy, to introduce to you the Marquis de Villars, the French ambassador to the court of Bavaria."

"There is no necessity for us to know each other," replied Eugene. "The marquis is a Frenchman, and I have no love for that nation; particularly for those who are favorites of Monsieur Louvois. Adieu, your highness."

And without vouchsafing a word to the French ambassador, Eugene entered his gondola.

"I must apologize for my friend," said the courteous Max Emmanuel to the marquis. "He has been sorely injured both by the King of France and his minister. Forget his bluntness, then, I beseech you, and forgive his unpleasant remark."

"He is your highness's friend, and that at once earns his forgiveness," replied De Villars. "But that the friend of the Elector of Bavaria should be the enemy of my sovereign I deeply regret; for he may prejudice your highness against the King of France. He may transfer his aversion to—"

"Let us rather suppose that I may transfer my love of France to him," said Max Emmanuel. "But let us eschew politics, and enjoy the bliss of the hour. To-day la bella Venezia puts forth all her charms. And as the swift gondolas skim over the green waters of the lagoon, so flies my heart toward my bellissima Venetiana!"

At twelve o'clock, Laura left her dressing-room to join the Marquis de Strozzi and his sister in the drawing-room below.

"Great heavens, how beautiful!" cried Lucretia, embracing her. "I have not been wise in placing myself so near you, bewitching Laura. Ottario, do look at her; did you ever see such a vision of beauty?"

"Pray do not force the marquis to praise me," said Laura; "you are perfectly aware that I am indifferent to his approbation. But as regards beauty in Venice, where beautiful women abound, the Countess Canossa is acknowledged to be la belleza delle belle. And to think that nobody will see you to-day in my closed gondola!"

"You adhere to your resolution to have your gondola curtained?" asked the marquis.

"Yes," replied Laura, without bestowing a glance upon him.

"And I rejoice to know it," exclaimed he, passionately, "for I alone will drink in all your beauty. For me alone have you worn this becoming costume."

"You know perfectly well that my dress was chosen by your sister."

"Catharine Cornaro was by adoption a Venetian," returned Strozzi, "and since you have willingly donned her dress, I must accept it as an earnest of your consent to appear as the wife of a Venetian noble."

To this taunt Laura made no reply. She gave her hand to the countess, and they passed into the corridors together. The walls were hung with *chefs-d'œuvres* of Titian, Tintoretto, Paul Veronese, and Gioberti, all gorgeously framed in Italian style; and between each picture was a mirror that extended from floor to ceiling. Through these magnificent halls went Laura, as regardless of their splendor as of the passionate glances of the man who walked by her side, so near and yet so far, so very far away from her heart.

The gondola that awaited them was an heir-loom of the Strozzis, and was never used except on gala-days. It was well known to the Venetians, every one of whom was accustomed to point to it with pride, saying, "There goes the bucentoro of the Strozzis!"

As Laura was about to step into this glittering bucentoro, the gondoliers around, delighted with her beauty, shouted, "Evviva la Marchesa Strozzi!" To their great astonishment, the marchesa, instead of bowing and smiling as is usual on such occasions, gave no other evidence of having heard their greeting than that which by a frown and a flash of her dark eyes might be construed into a signal of displeasure, as she disappeared behind the silken hangings of the bucentoro.

The centre of the gondola was supported by gilded pillars, surmounted by a canopy of silk and gold. Behind this canopy was a sort of pavilion, bordered by seats cushioned with gold brocade. In the centre was a table, of costly material and make, on which stood a golden vase of rare flowers. The pillars also were wreathed with flowers, which appeared to be carried from column to column by flying Cupids that were holding up the garlands in their chubby little hands. In short, the temple was worthy of the divinities, one of whom was light-hearted and coquettish, the other proud and serious. Between them was the Marquis de Strozzi, in the rich habit of a Greek corsair—a character which his handsome, sinister face was well fitted to represent. His gloomy black eyes were fixed upon Laura, while his hands toyed with a silken cord that hung from the pillar against which he was leaning.

The eyes of the countess were fixed upon the cord, and presently she raised them with a glance of inquiry to her brother. He nodded, and his sister smiled. Then throwing herself back among the cushions, she raised her little foot to a gilded stool that was before her, and leaning her head against the pillar, looked out upon the waters with an expression that might have become Danaë awaiting her shower of gold.

Laura, on the contrary, wore a look of resolve that seemed inappropriate to the scene and the occasion. But her thoughts were far away from the frivolities that interested Lucretia. She had determined that, in presence of all Venice and of the foreigners that had assembled there to celebrate the carnival, she would burst asunder the compulsory ties that bound her to Strozzi. Before the world she would give the lie to that simulated bridal, and fly to him who was, by all the laws of God, her true and only spouse.

Thus thought Laura, while far away from the crowds that from gondola to gondola were greeting one another, the bucentoro pursued its solitary way over the water. She had managed to draw aside the curtain and to look around for him who to her filled the world with his presence. At last she saw him. He was there—there ! and he saw her, for his gondola changed its course, and came nearer. Like an arrow it sped across the waters, taking heed of no impediments, dashing into the midst of other gondolas, as reckless as a pirate of the consternation it created among the bewildered gondoliers, who were forced to give it passage, or be dashed aside like so much spray ; while Eugene's gaze was fixed upon the golden bark of the Strozzi—the argosy that bore such precious freight. At

last they neared it, and Eugene could see the little white hand,
holding a bouquet of roses from between the crimson hangings of the pavilion.    His eyes brightened, and his whole being
seemed transfigured.   Gallant and comely he looked—a knight
worthy of any woman's love.

The Elector of Bavaria had seen all the movements of Eugene's gondola.   He had seen it suddenly change its course,
and had watched the prince pointing with uplifted hand to
some object in the distance, which, to judge by his bearing,
one would have supposed was a breach to mount.   Max Emmanuel had smiled and said to himself : " In yonder direction
lies Eugene's love-secret.   We had better follow, for we may
be useful in time of need.   He seems to me to be too bashful
to manage an intrigue with skill."

So the elector gave orders to follow the gondola of the
Prince of Savoy ; and now his gondoliers, too, were rowing
for their lives, while many a bright eye was turned admiringly
upon his tall, graceful form.

Laura was not the only person that was looking out from
the curtained bucentoro.   The marquis, too, had seen the two
approaching gondolas ; and now, as the foremost one came
full in view, he passed his arm outside, and, while Laura's head
was turned away, made a sign to Antonio, who responded with
another.

The gondolas were now so close that their occupants were
easily recognized.   Strozzi saw Eugene's passionate gaze, and
guessed that it had been returned, although the face of his
wife had been averted, so that he had not seen the act

At this moment Laura turned, and gave a quick, searching
glance around the pavilion.

" You are looking for me ? " asked Strozzi, with a singular
smile.   " I am here, my wife, to protect you from all danger ;
and as I am weary of standing, and as there is no seat for me
beside you, I will take the place that my heart covets most."

And, before Laura could prevent him, he had thrown himself at full length, had clasped her feet, and raised them over
his knee, so that they had the appearance of having been
placed in that familiar position by her own will.   He then
pulled the silken cord which he had held all this while in his

hand, and the curtains of the pavilion were rolled up, exposing its three occupants to the view of the whole Venetian world. On one side lay Lucretia, in her Danaë-like position, and on the other, gazing with the rapture of an accepted lover into the face of the marchioness, lay Strozzi. The picture was unequivocally that of a pair of lovers, and those who knew her not as his wife were convinced that in Laura they beheld the mistress of the Marquis de Strozzi.

"*Evviva!*" shouted the enraptured multitude, dazzled by the beauty of the tableau. No one heard Laura's despairing entreaty for release from a posture so humiliating. Nor had any one heard the exclamation of delight that burst from the lips of the elector, as in Lucretia he recognized his houri.

"There she is!" exclaimed he to the French ambassador.

"Who?" asked the latter, in astonishment.

"The most beautiful woman that ever distracted a susceptible man," was the reply. "Do you not know her?"

"I regret to say that I do not, but I will make it my duty to discover her abode, and communicate the discovery to your highness."

"Thank you," began the elector. But suddenly he stopped, and gazed intently upon Prince Eugene, who was standing at the stern of his gondola, only a few feet distant from the bucentoro of the Strozzis. The elector directed his gondoliers to approach that of the prince, and, springing from one boat to the other, he laid his hand on Eugene's shoulder.

"Friend," said he, "I do not desire to force myself into your confidence; but lest I become your unconscious rival, answer me one question. Is that lady there, in the red-velvet dress, the object of your unhappy attachment?"

"No, dear Max," replied Eugene, with his eyes fixed steadfastly upon Laura.

"Truly?"

"Truly, I do not know her; but if you ask Antonio, he will tell you."

With these few words Eugene turned away, and, in a low voice, promised a rich reward to his gondoliers if they would but touch the gondola of the Marquis Strozzi.

The elector beckoned to Antonio. " Who is that lady in the gilded gondola close by ? " said he.

" Which one, your highness ? "

" The one in red velvet."

" That is the Countess Lucretia Canossa, sister of the Marquis de Strozzi."

" Is she married ? "

" Yes, your highness, to a man who has squandered her fortune ; so that but for her brother she would be penniless."

The elector thanked Antonio, and leaped back into his own gondola. The Marquis de Villars, meanwhile, who knew that gondoliers were the news-givers of Venice, had ascertained quite as much of the position of the countess as Max Emmanuel had done during his short absence.

" I can answer your highness's question now," whispered he. " I have learned every thing concerning her that it is needful to know from the gondoliers."

" And I, too, know all that I care to know," replied the elector ; " so here am I, like Rinaldo before the enchanted gardens of Armida : I must and will enter ! "

" Of course you will. What woman can withstand the fascinations of the handsomest cavalier in Europe ? " observed the marquis ; adding to himself : " And thank Heaven that I know the Armida of his longings, for she must draw this Rinaldo, not only into her own toils, but into those of France."

Eugene was standing on the edge of his gondola, his passionate gaze fixed upon the group that had been disclosed by the rising of Strozzi's silk curtain. What could it mean ? Oh ! it was horrible ! To see Laura lying back in a position so voluptuous, her feet clasped in Strozzi's arms, his eyes so lovingly triumphant, was like a poisoned dagger to the heart of her unhappy lover. Had she called him thither to make him the sport of his successful rival ? The very thought was madness : and yet Laura feigned not to see him ; her eyes were steadily cast down.

Eugene was determined to know the worst ; he would not retreat until conviction had chased away this deadly suspense. Slowly his gondola came near and more near, while in that of his rival its approach was watched by two of its occupants.

both of whom knew equally well for what purpose it was coming.

Laura gathered up all her strength for one effort, and freed her feet from Strozzi's clasp.

"You are a wretch!" exclaimed she with indignation. "If you pollute me again with the touch of your hands, I will drown myself here, in your very sight."

"Oh no; you will throw yourself overboard, that Prince Eugene may plunge after you. Listen to me, Marchioness de Strozzi. I am perfectly acquainted with the nature of the stratagem you proposed to put into execution to-day. But I tell you that as sure as the gondola of the prince touches mine, and you make the least movement of your hand or foot, he dies."

"Vain threat!" exclaimed she, surveying him with contemptuous disbelief.

"You think so? Let me prove to you the contrary. Do you see the mask behind Prince Eugene? He is the man that will do the deed. Observe his motions while I speak a word or two, ostensibly to my rowers—really to him."

And the marquis called out, as though to his gondoliers, "Are you ready?"

The words were no sooner spoken, than the mask bowed his head, and drew from his cloak a poniard, which he raised and held suspended over the back of Eugene's neck.

Laura uttered a cry and fell back among the cushions, while Strozzi, hanging over her with the air of an enamoured lover, whispered: "The gondola almost touches ours. Make but the smallest sign—lift but a finger, and I swear that I will give the signal for his death!"

"O God! do not kill him!" was all that the wretched girl had strength to say.

The gondolas met. Eugene stood erect on the stern of his boat, his right arm extended toward her whom he loved. But alas! she came not. She did not even turn her head; for Antonio was there, his poniard uplifted, and Eugene's life depended upon her obedience.

"Traitress!" exclaimed the prince, as Strozzi's bucentoro shot ahead, and the red-silk curtains, falling heavily down,

20

shut out the fearful tableau that had been prepared to torture and exasperate him.

Laura had swooned, and her fall had been remarked by the gondoliers.

"Poor thing," said one of them, "she has a paroxysm of insanity."

"How insanity?" asked Conrad.

"Everybody in Venice has heard of the lunacy of the Marchioness de Strozzi," was the reply. "It is for that reason that she never goes out. The marquis perhaps thought she might be trusted to see the regatta; but he was mistaken. You must have remarked how closely he watched her for fear of some catastrophe."

"Insane, is she?" said Eugene, with quivering lip, to Antonio.

"Pazza per amore," replied he, with a shrug. Then, coming closer to the prince, he added, "The marquis gives out that his wife is crazy, and, as nobody ever sees her, nobody is any the wiser."

"And you? What think you, Antonio?"

"I do not believe it, for I know the signora well."

"You know her?" said Eugene, touching Antonio on the shoulder.

"Yes. She it is who recommended me to take service with your highness, and to tell you that you might trust me."

"Oh, I do trust you, good Antonio. Did I not say that the scar on your face was your best recommendation?"

"Yes, excellenza; and I will not forget it."

"Can you explain to me the mystery of the scene we have just witnessed?"

"Yes, excellenza. The marchesa intended to leap into this gondola and fly with you from Venice; but, as she attempted to rise, the marquis showed her a dagger, and swore that if she moved hand or foot he would spring into your highness's boat and kill you."

"And I cursed her!" thought Eugene, "and she heard my cruel words. Oh Laura, my Laura! when will I lie at thy feet to implore forgiveness? Home," cried he aloud, to the gondoliers. Then, in a whisper, he added to Antonio, "I must speak with you as soon as we are alone."

All this time Laura lay insensible in the bucentoro, her husband gazing intently upon her pallid face. The Countess Lucretia was wearied to death with the whole performance.

"Fratillo," said she, "I hope that you have done with me, and that you intend to return with your sentimental beauty to the palace."

Without removing his eyes from Laura, Strozzi bent his head, while the countess went on :

"My gondola, your handsome present, is just behind us, and I must say that it is worthy of Aphrodite herself. Pity that no goddess should grace such a lovely sea-shell. Have I your permission to occupy it, and leave this stifling atmos phere of love ?"

"Go, go," answered Strozzi, impatiently.

"Thanks ! " was Lucretia's heartfelt reply ; and, opening the curtains, she beckoned to her gondoliers, and stepped grace-fully from the bucentoro to her own dainty bark.

"It is rather tiresome to be without company," thought she, as she was rowed away ; "but solitude is better than conceal-ment behind those hateful curtains of Ottario's. I wonder who is the handsome cavalier that seemed to be struck with me a while ago ? One of the foreign princes, I imagine, for he had a star on his breast. Ah !—There he is, staring at me with all the power of his splendid eyes."

And the beautiful Lucretia, pretending not to see the elect-or, sank gracefully back among her white satin cushions.

"Row toward the piazetta," said she to her gondoliers, "but go in a direction contrary to that taken by yonder large gon-dola filled with cavaliers."

"That of the Elector of Bavaria ? Yes, signora."

"Ah ! " thought she, delighted, "he is the Elector of Bava-ria, son-in-law of the Emperor of Germany. It would be worth my while to entice so handsome a prince from his loyalty to an emperor's daughter ! "

Scarcely had the gondola of the countess altered its course, before the elector ordered pursuit.

"Do you see that gondola there, fashioned like a sea-shell,

and cushioned in white satin, Montgelas?" said he to his chamberlain.

"Yes, your highness."

"Say to the gondoliers that we follow in its track. Whether we see the regatta or not is of no consequence, so we keep in view of that Venus in the conch-shell."

The Marquis de Villars had pretended to be in earnest conversation with his neighbor, but he heard every word of this order.

"Yes, indeed," thought he. "The countess must be bought, if her price be a million."

Lucretia vouchsafed not a glance that could be detected at her pursuers ; but she saw every thing, and exulted at her conquest. "Oh, emperor's daughter, emperor's daughter.!" said she, "your husband is falling into my toils. They say you are handsome, but your elector's eyes tell me that I am handsomer than you !"

And so she beguiled her solitude, while in the bucentoro Laura still lay in her swoon, and Strozzi gazed enamoured upon her beauty.

"Beautiful as Aurora !" murmured he, "beautiful as a dew-gemmed rose ; beautiful as the evening star ! I love you—I love you to madness, and you must, you shall be mine !"

He bent over her, and, now that she had no power to resist him, he covered her face with passionate kisses. But his kisses restored her to life, and with a shudder she raised her hands, and threw him off.

"Touch me again, and I will plunge this dagger in your false heart !" cried she, drawing a poniard from her bosom.

"I would not care, so I could say that you were mine before I died !"

"Would that you _were_ dead, that I might fly to him whose wife I am, in the sight of Heaven !"

"Put up your dagger," said Strozzi, coldly, while a look of venom chased away the love that had beamed in his eye. "I will not trouble you again."

"You have betrayed me a second time, liar and impostor that you are !" exclaimed Laura, replacing her dagger. "You have deceived my lover into the belief that I am false to him, but, believe me, he shall know the truth. God will protect him from you and your bravi, and He will avenge my wrongs ! Now, order these curtains to be raised. It is better to be gazed at by the multitude, some of whom have hearts and souls, than to sit in this pavilion within sight of you ! And bid your gondoliers take me home to my prison, where, God be thanked! I can sometimes be alone with my own thoughts ! "

Strozzi obeyed like a cowed hound. He lifted the curtains, and ordered the men to row to the palace.

Laura's eyes sought the gondola of her lover, but she could not see it. It had left the regatta, and had already landed at the stairs of the Palazza Capello.

## CHAPTER VI.

### THE NEGOTIATOR.

COUNTESS LUCRETIA CANOSSA had just risen, and lay reclining on a faded ottoman, attired in a négligé, which was any thing but elegant, or appropriate to a beauty. She had rung several times for her breakfast, but her waiting-maid had not seemed to hear the summons, for nobody came at the call.

The countess, however, was so absorbed in her day-dreams, that she forgot her breakfast. For a time her thoughts dwelt upon the singular scene that had taken place in the bucentoro. She knew nothing of the complications relating thereunto ; she had but witnessed the approach of the gondola which she supposed to be that of her sister-in-law's lover ; had seen her brother's extraordinary excitement, and had guessed that some disappointment connected with the presence of the insignificant little personage in that gondola had caused Laura to fall into a swoon. She felt sincerely sorry for her unhappy sister-in-law, but the countess was not inclined to sentiment ; so she dismissed the mystery of Laura's troubles with a sigh, and fell to thinking of the Elector of Bavaria.

He had followed her all day, and well had she perceived that he had had eyes for no one but herself. And when she had affected to weary of his pursuit, he had left his own gondola for that of Count Cornaro, who had approached and asked permission to present his distinguished guest. The permission having been accorded as a matter of course, the elector had entered into an animated conversation with her, which lasted until the close of the regatta.

She had met him again that evening, at a ball given by Admiral Mocenigo to the foreign princes. Many a handsome, gay gallant was there ; but the handsomest and most admired of them all was Max Emmanuel of Bavaria. His dress, too, was magnificent in the extreme. It was so covered with diamonds that it was like a dazzling sea of light. But more splendid than his jewels were the flashing eyes which, during that whole festival, had been fixed in admiration upon the beautiful Lucretia ; and what was still more delightful was the fact that everybody had observed it, and that many a dame, who had eclipsed the Countess of Canossa, and slighted her because of her poverty, had envied her the conquest of the Bavarian prince's heart. It had all ended as it should have done. Max Emmanuel had asked permission to call upon her, and he was to make his visit at one o'clock that day.

Lucretia had advanced so far in her triumphal course, when she cast a glance of dismay at her mean, faded furniture.

"Oh, how forlorn it looks !" said she. "And to think that this is the only room wherein I can receive a visit ! for not another apartment in the palace contains a chair whereon a man might take a seat. I ought not to have yielded to my vanity, and consented to receive him at home, for, when he sees my poverty, he will no longer think my heart worthy of being won. He will believe that it can be bought, and I shall sink in his estimation to the level of an ordinary courtesan. I must be proud and reserved to-day with him ; and, as I have naught else to display, I must show off my wardrobe. But where can Marietta be ? Perhaps Count Canossa has gambled her away, and she has gone off like the rest of the appointments of this dreary palace."

Lucretia rang again ; still there was no answer.

"The poor girl must have gone out to get me some breakfast. I had forgotten that the cook left us because he had not been paid for a year; and, as there is nobody else here, I must e'en have patience until Marietta returns."

Lucretia sighed, and fell back upon her ottoman. For some time past she had been aware that there was considerable bustle in the palace, attended by hammering, and the sound of furniture either placed or displaced. She had paid very little attention to it, for the rooms were entirely empty, and she could only conjecture that her needy spouse might have rented them out for the carnival. But the noise came nearer and nearer, until she perceived that it had reached the adjoining chamber, whence she could hear the sound of voices, and distinguish much that was said.

She rang again, and this time the door was opened by some invisible hand, when Marietta, bearing in her hand a large silver waiter, advanced to a rickety table which stood near the ottoman, and placed upon it a most delicate breakfast, served in dishes of costly, chased silver. Not only the service was superb, but Marietta herself was attired in a costume which shamed the shabbiness of her high-born mistress.

Begging the countess's pardon for her unpunctuality, the maid proceeded to pour out the chocolate, which she handed in a cup of Sèvres porcelain.

Lucretia rubbed her eyes. "Where, in the name of Aladdin, did you get that dress?—And where this service?"

"The dress was brought to me this morning, my lady, and the mantua-maker told me that it had been ordered by yourself; the jeweller who brought the services of silver told me the same thing."

"I!" cried the countess. "I order such costly things?"

"Why, yes, my lady, for the upholsterers have almost arranged the beautiful furniture you bought yesterday."

The countess smiled. "This is a prank of some carnival-mad jester, child," said she. "There is not a word of truth in it. I wish there were!"

"It is as true as that there are at least fifty workmen in the palace at this very moment," was Marietta's reply.

Lucretia made no answer. She sprang from her ottoman, and, crossing the room, threw open the door leading into the next saloon.

Marietta had spoken the sober truth. There they were all
—fifty—some hanging satin curtains before the bare windows,
others placing lofty mirrors in the recesses ; one detachment
uncovering the gilded furniture, another arranging it, while
the last folds of a rich Turkey carpet were being smoothed in
the corners of the room, where dainty tables held vases of
costly workmanship, filled with rare flowers.

At first the countess had been struck dumb and motionless.
Recovering herself, however, after a moment or two, she went
hastily up to the person who seemed to direct the proceedings,
and accosted him :

" Will you oblige me by saying who ordered all this furniture ? "

" Her ladyship, the Countess de Canossa," was the man's
reply.

" Are you acquainted with the countess ? " asked Lucretia.

" No, madame ; I have not that honor."

" Then, how do you know that you are acting by her orders ? "

" I received them yesterday through her steward."

" Her steward ?   And have you seen him since ? "

" Yes, madame.   He came again this morning very early,
to see whether we were punctual.   It was all to be completed
by one o'clock, and, as it is not quite ten, you perceive that we
will certainly have done in time.   But I must ask you to see
the countess and request permission for the workmen to be admitted to her boudoir.   Will you be so good as to convey the
message ? "

Lucretia cast a glance of shame at her faded gown.   " He
does not know me," thought she, " and how should he in
such a guise ? "   Then she added, aloud, " I will apprise the
countess."

Marietta was now in the dressing-room, whither she requested the presence of her mistress immediately.

" What is it ? " asked the bewildered Lucretia.

" The dressmaker is there, signora, to see if your dresses are
to your taste," replied Marietta.

" Let me see them," cried she, impatiently.

Marietta drew from a box a dress of pink satin, which,

from its make, was evidently intended for an under-skirt. "There is another, just like it, of blue satin," exclaimed the enraptured lady's maid, "and here is a box containing two peignoirs of guipure, with morning caps to match. How beautiful your ladyship will look in these négligés ! "

"We will see at once whether I do," answered Lucretia, clapping her hands with joy. "Here Marietta—quick ! Help me off with this hateful gown, and hand me the pink-satin petticoat."

In a few moments the mistress and maid were equally happy, while the former was being decked in her magnificent négligé. The satin petticoat was loose ; and over it was thrown the guipure peignoir which reached to the throat, and was confined at the waist by a pink sash. The full sleeves were open, leaving half-covered, half-exposed, Lucretia's arms, firm and white as Carrara marble.

"Now this love of a lace cap," cried Marietta, placing it with great coquetry around the black braids of Lucretia's glossy hair ; while the latter, quite reconciled to the wonders that were being enacted around her, was profoundly engaged in admiring herself in a looking-glass.

"And now," said Marietta, "you are ready, and certainly you are as lovely as a fairy."

"Fairy, say you ? Yes ; that seems to be the appropriate name for one who is the recipient of such extraordinary riches as these. But now, Marietta, whence do they come ? Are they from my brother ? "

"Signora, I know no more than I have told you. Yesterday a gentleman (I think he must have been a Frenchman) came hither, announced himself as an architect, and told me that your ladyship had sent him to examine the palace, with a view to refurnishing it with great magnificence."

"Did you take him over the rooms ? "

"Of course I did, my lady. He took various notes as he went along, and remained longer in your boudoir than in any room in the palace. He sat down and made a drawing of it, asking me, now and then, a question as to your ladyship's tastes and habits."

"Gracious Heaven ! " exclaimed the countess, while a pain-

ful blush overspread her face, "has *he* been here to see my
need and hear of my privations ?   Can *he* have been the secret
giver of all this magnificence ? "

As the possibility that the Elector of Bavaria was her unknown benefactor, presented itself to Lucretia's mind, her
humiliation grew extreme ; for if these gifts were from him,
they proved that he held the daughter of the noble house of
Strozzi to be a creature that was to be bought with gold, without the poor pretence of one word of love.

"When came he, and what sort of looking man was he ? "
asked she, frowning.

"He came just after the regatta had begun, signora."

"Then, God be praised, it was not *he !*" said Lucretia to
herself, " for at that hour, he was with me, in Count Cornaro's
gondola."

A faint knock was heard at the door, and the décorateur
begged permission to enter.   His coming awakened the countess from her reverie, and she hastily bade him come in, "for,"
said she, "it must be almost one o'clock."

"The clock on the mantel of the drawing-room has just
struck eleven, your ladyship," replied the man, who, now that
she was richly dressed, recognized the lady of the house.

"So," thought Lucretia, "I have a clock ! " and she bounded off to the drawing-room to see it.   Marietta followed with
the chocolate, which, in the excitement of the moment, had
been forgotten.

"True," said the countess. "bring me my breakfast, and let
me take it here in this beautiful apartment.   Who is that at
the door ? " added she, as Marietta went forward to open it.

"Your ladyship's butler," replied she.   " He comes to know
whether the déjeuner à la fourchette is to be served in the boudoir or in the banqueting-hall."

"Let it be in the banqueting-hall, for I may have several
guests."

"The steward ordered it for one o'clock, my lady.   He said
that you expected some guests of distinction."

"My steward ? " repeated Lucretia, smiling.   "So it seems
that I have an entire household.   Let us go over our altered
domains, Marietta."   And the two went from room to room,

the femme de chambre as delighted as her mistress, until they descended as far as the kitchen. Here every thing gave evidence that the déjeuner was to be a rare one. Two cooks, in white, presided over the arrangements, and two scullions were busy carrying out the orders of the chief. They were so absorbed in their business, that they did not perceive the countess who stood in the door.

Presently from the storeroom opposite there emerged a man with baskets of bottles, which he deposited on the table, saying :

"Here is Burgundy for the Bayonne ham. The champagne, sherry, and constantia, are for the table."

The countess had now seen and heard enough. Not only was her palace fitted up, but her kitchen was in order, and her wine-cellar filled. So she returned to the drawing-room, where she was met with the tidings that her boudoir was ready for occupation, and nothing now remained to be done, unless her ladyship had any alterations to suggest, or deficiencies to point out.

Her ladyship professed herself satisfied, and then came a moment of embarrassment. "As regards the payment—"

"Oh, signora, the steward is to meet me at twelve o'clock, to arrange that matter." And with these words he took his leave.

"I ought to have followed him," thought Lucretia, "to solve this agreeable riddle, by making acquaintance with my steward. But pshaw ! I shall soon know all about it. Nobody has made me these presents without intending to get a word of thanks for the benefaction."

She had scarcely seated herself in a new and beautiful ottoman, which had replaced her faded, rickety old couch, before a servant appeared and announced,

"Her ladyship's steward ! "

"My ladyship's steward ! " echoed Lucretia. "Do let us make his acquaintance."

He came in—a small, slender man, apparently young, with a pair of twinkling black eyes, and a countenance expressive of great energy. With the air of a finished gentleman he bowed, advanced, and bowed again.

"Signor," said the countess, "you have been announced by a title which I have no right to bestow upon any person living —that of my steward. Pray tell me who you are."

"Gracious countess," answered he, smiling, "I have the honor to present myself. I am the Marquis de Villars, ambassador of his majesty the King of France to the court of Bavaria."

"And may I ask why, in addition to your other representative titles, you have assumed that of steward to the Countess of Canossa?"

"Because, signora, seeing that your habitation was not worthy of you, I have ventured to perform the duties of a faithful steward, by fitting it up in a manner which I hope is agreeable to the divinity at whose shrine the elector is now a worshipper?"

"Did the elector suggest—" began Lucretia, reddening.

"Oh no, signora; he knows nothing of the little surprise I have prepared for you. It does not concern him at all."

"Then I am to suppose that Count Canossa, having gambled away my very home, this palace has become your property, and I am here on sufferance. How long may I remain?"

"How long may you remain in your own home! Signora, all that you see has been done for you, in your own name, and I hope you will do me the honor to accept it."

"From whom?"

"You shall learn as soon as we understand each other, signora."

"Then let us come to an understanding at once, for the Countess Canossa does not receive princely gifts from strangers."

"Of course not, nor would a stranger take so unpardonable a liberty with a lady of her rank and birth. But before going further, let me assure you, signora, that you are under obligations to nobody for the little surprise I have prepared for you. Not in the least to me, for I am but the representative of him who begs your acceptance of it."

"You speak in riddles," said Lucretia, with a shrug. "But, at all events, I understand that this furniture, silver, and these rich dresses, are mine?"

"Assuredly yours, signora."

"Then let me inform you that in a week, at farthest, they will go, as they came, in the space of a few hours. Count Canossa will have lost them at the gaming-table, and the palazzo will be in the same condition as it was yesterday."

"Count Canossa is powerless to touch the least portion of your property, signora."

"Powerless? How! Are you a sorcerer, and have you changed him into stone? Or have you spirited him away?"

"I have spirited him away, signora. I have persuaded him by the eloquence of gold to forsake Venice, forever. As long as he remains in Paris, he is to receive a yearly pension from the King of France."

"Gone to Paris! Pensioned by the King of France!" exclaimed Lucretia.

"Gone, signora; and, in leaving, he desired me to say to you that he hoped you would forgive all the unhappiness he had caused you since your marriage."

"Gone! Gone! Am I then free?" cried Lucretia, starting from her ottoman, and grasping the hand of the marquis.

"Yes, signora. You are free to bestow your heart on whomsoever you will. Count Canossa will never molest you more."

"Oh how I thank you! How I thank you!" replied she, her beautiful eyes filling with tears of joy. "But tell me," added she, after a short pause—"tell me, if you please, the meaning of all this providential interference with my domestic affairs?"

"I am ready, signora," said the marquis, waiting for the countess to resume her seat, and then placing himself at her side. "Perhaps in your leisure hours you may have interested yourself in European politics."

"Not I," said Lucretia, emphatically.

"Then allow me to enlighten you on the subject," replied the marquis.

"To what end?" inquired she, impatiently.

"I will not detain you long, signora. Give me but a few moments of your attention. Doubtless you have heard that the Emperor of Austria, for several years past, has been at war with the Porte ? "

Lucretia nodded, and the marquis went on. " Perhaps it will interest you to know that the Elector of Bavaria is an ally of the emperor, and has distinguished himself greatly, particularly at the siege of Buda."

" Oh, I can believe it," cried she, with animation. " He looks like a hero. Tell me, pray, something about his exploits."

" Later, signora, with pleasure ; but for the present we must discuss politics. Now the Emperor of Austria is fast getting the better of the Sultan ; and if the latter should succumb in this war, the former would not only be left with too much power for the good of Europe generally, but would become a dangerous rival to the King of France. Now it is important for my sovereign that the victories of Austria cease, and that Austria's power wax no greater. Have I expressed myself clearly ? Do you understand ? "

" I begin to understand," was the reply.

" Now, there are various ways of crippling the resources of Austria ; for example, her allies might be estranged. Have patience, signora ; in a few moments my politics will grow personal and interesting. One of the emperor's most powerful allies is the Elector of Bavaria."

" Of course," cried Lucretia, delighted with the turn that politics were taking. " Of course he is, being the emperor's son-in-law. Tell me about the elector's wife. Is she handsome ? Does he love her ? "

" Signora, as regards your latter question, the elector himself will have great pleasure in answering it. As regards the former, the Archduchess Antonia is handsome, but sickly, and her ill-health has lost her the affection of her husband."

" Ah ! " cried Lucretia, relieved, " he does not love her."

" He loves her no longer," said the marquis. " But he was greatly taken by the charms of the Countess Kaunitz ; and as the elector's alliance with Austria was a matter of more importance than his conjugal relations with the archduchess, the husband of the fair countess was appointed ambassador to Bavaria, and his wife ambassadress. It was through the influence of this charming ambassadress that Max Emmanuel joined the forces of Austria."

"So he has a mistress, then? One whom he loves?"

"Whom he loved until he saw the Countess Canossa."

"Do you think I could supplant her?" exclaimed Lucretia, her large eyes darting fire at the thought.

"I do not doubt it," was the flattering reply. "If you choose, you can trample under foot this arrogant Austrian, who flatters herself that Max Emmanuel is all her own."

"I would like to try," cried Lucretia, with the air of an amazon about to go into battle.

"Then let me offer my services," said the marquis, bowing. "The elector is peculiar, and has pretensions to be loved for his own sake ; therefore he would never quite trust the disinterested affections of a woman whom he had power to raise from poverty to affluence."

"Ah !" cried Lucretia, with a significant bend of the head. "*Now* I begin to apprehend your meaning as well as your munificence."

"Signora," said De Villars, with equal significance, "the King of France seeks a friend who will alienate the elector from Austria, and win him for France. Will you accept the trust?"

"But you said that he loved another woman."

"So much the greater will be your glory in the conquest, for the countess is beautiful and fascinating."

"Is she in Venice?"

"Wherever the elector goes, thither she is sure to follow."

"She must leave Venice ; she must be forced to leave !" cried the vindictive Italian, ready to hate the woman whom Max Emmanuel loved.

"You must do better. Induce the elector to forsake her, and leave her in Venice like another Didone abbandonata, while you carry him in triumph back to Munich."

"I will, indeed I will !" exclaimed Lucretia, exultingly.

"Ah, signora," said the marquis, coaxingly, "what a magnanimous and disinterested nature you display ! You accede to my request without naming conditions. Allow me to admire your nobleness, and believe me when I say that my royal master shall hear of it."

"Well, tell him that, if it lies in my power, Max Emmanuel shall learn to dislike Austria and love France."

"Signora, you are the instrument of a great purpose. I give you a whole year wherein to work ; and if, at the end of that time, you have prevailed upon the elector to sign a treaty of alliance with France, *you*, as one of France's noblest allies, shall receive from my royal master one million of francs. Meanwhile you shall have ten thousand francs a month for pin-money."

" Alas ! " said Lucretia, " I am forced to accept ; for my husband has so effectually impoverished me that I live on the bounty of my brother.   And he is so arrogant that I am almost as glad to be independent of him as to be delivered from my detestable husband.   I shall endeavor to let my acts speak my gratitude for the deliverance."

" Allow me, signora, to present you with your pocket-money for this present month, and give me a receipt in the shape of your fair hand to kiss."

So saying, he laid a purse of gold at Lucretia's feet, and covered her hand with kisses.

" I shall want to consult you frequently, dear marquis,' observed Lucretia.

" I shall always be at your service."

" And now, I take it as a matter of course, that what has passed between us this morning is to remain a profound secret."

" As a matter of course, signora, it goes no further," returned De Villars,* " and to insure perfect secrecy, you must pretend not to know me when we meet abroad.   Not even the elector—or, perhaps I should say, above all men, the elector is not to know of my visit.   I must, therefore, take my leave, for—hark ! your clock strikes one, and lovers are sure to be punctual."

" I shall expect you every morning at eleven ; and so we can take counsel together, and I can report daily progress to you."

* " Memoirs of the Marquis de Villars," vol. i., p. 104.

"Aurevoir, then, signora. Allow me one word more. If, before the close of the carnival, you leave Venice in company with the elector, I shall take the liberty of refunding to you the entire cost of the refurnishing of your palace to-day, as compensation for its temporary loss. And now, fairest of the allies of France, adieu !"

The French ambassador had hardly time to make his escape, before the doors of the drawing-room were flung open, and the lackey announced, "His highness the Elector of Bavaria !"

## CHAPTER VII.

### THE LOVERS REUNITED.

Two weeks had elapsed since that unhappy meeting between Eugene and Laura—two weeks of expectation and hope frustrated. In vain had Eugene attempted to reach her with a message ; in vain had he remained for hours before her windows ; in vain had Antonio tried to penetrate into her presence. Day after day came the same sorrowful news : the marchioness was very ill, and no one was allowed to pass the threshold of the palace. Her husband watched day and night at her bedside, and, excepting Mademoiselle Victorine, no living creature was allowed to enter her room.

When, for the fourteenth time, Antonio returned unsuccessful from his mission, Eugene became so agitated and grew so pale that the bravo was touched to the heart, and, taking the prince's hand, covered it with kisses.

"Do not be so cast down, excellenza," said he, imploringly ; "have courage, and hope for the best."

"Oh, Antonio !" murmured the prince, "she is dead !"

"No, excellenza, no ! I swear to you that she lives, nor do I believe one word of this rumored illness."

"Why should you not believe it, my friend ?"

"Because I know the marquis well ; and this is merely a pretext for keeping his wife imprisoned."

"Thank you, Antonio, thank you," replied Eugene, " for

21

this ray of hope. Then I depend upon you to deliver my message sooner or later. Remember my words : ' The Prince of Savoy knows why the marchioness did not speak to him. He lives, loves, and hopes.' And if you will but return to me with one word from her lips, I will feel grateful to you for life, Antonio."

" I will serve you with my life, excellenza," said Antonio, bowing and leaving the room.

He had not been long away, before the door was opened, and Conrad announced the Elector of Bavaria.

" I have come to entice the hermit of the Capello out of his cell," cried Max Emmanuel. " My dear Eugene, was ever a man so obstinate a recluse ? Every time I come I am told that you are at the arsenal, the dock-yards, the armory, a picture-gallery, or some other retreat of arts and sciences."

" Well, dear Max, I am a student, and find much to learn in Venice."

" To whom do you say that ? " cried Max, laughing. " As if I, too, were not a student, only that my tastes lie not in the same direction as yours, and as if I were not making tremendous progress in my studies ! "

" No wonder : you are far advanced in every branch of learning, while I am but a neophyte."

" No such thing ; you are much more deeply learned than I ; but you are the victim of an unfortunate passion which you are striving to smother under a weight of study, while I—I, my dear fellow, am distancing you every hour of the day, for my studies are all concentrated upon the 'art of love.' "

" God speed you, then, and deliver you from the malady that is wasting away my life ! "

" You are an incomprehensible being, Eugene. I cannot comprehend your dogged fidelity to such an abstraction as a woman whom you never see. You have not trusted me with your secret, and yet I might have done you some service had you been more frank with me."

" You mock me," replied Eugene, gloomily.

" No, Eugene, I do not mock you. I know your secret, despite your taciturnity. I know that you love the Marchioness Strozzi, and that the jealousy of her husband is such that you have not been able to speak a word with her since your arrival in Venice."

"Who could have told you?"

"My houri—she whose love has made of Venice a Mussulman's paradise to me. Oh, Eugene! I am the happiest man alive! I am beloved and loved for myself. My beautiful mistress is noble and rich; she refuses all my gifts, and yet she is about to give me unequivocal proof of her love: she is about to leave her lovely Italian home, and fly with me to Munich."

"Are you about to leave Venice so soon?"

"The archduchess is dangerously ill, and yesterday a courier was sent to summon me home. And, would you believe it? my Lucretia consents to accompany me, on condition that I force no gifts upon her acceptance, but allow her to furnish her house in Munich at her own expense. Did you ever hear of such disinterestedness? Now I am about to give you a proof of my confidence, and tell you the name of my mistress. It is the Countess Canossa. Well!—You are not overjoyed? You do not understand!—"

"How should I be overjoyed or understand, when I do not know the lady, Max?"

"Great goodness, is it possible that this unconscionable snail has lived so closely in his shell that he does not know how fortunate for him it is, that the Countess Canossa loves me! Hear me, Eugene. My Lucretia is the sister of the Marquis de Strozzi."

"My enemy!" murmured Eugene, his brow suddenly darkening.

"Yes; but not his sister's friend; for although he makes a confidante of her, she hates him. Except Victorine, the countess is the only person permitted to have access to her sister-in-law's apartments."

Eugene's eyes now brightened with expectation, and he looked gratefully up into the elector's handsome, flushed face.

"Yes, Eugene, yes," continued Max, "and through her angelic goodness, you shall visit your Laura. To-day, Lucretia appears as Mary Stuart, at a masked entertainment given by

Admiral Mocenigo. Before she goes, she is to show off her dress to the poor prisoner of the Palazzo Strozzi. Her long train is to be borne by a page, who of course will have to follow whithersoever Mary Stuart goes. This page is to be yourself, my boy ! "

Eugene threw himself into the elector's arms. He was too happy for speech.

At noon, on the same day, the gondola of the Countess Canossa stopped before the Palazzo Strozzi. The countess, dressed in a magnificent costume, went slowly up the marble stairs, her long train of white satin borne by a page in purple velvet. His face, like that of his mistress, was hidden by a mask ; and the broad red scarf which was tied around his slender waist, confined a small dagger whose hilt was set in precious stones. His eyes were so large and bright that the mask could not entirely conceal their beauty ; and it was perhaps because of their splendor that the porter hesitated to admit him within the palace.

The countess, who had gone a few steps before, turned carelessly round, and asked why her page did not follow.

"Your ladyship," replied Beppo, the porter, " the marquis has forbidden the admission of strangers."

" And you call that poor, little fellow of mine a stranger ? You might as well ask me to cut off my train, as expect me to wear it without my page !—Come, Filippo, come ! "

Filippo passed on, while the old porter grumbled.

"Never mind, Beppo," said the countess, looking back kindly, " I will tell my brother of your over-watchfulness, and inform him what a love of a Cerberus he has for a porter." And on she went, having reached the top of the staircase, before Filippo and the train had gone half way.

Mademoiselle Victorine was awaiting their arrival, and made a profound courtesy to Lucretia.

"Signora, the marchioness awaits you in her boudoir."

" And the marquis knows that I am here ? "

"Yes, signora. He was anxious to accompany you in your visit to my lady ; but she would not consent ; and you know that he dares not go without it. He never has crossed the threshold of her dressing-room."

"I know it well. Now go and announce my visit to her. But first, go to the marquis and tell him that, as soon as I shall have returned from the apartments of my sister-in-law, I wish to see him in his cabinet, on important business."

This was spoken in an elevated tone, so that all the spies, whom Lucretia knew to be eavesdropping around, might hear her words and repeat them.

"I go, signora," replied Victorine, in the same tone; but she added in a whisper to the page, "For God's sake, be discreet!"

The lady's maid, in obedience to Lucretia's orders, went directly to the cabinet of Strozzi, while the countess proceeded in an opposite direction. At the end of the grand corridor was a lofty door, which, being shut, the countess remained stationary; while Filippo, who seemed not to have remarked it, went on with his train, until he stood immediately behind his mistress.

She chided him for his familiarity. "Back, Filippo," said she, impatiently. "When I stop, how do you presume to go on? You are too unmannerly for a page!"

Filippo murmured a few unintelligible words, and retreated, while the countess knocked several times at the door.

"It is I, Laura, the Countess de Canossa."

If anybody had been near, the beatings of poor Filippo's heart might have been heard during the pause that ensued before the door was opened. At length its heavy panels were seen to move, and a sweet, soft voice was heard:

"Come in, dear Lucretia."

The countess disappeared within; but scarcely had she entered the room before she grasped Laura's arm, and hurried her into the room beyond.

"Not here, not here," whispered she. "Go into your private apartment, Laura. In this one you would be unsafe. There will be listeners at the door."

Laura made no reply; she flew back and disappeared behind the portière that led into her boudoir. The countess looked back at her page, who leaned trembling against a marble column close by.

"Shut the door, Filippo," said she, "and await me here. I

will see the marchioness in her boudoir, and Mademoiselle Victorine will be back presently, to entertain you."

The door was shut, and Filippo, letting Mary Stuart's train drop without further ceremony, sprang forward and touched the arm of his royal mistress.

"Where is she?"

"In her boudoir." The page would have gone thither at once; but Lucretia stopped him. "Mark my words well. Speak low; and when Victorine summons you away, obey at once, for delay may cost you your life. And now, impatient youth, begone!"

They were together. Laura would have sprung forward to meet him, but emotion paralyzed her limbs, and chained her to the floor. He clasped her in his loving arms, kissed her again and again, and each felt the wild throbbing of the other's heart. Forgotten were the long years of their parting, forgotten all doubt, all anguish. It seemed but yesterday that they had plighted their troth in that moonlit pavilion; and nothing lay between, save one long night which now had passed away, leaving the dawn of a day that was radiant with sunshine.

"I have thee once more, my own! Close—close to my heart, and would to God thou couldst grow there, blending our dual being into one!"

"Not once more, my Eugene, for thou hast never lost me. I have kept unstained the faith I pledged, and never have I belonged to any man but thee!"

"But alas, my treasure, I may not possess thee! Let me at least drink my fill of thy beauty, my Laura!"

She drew him gently to her divan, and there, just as he had done in the pavilion, he knelt at her feet, and gazed, enraptured, in her face. With her little white hands she stroked his black locks, and lifted them from his pale, high brow.

"My hero," murmured she, tenderly. "Thou hast decked that brow with laurels since I loved thee, Eugene; and the world has heard of thee and of thy deeds of valor. I knew it would be so; I knew that the God of the brave would shield thy dear head in the day of battle, and lift thee to mountain-heights of glory and renown."

"And yet I would so gladly have yielded up my life, Laura! What was life without thee? One long night of anguish, to which death would have been glorious day! Oh, Laura! that day—that fearful day—on which I was bereft of thee!"

She laid her hand upon his lips. "Do not think of it, beloved, or thou wilt mar the ecstasy of the present. I, too, have suffered—more, it must have been more, than thou! And yet in all my anguish I was happy; for I was faithful, though sorely tried, and never, never despaired of thy coming."

"And yet thou art the wife of another."

"Say not so. When the priest laid my hand in his, *I* laid it in thine. To thee were my promises of fidelity, to thee I plighted my troth. That another—a liar and deceiver, should have inserted his odious name for thine, laid his dishonored hand in mine, has never bound *me!* I was, I am, I will ever be thine, so help me, God! who heard the oath I swore, and knew that, swearing, I believed thee there!"

"And I could doubt her, my love, my wife! Forgive me, Laura, that in my madness I should have accused thee."

"All is forgotten, for I have thee here!"

It was well for these impassioned lovers that a friend watched for them without. Lucretia had mounted guard for half an hour, when Victorine returned to say that the marquis would be glad to see his sister; her visit had lasted long enough.

"Take my place, then, Victorine; bolt the door, and admit nobody."

"Oh, signora, if the marquis finds us out, he will assassinate me!" said Victorine, trembling.

"He will not find us out; and you can very well endure some little uneasiness, when for a few nervous twitches you are to receive two thousand sequins. Think that, by to-night, you will be on your way to Paris."

"Would to God I were there, away from this frightful robbers' nest!"

Lucretia laughed. "You flatter the city of Venice. But I am not surprised that you are not in love with the Palazzo Strozzi, for when its master is contradicted, he is a raging tiger, whose thirst nothing save human blood will quench."

"O God ! O Lord ! I am almost dead with fright !"

"Have patience, mademoiselle. Look at yonder clock on the mantel. Precisely at the expiration of one hour, come with your message to my brother's cabinet. That will be the signal for your release. Are your effects out of the palace ?"

"Yes, signora ; they are all at the hôtel of the Marquis de Villars."

"And the gondola of the elector will be here to speak the prince's adieux. Now remain just where you are ; and, instead of opening your ears to what is passing in yonder boudoir, make use of your leisure to say your prayers, which you may possibly have forgotten this morning."

The countess lifted up her long train, and, passing it over her arm, went on her way to meet the amiable Strozzi.

"Really, Ottario," said she, entering the cabinet, "your palace is singularly like a prison. As I came through the corridor, I felt as if I were passing over the Ponte de' Sospiri. The atmosphere of the place is heavy with your jealous sighs."

"True ; there is little happiness under the marble dome of my palace. But let us speak of other things. What can I do to serve you ?"

"You seem to intimate that I can never desire to speak with you, except to ask a favor."

"I find that, generally speaking, the case."

"For once you are mistaken. I want nothing from you whatever."

"You seem to have grown rich by some legerdemain or other, Lucretia. I hear that you have refitted your palace with great magnificence. Has Canossa come into a fortune ? or has he been winning at the card-table ?"

"Neither ; but it was precisely of my newly acquired wealth that I came to speak with you. I am about to quit Venice, perhaps forever ; and before leaving I wished to have an explanation with you."

"Gracious Heaven ! who will take your place by Laura ?"

"Very flattering that my departure occasions no emotion in my brother's fond heart, save regret for the loss of his spy !

But never mind, I overlook the slight, and proceed with my confession."

So Lucretia went over all the humiliations and hardships she had undergone within the past six months ; and, after dwelling pathetically upon her own sufferings, she related the manner of her meeting with the Elector of Bavaria, and its consequences. They loved each other to adoration ; he lavished every gift upon her that his wealth could purchase, and now she was about to give him substantial proof of her attachment, by going off with him to Munich. No mention was made, in the recital, of her episode with the French minister.

The countess had barely arrived at the end of her confidences, when a knock was heard, and Mademoiselle Victorine walked in with a message from the marchioness.

" What message ? " cried Strozzi, rising at once to receive it.

" Pardon me, excellenza, it is only a message for the signora," said Victorine, courtesying. " My lady wishes to know if the countess has the French book that she promised to bring to-day ? "

" Dear me ! I had forgotten it," cried the countess. " But stay, Victorine, it is in the gondola below. Let little Filippo go after it."

" Who is Filippo ? " asked the marquis, frowning.

" My page, to be sure. Have you never seen him ? Of course I could not carry Mary Stuart's long train up the staircase without a page to help me."

" And he is here, in the palace ? "

" Of course he is : where else should the child be but here with me ? And, as I was not anxious to have him eavesdropping about your cabinet while we were conversing, I gave him in charge to Victorine."

" I shall discharge Beppo," growled the marquis. " How dared he—"

" Let me intercede for poor Beppo," laughed Lucretia. " He would have kept out Filippo, but I insisted that your prohibition could not extend to boys, and I insisted upon having him to carry my train. Since his presence here annoys you, he shall be made to leave, and await me in my gondola."

"But the book, signora," said Victorine, with quivering lip.

"True—the book for Laura. Will you permit Victorine to go with Filippo, and get it? But bless me! Without her protection, Beppo would not allow him to pass. You consent for her to accompany him?"

"Yes," said Strozzi, roughly. "But if ever you come again, leave your page at home."

"The watchword, signor?" asked Victorine.

"Venetia," returned Strozzi.

"What!" exclaimed Lucretia, "does Victorine, too, need a password to leave the palace? My dear brother, I admire your genius! You are qualified to make a first-rate jailer."

Mademoiselle Victorine had not tarried to hear the ironical compliment of the countess. She flew along the corridor to the apartments of the marchioness, and, first knocking at the door, she drew back the portière.

"Your highness," said she, "the hour has expired." Then dropping the portière, that the lovers might part without witnesses, she waited without.

Laura's arms were around his neck. Eugene drew her passionately to his heart. "Must I then go without thee?" murmured he.

"Yes, my Eugene; this time thou goest alone. But be patient and hopeful, and thy spouse will find means to escape from her jailer."

"I cannot go," cried Eugene, despairingly. "Nor can I leave my enemy's house like a frightened cur, while the woman I love remains to bear his anger. He must—he shall renounce my wife!"

"That is, you would see me murdered before your eyes!" exclaimed Laura, well knowing what argument would move him most to discretion. "Eugene, he has sworn to assassinate me, if I ever speak to you—and, believe me, he will keep his oath."

"And I must leave my treasure in his bloodthirsty hands?" cried the prince, pressing her still more closely in his arms.

"The tiger will do me no harm, Eugene, if thou wilt go before he sees thee,"

"Your highness," said Victorine, imploringly through the portière, "for God's sake, tarry no longer!"

Laura, freeing herself from his embrace, led him to the door. "Farewell, my beloved," said she. "God is merciful, and will reunite us."

"One more look into those dear eyes, one more kiss from those sweet lips."

"Oh, your highness!" whispered Victorine, a second time.

Laura raised the portière, and led him forward. She saw Victorine reach him his mask, and then, darting back into her boudoir, she fell upon her knees, and prayed for an hour.

Meanwhile the Countess Lucretia was still discussing her affairs; but she seemed to have become absent-minded, sometimes stopping suddenly in her speech to listen, occasionally directing anxious glances toward the windows.

The marquis was too keen for these symptoms to escape his penetration.

"Are you watching or waiting for any thing?" asked he.

"Yes," replied she, "I await something, and—oh! there it is!"

As she spoke these last words, a voice from the water called out three times: "Addio! addio! addio!"

"Do you know what that 'addio' signifies?" asked Lucretia.

"How can I understand the signals that pass between you and your loves?"

"I will tell you what it means," said she, looking full into her brother's face. "I—but no! your eyes glare too fiercely just now; you are ready for a spring, and I dare not wait to be devoured. Addio, Ottario, addio. Take this note, and swear that you will not open it before ten minutes."

"What childishness!" exclaimed Strozzi, rudely.

"You will not? Then you shall not see its contents, which, nevertheless, concern your Laura."

"Laura!—Then I swear that I will not open it before ten minutes."

"It is on the table. Be careful how you break your oath. You would not be safe were you to unfold that paper before ten minutes."

So saying, she kissed her hand, and tripped merrily away to her gondola.

At the expiration of the time required, Strozzi took up the paper, and broke its seal. It contained the following:

"MY DEAR BROTHER: You sold me to Count Canossa, and you have degraded me to the trade of a spy. You have forced me, more than once, to play the dragon by your poor, unhappy wife; but I have repaid her for my unkindness, and have avenged myself also. My little Filippo is Prince Eugene, and he is to remain alone with your wife, exactly as long as I converse with you in your cabinet. The three 'addios' which you will have heard ere this from the Canale, signify that the prince has reached his gondola, and is safe. Also that Mademoiselle Victorine, my accomplice, has fled. You gave her ten ducats for each betrayal of her mistress; we offered two thousand sequins, and of course she betrayed you. Addio!"

To describe the fury of the marquis would be impossible. But his paroxysm of rage over, he at once began to revolve in his mind the means of revenge.

"There must be an end to this martyrdom," said he. "It must end!" He looked at the clock. "'Tis time Antonio were here, and he shall do it."

He struck three times on his little bell, and the door in the wall glided back, giving entrance to Antonio.

---

## CHAPTER VIII.

### ANTONIO'S EXPIATION.

THE next morning Antonio asked admittance to the cabinet of his new employer.

"Your highness," said he, "I have seen the marchioness."

"What greeting does she send, good Antonio?"

"My lord, she awaits Filippo at eight o'clock this evening."

"She awaits me ! " echoed Eugene. " And you are to conduct me to her ? "

"Yes, my lord. I am acquainted with the secret passages of the palace. I will show you the way, and, as God in heaven hears me, I will bring you safely back."

"How solemnly you speak, Antonio ! "

"Ah, excellenza, it is easier to enter that palace than to leave it ! But you shall leave it in safety, as I hope to be saved from perdition ! "

"At what hour did you say ? "

"At eight this evening. And now, my lord, allow me to leave you for a time. The marquis requires me to remain at the palace, and I must be punctual, or he will suspect me. You will be obliged to engage another commissionnaire ; but, believe me, I shall better serve you in the palace than here."

Antonio was allowed to depart ; but instead of going toward the Strozzi palace, he betook himself to that of the Elector of Bavaria, where the household were in that state of confusion which precedes a departure. The elector had chosen to leave Venice by night.

"I have an important message from my lord, Prince Eugene of Savoy to his highness of Bavaria," said Antonio, making his way through the busy throng of servants. "Is he in his cabinet ? "

"Yes. The chamberlain is in the anteroom. He will announce you."

"His highness will receive the messenger of Prince Eugene," was the reply ; and Antonio, having been admitted, had a conversation of some length with the elector, which left the latter in a state of great agitation.

"I wish it were in my power to render assistance ; but I dare not. He made me promise that I would not interfere in any way ; and I must keep my word. I would but act in the dark, and might ruin him.—And now to Lucretia, to devise other means of rescue, if these should fail—"

After leaving the elector, Antonio directed his steps toward the prison near the palace of the doge. The porter that stood near the grated door looked searchingly at the mask that presumed to tarry before those dismal gates whereof he was the guardian.

"Would you earn a thousand sequins?" said Antonio, in a whisper.

"How?" asked the porter, opening his eyes like two full moons.

"Do you know in which cell Catherina Giamberta is confined?"

"Yes, I know."

"Take this flower to her.  It is her birthday, and she loves flowers.  Tell her it comes from Antonio, and ask her to send him the ribbon she wears around her neck.  If you return with it, I will give you one thousand sequins."

He handed the porter a large rose, whose stem was carefully wrapped in paper.  Christiano scarcely saw what it was, so dazzled were his eyes by the approaching glitter of a thousand sequins.  But he thrust it in his bosom, drew the bolts of his prison, and disappeared within its gloomy depths.

Antonio leaned his head against the clammy prison-wall and waited.  In half an hour the turnkey returned.

"Have you your thousand sequins with you?" asked he.

"Here they are," said Antonio, drawing from his cloak a purse, through whose dingy silk meshes the gold was visible.

The turnkey put his hand through the grate, and Antonio saw a faded, yellow paper, tied with a silken cord.  He took the packet, and in return gave Christiano the purse.  As he did so, he said : "Make good use of it ; I have passed through five years of misery to earn it.  Make good use of it, and if you will have a mass said for the repose of my soul, 'tis all I ask in addition to the service you have just rendered me."

He turned away, and, hurriedly taking the direction of St. Mark's, entered a side-door, and stood within its sacred walls.  The church was empty and dimly lighted.  Antonio knelt down behind one of the pillars, and opened the paper.

It contained a lock of golden hair—the hair of a child.  The bravo pressed it to his lips, and, murmuring a few fond words, laid it lovingly upon his heart, and began to pray.  When his prayer was ended, he approached a confessional wherein sat an old Benedictine monk, and, kneeling down, began his confession.

The recital was a long, and apparently a terrible one; for more than once the monk shuddered, and his venerable face was mournfully upraised as if in prayer for the penitent. When Antonio ceased, he remained silent, still praying.

"Reverend father," murmured the bravo, "may I not receive absolution for my sins!"

"Yes, my son, you shall receive such absolution as it rests with me to give. If, as I hope, you are truly repentant, God will do the rest. You have sinned grievously, but you are ready to expiate." And the priest performed the ceremony of absolution.

"Reverend father, give me your blessing—your blessing in *articulo mortis.*"

"Come hither and receive it."

Antonio emerged from the confessional, and knelt on the marble pavement, while the rays from a stained window above fell upon his head like a soft, golden halo. The priest, too, stepped out, and, laying his hand upon that bowed head, made the sign of the cross, and blessed him in *articulo mortis.* Then going slowly up the aisle, and kneeling within the sanctuary, he passed the night in praying for a soul that was about to depart this world.

---

## CHAPTER IX.

### THE DUNGEON.

THE clock on the Campanillo of St. Mark's struck eight. The day of longing expectation had at last worn away, and Eugene was once more to be admitted to the presence of his beloved.

Before leaving his cabinet he had sent for Antonio, and, reaching him a purse of gold, had said: "Here, my brave— here are two hundred ducats. Take this purse, and, when you

make use of its contents, remember that I gave it as a token of
my gratitude for your fidelity and friendship."

"No, your highness," replied Antonio, in a tearful voice—
"no, your highness, I need no gold. If you would give me a
souvenir, let me have the glove that has covered the right hand
of a hero whose sword has never been unsheathed save in the
cause of right."

"Singular man," exclaimed Eugene, "take them both, and
believe that I thank you for your attachment. And now, let
us away ! "

"Yes, my lord ; but I implore you, not this rich cloak of
velvet. Take this black wrapping of cloth ; it is more appropriate for an adventure such as ours."

The little gondola lay moored at the stairs, without gondolier or light. Nobody was there except Eugene and Antonio,
who rowed without help. They made for a channel leading
to a wing of the Palace Strozzi, whose dark, frowning walls,
unrelieved by one single opening, were laved by the foul and
turbid waters of the narrow estuary. Antonio's practised eye
discovered the low opening that gave access to the palace ;
and, after fastening his gondola to a ring in the wall, he
knocked three times at the door. It was opened, and they entered a small vestibule, dimly lighted, where they were confronted by a man who asked for the password.

Antonio whispered something in his ear, and they were
permitted to ascend a steep, narrow staircase leading to a passage so contracted that Eugene's shoulders touched on either
side, as he struggled along toward a second staircase. When
they had reached the last step, Antonio said : "We have no
farther to go. Pass in, signor, and, whatever ensues, remember that you must patiently await my return."

A door opened, Eugene passed through, and it closed behind him. He was in a room of singular shape and construction. It was a rotunda, whose blank walls were without opening whatsoever ; neither door nor window was to be seen
therein. Suspended from the lofty ceiling was an iron chain,
to which was attached a small lamp, whose light fell directly
over a table that stood in the centre of the room. On the table
lay a piece of bread and a glass of water ; near it was placed a

wooden chair, and this was all the furniture contained within the dismal apartment.

"A dungeon," said Eugene to himself. "One of those dungeons of which I have heard, but in whose existence I never believed until now."

He was perfectly collected ; but he comprehended his position, and knew that he had been betrayed. He had been lured into this secret prison, there to die without a sign ! But he must make one desperate effort to escape. Death he could confront—even the death that stared him in the face ; but to know that Laura would be doomed to a life of utter wretchedness, was a thought that almost unsettled his reason.

He surveyed the place, and then felt every stone, every crevice, that came within his reach. As he raised his mournful eyes to look above him, the wall just below the ceiling began to move, a small window was opened, and within its iron frame appeared a pale, sinister face—the face of the Marquis de Strozzi.

Eugene tore the mask from his face, and his large eyes flashed with scorn.

"Assassin !" cried he, "cowardly assassin !"

The marquis laughed ; he could afford to laugh. "Yes," said he, "I am any thing you may please to term me ; but *you*, Prince of Savoy, are no longer among the living. Your days are numbered : farewell !"

The window closed, and the wall moved slowly back until no trace of the opening was to be seen. A dungeon ! A grave ! Eugene of Savoy would die of hunger ! no human ear would hear his dying plaint ; within a few steps of one that loved him he would disappear from earth ; and, until the great day whereon hell would yield up its secrets of horror to the Eternal Judge, his fate would remain a mystery ! Alas ! alas ! And was this to be the end of his aspirations for glory ?

But hark ! What sound is that ? The invisible door, for which he had been groping in vain, was once more opened, and Antonio glided noiselessly into the room.

He raised his hand in token of warning. "Not a word, my lord," whispered he. "I come to save you."

22

"To save me, traitor! You, the despicable tool of Strozzi?"

"Oh, my lord! Have mercy, have mercy! Every moment is precious : listen to me, listen to me!"

Antonio sank on his knees, the mask dropped from his face, and his pale, suffering countenance wore any aspect but that of treachery.

"In the name of the Marchioness Laura Bonaletta, hear me," said he, imploringly.

"Laura Bonaletta!" echoed Eugene, in a voice of piercing anguish. "What can such as you know of Laura Bonaletta?"

Antonio gave him a folded paper containing these few lines : "If thou lovest me, do as Antonio bids thee. If thou wouldst not have me die of grief, accept thy life from Antonio's hands, and oh, love! believe me, we shall meet again. Thy Laura."

Eugene pressed the paper to his lips, and when he looked at Antonio again, his eye had lost its sternness, and about his lips there fluttered a sad smile.

"What does this mean, Antonio?" said he.

"Excellenza, it means that I was a hardened sinner until you rescued my soul from perdition. Would that I had time to lay before you the sins of my whole life, that you might know from what depths of crime you delivered me! But time is precious. I can only say that I am no brave soldier that was scarred in battle. This wound upon my face was from the hand of my father, and, for the crime of his murder, my right hand was hewed by the arm of the executioner. Nay— do not start, my dear, dear lord! 'Tis you that brought me to repentance ; 'tis you that inspired me to seek reconciliation with Heaven. I came to you a bravo—the emissary of the Marquis Strozzi ; but when you touched my mutilated arm with your honored hand—when you trusted me because you believed me to be brave—I swore in my heart that you at least I would not betray. 'Tis true, I led you hither where Strozzi would have left you to die of hunger. Ah, my lord! you are not the first that has looked upon these cruel walls. Giuseppi, the gondolier whom the countess loved—he, too, poor youth, came hither—and six days after I was sent for his corpse, and consigned it to the sullen waters of the lagoon, that covers the secrets of Strozzi's atrocious murders."

"But why, then, did you not warn me?"

"Because Strozzi would have murdered me, and employed another man to betray you into his hands. Or, if you had believed me, you might have remained in Venice, and you must fly this very night—this very hour. Until you are safe, Strozzi must believe that you are his prisoner."

"Am I, then, forever doomed to turn my back upon this man?"

"My lord, my lord, no vain scruples! The Marchioness Bonaletta will die if you do not live to rescue her from his tyranny."

Eugene grasped his arm. "Ah, yes, indeed! Then come, Antonio—let us fly."

"My dear lord, one man only can leave this room. The porter is ready with his dagger if both should attempt to pass."

"You would remain here in my place! You would sacrifice your life to liberate me, Antonio!"

"The parricide would fain be at rest," replied Antonio, gently. "The sinner would gladly suffer death, that, expiating his crimes, he may hope to be forgiven by his Maker."

"Never will I purchase life at such a price," was the reply of the prince.

"My life is accursed," said Antonio; "my death will be triumphant. My lord, if you knew how I longed for death, you would not refuse me the blessing I covet. My Catherina ere this awaits me in the other world; I long to rejoin her—I long to obtain the pardon of my murdered father."

Eugene's face was buried in his hands, and he was weeping. "I cannot, I cannot," gasped he.

"You would drive your Laura to despair, then? You would go to your grave without renown?"

"No; I would live. Come: we can overpower the porter —if nothing less will save us, we can kill him."

"Before he dies he will call for help, and help will be near. But one of us can escape; and, by my eternal salvation, I swear that I will not be that one! Away with you! Away! In a moment it will be too late! Do you not hear me? Whether you go or stay, I never will leave this place again!"

Eugene staggered against the wall, and sighed heavily. Antonio knelt at his feet. At last he murmured almost inaudibly, "I will go."

Antonio sprang from his knees, threw his cloak around the prince, and, with eager, trembling hands, adjusted his mask.

"Thank God!" said he, "we are of the same size and build. There is not the least danger of recognition. The porter will suspect nothing. The password is, 'One of two.' The gondola is moored in the place where we left it, and your friends are at the landing, awaiting you now. The marchioness knows that you are to leave Venice to-night. God in heaven bless you. And now away!"

"Antonio," replied Eugene, greatly affected, "with my latest breath I will bless and thank you."

Then folding the bravo in his arms, he would have spoken his thanks again, but Antonio hurried him away, closed the door, and then fell upon his knees to pray.

The password was spoken, the door was opened, and Eugene was saved! He sprang into the gondola, and it flew across those sullen waters like an arrow. As he reached the landing, a well-known voice called out, "Eugene!"

"Max Emmanuel, I am here!" was the reply, and the friends were locked in each other's arms.

At length the elector spoke:—"I have confronted death," said he, "but never in my life have I passed an hour of such anguish as this. Come, Eugene, yonder lies the ship that is to bear us away from this sin-laden city. Step into my gondola, we have not a moment to lose."

They rowed to the ship's side; they mounted the ladder, and before the dawn of day Venice with her palaces and their secret prisons had disappeared, and the friends were far on their way to Trieste.

# BOOK V.

## CHAPTER I.

### A TWOFOLD VICTORY.

THE winter of 1688 had gone by ; the snows were melting from the bosom of reviving earth ; and the trees that bordered the avenues of the Prater were bursting into life. At the court of Austria nobody welcomed spring ; for its approach betokened the cessation of gayety, and the resumption of hostilities. The year 1687 had been rendered illustrious in the annals of Austrian history, by Charles of Lorraine, who, on the 12th of August, had gained a signal victory over the Turks. The rebellion in Hungary, if not suppressed, was smothered ; for the weary and exhausted Magyars had been totally crushed by the iron heel of General Caraffa, and they had submitted to Austria. The conditions of the surrender were hard : they demanded the relinquishment of some of the dearest rights of the liberty-loving Hungarians. First, they were to renounce all right of resistance against the King of Hungary ; second, they were no longer to elect their own sovereigns ; the crown of Hungary was made hereditary in the house of the Emperors of Austria. The Archduke Joseph, then ten years of age, was crowned king ; and the Hungarians were compelled to take the oath of allegiance to this irresponsible sovereign.

This being a decisive victory, the campaign ended early, and the season of festivity had therefore been a prolonged one. Not only the aristocracy of Vienna had celebrated the heroism of the victors by balls, concerts, and assemblies, but the emperor himself sometimes prevailed upon his retiring and devout empress to participate in the national gayety, by giving entertainments to her subjects at the imperial palace.

It was the festival of the Empress Eleanora, and the day was to be celebrated by the production of a new opera, entitled "Il Pomo d'Oro." The rehearsals had been superintended by the emperor in person ; he had suggested and directed the scenery and decorations, and, to the great scandal of his confessor, Father Bischof, Leopold had more than once curtailed his devotions, to attend these rehearsals.

On the day of the performance the emperor retired early to his dressing-room, and, to honor the festival of his consort, arrayed himself with imperial magnificence. His doublet was of cloth of gold, edged with fringe of the same ; his cloak of purple velvet, richly embroidered, was fastened on the shoulder by an agraffe of superb diamonds. The breeches, reaching to the knee, were of velvet, like the cloak ; and the hose, like the doublet, were of cloth of gold. The shoes of purple velvet were fastened with buckles of diamonds to correspond with the agraffe of the cloak. His ruff was of gold lace, his hat was decorated with a long white plume, and on his breast he wore the splendid order of the Golden Fleece.

When Leopold entered his music-room, Kircherus, who was there, awaiting him, could not repress an exclamation of wonder at the dazzling apparition.

"You are amazed at my magnificence," said the emperor, laughing.

"Your majesty, say rather that I am struck with admiration than with amazement. You are as glorious as the god of day ; and if the Muses were to trip by, they would surely mistake you for their Phœbus, and, quitting Parnassus, make themselves at home in Vienna."

"And be driven away with contumely ; for, being heathen maidens, Father Bischof would speedily exorcise and exile them back to Greece. And now tell me what you think of the new opera. Do you expect it to be successful ? "

"Indeed I do, your majesty. It is, to my mind, heavenly."

"And to mine also. 'Tis the very music with which to lull the dying soul to rest. I have spared nothing to bring it out handsomely, and it has certainly been a golden apple to my purse, for it has already cost me thirty thousand ducats. But I tell you this in confidence, Kircherus : were my generals to hear of it, they would cry out that money is to be had for every thing except the army."

"I wish there were no army to swallow up your majesty's resources, and that we might be allowed to enjoy our music in peace," growled Kircherus.

"Hush, Kircherus; you are an artiste, and know nothing of the exigencies of political existence. I would I were such a heavenly idiot as you; but God has decreed otherwise. It is my duty to declare war or peace, as becomes the ruler of a great people; and so disinclined am I to strife, and so inclined to peaceful arts, that I sometimes think I have been purposely thwarted by God, and cast upon an epoch of perplexity and dissension, that my character might be invigorated by its exigencies. Even now I go reluctantly from art, to hold a council of war. I fear it is about to be anything but amicable; so, do your best to console me on my return, and see that all goes well as regards the opera."

The officers of the war department had been for more than half an hour awaiting the appearance of the emperor. One only was absent, the Duke of Lorraine, who had excused himself on a plea of indisposition.

"He is craftier than I had supposed," said the Margrave of Baden to his nephew. "He avoids the unpleasant responsibilities of debate, and shields himself behind the orders of the emperor."

"Because he awaits a reappointment to the chief command," replied Louis. "For him is the glory of our victories; for us the danger. But I have a missile to throw into the camp of the enemy; it is from Max Emmanuel, who votes with us."

"Ah, indeed!" said the margrave, with a satisfied air. "Then I think we may hope to thwart this insolent pretender, who considers me incapable of directing the war department of Austria."

"He has offered me a public affront," returned Louis, indignantly. "I had a right to command the Slavonian cavalry; and he bestowed it upon Dunewald, who is nothing but his creature. I have therefore followed the example of Max Emmanuel, and shall resign my commission to-day."

"I would give millions if, after your defection, he were defeated by the Turks. But he has the most unconscionable luck. And then, that silly Prince of Savoy, who blows such blasts in his praise. Louis, you ought not to be so intimate with Prince Eugene—he is one of our enemies."

"Oh no," replied Louis, smiling. "Eugene is the enemy of no man. Say nothing against *him*, uncle, if you love me. He is a youth of noble spirit, incapable of envy ; recognizing every soldier's merit except his own. Our cousin of Savoy is destined to become a great man."

"He is already a great man," replied the margrave, with a sneer. "Not twenty-five years of age, and a knight of the Golden Fleece—a protégé of the emperor, the favorite of Charles of Lorraine !"

At this moment the doors were opened, and Leopold, followed by a small, slender officer, entered the council-chamber.

"The Prince of Savoy !" muttered the margrave, impatiently.

"Eugene !" said Louis to himself, as, bowing his head with the rest, he wondered what could be the meaning of his cousin's presence.

"My lords," said the emperor, taking his seat, "I have invited Prince Eugene of Savoy to assist at this council—not only as a listener, but as one of us ; and I shall call upon him to give his opinion as such, upon the matters that come under discussion to-day."

"Pardon me, your majesty, if, as president of this council, I remind you that the Prince of Savoy is too young and inexperienced for such a discussion, and that no man in active service, under the rank of a field-marshal, ever participates in the debates of the war department."

"Your highness is quite right, and I thank you for the reminder. We have no desire to infringe the etiquette of the council-chamber ; and as we have invited the prince therein, we must repair our oversight by qualifying him to sit.—Prince of Savoy, we hereby create you field-marshal, and trust that, as such, you may win so many laurels that the world will pardon your youth in favor of your genius."

Eugene crimsoned to his temples, and kissed the hand

which Leopold extended. "My liege," said he, in a voice choked with emotion, "your majesty heaps coals of fire on my head. May God give me grace to earn these unparalleled honors!"

"You have already earned them," replied Leopold, "and Austria is proud to have won such a hero to her cause.—And now, my lords, to business. President of the council, what is the condition of our army at present?"

"Your majesty, the army is not, as yet, armed and provisioned; but it will be in a condition to oppose the enemy as soon as the marshes of Hungary are sufficiently dry to allow of an advance."

"That means simply that nothing has been done," replied the emperor, in tones of dissatisfaction, "and that the winter has been spent in total inaction. It means also that this year as well as last our soldiers are to feel the want of the necessaries of life; and that for lack of money, munition, and stores, our most advantageous marches will have to be relinquished."

"I see that the Duke of Lorraine has already accused and calumniated me," said the margrave, sullenly.

"The Duke of Lorraine has at times complained of the want of munition, stores, and forage; but he neither calumniates nor accuses any one. He has remarked that, instead of being sustained by the war department, he has been hampered and harassed by its opposition to his plans. Even his officers have manifested a spirit of such insubordination, that they have seriously interfered with his successes."

"That means that he has complained of me," interposed Louis of Baden.

"Yes, margrave, it does; and we are both surprised that a hero of your recognized ability and renown should fail in a soldier's first duty—obedience to orders."

"Your majesty," exclaimed Louis, "I am no subordinate officer to receive or obey orders from another! I am an independent prince of the German empire, in every respect the equal of the Duke of Lorraine."

"Except as an officer in the Austrian army," replied Leopold, "in which character the Duke of Lorraine is your chief.

You have not sufficiently considered this matter of your rank
as an officer in my service ; let me hope that, for the future,
you will acknowledge and respect the authority of your commander-in-chief. I myself have found him ever ready to
acknowledge and respect mine."

"The will of the emperor, to us, is law," said the Margrave
Herman. "But your imperial majesty has hitherto exacted
of your officers that they should receive your mandates
through the medium of the minister of war. The Duke of
Lorraine, who claims such strict obedience from others, has
set at defiance the mandates issued from this council-chamber.
As president of the same, I complain of the insubordination of
your majesty's commander-in-chief. He has not carried out
the orders received from the war department."

" He would have been more than mortal had he done so ;
for the war department has required of him feats that were
physically impossible. We can trace out upon this green
cloth before me any number of strategic movements, which,
supposing the enemy to be of one mind with ourselves, would
annihilate him beyond a doubt. But as he is apt to do the
very reverse of what we would prescribe, the man upon whom
rests the responsibility of confronting him, must use his reason, and modify orders according to circumstances. *What is
to be*, you cannot include in your paper plans of attack ; but
the Duke of Lorraine has met every emergency as it presented itself on the field, and every true Austrian should be his
friend."

"Your majesty," cried the margrave, greatly irritated,
" the president of this council must nevertheless persist in his
conviction that the highest court of military jurisdiction is
here, and that the commander-in-chief of the army is its subordinate."

" You mistake the extent of its power," replied the emper-
or, with composure. " It is merely expected of the general-
in-chief that he act in concert with the war department."

" Which the Duke of Lorraine has never done ! " cried the
margrave, impetuously.

" Perhaps the blame lay in the injudicious exactions of the
minister of war," replied Leopold, carelessly ; " and if, despite

of all the obstacles that were placed in his way, he has subdued Hungary, you have no part in his glory, my lord ; for in
every case your judgment has been contrary to his."

"It follows, then, that I have not filled my office to the satisfaction of your majesty," said the margrave, choking with anger.

"I regret to say that I have less confidence in your judgment than in your ability, my lord ; the former is unhappily
often obscured by prejudice," replied Leopold, calmly.

"Your majesty," cried the margrave, "in this case I shall
feel compelled—"

"I do not wish you to say or do any thing on compulsion,
my lord ; I prefer to assign you a position in which your talents, being unfettered by your antipathies, will shine with
undimmed lustre. You have complained of late that the
duties of the war department have become irksome to you ; if
so, I can give you an appointment less onerous to you, but
equally important to the state. I am just now in need of an
intelligent representative before the imperial Diet. This
charge I commit to you, premising that you must start for
your post immediately, that you may infuse some life into the
stagnant councils of the ambassadors of the princes of Germany."

"Your majesty wishes to banish me from court?" asked
the margrave, pale with anger.

"Certainly not, your highness," replied the emperor, gently. "I send you on an honorable embassy, and one whereat
I need a capable and fearless advocate. The question to be
decided before the imperial Diet is one of life or death to Austria, nay—to Germany. France is evidently preparing for
war with the German empire. Her fortresses on the eastern
frontier are all garrisoned ; her troops are approaching ; and
under some pretext or other, they will cross our boundary
lines. This being the case, the princes of the empire must
cease their everlasting petty dissensions, and band themselves
together for the defence of Germany. Be it your task to
strengthen the bond of unity between them, and to convince
them that in close alliance with Austria safety is to be found
for all. I know of no man who can serve my interests at
Regensburg as well as you, my lord ; while, happily, I can

find a substitute for your presidential chair at home, in Count von Starhemberg. And now, farewell ; and let me hear from you as soon as possible."

The emperor extended his hand to the margrave, who, scarcely able to control his dissatisfaction, barely raised it to his lips, and hurried away.

"My lords," said the emperor, "let us proceed to business. The spring is nigh, and a new campaign is about to be planned. Count von Starhemberg, as president of this assembly, will be so good as to impart his views."

Count von Starhemberg bowed :—"Your majesty, it appears to me that our policy is to avoid a general engagement. The end of this campaign is the reduction of Belgrade, and great precaution must be used if we are to succeed. I would divide the army, so as to begin operations at three points simultaneously, and weaken the enemy, by scattering his forces. By detaching, we can easily defeat them, and capture their arsenals. This accomplished, we proceed to Belgrade, and, with the conquest of this Turkish stronghold, we end not only the campaign, but the war."

As Von Starhemberg concluded this harangue, the emperor addressed himself to Prince Louis of Baden.

"Your majesty," replied he, "I have no opinion to offer, for my views coincide altogether with those of Count von Starhemberg."

"And you, Count von Kinsky ?"

"Your majesty, I sustain the president."

The same replies were forthcoming from Counts Liechtenstein and Puchta, and the emperor, having heard each one, relapsed into silence. After a pause, he spoke. "There reigns a remarkable unanimity of opinion here, among the councils of the war department," said he, with some emphasis. "Five members having but one mind as to the prosecution of the war ! Not one variation from the plan of the president— not one suggestion—not even from so experienced and able a general as Louis of Baden ! This is singular and surprising. We have yet to hear the youngest member of the council. Field-Marshal Prince of Savoy, speak without restraint, and fear not to express your own views."

"Pardon me, your majesty," said Eugene, blushing, "if I venture to dissent from the opinions expressed by those who are my seniors in years, and my superiors in experience. But it is the duty of a man, when called upon to speak, to speak honestly ; and I should be untrue to my most earnest convictions, were I to give in my adherence to the plan proposed."

Amazement was depicted upon the faces of the assembled councillors ; not only amazement, but disapprobation of Eugene's boldness. The emperor, however, looked kindly at the prince, and bade him proceed.

"With your majesty's permission, I am of the opinion that the entire army be concentrated in an attack upon Belgrade. To divide our forces will enfeeble them doubly ; their numbers would be inconsiderable, and their command by one chief, impossible. Division is weakness—concentration is strength. Belgrade is our goal, and to Belgrade let us march at once. Let us possess the key of Turkey, and then we can make conditions with the Sultan."

"I honor your frankness, prince," replied the emperor. "I should respect it, were my opinion on the subject adverse to yours. But it is not. My lords, I regret that we are not all of one mind ; but I must decide in favor of the campaign as proposed by Field-Marshal Eugene of Savoy. I cannot consent to have the army crippled by division ; we must put forth all our strength, if we are to lay siege to Belgrade, and to this one end let our warlike preparations be directed."

"Your majesty's will is law," replied Count von Starhemberg. "It only remains for you to name the one to whom the chief command of the Austrian forces is to be intrusted."

"It is to be intrusted to him who has commanded it with such signal ability—to the Duke of Lorraine, my lord.—And now, gentlemen," added the emperor, rising, "the sitting is ended."

"Your majesty," interposed Louis of Baden, "I crave a few moments more."

The emperor gave consent, and the young prince came forward and spoke.

"Your majesty, the *chief* command of the army being given to the Duke of Lorraine, it follows that neither the

Elector of Bavaria nor I have any independent position; we
are to obey the orders of the Duke of Lorraine. This being
the case, Max Emmanuel has commissioned me to announce
with the utmost respect that it does not become a reigning
prince to be the instrument of any other man's will. His
subjects have already complained of the subordinate rank of
their sovereign, and he cannot allow their sense of honor to be
wounded by a renewal of such affront. He therefore tenders
his resignation. He will withdraw the Bavarian troops, and
take no part in your majesty's projected campaign against the
Turks."

"We shall take time to consider the subject," replied Leopold, in a tone of unconcern, "and will speak with the elector
in person. Have you anything else to say?"

"Yes, your majesty," said Louis. "I, also, consider it beneath my dignity to serve under a foreign prince, and I owe it
to my own self-respect to act with the elector, and to tender my
resignation."

The emperor looked searchingly at the troubled countenance of the margrave, who blushed beneath his gaze, and cast
down his eyes.

"And you, too, would abandon your colors?" asked Leopold.

The eyes of the margrave flashed fire. "I false to my
colors!" exclaimed he.

"You," repeated the emperor. "With your rank, as Margrave of Baden, I have nothing to do. You are an officer in
my army, and have taken the oath of allegiance to me, as
your lord and emperor. I ask you if you deem it honorable
to desert your flag on the eve of a campaign? Do we not call
such conduct by the name of cowardice?"

"Your majesty," cried Louis, vehemently, "I a —!"

"I do not speak of you," interrupted Leopold, calmly. "I
ask you, if, at the moment of engaging the enemy, one of your
ablest officers were to come to you with the proposition you
have just made to me, by what word would you characterize
the act?"

"Your majesty—I—I—" stammered the margrave.

"You cannot answer, my lord, but I will answer for you.

You would say to such a man, 'He who deserts his post in the hour of danger is a coward.' But you, Margrave of Baden, are a man of honor, and therefore you will withhold your vaulting ambition. You will not strive with the destiny which makes Charles of Lorraine an older and more experienced, but not a braver man than you ; but you will return to your duty, and emulate his greatness. Ambition is inseparable from valor ; but it must be checked by reason, or it degenerates into envy. What would you think of a crown prince who should feel humiliated at his subordinate rank when compared with that of his father ? When you entered my service, the Duke of Lorraine was already general-in-chief of the armies of Austria ; and, as he has always led them to victory, it would be in the highest degree unjust to supersede him by another. He who would command, must first learn to obey. Margrave of Baden, I cannot accept your resignation."

"I will do my duty," replied Louis, bowing low before the emperor's reproof. "I submit myself to your majesty's decision, and remain. '

"Say, rather," returned Leopold, smiling affectionately upon the young prince, "say rather that you go, for the campaign must open at once. Be diligent, Count von Starhemberg ; inaugurate your preparations this very day ; and you, Field-Marshal Prince of Savoy, hasten to Innspruck, to communicate to the Duke of Lorraine the result of our council of war."

"I thank your majesty," replied Eugene, "for this gracious command. May I be permitted to retire, and make my preparations to leave ? "

The emperor bowed his head, and addressed the Margrave of Baden. "As there is no such urgency attending the movements of your highness, I will be happy to consider you as my guest, and shall expect the pleasure of your company at the opera.—You also, gentlemen," added he to the other members of the war department. "The empress is already in the theatre, awaiting our coming."

And with these words, the emperor, followed by his councillors, left the room. Without, the court was waiting to accompany him ; and, when the lord-chamberlain had announced to the world that his majesty the emperor was about to visit the opera, the long, brilliant cortége set itself in motion.

----

## CHAPTER II.

### THE DUMB MUSIC.

THE court entered the theatre. The emperor's suite took possession of the boxes on either side of the one appropriated to the imperial family, while Leopold, followed by Prince Eugene, whom he delighted to honor, entered the imperial box.

"I wish to present our new field-marshal to the empress," said he to his courtiers.

The empress was seated in one corner of the box, busily engaged with a piece of embroidery. She was so absorbed in the mysteries of silk and golden stitching, that she scarcely remarked the entrance of the court. For a moment her eyes met those of the emperor, to whom she bowed and smiled ; then, bending her head again, she resumed her work.

The emperor took a seat by her, and watched her flying fingers with affectionate interest. "Your majesty is unusually industrious to-day," said he, smiling, and touching the embroidery.

"I was merely beguiling the hour of expectation which has passed away with your majesty's presence, by completing a flower on this altar-cloth, intended for the chapel of the blessed Eleanor, my namesake."

"The blessed Eleanor must excuse you to-day if I claim your presence here," replied the emperor. "And let me implore you for a while to fold those busy hands, and give your attention to the music which has been gotten up for your especial gratification."

The empress quietly folded her work, and rose from her tabouret.

"Allow me to present to your majesty the youngest field-marshal in the army," said Leopold, signing to Eugene to advance.

"I congratulate your highness," replied the empress, while Eugene knelt and kissed her hand. "Are you, indeed, so very young, prince?"

"No, your majesty," said he, sadly. "I am so old, that I wonder my hair is not gray."

"Indeed! How old are you, then?"

"Your majesty, I am forty-six years of age," replied Eugene.

"Why, how can you say such a thing," exclaimed Leopold, "when everybody knows you to be just twenty-three?"

"Your majesty, are not the years of active service reckoned by the soldier as double?"

"Yes, assuredly, my young field-marshal."

"Then, my liege, I am forty-six years of age, for my life has been one long war with troubles and trials."

The empress looked sympathizingly into the deep, sad eyes of the young prince, and saw that he spoke the truth.

"Have you then had many sorrows?" asked she, gently.

"Ay, your majesty; I have struggled and suffered since childhood, for I have ever been a soldier of misfortune."

"But you are no longer one," said Leopold, laying his hand upon Eugene's shoulder; "you have taken the oath of allegiance to Austria, and misfortune has now no claim upon you."

Eugene looked up, and the face of the emperor was beaming with kindness. "Whatever betide, my liege," returned he, "I am yours for life, and Austria is my land of adoption."

"I am glad to hear it; and now there is but one thing wanting to make you a subject after my own heart. You must marry an Austrian wife that shall make you as happy a husband as myself, and transform earth into heaven, as her majesty has done for me. It is in commemoration of my own happiness that I have chosen the opera of 'Il Pomo d'Oro' to celebrate the empress's festival. 'Il Pomo d'Oro'—that is, a happy union—the golden apple of paradise."

And the emperor, enchanted to have turned the conversation to a subject which was to him of supreme interest, offered his arm to the empress, and conducted her to the front of the box.

As soon as their majesties appeared, the spectators rose and

23

cheered them enthusiastically. The imperial pair took their
seats, and behind them stood Prince Eugene, the only other
occupant of the box.

The emperor now waved his hand as a signal to the marshal
of the household, who, raising his gilded staff, conveyed the
imperial command to the leader of the orchestra. "His majesty is graciously pleased that the opera shall commence," cried
the lord-chamberlain.

The leader bowed to the emperor, and took his place, which
was conspicuously raised above that of the other musicians.

"His majesty is graciously pleased to allow all present to be
seated," was the second cry of the emperor's mouth-piece.
And now was heard a rustling of ladies' silks, and of cavaliers'
velvets, and the grateful spectators took their seats, while the
emperor, with a look of extreme satisfaction, opened the score
of the Pomo d'Oro, laid it on the ledge of the box, and began
to hum the overture.

"Have you your text-book?" asked he of the empress. "I
ordered one for your especial use ; a synopsis of the opera, with
the principal airs only. I hope that you received it. This one
is too heavy for you."

The empress pointed to a purple-velvet book at her side, and
slightly bowed her head.

Leopold nodded, much pleased, and then gave his attention
to the stage.

The audience breathlessly awaited the opening. The leader
flourished his baton. The violins raised their bows, the haut-
boys and horns were clapped to the mouths of their respective
performers, bass-viols were seized, harps were clutched, and
drumsticks were raised in the air.

Nevertheless, not a sound was heard from the orchestra !

The emperor looked up from his score, and there, to be sure,
was the leader, his baton going from left to right—there were
the violins busy with their bows ; the wind instruments were
blowing for dear life ; the harpists were tugging at their
strings ; the drumsticks were going with all their might—and
not a sound ! The musicians might just as well have been so
many phantoms.

The emperor, in his bewilderment, turned to the empress,

who was so profoundly engaged with her score, that she murmured the words thereof half aloud.

"Do you hear the music?" asked her husband.

She started a little, and, blushing deeply, looked very much confused. "Yes, yes," replied she, absently; "it is very fine."

"I must then have lost my hearing," said Leopold; "for I hear nothing." And a second time he glanced at the orchestra, where the music was proceeding with the utmost energy.

"I cannot unriddle the mystery," thought the emperor, "for the empress hears the music and pronounces it fine. Prince Eugene," added he, aloud, "Do *you* hear any thing?"

"Not a sound, your majesty."

The emperor, looking very much relieved, beckoned to the lord-chamberlain, and sent him to inquire into the matter.

The audience, meanwhile, were quite as astounded as their sovereign. However, after a time they began to whisper and smile; and finally, as the drummer performed an extra flourish with his drumsticks, a voice was heard to cry out, "Bravo! bravo!"

This was the signal for a general burst of laughter, which the marshal of the household, though he shook his baton furiously, was impotent to quell. While the merriment was at its height the lord-chamberlain returned, and his countenance was expressive of extreme indignation.

Leopold, who for a moment had forgotten his Spanish formality, and had retired to the back of the box, advanced eagerly to meet him.

"What says the leader?" asked he, hastily.

"The leader, your majesty, is in despair, and is as much at a loss to account for the eccentricity of his orchestra as the audience themselves. He says that the last rehearsal was perfectly satisfactory."

"Go, then, to the musicians. See the first violin, Baron von Rietmann, and tell him that the overture must commence."

The lord-chamberlain went off on his mission, while Leopold, in undisguised impatience, stood at the door of his box waiting. The empress, apparently not cognizant of any thing around her, kept her eyes steadfastly riveted on her book. Prince Eugene had risen, and stood behind the emperor.

"What think you of this opéra comique?" asked Leopold.

"It is past my comprehension, your majesty. I cannot conceive how they presume to—"

The emperor suddenly interrupted him. "I begin to apprehend the difficulty," said he, laughing. "My musicians are all of high rank, and, as noblemen and artistes, they have a two-fold pride. They know perfectly well that I cannot do without them, and they occasionally take advantage of the fact to annoy me. They have some cause of complaint, I confess, and—Ah! What says Baron Rietmann?"

"My liege,"—replied the chamberlain, pale and breathless.

"Do not look so terrified," said Leopold; "what says the baron?"

"Your majesty, I am ashamed to be the bearer of his message," sighed the chamberlain. "He says their instruments will be dumb until the arrears due the orchestra for the last three months are paid!"

At this the emperor burst into an audible fit of laughter; then, remembering himself, he glanced anxiously at his impassible empress, to see if she had overheard him. No; she was perfectly unconscious of any thing but her book.

"Rietmann is a bold fellow," said Leopold at length, "but he is a great artiste, and I forgive his presumption. He is quite correct, however, as regards the orchestra. The imperial treasury has been drained for the army, and nothing remains for my musicians."

"Your majesty must order the army to refill the treasury at the expense of the enemy," said Eugene, with a smile. "It is said that the grand-vizier has immense treasures in Belgrade."

"Capture them all, field-marshal, for we are sorely in need of them. But let us try first to compromise with these musical rebels here.—Go, my lord-chamberlain, to Baron Rietmann, and say that the arrears due the orchestra shall be paid to-morrow, and thereunto I pledge my imperial word.—Now, Prince Eugene, let us resume our seats. I presume that my golden promises will restore the dumb to speech."

And so they did. Scarcely had the lord-chamberlain whispered the emperor's dulcet words into the baron's ear, before a signal passed between the musicians, and the overture began.*

The scenic effect of the opera was beautiful. The fountains were of real water, and graceful naiads disported within their marble basins ; and there was lightning and thunder ; there were transformations of men into animals, and finally, there was a golden apple which fructified into a bewitching fairy. She sang so delightfully that the emperor, in his enthusiasm, let fall his score, and applauded with all his might.

The fairy was encored, and, as she was about to repeat her aria, the emperor turned to the empress and requested leave to be allowed the use of her text-book for a few minutes. In his eagerness he did not remark her exceeding confusion ; but as, taking the book from her hands, he gave a glance at its pages, he uttered an exclamation of surprise.

And no wonder ! For, instead of an opera-score, he found a prayer-book !

"I hope your majesty will excuse me," stammered the empress. "In absence of mind, I brought my prayer-book instead of the score."

"And your majesty was praying for us," replied Leopold, half-vexed, half-amused. "But in our sinful way, we, too, are praying ; for surely music such as this is both prayer and praise ; and He who taught the nightingale her song, must surely rejoice to hear from human tongues the strains which He has revealed to inspired human genius !"

---

## CHAPTER III.

### THE RETIREMENT OF THE COMMANDER-IN-CHIEF.

THE imperial army, in five divisions, had marched to the Turkish frontier. They had traversed Transylvania, taking, on their way, the fortresses of Grosswardein, Sziget, and Ca-

* This scene is historical.—See " Life and Deeds of Leopold the Great."

nischa ; and, farther on their victorious march, Peterwardein and Illock.

The Turks had pursued their usual mode of vengeful retreat, tracing their march with fire and blood, and, wheresoever they were forced to surrender, leaving to the victors naught but the smouldering ruins of the strongholds from which they had been driven.

The imperialists were eager to invest Belgrade ; but their general-in-chief was ill ; and for several days they had watched in vain to see the hangings of his tent drawn aside, and hear the welcome order to march.

Finally a courier arrived from Vienna, and it was rumored that instructions had been received to advance. The troops were all the more hopeful that, immediately after the dismissal of the courier, the Duke of Lorraine had sent a messenger to Field-Marshal the Prince of Savoy, requesting his presence at headquarters.

The prince obeyed the summons without delay, and, entering the tent, found the adjutant and the duke's physician, sitting together, discoursing mournfully to each other of the illness of the beloved commander.

"I fear," said the surgeon, "that his highness is attacked with nervous fever ; his symptoms indicate it. He passed a restless night, and is suffering from intense headache. He must not be excited ; he can therefore see nobody."

"But he has sent for me," objected Eugene.

The surgeon shook his head. "Your highness has heard my opinion, and, if you approach him, it must be on your own responsibility."

"I am a soldier," replied Eugene, smiling, "and must obey orders. I have been sent for by the general, and must at least be announced."

At this moment the hangings of the inner tent were drawn aside, and Martin, the duke's old valet, came forward.

"Am I wanted ?" asked the surgeon.

"No, sir," replied Martin. "His excellency bade me see if the—Ah ! There he is ! Your highness, the duke begs your presence at once, and requests these gentlemen to leave the tent until his conference with your highness is at an end. He is very nervous, and the least rustling affects his head."

"Just as I feared," sighed the surgeon. "Martin, in one hour I shall return, to change the cold compress."

Eugene entered the sleeping apartment of the duke, and his pleasure at being admitted to see his commander, was changed into anxiety, when he beheld the pale, careworn face of the duke, and saw his head enveloped in bandages.

"Martin, have they left the tent?" inquired he, languidly.

"Yes, your highness; and I shall remain and keep watch that no one may enter."

"Do it, good Martin, for indeed I do not wish to be disturbed."

Martin disappeared, and the duke, removing his bandages, rose from the couch, and sank into an arm-chair.

"We are alone, and I may as well dispense with all this; it is needless."

"Then, your highness, God be thanked, is not sick?" exclaimed Eugene.

"Yes, I am sick," replied the duke, sadly, "but not in the sense in which my physician supposes. A malady of the mind is not to be cured by compresses."

"Have you bad news?" asked Eugene, with tender sympathy.

"Ah, yes," sighed the duke. "Bad news for him who, loving his fatherland more than self, is withheld from willing sacrifice by the unworthy strivings of ambition with duty. But of that anon. I have sent for you to confer of the affairs of the Austrian army; for I know that I can count upon your sincerity, and trust to your discretion."

"Your highness knows how unspeakable is the love I bear you; you well know that it is the aim of my life to imitate, though I may never hope to rival, your greatness."

"I thank you for your honest affection, dear Eugene," replied the duke, looking fondly into the speaking face of his youthful worshipper. "I thank God that you are here, to complete what I am forced to leave unfinished."

"Your highness would forsake Austria!" cried Eugene, alarmed.

"Ask rather, my son, whether Austria has not forsaken me," was the mournful reply. "It is of this that I would speak with you. You are the only officer in the army that does not bear me ill-will ; and to your sound and impartial judgment I am about to submit the question of my resignation."

"Resignation !"

"Yes ; but first let us talk of the campaign which is before us. You know that its main object is the capture of Belgrade."

Eugene bowed assent.

The duke laid his finger on a topographical chart that lay on a table close by. "Here is the key which opens the door to Turkey. Unless we obtain this key, our past victories are all without significance, and for years we have been pouring out Christian blood in vain."

"But we shall take Belgrade," cried Eugene. "We have sixty-six thousand well-armed men, all eager for the fray."

"And the Turks have one hundred and fifty thousand."

"But they are not a consolidated army, and we must prevent them from uniting their forces."

"True ; and for this end I have sent Prince Louis of Baden to Bosnia with six thousand men, that he may keep them busy at Gradiska. But the long march has exhausted his troops, and he has written to ask for re-enforcements. I must grant them ; and to-morrow I send him four thousand men. How many does that leave us ?"

"About fifty thousand, general."

"Suppose the enemy oppose fifty thousand to our ten, in Bosnia, there still remain to him twice as many as we can oppose to him."

"Yes ; but they are not commanded by a Duke of Lorraine," exclaimed Eugene, with enthusiasm. "A great general outweighs the disparity of numbers."

A sad smile played about the duke's features. "I am not indispensable to Austria's success," said he. "My men will fight as bravely under another commander as they have done under me ; but I do not say that I relinquish them to that other without a pang."

"Has such a question been raised ?" asked Eugene, sadly.

"You are too close an observer not to have suspected it. Do you remember my telling you that I would be obliged to succumb to the hatred of my enemies?"

"Yes, your highness."

"I did not overrate their influence. Even those who hate each other forget their hatred, to persecute me. And yet I have never done them the least wrong. There is Prince Louis of Baden—I have shown him every mark of distinction in my power, and yet he hates me."

"Too true," sighed Eugene. "And I confess that since I have known it, I love him less."

"You are wrong. He is merely an echo of his uncle, who has some right to hate me, for to me he owes the loss of his place as president of the war department. He was not fit for the office, and I convinced the emperor of his incapacity. This, I allow, to be a ground of dislike. But there is another distinguished officer, too, that hates me. What have I done to Max Emmanuel?"

"You have not only given him every opportunity to gain renown, but often have I admired your magnanimity when he has conspicuously paraded his ill-will."

"I thank you for that avowal, Eugene; for well I know how unwillingly you blame the elector. And he deserves your friendship, for he loves you sincerely. He has a noble heart, although I have not been able to win it; he is a fearless hero, and a great military chieftain. It is a pity that we were contemporaries. Were I to die to-day, no man would be louder in my praise than he; but I live, and he cannot brook a rival."

"Nay, your highness, he is not so presuming as to suppose that he is worthy to supplant you."

"He is about to supplant me, Eugene. I forgive him; for he is young, ambitious, and conscious of his own genius, which, while I enjoy the chief command, is hampered by a subordinate position. He is just as capable as myself; but I do not feel that he is my superior, and therefore it pains me to be obliged to resign my command to him."

"You do not think of such a thing! What would be the effect of your retirement upon the troops?"

"They would cry out, as the Frenchmen do, 'Le roi est mort,

vive le roi !'  I am not self-deceived as to the ephemeral nature
of military popularity.  It is always directed toward an object present and tangible, and speedily consoles itself for the
loss of one idol by replacing it with another.  But now, listen
to me.  A courier has just arrived from Vienna.  The presi
dent of the war department declares himself unable to put any
more troops in the field ; he has neither money nor munition
more.  The emperor writes under his own hand that he has
several times called upon the Elector of Bavaria to join his
command, and place himself at the head of his Bavarians."

"And he has refused !" cried Eugene.

"No.  He has accepted, but conditionally only.  Can you
guess his conditions ?"

Eugene turned pale and stammered : "Your highness, I
cannot—I hope that I do not—"

"Well, I see that you have guessed.  He demands the
chief command of the entire army."

"But if the emperor, as a matter of course, refuses this unreasonable and presumptuous demand ?"

"Then he withdraws his troops.  Peace—peace !  I know
that you love the elector : let us not discuss his acts, but consider their bearings upon the welfare of Austria.  For months
the emperor has been trying to arrange matters, but all in
vain.  Count Strattmann, the last envoy, who had a long personal interview with Max, says that he will not retreat from
his exactions.  He assumes the chief command, or his troops
are this day ordered to Bavaria."

"The emperor will never yield.  He ought not to yield."

"The decision of this difficulty has been left with me.  Max
is close at hand, in Essek, awaiting my determination.  And
now, Eugene, what answer shall I send him ?"

"There is but one.  The Austrian army cannot spare the
Duke of Lorraine."

"But still less can it spare the Bavarian troops.  How many
men did you say that we counted in all ?"

"Fifty thousand, your highness."

"And of these, how many are from Bavaria ?"

"Eight thousand infantry," said Eugene, with a sigh.

"And four thousand cavalry.  In all, twelve thousand ; and

let us do him justice : the troops of the elector are an admirably disciplined and efficient body of men. Now, if we lose this number, our forces are reduced to thirty-eight thousand. Can we confront a hundred thousand Turks with such a handful ?"

Eugene spoke not a word. His face was bent over the chart, but it was easy to see that he was powerfully agitated. After a long silence, the duke pointed with his finger to the spot on the map which the prince had apparently been examining.

"This tear is my answer," said he. "We cannot spare the Bavarians."

"Too true," murmured Eugene, "too true."

"Then the general must sacrifice his ambition to the national welfare ; he must retire from his command."

"Oh, no ! Not yet. Let *me* go to the elector. We are intimate friends, and I will persuade him to retract his unrighteous exactions."

"You will not succeed. Moreover, I would not accept the sacrifice. Could we have done without his troops, I would joyfully have retained my command ; but we have no right to ask of Max Emmanuel, who cannot be spared, to yield to me, who can be spared. I repeat it, then : I accept no sacrifice from the elector, nor will I be outdone by any man in magnanimity. The wound smarts, I am not ashamed to confess it ; but my duty is too clear before me for hesitation ; and in its fulfilment I have great consolation. To you, dear Eugene, this hour will afford a valuable lesson."

"Ay, indeed," replied Eugene. "It will teach me high resolve and holy resignation. If I ever should be tempted to envy the greatness of a rival, I will remember the day on which my friend's mad ambition deprived an army of its great and renowned commander."

"You are not apt to have rivals, Eugene, for you will surpass all your contemporaries in military genius. As for me, I retire, but I shall probably find other opportunities of using my sword for Austria. If—as God grant !—we should be victorious again this year, the King of France will show his teeth, and perhaps the laurels I have lost on the Save I may recover

on the Rhine.  And now, son of my heart, farewell !  God be
with you, now and evermore !"

He embraced Eugene with affection, and, returning to the
table, rang for Martin.  The old man answered the summons,
whereupon the duke began at once to give orders for his departure.

"Say to the surgeon that my head is worse, and that I
crave his attendance.  Then see the imperial couriers, and
send them hither."

"The surgeon is here," said that individual, coming forward.  "But what do I see ?  Your highness has risen ?"

"Yes, doctor, for I am too ill to remain in camp any longer,
and we must start to-day for Innspruck, where you will find
me an altered man, and the most submissive of patients."

"Thank Heaven !" replied the surgeon, "for your highness
needs rest."

"I will take as much as is needful," said the duke.  "And
now," added he to Eugene, "will you do me a last favor ?"

"What can I do for your highness ?"

"Seat yourself at my escritoire, and write what I shall dictate."

Eugene took up his pen and wrote :

"*Instructions for my officers :*

"My health being too weak to allow of my remaining any
longer in active service, I am compelled to resign the command of the imperial armies to another.  My successor, his
highness the Elector of Bavaria, is at Essek, and will be with
the army in a few hours.  Until his arrival, I appoint Field-
Marshal Count Caprara my representative.  God protect the
emperor and his brave army !"

"Thank you, prince," added the duke.  "Now be so good as
to reach me your pen, that I may sign my name."

When his signature had been appended to this short proc-
lamation, the duke, sighing heavily, said, "Eugene, do you
know what I have just signed ?  My death-warrant !"

"Oh, my general !"

"Hush !  Here come the couriers."

The duke bade them welcome, adding, "Did his imperial majesty charge you with any letter subject to my order?"

"Yes, your highness. We have one to the Elector of Bavaria, which, according as your highness commanded, was to be delivered to the elector, or returned to his majesty."

"Hasten to Essek, and deliver it to the elector.—And you, baron," said he, addressing the other courier, "return to Vienna, and say to the emperor that, as you were leaving the camp, I was departing for Innspruck; and, that you may be able to speak the truth literally, you shall see me go. If I mistake not, Martin is coming to say that my travelling-carriage awaits me."

"Yes, your highness, we wait for nothing but your commands."

"Then let us depart. Doctor, you will bear me company as far as Innspruck, will you not? Give me your arm, Prince Eugene."

With these words, he put his arm around the prince's neck, and, supporting himself on that slender frame, the duke, who was a man of tall stature, left his tent, and walked slowly to the carriage.

Behind him, in solemn silence, came the physician and the two couriers. At the door of the chariot he let his arm glide away from Eugene's neck, gave him one last fond look, one last friendly pressure, and then was gone!

The prince followed him with his eyes, until the chariot had disappeared from view. Then, sad and solitary, he returned to his own tent.

"And thus I am doomed to lose all that I love!" was his bitter reflection. "The Duke of Lorraine—Laura!—Oh, my Laura, how light to me were other losses, wert thou but here to smile me to forgetfulness!"

And, with his head bowed down between his hands, Eugene forgot all time, to dream of his love. For several hours he sat thus—his spirit all unconscious of the day, the hour, the place—when suddenly he was aroused from his reverie by a familiar voice.

"Eugene," cried Max Emmanuel, "where are you? The whole army is shouting me a welcome, and my friend has no greeting for me! He waits until I force myself into his tent to claim his congratulations!"

"I was not awrae that your highness had arrived. I—I—"

"And is this my welcome!" cried the elector, disappointed. "Are you displeased with me for superseding your master and hero?"

"Yes, proud, ambitious Max, I am grieved; for you are right, he was my master and my hero."

"Proud, ambitious, am I? Yes, I acknowledge it, and acknowledge it without shame. The day for hero-worship has passed away, and that of heroic action has dawned for both of us. Forgive me if I have usurped the place of your demi-god; and, in his stead, accept your friend and companion-in-arms. Think of the pledge we made before Buda, and refuse me not the advantage of your support. Without you, I cannot capture Belgrade; with you, I feel that I am invincible. Will you not sustain me?"

"I will, dear Max, and, sorely though you have grieved me, I bid you welcome."

---

# CHAPTER IV.

### THE FALL OF BELGRADE.

Two months had passed away since Max Emmanuel assumed command of the imperial army. During this time the besiegers had dug trenches and thrown up embankments; had demolished fortifications, and thrown bridges across the Save, with a view to attacking the Turks both in front and rear. The latter had been obliged to look on while all this had been progressing, impotent, in spite of their valor, to stop proceedings. Of course they had thrown bombs and sprung mines under the feet of their enemies, but nothing dismayed the Austrians, and finally they were prepared to assault the city.

The duke had twice called upon Achmed Pacha to surrender. The first summons, sent by a Turkish prisoner, was laconically answered by the gibbeting of the unfortunate messenger within sight of the Austrian camp. To the second, Achmed Pasha replied by a thousand greetings to the brave Duke of Lorraine ; adding that the siege would terminate as it pleased God.

"And we are here to carry out His will," observed the duke, laughing. "The miners must cease their work neither day nor night ; they may be relieved, but must not stop. Tell them that if they work me a passage to the fortress by the 16th of September, I will give to each one of them from this day forward a gratuity of two ducats a day."

On the 15th of September the Turkish commander was a third time summoned to surrender. This last summons was treated with contemptuous silence. It had been delivered to Achmed Pacha, while, accompanied by his Janizaries, he was on his way to the mosque. When he had finished its perusal, he addressed two of his officers that were walking on either side of him.

"What answer would you advise me to make to the Christian commander-in-chief ?" asked he of the first. "In the name of Allah and the Prophet, I call upon you to speak according to your convictions."

"The two Janizaries exchanged glances of uneasiness ; but Achmed Pacha's stern, handsome face was inscrutable in its composure.

"We are sorely pressed," replied the officer, mustering courage to speak. "Unless Allah work a miracle in our favor, we must succumb ; it seems to me, therefore, that a useless defence will but exasperate the enemy."

Achmed Pacha turned to the other. "And you ?" said he, mildly.

"Most illustrious leader of the armies of the faithful," said the second officer, quite reassured as to consequences, "if you insist upon hearing the candid opinion of the least of your servants, I must venture to say that our garrison is exhausted and spiritless. Allah has forsaken us, and it were better to stop further effusion of blood by an honorable surrender."

Achmed's eyes now darted fire, and the angry blood rushed to his pale brow. He signed to a third officer to advance.

"You have heard these traitors," said he in a loud, distinct voice. "Off with their cowardly heads, and bear them through the city on pikes, while a herald shall come after you, crying out to all who choose to profit by the warning, 'Such is the fate of the traitors that counsel submission to the Christian!'"

The officers were thrown to the ground, and, in a few moments, their headless trunks lay stretched on the earth, while their heads were borne aloft through the streets of Belgrade.

"Justice is satisfied," said Achmed Pacha, solemnly; "now let us betake ourselves to prayer. Let us thank Allah, who has turned away the perils by which we were threatened, and is preparing for the faithful a great triumph over their unbelieving foe. The grand-vizier is at hand with re-enforcements, and ere long the Christians will be put to ignominious flight."

This declaration of the general soon made its way to every house in the city, and caused universal joy. The soldiers crowded around their chief and swore to defend Belgrade until the grand-vizier arrived.

"And the Sultan will reward you all," said Achmed. "The booty will be left to the soldiery, and the commander of the faithful will pour out the treasures of his generosity from the horn of his beneficence. The defenders of Belgrade will be the nearest to his throne and his heart, and to your children shall descend the honors he will confer! Now come and let us praise Allah for the glory you are about to win'!"

And with this flourish of promises, Achmed Pacha entered the mosque. Once there, he fell upon his knees, and prayed after the following fashion:

"Allah, forgive me the lies which I have just uttered before the gates of Thy holy temple. Allah, make true my words: send hither, I implore Thee, the help I have ventured to promise to my unhappy garrison; for the two unfortunates whom I have just executed were the speakers of truth; if a miracle is not vouchsafed to us, we are lost."

In the Christian camp Max Emmanuel was making ready to storm the city; and his troops, with beating hearts, were eagerly awaiting the signal to begin the assault.

"You are really going to commence your attack?" asked the Duke of Mantua of the elector.

"Not only to commence, but to finish it," was the reply. "Before the sun sets, Belgrade must be ours."

"Very fine and sententious," replied the duke, with a shrug, "but, unfortunately, impracticable."

"Well—nobody can deny that your highness is a *far-seeing warrior*," said Max, laughing, and remembering Mohacz.* "You have an eagle-glance for a field of battle, and I propose to renew for you to-day the spectacle which last year you enjoyed looking on, while the rest of us were fighting."

"Think you that Belgrade is a bee-hive, and that the Turks are to be smoked therefrom, like a swarm of bees?"

"I think that Belgrade is peopled by Turks, not bees; and yet I shall smoke them out of it this very day. Will you bet me five thousand ducats that I do not?"

"Yes, I take the bet; and although five thousand ducats is a considerable sum, I sincerely hope I may lose it. I shall make haste to return to my villa, whence I can look on the assault, while I pray for the success of your arms."

"We shall have unspeakable comfort in the thought," cried the elector, galloping off to join his staff.

"A pious Moses that," said he to Prince Eugene. "I am really glad that he has again taken his leave. I lose all my pride of manhood when I look upon such a poltroon, and think that we are of the same species."

"He is a natural curiosity," said Eugene, "a mere exception to his race. I rather enjoy the contemplation of such a sporadic case of cowardice."

The attack was to begin at five points simultaneously.

---

* The Duke of Mantua had promised to come to the assistance of the emperor. In 1687 he visited the imperial camp, where he was received with every mark of consideration. On the morning of the battle of Mohacz, as the troops were about to make the attack, he came up to General Caprara, and in the coolest manner asked from what point he could best observe the fight. The general replied, " Your highness must join the staff of the commander-in-chief if you wish to look on without being mixed up in the general engagement."—" But the staff are in constant danger, as well as the rest," was his answer, " and I might be struck by a ball or a bomb-shell."—" Oh!" cried Caprara, " you wish to look on without endangering your life! Then go up to the top of yonder mountain." The duke went, and remained there until the battle was ended.

24

When the fifth courier had reported his division to be in readiness, the elector, giving orders to his staff which dispersed them for a while, turned to Eugene and began in a low voice :

"Eugene, I feel like a lover who has just become a husband. My heart beats with anticipation of bliss, and is all aflame with desire."

"I should think you had clasped Bellona to your heart so often, that you would have learned to accept her favors without excitement or anxiety," returned Eugene, playfully.

Max glanced at the calm and self-possessed prince, and replied : "You shall teach me self-control, dear Eugene, for you have wonderful mastery over your emotions.  Did I not know what a warm heart is throbbing under that composed demeanor, I should imagine Prince Eugene to be a mere compound of wisdom and self-possession ; and yet I know that, at this very moment, that heart is burning with love for one who, in the hour of battle, is dearer to him than ever.  Eugene, this is a moment of solemnity enough for me to ask you whether Laura lives ? "

"I do not know," murmured he, nervously grasping his reins, and becoming very pale.  "I have no news, and yet, if she were dead, my heart would tell me so ; I believe, then, that she is alive, and, should I fall to-day, there hangs a medallion around my neck (her dear portrait), which must be sent to her.  Say that I died loving her beyond all power of speech to convey ; that for her love, I bless and thank her, trusting that she will forgive me for having been the cause of all her misfortunes.  I am grateful to you, Max, for having spoken of her to me.  If I die, this is my last will."

"Enviable saint, that has but one legacy and one love !  I shall take very good care not to entertain you with the history, in many volumes, of all *my* various loves.  But the last of them you can greet for me, should I fall to-day ; and you will do it cordially, for she is Laura's sister-in-law.  Tell my beautiful Lucretia that I have been happy in her love ; and, although I would not have her mourn for me, I hope she will sometimes waft me a thought or a gentle sigh.  And now—to arms, and to victory! You promise to fight at my side, do you not?"

"Yes, Max—nothing but death shall part us, until Belgrade is ours."

"Give me your left hand, while, with the right, I give the signal for the attack."

So saying, the elector held aloft a silken flag, which fluttered for a moment, and then boldly caught the breeze.—There was a short silence; then every Christian gun proclaimed defiance to the Turk.

Early in the action, General Scarffenberg was mortally wounded; but he had carried his point of attack, and with his dying eyes he saw the Austrians mount the breach, and drive away the enemy at the point of the bayonet. The bastion once reached, the men, almost reeling with fatigue, paused for a moment to regain breath. The enemy taking advantage of the halt, returned and poured out such numbers of fresh assailants that the Christians from sheer exhaustion began to falter, and were about to be driven back, when Prince Eugene, seeing their danger, sprang forward to General Sereni, and called for re-enforcements.

Placing himself at their head, the bastion was recaptured, and the Austrians rushed eagerly forward to follow up their success.

But just beyond the breach lay a deep, wide trench, behind which the enemy had fortified themselves, and were now pouring out a murderous fire.

"The line of these breastworks must be broken," said the elector.

But the question was—how were they to be broken? Not a path was to be seen conducting thither; and the imperialists, hurried forward by the eager troops behind, who were unaware of the impediment in front, seemed to have no alternative but that of inevitable death or retreat.

Retreat! odious word, which the officers could not bring their lips to pronounce. And yet there was no possibility of advancing; and to remain stationary was to offer themselves for massacre. The soldiers were so closely packed together that they could make no use of their weapons, while the Turks were shooting them down like so many birds in a battue. The elector stood by the side of the breach, and called a hasty council of his officers.

"We have done enough for to-day," said General Sereni. "We can intrench ourselves behind the breach, and renew the attack to-morrow."

"The men are exhausted," urged another. "We will surely capture the fortress to-morrow."

The elector had listened in perfect silence to the various changes rung on the same idea ; but he was not altogether convinced. He now turned to Eugene, who spoke not a word, but gazed sharply from the trench to the serried ranks of Turks on the opposite side. He raised his eyes with a mournful, questioning look, to the face of the perplexed commander. Their glances met, and a smile of perfect understanding passed between them.

The elector hurried forward to the brink of the trench ; behind him came Eugene. Both drew their swords, and, brandishing them above their heads, Max Emmanuel called out in clear, distinct, and ringing tones :

"Comrades, look, and follow me !"

Then the two heroes sprang into the trench, and the troops rushed forward to follow them. Many dislocated their limbs, as they leaped down ; but such as escaped without broken bones went onward, fighting like tigers.

Suddenly an arrow pierced the cheek of the elector, and his face was covered with blood.

"You are wounded, dear Max !" cried Eugene, affrighted.

The elector laughed, and, drawing out the arrow, replied, "Not at all ; this is Bellona's first kiss."

And, like a furious lion, he dashed ahead, and avenged the kiss by many a stout blow of his sword.

The Janizaries were driven from their breastworks, but, ere they went, one of them, astonished at the prowess of Eugene, whom he took to be a lad, was determined to make short work of the insolent boy that was slaying right and left like another David.

He raised his brawny arm, and smiled contemptuously upon so puny an adversary. But when he would have dealt his blow, it was parried by a thrust of such power that he reeled and almost lost his balance. In his fury he raised his cimeter and cleft the helmet of the prince in twain.

For a moment Eugene was dizzy, though uninjured ; but, quickly recovering his senses, he made a lunge at the Janizary and ran him through the body. Without waiting to see him die, the prince drew out his sabre and darted onward. The imperialists shouted and cheered him as he went, but the Turks, too, had witnessed the deed, and more than one musket was vengefully aimed at the slayer of the Paynim Goliath. One—one, alas ! has reached the mark. It has pierced his foot, and he is no longer in a condition to make another step. Heaven be praised that the Turks have taken flight, and that the Christians have possessed themselves of the trench ! Eugene has the comfort of knowing that he will not be a captive, and this assurance gives him strength to drag himself within speaking distance of a group of soldiers.

" Bear me away, if you please," said he ; " I cannot walk."

Two of them hastened to his relief, and bore him tenderly away to the spot where a field-surgeon was attending to the wounded.

The town and citadel have fallen ; nothing now remains to the Turks but the castle, from the windows of which a white flag is proclaiming their defeat and surrender. But the Christians do not see it ; and the elector, followed by his victorious troops, rushes, sword in hand, to the prison wherein the Christian prisoners are confined. The dungeons were crowded with fugitive Turks, who had betaken themselves thither as the safest place to be found. They cried for mercy, and it was granted them. Their lives were spared, but they were prisoners. Achmed Pacha was among them. He came forward and bent the knee before his conqueror.

"Allah has willed it," said he, "and may his name be praised ! General, thou hast prevailed, and I am thy prisoner. I ask but one favor of thee. Give me no Greek or Rascian for my master ; let me serve a German."

The elector smilingly raised him, and explained that Christians did not enslave their prisoners of war. "You have defended yourself heroically," added he, " and we honor a brave enemy. The Emperor of Germany alone is the arbiter of your fate."

"Allah will decide what that fate is to be," was the pious response of the Mussulman.

The Elector of Bavaria has won his wager ; but what cares a victorious hero for ducats or dastards like the Duke of Mantua?

"Where is Eugene?" was his first inquiry. And, not seeing him among his followers, he darted out of the castle in search of his friend.

The question passed from man to man, until one was found at last to answer it. The prince was in the hands of the imperial surgeons, who were vainly endeavoring to extract the ball.

The elector dragged one of them aside. "Is he dangerously wounded?" asked he, anxiously.

"He may not die of the wound," was the surgeon's reply ; "but it will be tedious and very painful."

"He will live !" cried Max, wiping away a tear, and hastening to the litter whereon Eugene was lying.

He bent over him, and gently touched his forehead.

Eugene raised his large, melancholy eyes, and looking upon the beaming face that encountered his, he pointed to the wound, around which the blood had already coagulated, and said :

"Happy Max, whom Bellona has kissed ! Me she has trodden under foot."

---

## CHAPTER V.

### THE MARCHIONESS.

"Strozzi, take my advice, and give up this miserable life. Of all earthly bores, solitude is the greatest."

"No, Barbesieur, in solitude I find my only comfort," returned Strozzi, with a weary sigh. "Here, at least, Laura is indubitably mine ; here she is Marchioness de Strozzi."

"She is Marchioness de Strozzi throughout the entire world,

as I am ready to prove, who saw your hands joined together, and heard your reciprocrated vows in Paris."

"Yes, yes ; but you know that she denies the marriage, and persists that she is the wife of Eugene of Savoy."

"She is a sentimental fool," cried Barbesieur, with a coarse laugh. "And devil take me but I would cure her of her folly were she my wife ! If she will not love you, man, why do you not force her to fear you ?"

"Fear me ! Her soul knows not fear. Have I not tried to intimidate her over and over again ? and every threat I hurl, she thrusts back into my teeth, as though her spirit were defended from harm by some invisible, enchanted armor."

"And you love her ! You, the master and jailer, creep about, with sallow cheek and sunken eye, while your prisoner is the very impersonation of hopeful happiness. At every unexpected step she listens with a smile ; if a cloud stray across the window, she mistakes it for the shadow of deliverance ! Verily, my excellent father, who sent me hither to find out whether you were slowly killing his daughter by your cruelty, will scarcely believe me when I tell him what a beneficial effect has been produced upon her by your wholesome restraint. You must know that, although not remarkable for his social virtues, Monsieur Louvois has intervals of puling sensibility, at which times he reproaches himself with the part he took in the comedy of your marriage, and, since Prince Eugene has grown famous, almost repents that he did not accept that fascinating individual for his son-in-law. He is beginning to be absolutely afraid of the little ex-abbé."

"And I too fear him," said Strozzi, gnashing his teeth. "He bears a charmed life, or he would not see the light of heaven to-day. I thought I had him beyond all power of rescue, once in Venice. So sure was I that he must die, that I hastened to Laura and announced his demise. That night I took her away, hoping by change of scene to induce forgetfulness, where hope, of course, was extinct. One day, in Milan, a group of men were talking of some recent victory of the imperialists, and to my amazement I heard the name of the Prince of Savoy among those who had most distinguished themselves,"

"Was Laura with you ?" asked Barbesieur.

"Alas, she was ! And her beautiful face was transfigured with joy. I felt as if I could have swooned with jealousy. I hurried her home, and in half an hour she was on the road to this castle. Here I knew that no news could ever reach her of the world or its heroes ; here I could leave her, and fear not to absent myself, for this is a lonely forest, no strangers ever wander hither, and I have good, watchful dragons to guard my treasure. I posted then, with all speed, to Venice, entered the palace at night, and made my way to the secret prison of which you have heard, to see for myself if it could possibly be true that Eugene of Savoy was living."

"Did you find any one ?"

"Of course, some man was bound to be there : else he could not have escaped. Conceive my fury when I recognized my own hired bravo, Antonio, who must have betrayed me, and remained instead of the prince. I opened a niche in the wall, kicked his rotten carcass into the lagoon, and, more wretched than ever, returned to this hell wherein I languish, while paradise is within sight."

"How long do you intend to make a voluntary Tantalus of yourself."

"I shall stay until she forgets Prince Eugene, and loves me."

"I wish you joy ; meanwhile I shall await your bulletins at my delightful residence—your generous gift. I must remain until the arrival of my father's couriers ; and, having seen them off with the glad tidings of my fair sister's flourishing condition, I will be off for Bonaletta. I wonder which of us two she hates the more ? Come—we may as well go at once to her rooms, that my visit may be over."

So saying, Barbesieur put his arm within that of the marquis, but the latter, drawing back, pointed to the clock on the mantel.

"It is too early : she never permits me to come before eleven."

"And you—her husband, suffer such impertinent dictation from your vassal—your wife !"

"I dare not thwart her by any intrusion of myself except

at her will. If I were to lay my hand on her, she would kill herself, like another Lucretia, to save her honor. And if I contradict her by coming before my time, she will start and grow pale, perhaps faint, and be sick ; and oh, Barbesieur ! the idea of losing her, makes me frantic."

"As you please," returned Barbesieur, with a shrug and a loud laugh. "But as I am not pining for a sight of her beauty, I shall go rabbit-hunting, while you stay at home and look wistfully at what you dare not take."

So saying, Barbesieur shouldered his gun, whistled to his dogs, and went off to the chase ; while Strozzi, his eyes on the dial of the clock, awaited the hour for visiting his inapproachable wife.

The marchioness was in an apartment situated in the centre of the wing which her affectionate husband had fitted up for her incarceration. No one that entered this magnificent suite would ever have imagined that it was a prison. The walls were covered with hangings of satin and gold ; the floors were hidden by Turkey carpets as soft as turf ; the windows were festooned with curtains of velvet and lace ; and their recesses filled with tall Venetian mirrors. Paintings of value adorned the walls, and frescoes ornamented the ceilings ; while every object of *vertu* that was known to the age, lay in elegant profusion about this luxurious abode.

And yet it was veritably a prison, wherein the Marchioness de Strozzi was confined "because of her hopeless lunacy," and the windows thereof were guarded by a strong trellis-work of iron, which might clearly be seen through their panes, while without, in an anteroom, two she-dragons kept watch over the doors which led from the prison to the world without.

The parlor of Laura's habitation opened into a boudoir which led to the bedroom. This apartment was as sumptuously fitted up as the others, but its windows were similarly guarded. Opposite, and beyond the parlor, was a small room occupied by the duennas, so that the prisoner could not leave her apartments without encountering one or both of them.

Tonietta, the second lady's maid, was busy with her needle

when the marquis entered, and began his usual routine of in quiries.

"How is the marchioness to-day? Is she quiet and well-disposed? Has she breakfasted? Does her health seem good?" and so on.

The woman's lip curled, but she controlled herself and made reply. "Her ladyship is as usual. She has played on the harp, sung, and taken her chocolate. But she was unusually cheerful while we were occupied with her toilet, and I do not like this humor."

"Why, why?" asked Strozzi.

"Because it is a very sudden change—too sudden to portend good. She has always been reserved, and showed no disposition to be friendly. All of a sudden, she becomes talkative and gay."

"So much the better. That proves that she is becoming accustomed to her lot."

"It might prove just the contrary," returned the duenna, with a crafty glance at her master. "It might be intended to blind us, or it might prove that she has hopes of escaping."

"Great God!" shrieked Strozzi, "you terrify me. What hope can she possibly indulge of escape?"

"I do not know, but I like not her cheerfulness, nevertheless. However, be under no apprehension, my lord; we keep strict watch, and there is no mode of egress save through one of these two doors. I am not afraid during the day—but at night! Who knows? Your lordship was wrong to allow her to sleep in a room without us, and to permit her to fasten her door against us."

"She would have it so," sighed Strozzi; "but what does it signify? Had she wings, she could not fly out of her prison."

And, with these words, he passed into the parlor.

Laura sat by a window before her easel, and was so absorbed with her work that she was, or affected to be, unconscious of her husband's entrance. Not daring to advance, he stood in the doorway, devouring her with his eyes, almost mad with desire to clasp her to his heart. She, on her side, sat painting, and humming a song, her blue-satin dress defining the graceful contour of her bust and slender waist, then swelling out beneath into rich folds that shimmered like silver under the sunbeams that fell upon them from the window above. The long lace sleeves drooped in gossamer waves over the dress, leaving bare her round, fair arms, firm and white as those of the Venus of Milo. Her hair was gathered into a Grecian knot behind, and her delicate profile, illumined by the morning sun, was so marvellous in its beauty, that Strozzi's eyes filled with tears as he gazed, and his sallow, sunken cheeks glowed with mingled love and hate.

He made a few steps forward, and encountered the cold glance of her splendid eyes, and saw the slight bend of her haughty head, as she became aware of his presence.

" What brings you hither, sir ? " said she. " But I need not ask. You have come to satisfy yourself by ocular demonstration that your prisoner has not flown up the chimney. You need not trouble yourself to remain—I am here."

" Prisoner, say you, cruel Laura ! 'Tis I that am a prisoner ; prisoned by your coldness, and yet I love you—I love you to madness ! "

" You are quite right thus to define your love ; and perchance it may lead you to that lunacy which is your lying pretext for incarcerating me alive in this lonely castle."

" Oh, I fear it, I fear it ! " cried he, despairingly, " for day by day my reason fails me. Have mercy, have mercy ! "

" Mercy ! You who would have taken the life of the man I love. You are an assassin, whose just portion would be the scaffold. But enough—why renew each day the mournful duo of your love and my contempt ? Let me be silent and wait."

" Wait ! Oh, then, there is hope for me, and you bid me not despair ! "

" You !—I spoke of myself ; for, as there is a just God above us, I believe that He will open the doors of my prison, and send His angel to deliver me."

" Then you are entirely without sympathy."

" Entirely,—for the man that obtained possession of my person by a fraud, and who, for five long, bitter years, has laden me with the chains of this lie which he calls our marriage."

" I know that you have suffered, and I have wept for your sufferings, while I have been impotent to lessen them. Speak but the word—say that you are that which, by the laws of God and man, you have been for these five long years, and I open your doors and restore you to freedom. I ask you not to love me; but I implore you to accept my love, and acknowledge yourself to be my wife; for well I know that, the acknowledgment once made, you are too honorable, too virtuous, to sully the name you are willing to bear. Oh, Laura, my peerless Laura! I will make amends for all that I have inflicted upon you through the madness of my love. I have wealth unbounded—a noble name, high station: all shall be yours. See—I am at your feet. Call me your husband, and henceforth I live to be your willing slave!"

"Never!" exclaimed she, starting from her seat, and receding in horror from his touch. "My body you hold in bondage, but my spirit is free; and it is away from this gloomy prison, far away, mingling with that of my spouse before Heaven, my Eugene, my lord and husband."

"Silence!" shrieked Strozzi, starting to his feet. "Silence! or you will drive me mad! And be assured that as long as you defy me, just so long will I hold you in bondage."

"You may not live forever, marquis, for the Strozzis, like other men, are mortal; and death, perchance, may liberate me, without your permission. But live or die, as you choose; I shall find means to rejoin Eugene, and this conviction gives me strength to endure your persecutions."

"The Marchioness Bonaletta is too proud and chaste to be the mistress of any man," returned Strozzi, with some return of courtesy.

"What do you know of me?—I counsel you not to build your hopes upon any estimate you may have formed of my notions of honor, for they will sorely deceive you, if you do."

Before the marquis had time to reply to these defiant words, the door opened, and Barbesieur, holding a letter in his hand, entered the room.

Laura frowned, and asked Strozzi by what right her room was thus invaded by a stranger. "I do not desire his presence," she said. "Be so good as to conduct him to your own apartments."

"I am not so easily conducted, most amiable sister," returned Barbesieur. "I have come to deliver a message from your father, after which I shall take my leave without the least regret. *We* are about to go to war with Germany, and *I* am about to receive a general's commission in the French army, so that I have no time to lose in forcing my company upon you."

"You a general's commission! You that were once publicly disgraced by—"

"Your marriage has long ago consoled me for that trifling mishap," interrupted Barbesieur, "and in Paris nobody has ever presumed to think less of me on account of it. I think that, in every way, the sufferer therefrom was the valiant Eugene. And, by-the-by, that leads directly to the business that brought me hither. That Emperor of Austria has been entirely too lucky in war to please the King of France; and Max Emmanuel, whom we had expected to win over to our side, is the commander-in-chief of the imperial armies. Max—your *quasi* brother-in-law, Strozzi; for doubtless you are aware that Lucretia, the left-handed electress, is the first person in importance at the Bavarian court."

"May she be damned for it!" muttered Strozzi, between his teeth.

"Not on her head as much as on yours rests the shame of Lucretia's act," said Laura, reproachfully.

"Ah!" cried Strozzi, a gleam of joy darting athwart his meagre face, "you acknowledge, then, that a woman is disgraced who loves a man whom she cannot marry!"

"A truce to this nonsense, my turtle-doves," interposed Barbesieur. "I bring you tidings which henceforth render such discussions superfluous. Listen to me, both of you. My father has sent me a bit of news which, coming direct from the Marquis de Villars—that is, from Munich—is positive and authentic. Here it is."

Laura turned away her head that they might not see her emotion, while Strozzi besought Barbesieur not to be so long-winded.

"Well, I will gratify you both. Belgrade is taken; Prince Eugene, as usual, was foremost in the fight; but unhappily for some people, and happily for others—"

Here Barbesieur paused to enjoy the agony of his sister's suspense. Her face he could not see, but her trembling figure gave evidence of the poignancy of her anguish.

"Well—" said Strozzi, "what befell him?"

"Something not at all uncommon—he was killed."

Laura turned quickly around and caught the diabolical glance of Barbesieur's eyes. "I—I do not believe it," murmured she.

"Did you say that you had the original letter from the Marquis?" asked Strozzi, eagerly.

"Yes, here it is; the marchioness can see for herself."

Laura took the paper and glanced hurriedly over its contents. She raised her eyes to heaven in thanksgiving. "He is not dead," said she, almost inaudibly.

"Then you have read very carelessly," returned Barbesieur. "The letter says, 'so dangerously wounded that he was transported in a dying condition to Vienna.'"

"Had he been dying, he would not have been transported to Vienna," exclaimed Laura, with a smile of returning hope. 'No, no! Had Eugene been dead, the air I breathe, the clouds that I watch as they pass by yonder grated windows—my heart, whose beatings are responsive to his—every thing in nature would have revealed the terrible truth. Eugene lives—and lives to fulfil his great and glorious destiny. Pardon me, O Lord, that, for a moment, my faith was weak!"

She looked so transcendently lovely as she spoke, that Strozzi's heart sank within him. He turned his face away, and groaned.

"My charming sister is easily consoled, you perceive," said Barbesieur to Strozzi. "And now that, according to her own interpretation of the marriage ceremony, she is widowed, I hope to hear before long that you have effectually dried up her tears. Come—let us leave this hopeful widow to herself."

"I come," replied Strozzi, "for you must take some refreshment before you go. Until the hour of dinner I take my leave, marchioness."

"Marquis," said Laura, following him to the door.

Strozzi dropped Barbesieur's arm, and returned to her at once.

"You have something to command?" said he, humbly.

"I do not wish to dine to-day," said she. "It will be useless, then, for you to return."

"I cannot deny myself that pleasure," was the reply.

Laura constrained herself to soften her tone, and to implore. "Only this one day," said she, in trembling tones. "I need repose—quiet—"

"To weep out the first pangs of widowhood," interrupted Barbesieur, with one of his coarse laughs. "Come, Strozzi—let her cry it out to-day, she will be all the more smiling for it to-morrow."

"Then as you please," said Strozzi, bowing respectfully. "I will not return until to-morrow before noon."

"Tell my turnkeys that they need not disturb me," said Laura. "Let me be veritably and entirely alone."

"You cannot dispense with their help," objected the marquis.

"I can and will dispense with their presence," returned Laura. "And may I ask of you, as a guaranty that I shall not be disturbed, to leave the keys inside? The bolts without are secure, and the women can watch by the doors to see that I do not attempt to escape."

"Your will shall be my law, to-day," said Strozzi, "for I am but its slave. When will you reward my love—when, Laura?"

"Leave me, I implore you," was the faltering reply of his stricken wife; "leave me for this one day!"

"I will," cried Strozzi, casting passionate glances at her, "but to-morrow?"

"To-morrow," replied Laura, solemnly, "to-morrow is in the hands of God!"

"There, now," exclaimed Barbesieur, "she is making promises already. Come along—I am really hungry."

The voice of Strozzi was heard in the anteroom, and in a few moments Carlotta removed the key to the inside. With one bound Laura reached the door, and fastened it within. Then crossing the parlor, she locked herself within her boudoir, and, falling on her knees, besought the blessing of God upon her flight—for she was resolved to fly that very night.

## CHAPTER VI.

### THE FLIGHT.

FOR one year—from the day of her meeting with Eugene—Laura had been revolving in her mind the possibility of escape, and again and again had she been compelled to acknowledge that escape was impossible. At night, lest sleep should overpower their senses, her untiring spies had barred the doors that led from the anteroom with their beds. Sometimes Laura had proposed to bribe them; but in the event of success with the women, a watchman kept guard at the head of the staircase; and at the entrance of the castle was stationed a porter, whom no one could pass without the watchword. If all these obstacles had been overcome, and the prisoner had found egress to the park, she was met by four watchmen, whom neither promises nor bribery had power to conciliate. These were four bloodhounds who were loosed at night by the marquis's own hands, and on whose fidelity he knew that he might count.

Flight through the doors was out of the question; flight from the windows, had they been free, was equally so; for whoever had dared their dangerous descent, would have been devoured the very moment he touched the ground below.

Plan after plan was made and rejected, and yet she must—she would escape.

In her parlor was one of those large chimneys found in old castles, chimneys that were intended to consume an entire load of wood at once. On one occasion, Strozzi being present at the time, a chimney-sweep went up its grimy walls, to cleanse them from the accumulated soot of the winter. Strozzi, forgetting that the sweep had to return, began to make declarations to Laura, and finally became so lovelorn as to throw himself at her feet. He was on his knees, whining for forgiveness, when the little sweep, like a *deus ex machina*, alighted suddenly in the middle of the hearth, and surprised him in his abject and ridiculous posture.

Laura laughed outright; but the marquis, of course, did

not share her mirth. He turned furiously upon the sweep, threatening to take his life for his impertinent intrusion. The poor fellow pleaded the impossibility of getting out by any other means, when the marquis, stamping his foot with rage, bade him begone up the chimney, and ordered him to find his way over the castle-roof to another chimney at the farthest extremity of the building, which led into an ancient buttery, and thence to the park.

From that day, Laura had revolved in her mind the feasibility of escape through the chimney. If a boy like that had so often gone up and down in safety, why not she, when urged by the double incentive of liberating herself from Strozzi, and making her way to Eugene? The more she pondered the scheme, the easier it seemed of execution, and she began seriously to resolve means for carrying it out.

Accident soon befriended her. One day, in stepping back from a window, whence she had been watching the flight of a flock of birds, her foot became entangled in the carpet, and she fell. This carpet did not cover the entire room. Within a foot of the walls it was fastened by little brass rings, to nails of the same metal, which caught and confined it to the floor.

Laura naturally looked to see the cause of her fall, and, while examining the loosened nails, she perceived that the carpet—a magnificent product of the looms of Turkey—was lined underneath with a species of black cotton cloth, very similar to that of which the sweep's garments were made. When she saw this, her heart beat so wildly that she felt as if it were about to burst. Here was the material of which her dress should be made! Providence had sent it to her, and the enthusiastic girl knelt down and thanked God for His goodness.

She now began to loosen it, and night after night, when her door was locked inside, she worked as prisoners alone are gifted to work, until she had stripped off enough cloth for her purpose. She gave out that, to beguile her solitude, she was desirous of embroidering an altar-cloth of black velvet, and Carlotta was dispatched to the nearest town, to procure materials for the work.

Carlotta was absent three days, whence Laura concluded

25

that the "nearest town" was at some considerable distance
from the castle, of whose situation the marquis had taken
good care that she should remain ignorant. But another accident revealed to her the name of the town. She found it
in a small paper which enveloped some thread, and contained
the name of the merchant from whom it had been purchased,
with the place of his residence in a street which Laura knew
to be the great thoroughfare of Turin. She was then not two
days' journey from Turin, and no longer on Venetian soil.

Once in Turin, she was safe from pursuit, for her estates
lay in Savoy, and the duke was obliged to give her protection.
She was his subject, and he could not refuse it.

And now began that change of manner and of life which
had awakened the suspicions of the two duennas. For several
hours of the day she worked at her altar-cloth ; but when
night set in, and her doors were locked, the needles, thread,
and scissors, disappeared from the frame in the parlor, and
the black cloth was gradually converted into a jacket and
pantaloons like that of the sweep. This accomplished, Laura
set about devising a cord and weight, by which she might descend into the buttery. She had so closely observed the little
lad she was resolved to emulate, that she had succeeded in
fashioning out of the heavy bindings of some old hangings,
that lay in a sort of rubbish closet, a stout rope, of strength
sufficient to bear her weight.

It was at this juncture of her preparations, that Barbesieur
broke in upon her happy solitude, with his terrible tidings of
Eugene's misfortune. She was ready to risk her life to meet
him, and perchance he was mortally wounded, and she might
never see him more ! A woman less resolute might have
faltered in her purpose ; but to Laura the news of her lover's
danger had imparted new strength, and she would liberate
herself that very night, or perish in the attempt.

She had no money ; the marquis had considered it prudent
to relieve her of the custody of her wealth, and to put it out
of her power to bribe his spies. But she had jewels, and such
of these as could be concealed about her person she took.

During the day she had played upon her harp, and improvised melodies so ravishing, that Strozzi had been on his knees

outside, listening and weeping by turns. Finally, when she had ceased singing, he knocked, and besought her to let him look for one moment upon her face, to let him imprint one kiss upon her hand.

Laura thought it prudent to comply, so she opened the door and allowed him, for the first time in his life, to hold her hand and press it to his lips, and to thank her for the heavenly music. Not to overdo the matter, she allowed him to remain but a few moments ; and the marquis retired, perfectly convinced that all was right, and that he had a hope of winning that obdurate heart at last.

Night was at hand ! The skies were overclouded, with here and there a star struggling through the darkness. Gradually the castle grew silent, the closing of doors and drawing of bolts ceased at last, and all was still.

All, except those two duennas ; and Laura saw that if she ever was to lull them to bed, she must call them in to undress her. So opening the door, she beckoned to Carlotta, who, to her great joy, appeared in a dressing-gown. Finally, the comedy being over, and the duennas completely hoodwinked, Laura locked her doors a second time, and, retreating to her bedroom, raised the carpet and drew forth her black disguise. She tore off her white night-gown, clasped a pearl necklace around her neck, and several diamond bracelets on her arms, and then arrayed herself in the costume of the chimney-sweeper. She took up her rope, and, fastening a small iron casket to the end, slung it over her shoulder, and began her dark, perilous ascent. Away ! away ! Over the castle-roof to liberty and love !—

With her delicate little hands she seized a hook that projected from the chimney. She reached a second and supported her foot on the first ; a third, a fourth ; and now the opening grew narrow and more narrow, and she struggled along through the black, suffocating hole, until her breath had almost failed her, and she had nigh been choked to death ! Poor girl ! She could not reach her eyes to clear them of the soot that was blinding and maddening her with pain, and she began to tremble lest she should lose her senses. But she prayed to God to deliver her, and made one supreme effort to free herself. She felt the air from above ; the hole began to widen, and she could lay her head backward and breathe. She raised her smarting eyes and saw a light—a star ! A greeting from heaven !

But she felt that at such a moment she must not indulge in sensibility. The extremity in which she found herself required resolution, daring, and coolness. She called up all her courage, and struggled on. At last—at last, her hands rested on the top of the chimney : she drew herself upward, and with one bound sprang upon the roof.

For a moment or two she leaned her weary arms upon the edge of the chimney ; then, placing her ear at the opening, she listened to hear if there was any stir below. No—all was silent ; not a sound broke the profound stillness of the night. She must be going then—over the castle-roof to liberty and love !

She groped, with hands outstretched, for some support, but found nothing. Nevertheless she must tread the dark and mysterious way that was to lead her to freedom, and she made a few steps forward. Suddenly she grew faint and dizzy, and a shudder ran through her limbs ; she tried to rally her strength and put out her foot. It encountered some obstacle which sent her reeling backward ;· and, murmuring a prayer to Heaven, she swooned and fell. When she recovered her senses, she was lying, she knew not where, perhaps she had fallen from the battlements to the ground, there to be devoured by the savage bloodhounds, or to become again and forever the prisoner of the abhorred marquis. But she felt no pain, and, stretching out her hand to make an effort to rise, she perceived that she was on a smooth, hard surface, and lay against the battlements, or rather against a heavy stone balustrade that surrounded the castle-roof. With this balustrade to grasp, she could arrive at the chimney she was seeking ; all she had to do, was to use it as a guide to the remote wing she was trying to reach. If there had been but a few friendly stars to smile upon her perilous pilgrimage ! But the night was fearfully dark ; so dark that she had no reliance beyond her sense of touch. This alone admonished her of her approach to the angle where she was to turn into the wing. Now and then she paused and looked back to see if there was light or sign of life along that broad castle-front. But all was safe, and she went slowly on. She felt hopeful now, and strengthened, for the wing was quite remote from the inhabited parts of the castle ; its windows opened low ; and a pathway, now overgrown with weeds, led from one of these windows to a gate which, as the marquis had never dreamed of danger in that quarter, was always left unlocked for the accommodation of the foresters and wood-cutters. Oh, that she were but there ! On ! on ! she must hasten, or she might be discovered ! She was about to press forward, when, to her unspeakable horror, she perceived that her hand rested no longer on the balustrade. She had passed the chimney and stood upon the unprotected battlements ! Shuddering, she drew back—her feet almost giving way under her trembling limbs ; but in the might and vigor of her strong, firm will, she drew herself up and retreated. The roof was not steep—it had merely descent enough to carry off the rain ; but the tiles were so smooth that more than once she slipped back, and she was becoming timorous and weak. While she was resting for a moment from her fatigue, however, she saw something looming up above the roof the sight whereof restored her courage and her strength. It was the long-sought chimney.

She darted toward it, and in a few moments had made fast her rope, and dropped it within. She caught it in her hands, and then, carefully sliding into the chimney, began her frightful descent. In vain she tried to resist ; the rope slipped through her fingers with such fearful rapidity that, by the time she had reached the hearth, her delicate hands were all streaming with blood. She scarcely felt the pain, she had but one absorbing thought—she was free !

Folding those poor, quivering hands, she whispered a thanksgiving to God, and rose, full of hope and joy. Not a sound was to be heard ; and now, blessing the obscurity that shielded her from view, she opened the window, and darted down the pathway. The gate yielded to her touch, and, like a frightened doe, she fled through the woods, until the castle was out of sight, and she could venture to breathe.

## CHAPTER VII.

### THE FORESTER'S HUT.

MORNING had not yet dawned ; nevertheless there was light and life in a little hut that nestled in the woods near Strozzi Castle. The forester, in hunting costume, stood in the middle of the hearth ; while his young wife, by the light of a flaming pine torch, prepared his breakfast.

The whole room was illumined by the torch, whose red rays flickered even over the face of the infant that lay sleeping in its cradle, and shone far down the forest glade, a kindly beacon to guide the footsteps of the fugitive of Strozzi Castle.

The forester rose from his breakfast, and slung his gun across his shoulder. "Now I must go, Marcella," said he, "or the stag will have left the brook before I get there. By sunrise it will be off."

"Go, then, Luigi, and may the holy Bernard protect you ! I do hope you will bring down the stag, and please the marquis by your skill as a huntsman."

"Please him ? He looks as if nothing on earth would ever please him again. He is the crossest-looking man you ever saw ; so unlike his wife. They say the marchioness is crazy ; but I do not believe it."

"Why, Luigi ? Did you ever see her ?"

"Once, when I went to the castle to tell the marquis that his hounds were ready for the hunt. He was out walking in the park, and I had to wait for him to come back. Presently he came with two lackeys before him, and two behind, and at his side the most beautiful woman you ever laid your eyes upon. I could have fallen on my knees before her, she looked so lovely ; while he—bless me, Marcella, with his fierce eyes and his thick brows frowning over his long, sallow face, he looked like Love's headsman—such a face.—But I must go ; I will tell you the rest another time."

"Oh no ; do tell it to me now, I love so to hear you talk, dear Luigi. But I will not keep you from your work. Let me go a bit with you into the forest, as far as the blasted oak.

It is too late for me to sleep, and the baby will not wake for half an hour."

"Very well," said Luigi, kissing her; "come, for morning will soon dawn."

So, with their arms entwined about each other, the young couple went out into the woods, and the sound of their loving voices was sweet to the ear of the wanderer that stood upon their threshold. Laura pushed open the door, and entered the little room, looking around to see if any one was nigh.

Her dress was torn, and her hands and feet were bleeding; but her countenance beamed with hope, as, approaching the fireplace, she rested her stiffened limbs.

After enjoying for a few moments the reviving glow of the fire, she rose and looked around to assure herself that no one was near. "She is to be absent for half an hour," said Laura to herself. "By that time I will have destroyed this garment, and God will forgive me the substitution of my bracelet for one of the peasant's gowns."

Opening a chest that stood by the side of the bed, the marchioness took out a petticoat and kirtle of coarse, dark stuff; stripped off her sweep's dress, and, in a trice, was transformed into a country-maid, very beautiful, but sooty still. Then throwing her disguise into the fire, she rejoiced to think that no human being would ever find out the manner of her escape.

Half an hour after, Marcella returned, and rekindling the fire, prepared to warm her baby's milk. As she rose from her knees, she looked instinctively around at the child's cradle, and there, to her extreme astonishment, she saw the figure of a woman with hands outstretched, and eyes that seemed to plead for mercy. Marcella darted toward the cradle, her fears being entirely for her child. But it lay peacefully slumbering with a smile on its face, and the mother began to be apprehensive for her wares.

"Who are you?" said she, sharply, to Laura.

"Marcella," replied the marchioness, coming forward and taking her hand, "I am an unhappy woman, that implores you, by all your hopes of heaven, to rescue her from persecution."

But Marcella heard not a word of this petition. She had

recognized her petticoat and kirtle, and screamed with all her might :

"Those are my clothes, you thief·! You have been robbing me ! Thief ! thief !" cried she. "Oh, why is Luigi not here ? Give me my kirtle ! Off with my clothes, this instant, you rogue !"

Laura was somewhat alarmed, and not a little hurt ; for the grasp of the peasant was rough, and her voice, as she called for help, was loud and piercing.

"Marcella," said she, when she had opportunity to speak, and her tones were so pleading, that the woman listened in spite of herself—"Marcella, as I stood beside your threshold to-night, I heard your husband telling you of the misfortunes of the Marchioness Strozzi. He broke off to go into the forest ; you followed him, and now I can tell you what he related after you left the cottage. Your husband came respectfully up to the marquis, who repulsed him rudely, and asked what business he had in the court of the castle. Luigi replied that Battista had admitted him, whereupon the marquis discharged Battista on the spot, and drove him from the castle. Then he dragged the marchioness forward and hurried her up the steps of the portico."

"Just so," murmured Marcella. "But what else ? Do you know what else occurred ? What the signora did ?"

"Of course I do. Slipping from her finger a diamond-ring, she presented it to Battista, saying, 'Forgive me ; it is I who am the cause of your dismissal.'"

"So she did !" cried Marcella. "But how came you to know ?"

"Alas ! I am that unhappy marchioness."

"The Marchioness Strozzi !"

"Yes ; but believe me, Marcella, I am not crazy. For five years I have been a prisoner, and now that God has willed my liberation by means so marvellous as almost to partake of the character of a miracle, He has sent me to you that you might aid in the blessed work of my deliverance. See my hands bleeding and cut—see my feet torn by thorns, and bruised by stones ;—and oh, as you hope for mercy, help me on my way to liberty !"

"I do not believe you," was the reply of the cautious Marcella. "The Marchioness Strozzi would not come out of her grand castle by night to steal a poor peasant-woman's clothes. Where are your fine garments, if you are the marchioness? Let me see them."

"I came disguised, and burnt up the dress in which I made my escape. I needed another disguise, and have taken your clothes; but I will reward you richly for the forced loan. Take this bracelet; your husband can sell it, and, with the money, buy you a pretty farm."

"Ah!" screamed Marcella again, "now I know you to be a thief, perhaps worse than a thief! You have been stealing the jewels of the signora; for aught I know, murdering her with those bloody hands, and now you want to bribe me to help you away! No, no, you shall not escape—that I promise you."

"Oh, Marcella, how shall I convince you that I am no impostor? I swear, by God who made, by Christ who redeemed me, and by His holy mother, the Blessed Virgin, that I am the Marchioness of Strozzi, the unhappy prisoner of yonder gloomy castle. It is impossible that you can be so cruel as to deliver me into the hands of its wicked lord! A woman that loves—that loves her husband and child, must surely have a compassionate heart! See—I am at your feet!—In mercy, help me to escape!"

Marcella slowly shook her head. "I cannot, I cannot, I dare not."

"Yes, yes, you can, you dare do a good action. Think of the joy you experienced when the pangs of your travail were past, and you had given birth to a child whom you loved even before it had seen the light of life. Think, if your child should be in distress like mine, and kneel in vain at the feet of another woman who might deliver it from peril, and would not! —Oh, if you were in your grave, as my dear mother is, would you not curse the heartless being that repulsed your orphan! —Oh, mother! my dead mother! soften this woman's heart, that she may help me!"

Just then the voice of the baby, cooing in its cradle, reached Marcella's ear, and strangely moved her heart.

"Ah, the child—the dear child will plead for me," cried Laura. And, stooping to the cradle, she raised the baby in her arms, and brought the little rosy, smiling thing to its mother's feet.

"Let this baby, whom you love, be my advocate. I lay my hand upon its head and swear before Heaven that I am an innocent fugitive from persecution. Do unto me as you would have others do unto your own child."

And Marcella, no longer able to resist the pleadings of that melodious voice, burst into tears, and, encircling both Laura and the baby in her arms, clasped them close to her heart.

"My child, my child!" cried she, tenderly. "As I do to this unhappy lady, so may others do unto you."

"Then you will not betray me!" cried Laura, joyfully. "Oh, good, good Marcella, may God bless you for those pitying words!"

Marcella wiped her eyes, kissed her baby, and, replacing it in its cradle, said, "Now, signora, that I consent to assist you, tell me at once what is to be done, for it must be done quickly."

"Give me these clothes and a little money; guide me out of the forest to a post-station whence I may travel to Turin; and for these services take the bracelet: it is honestly mine, and therefore yours."

"It is now four o'clock," observed Marcella, looking toward the east.

"And precisely at eight the marquis will visit my rooms and discover my flight. Come—come—we have indeed no time to lose."

"We can reach the station in an hour," replied Marcella, "and the postilions will start early this morning for—to what point did you say you wished to travel, signora?"

"To Turin."

"That is a pity," murmured Marcella.

"Why?" asked Laura, anxiously.

"Because, if you were going northward, we might find you an escort. Luigi and I met a courier who was going to the next station to order post-horses for a traveller who is to leave for Vienna this morning. The man stopped to ask us the way."

"For Vienna!" cried Laura. "Who is going to Vienna?"

"The physician of the Duke of Savoy, whom his highness is sending to see a kinsman of his who is very ill in Vienna."

Laura uttered a cry of joy. "O God! my God, I thank thee!—Come, Marcella: I know the duke's physician, and he, of all other men, is the one I prefer for an escort."

"But your poor, bleeding feet, signora," cried Marcella, piteously.

"Never mind them. May they bleed anew, so I but reach the station in time to meet the physician! God has sent him to my deliverance. Come—let us away!"

# BOOK VI.

## CHAPTER I.

### SISTER ANGELICA.

Two months had passed away since the fall of Belgrade, and Prince Eugene of Savoy was still suffering from his wound. Nothing had been spared that could contribute to his recovery ; he was attended by the surgeon-in-chief of Max Emmanuel, visited daily by the physicians of the emperor, and nursed by his untiring secretary, Conrad. More than once the report of his death had been spread throughout Vienna, and then contradicted.

But, until the arrival of the physician of Victor Amadeus, all medical skill had proved unavailing. Whether through the agency of Doctor Franzi or of the nurse whom he had brought with him, Prince Eugene began, at last, to improve.

Sister Angelica, the nurse, had watched her patient with preterhuman vigilance. Day and night she sat by his bedside, dressing his wound, administering his medicine, and resting his fevered head on her shoulder ; laying her soft, cool hand upon his brow, until to wild delirium succeeded tranquil sleep, or a calm, placid wakefulness. At such times the nun was accustomed to sing ; and at the sound of her voice, Eugene smiled, and resigned himself to rest.

At last, the glance of his eye grew intelligent, and he returned to a consciousness of his position. Doctor Franzi remarked with regret, however, that he was apathetic, listless, and quite indifferent to his recovery. He made no complaint, seldom spoke, and seemed to be sinking gradually into a state of nervous prostration.

"Your highness," said the surgeon, one day, "you are now

convalescent, and it is time you made some effort to receive your friends."

Eugene turned wearily away, and sighed. "No, no," murmured he, "I am averse to the sight of any man, friend or foe."

"Nevertheless, I prescribe it," urged the doctor. "You are now less sick in body than in mind, and you must have change of scene to cheer you."

"Change will not cheer me," replied Eugene, languidly. "I feel nothing but absolute weariness of life."

"A morbid state of mind resulting from your long confinement to this room, and it must be overcome by yourself. A pretty thing it would be, to be sure, if, after saving your life, we should allow you to fling it away because you are as melancholy as a lovesick maiden!"

"Doctor," cried Eugene, flushing, "choose your words more carefully!"

"Good, good," returned the doctor, with an approving nod. "You have some spirit left, I perceive, and if you would but see one or two of your most intimate friends—"

"I will not see them," interrupted Eugene, peevishly. He would have said something more, but his speech was checked by a paroxysm of coughing. In a moment, the door opened noiselessly, and the nun gliding in hastened to support his trembling frame; and, while he suffered his head to fall upon her shoulder, wiped the dews from his clammy forehead. Then, gently placing him on his pillow, she warmed his drink over a lamp, and held it to his lips while he partook of it.

"Thank you, dear sister," said the invalid, faintly.

The next morning a consultation was held by the physicians of the prince, and it was decided that he must have change of air without delay. Eugene, reclining in an arm-chair, looked wearily on, until the conference was at an end; then, shaking his head and frowning, he turned away and gazed fixedly at his nurse, who, with arms crossed over her breast, stood close at hand, ready to anticipate his wants ere he could give them utterance.

"Your highness must not resist," said the imperial court physician. "Change of air and of scene is indispensable to your recovery."

"Let me die here," was Eugene's languid reply.

"Your highness is not going to die," observed Doctor Franzi ; "but I am afraid that you are about to cause the death of another person."

"Whom can you mean ?" asked Eugene, interested.

"I mean Sister Angelica, your nurse."

"Surely she is not sick," said the prince, turning anxiously around. "No !" said he, smiling, "no—she is here."

"And yet she is sick," persisted Doctor Franzi. "For a month past, she has lived without sleep, scarcely snatching a moment to change her clothing, and never once breathing any but the air of this sick-room." The nun made a deprecating gesture. "You need not deny it," continued the doctor. "Prince, when Sister Angelica was allowed by the prioress of her convent to accompany me to Vienna, she made a vow never to leave my patient until he recovered from his illness or died. Now you are neither dead nor about to die ; but if you do all you can to frustrate our endeavors to cure you, your nurse will succumb long before you are well enough to dispense with her valuable services."

"In that case, I cease to oppose you," said Eugene. "Do with me what you will. God forbid that I should harm my ministering angel !"

"In view of your highness's submission to our orders," observed the court physician, "his majesty the emperor has offered the use of his palace at Schönbrunn, and we have taken the liberty of preparing every thing for your immediate departure."

"His majesty is too kind," was the reply, "and my first care shall be to thank my gracious sovereign for so signal a proof of his beneficence. Let us then depart for Schönbrunn. You are satisfied, dear sister, are you not ?"

The sister bowed her head, and passed her hand over Eugene's glossy, black hair, while Doctor Franzi came in and out, making preparations for the accommodation of his patient.

A litter was brought, and when the prince had been carefully placed upon it the doctor inquired whether he felt comfortable enough therein to bear the journey. Eugene, on his part, asked how his physician and the nun were to travel.

"We expect to occupy your highness's carriage, and to precede you, by a half hour, to Schönbrunn."

"Would it be inconvenient or uncomfortable for Sister Angelica to occupy the litter with me?"

"By no means; but if she accompanies your highness, things will not be quite so comfortable for your reception."

"Then let me have less comfort, and more content. She supports my head so delightfully when I cough, and moves my wounded foot so gently—"

The nun no sooner heard these words than she put aside the doctor who was standing before her, and hastened to the litter, altered the inclination of Eugene's pillow, and very gently changed the position of his wounded foot.

"Oh, how I thank you, dear sister!" murmured the prince, with a sigh of relief. "When you are by, pain seems to vanish, and night breaks into joyful day."

The bearers raised the litter, and the little cortége set out for Schönbrunn. Two runners went before, to make way, crying as they went along:

"Room for the litter of his highness the Prince of Savoy!"

The hurrying wayfarers retreated at the sound; a passage was opened through the crowded thoroughfares; and, while the hero of Belgrade was borne along the streets of Vienna, the people stood respectfully aside to let him pass.

The air of Schönbrunn was pure and delightful. Every morning the prince was conveyed to its lovely gardens, where he spent at least an hour in inhaling the sweet breath of coming spring. He drank goat's milk for his cough, and partook submissively of the food prescribed for his nourishment; but his fever was not subdued, and his cheeks grew paler and thinner each day.

"We must use other means," said Doctor Franzi to the nun, who had been anxiously questioning him as to the result of a consultation held that day over the sinking patient. "My colleagues are of opinion that his fever is hectic, and therefore incurable; but I differ with them. I really believe that if he could be roused from his apathy, we could save him yet.

Corporeal remedies have done their best ; we must try a moral reaction."

"What do you mean ?" murmured the nun.

"I mean that Sister Angelica must raise her veil, and break her long silence," replied the doctor, raising her delicate white hand to his lips.

The nun trembled, and caught her breath, the doctor viewing her with amazement. "What !" said he, "you who have displayed such fortitude and endurance, are you about to become faint-hearted ?"

"Doctor," whispered she, "joy has its agitation as well as grief. And if the shock should be too great for him !"

"If too great now, he will never be able to bear it, my dear child. It is possible that it may deprive him for a time of consciousness, but he will awake to life another man. At least, such is my impression. I consider that his fate now lies in your hands, and you must decide it to-day—nay, this very hour."

"Oh, doctor, I am so unprepared ! I have no self-command ; let us wait until to-morrow. If we should fail—"

"We shall have done him no injury. I am ready to answer before God that—"

The door was partially opened, and the valet of the prince apologized for interrupting them. "His highness feels very much exhausted, and calls for Sister Angelica."

"She will be there in one moment," replied the doctor.— "You see," whispered he, "that his heart has divined your presence. As soon as you leave the room, he begins to suffer."

So saying, he gave her his hand, and she submitted to be led as far as the door of the prince's sitting-room. There she paused, and laying her hands upon her heart—

"Oh, it will burst," murmured she. "Doctor, you will remain with me—will you not ?"

"I will remain as long as my presence is beneficial, and depart as soon as it becomes oppressive. Come !"

He opened the door, and, with gentle constraint, compelled her to advance. The prince, extended on his couch, looked very ill. "Have you given me up ? Have you, too, forgotten me ?"

" ' You too,' " echoed the doctor, while the nun was engaged in preparing the patient's drink. " Why, has anybody else ever forgotten your highness ? "

" No," sighed Eugene ; " I was unjust. But I have lost her, and that loss is killing me."

" You hear him," whispered the doctor, while the nun, scarcely able to hold the glass, presented it to the lips of her patient.

" Drink, Prince Eugene," said she, in low, trembling tones. At the sound of her voice he started, and raised his head to listen.

" Great Heaven ! Who spoke ? "

The doctor smiled, and, slightly raising his shoulders, replied : " Nobody but Sister Angelica, I presume, for nobody else is here."

" Sister Angelica ! " repeated Eugene, slowly. " I thought she had made a vow of silence, to last until her return to the convent ? "

" You are quite right ; but it appears that she has forgotten herself for a moment, in her anxiety to serve you. Drink, then, to oblige her."

Eugene clutched the glass and emptied it of its contents.

" Good," said the doctor. " Now that you are somewhat refreshed, I must entertain you with a little outside gossip. I have letters from Turin to-day. Victor Amadeus has disenthralled himself from his filial bondage. His mother, having been regent during his minority, has been struggling since his majority to retain her supremacy over him and the duchy. She insisted upon taking precedence of her daughter-in-law, the reigning duchess, and was equally bent upon dismissing one of the ministers. There was considerable strife, and no little intrigue in Turin, until the defection of one of the dowager's adherents, which so strengthened the opposite party, that she was obliged to succumb, and retired in high dudgeon to her estates. The duke, on his side, out of gratitude to his new friend, has created him prime minister—an appointment which is very popular in Savoy—for there is not a worthier man in the dukedom than the Marquis de Bonaletta."

26

At sound of this name, Eugene started up, and leaning his head upon his hand, prepared to listen.

The doctor continued : " By-the-by, he is the uncle of the unfortunate young marchioness of that name who was forced into a marriage with a depraved Venetian nobleman called Strozzi. Your highness has heard her history ? "

Eugene murmured something in reply, and sank back upon his pillow.

" A very melancholy affair," pursued the doctor, signing to the nun to approach, " and it has ended most singularly."

"Ended ! How ? " cried Eugene. " Speak, doctor, I implore you : is she dead ? "

" She ? The marchioness ? Quite the contrary, she is alive and well. Her husband suddenly disappeared with her from Venice, last spring ; and it was discovered that he had confined her within a solitary castle, somewhere in a forest ; having previously given out to the world that she was a raving lunatic."

" The accursed liar ! " muttered Eugene. " May God grant me life to avenge her wrongs ! "

" Your highness is much moved at the recital," continued the doctor, " and no wonder, for it is a fact much stranger than fiction. But I will defer the conclusion of my story to some other day. You are too much excited to hear it now."

" Oh no, indeed ! I am strong—well. Look at me, doctor ; and believe me when I say that your conversation is more healing than all the medicines you have ever administered."

" In truth, your highness seems quite invigorated within the last half hour. Do you not perceive the change, Sister Angelica ? "

She bowed her head, and approached the couch.

" Then, in mercy, let me hear the rest," cried Eugene, his eyes flashing with eagerness.

" Be it so, then. In spite of bolts, bars, and her miserable husband's spies, the marchioness has managed to escape."

" Escape ! " exclaimed Eugene, starting from his couch, and standing upright upon the floor. In a moment the nun was behind him, ready to support him in case of need ; but he walked hurriedly to the window, threw it wide open, and inhaled the fresh morning air. For a while, not a word was spoken. The prince looked upward at the blue and silver clouds that were floating silently by ; his large, dark eyes wandered lovingly over the beautiful landscape that lay below, and then, bowing his head, he lifted his heart to heaven, and thanked God.

"Doctor," said he, at last, "whither fled the marchioness?"

"No one knows, your highness. But you must excuse me if I take my leave. I must attend a consultation of—"

"Doctor," cried the prince, grasping him by the arm, "you cannot go : I must know all that you have to tell."

The doctor smiled. "Upon my word, your highness speaks as if you were ordering a charge against the Turks. But I cannot obey : Sister Angelica has heard the story from beginning to end, and she will relate the rest of it. Adieu."

So saying, Doctor Franzi left the room.

"Oh, dear sister," cried Eugene, "can you tell me whether she fell into his hands again?"

"She did not," replied the nun, in a low, tremulous voice ; 'but the shock of her disappearance was so terrible in its effects upon the marquis, that he is now a maniac in the very apartments wherein he had confined his wretched wife."

Eugene had listened in breathless amazement to these low, fluttering words ; and when they ceased he seemed still to listen. His face had become excessively pale ; his lips were slightly parted, and his eyes riveted upon some imaginary object at a distance, which seemed to obliterate from his mind the presence of his companion. She meanwhile became so terrified that she clasped her hands, and knelt at his feet.

He saw—he understood it all, and, raising her in his arms, he pressed her rapturously to his heart. The veil had fallen, and she was there ! His Laura ! his long-lost Laura !

## CHAPTER II.

### LOUIS THE FOURTEENTH.

THE morning service was at an end, and King Louis XIV., attended by his courtiers, left the royal chapel. His countenance was troubled, and it followed, as a matter of course, that everybody else wore a woe-begone expression. The fact is, that things were very dull and solemn at the French court. Feasts and festivals were forbidden, and nobody was allowed to look cheerful. La Vallière, in a Carmelite convent, was doing penance for the sin of her love for Louis ; while De Montespan, in the world, was expiating hers within sight of the king's indifference. He had tired of her long ago, but had permitted her to remain at court, where her saloons were as stupid, as silent, and as empty, as they had once been bright and crowded.

The reigning favorite was De Maintenon, who might have had followers innumerable, had she desired them. But she appeared to be perfectly unconscious of her own power ; going about, now as ever, with modest mien and simple dress, with folded hands and downcast eyes, apparently unaware of the existence of any mortal whatsoever, save that of her well-beloved Louis. And her course of action had been triumphantly successful, for by many she was believed to be the legitimate spouse of the King of France.

From the chapel, Louis betook himself to the boudoir of the marquise, and greeted her with a slight inclination of his royal head.

" Why were you not at mass to-day, madame ? " inquired he, curtly, as, hastily crossing the room, he flung open the window. and admitted the sharp air of a raw autumn morning.

De Maintenon stifled a sigh, and compelled herself to smile. " You know, sire," replied she, gently, " that I am indisposed. My physician has forbidden me to breathe the air, and for this reason I dared not follow the impulse of my heart, and join my prayers to those of your majesty this morning. The autumn winds are too keen for me."

The king paid no attention to De Maintenon's allusion to the "autumn winds." The window remained open, and she was obliged to stand directly in front of it as long as Louis was pleased to enjoy the breeze.

"You are becoming sickly, madame," observed he, coldly.

"True, sire, I suffer of late," sighed she.

"You are getting old," replied he, tartly. "Old age is a sorry companion; it makes people peevish and disagreeable."

The marquise grew as pale as ashes, and the sharp glance of her black eyes was turned quickly upon the countenance of the king, who, instead of looking at her, was staring out of the window at the marble Naiads, over whose white limbs the waters of a fountain were foaming and plashing, in myriads of pearly drops. He appeared to be quite unconscious of having wounded the feelings of his sensitive companion.

She, on her part, felt that a crisis was at hand, and that, to waken the king from his apathy, desperate measures must be adopted. She plunged into her remedy at once.

"I see," sighed she, "that my presence is irksome to your majesty. It is better, therefore, that I gather up my strength, and sacrifice my happiness to yours. I will retire to St. Cyr."

Louis raised his shoulders. "I think not. People often say such things, but never mean what they say."

"Sire, Madame de la Vallière is a proof of the contrary, and I—although (as you remarked just now)—I am old, possess a heart over whose emotions time and age have no power. I love as I have ever loved, passionately, profoundly; but my love is disinterested, and soars high above all self-gratification. Now that it has become obtrusive, its current shall be turned to heaven, and in the sacred walls of a cloister I will spend the remainder of my days in prayer for him whose image I shall cherish unto death. Sire, I respectfully request permission to enter the convent of St. Cyr."

Louis began to be uneasy. He knew very well that De Maintenon had a vigorous and resolute soul, quite capable of carrying out any purpose dictated by her head; and, if once she appealed from her affections to her pride, he felt that no ulterior persuasions of his would avail to deter her from the step she meditated.

"Are you serious, madame?" said he, reproachfully. "Would you, indeed, forsake me?"

"Sire, I am so earnest in my intention to free you from the presence of an infirm old woman, that I repeat my request to be allowed to depart now—this very hour."

The king hated nothing on earth like surprises; he disliked to have the sluggish waters of his every-day life stirred by unaccustomed occurrences. He turned around at once to remonstrate, and, instead of the pallid face he had encountered just a few minutes ago, he saw a pair of glowing cheeks and flashing eyes, from whose lustrous depths there darted a light that warmed up his tepid old heart, and set it to beating as it had been wont to do, when La Vallière smiled and De Montespan coquetted.

"Surely," said he, "you would not set a bad example to the wives of my courtiers, Françoise! You would not teach them that when they tire of their husbands they may desert them, and bury their ennui in a convent!"

"Sire, I cannot accept the responsibility of other women's derelictions. My duty points out to me a convent as the proper refuge for a woman who has outlived her husband's love."

"I will not release you from your marriage-tie, madame; and, should you brave my displeasure, and attempt to leave me, I would follow you to St. Cyr, and drag you from the altar, were you in the very act of making your vows!"

The marquise dropped on her knees. "Oh, sire, do I hear aright! I am not odious to you!—You will not drive me away from my earthly heaven! I may yet be happy, yet be loved!"

The king bent over her, and raised her tenderly in his arms. "Rise, madame," said he, "it does not become the wife of the King of France to bend the knee to any man. You know full well, Françoise," continued he, affectionately, "that without you my life would be an aimless, burdensome one. Who could replace you, my wife, my counsellor, my prime minister?"

"Ah, sire, what words! They thrill me to the depths of my heart, and restore me to bliss unspeakable!"

"Then the cloud of your discontent has passed away, has it not?"

"Oh, sire, it is day, bright day, and my soul is flooded with sunshine!"

"Then let us sit down on yonder divan, and talk of the affairs of France. Do you know that I have bad news from Germany?"

"I feared as much, sire, when you entered the room with such a troubled aspect."

"These German princes will not come to a decision as to my claims. For four years my envoys have been before the imperial Diet, vainly urging them to define our boundaries."

"They are procrastinating in the hope of receiving succor from the emperor, who, as soon as he has sufficiently humbled the Porte, will make an attempt to humble France. With Leopold to sustain them, the Diet will claim Strasburg and Alsatia, and exact of your majesty the withdrawal of the French troops from all the Rhenish provinces."

"They shall not be withdrawn," returned Louis. "When France has her grasp upon a province, she never relaxes her hold. And so far am I from any intention to temporize, that, if the Diet decides against me, I will not scruple to break the twenty years' truce, and appeal to arms. This I have long ago decided to do, so we need not discuss the question any longer. I have other matters to confide to you, which harass me."

"Has the emperor refused to recognize the new Elector of Cologne?" asked the marquise, indignantly.

"Yes, he has had the assurance to reject the lawful election of Egon of Furstenberg; and to appoint, in his stead, Joseph Clemens, the brother of the Elector of Bavaria. Out of four-and-twenty prebendaries of the archbishopric of Cologne, fourteen votes were given to Egon, while Joseph received but ten. And what, do you suppose, is the ground of the emperor's insolent rejection of my nominee? He pretends that the fourteen voters were bribed by France, and that the candidate himself is disaffected, and under French influence. This is tantamount to a declaration of war; and, what is worse than all, Pope Innocent sustains the emperor."

The marquise folded her hands in pious resignation. "That is a sad proof of the unfriendliness of his holiness toward France," murmured she. "But that is the fault of the Minister Louvois. He has deserved the displeasure of his holiness by the forcible occupation of Avignon (so long the residence of the successors of St. Peter), and by the arrest of the papal nuncio."

"He could not help it," cried Louis, impatiently ; "it was an act of reprisal. Our ambassador at Rome had been affronted ; the spies of the pope had forced themselves into the hôtel of the embassy and had arrested two men that had sought protection from the French flag."

"Sire," said the marquise with determination, "they were papal subjects and criminals, who had no right to the protection of the French flag. It should never be said that Louis of France shields from justice the theives and murderers whom the Vicar of Christ would punish. You know, sire, that these men had committed sacrilege. They had plundered the altar of St. Peter's of its golden pyx and candlesticks, and had poniarded the sacristan that had them in charge."

"It was a crime—that I cannot deny," said Louis with a deprecating sigh, "but the right of asylum is sacred, and we were forced to defend it."

"Sire, do you, an earthly monarch, pretend to believe that you can shield a criminal from the all-seeing vengeance of the Lord ? Had the sinner the wings of the morning, wherewith he might fly to the uttermost limits of the earth, the arm of God would overtake and arrest him in his flight ! How, then, do *you* pretend to cover his crimes with the folds of the French flag ?"

The king was cowed by the bold and uncompromising voice of truth. He folded his hands and bowed his head.

"Alas, alas ! you are right and we were wrong ! We should not have given refuge to these murderers and plunderers. I am truly repentant, Françoise, and will do my best to expiate the sin."

"Sire, you are right to bewail the sin, but it lies not on your conscience ; it is the fault of your arrogant minister, who, without consulting you, demanded satisfaction of his holiness ; and, when it was righteously refused, took possession of Avignon, and imprisoned the papal nuncio. Then, when the deed was done, and not until then, he dispatched a courier to Paris, to inform you of what had taken place."

"That is true, dear Françoise," said Louis, mildly ; "but, after all, Louvois had no alternative. Had he consulted me, I might have felt myself bound to temporize ; whereas, by his assumption of the act, he renders apology on my part possible. The thing is done ; the honor of France is satisfied, and I can now release the nuncio, and make all necessary excuses to his holiness."

The marquise gazed searchingly at the countenance of the royal casuist, who bore her scrutiny without flinching, and, with a slight clearing of his throat, went on :

"I am not yet at the end of my chapter of vexations. A courier has arrived to-day from the Marquis de Villars. In spite of all his petty intrigues, and the millions with which he bribed the mistress of the elector, Max Emmanuel has never been estranged from Austria. So far from it, he has assumed the chief command of the imperial armies, and is about to lay siege to Belgrade."

"He will come to grief, sire," cried the marquise. "The Turks and Hungarians greatly outnumber the imperialists, and—"

The king raised his hand and shook his head. "I would you were right ; but, Françoise, you are a false prophet—my last and worst tale is told—Belgrade has fallen !"

"The will of God be done !" cried the marquise. "Christianity has triumphed, and the unbelieving Moslem has bitten the dust !"

"Pray," interrupted Louis, fretfully, "put aside your piety for a while and look at the thing through the medium of good sense and earthly foresight. The Emperor of Germany is victorious ; he is gradually weakening the Sultan, so that it is within the range of possibilities that he overturn the Ottoman power, and consolidate the Germanic confederations into one great empire. This done, he will turn his attention to France —of that you may be sure."

"My beloved sovereign speaks of events that will never

come to pass," replied the marquise, with one of her most enticing smiles. "Long before the Emperor Leopold will have exterminated the Turks, we will force him to defend his own territories from the invading armies of France."

"You approve me, then, and think that it is time I began to be aggressive in my warfare," exclaimed Louis, eagerly.

"I am always of the opinion of my lord and sovereign," was the courteous reply of the marquise, who had already forgotten the discussion relating to Avignon. "It remains to be seen if Louvois acquiesces."

"Louvois will do as he is bid," said Louis, frowning.

"Remember, sire, that he said publicly, yesterday, that the French army was not in a condition to open a campaign, and that it could not be equipped before spring."

"Before spring!" echoed the king. "While the generals of Leopold carry every thing before them!—for he has distinguished generals in his service, madame; one of whom is that same Eugene of Savoy whom you pronounced unworthy of a bishopric. Whatever he might have done as a churchman, I would he were an archbishop rather than what he is to-day!"

"Oh, sire!" said the marquise, reproachfully. "True—I never thought Prince Eugene had any vocation for the priesthood; and, knowing his disinclination to the church, I myself advised him to ask for a commission in the army. He did ask it—a mere captaincy—and your majesty well remembers who it was that influenced you to refuse him so small a boon. To Louvois France owes the loss of this great military genius."

"Right, right, you are always right, and I have unwittingly given you another pretext for blaming him."

"Although he is my bitter foe, I would not blame him, sire, were he not culpable."

"Your bitter foe, Françoise? How?"

"Ah, sire, was it not he that opposed our marriage?"

"Forgive him, dear Françoise, he acted according to his own notions of duty. But you see that my love was mightier than his objections, and you are, before God, my own beloved spouse."

"Before God, sire, I am ; but the world doubts my right to the name. In the eyes of the court, I am but the mistress of the king ; a humiliation which I owe to Louvois, who bound your majesty by an oath never to recognize me as Queen of France."

"I rejoice to think that he did so," was the king's reply, "for the tie that binds us is sacred in the sight of Heaven, while in the eyes of the world I am spared the ridicule of placing Scarron's widow upon the throne of Charlemagne the Great. In your own reception-room you act as queen, and I am perfectly willing that you should do so, for it proves that you are the wife of the king, and not his mistress. Be magnanimous, then, and forgive Louvois if, above the ambition of Madame de Maintenon, he valued the dignity and honor of the French throne. But the hour of my interview with you is at an end : I hold a levee this morning, and must leave you."

Kissing the hand of the marquise, Louis bowed and left the room.

---

## CHAPTER III.

### THE KING AND THE PETITIONERS.

WHEN the king entered the audience-chamber, the courtiers, dispersed in groups about the room, were all in eager conversation. So absorbed were they in the subject under discussion, that those who stood at the opposite end of the room were not aware of the royal presence until the grande tournée forced it upon their attention.

The king joined one of these groups. "Gentlemen," said he, "what interests you so deeply to-day ? Have you received any important news ?"

"Yes, sire," replied the Prince de Conti. "We are speaking of my cousin Eugene. He has been severely wounded, but not until he had materially assisted the Elector of Bavaria to capture Belgrade."

"Ah ! you have heard of the fall of Belgrade !" said the king, frowning, as he perceived that Louvois was approaching. "Is it you," asked he, curtly, "that has been in such hot haste to spread the news of the successes of the imperial army ?"

"Pardon me, sire," replied Louvois, "I am no gossip ; nor do the successes of the Emperor of Austria interest me suffi- ciently for me to deem them worthy of announcement here."

"Nevertheless, they are for you a cause of no little humilia- tion ; for they remind the world that you were once guilty of a blunder in your statesmanship.  If I am not mistaken, it was you who caused me to refuse Prince Eugene a commission in my army—that same Prince Eugene who has turned out to be one of the greatest military geniuses of the age."

"Sire," returned Louvois, reddening with anger, " you your- self were of the opinion that Prince Eugene of Savoy—"

"Sir," interrupted the king, haughtily, "I am of opinion that when you scorned Prince Eugene, you were lamentably deficient in judgment ; and that, if he is now shedding lustre upon the arms of Austria, it is because you repulsed him when he would have entered the service of France."

And the king, whose wounded vanity was greatly com- forted by a thrust at that of his prime minister, turned on his heel, and addressed himself again to the Prince de Conti :

"Whence came your news of the taking of Belgrade ?"

"From the Duke de Luynes, your majesty, who, you may remember, has joined the imperial armies.  But Eugene is not the only Frenchman who has distinguished himself at the siege ; the Prince de Commercy behaved in a manner worthy of all admiration."

"Yes, indeed," added the young Duke of Maine (the royal son of De Montespan).  "It is such deeds as his that have earned for Frenchmen the title of the 'Knightly Nation.'"

And the little hobbling duke, who had never drawn a sword from its scabbard, struck himself on the breast, as if he had represented in his own person the united chivalry of all France.

"I am curious to hear of the valiant deeds of the Prince de Commercy," said the king, carelessly.  "Pray relate them to us, prince."

The prince bowed : "Sire, as the Prince de Commercy was charging a body of Janizaries stationed at one of the gates of Belgrade, a Turk made a sudden dash at his standard-bearer, and captured the regimental flag.  The men were disheartened at their loss, when the prince, crying out, 'Wait a moment, boys, and you shall have another,' galloped right into the enemy's midst, and raised his pistol to bring down the standard-bearer of the Turks. The latter, taking immediate advantage of the position of the prince, thrust a lance into his right side. Without giving the least attention to his wound, Commercy grasped the spear with his left hand and held it fast, while with his right he drew out his sabre, killed the standard-bearer and bore away his flag. Then, withdrawing the lance from his side, he gave the blood-besprinkled banner into the hands of the German ensign, saying, as he did so, 'Pray be more careful of this one than you were of the other.'"

The king slightly bowed his head. "Indeed, the Prince de Commercy does honor to the country that gave him birth. I will take care that he is suitably rewarded."

"Sire," replied the Prince de Conti, "the Emperor of Germany has already done so. He has been promoted; and the flag which was stained with his blood now hangs within the cathedral walls of St. Stephen's; while, with her own hands, the empress is embroidering a new one for the regiment, which, in honor, of the prince, is called the Commercy regiment."

"The Emperor of Germany knows how to reward valor," exclaimed the Duke de la Roche Guyon, " for Eugene of Savoy is only five-and-twenty years of age, and yet he has been created a field-marshal."

The king affected not to have heard this remark, and passed on. His courtiers saw, with consternation, that he was annoyed at something, and every face in the audience-chamber gave back a reflection of the royal discontent. Louis sauntered along, occasionally addressing a word or two to such as he "delighted to honor," until the grande tournée had been made.

When the two Princes de Conti saw that he was disengaged, they advanced with a mien so respectful, that Louis knew perfectly well the nature of their errand, although he little guessed its purport.

"Well, gentlemen," said he, " for what new escapade have you come to crave our royal indulgence? I see, by your demeanor, that you are about to ask a favor of your sovereign."

"Yes, my liege," replied the elder of the two ; "we have come to ask a favor, but not such a one as your majesty supposes. We have grown melancholy, and your royal hand can heal us."

"Grown melancholy ! You, the boldest, gayest cavaliers in Paris !"

"Yes, sire," sighed De Conti. "We cannot sleep for thinking of the laurels of our kinsman of Savoy, and we humbly crave your royal permission to join the imperial crusade against the Turks."

Louis frowned, but quickly recovered himself. "Of course —of course," replied he, condescendingly; "if the laurels of the little prince disturb your slumbers, you have my full consent to go after him. 'Twere a pity to deny you so small a boon."

And, without giving opportunity to the two princes to thank him, the king turned around and addressed Marshal Créqui :

"Who knows," said he, raising his voice, " whether these two silly boys have not chosen the wiser part ? Though they may never earn any laurels, they may fight away some of their folly—which loss would be to them great gain."

"Sire, it is perfectly natural for youth to desire glory," returned the old marshal. "I think that thirst for fame is honorable to a young nobleman, and for this reason I have consented that my son, the Marquis de Blanchefort, should join the imperial crusade, provided he obtains your majesty's consent. I venture to hope that your majesty will not refuse to him what you have conceded to the Princes de Conti."

Louis looked with amazement at the smiling countenance of the old marshal, but he answered as before :

"I certainly will not do less for your son than for the De Contis. He has my consent to accompany them on their journey after glory."

The young Marquis de Blanchefort, who was near at hand, would have expressed his gratitude for the royal permission to leave France, but the king turned coldly away, and darted a peremptory glance at Louvois.

The minister understood, and came forward at once.

De Blanchefort, meanwhile, hurried off to join the De Contis, who, surrounded by a group of young noblemen, were engaged in a low, but earnest conversation.

"I have my discharge," whispered he.

"Then you are the third one upon whom fortune has smiled to-day," sighed the young Duke de Brienne. "I wish I were as far advanced as you."

"Allow me to give the three lucky knights a bit of advice," whispered the Duke de la Roche Guyon, Louvois's son-in-law. "Make use of the king's permission without delay. Who knows, but when the rest of us prefer our petitions, he may not withdraw his consent from you?"

"My dear friend," said the younger De Conti, "our trunks are packed, and our travelling-carriage awaits us at the corner of the Rue St. Honoré. Nobody knows what may happen; so that we are about to depart without parade, bidding adieu to our friends by notes of farewell."

"You have acted with foresight," replied the duke. "And you, De Blanchefort, when do you start?"

"My father is a soldier, and admires punctuality," answered the marquis. "Yesterday afternoon he presented me with a new travelling-chariot, and this morning he ordered it to be ready for my departure, at the corner of the Garde Meubles. That is even nearer than the Rue St. Honoré, and if you will allow me, I fly to see if it is still there."

"Do so," returned the duke, "and our dear princes would do well to follow your example."

"We were about to take our leave, and now—" began young De Conti.

"Away with you!" was the reply; and the three young men, murmuring, "Au revoir," disappeared behind the portière which led to the antechamber, and sped away from the Louvre to their carriages.

"Messieurs," said the Duke de la Roche Guyon, taking out his watch, "we must give them a quarter of an hour, before we irritate his majesty by preferring our own petitions."

When the quarter of an hour had elapsed, the duke replaced his watch, and resumed : " Now let us go and try our luck."

" Shall we go together, or one by one ?" inquired the Duke de Liancourt.

" We are four, and the king's good-nature is soon exhausted. The last two petitioners would indubitably be rebuffed, so I think we had better go in a body."

" With yourself as spokesman," said De Brienne.

" Right !" echoed the others, and they are all approached the king. He was engaged in conversation with Louvois, and interrupted himself to stare at the four young men, as if he had been greatly astonished to see them.

" Here is your son-in-law," observed he to Louvois. " What can he want ?"

" Indeed, sire, nobody knows his wants less than I. He is my daughter's husband, but no friend of mine."

" Here are De Turenne, De Brienne, and De Liancourt at his heels," replied the king, trying to stare them out of countenance, while the poor young men waited in vain for the royal permission to speak.

At last the Duke de la Roche Guyon gathered courage to begin.

" Your majesty, we come with all respect—"

" We !" echoed the king. " Then you represent four petitioners."

" Yes, your majesty, the three here present and myself. May I be permitted to state the nature of our petition ?"

The king bowed, and De la Roche Guyon resumed : " Sire, we are all, like the Princes de Conti and the Marquis de Blanchefort, envious of the laurels of Eugene of Savoy. We are athirst for glory."

" And you come to ask if I will not make war to gratify your greed for fame ?" asked the king, eagerly.

" Sire !" exclaimed the duke, " can you imagine such assurance on the part of your subjects ? No—we merely ask permission to join the imperial army."

" The army of the Emperor of Germany !" cried Louis, in a voice so loud and angry that his courtiers grew pale, and almost forgot to breathe. But the Duke de la Roche

Guyon had steeled himself against the bolts of this Jupiter Tonans.

"Yes, sire," replied he, courteously, "the army of the emperor who represents Christendom doing battle with Mohammedanism. It is a holy cause, and we hope that it has your majesty's sympathy and approbation."

"It would appear that the youth of my court are drifting into imbecility," replied the king, with a contemptuous shrug. "They need a physician ; and it will be time enough to listen to any request they may have to make, when they shall have returned to their senses."

"Your majesty refuses us !" said the duke, bitterly.

"When the king has spoken, sir," replied Louis, haughtily, "it becomes his subjects to obey and be silent. The court is dismissed ! Monsieur de Louvois, you will go with me to Trianon, to inspect the new palace. The court are at liberty to accompany us."

This "at liberty" being a command which nobody dared resist, the king had no sooner left the room than the courtiers hastened to their carriages and gave orders to their various coachmen to join the royal cortége.

## CHAPTER IV.

### THE WINDOW THAT WAS TOO LARGE.

MEANWHILE the king had made his way to the boudoir of his marquise, who advanced joyfully to meet him.

"Madame," said he, "I am about to drive to Trianon ; will you accompany me ? Decide according to your own judgment ; do not inconvenience yourself on my account."

"Your majesty knows that I live in your presence," sighed the marquise, "but—"

"But you dare not leave your room. Well—I am sorry ; you would have enjoyed the drive."

"The drive to Trianon," replied the marquise, "where, as an architect, Louvois will be the theme of your majesty's encomiums."

27

The king's lip curled. "Scarcely"—said he. "I do not think that Louvois will enjoy his visit to-day. I am not at all pleased with his plans, nor will I be at pains to conceal my displeasure."

The marquise looked inquiringly into the face of the king. It was smiling and significant.

"Sire," said the marquise, "are you in earnest? May I indeed be permitted to accompany you to Trianon?"

"Indeed, you cannot conceive how much I regret your inability to go," returned Louis.

"Oh, sire, my love is mightier than my infirmities; it shall lend me strength, and I shall have the unspeakable bliss of accompanying you."

"I counted upon you," returned Louis. "So let us go at once; the court waits, and punctuality is the politeness of kings."

Without paying the least attention to Louvois, who, as superintendent of the royal edifices, stood close at hand, the king entered his coach, and assisted Madame de Maintenon, as she took her place at his side. Louvois had expected to be invited to ride with the king, and this oversight, he knew, betokened something sinister for him.

And what could it be? "The old bigot has been sowing her tares again," said he to himself. "There is some mortification in store for me, or she would not have exposed herself to this sharp autumn blast to-day." And he ran over all the late occurrences of the court, that he might disentangle the knotted thread of the king's ill-humor. "It must be that accursed business of the Prince of Savoy, and the king is no better than these silly lads; the laurels of the little abbé keep him awake at night, and he vents his spleen upon me. What an oversight it was of mine, to let that Eugene escape! Had I caused him to disappear from this wicked world and given him an asylum in the Bastile, he never would have troubled us with his doings in Germany. *There* was my blunder—my unpardonable blunder. But it cannot be recalled, and the king's vanity is so insatiable, that there is no knowing how it is ever to be appeased. I must succumb for the present, and—Ah!" cried he, interrupting the current of his despondency, "I think

I can repair my error. We must allow his envious majesty to gather a handful of these laurels for which he has such a longing. We must put the Emperor of Germany in check, and—"

Just then the iron gates of Trianon opened to admit the carriage, and the superintendent of the royal edifices made haste to alight and wait the arrival of the king.

For the first time, his majesty condescended to seem aware of Louvois' presence. "Monsieur," said he, to the tottering favorite, "I have come to inspect this château. Madame la marquise, it being intended as a pleasure-house for yourself, you will oblige me by speaking frankly on the subject."

So saying, he gave his arm to madame, and the court, with heads uncovered, came submissively behind.

"Follow us," said the king.

This "us" delighted the marquise, for it was an informal acknowledgment of her right to be considered as the king's consort. With her large eyes beaming with joy, and her face radiant with triumph, she went, hanging on Louis' arm, over the château which his munificence had prepared for her occupation in summer. Immediately behind them walked Louvois; and after him a long procession of nobles, not one of whom dared to utter a word. The central building was pronounced satisfactory; its front and marble colonnade received their due meed of praise, and the king ended by these words:

"I am perfectly satisfied with Mansard; he is really a distinguished architect."

"Sire," returned Louvois, to whom this eulogium had been addressed, "Mansard will be overjoyed to hear of his sovereign's approbation. But your majesty will pardon me if I appropriate some portion of your praise; the ground-plan of the building is mine. I furnished it to Mansard."

The king made no reply to this attempt to extort a word of approval; he merely nodded, and went on his way. They had now reached a point whence the right façade of the building was brought to view.

"Monsieur," said Louis, pointing to the central window, "this window is out of proportion."

"Pardon me, sire," returned Louvois, submissively, "it is

exactly of the size of the central window in front, and only
appears larger because of the absence of a colonnade."

"Sir," said the king, indignantly, "I tell you that this window is much too large, and unless it be reduced the entire
palace is a failure."

"I must, nevertheless, abide by my judgment, sire," replied
Louvois, respectfully. "The two windows are exactly alike;
this one being more conspicuous than the other, but not one
inch higher."

"Then you have been guilty of some great oversight by
*allowing* it to appear higher than the other," returned the
king, rudely. "Your plan is ridiculous, and the sooner you
set about mending it the better."

"Sire," said Louvois, bitterly, "when praise was to be
awarded, the credit of the plan was Mansard's—"

"But as you did not choose to concede it, you must accept
the blame of your blunder. Your vision is not acute, sir, a
defect that is as unbecoming in an architect as in a war minister. You have been equally blind to the monstrous size of
yonder window, and to the great genius of my kinsman, Eugene of Savoy. Unhappily, your want of judgment, as regards the man, is irreparable; the defect in your window you
will be so good as to correct."

"Sire," said Louvois, trembling with anger, "I beg to be
discharged from my duties as architect to your majesty. Under the circumstances, I feel myself inadequate to perform its
duties."

"You are quite right," replied the king. "You will then
have more leisure to devote to the war department, and to devise some means for gratifying the national love of glory,
without driving my French nobles to foreign courts for distinction.—Come, madame," added the king, to the marquise, who,
all this time, had been standing with eyes cast down; the very
personification of humility.—"Let us proceed to Versailles;
for this ungainly window has taken away my breath. I must
have change of scene for the remainder of the day."

As they took their seat in the coach, the marquise whispered: "Oh, sire! how overwhelming, yet how noble, is your
anger! I should die under it, were it directed toward me;

and, in spite of all Louvois' ill-will toward me, I pitied him so sincerely that I could scarcely restrain my impulse to intercede for him."

"You are an angel," was the stereotyped reply.

Meanwhile, the court were preparing to follow the royal equipage. Louvois stood by, but not one of the nobles seemed aware of his presence; he was out of favor, and thereby invisible to courtly eyes.

On the afternoon of the same day the minister of war, with brow serene and countenance unruffled, entered the council-chamber of the king. He had found a remedy for his annoyances at Trianon, and he pretended not to see the marquise, who, as usual, sat embroidering in the deep embrasure of a window, almost concealed from view by its velvet curtains.

"Sire," said Louvois, "I come before your majesty with proposals of great moment, and I await with much anxiety your decision."

"Let us hear your proposals," said the king, languidly. "Have more couriers arrived with news of Austrian successes?"

"No, sire, we have had enough of Austrian victories, and I am of opinion that the emperor must receive his check from the powerful hand of France. It is time that your majesty interposed to change his fortunes."

The king was startled out of his indifference. He raised his head to listen, while the marquise dropped her work, and applied her ear to the opening in the curtains.

"Your majesty has acted toward this arrogant Austrian with a forbearance that is more than human. Well I know that your humane aversion to bloodshed has been in part the cause of your unparalleled magnanimity; but you have been thwarted in your choice of an Elector of Cologne; your claims to Alsatia and Lorraine have been set aside; the dower of her royal highness the Duchess of Orleans has been refused you; and patience under so many affronts has ceased to be a virtue. The honor of France must be sustained, and we must evoke, as a last resort, the demon of war."

"Gracious Heaven!" said the marquise, behind her curtain, "if he rouses the king's ambition, I shall occupy but a secondary position at the court of France, and he will be more influential than ever! Louis has already forgotten me, else he would call me to his side before he decides so weighty a matter."

The marquise was shrewd, and did not err in her speculations : Louis had indeed forgotten her presence. His heart was full of covetousness and resentment at the opposition of that presuming Leopold, who penetrated his designs upon the Rhenish provinces of the empire, and he thirsted for vengeance.

"Yes," replied he, "I have given an example of forbearance which must have astonished all Europe. I would have been glad to settle our differences in a Christian-like manner ; but Leopold is deaf to all reason and justice—"

At this moment the king's voice was rendered inaudible by a loud cough which proceeded from the window wherein the marquise had retired from observation.

"My dear Françoise," exclaimed Louis, "come and take your part in this important council of war."

The hangings were parted, and out she stepped ; slightly acknowledging the salute of the minister, she passed him by, and took an arm-chair at the side of the king.

"You have heard us discussing, have you not ?" asked Louis.

"Yes, sire," sighed she, "I have heard every thing."

"Then you understand that it concerns my honor to make war upon Germany ?"

The marquise turned her flashing eyes upon the one that held this royal honor in his keeping. "Sire," said she, "I am slow of comprehension ; for it has just occurred to me that your majesty's criticism upon a window at Trianon is to be productive of results most disastrous to the French nation."

"This criticism concerns nobody but Mansard," observed Louvois, carelessly. "I am no longer superintendent of the royal edifices."

"I do not understand you, madame," interposed the king. "What has a window at Trianon to do with the affairs of the nation ?   Pray let us be serious, and come to a determination."

"Sire," asked the marquise, " is not this matter already determined ?"

The king kissed her hand.   "It is—and your inquiry is a new proof of your penetration.   How truly you sympathize with my emotions !   How clearly you read the pages of my heart !   Yes, dear marquise, war is inevitable."

"Then our days of happiness are at an end," returned she, sadly ;   "and your majesty's heart will descend from the contemplation of heavenly things, to thoughts of strife and cruel bloodshed."

" The war is a holy one," interrupted Louvois, " and God Himself holds a monarch responsible for the honor of his people."

"Well spoken, Louvois," replied the king, approvingly. " The cause is just, and the Lord of hosts will battle for us. You, marquise, will be our intercessor with Heaven."

" But your majesty will not be nigh to pray with me," said the marquise, in regretful tones.

The king made no reply to this affectionate challenge ; he continued to speak with Louvois, enjoining upon him to hasten his preparations.

"Sire, my plans are laid," replied Louvois.

" Already ! " cried Louis, joyfully.

" Already ! " echoed De Maintenon, affrighted.

"Sire," continued Louvois, " as soon as your majesty has approved my plan, the couriers, who are waiting without, will transfer your royal commands to the army.   It is my design to march at once upon the Rhenish provinces, and to take possession of the Palatinate."

" Good ! but will our army be strong enough to fight the emperor and the Germanic confederation at once ?"

" Sire, the emperor shall have occupation elsewhere, and the princes of the empire must be terrified into submission."

" But how, now ?"

" Both ends may be reached by one stroke.   The Rhenish provinces, Alsatia, and the Palatinate, must be transformed into a waste. We must wage against Germany a war of destruction, whose fearful consequences will be felt there for a century to come."

" Oh, sire," exclaimed De Maintenon, such a war is contrary to the laws of God and man ! Shall France, the most refined country on the globe, set to civilized Europe an example of barbarity only to be equalled by the atrocities of the Huns and Vandals ? "

" My dear marquise," cried Louis, fretfully, "do be silent. —Go on, Louvois, and let me hear your plans."

"Sire, they are very simple. We have only to march on the German towns, sack and burn them, and put to the sword all those that presume to defy the power of France. We must spread consternation throughout all Germany, that your majesty's name may cause every cheek to pale, and every heart to sink with fear. The enemy shall provision our army, and forage our horses. We will take possession of their magazines, stores, and shambles ; and to every house that refuses us gold, we will apply the devouring torch. Thus we will make it impossible for the emperor to advance to Lorraine ; and the wide desert that intervenes between us will become French territory."

" I approve your mode of warfare, Louvois ; it is good. If the emperor had ratified my choice of an Elector of Cologne, and had sustained my claims to Lorraine and Alsatia, I would have conceded him as many triumphs as he chose in Transylvania. As he opposes me, let him take the consequence—war with all its horrors !"

"Your majesty empowers me, then, to dispatch my couriers ? " said Louvois.

"I do, my dear marquis," was the gracious reply, while the royal hand was held out to be kissed.

Louvois pressed it to his lips, as a lover does the rosy fingers of his mistress, and, hastening away with the agility of a young man, sprang into his carriage, and drove off. " ' My dear marquis,' " murmured he, with a smile of complacency. " He called me his dear marquis, and the storm of his displeasure has passed away. I came very near being struck by its lightning, nevertheless. That De Maintenon is a shrewd woman, and found me out at once. Yes!—yes, your majesty! Had you admired my window at Trianon, I should not have been obliged to involve you in a war with Germany."

---

## CHAPTER V.

### THE IMPERIAL DIET AT REGENSBURG.

In 1687 the imperial Diet assembled at Regensburg, to examine the claims of the King of France to Alsatia, Lorraine, the Palatinate, and other possessions, which his majesty longed to appropriate out of the domains of his neighbors.

On the 2d of October, 1689, a travelling-carriage might have been seen standing in front of the large, antiquated building occupied by Count Spaur, the envoy of the Emperor Leopold.

The postilion sounded his horn, and cracked his whip with such vehemence, that here and there an inquiring and angry face might be seen at the neighboring windows, peering out upon the untimely intruders, who were making dawn hideous by their clattering arrival. The footman sprang from his board, and thundered with all his might at the door, while, between each interval of knocking, the postilion accompanied him by a fanfare that stirred up the sleeping echoes of that dull old town in a manner that was astonishing to hear.

Finally, their zeal was rewarded by the appearance of a man's head at the window on the ground floor, and the sound of his voice inquiring who it was that was making all this uproar.

"Who we are?" echoed the footman. "We are individuals entitled to make an uproar, and shall continue to make it until we obtain admission to the presence of Count Spaur for his excellency Count von Crenneville, who comes on important business from his imperial majesty the emperor."

This pompous announcement had the desired effect; it awed the porter into civility, and he hastened to inform the footman of his excellency, that Count Spaur being in bed, he

would inform the valet, and have the Austrian ambassador apprised of the visit of Count von Crenneville.

"Open your door before you go, and admit his excellency
into the house," cried the footman, imperiously.

"I dare not," replied the porter, shaking his head. "I am
not at liberty to admit anybody, until I have orders to do so
from the valet of Count Spaur."

"Not admit the emperor's envoy?" exclaimed the indignant lackey. "That is an affront to his excellency."

"I do not know the person of his excellency," persisted the
porter, "and how do I know but some petty ducal envoy may
not be playing a trick on me, and so obtain fraudulent entrance to the house of the Austrian ambassador?"

"You presume to apply such language to Count von
Crenneville!" cried the footman. "I shall—"

"Peace, Caspar!" said a voice from the carriage; "the
honest fellow is quite right, and deserves no blame for his
prudence. Nevertheless, as we are no impostors, hasten, my
good friend, to the valet, and let me have entrance, for I am
very tired."

At this moment the porter was put aside, and a man in rich
livery came forward.

"Count Spaur has risen, and will be happy to receive his
excellency Count von Crenneville," said he. At these magical
words the heavy doors were opened, and the envoy sprang
lightly from his carriage, and entered the house. At the head
of the staircase he was met by Count Spaur, who apologized
for being compelled to receive his guest in a dressing-gown.

"It would not be the first time that I have seen you in a
deshabille, my dear comrade," replied Von Crenneville, "for
you cannot have forgotten the old days when we were quar-
tered together in Hungary. As I presume you have not breakfasted, I will take the liberty of inviting myself to breakfast,
for I am hungry and exhausted by travelling all night."

Count Spaur offered his arm, and conducted his guest to
the dining-room, where breakfast was about to be served.

Count von Crenneville threw aside his military cloak, un-
fastened a few buttons of his uniform, and took his seat at the
table.

"I am delighted to see you," said Count Spaur, handing a cup of chocolate. "Your arrival is a delicious interruption to the stupid life I had in Regensburg."

When they had breakfasted, Count Spaur led the way to his cabinet, and the conference began by Count von Crenneville handing a packet to his friend from the emperor.

The latter received it with a profound inclination, and carefully cutting it, so as to avoid breaking the seal, he opened it, and prepared to make himself master of its contents.

He shook his head dolefully. "His majesty asks impossibilities of me," sighed he. "Do you know what this letter contains?"

"Be so kind as to read it to me."

So Count Spaur began : "My dear Count,—It is time this imperial Diet end their petty quarrels, and go seriously to work ; for these are no days wherein important interests may be neglected for the sake of etiquette. Announce to the Diet that I require of them to be serious, and to come to the assistance of their fatherland. Count von Crenneville, who will deliver this to you, is empowered to declare the same to the assembled representatives of the Germanic Confederation.

(Signed) "LEOPOLD, Emperor."

"It seems to me that the demand is a reasonable one," remarked Count von Crenneville.

"But impossible of compliance. Do you know how long the Diet has been sitting at Regensburg?"

"Two years, I believe."

"Well : do you know what they have been doing for these two years?"

"No, count ; it is precisely to learn this that his majesty has sent me here," said Von Crenneville.

"I will tell you then. They have been profoundly engaged in settling questions of diplomatic etiquette. You may laugh, if you like ; but for one that has been obliged to hear it all, it is wearisome beyond expression. The first trouble arose from the etiquette of visiting. As imperial envoy, I received the first visit from them all, I returned my calls, and so far all was well. But when the other envoys were to visit among themselves, the dissensions began. Each man wrote to his sover-

eign, and each sovereign upheld his man ; couriers came and
went, and for a time Regensburg was alive with arrivals and
departures."

"And meanwhile the King of France was allowed to build
his bridges across the Rhine," observed Count von Crenneville.

"My dear friend, the King of France might have dethroned
the emperor, meanwhile, without a protest. Nothing under
heaven could be attended to, while this visiting question was
on the tapis."

"Is it decided ? "

"After three months of daily conferences, during which I
exhausted more statesmanship than would overturn an empire,
it was decided that the envoys of the princes would call on the
envoys of the electors, provided the latter would come half
way down the staircase to meet the former."

"God be thanked !  They could then proceed to business !"

Count Spaur replied by a melancholy shake of the head.

"You are not aware that, before the Diet assemble, a banquet is given, at which all are expected to be present.  You
are furthermore not cognizant of the fact that every concomi-
tant of this banquet has been made a subject of strife, from
the day on which the visiting question was arranged, until
the present time."

"My dear count, I pity you."

"You may well do so.  The electoral envoys claimed the
right of using gold knives and forks, while they exacted that
the ducal representatives should be content with silver.  These
latter resented the indignity, and of course the banquet had to
be postponed."

"This is pitiful indeed ; but go on."

"Then came the question of the color of the arm-chairs
around the table.  The electoral envoys claimed the right of
having their seats covered in red ; and contended that the
others were obliged by etiquette to cover theirs with green.
The others would not accept the green, and so arose the third
point of discussion.  The fourth disagreement was about the
carpets.  The electorals would have the *four* legs of their
chairs on the carpet (which is narrow), and the others should

have but the *fore*-legs of theirs.   The fifth regarded the May-bougns.   On May-day, the electorals exacted that the superin-tendent of public festivities should put six boughs over their front doors, while the others must content themselves with five.   Now, my dear count, you are made acquainted with the subjects of discussion which for two years have detained the imperial Diet in Regensburg ; which have imbittered my days, and made sleepless my nights ; which have nigh lost the cause of German nationality, and have made us the laughing-stock of all Europe."

"My friend, I sympathize with you.—But are these five questions not decided ?"

"No, they are not.   The ducal envoys indignantly refused to yield to the pretensions of their colleagues, and no banquet could be given.   After much exertion on my part to bring about an understanding, the banquet was set aside, and a com-promise was effected.   *All* the arm-chairs were covered with green—this was a concession to the ducal envoys ; while they, on their part, consented that the hind-legs of their chairs should rest on the bare floor !"*

"What a victory !   I congratulate you from my heart ; for I would much rather have charged a regiment of Jani-zaries."

"And at least have earned some glory thereby," returned Spaur, grimly.   "But the only reward I shall ever reap will be the unpleasant notoriety I shall have acquired as a member of this stultified assembly."

"My dear friend, be under no uneasiness as to that.   The King of France has crossed our frontiers, and you are about to throw aside diplomacy and take up the sword.   This is the message with which the emperor has charged me, both to yourself and to the imperial Diet."

"I am happy to tell you that to-day the Diet opens its sit-ting.   Hark ! the bells are ringing !   This announces to Re-gensburg that the envoys are about to proceed to the hall of conference.   Excuse me while I retire to change my dress."

"I will betake myself to the nearest hotel to follow your example," replied Von Crenneville.

* Pütter, " Historical Notes on the Constitution of the German Empire."

"By no means. Your room is prepared, and I will conduct you thither at once, if you wish."

Fifteen or twenty minutes elapsed, when the two imperial envoys met again, and drove, in the state-carriage of Count Spaur, to the hall of conference. The other envoys were all assembled, and, scattered in groups, seemed to be earnestly engaged in discussing some weighty matter.

Count Spaur remarked this, and whispered to his colleague : "I am afraid there is trouble brewing ; the electoral envoys are all on one side of the hall—the ducal on the other."

"The electorals are those with the red cloaks—are they not ?"

"Yes, they are ; and I fear that these red cloaks signify war."

"What do you mean ?"

"I mean war with—but, pardon me, I see that they are waiting for me to open the council."

With an inclination of the head, Count Spaur passed down the hall, and took his seat under the red canopy appropriated to the imperial ambassador. A deep silence reigned throughout the assembly, broken by the sweet chime of the bells that still continued to convey far and wide the intelligence of the opening of the conference.

Count Spaur took off his Spanish hat, and, bowing right and left, addressed the envoys :

"My lords ambassadors of the electors, princes, and imperial cities of the German empire, in the name of his majesty Leopold I greet you, and announce that the imperial Diet is opened. Long live the emperor !"

"Long live the emperor !" echoed the ambassadors.

"The Diet is opened," resumed he, "and I have the honor to introduce an envoy of his imperial majesty, who has this day arrived from Vienna."

At this, Count von Crenneville advanced, and the master of ceremonies placed an arm-chair for him under the canopy, at the side of Count Spaur.

At a signal from the latter, the other envoys took their seats, and Count von Crenneville addressed the assembly :

"My lords ambassadors of the electors, princes, and imperial cities of the German empire, his majesty greets you all. But he is deeply wounded at the indifference manifested by the Diet to the dearest interests of Germany, and he implores you, as you value your nationality and liberty, to lay aside your petty dissensions, and to unite with him in defence of your fatherland. The King of France has marched his armies into Germany—and disunion to Germans is defeat and ruin."

This prelude appeared to cause considerable emotion. There was visible agitation throughout the assembly.

Count von Crenneville felt encouraged, and was about to continue his appeal, when one of the electorals started from his seat and spoke:

"I beg pardon of the imperial envoy; but I must ask permission of the imperial representative-resident to make a personal remark."

"The permission is granted," replied Count Spaur, solemnly.

The envoy then continued, in loud and agitated tones: "I must, then, call the attention of this august assembly to a flagrant violation of the compact agreed between the first and second class of these ambassadors, by the latter. They have advanced their arm-chairs until the four legs of the same are now resting upon the carpet."

"We merely advanced our seats, to hear what his excellency had to say," remarked the envoy from Bremen.

"Nevertheless," replied Count Spaur, "I must request these gentlemen to recede. The understanding was, that their chairs were to rest partly on the carpet, partly on the floor."

Back went all the chairs, but their occupants looked daggers at the envoy from Mentz.

Count von Crenneville then resumed the broken thread of his discourse: "I earnestly request the assembly to come to a decision this very day. The country is in imminent danger, and can only be saved by unanimity and promptitude of action."

Here he was interrupted by the envoy from Bremen, who rose and begged to be allowed to make *his* personal remark.

Count Spaur gave the required permission, and Bremen began to protest against Mentz & Co.

"I beg to remark, that the electoral envoys have spread out their red cloaks over the backs of the chairs, in such a way as to conceal the green covering entirely from view."

"It is exceedingly warm in the hall," replied electoral Cologne; "we were compelled to throw off our cloaks."

"Why, then, did the electoral envoys wear their cloaks?" was the inquiry of the other side.

"Because we had a right to wear them hither, and violate no compact by throwing them over our chairs."

"But the electoral envoys had no right to use them as upholstery," objected Bremen, in tragic tones. "They have now the appearance of being seated on red arm-chairs."

"So much the better," replied Cologne. "If accident has re-established our rights of precedence, nobody has any business to complain." *

This declaration was received with a burst of indignation, and the princely envoys rose simultaneously from their seats. A noisy and angry debate ensued, at the conclusion of which the offended party declared that they would rest every leg of their chairs upon the carpet; and, as if at the word of command, every man dragged his arm-chair most unequivocally forward, and surveyed the enemy with dogged defiance.

There was now a commotion on the side of the electorals, in the midst of which Count Spaur, in perfect despair, cried out at the top of his voice:

"In the name of the emperor, I demand, on both sides, the literal fulfilment of your conditions. The electoral ambassadors must withdraw their red cloaks from the backs of their chairs, and throw them over the arms, and the other envoys must draw back their chairs until the hind-legs thereof are on the floor."

"My lords," added Count von Crenneville, "I demand also, in the name of the emperor, that all personalities be cast aside, and that we give our hearts to our country's cause. France is upon us. She knows how disunited are the princes of Germany, and their discord is her sheet-anchor. She knows that

* Historical.—See Pütter.

you are unprepared to meet her, and the emperor, being at present too far to come to your rescue, she will attack you before you have time to defend yourselves. Is it possible that you have sunk all patriotism in contemptible jealousies of one another? I cannot believe it! Away with petty rivalry and family dissensions : clasp hands and make ready to defend our fatherland !"

At this moment there was a knock at the main entrance of the hall, and two masters of ceremonies appeared.

"I announce to the imperial commissaries, and the envoys of the German empire here assembled, that a messenger, with important tidings, requests admission to this illustrious company."

"Whence comes he?" asked Count Spaur.

"He announces himself as Count de Crecy, ambassador extraordinary of the King of France to the imperial Diet."

This communication was received in profound silence. Dismay was pictured on many a face, and every eye was turned upon the presiding envoy, the representative of the emperor.

"I lay it before the imperial Diet," said he, at last, "whether the French ambassador shall be allowed entrance into the hall during the sitting of its members."

"Ay, ay, let him enter," was the reply—the first instance of unanimity among the envoys since the day they had arrived at Regensburg two years before !

The masters of ceremonies retired, and Count Spaur, putting on his hat, said : "I declare this sitting suspended. My lords, cover your heads !"

The French ambassador, followed by a numerous retinue, now entered the hall. He advanced to the canopy where the imperial envoys were seated, and inclined his head. Not a word was spoken in return for his salutation ; and, after a short pause, he raised his voice, and delivered his message :

"In the name of his most Christian majesty, Louis XIV., King of France, I announce to the Diet of the German empire that he has taken possession of Bonn, Kaiserswerth, and other strongholds of the archbishopric of Cologne ; that Mentz has opened her doors to his victorious armies, and that war is de-

28

clared between France and Germany. The sword is drawn,
nor shall it return to its scabbard until the inheritance of the
Duchess of Orleans is given up to France, and the King of
France is recognized as lord and sovereign of Lorraine, Alsatia,
and the Netherlands! War is declared!"

---

# CHAPTER VI.

### THE JUDITH OF ESSLINGEN.

It was a clear, bright morning in March. The snow had
long since melted from the mountain-tops, flowers had begun
to peep out of the earth's bosom, and the trees that grew upon
the heights around Esslingen were decked with buds of tender
green.

But the inhabitants of Esslingen had no pleasure in contemplating those verdant hills ; for the castle that crowned
their summit was in possession of the French. Within its
walls the enemy were feasting and drinking, while the owners
of the soil, plundered of all they possessed, had naught left to
them on earth save the cold, bare boards of their homes, wherein, a few weeks before, peace and plenty had reigned.

On the 2d of March, 1689, the French reduced the castle of
Heidelberg to a heap of ashes, and for more than a century its
bleak ruins kept alive the hatred of Germany toward their
relentless enemies.

God had permitted them to spread desolation over the land.
He had withdrawn His help from the innocent, and had suffered the wicked to triumph. After plundering their houses
of every necessary of life, General Melac now required of them
tribute in the shape of twenty thousand florins. To raise one-
fourth of the sum was an impossibility in Esslingen ; and the
burghers of the town had gone in a body to the castle to beg
for mercy.

Two hours had elapsed since they had departed on their
dangerous mission, and the people, with throbbing hearts,
awaited their return. Up to this day, they had mourned and

wept in the solitude of their plundered homes; but in this hour of mortal suspense, they had instinctively sought companionship; and now the market-place, in whose centre was the ancient town-hall, was thronged with men, women, and children, of every degree. Misfortune had levelled all distinctions of rank, and the common danger had cemented thousands of human beings into one stricken and terrified family.

They stood, their anxious looks fixed upon the winding path which led to the castle, while all around at the open windows pale-faced women hoped and feared by turns, as they saw light or shadow upon the faces of the multitude below.

Just opposite the council-hall was a house of dark-gray stone, with a bow-window and a richly-fretted gable. At the window stood two persons; one a woman whose head was enveloped in a black veil which set off the extreme paleness of her face, and fell in long folds around her person. Near her stood a young girl similarly attired; but, instead of the hair just tinged with gray, which lay in smooth bands across the forehead of her companion, her golden curls, stirred by the breeze, encircled her young head like a halo, and the veil that fluttered lightly around her graceful person lay like a misty cloud about a face as beautiful in color as it was in feature. Spite of suffering and privation, the brow was smooth and fair, the cheeks were tinged with rose, and the lips were scarlet as autumn berries. She, like the rest, had endured hunger and cold; but youth is warmed and nourished by Hope, and the tears that dim a maiden's eyes are but dew-drops glittering upon a beautiful rose.

Her face was serious and anxious, but her large black eyes flashed with expectation, and the parted lips showed that hope was stronger than fear in her young heart. Marie was the only child of the chief burgomaster of Esslingen, and the lady at her side was his honored wife.

"Do you see nothing, my child?" said the mother. "Great God! this suspense is worse than death! Your father expected to be back within an hour, and more than two hours have gone by!"

The young girl strained her eyes, and looked up the castle-road, which was just opposite the house. "Mother," said she, "I see something dark issuing from the gates."

"Oh, look again! Is it they?"

"Yes; I think so, dear mother. I see them advancing: it must be father and the deputies. Now I begin to distinguish one from the other. There are one—two—three. Great God, mother! were there not seven? I see but six!"

"Yes—seven. Your father, two burgomasters, and four senators. Are you sure? Look—count once more."

"I see them distinctly now: there are six. They will be hidden presently by the winding of the road; but I see them each one as he turns aside."

"And there are but six! One of them is missing! Oh, merciful Father, which of them can it be?"

"I see them no longer. Alas! they are too far for recognition, and we must wait. Oh, mother, how my heart pains me!"

"Let us pray, my darling," returned the mother, clasping her daughter's trembling hands.

"Dear mother, I cannot! I am too miserable to pray. If Caspar were but here, I should feel less wretched."

"And yet, as a soldier of the imperial army, he is in less danger than he would be, as a civilian of Esslingen. I thank Heaven, dear Marie, that your betrothed is not here. At least he fights face to face, with arms in hand; while we—oh, what weapon can avail against midnight murder and incendiarism?"

"And yet," sighed Marie, "I would he were here to protect me!"

"He would not be allowed to protect you, for, had he seen the familiarity of that despot yesterday, he would in all probability have lost his life in your defence."

"I had not thought of that, I had only yearned for his protecting arm. Yes, mother, he would have done some desperate deed had he seen the blood-stained hand of that accursed Frenchman when it touched my cheek, and heard his insolent tones as he asked whether its roses were colored by nature or art. Oh, mother, what a misfortune for us that we were on the street when he arrived!"

Mother and daughter now relapsed into silence, for the

deputies, their heads despondingly held down, were to be seen making their way through the crowd. Frau Wengelin could not articulate the words she longed to speak ; but Marie, clasping her hands in agony, cried out :

" He is not there ! My father is missing ! "

With one faint shriek, her mother fell senseless to the floor, while Marie, darting out of the house, made her way through the throng to the market-place, and overtook the deputies as they were ascending the steps that led to the hall of council. Grasping the arm of the first she encountered, she looked wildly into his eyes, while her quivering lips vainly tried to murmur, " Where is my father ? "

The old man understood those pleading looks, and answered them with tears.

" Where is my father ? " cried Marie, with the strength of her growing agony ; and, as the deputy was still silent, the multitude around took up the young girl's words and shouted : " Where is her father ? Tell us where is the Burgomaster Wengelin ? "

" Is he dead ? " murmured Marie, her teeth chattering with fear.

" No, Marie," replied the senator, " he is not dead, but if no help is vouchsafed from above, he will die to-day, and we must all die with him."

The people broke into a long wail, and Marie fell upon her knees to pray. She could frame no words wherewith to cry for mercy, but her soul was with God ; and for a few moments she was rapt in an ecstasy that bore her far, far away from the weeping multitude around. She was recalled from her pious transport by the voice of her uncle, one of the deputies, who was addressing the people.

General Melac had mocked at their petition. They had humbled themselves on their knees for the sake of their suffering fellow-citizens, but the heartless Frenchman had laughed, and, laughing, reiterated his command.

If before sunset the five hundred thousand francs were not forthcoming, the French soldiery would be there with fire and sword. The inhabitants should be exterminated, and Esslingen laid in ashes.

This horrible disclosure was received with another burst of woe, except from the unfortunate Marie, who stood like a pale and rigid Niobe—her grief too deep for tears or sighs.

When the tumult had somewhat subsided, the senator resumed his sad recital. At sound of the Frenchman's cruel mandate, the Burgomaster Wengelin had risen from his knees, and raising his head proudly, had cried out: "Give us back that of which you have robbed us, and we can pay you ten times the sum you ask. We were a peaceful and prosperous community until your plundering hordes reduced us to beggary. Be content with the booty you have already; and be not twice a barbarian, first stealing our property, and then, like a fiend, requiring us to reproduce and lay it at your feet."

The noble indignation of the burgomaster excited nothing but mirth on the part of the Frenchman. He laughed.

"Well, it makes no great difference, after all. Your lives will do quite as well as the ransom you cannot afford to pay for them. My soldiery like fire and blood and pretty women almost as well as they do gold, and I shall enjoy the spectacle from the castle-walls. As for you, burgomaster, you have something that I covet for my own use—your beautiful daughter."

"My daughter!" shrieked Wengelin, defiantly, "before she should be delivered to you, monster! I would take her life as Virginius took that of his well-beloved child!"

The general said not a word. For a time the two men eyed each other like two enraged tigers; but General Melac wasted no time in vain indignation. He signed to his guards, and ordered them to take away the prisoner, and retain him as a hostage until sunset.

"When our well-beloved citizens of Esslingen shall hear the report of the musketry that ends *his* life, they will know that the signal for pillage has been given. The execution will take place at sunset."

Then, addressing himself to the six remaining deputies: "Go," said he, "and relate what you have seen and heard to your fellow-citizens; and tell them that my Frenchmen are skilful both with sabre and torch; they have been practising for several weeks past in Heidelberg, Mannheim, and other German cities. Do not forget to communicate all this to the fair daughter of the burgomaster."

This time there was no outburst of grief from the people; they felt that all hope was vain, and they were nerving themselves for martyrdom. Presently there was a sound of voices, and the fugitives from Wurtemberg and the Palatinate were heard relating their frightful experience of the warfare of a monarch who styled himself "Most Christian King."

One of them mounted the steps of the council-hall, and described the entrance of the French into his native town. The people were driven with bayonets from their beds into the snow, children were tossed into the flames; old men were butchered like cattle; maidens were torn from the arms of their parents, and given over to the soldiery; and the narrator, who had escaped, had been for days without food—for weeks without covering or shelter!

As the man concluded this frightful picture of carnage, a voice from among the crowd was heard in clear, loud, ringing tones:

"There is rescue at hand—we must make use of it!"

At the same moment, Marie felt a grasp upon her arm, and turning beheld herself in the custody of a tall, pale man, who continued to cry out:

"She can rescue us! I saw the French general stroke her cheeks yesterday, and look at her with eyes of love. Did he not demand her of her father? And were his last words not a message to her? I hint that she might ransom us if she would!"

"Ay, ay," responded one of the crowd. "Ay!" echoed another and another; and now the chorus gathered strength, and swelled into a shout that penetrated the walls of Esslingen Castle, and reached the ears of Marie's unconscious father.

Marie covered her face with her hands, and sank upon her knees. "Oh, Caspar!" was the unspoken thought of her affectionate soul.

"Friends!" exclaimed her uncle, "you are drunk with

cowardly fright.  Know ye that ye ask of this maiden her own ruin for your lives ? "

"But if Melac's soldiery are set upon us," replied a young woman in the throng ; "we shall all be ruined—mothers, wives, and maidens.  And is it not better," continued she, raising her voice, and addressing the mob, "is it not better that one woman should suffer dishonor than a thousand ? "

"Marie Wengelin will have her father's life to answer for, as well as the lives of her fellow-citizens," cried another voice. " It is her duty to sacrifice herself."

At this moment the loud, shrill tones of an affrighted voice were heard calling out, " Marie ! Marie ! my child ! " and the figure of Frau Wengelin, with outstretched arms, was now seen at the window, whence the mother and daughter had watched the return of the deputies.

Marie would have responded to that pathetic appeal, but as she rose from her knees, and attempted to move, she was forced and held back by the crowd.  They were lost to all sense of humanity for the one segregated being by whose immolation the safety of the aggregate might be effected.

"Have pity ! have pity ! " cried the poor girl.  "Do you not hear my mother calling me ?  Think of your own children, and hinder me not, I implore ye ! "

" We think of our children, and therefore you shall not go !  You shall sacrifice yourself for the suffering many ! "

And they lifted her back to the peristyle, where she stood alone, confronting the pitiless crowd that demanded her honor wherewith to buy their lives.  What was the fate of the daughter of Jephthah, compared to that which threatened poor Marie of Esslingen ?

Suddenly a cloud seemed to pass over the sky, and the faces of her enemies were no longer distinct.  Marie raise her arms wildly over her head, and screamed, for too well she understood the shadow that rested upon the market-place.  The sun had sunk behind the heights of Esslingen, and one half hour remained ere her father lost his life.

The crowd renewed their cries, entreaties, and threats. Some appealed to her patriotism, some to her filial love, some called her a murderess,—the meanest among the multitude at tempted to terrify her—as if any doom could equal the horror of the one they were forcing upon an innocent, pure-hearted, and loving girl !

She raised her hand to obtain a hearing.

" You shall not perish if my prayers can save you ! I will go to our oppressor, and try to move his heart to pity."

She heard neither their shouts of joy nor their thanks. She was hardly conscious of the blessings that were being poured on her head, the kisses that were imprinted on her rigid, clammy hands. She stood for a while, her teeth clinched, her eyes distended, her figure dilated to its utmost ; then suddenly she shivered, thrust away the women that were clustering about her, and began her *via crucis.*

At the gate of the city she encountered the pastor that had baptized and received her into the church. He had placed himself there that he might pour what consolation he could into that bruised and bleeding heart. The old man laid his hand upon her golden curls, and she fell at his feet. The multitude that had followed their victim simultaneously bent the knee and bowed their heads ; for, although they were too far to overhear his words, they knew that the pastor was blessing her.

" As Abraham blessed Isaac, and as the Israelites blessed Judith, so do I bless thee, thou deliverer of thy people ! May God inspire thy tongue, and so soften the heart of the tyrant, that he may hearken to thy prayers, and, looking upon thy pure and virgin brow, he may respect that honor which is dearer to woman than life. God bless thee, Marie ! God bless thee !" He bowed his head close to her ear. "Marie you are a Christian. Swear to me that you will not stain your hands with blood."

Marie's eyes flashed fire. "Did not the Israelite kill Holofernes ? "

"Yes, my child ; but Israel's heroine was called Judith, and ours bears the blessed name of Mary ! 'Vengeance is mine, saith the Lord ; I will repay.'"

Marie's eye was still unsubdued, and she looked more like Judith than like Mary. The old pastor was agitated and alarmed.

"Marie, Marie, you are in the hands of God. Come weal, come wo, can you not trust yourself to Him? See, the sun goes lower and lower; but before I release your hand you must swear that it shall shed no blood."

Alas! Yes—the sun was rapidly sinking, and she must hasten, or her father's life would be lost. "I promise," said she, "and now, father, pray—pray for—"

She could say no more; but rising she went alone up the steps that led to Esslingen Castle. The people, still on their knees, followed her lithe figure till it was hidden for a time by the fir-trees that grew along the heights; then, as she emerged again and appeared at the hill-top, the multitude gave vent to their feelings in prayer.

Higher and higher she mounted, until they saw that she had reached the gates, and disappeared.

---

## CHAPTER VII.

### HER RETURN.

HOURS went by and darkness set in. It was a cold night in March; the wind howled in fitful gusts along the streets, but the people could not disperse. They sat shivering together in the market-place; for how was it possible for sleep to visit their eyes, when every moment might hurl destruction upon their heads. The old priest went from one to another, encouraging the desponding, and comforting the afflicted; praying with the mothers, and covering their shivering children, who, stretched at the feet of their parents, or resting within their arms, were the only ones there to whom sleep brought oblivion of sorrow.

At last that fearful night of suspense went by. A rosy flush tinged the eastern sky, it deepened to gold, and the sun rose. The people raised a hymn of thanksgiving, and, as they were rising from their devotions, the roll of a drum was heard, and a file of soldiers were seen issuing from the castle-gates. They came nearer and nearer, until they reached the city;

but by the time they had neared the market-place, not a human being was there to confront them : the people had all fled to their houses.

They stopped before the residence of the burgomaster, and from an opening made in the ranks there issued two persons ; the one a man, the other a woman. The latter was veiled, and her head rested languidly upon the shoulders of her companion.

A group of French officers escorted them to the door, where they took off their hats, and, bowing low, retired. The father and daughter were lost to view, the drum beat anew, and the men, without exchanging a word with the inhabitants, returned to their quarters at Esslingen Castle.

The people were no sooner reassured as to the intentions of the soldiers, than they poured in streams from their homes, and took their way to the burgomaster's house. Congratulations were exchanged between friends, parents embraced their children, husbands pressed their wives to their bosoms ; every heart overflowed with gratitude to Marie, every voice was lifted in her praise.

But she ! Scarcely enduring her mother's caresses, she had torn herself from that mother's embrace, and, hastening away to the solitude of her own room, had bolted herself within.

Two hours went by, and the house of the burgomaster could scarcely contain the friends that flocked thither to welcome his daughter. Without, a band of music was playing martial airs, while within, halls, parlors, and staircases, were crowded with magistrates in their robes of office, churchmen in their clerical gowns, and women and maidens in gay and festive apparel.

A deputation of citizens now requested to be permitted to pay homage to the heroine that had rescued her townsmen from death ; and Frau Wengelin ventured to knock at the door of her daughter's chamber. She was so earnest in her pleadings, that at last the bolt was withdrawn, and Marie, with bloodshot eyes, and mouth convulsed, appeared upon the threshold.

" Come, my child," said the poor mother, " the citizens will not leave the house until they have seen you." And compelling her forward, Frau Wengelin, with some difficulty, brought her as far as the foot of the staircase.

She was greeted with loud and repeated cheerings, which scarcely appeared to reach her ear, while her eyes, fixed upon the throng before her, seemed to ask what meant this turmoil.

Suddenly she heard her name whispered, and, with a fearful shriek, she recoiled from the outstretched hand of a young man, who had just rushed forward to clasp her in his arms.

"What ails my Marie on this festive day, where all is joy around?" said he. "I have just this moment arrived, to say that help is nigh, my countrymen," added he, addressing the crowd. ".Our army is at hand, and the French shall suffer for their deeds of violence in Germany. But what means this large and gay assemblage? And who are these?" asked he, as a group of young maidens came forward with a crown of laurel, and some of the principal burgomasters, leading the bewildered Marie to a throne decked with flowers, seated her on a chair under its green and fragrant canopy.

No answer was made to his inquiry, for one of the deputies began an address, in which Marie was hailed as the heroine that had rescued her fellow-citizens from death, and her native place from destruction. Her portrait was to grace the council-hall of Esslingen, and such honors as it lay in the power of its magistrates to confer, were to be hers forever.

At this moment Marie rose suddenly from her seat, gasped for breath, and fell as suddenly back, for the first time lifting her face, which, as she lay against the wall of flowers that concealed her chair, was marble-white, and strangely convulsed.

Her mother started forward, and Caspar, catching her in his arms, covered her face with kisses.

"What ails thee, my beloved? Oh, do not look so wildly at thy Caspar! Marie, my own one, what is it?"

"It is over," murmured she, almost inaudibly.

"What is over?" cried the frightened mother, bending over her child's writhing form.

" Life ! " sighed the girl, and her eyes closed wearily.

The frightful stillness was unbroken by a sound.  Frau Wengelin suppressed her sobs, that she might gaze upon her dying child ; while her father stood by, the picture of dumb despair.  Caspar held her to his heart, dimly apprehending the fearful tragedy of the hour, and the guests pressed noiselessly around, vainly striving to catch a glimpse of their victim's face.

The crowd opened to allow passage to the priest, who, approaching the throne, came and knelt beside Caspar.

" Marie," said he, in a loud, distinct voice, that reached the portals of her soul, and aroused her departing senses.

Marie slowly opened her eyes, and gazed upon the speaker.  " I have kept my oath," said she, hoarsely.  " No blood was shed, but I have returned to die."

" Wherefore to die ? " cried several voices at once.

" Ask my Caspar," murmured she, looking fondly into the face of her betrothed, and, with her eyes fixed upon his, Marie's soul took its flight to heaven.

# BOOK VII.

## CHAPTER I.

### THE ISLAND OF BLISS.

THEY were together in the little pavilion of the garden at Schönbrunn. With clasped hands, and eyes that sparkled with happiness, they sat in that sweet silence which to lovers is more eloquent than words. The door that led to the park was open, and the balmy breath of May wafted toward them the perfume of the flowers and trees without.

The park, too, was undisturbed by a sound. The laborers had gone to their mid-day meal, and the birds had hidden themselves away from the sunbeams. The great heart of Nature was pulsating with a joy like that of the lovers, too great for utterance. There was something in the appearance of this youthful pair which would have convinced a looker-on that there was a mystery of some sort surrounding the romance of their love. For the one was in the garb of a nun, her head concealed by a coif, and her person enveloped in a long white veil ; while the other was attired in a splendid Spanish dress. Over it hung a heavy gold chain, to which was attached the order of the Golden Fleece. His soft black hair lay on a forehead white as snow, and made a pleasant contrast with a face which was pale, not with sickness or suffering, but with that suppressed sensibility which leaves the cheek colorless because its fires are concentrated within the heart. No ! It was not for sorrow that Eugene of Savoy was pale ; it was from excess of joy ; for *she* was at his side, and the world had nothing more to bestow !

So thought he, as, with caressing hand, he lifted her long veil from her shoulders and threw it behind, in imitation of the drapery that hangs around Raphael's Madonnas.

"Oh, how I love you, Sister Angelica!" murmured he; "and, in my feverish visions, how often I have mistaken that white veil for the snowy sail of a ship of which I used to dream in my delirium—a ship that was bearing me onward to an island of bliss, where my Laura stood with outstretched arms, and welcomed me home! But what were imagination's brightest picturings to the reality of the deep joy that flooded my being, when the veil was flung back, and my love stood revealed! Oh, Laura—my life will be all too short to reward you for your fidelity."

"You love me, Eugene, and therein is my unspeakable reward."

"And will you never leave me, dearest?"

She laid her small hand upon his head, smoothed his hair fondly, and gazed passionately into his eyes. You ask, as if you required an answer," said she, in tones that were tremulous with love.

"I do require an answer, for I am continually fearing that this is a blissful dream; and that some morn I shall awake to find thee flown, and Angelica the nun all that is left of thee! When thou art absent from my sight, I shiver with dread lest I should see thee never more."

She laughed, and oh, how musical was her laugh! "Is this the hero of Belgrade, that talks of shivering with dread?"

"Yes; and when he thinks that he might lose you, he is no hero, but a poor coward. And in truth, my Laura, I am tired of a soldier's life—it is too exciting for my health; and I am tired of the world and its frivolities, too. If you love me as I do you, you will be happy in our mutual love, without other companionship than mine."

"Over castle-roof, and through the dangerous descent of that castle-chimney, came I to meet you, Eugene; how then should I pine for other companionship?"

"When I think how mysterious was your escape, I dread lest you should disappear from me as mysteriously. The very thought presses on my brain like the first horrid symptoms of madness; then my body begins to suffer, my wounds seem to open, and bleed anew. Laura, prove to me your love by going with me into solitude. I am tired of being a courtier, and have asked the emperor for my discharge."

"Did he grant it, Eugene?" asked she, fixing her large, penetrating eyes upon his, with an earnestness that forbade him to avoid her glance.

"He will grant it to-morrow. To-morrow for the last time, I go to the imperial palace as a field-marshal; I shall return thence nobody but Eugene of Savoy, your lover, who lives but to serve you, and repay if he can all that he owes to your courageous and heroic affection."

"The emperor has refused," replied Laura. "He gave you time for reflection," added she, looking intently again into her lover's eyes.

"Perhaps he may have wished me to reflect," replied he, smiling, and trying to endure her scrutiny. "But my resolve is not to be shaken. I shall retire to the estate presented me by the emperor in Hungary, there to live with my darling on an island of bliss, upheaved so far above the tempestuous ocean of the world's vicissitudes, that no lashing of its waves will ever reach our home. Will you go with me into this island, where you shall not fear the world's censorious comments on our reunion—where you may throw aside that false vestal garb, and be my own untrammelled bride?"

Laura said nothing; a deep glow suffused her cheeks, and her eyes filled with tears. Gliding from her seat to her knees, she took her lover's hand and covered it with kisses.

"Laura!" exclaimed he, "what can this signify?"

Laura wept on for a time in silence; then, when she had recovered herself sufficiently to speak, she replied:

"It signifies that I bow down before the magnanimity of him who, to shield me from the world's contumely, would relinquish that which he holds most dear on earth, his hopes of glory."

"Laura, give me an answer to my prayer. Will you go with me to my estates in Hungary?"

Laura smiled, but said nothing.

"Answer me, Laura, answer me, my own love."

"The emperor gave you a day to reflect upon your sudden

desire for retirement. Give me but one hour for my decision."

"You hesitate!"

"Only *one* hour, Eugene; but during that hour I must be alone with my Maker. Await me here."

Drawing the veil over her face, Laura bounded lightly down the pavilion steps, and walked hurriedly toward the palace. Eugene looked after her with eyes that beamed with love ineffable, sighing as he did so: "She is worthy of the sacrifice; I owe it to her."

The hour seemed interminable. At first, he fixed his eyes upon the walk by which she must return; then he turned away, that he might wait until he heard her dear voice.

At last a light step approached the pavilion; he heard it coming up the steps, and a beloved voice spoke:

"The Marchioness de Bonaletta."

Eugene turned, and there, instead of Sister Angelica, stood his beautiful Laura in rich attire—so beautiful that he thought he had never sufficiently admired her before.

He started forward, and, dropping on one knee, took her little hand, and covered it with kisses. Then, rising, he flung his arm around her waist, and drew her to a seat.

"Now read me the riddle," said he.

"My beloved, do you think me so blind as not to have comprehended the immeasurable sacrifice you would have made to my womanly pride? Oh, how I thank you, my own, peerless Eugene! But I will not accept it. I may not bear your name, but God knows that I am your wife, as Eve was the spouse of Adam; and it is for me to show that our bond is holy, by enduring courageously the stigma of being considered as your mistress. Enough for me to feel that to you I shall be an honored and beloved wife, incapable of sharing your fame, but oh, how proud of my hero! Gird on your sword, my Eugene, and fulfil your glorious destiny. Go once more into the world, and let me share your fate."

"Let her share my fate! She asks me to let her share my fate," cried Eugene, pressing her to his heart. And God and Nature blessed the union that man refused to acknowledge.

## CHAPTER II.

### THE FRENCH IN SPEIER.

GENERAL MELAC and his murderous hordes were in the old city of Speier, squandering the goods and money of which they had robbed the unfortunate inhabitants. Scarcely two months had elapsed since the departure of the French from Esslingen, and in that short interval they had laid more than one hundred towns in ashes.

But Melac was insatiable ; his eyes feasted on the scarlet hue of German blood, his ears were ravished with the sounds of German groans and sighs ; and oftentimes, when the poor hunted fugitives were flying from his presence, he made a pastime of their misery for himself, by aiming at them with his own musket, to see how many he could bring down before they passed out of sight.

He was holding a council of war with his generals ; but, while he made merry over his cruelties of the day before, and projected others for the morrow, his officers frowned and averted their eyes.

His thick, sensual lips expanded with a hideous smile. "It would seem that my orders are not agreeable," said he. "Pray, gentlemen, am I so unlucky as to have earned your disapproval ? "

There was no answer to this inquiry, but neither was there any change in the aspect of the officers.

"General Feuquière," cried Melac, "you are not usually reticent ; pray, let us hear your opinion of my mode of warfare."

"I cannot approve of cruelty," replied Feuquière, bluntly. "Our men act much less like the brave soldiers of a Christian king, than like demons that have been let loose from hell."

"You do not flatter us," replied Melac. "And I am curious to know whether anybody else here present shares your opinion."

"We are all of one mind," was the unanimous reply.

"We are assassins and incendiaries, but we have never yet fought a battle like men," resumed De Feuquiere.

"No," added Montclas. "We have longed in vain for honorable warfare ; for a fair combat before the light of heaven, face to face with men armed like ourselves ; and we are sick at heart of midnight torches and midnight murders."

"No doubt ; you are a sentimental personage, I hear : one who shed tears when the order was given to sack Mannheim."

"I am not ashamed of those tears," returned Montclas. "For three months these much enduring people have exerted themselves to do our bidding, treating us like guests who had come to them as foes. And when, in return for their kindness, our soldiery were ordered to sack their beautiful city, I wept while I was forced to obey the inhuman command of my superior officer. May Almighty God not hold me responsible as a creature for what I have been forced to do as a soldier !"

"You can justify yourself by referring the Almighty to me, as I shall certainly justify myself by referring Him to Monsieur Louvois. It is true that I do not weep when I carry out his orders ; but you may judge for yourselves whether I transcend them.—General Montclas, be so good as to read aloud this dispatch."

General Montclas took the paper, and read in an audible voice :

"'It is now two weeks since I have seen a courier from the army. What are you about that I receive no more accounts of the destruction of German cities wherewith to entertain the idle hours of his majesty ? You have been ordered to devastate the entire German frontier. You began bravely, but you are not keeping the promise of your opening. The Germans are full of sentiment, and you must wound them through their affections and associations. Burn their houses, sack their fine churches, deface and destroy their monuments and public buildings. When next you write, let me hear that Speier with its magnificent cathedral is a thing of the past ; and be expeditious, that Worms and Trier may share the same fate.

'LOUVOIS.'"

"You see, then," observed Melac, "that I do but obey orders.

"That may be," sighed De Feuquière, "but all Europe will
rise in one indignant protest against our inhumanity."

"Let them protest; we will have raised such a barrier of
desolation between themselves and France, that we can afford
to laugh at their indignation. I for my part approve of the
method of warfare traced out for us by the minister of war,
and I shall carry it out from Basle to Coblentz. The time we
allowed to the people of Speier for reflection, expires to-day.
To horse, then! The burgomasters are waiting for us in the
market-place by the cathedral."

Yes! The burghers, the clergy, the women, and the children, were on their knees in the market-place, crying for mercy.
Melac, laughing at their wretchedness, spurred his horse onward, and plunged into their midst, scattering them right and
left like a flock of frightened sheep; and the clang of his
horse's hoofs on the stone pavement sounded to his unhappy
victims like the riveting of nails in the great coffin wherein
their beautiful city was shortly to be buried.

But they were not noisy in their grief. Here and there
might be heard a slight sob, and, with this exception, there was
silence in that thronged market-place.

Suddenly the great bell of the cathedral began to toll, and
after it all the bells in Speier. General Melac slackened his
pace, and rode deliberately along the market-place, as if to
give that weeping multitude the opportunity of looking upon
his cruel face, and reading there that from him no mercy was
to be expected.

The bells ceased, and their tones were yet trembling on the
air, when the women and children lifted up their voices and
began to chant: "In my trouble I called on the Lord!"

The strain was taken up by the musicians who stood at the
open windows of the council-hall, and now the burghers, the
magistrates, and the clergy, joined in the holy song. The
French uncovered their heads and listened reverentially, while
many an eye was dimmed with tears, and many a heart bled
for the fate of those whom they could not rescue.

Every man there felt the influence of the blessed words,

except one. General Melac was neither awed nor touched ; his pale eye was as cold, his sardonic mouth as cruel as ever.

"He is perfectly hardened," murmured a monk, who was leaning against one of the columns of the cathedral. This monk was a young man, of tall, muscular build. His wide shoulders and fine, erect figure, seemed much more suitable to a soldier than to a brother of the order of mercy. Even his sun-burnt face had a proud, martial look ; and as his dark, glowing eyes rested on Melac, they kindled with a glance that was not very expressive of brotherly love.

"He is without pity," thought he, "and perhaps 'tis well ; for I might have been touched to grant him a death more merciful."

He moved away that he might distinguish the words that were now being poured forth from the quivering lips of the white-haired prebendary of the cathedral ; but the poor old priest's voice was tremulous with tears, and the monk could not hear. He then made a passage for himself through the crowd and approached General Melac. The prebendary had ceased to speak, and there was a solemn stillness in the market-place, for every sigh was hushed to catch the words that were to follow.

Melac looked around that he might see how many thousand human beings were acknowledging his power, then he drew in his rein and smiled—that deadly smile !

"My orders must be carried out," said he, in a loud and distinct voice. "Speier must be razed to the ground, and I am sorry that its inhabitants were unwilling to profit by the permission I gave them to emigrate to France. They would have been kindly received there."

"We hope for mercy," was the reply of the prebendary. "Oh, general, let us not hope in vain !"

"No mercy shall be given you," said Melac, who, turning to General Montclas, remarked, "What an advantage I have over you ! I know their language, and can understand all their expressions of grief ! It is a comic litany !"

"Demon, I will repay thee !" muttered the monk. And, coming close to the general's horse, he laid his hand upon the rein.

"What do you mean, sirrah?" cried Melac. "Withdraw your hand."

"Your excellency," replied the man in pure French, "allow me to station myself at your horse's head, for you may need my help to-day."

"Your help? Wherefore?"

"The work in which you are engaged is apt to provoke personal hostility. I dreamed last night that I saw you weltering in your blood, enveloped in flames. I am superstitious —very; particularly as regards dreams, and I left the hospital where I was engaged in nursing the sick, on purpose to protect your excellency from secret foes."

"Protect *me!* Who do you suppose would be so bold as to attack me? Not this whining multitude around us."

"Nobody knows to what acts despair may drive the meekest of men," was the monk's reply.

"Very well; I believe you are right," said Melac, a little disturbed. "Station yourself at my rein, then."

At that moment there was a general wail, and many a voice was lifted up in one last effort to soften the heart of their persecutor.

"Speier must be destroyed," was his answer, "but to show you the extent of my clemency, I will now announce to you that without the gates are four hundred forage-wagons, which I have provided for the removal of your valuables (if you have any) to any point you may select within the boundaries of France. Those who prefer to remain, are allowed to deposit their effects in the cathedral, and to guard them in person. The temple of Almighty God is sacred, and the hand of man shall not profane its sanctity by deeds of violence. Take your choice of the cathedral or the army-wagons: I give you four hours' grace. If, after that time, I find a German on the streets, man, woman, or child, the offender shall be scourged or put to the sword."

In a few moments the market-place was empty, and the people, exhausted and cowed though they were, by two months of oppression, had flown to take advantage of this last act of grace.

"Now, my excellent brother," said Melac to the monk,

" you see that I am quite safe, and can dispense with your protection."

" The day is not yet at an end," said the monk, solemnly.

" You are right," cried the butcher, " it has scarcely begun ; but by-and-by we shall see a comedy that will raise your spirits for a month to come. The actors thereof are to be the people of Speier, and the entertainment will close with an exhibition of fireworks on a magnificent scale. Send me two ordnance officers !" cried he to his staff.

Two lancers approached and saluted their commander.

" Let two companies of infantry occupy the market-place," said Melac. " Let four cannon be stationed at the entrances of the four streets leading to the cathedral. For four hours the people shall be allowed to enter with their chattels. At the end of this truce, two more companies of infantry shall be ordered hither, one of which shall surround the cathedral, the other march inside. A detachment of miners must encompass the columns and cornice of the roof with combustibles ; but use no powder, for that might endanger ourselves. There are straw, hemp, pitch, tar, and sulphur enough in the town to make the grandest show since Rome was burned. The infantry that enter the church, will massacre the people, and if they are dexterous the booty is theirs ; but they must do their work swiftly, or there will be no time to save anything, for I intend that the entire building shall be fired at once.

The monk started, grasped the mane of the horse with a movement that caused him to shy, and his rider to cry out in great irritation :

" What are you doing, fool ? "

" Pardon, your excellency, my foot was under your horse's hoof, and I could not help catching at his mane."

" Keep farther away, then ; I do not believe in dreams.— Away !" cried he, to the lancers, who, horror-stricken but powerless to refuse, went on their diabolical mission.

" And now," continued Melac, " we will ride to the gates to see what sort of entertainment our hospitable hosts of Speier are preparing for us there."

He galloped off with such swiftness that his guardian-angel was left behind. But he followed as fast as he could ; when ever he met a man hastening with his goods to the cathedral, bidding him "Beware !" and passing on. Some heeded the warning, others did not. They were so paralyzed by despair that the monk's words conveyed no meaning to their minds, and they went humbly on to their destruction.

He meanwhile hurried to the gates through which the weeping crowds were bearing, each one, what he valued most on earth. There were women, scarcely able to totter, whose dearest burdens were their own helpless children ; there were men carrying sickly wives or decrepit mothers ; there were others so loaded down with the few worldly goods that the odious Frenchman had left them, that their backs were almost bent in two, and they were scarcely able to drag themselves along ! The nearer the gates, the denser the throng, many of whom were fainting with misery and exhaustion ; but many also to whom despair lent strength.

Melac was there, enjoying the scene ; sometimes glancing toward the gates, sometimes toward the wagons which, for miles around, covered the extensive plain outside of the city. The poor fainting wretches that reached them let their burdens drop, and would have made an effort to follow them, but they were told that no one would be allowed to enter the wagons until all had been filled with their wares.

---

## CHAPTER III.

### THE TREASURE.

FOR three hours the monk strove in vain to reach the gate ; but the time of grace was fast approaching its close, and now, the press becoming less, he sped along as if he had been flying for life, until he came panting, almost breathless, to the spot where the French general, surrounded by his staff, was sitting on his horse, enjoying himself immensely.

"Ah !" said he, "our pious brother here ! Well—you see that I am alive."

"Yes, and I am glad to know it," replied the monk, resuming his place at the bridle.

Melac turned to one of his adjutants : " Give orders to the drivers to go on, and let the soldiers cut down every man that attempts to mount the wagons or withdraw his effects. To get the honey, we must kill the bees. When they are all dead, the men can divide the spoils." *

" As soon as the sport is over," continued he, to another adjutant, " I will repair, with my staff, to the council-hall, there to see the illumination. Ride on, and tell the superintendent that, when he sees my handkerchief waving from the great window in the second story, he must apply his matches."

So saying, Melac put spurs to his horse, and, followed by his staff, approached the wagons, and gave a signal with his sword.

The whole train was set in motion, and the horses were urged to the top of their speed.

The unhappy victims of this demoniac stratagem gave one simultaneous shout of indignation. Those nearest the wagons strove to clutch at them with their hands. Some held on even to the wheels, some mounted the horses, some snatched the reins. But sharp swords were near ; and, at the word of command, every outstretched arm was hacked off, and fell, severed, to the ground.

A struggle now began between the soldiery and the companions of those who had been so cruelly mutilated. They were unarmed, but they had the strength of brutes at bay ; and by-and-by many a sword had been snatched from their assassins, and many a Frenchman had bitten the dust. General Melac was so interested in a fight between two soldiers and two women whose children had been driven off in the wagons, that, before he was aware of his danger, a sword was uplifted over his head, and a frenzied face was almost thrust into his own. At this moment his reins were seized, his horse was forced back, and the stout arm of the monk had wrested the sabre from the enraged German, who fell, pierced by a bullet from the holster of an officer close by.

" Was it you, pious brother, that so opportunely backed my steed ? " inquired Melac.

* Historical.—See Zimmermann, " History of Wurtemberg," vol. ii.

The monk bowed, and the general saw that his forehead was bloody.

"Are you wounded?"

"Yes, general; I received the stroke that was intended for you, but parried it, and the blow was slight."

"I am a thousand times indebted to you for the service you have rendered me, and hope that you will not leave me a second time without your sheltering presence.—Ho! a horse there for the Bernardine monk!"

No sooner were Melac's commands uttered than they were obeyed, for he that tarried when the tyrant spoke was sure to come to grief. The monk swung himself into the saddle with the agility of a trooper, and, although the horse reared and plunged, he never swerved from his seat.

"Verily you are a curious specimen of a monk," laughed Melac. "I never saw a brother so much to my taste before. Come, follow me to the market-place, and you shall see my skill in pyrotechnics. If I had but Nero's field of operations, I could rival his burning of Rome. Happy Nero, that could destroy a Rome!"

"Do you, also, envy Nero his sudden death?" asked the monk.

"Why, yes; though I would like to put off the evil day as far as may be, I hope to die a sudden and painless death."

"Sudden and painless death," muttered the monk, between his teeth. "You allude to death on the field of battle?"

"Ay, that do I; it is the only end befitting a soldier. See —we are at the gates. The way is obstructed by corpses," continued he, urging his horse over a heap of dead that lay in the streets. "Luckily, they will not have to be buried; they shall have a funeral pile, like that of the ancients."

"Is the entire city to be destroyed?" asked the monk.

"Yes, the whole city, from one end to the other; and these tottering old buildings will make a brave blaze."

"A brave blaze," echoed the monk, raising his mournful eyes to the long rows of houses that so lately were the abodes of many a happy family, were as empty as open graves. They continued their way along the silent streets—silent even around the cathedral, where, early in the morning, so many thousand supplicants had knelt before God and man for mercy, but knelt in vain.

Some few were within the cathedral walls, some were lying, their ghastly faces upturned to heaven, and those who had survived were wandering across their blasted fields, bereft of kindred and home, houseless, hungry, and almost naked.

General Melac glanced at the cathedral porch. That, too, was empty and still.

"I wonder whether our men have done their work over there?" said he. "I must go and see."

Then dismounting, and flinging his bridle to his equerry, he called upon the monk to follow him. The staff also dismounted, and an officer advanced to receive orders.

"Gentlemen, betake yourselves to the hall of council, and await my return at the great window there, opposite."

The staff obeyed, and the general, followed by his preserver, ascended the steps that led to the cathedral.

"Your excellency," whispered the monk, coming very close, "before we enter, will you allow me to say a word to you?"

"I should think you had had opportunity enough to-day to say what you wish."

"Not in private, general. Until now we have had listeners."

"Well, is it anything of moment you desire to communicate?"

"Something of great importance."

"Speak on, and be quick, for time presses."

"Your excellency is resolved to burn down the cathedral?"

"Have I not told you that I would?" replied Melac, with a frown. "Nothing in heaven or on earth shall save it."

"Then," said the monk with a deep sigh, "for the sake of our brotherhood, I must violate the sanctity of the confessional. But you must swear to preserve my secret, otherwise you shall not hear it."

"A secret of the confessional! How can it concern me?"

"You shall hear. It relates to the concealment of two millions' worth of gold and precious stones."

The covetous eyes of Melac glittered, and the blood mounted to his brow. "Two millions !" gasped he.

"One for you and one for our brotherhood. Do you swear to keep the secret ?"

"Most unquestionably."

"And also swear that no one but ourselves shall know the place of its concealment ?"

"I swear, most willingly, for I do not intend to divide my share of the booty with anybody living. How soon do you expect to come in possession of it ? "

"Now—at this very hour."

Melac drew back, and eyed the monk suspiciously. "How ! These lying wretches had two millions of treasure, and not one of them would yield it up ?"

"General, the people of Speier have nothing—nothing. Nobody knew of it save the bishop, who died day before yesterday, and the sacristan, who died to-day. You remember that I was absent from your side during two hours to-day ?"

Melac nodded, and the monk went on : "Those two hours I spent by the dying-bed of this sacristan, the only depositary of the secret. He was wounded among the rest, was conveyed to a neighboring house, and there I received his last confessions. All the treasures of the cathedral—its gold, silver, and jewels—were, at the approach of the French army, conveyed to a place in the tower, which place the sacristan designated so plainly, that I can find it without difficulty."

"But what has induced you to share it with me ?" asked Melac, with a glance of mistrust.

"Imperative necessity, general. I cannot obtain it without your protection. You have given orders that no man shall be suffered to escape from the cathedral to-day, and, unless you go with me, the treasure must be given up to the flames. Certainly, if I could have gotten it without assistance, it would have been my duty to give it over entire into the hands of the brotherhood. But if you help me, I will divide it with you. It lies in the tower of the cathedral, close by the belfry."

"Come, then, come ; show me the way."

They entered the massive doors. The sentry saluted the general, and they passed on.

"Let nothing more be done until I return," said Melac to the sentry. "I wish to go over the old building before we consign it to the flames."

## CHAPTER IV.

### CASPAR'S VENGEANCE.

DEEP silence reigned within the walls of the holy temple, broken occasionally by an expiring sigh, or the faint sound of the death-rattle. For the French soldiery had done their work. The poor wretches that had been ensnared into seeking refuge there, had all been murdered, and their possessions removed to a place of safety. One hour earlier, the vaults of the house of God had rung with shrieks and groans, but the victims were now dying or dead.

General Melac went among the prostrate bodies, looking here and there behind the pillars, to see whether any thing of value had been overlooked by his subordinates. The monk meanwhile bent over the prostrate forms that lay in hundreds upon the marble pavement, and so absorbed was he in soothing their last moments, that he almost started as the rough voice of General Melac reached him from the opposite end of the nave.

"Come, come," cried he, in thundering tones. "Enough of useless sentimentality!"

Without a word the monk rose, and, pointing to the grand altar, the general entered the chancel, and followed his conductor to a small door cut in the wall. This the monk opened, and, stepping back, signed to Melac to advance.

"Does this winding-stair lead to the tower?" asked the latter.

"Yes, general, and as there is but one way to reach it, I resume my proper place, and follow you, as in duty bound."

Melac began to ascend the stairs, the monk coming behind

him, with an aspect the very opposite of that he had endeavored to maintain all day. His stooping shoulders were flung back, his head was erect, and in his eyes there sat a threatening devil, which, if Melac could have seen it, would have made his heart grow chill with apprehension. But Melac, too, was no longer the same. Up to this moment he had assumed an appearance of friendliness toward his companion. But now his eye flashed, and his hand clutched his sword, while deep in his heart flowed a current of treachery, which, translated into words ran thus :

"I do not see why he should have any part in this treasure. As soon as he has pointed out the spot, I will catch him in my arms and hurl him down into the body of the church. By Heaven ! the life of one miserable monk never was worth a million of treasure !"

Did the monk suspect what was passing within the mind of the general ? Perhaps he did ; for well he knew that he was capable of any amount of atrocity.

On they went, sometimes stumbling in the dark, sometimes emerging into the light, until at last they reached the topmost step where Melac halted to breathe.

"Are we almost there ?" asked he.

"Almost there," echoed the monk, while with a swift movement of his hand he drew from under his cassock two long, stout thongs of hide.

"What are you doing there ?" asked Melac.

"I am making ready my lasso," replied he, throwing one of the thongs over the head of the general ; and, before the latter had time to recover from his surprise, it was passed around his body, and his hands were pinioned fast behind.

Melac comprehended that he was betrayed, and making desperate efforts to free himself, he lost his footing, and fell at full length on the granite pavement of the tower. The monk now sprang upon his body, and drawing from his bosom a long handkerchief, he tied it fast over his victim's mouth.

"Your cries might be heard, and some fool might come to the rescue," said he. "You shall die without being allowed to give utterance to your despair."

Melac's eyeballs almost started from their sockets, but the monk looked on without pity. He dragged him to that part of the tower whence the gilded weathercock could be seen toying with the free air of heaven. The sky shone blue and bright; never had it seemed so fair to the wretch that was looking his last upon its azure dome. He felt himself raised in the arms of the monk, firmly fastened with a second thong, and then tossed outside the tower, where he hung, a small, dark speck in the eyes of the officers that were awaiting his return to the hall of council.

And now the monk cast himself down upon his knees. "O God, I thank Thee that Thou hast granted my prayer, and delivered this monster to my hands! 'Tis Thy will that I should be his executioner, and may Thy holy will be done forever and forever!"

He rose and approached Melac, whose face was ghastly pale, and whose eyes were overflowing with tears. "Now," said he, "know why I have delivered you unto a cruel and agonizing death. For months I have tracked your path, with power to have stricken you every hour of the day. But sudden death was too merciful for such a brute as you! The Hyena of Esslingen shall have the horror and apprehension of a slow, torturing, and solitary death. Without sympathy and without witnesses shall he die, and in his last moments, when his flesh quivers with agony, and the devouring flames shall consume his odious body, let him think on Marie Wengelin, and on me, her lover and betrothed husband—Caspar!"

Without another word, he drew from Melac's finger his signet-ring, and began to descend the winding-stair. The eye of his victim followed his tall, manly figure until it disappeared forever from his sight; and then he listened to his retreating footsteps until they grew faint and more faint, and all hope was lost! An hour of mortal agony went by; the sun sank slowly to rest, and a few stars brightened the sapphire vault above him. Suddenly a red glow brightened the heavens, and gilded the dark waters of the Rhine—that Rhine which he had so incarnadined with blood! Avenging God! It was the fire himself had kindled! It leaped up from every point of Speier—and now—now the cathedral was in flames, and death—slow, lingering, and agonizing—had overtaken the Hyena of Esslingen !

---

## CHAPTER V.

### THE DUCHESS OF ORLEANS.

"I CAN never consent to such a disgraceful marriage for my son," cried Elizabeth-Charlotte to her husband.

"Madame, I look upon it as a great honor that my son should espouse the daughter of the king."

"The daughter of shame and infamy—the daughter of a man who, violating his marriage-vow—"

"Madame," interrupted the duke, "you forget that you are speaking of his majesty the King of France !"

"King of France ? There is no question of a king, but of my brother-in-law, of whose faults—nay, sins, I may surely speak, within the walls of my own cabinet, I suppose."

"Madame," replied the duke, trying to draw up his small person until he fairly stood on tiptoe, "madame, I forbid you to express yourself in such terms of your sovereign and mine."

"Forbid me to speak the truth, you mean. And to be sure, at a court like this, where everybody feeds on flattery, truth is strangely out of place."

"Like yourself, for instance," observed the duke.

"Yes, like myself," replied the duchess, with a sweet smile that illumined her plain features, and lent them a passing beauty. "I believe that I am most unwelcome among the fine and fashionable folks of Paris ; but it is not my fault that I am here, a poor, homely sparrow in a flock of peacocks and parrots."

"Madame," replied the duke, pompously, "if you choose to consider yourself as a sparrow, you have my full consent to do so, although I must say that it is somewhat presuming for any one so to designate the woman whom I honored with my hand. But I must always regret that you have never displayed enough tact to lay aside your plebeian German manners, and resume those of the courtly and elegant entourage of the refined King of France."

The eyes of the duchess shot fire, and the hue on her cheeks deepened to scarlet.

"Your manners may be refined, monseigneur ; but God shield me from your morals ! The war you are waging against my native land is one of assassination and rapine ; and oh ! how I wish that I were free to leave France forever, that I might suffer and die with my dear, slaughtered countrymen ! But dearly as I love my native land, I love my children still more. Maternal love is stronger in my heart than patriotism, and my Elizabeth and my Philip are more to me than Germany !"

"You say nothing of me," observed the duke, sentimentally. "Am I, then, nothing to you ?"

"Yes, monseigneur, you are the father of my children. I plighted my faith to you, and I have kept my marriage-vows. But you know, as well as I, that we were both nothing but royal merchandise, bartered for reasons of state, and that we have never been congenial. Nevertheless, I love you as the father of my Philip ! for he has your handsome face and your refined and courtly bearing."

"Madame," returned the duke, blushing with gratification, "I thought you disdained to flatter."

"I do not flatter you, monseigneur," cried the duchess, cordially grasping his hand, and leading him to the mantel, over which hung a full-length portrait of the youthful Duke de Chartres. "See," exclaimed she with affectionate pride, "see what a beautiful picture Mignet has made of him. It was done in secret in Mignet's studio, and was brought to me yesterday as a birthday present from my boy."

"It was very thoughtless of Philip to visit Mignet," objected the duke. "He too often forgets his rank and relationship to the king."

"Forgive him, monseigneur. He forgot his station, to remember his filial affection," and for several moments the mother's eyes were fondly fixed upon the portrait. "Look !" resumed she ; "these are your eyes, your well-developed forehead, your aquiline nose, your pleasant and expressive mouth. In your youth, you were as handsome as he—I have often heard it said that you were the handsomest cavalier in Paris."

"Except the king, madame—except the king! I am too loyal a subject to excel his majesty in anything. I am glad, however, that you think my son resembles me; to me there is a blended likeness of both his parents in his countenance."

"Never, never!" exclaimed Elizabeth-Charlotte, with animation. "There is no trace of my coarse features in that aristocratic face; and yet, like the owl that hatched the eagle's egg, I am proud of calling him my son. And now, monseigneur, let me implore of you not to cross the escutcheon of our eaglet with the bar-sinister that disgraces the arms of Mademoiselle de Blois."

"Madame," exclaimed the duke, much irritated, "speak more respectfully of the daughter of Louis XIV.! She has been recognized by his majesty, and there is no stain upon her arms."

"Pardon me—it is not in the power of any sovereign to erase the foul blot of her birth; and I shudder when I think of an alliance between the son of the Duke of Orleans and grandson of the Elector Palatine, and the daughter of a king's leman. If his majesty mentions the subject to me, I shall tell him as much."

"Impossible!" cried the duke, aghast. "I have already promised that you would solicit the honor of an alliance with Mademoiselle de Blois."

"You promised what I will not perform. Do you suppose that I, by birth and marriage a royal princess, would debase myself so far as to ask for my son's wife the daughter of a harlot who drove the hapless queen to her grave? and to take her by the hand, and present her to the court as *my* daughter? I would rather absent myself forever from court, and I will certainly not attend the king's ball to-night."

"You cannot do that, for you accepted the invitation yesterday."

"Yesterday I knew not the humiliation implied in my acceptance. To-day I know it, and I will excuse myself, and be sick."

"Madame, I command you to appear at the ball," cried out the enraged duke, "and we shall see whether you presume to rebel against my conjugal authority."

"I shall not rebel," replied the duchess. "Since you command my presence, you shall have it; but I warn you that I shall mortally offend the king, for—"

The duke was about to protest anew against his wife's blasphemy, when the old German lady of honor, who presided over the toilet of her highness, rushed into the room in a state of great agitation.

"What is the matter, Katharina?" asked the duchess.

"Your royal highness," replied Katharina, panting, "a courier has just arrived from the Countess Louise. He has ridden day and night to deliver his message, and, although he is covered with mud and dust, he insisted that I should announce him to your royal highness."

"A courier from Louise!" murmured the duchess. "Something must have happened! Go, Kathi, bid him come into my little parlor.—Will monseigneur excuse me? I am deeply concerned lest some misfortune should have befallen my sister."

"Sister! Is the Countess Louise the daughter of a princess Palatine?"

"No, monseigneur; you know that she is the daughter of the Countess Dagenfeld, my father's wedded wife—although never acknowledged as such—because she was not of royal birth. There is no bar-sinister on Louise's shield; she is truly and honorably my half-sister."

The duchess bowed and hastened to her parlor, where the courier was awaiting her arrival.

"Has anything happened to the countess? Is she ill? Have I lost my dear relative?"

"No, your royal highness. Your princely relatives are well, and here—here is—"

He made an attempt to place a letter in her hand, but reeled and fell, exhausted, at her feet.

"Pardon me, madame," said he, "I have been for three days and nights in the saddle. My strength has given way—I cannot rise. But read your letter, I implore you."

The duchess stooped, and took it from his nerveless hand ; then, commending him to the care of Katharina, she broke the seal and began to read.

Its contents affected her so terribly, that her teeth chattered, her knees trembled, and, throwing herself upon the sofa, she covered her face with her hands and wept.

But she wept for a moment only.

"Katharina," cried she, to her old confidante, who was chafing the temples of the courier, "leave that poor youth for a moment, and fetch me a mantilla and hood. I must go to the king at once ! "

"Your royal highness is in a négligé," remonstrated Katharina ; "I will have to dress you."

"I cannot wait to be dressed," cried Elizabeth-Charlotte ; "speed away, and bring me my wrappings. God be praised, the king will be at home ! Thousands of lives depend upon my intercession ! "

Katharina returned with the mantilla, which, without the least regard to grace, her royal highness flung over her stout figure, while she jerked the hood over her head with an impetuosity that made the old lady wring her hands.

"Oh, her hair is down, and the hood all twisted to one side," murmured the mistress of the toilet, as the duchess, indifferent to all forms of civilization, dashed down the staircase and leaped into her carriage.

## CHAPTER VI.

### THE DELIVERANCE OF TRIER.

THE equipage thundered along the streets of Paris, and drew up before the hooded door, at the side entrance of the Louvre, which was especially reserved for the use of the royal family.

The duchess sprang from her carriage, hurried up the staircase, almost stumbling over the sentry as he made an attempt to present arms, and flew into the antechamber that led to the cabinet of the king.

She came in like a frigate under full sail, but was encountered by a gentleman of the privy chamber, who barred the entrance.

"Make way for me—do !" said she, clasping her hands. "I must see his majesty this very moment."

"His majesty is in secret conference with the Marquis de Louvois and Madame de Maintenon," was the reply. "Not even your royal highness can obtain admittance."

"So much the better if Louvois is there. Let me pass—I command you, let me pass !"

"Indeed, madame, you know not what you ask. I have received stringent orders to admit nobody."

"The royal family are never included in these prohibitions," cried the duchess.

"But to-day, your royal highness, I was placed here to prevent their coming ! You well know that none but the princes and princesses of the blood would presume to make use of this entrance."

"It concerns the lives of thousands !" urged the duchess.

"Did it concern that of my own son, I would know better than to seek to save it by disobeying his majesty's orders."

"You will not—positively will not let me pass ?"

"I dare not, madame."

"Then you must excuse me, but I shall force my way," returned Elizabeth-Charlotte, grasping the slender form of the king's gentleman, and, with her powerful hands, flinging him into the corner of the room, while she strode rapidly to the opposite door, and opened and had closed it again before her opponent had recovered his breath.

Before touching the bolt of the door which opened directly into the king's cabinet, she paused to recover her breath, and to gather courage for the coming interview. She trembled from head to foot, and leaned against the wall for support. But Elizabeth-Charlotte was not a woman to be deterred, by fear of kings, from what she deemed her duty. With the resolution that characterized her, she uttered one short ejaculation for help from above, and opened the door.

Louvois was in the act of speaking. "Sire, our arms are as successful in Italy as they have been in Germany, where town after town has been taken without the drawing of a sword—where the people have offered the keys of all the fortresses to your generals, and have welcomed the advent of our troops with joy."

"Your majesty," cried the duchess, coming forward, "do not believe him ! He tells a falsehood—O God ! what a falsehood !"

The astonishment of that cabinet-council is not to be described. The king rose from his seat and confronted her with eyes that flamed with anger.

"Madame," exclaimed the grand monarque, in a rage, "were you not told that I would see nobody this morning ?"

"Yes, your majesty ; so emphatically told, that, before I could make my way to your presence, I was obliged to hurl your gentleman to the other side of the room. It is not his fault that I am here !"

Madame de Maintenon rolled up her eyes, Louvois sneered, and Louis, looking as if he wished that he could consume his sister-in-law with a glance, turned around to his minister.

"Monsieur Louvois, be so good as to forget the imprudent words that madame has just spoken. It is impossible that a princess of the blood should so far forget her own dignity as to lay hands on an attendant of the king. Take care that the indiscretion of her royal highness go no farther than these walls ; and, if you hear it spoken of, contradict it flatly."

"Your majesty," exclaimed the duchess, "that is the very way to make everybody believe it, for surely nobody will believe Monsieur Louvois."

"Sire," said Louvois, shrewdly, "I was about to communicate tidings of the greatest importance to your majesty. I would be glad of your permission to resume our conference. It is late, and—"

"Madame," cried Louis, " once for all, leave this room, and interrupt us no longer."

"Does your majesty suppose that, after forcing my way to your presence, I intend to retreat without accomplishing the object for which I came ? I entreat of you, hear me, and judge for yourself whether my pertinacity is not justified by the occasion of my intrusion."

"Very well, madame," replied Louis. "I will remember that you are my brother's wife, and forget an excess of presumption which, were you not my sister-in-law, would merit the Bastile. Speak, and let us hear your petition. It needs to be one of moment to earn your pardon."

With these words, Louis threw himself into his arm-chair, and, pointing to a tabouret at hand, requested her royal highness to be seated. The duchess looked around the room, and, seeing a vacant arm-chair a little farther off, she rolled it forward, and seated herself with great grandeur. This chair belonged to Madame de Maintenon, who, a moment previous, had risen and walked to the window.

She became very red in the face, and, coming directly in front of the duchess, said : "Madame, this is my own armchair ; be so good as to excuse me if I ask you to rise."

"Impossible, my dear marquise, impossible !" was the rejoinder. "His majesty requests me to be seated, and this is the only seat in the room that accords with my rank. If his majesty allows you to seat yourself in his presence, and that of a princess of the blood, there is a tabouret which doubtless was placed for your accommodation on such occasions."

Madame de Maintenon looked imploringly at the king, hoping that he would interfere ; but he did not. His eyes were cast down, and it was plain that no help was to be expected from him. His unacknowledged spouse was therefore obliged to yield the point, and put up with the tabouret.

"Now, madame," said Louis, as though rousing himself from profound meditation, "I await your pleasure."

"Sire," cried the duchess, "I have come hither to accuse yonder traitor, who, in your majesty's name, is perpetrating deeds of horror that are enough to brand any sovereign with infamy. Did I not hear him say, as I entered this room, that the French army was received with open arms by the Germans ?"

"You did, madame. As a proof of the truth of this assertion, here are the very keys of all the towns and fortresses we have besieged."

The king pointed to a basket wreathed with flowers, wherein lay a heap of gigantic keys.

"Oh, sire," exclaimed the duchess, "these keys were purchased with blood and pillage. Your soldiers have not
marched into Germany like the invading armies of a civilized
nation ; they have come as incendiaries and assassins. Witness my father's castle, which they reduced to a heap of ashes."

"My dear madame," said Louis, deprecatingly, "war is not
a pastime. I regret that it was necessary to burn your father's
castle ; but you perceive that it was not burned in vain, for
your countrymen, since then, have shown themselves amen-
able to reason."

"Sire, you are shamefully deceived ; and I have come to
lay at the foot of your throne the plaint of an unhappy people.
Ah, you little know what crimes are being committed in your
name ! General Montclas himself shed tears when Mannheim
was sacked and destroyed ; and, when the people of Durlach
were driven by your soldiery into the very midst of the flames
that were consuming their homes, the Duke de la Roche remonstrated with the Marquis de Crequi on the atrocity of the
crime. What do you suppose was the answer of the marquis ?
'Le roi le veut !'"

"Is this so ?" asked the king, turning to Louvois, who
was hiding his troubled countenance in the embrasure of a
window.

"Sire, I have never heard of it before," replied the minister.

"Well may he say that he never heard of it, if he means
that your majesty never gave such an order to him !" cried
Elizabeth-Charlotte. But if he means that he did not order
these massacres, he tells an untruth. He is avenging on the
people of Germany the laurels which Prince Eugene has
earned in the service of the emperor, and which, but for him,
would have redounded to the glory of France. Oh, sire ! this
war is one of personal vengeance on the part of your wicked
subject ; it is not waged for your honor or advantage. I ask
in his presence, did the King of France order the destruction
of Worms and Speier ? Was it by the order of our gracious
sovereign that the very house of God was committed to the
flames ?"

"Can such a crime have been perpetrated in my name ?"
cried Louis, with indignation.

"Sire," replied Louvois, "your majesty has said it—'War is no pastime.'"

"He does not deny it," cried the duchess, wiping away her tears, and struggling for composure to go on. "But what is done, is done—Worms and Speier are in ashes, and their murdered inhabitants at rest. But, oh, my liege, my gracious lord, the city of Trier is threatened with the same fate! For three days the people have been crying in vain for mercy.—At your feet, sire, I implore you, have pity, and save them from butchery!"

And the duchess, with hands upraised, and eyes that were streaming with tears, sank on her knees before the king.

Louis rose hastily from his seat.

"Rise, madame," said he, "and let us retire to yonder embrasure. I wish to speak with you in private."

So saying, he gave her his hand, and conducted her to a deep recess at the farther end of the room, which was, in fact, a small apartment furnished with seats—a cabinet within a cabinet. He loosened the gold cord that confined the curtain to the side, and it fell to the floor—a thick, heavy portière that shut all sound from the apartment without. Not satisfied with this, the king opened the casement, that the hum from the street below might effectually drown their voices.

"Now, madame," said he, "we will converse openly and without reserve, as it befits near relatives to do. Has your husband confided to you my wishes?"

"What wishes?" asked the duchess, who, in her anxiety for the fate of Trier, had forgotten the occurrences of the day.

Louis was piqued. "I allude to my matrimonial plans for your son and my daughter; and I beg you to observe that where I have a right to command, I am gracious enough to request their fulfilment. It is understood that the Duke de Chartres is to be betrothed to Mademoiselle de Blois this evening?"

"Sire," murmured Elizabeth-Charlotte, who began to understand how much she was risking by her mediation in favor of Trier, "sire, I implore you to save the lives of thousands of human beings, and you answer me by questions as to the marriage of my son!"

"My dear sister," returned the king, with a smile, "surely you take more interest in the fate of your child, than in that of a remote town in Germany. My brother has already consented that our children should be united; and, as you are here, I wish to hear from your own lips that the union gives you as much satisfaction as it will afford to me."

"Sire, the Duke de Chartres is but a lad—wild and untamed. He is not fit to be the husband of any woman."

The king frowned. "What do you mean?"

"Sire, he is but sixteen years of age—a boy; and it is not customary for princes of the blood to marry before the age of eighteen."

"I know that as well as yourself. It is no question of marriage, only one of betrothal. Mademoiselle de Blois is but twelve, and no fitter to be married than your son. But it is well for young people to know that they are bound by honor to restrain their passions and curb their irregularities. If the Duke de Chartres is untamed, you have the means of keeping him within bounds, and of forcing him to lead a chaste and virtuous life."

"Oh, sire, you know full well that the promises of their parents do not bind youthful hearts. My Philip is inclined to dissipation, and it would be an unfortunate match for Mademoiselle de Blois."

"Give me a direct answer to my inquiry. Do you consent to the betrothal of your son with my daughter?"

Elizabeth-Charlotte burst into tears. "Sire, I—I—cannot," murmured she.

The king flushed with anger. "I thought so," said he. "You are nothing but a mass of prejudices, which you would rather die than relinquish. Very well, madame; I bow to your prejudices, and will make no vain efforts to overcome them. Excuse me if, as regards your petition, I echo your words, 'I cannot.'"

"Oh, sire," cried the duchess, "the cases are not parallel. I plead for the lives of so many unfortunates!"

"And I for my own gratification; and assuredly a wish of the King of France is of a little more importance than the fate of a miserable German town."

"Your majesty, it would cost you but a word to earn the blessings of so many grateful hearts."

"And it would cost you but a word to give rank and an unequivocal position to my favorite daughter. For if a woman like yourself, recognized as a model of propriety, acknowledge her as your son's bride, you insure an honorable future to all my children not born to the throne. It is in your power to raise Mademoiselle de Blois to the rank of a legitimate princess of the blood, and thereby to confer a favor upon her father."

"Oh, sire, indeed I cannot! Ask any thing of me but that! It would give the lie to all the teachings of my life! It would be an acknowledgment of the worthlessness of chastity—of honor! Oh, forgive me! My brain reels; I know not what I say!"

"*But I do;* and I have heard enough. I shall countermand the soirée, and seek another bridegroom for Mademoiselle de Blois. But Trier shall fall, and on your head be the fate of its inhabitants!"

He rose and would have put aside the portière, but his hand was convulsively clutched, and the duchess, in a voice that was hoarse with agony, gasped:

"Have I understood? You would barter the fate of Trier for my consent to this unnatural marriage!"

"Yes, by God, I do!" was the profane and passionate reply of the king.

"Stay—stay," murmured she, trembling in every limb. "Would you rescue the city if I consented?"

"I will do so, with pleasure."

The duchess shivered, clasped her hands together, and, closing her eyes as though to hide her humiliation from Heaven, she retracted her refusal, and then fell almost insensible into an arm-chair.

The king approached her and kissing her, said, "Madame, from my heart, I thank you."

The poor duchess scarcely heeded these gracious words. She had received a blow that well-nigh blunted her heart to the sufferings of her countrymen. But she had made the sacrifice of her principles, and she must reap the reward of that terrible sacrifice.

"Sire," said she, as soon as she had recovered strength enough to articulate, "sire, fulfil your promise immediately, or it will be too late."

"Give me your hand, dear sister," replied Louis. "Once more I thank you for the happiness you have conferred upon me, and the first gift of Mademoiselle de Blois to her mother-in-law shall be the safety of Trier. I implore you, try to love the poor child, for my sake."

## CHAPTER VII.

### THE FIRE-TONGS.

RAISING the curtain, Louis XIV. offered his hand, and the royal brother and sister-in-law re-entered the cabinet, where their return was eagerly awaited by Madame de Maintenon, and uneasily expected by the minister of war.

"Monsieur de Louvois," said the king, "I am in possession of all the details that relate to the shameful abuse that has been made of my name in Germany. The cruel practices which you have authorized toward an innocent population must cease at once, and our troops be commanded to prosecute the war as becomes the army of a Christian nation."

The king, while he spoke these words, was gradually advancing to his writing-desk, which stood close to the mantel. Seating himself in his arm-chair, he turned his countenance away from the penetrating glances of De Maintenon, and began to play with the bronze shovel and tongs that lay crossed upon the fender.

After a pause, during which he waited in vain for a reply from Louvois, he resumed : "Why do you not answer me, Louvois ? "

"Sire, your wishes shall be fulfilled. The next courier that leaves for Germany, shall bear your royal commands to the army, and they shall be ordered to remain altogether on the defensive."

"What do you mean, sir ? " cried the king.

"If your majesty intends to treat your enemies with clemency, you must expect no more victories, but remain content with the territory you have already acquired. What are we to do, if we are crippled by injudicious and false humanity? Must we relinquish our claims? Shall we content ourselves with having made threats which we are too pusillanimous to execute?"

"Monsieur," said Louis, haughtily, "you are becoming impertinent. Cease your questions, and obey my commands. Send off your couriers at once. Trier shall not be destroyed; nor shall its inhabitants be driven from their dwellings. Private property shall be respected, and the temples of the Most High held sacred."

"Sire," said Louvois, "I will obey; but, unhappily, as regards Trier, your clemency comes too late. I cannot save it."

"Cannot!" shouted Louis, who to please his sister-in-law had worked himself into a veritable fury. "Who dares say he cannot, when I command?"

"Your majesty, what is done cannot be undone."

At these words the king sprang from his chair, still holding the tongs in his hand.

"Do you mean to say that you have ordered new atrocities to be commited in Germany?" exclaimed he.

"Sire," replied Louvois defiantly, "if it pleases you to term the necessities of war atrocities, so be it. The people of Trier having imitated the stubbornness of those of Speier, I ordered them to be subjected to the same treatment."

"Sir," cried Louis, raising the tongs, as if he intended to assail his minister with them, "you shall countermand this order at once, or I will smite you as the lightning blasts the oak!" All this time he was advancing, until the tongs were in dangerous proximity with Louvois' head.*

The minister was thoroughly frightened. "Sire," exclaimed he, receding in terror, "would you murder me?"

"It would be too honorable an end for you to die by my hands," replied the king, letting fall his tongs. "But this I say to you: if Trier is destroyed I will make an example of

* Historical.—See "Memoirs of the Court of France," by the Marquis de Dangeau.

you that shall deter any other traitor from using my name to gratify his wicked revenge. Send off your couriers; nor return to this palace until you come to inform me that Trier is safe." So saying, the King turned his back, and began to converse with Madame de Maintenon on the subject of an afternoon ride; after which he offered his arm to his sister-in-law and conducted her himself to the head of the private staircase.

He had no sooner left the room than Louvois darted to the side of Madame de Maintenon, who was just about to raise a portière leading to her own apartments.

Catching her dress in his agitation, Louvois implored her to remain.

"Wherefore, monsieur?" asked she, coldly.

"Oh, madame, I fear that I shall never be able to rescue this accursed city, and, I implore you, be my mediatrix with his majesty."

"On what grounds, monsieur?"

"Oh, madame, you have enemies as well as I: let us make a compact together, and crush them all. Uphold me for this once, and you will not find me ungrateful."

"I fear no man's enmity," was the reply of the marquise. "My trust is in God, who ruleth all things."

"You refuse me then?" said Louvois.

"I am not in a position to defy the king, and uphold his rebellious subjects. Were I Queen of France, my influence would, perhaps, avail; as it is, I would advise you to make all speed to dispatch your couriers, and thereby rescue Trier and yourself."

With these consolatory words, the marquise disappeared; and Louvois, taking her advice, unpalatable though it was, rushed in undignified haste through the corridors, and plunging into his carriage, was driven at full gallop to his hotel.

Twenty minutes later his couriers were on their way. To him who arrived at Trier first, Louvois promised a purse of one thousand louis d'ors, and, if he reached the city in time to save it, the sum was to be doubled.

Thanks to this reward, as well as to the dilatory movements of the courier that had borne the order for destruction, Trier was saved on the very morning of the day which should have been its last.

Louvois was ordered to bring the news to the duchess in person.

She was in her cabinet with the Duke de Chartres, who had been complaining of the ugliness and stupidity of his affianced bride. Louvois was announced, and the duchess, in her impetuous way, hurried to the door and met him—not by way of welcoming him, however.

"I never expected to see you here under my roof," said she, "nor would I receive you had you not come from his majesty."

"Madame, I will withdraw as soon as my message is delivered," replied Louvois, haughtily. "His majesty has sent me to announce to your royal highness that Trier is safe."

"Now, God be thanked!" exclaimed Elizabeth-Charlotte solemnly.

"With your leave, madame, I withdraw," observed Louvois.

"Not yet. You have brought me tidings of one deliverance—I will impart to you another. Have you any news from my poor Laura?"

A cloud overspread the minister's brow. "I have not heard from her for more than a year, at which time she fled from her husband's castle, how or whither he has never been able to discover."

"And you—have you no idea of her whereabouts?"

"She must either have died, or have retired to a convent."

"She has done neither," replied the duchess.

"She lives!" cried Louvois, with more terror in his voice than joy.

"Yes; dear, ill-used Laura! She lives, and lives happily with him whose arm will protect her against future persecution."

"Your royal highness does not mean to say that my daughter has sought the protection of Prince Eugene?" cried Louvois.

"I do, indeed: they are united at last, whom you sought to put asunder."

"Great God!" was the minister's exclamation. "She has given herself up to shame! She lives publicly as the mistress of a man who was not worthy to become her husband! Your royal highness must have been misinformed."

"I have it from herself, nevertheless."

"And your royal highness, that bears the name of the most virtuous woman in Paris, is not shocked at her unchastity?"

"Unchastity! You talk of unchastity, who, while she was plighting her troth to this same Eugene, were not ashamed to prostitute her to Strozzi! Cease your disgusting cant, and learn that I acknowledge and respect the tie that binds your daughter to her real spouse: and woe to you, if you dare trouble the current of her peaceful life! Farewell. Say to his majesty that I shall be forever grateful for the deliverance of Trier."

"Philip," added she, when Louvois had left the room, "forgive me, beloved son, if I sacrificed you to the well-being of my oppressed countrymen! You say that your affianced is stupid; but every weary hour you spend in her society shall be repaid to you by the blessings of those whom you have saved from assassination. Moreover, Mademoiselle de Blois is not yet your bride, and many a thing may intervene to prevent you from being forced to espouse her. If your mother can do any thing to frustrate it, be sure that she will come to your assistance. Her consent was wrung from her, 'tis true—but not her willingness."

"Laura the mistress of Eugene of Savoy!" muttered Louvois, as he descended the marble staircase of the ducal palace. "And to propitiate that royal virago, I dare not revenge myself! But no!" said he suddenly, "no—I need not lift a finger. I will leave it to Barbesieur; *he* will attend to it. He will put an end to her infamous life!"

## CHAPTER VIII.

### BRAVE HEARTS.

THE embassy of Prince Eugene to Turin had been attended with the happiest results. His arguments in favor of the emperor had proved irresistible, for he had worked upon the pride as well as the ambition of his kinsman. He had addressed him as a "royal highness ; " had promised him accession of territory ; and finally had imparted to him a diplomatic secret which decided him at once to join the imperialists. In the event of any manifestation on the part of Victor Amadeus that was friendly toward the emperor, Louvois had ordered Marshal Catinat to take him prisoner, confine him in the fortress of Pignerolles, and appoint the duchess-dowager Regent of Savoy.

The astounding insolence of the French minister gained a zealous partisan for Leopold. " I am yours and the emperor's forever," cried the indignant duke. " And from my heart I hope that we may both have speedy opportunity to avenge the wrongs we have sustained at the hands of Louis XIV. and that atrocious villain—Louvois."

" As for my wrongs," replied Eugene, with a beaming smile, " they are all forgotten in my excess of happiness."

" So, then, you are happy at last ? " asked Victor Amadeus, kindly.

"Supremely blest," was Eugene's emphatic reply.

"Supremely blest ? " repeated the duke, shaking his head. " Pardon me if I think otherwise. Do you not think that you could be made happier by obtaining the sanction of the church to your liaison with the Marchioness de Strozzi ? "

" I would be the proudest and happiest of created beings if I could call her my wife," sighed Eugene. " And since the subject has been broached between us, I will confide in you. I have written to the pope an account of Laura's fraudulent marriage with Strozzi, and I hope that his holiness will recognize the unlawfulness of that wicked transaction. It seems to me impossible that Religion should look upon it otherwise than as an act of falsehood."

31

"You have no answer as yet from Rome?"

"I expect an answer to-day; and now, that the crisis of my Laura's destiny is at hand, I begin to be timorous as to the success of my petition. The pope is not my friend; I have upheld the Waldenses against the church, and have sought their alliance for Austria. These, I know, are serious offences; and not less displeasing to his holiness will be the news of your defection from France to Austria through my intervention."

"True—true," said Victor Amadeus, thoughtfully. "Your embassy to Turin will prove prejudicial to your own interests at Rome. I am afraid they will suffer. And if his holiness will not grant a divorce, what is to become of the marchioness? You will not continue to live with her out of wedlock?"

"Pardon me," replied Eugene. "She is mine in the sight of God, and man shall not part us. Our union is holy in our own eyes, and we shall maintain its sanctity against the whole world. It will very soon forget us, and consign us to the oblivion we covet."

"You are not so easily consigned to oblivion, my dear cousin; you occupy a prominent position before the world, and the brighter your fame as a hero, the darker will be the shadow that falls upon your mistress. My wife and I have talked this matter over, and we have determined to make a joint effort either to have you formally united at the altar, or to use our honest endeavors to induce you to separate. The duchess has sent three invitations to the marchioness, every one of which has been refused."

"The marchioness desires no intercourse with the world. She is independent of its sanction or its blame."

"Because, for the present, her world is concentrated in you. But it will not always be so; and the duchess has gone this very morning to pay her a visit, hoping to prove to her that a woman should not only avoid wrong, but the appearance of wrong. At the same time, we both render ample justice to the purity of intention of the marchioness."

"Not only of intention, but of conduct," replied Eugene. "But let us discuss other matters. The elector, Max Emmanuel, has arrived at Montcaliers, the imperialists have joined him, and the Spanish troops are on their way."

"My army also shall march to Montcaliers to-morrow. It is time that the atrocities of Louis XIV. should cease. His soldiers have been worse than an irruption of the Goths both in Germany and in Italy."

"With the help of God, we will emulate their deeds in France."

While the two Princes of Savoy were in their cabinet together, the duchess was on her way to visit the marchioness. She was determined not to give Laura the opportunity of denying herself. To this end she followed the lackey that announced her, and as he opened the door, and was about to pronounce her name, she passed him by, and, going directly up to Laura, introduced herself.

She was calmly and courteously received, and, after some desultory conversation, entered upon her delicate mission.

"I have but one rule of action," said Laura, in return, "and I cannot wound my own convictions by shaping my conduct according to the standard of others."

"But surely you do not apply this rule to your unlawful liaison with Prince Eugene !" exclaimed the duchess.

"It is no unlawful liaison," replied Laura, simply. "I am Eugene's wife in his eyes and in mine : we have plighted our troth, and will be faithful to our vows until death !"

"And to this fidelity you sacrifice your honor and your peace of mind. Prince Eugene is but a mortal man. He is, for the time, desperately in love, and scorns all possibility of change. But by-and-by he will begin to be annoyed by the world's censure ; he will be ashamed to be seen with you—"

"Madame," interrupted Laura, proudly, "by what right do you thus prejudge the conduct of Prince Eugene ?"

"By the right of experience, my poor child, and of a knowledge of the human heart, whose inconsistencies are all unknown to you. Let me relate to you a history that concerns me nearly, and has caused me many a burning tear. My husband was once beloved by a beautiful woman, who, for his sake, left her husband, the court, and the grand monde, to be the solitary inhabitant of a castle, which, to be sure, was fit to be the abode of a goddess. She became the mistress of the Duke of Savoy, who loved her to distraction. I, his unhappy wife, had no right to remonstrate, for our union was like that of princes generally, an affair of state ; and Victor Amadeus never knew that my poor heart was racked by jealousy, and that many a time I prayed for death as the only remedy for my anguish. For a time the duke was contented to see the Countess de la Verrue in her castle, but by-and-by he exacted of this poor devoted creature another sacrifice—that of returning with a brow of shame to the world. He fitted up a residence for her in Turin ; passed all his time at her side ; drove out with her, and finally held his levees at her palace. Now, there were certain festivals *de rigueur* that were obliged to be given at the ducal palace ; and from these festivals the countess would be excluded unless she was invited by myself. I had nothing to lose, and hoping to win an approving smile from Victor, I invited his mistress, and, when she entered the hall of reception, placed her above all possibility of slight by advancing to meet her."

"That was magnanimous indeed !" exclaimed Laura.

The duchess smiled. " Do not overestimate the act, my dear child. There was quite as much policy in it as magnanimity. I know men well : they are greater slaves to opinion than women ; they have not half our moral courage, and not one of them can long confront the disapprobation of the world. From this day, a change came over the spirit of my husband. Seeing that the world held me in high esteem for my sacrifice, and held his mistress very cheaply, he began to feel uncomfortable when he brought her before its scrutiny. From discomfort he proceeded to shame, and finally the day came—the inevitable day that dawns for every woman who lays her honor at the feet of her lover. The poor countess was reproached for the sacrifices she had made, and blamed for her weakness in yielding to the importunities of her seducer ! She fled, brokenhearted from his presence, and, like poor La Vallière, took refuge in a convent. Oh, my dear young lady !" continued the duchess, taking Laura's hand in her own, " be warned, and do not court the fate of these unfortunate victims of man's inconstancy !"

"Madame," returned Laura, "their fate in no way can affect *me*, for I am not the mistress of Prince Eugene. He can never reproach me with weakness, for he, like myself, believes in the holiness of our union. We have been sinned against, but are not sinning. No woman can say of Eugene that he has broken his vows to her ; no man can say of me that I have been unfaithful to him ! "

"You forget the Marquis de Strozzi."

"Forget him ! Great God ! Forget the villain who, under cover of night, stole the vows I pledged to Eugene, and kept me his prisoner for five long years ! No, madame, I have not forgotten the Marquis de Strozzi ; but he is no husband of mine. My spouse before Heaven is Prince Eugene —and, so help me God, I will be true to him in life as in death ! "

"You are a noble woman ; and your love, I admit, is as pure as that of Eve for Adam. But, for your exalted ideas of duty, you will receive naught from the world save scorn and contumely."

"So be it. In my Eugene's love will be my exceeding great reward. The arrows of the world's contempt will fall harmless at my feet, for his dear arm will shield me from their sharpness. My world is Eugene ; he alone is my husband, and my judge."

The duchess looked compassionately at the beautiful enthusiast, and heaved a sigh. "I cannot save you, my child : your resolution is mightier than my arguments, and I can only pity and love you. Farewell ! May your heroism meet with the reward it deserves."

Laura accompanied the duchess to the door, and returned, calm and serene, to her embroidery-frame. She was working a standard for her beloved Eugene, and appeared quite to have forgotten the visit of the duchess, when, suddenly her cheeks flushed, and she raised her head to listen. She sprang from her seat, crossed the room and opened the door. Eugene came in, clasped her in his arms, and imprinted a kiss on her fair brow.

"My own love, my white swan," whispered he.

She lifted her magnificent eyes to his, there and he read the history of her deep, deep love. They sat down together, his arm still around her waist.

"Has the Duchess of Savoy been here?" asked he.

"Yes. She was here to persuade me, for the world's sake, to leave you."

"The duke has been doing the same by me," said Eugene.

And then they smiled. Neither one made protestations to the other; neither one had any thing to relate. The heaven of their mutual trust was without a cloud.

Their silent, solemn happiness was interrupted by a knock. Conrad came in with two dispatches—one from Germany, and one from Rome. Eugene took them from the golden salver on which they lay, and said:

"With the permission of the marchioness, I will read them."

She bowed and smiled; then, passing her arm through his, led him to a divan, and would have had him take a seat by her side.

"No, darling," said he, gently putting her down upon its satin cushions. "Lie there, while I sit at your feet and read the fiat of Rome."

He unfolded the letter, and read, Laura watching him the while; smoothing his hair with her loving hands, and gazing in his face with tenderness unspeakable. As she gazed she saw a cloud pass over his features; he looked up at her, and his eyes wore an expression of strange compassion and sorrow.

Laura bent forward and kissed him. "What ails my love?" said she.

"This letter has destroyed a blessed dream, beloved. I had hoped that we had propitiated Fate, and that misfortune had ceased to follow us."

"Why, what have your political papers to do with our fortunes?"

"This is not a political dispatch," replied Eugene. "It is the answer to a letter I addressed to Pope Innocent. Will you read it, dearest?"

She took the paper from his hands, and then began to laugh.

"I do not read Latin," said she. "Translate it for me."

Eugene then rose, put his arm around her and read :

"The sacrament of marriage is holy and inviolable, and it cannot be set aside. Woe be unto those who deny its sanctity and its irrevocable pledges ! The marchioness Strozzi was married by a priest, and her witnesses were a father and a brother. We are under the necessity of refusing the petition of the Prince of Savoy ; for, no representation of intentions misdirected, can stand against the deliberate consent of the parties to wedlock, witnessed by honorable relatives. We, therefore, call upon the Prince of Savoy to humble himself as beseems a man that has sinned against God and the Church, lest he incur her malediction, at the hands of the vicar of Christ on earth."

The paper fell from his hands and fluttered to her feet.

"You appealed to the pope to annul my marriage with Strozzi ?" asked she.

"Yes, my beloved. I would have aspired to the bliss of seeing the beautiful Laura Bonaletta my own wife—my wife before the world."

"How good, how noble of you !" murmured she. "You would have elevated poor Laura Bonaletta to the height of your own greatness, and would have had her bear your glorious name ! It would have been too much bliss for me to bear that honored name, Eugene : and yet ! oh, how I wish I might have called myself Princess of Savoy ! This happiness is denied me, and I must submit ; but I will not sin against my conscience, by allowing any judgment of mortal man to drive me from your side. Once more I lay my hand in yours, and what God has joined together, no power of man shall ever put asunder."

Eugene clasped her trembling hand in his, and, raising his eyes to heaven, recorded their vows.

After a pause, Laura resumed : "You have another letter to read, dear Eugene. Perhaps it may console you for our own disappointment. It is from Germany, and will, doubtless, bring pleasant tidings."

Eugene unfolded the dispatch, with a smile ; but scarcely had he glanced at its first words, when his face grew pale, and his hands trembled so that he could scarcely hold the paper.

"Ah!" cried Laura, "another disappointment!"

"Oh, Laura," sighed he, "Charles of Lorraine is no more."

"Your dearest friend?"

"Ay—my dearest friend! Charles of Lorraine dead!— And dead of a broken heart. Not on the battle-field, as became the greatest hero of his age, but on a bed of sickness. No officer by to do him honor—no soldiers there to weep for their adored commander! Oh, I would be a happy man, could I but win the love of my men as he did, and earn but one of the many laurels that were wreathed around his honored head!" *

"Your laurels will surpass his, my Eugene," exclaimed Laura, with prophetic love. "You are destined to achieve immortality."

Eugene shook his head, and, almost unconsciously, murmured these lines of Homer:

> "Like leaves on trees, the race of man is found,
>    Now green in youth, now withering on the ground;
>    Another race the following spring supplies,
>    They fall successive, and successive rise.
>    So generations, in their course, decay,
>    So flourish these, when those have passed away!"

"Any admission within these enchanted walls?" said a gay voice, behind them; and, starting up in amazement, they beheld the tall figure of the Elector of Bavaria, and behind him, Conrad, with a perplexed and most distressed countenance.

"Before I say another word, let me exonerate Conrad from any complicity in my indiscretion," said the elector; "for, I must say, that he told a series of falsehoods on your account, that will keep him out of heaven for many a month. But I surprised him glancing uneasily toward this door, so I took your Peter by the shoulders, put him aside, and walked into paradise without his permission."

---

* Prince Eugene's own words.—See Zimmermann.

"Very well, Conrad," said Eugene ; "you are excused." And, taking the hand of the elector, he led him to the marchioness, and presented him as his dearest living friend.

The elector kissed her hand and bent the knee before her as he would have done before an empress.

"Madonna," said he, "I bow before your beauty and your worth. I am a poor, sinful mortal, but I have, at least, an appreciation of heavenly goodness, and I come to do homage to the innocence, the purity, and the courage of my friend's guardian angel."

"You are most welcome, prince ; but, I pray you, rise. It becomes not a hero like you to kneel before poor Laura Bonaletta."

"I would have died but for her care," said Eugene, when the elector had accepted a seat at Laura's side. "She came to me through perils that shame our every-day deeds on the field of battle."

"I have heard of her miraculous flight from one who loves her dearly. We rejoiced together over the news of her escape."

"You allude to Lucretia," said Laura—"how is she ?"

"Like other mortals," laughed the elector ; "loving to-day and hating to-morrow, and, finally, discovering that lovers' hate is love. Neither you nor Eugene can understand these vicissitudes of sublunary attachments ; for you have nothing in common with the stormy and changeful sea of ordinary loves. Heaven created you one for the other, and your lives are a development of that divine charity which 'believeth all things, hopeth all things, and endureth all things.'"

# BOOK VIII.

## CHAPTER I.

### THE ADVANCE INTO FRANCE.

THE war in Italy had lasted for three years without any decisive result on either side. Here and there some unimportant advantages had been gained by the imperialists, which had then been balanced by some equally trifling defeats. The campaign had opened unfortunately. Against the advice of his generals, Victor Amadeus had given battle to General Catinat, near the abbey of Staffarda, and in spite of all that his kinsman Eugene could do by personal bravery to repair the blunder, the imperialists sustained a most humiliating defeat. Eugene, however, had the melancholy satisfaction of knowing that he had predicted the result, although his remonstrances had been unavailing to avert it.

This disaster had the effect of cooling the zeal of Victor Amadeus to such an extent, that he actually began to repent of having taken sides against the French. He was too wary to betray his state of mind ; so he pretended great ardor, and called urgently for re-enforcements. Backed by the importunities of Prince Eugene, he succeeded in obtaining them, and at their head the Elector Max Emmanuel, commander-in-chief of all the imperial forces.

In spite of all this, the war was not vigorously prosecuted. Max Emmanuel, although brave and true, seemed to have lost the qualities that had made him a wise and energetic commander : he lacked coolness when plans were to be conceived, and decision when they were to be carried out. He left all supervision to the care of his subordinates, and spent his days in the pursuit of pleasure.

All this Prince Eugene perceived with unavailing regret. He was powerless to prevent it, for, as the youngest of the field-marshals, his duty was restricted to the mere execution of the orders of his superiors. The war dwindled down to an insignificant though bloody contest with the mountaineers of Savoy and the Italian peasantry, and things continued in this state until the allies of the emperor manifested their discontent, and called for the removal of Max Emmanuel. Field-marshal Carassa was recalled, and, at the beginning of the campaign of 1692, the command of the allied forces was given to Victor Amadeus, while Field-Marshal Caprara was appointed second in command.

Circumstances now seemed favorable to an earnest prosecution of the war. The imperialists were assembled at one point ; they were superior in numbers to the enemy, and at their head stood a man who lost no opportunity to publish to the world his devotion to Austria, and his detestation of France.

Eugene was not as hopeful as the rest. He had had enough of valiant words, and was longing for valiant deeds.

"We must advance into France," said he, when the generals next assembled in council. "We must retaliate upon the people the persecutions of their army in Germany and Italy. We must enter by the pass of Barcelonetta, which for the present is unguarded. Before troops can arrive to succor the garrison, we shall have taken several more posts of importance."

"But should we take, will we be able to hold them ? " asked Victor Amadeus, affecting wisdom.

Eugene's large eyes looked searchingly into the sealed book of his cousin's shrewd countenance.

"Your highness," replied he, "above all things let us have confidence in ourselves, and let us place some trust in the fortunes of war."

"Catinat is very sagacious," observed General Laganay, the leader of the Spanish forces. "As soon as we move in the direction of Barcelonetta, he will re-enforce the garrison."

"Then so much the more necessity for speed on our part," cried Eugene. "We must mislead the enemy, and make a feint on Pignerol. To this end, let us send a corps of observation into Piedmont, while we order a detachment of dragoons and infantry to possess themselves in all haste of the pass."

The Duke of Savoy looked thoughtful, and there was profound silence among the members of the war council. After a pause of some duration, Victor Amadeus raised his head, and gave a long searching look at the excited countenance of his cousin.

"The Prince of Savoy is right," said he, at length. "We must avenge our wrongs, and carry the war into France. Our way lies through the vale of Barcelonetta, and we must move without delay."

The face of Eugene was so lit up by joy that his cousin smiled, and gave him a significant look.

"I have an account of my own to settle with France," added he, "and personal affronts to resent. So has my cousin, who longs to avenge the injuries he has received from Louvois."

"I assure your royal highness," answered Eugene, eagerly, "that personal feeling has naught to do with my opinions as to the prosecution of this war. I would despise myself if, in what I have spoken regarding the interests of the emperor, I had been actuated by any secret motive of aversion toward his enemies."

There was something in this protest that annoyed Victor Amadeus, for his eyes flashed, and his brows were momentarily corrugated. But no one knew better than he how to suppress any symptoms of vexation. It was not convenient to evince displeasure, and he composed his features back to serenity.

"Members of this council of war, and officers of the imperial army," said he, with an appearance of solemn earnestness, "we must act promptly and energetically. Let us prove to our allies, and to all Europe, that we know how to avenge the wrongs of our countrymen. We pass the boundary-lines of France!"

And every preparation was made to carry out this determination. The army was to advance in three divisions, and Prince Eugene was to lead the vanguard.

His way lay through the mountainous districts of Savoy ; but, with experienced guides to lead them, the dragoons were able to defile through secret passes unknown to any but the natives, and to arrive unsuspected upon the frontiers of France.

The peasant that preceded Prince Eugene stopped for a while, and, raising his arm, pointed onward.

"This is France," said he. "Yonder is Barcelonetta, and the towers you see beyond are those of the fortress of Guillestre."

Eugene thanked him, and put spurs to his horse. On the frontier he drew in his rein, surveyed the lovely green plain before him, and addressed the Prince de Commercy.

"I have kept the promise I made in Hungary," said he.

"I remember it," replied De Commercy. "I had been telling you that, after hearing of your heroic deeds in the emperor's service, Louvois had said : 'Let Prince Eugene beware how he attempts to return to France !' And your reply was this : 'I shall return, but it shall be sword in hand.'" *

"And we are here—my good sword and I. Nine years ago, I left my native country, a miserable and despairing youth."

"And you return a great general, and one of the happiest men alive," cried De Commercy.

"Ay," murmured Eugene, "one of the happiest men alive ! —so happy, that methinks the contrarieties of life are so many vaporous clouds, that throw but a passing shadow over the face of heaven, and then melt into the azure of resplendent day. From my heart I thank indulgent Destiny for her blessings !"

"Destiny that was mightier than the puny enmity of a Louvois ! Well—we have had our fill of glory in Hungary and Italy. I hope we shall find a few laurels here in France."

"I hope so," said Eugene, moodily, "though oftentimes I—"

"Why do you hesitate ? What do you fear ?" asked De Commercy.

"I fear," replied Eugene, lowering his voice, "that we will not be allowed to pluck laurels that grow on French soil."

"Do you think the French will outnumber us ?"

"No," sighed Eugene, "the enemy's numbers give me no

* Historical.—See Armath, "Prince Eugene of Savoy," vol. i.

uneasiness : I am afraid of our own weakness. We lack the *morale*—the will to conquer."

" Why surely, Eugene, you lack neither," replied De Commercy.

" As if *I* had any voice in these councils ! Were it left with me to manœuvre this army, I would lead it to Paris in two weeks. But, unhappily, you and I are but the instruments of the will of our superiors. I will not conceal from you, my friend, the impatience with which I submit to carry out orders against which my judgment continually rebels ; and how weary I am of serving, where I feel that I ought to command. You know me too well to suspect me of the meanness of a mere lust for distinction. Had we a true or competent leader, I would be content to remain where I am, as youngest field-marshal in the army—in the fifth rank ; but—"

"But you consider Victor Amadeus as incapable as Max Emmanuel ? "

" Max was not incapable," said Eugene, as though speaking to himself. " True, he exhibited none of those great qualities which distinguished him in Hungary ; or perhaps he was shrewd enough to perceive that no amount of generalship could prevail against the dulness of his German officers. the ill-will of the Spaniards, and the irresolution of the Duke of Savoy. I believe he concluded to let things take their course, and cause his own removal. But he, at least, was honest. He was not casting his eyes about, to see on which side lay his own interest. His countenance is a true reflex of his soul— and what he says, he means."

" And by this you wish me to infer that such is not the case with our present commander-in-chief ? " asked De Commercy.

Eugene bent his head in token of assent, and gazed for a moment at the country which lay before them. " We will capture Barcelonetta," said he, " Gillestre, and perhaps Embrun, provided we are too rapid in our movements for the duke to circumvent us by countermanding orders. We must strive to make retreat impossible, but we must not lose sight of Victor Amadeus. We must watch him closely, and be on our guard against—"

" Against what ? " asked De Commercy.

"Against treason," whispered Eugene.

"How! You think it possible that—"

"That while the road to Paris is open before us, we never get farther than Embrun. Unless we are wary, De Commercy, we shall be betrayed and sold to the enemy.—But look! Here come our vanguard. You can indulge your fancy for rural scenery, while I go to receive them." And Eugene galloped back to his men, who received him with shouts of enthusiasm.

"My braves," said he, unsheathing his sword, and pointing to the smiling plains beyond, "my braves, this is France! the enemy's country, which we are here to conquer!"

The troops responded with a yell that betokened their readiness for the bloody work.

## CHAPTER II.

### THE RAVENS.

The men were allowed an hour's rest to feed their horses and prepare their dinners. Fires were lighted, vivandières went hither and thither, wishing that they could multiply themselves to answer the demands of the hungry soldiers. Here and there were picturesque groups of men reclining under the trees, some chatting, some smoking, others singing songs of home.

This bivouac was a pleasant scene to look upon; but its peace was like the stillness that precedes a storm. A few hours might change these light-hearted human beings into mangled corpses, and dye this velvet sward with human blood.

Eugene had dismounted, and, accompanied by one of his staff-officers, mingled with the merry crowd. Everywhere he was greeted with demonstrations of affection and contemplated with unmistakable admiration. Sometimes he paused awhile to chat with the soldiers, of their families at home; often accepting the bread they offered, and tasting of the soup that was being distributed by the vivandières.

Now and then a gruff voice was heard calling out to the "little Capuchin," as the soldiers were accustomed to designate Eugene, through fondness. At such times, he smiled, nodded, and, when his officers would have chided the men for their familiarity, besought them not to reprove them for a jest so harmless.

"Why do you look so melancholy, lieutenant?" asked he of a young officer, who, apart from his comrades, was leaning against a tree, gazing intently in the distance.

The officer appeared to waken from a fit of abstraction, for he gave a slight start, and removed his cap.

"Are you not pleased at our invasion of France?" asked Eugene.

"Ay, that am I," replied he, with a bitter smile. "I have long hoped for this invasion, and I thank God that it is at hand."

"You are ambitious to wear the epaulets of a captain, I presume?"

"No, general, no. I care nothing for military finery."

"Why, then, have you longed to march to France?"

"Because I hunger and thirst for French blood. General, I implore you, give me a body of men, and let me initiate our invasion of France by giving the French a taste of guerrilla warfare."

"Are you so sanguinary, young man?" asked Eugene, in amazement. "Do you not know that war itself should be conducted with humanity, and that we should never forget our common brotherhood with our enemies!"

"No, general, I know it not, nor do I wish to know it. I know that the French have left me without kindred, without home, without ties; and that they have transformed me—a man whose heart once beat with sympathy and love for all living creatures—into a tiger, that craves blood, and mocks at suffering."

"Unhappy man!" exclaimed Eugene, sadly. "Then you have suffered wrong at the hands of the French?"

The young man heaved a convulsive sigh.

"I come from the Palatinate," said he. "My parents' house was fired, my father murdered, and my mother driven out into the woods, where she perished. But this is not all. I loved a maiden—a beautiful and virtuous maiden, to whom I was betrothed. O God! that I should have lived to see it! General, the name of my betrothed was Marie Wengelin."

"Marie Wengelin!" echoed Eugene, with a shudder. "I have heard of her tragic end. It was she that delivered Esslingen, but was—"

"Marie! Marie!" cried Caspar, hiding his face with his hands.

Eugene kindly touched him on the shoulder. "Unfortunate young man," said he, "from my soul I pity you, and well I understand your hatred of the Frenchman."

"Dear general, give me the command of a body of marauders that shall clear the way for our army. There is many a man in our regiment as eager for revenge as I; let us be consolidated into one corps, and where bloody work is to be done, confide it to us."

Eugene thought for a moment, and then replied: "So be it; you shall have your wish. Select one hundred men, of whom you shall be captain, and come to me, individually for your orders, reporting also to myself, and not to my officers. I will give you opportunity to distinguish yourself, young man; but remember that it is one thing to be a hero, and another to be a cutthroat. Retaliate upon the men, but spare the women. If, in every Frenchman, you see a Melac, look upon every woman as your Marie. Will you promise me this?"

"I will, general. At last I shall have vengeance, I shall serve my country, and when my work is done, may God release me from this fearful earthly bondage!"

"Utter no such sinful wishes. Believe me, there is balm for every wound; and I, who tell you this, have suffered unspeakably."

"General, my Marie is dead, and died by her own hand."

"She died the death of a heroine. But for you, it is heroism to live, and so to live that the world may esteem you worthy of having been loved by Marie Wengelin. Ah! you are no cutthroat. I see it in the glance of your eye, in the tremor of your lip. You shall have command of the guerrillas;

32

for you will not be barbarous in your warfare. What is your name ? "

" Caspar Werner."

" Give me your hand, Caspar Werner, and promise me that you will go through life with the fortitude that becomes a brave man."

Caspar grasped Eugene's extended hand. "Yes, general, I promise. I will be worthy of my Marie—worthy of your kindness to-day ; and from this hour forth I am yours for life or death."

Eugene gazed admiringly into the handsome face of the trooper. "I will do all that lies in my power to lessen your troubles, Caspar, and you shall be under my own special protection. How soon will you be able to organize your corps ? "

" In ten minutes, general."

Eugene shook his head incredulously.

" You will see, general," said Caspar. "We are all prepared, and awaited nothing but your consent. Now look ! The men have just risen from dinner. Will you allow me to present them now ? "

" Certainly. I will wait for them here."

Caspar leaped on his horse, which was close at hand, grazing, and galloped to the spot where the soldiers had bivouacked. Eugene, who was now joined by several of his staff, followed his movements with great interest.

The trooper came so suddenly upon his comrades, that not one of them had been aware of his approach. They went on chatting and smoking until, all of a sudden, were heard these few words : "Ravens, to horse ! "

In the twinkling of an eye, every man stood erect. For the second time, Caspar called out, "Ravens, to horse ! " when their hands were on the bridle, and in less than five minutes they were all mounted.

Before ten minutes had expired, the Ravens had defiled before Prince Eugene, who contemplated, with a sort of grim satisfaction, their stalwart forms, their resolute, bronzed faces, and their fiery, flashing eyes.

He signed to Caspar to approach.

" Gentlemen," said he to his officers, "let me present to

you Captain Werner of the —th. He is in command of an independent corps who call themselves 'The Ravens,' but in their aspirings emulate the eagle."

"General," said Caspar, "give the word, and let your Ravens fly."

"You have it," replied Eugene, smiling. "Yonder are the towers of Barcelonetta. On our march thither are two forts; they would inconvenience our advance, and must be taken."

"They shall be taken," was the reply, and in a few moments the Ravens had flown, and were no longer to be seen.

One hour later the vanguard of the imperial army resumed its march. Nothing checked their advance, for the Ravens had carried every thing before them. Barcelonetta, terrified at the fate of the two other forts, held out the white flag; and, by the time Prince Eugene had arrived, a procession was on its way to deliver into his hands the keys of the fortress. The clergy, in full canonicals, were at their head, and after them a troop of young girls dressed in white, the first of whom presented the keys on a silk cushion, and petitioned "the great hero" for mercy.

"Oh, my mother!" thought he, as he took the keys, "you are avenged. The despised abbé has proved to the King of France that he is not a weakling unworthy of wearing a sword!"

They tarried but a night at Barcelonetta. On the morrow they captured Guillestre, and set out for Embrun, where they expected to be joined by the main army.

Embrun resisted for twenty-four hours, but at the end of that time it fell, and Victor Amadeus took up his headquarters there, while Eugene marched on to Gab. He had been preceded by the Ravens, who, in imitation of their enemies, had driven the people from their houses, and had set fire to whole villages, cutting down all who offered resistance.

And, while they transformed the beautiful plains of Dauphiné into a waste, and marked their path forward by smoking ruins, they shouted in the ears of the unhappy fugitives: "Revenge! Revenge for the woes of Germany!"

"Revenge for the woes of Germany!" cried the Ravens, as they leaped from their horses to storm the walls of Gab.

But no answer was made to their challenge, for not a soul was there to give back a defiant word. The gates stood open, the walls were unguarded, and, when the dragoons entered the town, they found not one living being whereon to wreak their vengeance. So hasty had been the flight of the inhabitants that they had left their worldly goods behind, and their houses looked as though the owners had but just absented themselves for an hour or so to attend church, or celebrate some public festival.

The Ravens took possession, and, when Prince Eugene arrived, he found the Austrian flag waving from the towers, and that of Savoy streaming above the gates.

"You have done your work quickly," observed he to Caspar.

"There was nothing to do, general," was the reply. "There is not a living soul of them within the walls. And now, your highness—a boon!"

"What is it?"

"General, recall to your mind Speier and Worms, and grant us leave to find our retaliation for their destruction in Gab."

"You say there is not a living soul in Gab? Are there, then, no women, no children, no superannuated or infirm?"

"General, every house is empty. I found but one living creature in Gab—a young girl who lay sick in bed—too sick to move."

"Alone? forsaken?"

"Forsaken, general, save by one little dog that had just expired at the side of her bed, for its body was warm and supple."

"And the poor girl?"

"She was dying."

Eugene's large, questioning eyes were upon Caspar's face, and their expression was anxious and painful. "Caspar, did you remember your promise?"

"Yes, general, I did. The maiden asked for water, and I held the cup to her lips. I seated myself at her bedside, and while my comrades sacked the town, I soothed her last moments. When all was over, I covered her face, and left the house."

Eugene extended his hand. "You acted nobly, Caspar."

"Nay, general," replied Caspar, his eyes filling with tears, "her name was—Marie !—But now, that I can assure you on my honor that there is no creature to molest in the town, I once more present the petition of my men. They ask for permission to destroy Gab."

Eugene pondered for a moment, and then gave his consent. "Let them do what they choose with the town."

Then, turning to the Prince de Commercy, "I begin to think," said he, "that I have done injustice to Victor Amadeus. It was he who, contrary to the opinions of his officers, ordered the advance to Gab. He will be delighted and surprised to hear that we have possession of the fortress already, for he was anxious to be with us at the siege."

"I can believe it : he may well desire the honor of capturing one stronghold in France, when his cousin has already reduced two.—But look, Eugene, at yonder courier coming toward us—he seems to be in haste."

The courier came on, his horse flecked with foam, himself covered with dust ; and, no sooner had he approached within hearing, than he called in a loud voice for "Field-Marshal, the Prince of Savoy."

An orderly conducted him at once to the prince, to whom he delivered a package from his highness the Duke of Savoy.

Eugene broke the seals, and began to read. His brows met, and, as he looked up from the perusal of his dispatches, his face was expressive of extreme annoyance.

"It is well," said he to the courier. "Say to his highness that we will obey. Monsieur de Commercy, let us ride together up the heights, whence we may have a full view of Gab and our troops."

They set their horses in motion, and in a few moments had reached the summit of the hill. Here Eugene reined in his horse, and reopened his dispatch.

"Here we are alone, Commercy. Let me read you the letter of my well-beloved cousin and commander-in-chief :

"'My dear kinsman and distinguished field-marshal: To my unspeakable regret, I am deprived, by a serious illness, of taking part in the attack upon Gab. My physicians have ordered me back to Embrun, there to await the result. These presents will convey to the advance guard my command to retreat to Embrun until further orders. It is my intention (unless I succumb before your arrival) to hold a council of war ; and, to this intent, I require the presence of all the general officers. Hasten, therefore, my dear Eugene, lest you should find me no longer alive ; and believe that, living or dying, I am, as ever, your devoted kinsman and friend.

(Signed)          "'VICTOR AMADEUS, Duke of Savoy.'"

"Do you believe all this?" asked De Commercy.

"Stay till you hear the postscript from his own hand :

"'My dear cousin : You must pardon my egotistic ambition, if I do not allow the siege of Gab to be prosecuted without me. I am very desirous of glory, and perchance your laurels have contributed to my indisposition. At any rate, before you take a third fortress, I must have my opportunity of capturing two. So, instead of attacking Gab, come to Embrun to the relief of

"'Yours, besieged by illness,          V. A.'"

"I repeat my question—do you believe in his illness?"

"And you—do you believe in his ambition?"

"Why not? He avows it openly."

"For which very reason, it has no existence. Victor Amadeus is too crafty to make such an avowal in good faith. He never says what he thinks, nor does he ever think what he says. No, no—my poor little leaflets of laurel would have given him no uneasiness, had they not been plucked on French soil !—But we must wait and see. The main point is to retreat to Embrun."

"And Gab? Will you retract your gift of its empty houses to the Ravens?"

"No. My instructions were not to besiege Gab. It surrendered before they reached me, and I shall leave it to the soldiery. As for you and me, we must hasten to Embrun to try to break the seal of my cousin's impassible countenance, and read a few of his thoughts. Did I not tell you that we would march no farther than Embrun?"

## CHAPTER III.

### SICK AND WELL.

THE Duke of Savoy had taken up his residence at the castle of Embrun, where, as soon as the officers had arrived, his highness called a council of war. They were assembled in the council-chamber, awaiting the appearance of the invalid.

The doors leading to a room beyond, were opened to give passage to a huge arm-chair on rollers, which was wheeled by four lackeys, to the centre of the hall. The duke's head reclined on a cushion which had been fastened for the occasion to the back of the chair: the remainder of his person was buried under a purple velvet coverlet, except his neck and arms, which were clothed in a black doublet, the whole costume being eminently calculated to heighten the pallor of the duke's cheeks, and increase the whiteness of his hands as they lay limp and helpless on the velvet covering. His eyes were half-closed, and as he made a feeble attempt to survey the assemblage before him, they appeared to open with difficulty. With a faint motion of the hand, he signed to the lackeys to retire, and then made a painful effort to raise his head.

Deep silence reigned throughout the council-chamber, but the gaze of every man there was fixed upon the pallid face of him in whose trembling hands lay the destinies of four different armies. His dim eyes wandered slowly about the room until they rested on the person of Prince Eugene, who, hot and dusty, presented an appearance that contrasted strongly with that of his brother-officers.

"Our dear kinsman Eugene has arrived, I see," said the duke, in a faint voice. "We were afraid that we would be obliged to hold this important council without your presence."

"I hastened with all speed to obey your highness's summons," replied Eugene, "and I must avail myself of this opportunity to apologize for my dress. I have just dismounted, and hurried to the council-chamber that I might myself announce to your highness the good news of which I am the bearer."

"Let us hear it," murmured the duke, closing his eyes, and letting his head droop upon the pillow.

"Your highness, we were not obliged to storm Gab: it surrendered without a shot."

The duke's eyelids moved, and a flush overspread his face. No one remarked this save Eugene, for all other eyes in the hall were riveted upon himself.

"This is very good news," said the duke, feebly.

"Your highness sees, then, what a panic is produced by the mere mention of your name. It is a talisman that will lead us to Paris without opposition or loss of life. Like Cæsar, you come, see, and conquer—and that—not by your presence, but by your reputation."

"Your highness is too modest," said Victor Amadeus, somewhat recovering his voice. "I cannot accept the laurels you have so honorably won. Alas!" continued he, "I fear that I shall never lead an army into battle again!"

And, as if exhausted by the thought, he fell back and was silent. In a few moments, he raised his head and spoke: this time with open eyes, and with some distinctness.

"Gentlemen take your seats. The council is opened."

The great question of the next movement of the army was now to be agitated. The council were divided in their sentiments. Some were for rapid advance, others were of opinion that great discretion was to be exercised, now that they stood on the enemy's territory, and that not one step should be made without great deliberation as to its expediency.

At the head of the latter party stood General Caprara. "We have no right to trust to luck in war," said he. "We must take into consideration all the mischances that may befall us in the enemy's country, and act accordingly. Prince Eugene's advance-guard, for example, had the good luck to find Gab abandoned by its inhabitants. Had they remained to defend their city, we would have lost our men to no purpose whatever."

"My advance-guard is composed of young and brave men, who, to avenge the injuries of Germany, have devoted themselves to death ; but they are so fearless, and therefore so terrible, that I believe they will live to perform many a gallant deed."

"If they are not hanged as marauders," retorted Caprara ; "for my edicts against plunderers and incendiaries remain in force here as well as at home."

"Your excellency has, then, changed your mode of warfare since your soldiery devastated the towns of Hungary," said Eugene.

"Field-Marshal !" cried Caprara, reddening.

"What, your excellency ?" asked Eugene, with a provoking smile.

"Gentlemen," interposed the Duke of Savoy, "distract not our councils with your personal differences. Field-Marshal Caprara, you are, then, of opinion that it would be perilous for us to advance farther into the enemy's territory ?"

"Yes, your highness," growled Caprara, looking daggers at Eugene. "A rapid march might give opportunity for the display of personal prowess, which, while it redounded to the credit of the few, would imperil the safety of the many."

"I heartily second the views of General Caprara," said General Legnaney, the leader of the Spanish division. "If we march on, we leave our base of operations far behind, and render unforeseen calamities irremediable."

"That is my opinion ;" "And mine," cried several voices together, but among the younger officers there was dissenting silence.

Victor Amadeus gave a long sigh, and, turning his head slowly, addressed Eugene :

"Field-Marshal, Prince of Savoy, it is your turn to speak."

"I, your highness, am of opinion that we push our conquest with vigor. All the talent and strength of the French army has been sent to the Netherlands, and France is, so to speak, at our mercy. We have no obstacles before us in the shape of men in the field or garrisoned strongholds. As we

captured Barcelonetta, Guillestre, and Gab, so will we capture
every place that lies on our march. There is absolutely nothing of the proportions of a mole-hill to prevent us from going
as far as Grenoble—nay, as far as Lyons."

"The Prince of Savoy has spoken like a sagacious general,"
said the Prince de Commercy. "Nothing prevents us from
marching to Lyons."

"I sustain his views," added the Duke of Schomberg. "We
must advance. Let us promise protection to the Waldenses,
and so foment civil discord among the enemy. To create
disaffection in the enemy's country is good policy—and it is a
policy that will bear us on to Paris."

"We are of the same mind," said the other officers, who
had kept silence.

And now ensued another pause. The casting vote on this
momentous question was to be given by Victor Amadeus. He
had recovered his strength in a wonderful manner, for his
face had lost its pallor, his eyes their dimness, and his whole
countenance beamed with resolution.

"Gentlemen," cried he, as, in his excitement, he rose from
his chair, "to youth belong fame and conquest ; to youth belongs the strength that casts away impediments, and overleaps
all hindrances to success. Forgive us, who, being young,
thirst for glory, and long to quench that thirst in the sparkling waters of military success. Forgive me, you who are sa-
tiated with ambition gratified, if, rather than be discreet with
you, I would be rash with my young kinsman. I am of Prince
Eugene's opinion. Nothing hinders our march to Grenoble.
I am impatient—"

Suddenly he paused, and grasped the arms of the chair. A
shudder pervaded his whole body, and, with a convulsive gasp,
he fell back, apparently insensible.

The assembly broke up in confusion. Physicians were
summoned, and, at their bidding, the duke was slowly borne
back into his chamber. His head was enveloped in damp
cloths, his temples were rubbed with stimulants, and, after
various restoratives had been applied, he slowly opened his
eyes, and looked bewildered about him. Nobody was near except Doctor Mirazzi. The other physicians had retired to the

embrasure of a bay-window, and the lackeys had gathered about the door, where they were awaiting further orders from their superiors. All this the duke had seen at a glance. He closed his eyes again, but, as he did so, he made a sign to Doctor Mirazzi.

The latter bent his head to listen, but in such a manner as to convey the idea that he was watching his patient's fluttering breath.

" Dismiss them all," whispered the sick man.

The doctor gave no ostensible sign of having heard. He still kept his ear to the patient's mouth ; then, after a while, he placed it close to his heart. The examination at an end, he went on tiptoes toward the window where his colleagues were standing.

" He sleeps," whispered he. " When he awakes, his malady will probably declare itself. I will remain here to watch him ; it is unnecessary for you to confine yourselves with me in this close sick-room. Will you oblige me by returning this evening for a consultation ? "

" Certainly," was the reply of the others, who were grateful to be relieved from duty. " Shall we appoint seven o'clock ? "

" Yes," answered Mirazzi ; " and we will hold our consultation in the duke's sitting-room. Our presence here might be prejudicial."

And, with injunctions for silence, the doctor accompanied his colleagues to the door, which was noiselessly opened by the lackeys ; but, before they had time to close it again, Mirazzi shut it with his own hands, loosening simultaneously a thick velvet portière, through whose heavy folds no sound could penetrate without.

Victor Amadeus, meanwhile, lay motionless in his armchair.

" Your highness," said Mirazzi, " we are now safe and alone."

The duke arose, kicked off his coverlet, and stood erect. " My dear doctor," said he, " you must prove to me that I may trust you."

" For thirty years I have served your royal highness's family, and I am ready to do so, be it with my life," replied Mirazzi.

"I believe you, Mirazzi ; and therefore I, who am insincere toward everybody else, am honest in my intercourse with you. Now listen to me.  In the science of medicine there are many remedies for diseases.  Are there any potions, known to physicians, that have power to *produce* maladies ? "

"That is a dangerous inquiry, your highness ; for it regards the most tragic secrets of the craft.  There are many, many things known to us that will produce sickness, followed by death, immediate or remote ; but unfortunately there are not as many as you suppose, that will restore the vital energies where they are impaired by disease."

"But, doctor, surely you have some way of simulating disease without injuring the patient.  Cutaneous maladies, for instance, must be very easily induced."

"They can more easily be induced than simulated.  I can raise a scarlet eruption on a man's skin ; but when it appears, it will bring with it fever and thirst."

"So much the better, so much the better ! " exclaimed Victor Amadeus, eagerly.  "How long will the symptoms last ? '

"If proper remedies are administered, they will disappear in five or six days, your highness."

"Good, good," murmured the duke to himself ; and then he began to pace forth and back the length of the apartment. After a while he came and stood directly in front of the doctor, who with his sharp eyes had been watching him as he walked, and perfectly apprehended the nature of the service he was expected to render to his distinguished patient.

"Doctor," said the sick man, " I feel the premonition of some serious illness.  My head swims, my limbs ache, and cold chills are darting through my body.  My fever will be high, and perchance I may grow delirious.  Let me then use the rational interval left me, to make such dispositions as might be necessary in case of my demise."

" Then let me advise your highness to get to bed as speedily as possible," replied the doctor, solemnly.  " This done, I will call in our consulting physicians—"

" By no means : I hate consultations.  Nobody shall come

into my room but yourself, and, when you need the advice of your coadjutors, you must assemble them in some other part of the castle."

"I thank your highness for so signal a proof of confidence," said Mirazzi, "but I am not at liberty to assume the undivided responsibility of your nursing; for you may become really sick, and you must have all needful attention. Were we in Turin, her highness your noble spouse would suffer no one to attend you except herself; but here—"

"Here she shall not come; and to make sure of this fact, I will write her a letter in my own hand that will allay any anxiety she might feel on my account. Write yourself to the duchess, and ask her to send my old nurse—her that has always tended me in sickness. But I feel very ill, doctor. Call my valet to undress me. When I am comfortably arranged in bed, I will send for my secretary, and afterward for my staff-officers. They must receive their orders from *me*, before I lose my senses."

"To bed, to bed, your highness—that is the main thing!"

"Yes, that is the main thing," echoed the duke, falling into his arm-chair, and drawing up his velvet coverlet. "Now, doctor," added he, in a very faint voice, "call my valets, or I shall swoon before they get me to bed."

---

## CHAPTER IV.

### THE DUKE'S DANGEROUS ILLNESS.

THE news of the duke's terrible illness spread through the castle, over the town, and reached the barracks of the soldiers, who, like their officers, received the intelligence with blank looks of disappointment.

The staff-officers hastened to the castle, and some of them made attempts to penetrate the sick-chamber. But all in vain. Doctor Mirazzi's orders were stringent, and the nerves of his patient were not to be tried by the presence of any man, were that man his own brother.

"We can determine nothing, nor can we administer any remedies," said he, "until the malady declares itself. We must wait."

"We must wait," said the duke's physician, and the whole army was doomed to inaction, while urgent and more urgent grew the necessity for active operations.

Throughout the castle reigned profound stillness : not the least sound was permitted to reach the duke's ears. The officers that called were kept at a distance from his apartments, and to all their inquiries there was but one and the same reply—the duke was delirious, and incapable of giving orders.

Finally, after three days of mortal suspense, it was announced that his highness of Savoy had malignant scarlet fever.

During the four days that followed this announcement, nobody was allowed to enter the room except Doctor Mirazzi, and the old nurse that sat up with the duke at night. But, on the fifth day, two persons were admitted. Of these, one was the marshal of the duke's household, the other was his cousin Eugene.

They were received with mysterious whisperings, and were warned not to excite the patient. He had, in the incipiency of his illness, insisted upon making his will, and these two confidential friends had been summoned to witness it.

The old nurse now joined them to say that his highness was awake, and would see Prince Eugene.

"My dear cousin," said the duke, languidly, "come and receive my last greeting."

Eugene entered the alcove, and stood at the bedside. The bed was curtained in purple velvet, and the hangings were so arranged as to leave the duke's face in obscurity. Eugene perceived, nevertheless, that there was no emaciation of features, nor any alteration in the expression of the sharp, restless eye.

"My dear kinsman," continued the invalid, "it is all over with me. I die without fame ; I have fought my last battle and am vanquished by invincible death."

"No, your highness, you have not the aspect of a dying man ; and I have strong hope that you will live to perform great deeds yet. Young, wise, and brave as you are, your strong will may vanquish not only death, but our common enemy—the King of France."

"May your words prove prophetic!" sighed the duke, "but something tells me that I must prepare for the worst. I have made my will, and—"

He paused, gasped for breath, and closed his eyes. Then motioning to Eugene to come nearer, he whispered: "I have appointed you my executor until the majority of my heir. Promise me to do all in your power to make my subjects happy."

"Your royal highness amazes me, and I know not—"

He was interrupted by a loud groan which brought Doctor Mirazzi to the bed in a trice. The duke was trembling; his teeth were clinched, and his hands were pressed upon his temples.

Restoratives were used, and at the proper time the patient unclosed his eyes. With a great effort he raised himself in bed, beckoned to the marshal of the household to approach, and, supported by Mirazzi, he put his name to the will.

"I request my minister and the marshal of my household to approach and witness the signing of my will."

They came in, and, taking up a document which lay on a table close by, the duke raised himself in bed, and, supported by the doctor, gave his signature.

"Take it," said he, "to Turin. Place it in the archives, and when I am dead let it be opened in the presence of the duchess and of my well-beloved kinsman here present, the Prince of Savoy. And now," said he, "farewell. My strength is exhausted! The end is nigh!"

And with these faintly-articulated words, Victor Amadeus fell back upon his pillow and swooned.

Eugene returned to his quarters in a state of extreme perplexity.

"How is the duke?" cried De Commercy, who shared his lodgings.

"I do not know," said Eugene, moodily. "But this I know: we march, not to Grenoble, but back to Turin."

"Indeed!"

" Yes ; such are the duke's latest orders, and, as he has appointed no one to represent him, the army is still under his sole control. I told you, we should get no farther than Embrun ! "

" But the duke ? It is not possible that he is acting the sick man all this while ? "

" Not possible ! Nothing is impossible to such a crafty, vulpine nature as his ! "

" The bulletins say that he is attacked with scarlet fever, and you must have seen whether he bears its marks on his skin or not."

" He has them, but—this shrewd kinsman of mine has many a secret unknown to such as you and myself, Commercy. Perhaps I do him injustice ; for, in good sooth, I am provoked, and in a humor to suspect everybody. His voice is very weak, and indeed, Commercy, I would feel very uncomfortable should he prove to me, by dying, that I have suspected him unjustly. I must go again ; I *must* satisfy my doubts."

The duke's condition was declared to be so precarious that sentries were stationed at every entrance of the castle, to prevent so much as the lightest footstep from being heard by the noble patient. He was passing a crisis, and, during the transition, not a soul must be admitted within the castle gates.

Prince Eugene, nevertheless, at dusk, betook himself thitherward. The sentry saluted him, but barred the entrance.

" You do not know me," said the prince. " I am the duke's nearest kinsman, and, unless you have orders to exclude me personally, I have the entrance to his chamber."

" We have no orders with reference to your highness," was the reply.

" Then I must pass, and I shoulder the responsibility."

The officer signed to the sentry to stand aside, and Eugene entered the castle, crossed the tessellated vestibule, and ascended the wide marble staircase. Here he was stopped a second time, but he referred the guards to the officer below, and was again allowed to pass. " I must try to solve this riddle," thought he. " The emperor's interests hang upon the solution.

Luckily, I have a pretext for my unexpected visit in these dispatches."

He had now traversed the long, lofty hall ; had entered a smaller one that led to the duke's antechamber, and had reached the opposite end of the room, where stood two more sentries, one before each door that opened into the duke's chamber. They had seen him in the morning, and taking it for granted that, having penetrated thus far, he had authority to go farther, they saluted him, and stepped aside.

Eugene whispered, "Is this the door by which I entered this morning ? "

The sentry bowed.

"Whither does it lead ?"

"To his royal highness's alcove, my lord."

"Right," said Eugene, laying his hand on the lock. It turned, and he was in a small recess which opened into the alcove. The portière was down, and Eugene stood irresolute before it. He felt a nervous dread of he knew not what, and almost resolved to retrace his steps. He thought he could not bear the shock of the duke's treachery, should the illness prove—as he feared it would—a sham. He wondered what he would do ; and began to think it better not to penetrate into the secrets of his kinsman's acts, but—

No, no ! He had gone too far to lose his opportunity, and, ashamed of his irresolution, he raised the portière. The alcove was darkened by draperies, but as soon as Eugene's eyes had accustomed themselves to the obscurity of the place, he drew near the bed, opened the curtains, and beheld—nobody ! nothing !

"I was right," muttered he, grinding his teeth ; "it was a comedy ! " As he retreated, he stumbled against the little table, and the chink of the phials that stood upon it was audible.

"Is that you, my good Annetta ? " said the voice of the duke.

Eugene emerged from the alcove, and entered the sitting-room. There, in an arm-chair, before a table laden with viands, fruits, and rare wines, sat the expiring patient that had made his will in the morning.

33

The duke was in the act of raising a glass of wine to his lips. He laid it hastily down, and his keen eyes darted fire at the intruder.

"What means this?" asked he, in a voice that was somewhat uncertain.

"If I may be permitted to interpret what I see before me," replied Eugene, "I should say that your highness is merely carrying out military customs. We were at a funeral this morning, to the tune of a dead march—we return, this afternoon, to that of a quick-step."

"I hope you are agreeably surprised to find that instead of being left behind, I have come back with the music," said the duke, recovering his self-possession. "Come and join me in a glass of good wine. I am as yet too weak to do the honors of my house, but I shall enjoy my repast twofold, now that I have a guest. Sit down. My physician, having ascertained that what I mistook for approaching dissolution was a favorable crisis, has prescribed a generous diet for me, and I do assure you that, with every mouthful, I feel my health return. Ah, Eugene! life is a great boon, and I thank God, who has generously prolonged mine. I hope that you, too, are glad to see me revive; the army, I know, will rejoice to hear of my recovery."

"I do not doubt their joy," replied Eugene, "for your highness's quick convalescence will spare them the mortification of a retreat to Piedmont. I presume you will now march to Paris."

"My fiery, impetuous Eugene," replied Victor Amadeus, with an air of superiority, "you forget that convalescence is not health. I am here for three weeks at least, and by that time the season will be too much advanced to make a second invasion of France. So, God willing, we shall return to Piedmont, there to prosecute the war against Catinat and his incendiaries, whom I hope to drive ignominiously from Italy."

"That is—we are to hold ourselves on the defensive," replied Eugene, bitterly. "Your highness is truly magnanimous! All France lies within your grasp, and, instead of taking advantage of your good fortune, you lay it humbly at the feet of Louis. We have it in our power to dictate terms, while this retreat exposes us to have them dictated to ourselves."

"Field-marshal," said the duke, haughtily, "you forget that you speak to your commander-in-chief."

"Yes—to remember that I speak to the Duke of Savoy—"

"With the head of your house," interrupted the duke, "to whom you owe respect."

"I accord it with all my heart. Precisely because the Duke of Savoy is the chief of our house, do I implore him not to turn his back upon the road which lies open to fame and renown, but to advance bravely to the front, as becomes the friend and ally of the emperor."

Victor Amadeus put his hand up to his head. "Excuse me —I am not equal to the holding of a council of war, nor do I intend to have my commands discussed. We go back to Piedmont."

"Then I must submit," said Eugene, mournfully. "But I crave permission to ask one question of my kinsman."

"Say on," answered the duke, wearily.

"Does your highness propose to desert the cause of the emperor, and renew your alliance with France? Ah, you smile! You smile to think that I should be so unpractised in the art of diplomacy, as to expect a direct answer to such an inquiry. But I entreat you to remember, that your defection concerns not only your honor but mine also."

"My dear Eugene," said the duke, mildly, "you are anxious without any grounds for anxiety. At your solicitation, and from my own convictions of duty, I became the ally of the emperor; I have never reaped any advantage from the alliance, and yet I have remained perfectly loyal. France has made me many offers, every one of which I have rejected. So, make yourself easy on the score of my good faith, and let us change the subject. To what chance do I owe the pleasant surprise of this visit from you?"

"I have the honor to bring letters to your royal highness from the emperor," answered Eugene, presenting his dispatches. "I owe it to my relationship with your highness, that I was allowed by your sentries to effect my entrance here."

"Of course, of course. Everybody knows in what high esteem I hold Prince Eugene.  Verily I believe you to be the most popular man in the army, and your brown cassock to inspire more respect than my field-marshal's uniform.  And now to study the emperor's letter.  I say *study*, for his majesty will write to me in Latin, and I am no great scholar."

"While your highness is occupied," said Eugene, rising, "I will retire to the window."  He crossed the room, and, entering the embrasure, was completely lost to view behind its hangings.

There was a silence of some duration.  The duke studied his Latin, while Eugene looked out of the window.  Suddenly, without any previous formality of knocking, the door leading to the antechamber flew open, and the voice of the old nurse was heard.

"Your highness," said she, as though communicating a most agreeable piece of news, "your highness, here is the French ambassador.  I—"

"Peace, Annetta, peace!" cried Victor Amadeus.  But Annetta was too much interested to hear, and she went on with great volubility :

"Here he is ; I passed him through.  Everybody mistook him for Prince Eugene—"

"Annetta, hold your tongue!" cried the duke, in a thundering voice.

"Ay, your highness, ay," was the reply of the old woman, who, stepping back, opened the door and called out :

"Count Tessé, his highness expects you ; come in."

And, to be sure, there walked in a gentleman wearing the identical brown cassock, with its brass buttons, which was known as the costume of Prince Eugene of Savoy !

Victor Amadeus, in despair, sprang from his chair, and made a deprecatory movement by which he hoped to prevail upon the count to retreat.  But he only looked bewildered ; and his bewilderment increased to positive consternation, when the curtains opened, and the veritable Eugene stepped out and surveyed him with undisguised contempt.

"My dear Eugene," said the duke, in a conciliatory voice, "you see how pertinaciously I am besieged by these Frenchmen.  Here, for instance, is Count Tessé.  This is his third attempt to force an interview with me, and he has gained his end by bribing my silly old nurse to admit him under the garb of one to whom no one here would dare deny entrance. Count Tessé is an envoy of the King of France, and in your presence I intend to show him that no offer, however brilliant, can induce me to forsake my imperial ally of Austria."

"I am perfectly convinced of your loyalty," said Eugene, with an ironical smile, "and, to prove my trust, I beg permission to withdraw. I have the honor to bid you good-evening."

So saying, Eugene inclined his head to the duke, and, paying no attention whatever to his double, passed on.

With a saddened heart he returned to his barracks. He was met by the Prince de Commercy, holding aloft a huge placard. "The bulletin! The bulletin!" cried he. "The crisis is past, and the duke is safe."

"We, however, my friend, are in great danger. We are not driven from French territory by our enemies, but by our pretended friends. Ah! Victor Amadeus has this day inflicted upon me a wound more painful than that of the Janizary's arrow at Belgrade. He has withered my laurels at the very moment when my hand was extended to pluck them."

"Then he abandons us, and declares himself for France?" asked De Commercy.

"If that were all, we could bear his defection, for we would have one enemy more—that is all. Instead of which, we have a double-faced friend who will have far more power to injure us by his treachery in our own camp, than by his hostility in that of the enemy. I will warn the emperor, as it is my duty to do ; but he will be dazzled by the fine promises of the duke, and disregard my warning.* Meanwhile, as long as Victor Amadeus wears his mask, should we even wrest a victory in

---

* Every thing happened exactly as Eugene predicted. The Duke of Savoy retained command of the imperial army for three years, during which he played into the hands of Louis XIV., condemning the allied forces to total inaction, until France had complied with all his exactions, when he declared himself for Louis, and accepted the rank of a general in the French army. The Prince de Commercy was so exasperated that he challenged the duke, but the challenge was refused.

spite of his intrigues, he will manage to deprive us of all its advantages. He will sell us to France, of that you may be sure."

---

## CHAPTER V.

### THE MARQUIS STROZZI.

"THEN you think that Strozzi will not recognize me?" asked Barbesieur de Louvois.

"I know it," replied Carlotta. "His memory is a blank from which every image, except that of his wife, has been effaced."

"Does he love her still?"

"Unhappily he does," sighed Carlotta.

"My good girl," said Barbesieur, trying to look amiable, "pray don't be so concise. Tell me the condition of the marquis, at once : I did not come to this old owl's roost for pastime. I came to see what could be done to restore its unhappy lord to reason. That you are observing, I remember ; you proved it by the good care you took of my sister Laura."

"My lord, you jest ; but the flight of the marchioness has disgraced me. She outwitted me, and I shall hate her to the end of my days."

"Verily I believe you," laughed Barbesieur, as he saw the glitter of her pale-green eyes. "I see in your face that you know how to hate. But you must excuse me if I am amused when I think I see you watching the doors like a she-Cerberus, while that sly creature was flying out of the chimney. But never mind her : I want to talk with you of her husband. I know that he was confined in a mad-house ; but, having occasion to see if he was sane enough to do me a service, I found out that he had been discharged as cured, and had retired within himself. Now, good Carlotta, tell me his veritable condition."

"He never has been sane since the flight of the marchioness. The morning after, when, in spite of our knocking and calling, we received no answer, I set Julia to watch the doors (for I thought she was merely trying to frighten us, and would make her escape while we were away), and went to consult the marquis as to what we must do. When we returned, Julia assured us that she had not heard a breath since I had been away."

"And I suppose that the marquis forced the doors?"

"Oh, no, my lord," replied Carlotta, bitterly. "He was so fearful of displeasing her that he resisted all my importunities to break them open. He knocked and begged so humbly for admission, that I fairly cried with rage. This lasted for hours. Finally he fell on his knees and cried like a child, promising, if she would open the door, to give her her freedom, and never imprison her again. Then he swore by the memory of his father that he would go to Rome and get a divorce for her. It was shameful; and at last I cried out for passion, and told him to get up and behave like a man. But all in vain. Suddenly Julia came running to say that, while the marquis had been lying before the parlor door, she had forced the one that led to the sitting-room, and that the marchioness had escaped."

"What did Strozzi do when he heard this? Whine louder?"

"Oh, no! He sprang up, rushed into the rooms, and began to search for her."

"I suppose you helped, like good dogs after their game?"

"Of course, for it seemed impossible that she should have gotten out by any but supernatural means. But at last we were obliged to accept the fact of her flight, wonderful as it was, and we sat down. Not so the marquis. He appeared to think that she had been transformed into a mouse, for he ran about, opening boxes, looking under tables, occasionally stopping to roar like a wild beast, or falling on his knees and weeping. Then he would begin his hunt again, and this lasted the whole day. We asked him to take some rest, and let his servants be sent out to search the woods, but he gave us no answer, still going round and round until dusk, when he called for lights. He kept up his search the whole night; and when the sun rose, and we awoke, we found him running to and fro, from one room to the other. In vain we pressed him to eat or to rest, he spoke not a word to any of us. Finally, one of the men laid hands on him to force him to sit down, when he drew back and struck him with such force that the blood spirted from his face, as he fell full length on the floor. The marquis went on in this manner for a week, each day growing paler and feebler, until at last he staggered like a drunken man."

"Unhappy lover!" exclaimed Barbesieur, with a shrug.

"Finally, the physician we had sent for came from Turin. By this time the marquis had fallen from exhaustion, and lay asleep. He was lifted to bed, and four men were set to watch him; for the doctor expected him to be violent when he waked. And so he was. He tried to leap out of bed, and was finally bound hand and foot. After a while, came his cousin from Venice, who took charge of him and of his property."

"Yes, to my cost," growled Barbesieur, "for he swindled me out of my pension."

"The Marquis Balbi-Strozzi inherits the estate, if the Marquis Ottario dies without heirs," said Carlotta.

"The Marquis Ottario will not be such an ass as to die without heirs," cried Barbesieur, impatiently. "He shall be reconciled to his wife, or he shall marry some other woman, and beget children. The devil! He is a young man, and nobody dies of love, nowadays."

"He looks like a man of eighty," said Carlotta.

"He is much changed, then?"

"You would not know him, my lord."

"Perhaps not, but he will recover his youth with his health. What does he do all day, Carlotta? What does he say?"

"My lord, he says nothing, except an occasional word to his valet. As for what he does, he is forever shut up in his laboratory."

"Laboratory? What sort of a laboratory?"

"A room which, immediately after his return, he had fitted up like a great kitchen. When the alterations had been made, he went to Turin, and came home with the entire contents of an apothecary shop, with which the shelves of his laboratory are filled. I helped him to place his jars and phials, but much against my will, for he calls me ugly names."

Barbesieur laughed. "Do tell me what he calls you?"

"My lord, you may laugh, but you would not like to answer to the name of 'Basilisk.'"

"To be sure, 'Floweret' would be much more appropriate to your style of beauty, Carlotta; but let that pass, and go on with your narrative. What is Strozzi about, in this laboratory?"

"How do I know, my lord? He cooks and evaporates his messes; then runs to his table and reads in some mouldy old parchments; then hurries back to the chimney and stirs his pipkins—then back to the table—and so on, all day long."

"But, my angelic Carlotta, if nobody is allowed to enter the laboratory, how came you to be so admirably posted as to Strozzi's movements?"

Carlotta looked perplexed. "My lord, there is a little hole in the door that leads out to the corridor, and sometimes I have thought it but right to watch our dear lord, that he might do himself no harm."

"Which means that you bored a hole in the door by way of observatory. Nay—do not deny it; I respect your thirst for knowledge. Does he never leave his laboratory?"

"Oh, yes, my lord. He writes a great deal in his cabinet. All his orders are transmitted in that way. Last week the steward made a mistake in his accounts—"

"To his own prejudice?"

"My lord," said Carlotta, with a hoarse laugh, "no, to that of the marquis. When he discovered it, he wrote underneath, 'Two thousand florins unaccounted for. If this occurs a second time, you are discharged.'"

"Good, good!" cried Barbesieur. "Then he is returning to his senses. He receives no company?" added he.

"How should he? He knows nobody, and has forgotten every thing connected with his past life."

"But you told me that he still remembered the marchioness?"

"As for her, my lord, he loves her as madly as ever. He stands before her portrait, weeping by the hour, and the table is always set for two persons. Every morning he goes into the garden and makes a bouquet, which he lays upon her plate before he takes his seat."

"Poor Strozzi! Sane or mad, he will always be a dreamer!" said Barbesieur. "Where is he now?"

"In the garden, my lord; for it is almost the hour for dinner, and he is in the conservatory gathering flowers for the empty plate."

"Show me the way. I am curious to know whether he has forgotten his brother-in-law and benefactor."

## CHAPTER VI.

### INSANITY AND REVENGE.

BARBESIEUR followed Carlotta to the garden. They were walking silently down the great avenue that led to the conservatory, when, at some distance, they beheld advancing toward them the figure of a man. His step was feeble and slow; his black garments hung loosely about his shrunken limbs; his face was bloodless, like that of a corpse, his cheeks hollow, his large eyes so sunken that their light seemed to come from the depths of a cavern. His sparse hair, lightly blown about by the wind, was white as snow; his long, thin beard was of the same hue.

"Who is that strange-looking old man?" asked Barbesieur.

"That, my lord, is the Marquis Strozzi!"

"Impossible!" cried Barbesieur, with a start.

"I told you, my lord, that he looked like a decrepit old man," said Carlotta.

"And truly he is not a very seductive-looking personage," answered Barbesieur. "But we must try if, in this extinguished crater, there be not a spark by which its fire may be rekindled. Leave me, Carlotta. I must have no third person here to divert Strozzi's attention from myself."

"Shall I not announce you, my lord?" asked Carlotta, who was dying of curiosity to see the meeting.

"Not at all, my angel. Go back to the castle—not by that winding path, if you please, but by this wide avenue. And—be alert in your movements, for I shall watch you until yonder door closes upon your youthful charms, and hides them from my sight."

Carlotta looked venomous, but dared not tarry, and Barbesieur followed her with his eyes until he heard the clang of the ponderous castle-door behind her. He then confronted the living spectre that, by this time, was within a few feet of him.

"God's greeting to you, brother-in-law," cried he, in a loud, emphatic voice, while he grasped Strozzi's poor, wan hands, and held them within his own.

The marquis raised his dark, blank eyes, then let them fall again upon the bouquet which Barbesieur had so unceremoniously crushed.

"Sir," said he, gently, "do release my hand, for see—you are bruising my flowers."

"Sure enough, he does not recognize me," said Barbesieur, relaxing his hold; while Strozzi, unmindful of his presence, caressed his flowers, and smoothed their crumpled leaves.

"She loves flowers," murmured the poor maniac.

Barbesieur took up the words. "Yes," said he, "yes; my sister Laura loves flowers. Pity she is not here to see them."

The marquis shivered. "Who speaks of my Laura?" said he.

"I,—I, her brother," bawled Barbesieur, looking straight into Strozzi's eyes. "I spoke of her, and, by G—d, I have a right to call her, for I am her brother Barbesieur!"

Strozzi extended his hand, and an imbecile smile flitted over his ghastly face. "Ah! then, you love her?" asked he, mournfully.

"Of course I love her," was the lying response. "You remember—do you not—that you were indebted to me for your marriage with Laura Bonaletta?"

"Bonaletta!" screamed Strozzi. "There is no Laura Bonaletta; her name is Laura Strozzi, the Marchioness Strozzi, my wife! Remember that, sir—remember it."

"To be sure, to be sure," murmured Barbesieur; "he has

forgotten everybody but that tiresome Laura.   Let us see if we
cannot stir up his memory to another tune."

Strozzi meanwhile had passed on, and, with his eyes fixed
on his flowers, was slowly making his way to the castle.   Barbesieur followed, though the poor lunatic seemed to have no
consciousness of his presence.   They walked on together in
silence, until they had reached the castle, and entered the dining-room, where dinner was served.

Strozzi went up to the table, laid his offering on the plate,
and bowed :

"Will you allow me to take my seat?" said he, humbly,
while he took a chair opposite, which old Martino had drawn
back for his accommodation.

"Do you see, my lord?" said Martino to Barbesieur; "he
imagines the marchioness present at all his meals."

"He must be undeceived," said Barbesieur, roughly.

"I beseech you, signor," said the old man, "leave him in
error ; for, if you undeceive him, you will rob him of the only
glimpse of happiness that remains to him."

"I shall make the attempt, nevertheless," replied Barbesieur, in a tone that admitted of no further remonstrance,
while he advanced to the table, and seated himself in the
empty chair.

The marquis started, and his brow darkened.   "Sir," said
he, "that is the head of the table—the place of the Marchioness
Strozzi."

"I know it," was the reply, "and, as soon as she makes her
appearance, I will give it up.—Martino, serve the soup ; I am
hungry."   So saying, he tossed the bouquet to the valet, and
poured out some wine.

At this, Strozzi sprang up, and, staring at Barbesieur, with
eyes that glowed like the orbs of a wild animal—"Sir," exclaimed he, "you are an insolent intruder !"

"I know it," cried Barbesieur—"and what next?"

The marquis gazed in bewilderment at the threatening face
of his self-invited guest, and then, slowly turning around,
prepared to leave the room.   Barbesieur rose and followed
him.

At the door of his cabinet he stopped and cried out :

"Let the marshal of the household see to it that no one intrudes upon my privacy!"

And, with a gesture of offended dignity, he entered the room. Barbesieur, however, was immediately behind him, and they had no sooner crossed the threshold than he locked the door, and put the key in his pocket.

"Now, I have him," thought he, "and I shall begin my experiments."

"Sir," said Strozzi, alarmed, "why do you persecute me?"

"I want you to say if you know me," answered Barbesieur, dominating the madman with the calm, powerful glance of reason.

Strozzi shook his head, murmuring, "No, sir, no. I do not know you."

"But I know *you*, Strozzi, my good fellow. You are my beloved brother-in-law, the husband of my sister Laura, who forsook you so shamefully, because she did not love you."

The shaft had pierced. A gleam of returning reason shot athwart Strozzi's face, and a faint color rose to his cheek.

"Not love me!" echoed he, tearfully; "whom, then, does she love?"

Barbesieur laid the weight of his great hands upon Strozzi's shoulders, and looked steadfastly in his eyes. Raising his voice to the utmost, he shouted: "I will tell you whom she loves, and mark me well, Strozzi. She loves Prince Eugene of Savoy!"

"Eugene of Savoy!" shrieked the wretched creature. "Eugene of Savoy! Ah, yes, I remember. I hate him, and he must die!"

"Ay, that's it!" cried Barbesieur, cheerily, "that's it. He must die; and when he is dead, Laura will love the Marquis de Strozzi."

"You think so?" asked Strozzi, laying his tremulous hand upon Barbesieur's great firm arm.

"I know it. The very moment Prince Eugene dies, Laura's heart is yours."

"He must die! He must die!" murmured Strozzi, clasping his attenuated fingers, and looking imploringly into Barbesieur's face.

"Ay, that must he, and you are the man that shall take his life. Your honor demands it of you."

"Yes, my honor," repeated Strozzi, "my honor. I thank you, sir, for your goodness to me. You are the first person that ever advised me to avenge myself on Eugene of Savoy. You are the only person that ever advised me to take his life, and I believe you, and trust you. Yes, sir, take my word for it, Eugene of Savoy shall die!"

"How will you go about it?" asked Barbesieur.

An expression of cunning was seen to steal over the face of the madman, as he replied, "That is my secret, sir."

"I will tell you how to make an end of him," cried Barbesieur, patting him on the shoulder. "Poison him!"

Strozzi gazed with astonishment at his brother-in-law, and forthwith conceived a profound respect for his cleverness. "Did you know that?" said he, with a silly smile. "Did you know that I meant to poison him?"

"To be sure I did, and I came here to work with you in your laboratory, until we concoct the right dose for him."

"Did you know that I had a laboratory?" asked Strozzi, in a whisper. "And did you know that I was trying to find a brave, beautiful poison that would kill him like a pistol-shot, or a good stab under the ribs?"

"I knew it all, and I came to help you."

"I thank you, sir, I thank you! Give me your hand. I take you for my friend, and trust you. Come with me to my laboratory."

So saying, he passed his arm within that of his brother-in-law, and led him to the opposite end of the room. Barbesieur laid his hand on the bolt, but the door was locked.

"You see," said Strozzi, waxing confidential, "I keep this door always locked, for let me tell you, my dear friend, that Eugene of Savoy has surrounded my castle with a regiment of dragoons, who are his spies. That is the reason why I never talk to anybody—I am so afraid that my people will betray me to Prince Eugene's dragoons. Luckily, they have never found out the secret of my laboratory, for I always carry the key in my pocket. Here it is." He took out his key and unlocked the door, but before opening it he addressed Barbesieur in a solemn whisper :

" My dear friend, before you enter my sanctuary, swear to me, by the memory of my dear departed wife, that you will not betray its secrets to Prince Eugene's dragoons."

"I swear, my dear Strozzi, by sun, moon, and stars—"

Strozzi shook his head, and folded his hands reverently. " No, no ; swear by the memory of my sainted Laura."

Barbesieur swore, and the door was opened.

" Come in," said Strozzi.

" And may all the gods of vengeance bless my entrance hither !" muttered Barbesieur, between his teeth.

The room was as Carlotta had described it. Its long shelves were filled with jars and phials, and over the chimney was a wide mantel, with porcelain pipkins, retorts, glass tubes, and flasks.

" Ah," cried Barbesieur, taking a phial from its shelf, " this is a precious beverage, that lulls one to sleep or to death, as one's friends may prescribe."

" Yes—it is laudanum," replied Strozzi. " A painless dagger, an invisible sword of justice in the hands of the elect. It was the basis of all the wonderful preparations of Katherina de Medicis. There was a woman ! Why did I not know her, and learn of her the precious secrets of her laboratorium ? From my youth, I have studied chemistry, and I had a beautiful room in Venice, where I used to work with the famous Chiari. But we never discovered Katherina's secret."

" What secret, dear Strozzi ?" inquired Barbesieur.

" The secret of killing people by fumes, which left no trace whatever of their action on the body," answered Strozzi, with an awakening gleam of wickedness in his eyes.

" And you believe that there are such delicate, ethereal little ministers of vengeance ?"

" Do I believe it ?—Why, to their agency, Katherina owed her elevation to the throne of France. Nobody knows this better than I, for my ancestor Filippo Strozzi was her friend and relative, and their correspondence now is in the archives of the family, at Venice. I am indebted to the letters of Katherina for much of my knowledge of chemistry."

"And so you found out from her correspondence how she managed to become Queen of France?" asked Barbesieur, anxious to indulge Strozzi's sudden fit of garrulity.

"I did," was his complacent reply, while he nodded his head repeatedly, and stroked his long, white beard. "When Katherina came to France, she came as the bride of the Duke of Orleans, the second son of Francis I. There seemed no chance for *her* to be a queen, for the dauphin was a lusty young fellow who was already betrothed to the beautiful Infanta of Spain. But Katherina had no mind to let the infanta reign in France, so she invited the dauphin to her castle of Gien, and took him to her conservatory. There was a beautiful rare flower there, which had a strong perfume. Katherina directed his attention to it, but advised him not to hang over it too long, as it never failed to give *her* the headache, if she approached it too closely. The dauphin laughed, and was not to be frightened away from a flower, because of the headache. Moreover, the odor was delightful, and he would not be warned. That day he had a headache; the next, he was pale and feeble, and in less than a week, he died, and nobody the wiser, except Katherina."

"And he died, really from the odor of a flower?"

"Yes, from a flower which Katherina had perfumed for his use, my dear friend. And do you know how she made away with Joanna of Navarre, who had guessed the secret of the dauphin's death, and had already hinted her suspicions to her brother Francis?"

"No, I never heard of it. Upon my word, Strozzi, you interest me exceedingly."

"Do I? Well, I will tell you more, then. Katherina made a present to Joanna of a pair of embroidered gloves. The day after she wore them she was dead. What do you think of that?—And did you ever hear how the Prince of Porcia died—he who advised the dauphin to divorce his wife because she had been married for eight years and had borne him no children?" continued Strozzi, with increasing volubility.

"I confess my ignorance, Strozzi; do enlighten me."

"I will, sir. The prince received a present from Katherina (she was a great hand to make presents). This time it was a flask of fine Italian oil for his night-lamp, which oil, in burning, emitted a delicate perfume. By the time the flask was emptied, the prince had gone the way of all flesh."

"And all this because of Queen Katherina's science?"

"And all this because of Queen Katherina's science!" echoed Strozzi.

"But you have not yet hit upon her secret yourself?"

"Not yet; but I think I am on the track, and hope to discover it in time to try it on Prince Eugene."

Barbesieur rose from his seat, and, coming toward Strozzi, struck him on the shoulder. "Now, Strozzi, look at me attentively, and try to understand what I am about to say to you. I will help you to seek this poison. Do you hear?"

"Yes," said Strozzi, with a cunning leer. "Yes, I hear. You will help me to seek the poison for Prince Eugene."

"Good," replied Barbesieur. "Now, look at me full in the eyes. Look, I tell you!" repeated he, as Strozzi's face began to relapse into imbecility. "I have found the poison."

Strozzi uttered a triumphant yell, but Barbesieur silenced him. "Pay attention while I tell you how I became possessed of it. I was by, when La Voisin was put to the torture in *La Chambre ardente*, and I heard her confession. I was deputed to search for her papers; and before I delivered them up you may be sure that I examined them, to see what I could make out of them for my own profit. I found various receipts for love-potions, as well as for the renowned *poudre de succession* of the Countess Soissons; but of that anon. Do you mark me, Strozzi?

"Oh, sir," cried Strozzi, trembling in every limb, "speak—speak quickly, or I shall die of suspense!"

Barbesieur then, emphasizing each word, replied: "I found a parchment on which were inscribed these words: 'Receipt for procuring death by inhalation. Queen Katherina de Medicis.'"

"That is it, that is it," howled Strozzi, and in his ecstasy he flung his arms around Barbesieur's great body. But suddenly his countenance became expressive of distrust, and his eye had a deadly glitter, like that of a snake.

"But will you give it to me? Where is it? I warn you,

34

do not trifle with me, for you never shall leave this laboratory until I have it !"    Meanwhile he made a furtive movement toward his breast.

But Barbesieur had seen the gesture, and with his powerful
grasp he clutched Strozzi's hand, and withdrew it armed with
a poniard of fine, glistening steel.   Flinging it with such force
against the wall that it buried itself in the masonry, Barbesieur
gazed for a moment at the poor fool whose teeth were chattering with fear ;  then leading him to a seat—

"Come," said he, "let us talk like men.   We are neither
enemies nor rivals ;  we are brothers, having one and the same
interest at stake."

"Yes, sir," murmured Strozzi, obsequiously.

"Well, then, look at me.   Did you ever see me before ?"

Strozzi raised his obedient eyes and looked—for a while, in
blank amazement.   But gradually his black orbs dilated, and
a sudden flash of intelligence crossed his face.   He breathed
hard.

"I think, sir, I think you are—are—ah, yes !  I know.
You are Count Barbesieur de Louvois."

"Right, right," cried Barbesieur.   "Laura Strozzi's brother."

"Are you the brother of my darling Laura ?" cried Strozzi.
"If you are, you are welcome, sir.   Oh, if she were but alive
to see you !"

"Alive ?  What do you mean ?  Where do you suppose her
to be ?"

"She is dead," replied Strozzi, his eyes overflowing with
tears.   "Dead—my own, my precious angel !"

"Of what did she die ?" asked Barbesieur, highly amused
at poor Strozzi's grief.

Strozzi shook his head.   "No one on earth knows, sir.   She
must have dissolved in a sunbeam, and gone back to heaven,
for her corpse was never found here below."

"Strozzi, you are mistaken," exclaimed Barbesieur, with an
authoritative gesture.   "Mark my words, and believe them,
or I shall be very angry.   The Marchioness Laura is *not* dead.
She lives here on earth, not far away from you."

"She lives !" repeated Strozzi, starting from his seat and

falling at Barbesieur's feet. "Tell me where she is. Let me go, let me go, and bring her home. Come—come with me!"

"Wait a minute. She is living with Eugene of Savoy, disgracing you and me both. Before you bring her home, you must take the life of her paramour, and just as soon as you have done that, she will be freed from the spell that binds her, and will love nobody but you."

"Ah, he shall die," muttered Strozzi.

"Yes, he must die, and *you* must kill him. But *I* shall furnish the means. And now to work, to prepare the ambrosia that shall give him immortality!"

## CHAPTER VII.

### THE AMBROSIA.

THANKS to the illness of the Duke of Savoy, the summer campaign of 1692 was of short duration. The allies had dispersed and retired to winter-quarters; the imperial army had retreated to Piedmont; and the officers in command of the several divisions had betaken themselves to Turin to enjoy the festivities that followed the recovery of Victor Amadeus.

Eugene had been invited with the rest; but he gave his health as an excuse for avoiding the changeable winds of Turin, and seeking the balmy atmosphere of Nice, where, having found comfortable quarters for his troops, he proposed to pass the coming winter.

Victor Amadeus made great pretence of regret at Eugene's absence; but, truth to tell, he was not sorry to escape the scrutiny of his clear-sighted cousin, who, for his part, was happy beyond expression in the devotion of his men, and the companionship of his Laura.

Here in the peaceful seclusion of the obscure little village of Nice, Eugene and Laura enjoyed unalloyed happiness. The fishermen and sailors, that formed the principal part of its population, knew nothing of the history of the grand Austrian officer that had come to live among them. In their eyes, the beautiful signora was his wife, as a matter of course ; and they sunned themselves in the radiance of her beauty, without ever giving a thought to the nature of the ties that bound her to the field-marshal.

They were without an obstacle to their happiness. Eugene, sitting at a table covered with paper and charts, wrote dispatches, and planned his next campaign ; while, on an ottoman at his side, Laura read or embroidered, often interrupting her occupation to gaze at his beloved countenance.

As for him, his mind was clearer, his hand was firmer, his spirit seemed to dominate every subject of its contemplation, when she was by. Oftentimes he paused in his labors to watch the delicate outline of her sweet face, and, when their eyes met and they exchanged a loving smile, he felt that there was a communion of hearts that beggared language, and would have no interpreter but a glance.

They were sitting together on the perron of their villa, which looked out upon the shores of the Mediterranean. The door leading to the drawing-room was open, exposing to view a harp from which Laura had just risen. Before them lay the boundless expanse of the ocean, blue with reflected azure from heaven ; and, like some soft, weird melody to their ears, was the murmuring of the waves, that kissed the smooth, white beach before them. Elsewhere all was silent, for Nature seemed to listen—unwilling, by a sound of stirring leaf, to break the delicious stillness.

On a sudden, a wild scream was heard in the air above, and a vulture, cleaving the clouds, flew over their heads. Laura's smiling face was upturned to reply to some loving expression of Eugene's ; but when the vulture's scream was heard, she rose to her feet, and with a slight shudder followed its flight until it lessened to a dim speck on the horizon.

" What has disturbed you, dearest ? " asked Eugene.

"Nothing," whispered she. "And yet I am a miserable coward. Even this vulture's scream has startled me. It seems like an ill omen."

" Why, my darling, why should a vulture's scream be ominous ? "

" Do not laugh at me, Eugene ; but my old nurse used always to cross herself when a vulture was in sight, and if it screamed, she wept, for she said it betokened the approach of misfortune."

"Why should you share the superstition of your nurse, dearest?"

"Because I myself once heard the scream," said Laura, growing very pale. "I was standing with my nurse on a balcony of Bonaletta Castle, and she was making wreaths of pomegranate and orange from the blossoms I plucked. Meanwhile she was telling me a tale about some enchanted princess, to which I was listening with my whole heart. Suddenly I heard the cry of a vulture, the old woman dropped her flowers, clasped her hands, and cried out: 'Oh, my God! there is woe at hand! Come, child, come to the chapel, and pray the Lord to avert it.'"

"And it was averted by your dear prayers, was it not?" asked Eugene, kissing her.

"Alas, no! Not many hours afterward, I was called to my mother's room. "She lay on her bed, dying,—in her hand, a crumpled letter. The letter was from Barbesieur, and its contents were her death-blow! Eugene, she never opened her eyes again!—And oh, how she loved me—that dear mother!"

"Who that knows you can help loving you?" said Eugene, tenderly. "Look at me, my treasure—look at me, and smile. What—tears?"

"I am thinking of my mother, dear, and of her wretched life. It humiliates me to remember that she, who was a saint, suffered so many sorrows, while I, her child, who have done nothing to merit it, am too, too happy."

"Nothing to merit happiness? You, whose constancy and heroism I could not dare to imitate? Ah, Laura, remember that before I knew you, I was without hope, without trust, without love. You crossed my path, and then my soul began to soar to God; for God is love, and he that knows not love knows not what it is to adore his Creator. You are not only the architect of my happiness, beloved, but that of my religion."

Laura flung her arms around his neck, and rested her cheek

against his. "And you—you are my sun—the luminary of my life! Without you, all is dark and void. Oh, Eugene! be prudent, love, and beware of your enemies; they encompass you with snares. Do not go unarmed to the barracks, for not long ago the soldiers saw a man following you after dusk. They searched him, and found on his person a poniard, and in his possession a purse of gold."

"We cannot deny that the dagger and bowl seem to be the order of the day, in this land of bravi," returned Eugene, "and I am continually warned that, dead or alive, the French are resolved to possess themselves of my body. But between intention and execution there lies a wide path, and, in spite of prison and steel, I hope to tread it safely.* So do not be unhappy on my account, sweet one. Let me look in those dear eyes, and there read the poem of our love—a love that death itself shall not overcome."

"No, not death itself," said Laura, repeating his words, and nestling close to his heart. He laid his hands upon her head, and blessed and kissed her.

"So would I love to die—so—resting on thy heart, and gazing into thy face," murmured she, her eyes filling with tears of joyful emotion.

"Die!" exclaimed he, shuddering. "Love cannot die. Through all eternity, its choral hymn—"

He unclasped his arms, for steps were heard along the corridor, and presently, within the frame of the open door, was seen an orderly attached to the household. Laura retreated to the parlor, while Eugene demanded the reason of an intrusion so untimely upon his privacy.

"Your highness, a courier has arrived, with dispatches from the Duke of Savoy. They are so important as to require immediate attention, and he will deliver them to no hands but your own."

"Admit him," said Eugene, entering the drawing-room, and joining Laura, who had taken a seat before her easel, and was preparing to paint. "Shall I see the courier in my cabinet, or receive him here?" said he.

* Eugene's own words.—See Armath, "Life of Prince Eugene," vol. i. p. 51.

"Remain here, my dearest, and let me hear the sound of your voice." So saying, she drew the hangings together, and, in the deep embrasure of the bay-window, was entirely concealed from view. Gliding back into her seat, she raised her loving eyes to the canvas whereon she was painting a portrait of her Eugene.

"I shall never, never catch the expression of those wonderful eyes," said she to herself. "This is their color, but where is their heavenly light? How shall I ever transmit—"

She started, let fall her palette, and gazed, horror-stricken, at the hangings. She had heard a voice, the tones of which, she knew not why, made the blood freeze within her veins. These were the words she heard: "Here, your highness, are my dispatches." Words without significance, but Laura shivered from head to foot. With trembling hand, she parted the hangings and looked out.

There, in the centre of the room, stood Eugene, in the act of opening a sealed paper. For one moment, her eye rested tenderly upon the beloved image; then she glanced quickly at the person who stood by the door. He wore the Sardinian uniform, and stood in a respectful posture, his eyes cast down.

But Laura? She stared at his swarthy face and bloodless lips, the sunken cheeks, and beetle brow, with a strange repugnance that almost shaped itself into some old, forgotten dislike.

"I must have seen him somewhere," thought she, "and the dim remembrance of the countenance pains me terribly. If he would but speak again! I surely would recognize that voice—that voice which sounds to my ear like some retrospective agony of which I may have dreamed long years ago."

Eugene still held the paper. He had opened it, and was turning it in and out, with an expression of great surprise. "What am I to understand by this mystification?" said he.

"Your highness," returned the courier, "the dispatches are secret, and written with sympathetic ink. If you will hold them over a light until a vapor begins to rise from them, the writing will appear."

Eugene rang and ordered a light. He stood smilingly, scrutinizing the blank pages of his letter; the courier kept his eyes on the floor, and Laura behind the hangings stood contemplating the scene, her heart throbbing as though it would burst. She saw the orderly place the wax-light upon the table, and Eugene advance and hold the dispatch above it. She turned unconsciously toward the courier. His eyes, no longer riveted on the floor, glared horribly at Eugene ; and in their glance were written manifest hatred and exultation.

For one moment Laura felt as though she were stiffening to stone ; then, dashing aside the curtains, she bounded to the table, crying out with all the strength of her love :

"Eugene, 'tis Strozzi !" And, tearing the poisoned paper from his hands, she flung it at the feet of the courier.

He sprang forward, and seized her in his arms. Eugene darted to her rescue, and strove with all his might to free her from Strozzi's grasp. But despair and insanity had lent him strength, and vain was all striving to unlock his hands as they clutched her slender throat, and threatened her with speedy death.

Eugene made one bound to the table, and snatched up his pistols. At the same moment, a dagger gleamed in the air. Laura fell back with a piercing cry. and Strozzi, kneeling over her prostrate body, covered her face with kisses.

The sharp report of the pistol was heard—the murderer leaped up into the air, and then dropped dead upon the floor. And close beside him lay Laura with a poniard in her breast, whose hilt of diamonds rose and fell with her quick breathing, and glistened brightly in the rays of the setting sun that gilded the terrible picture.

Instinctively Eugene would have withdrawn the murderous weapon from his darling's heart, but he felt his arm withheld, and turning beheld Doctor Franzi.

The doctor shook his head, sadly. "Do not touch it," whispered he, " or her life-blood will gush out, and she will die at once."

With a look of despair, the wretched man arose, and beckoned to the doctor to follow him to the balcony.

"The truth," gasped he, while his eyes glared as if they would have started from their sockets. "Must she die ?"

"She will die instantaneously if the dagger is withdrawn.

I am familiar with the thrusts of these Venetian bravi—when they aim at the heart, death follows the stroke immediately ; but when they strike the breast, it ensues with a gush of blood, at the withdrawal of the weapon."

"Is there any—hope ? "

The doctor knew not how to shape an answer to this heart-rending appeal. He turned away his face, and Eugene understood the mute reply.

"How long ? " asked he, almost inaudibly.

"If it were any other woman, I should expect internal hemorrhage to ensue within half an hour ; but the strong will of the marchioness will ward off death for the space of an hour."

Eugene stifled a groan. "O God ! is there no, no help ? "

"None. Science cannot prevail against the well-directed blow of a Venetian dagger. But the marchioness will not suffer."

"No," sobbed Eugene, "for she dies ; but I—I—"

"Go to her, my dear friend—go before she calls, for every exertion she makes will hasten the end."

Eugene wrung his hands. "Not yet—I cannot. I must have a moment to conquer this overwhelming anguish. Go to her yourself, doctor—tell her—I—"

But the doctor was already in the parlor, and Eugene was alone. He leaned over the balcony and stared out at the sea ; the breeze had freshened, and the sound of the waves as they dashed against the shore seemed to mock at his agony. He looked above : the skies were serene and indifferent to his misery. The sun was setting in a flood of red and gold. Alas ! alas ! For Laura, it would rise no more !

But Eugene remembered that she had but an hour to live, and, shuddering, he overcame his weakness and approached the dying girl. She held out her hands, and smiled.

"Eugene," said she, "I long for air and light. May I be lifted out upon the balcony ? "

Eugene looked at Doctor Franzi, who beckoned to the servants. They rolled a divan to the spot where the marchioness lay, and she was placed upon it, and gently removed to the balcony. She thanked them all for their kindness, and each member of her household kissed her hand, and went away weeping. No one now remained with her save Eugene and the doctor.

"Step aside for a moment, beloved," said she. "I would speak a few words with our dear friend."

He obeyed, and retired out of hearing, but not out of sight. He could not do that. They had but half an hour !

"Doctor," said Laura, "I must die, must I not ? "

"All things are possible with God, but—"

Her eyes filled with tears. "Does Eugene know it ? "

"Alas, he does ! "

"Doctor, promise me that if in his grief he should forget to care for his own welfare, you will watch over it as I would have done, had Heaven permitted. As long as sorrow predominates over reason, you will enter his room every morning, and speak these, my dying words : 'Laura sends you her greeting, and bids you do all that you can to preserve your health, and to overcome your sorrow.' Promise me this."

"I promise," replied the doctor.

"And now, tell me. Is my enemy—is Strozzi dead ? "

"The bullet went through his brain."

"May God forgive him, as I do ! " murmured she. "And now, dear friend, farewell ! I thank you for all my happiness on earth, and bless you with my latest breath for your kindness to Eugene and to me." *

She gave him her hand, which he kissed, and, no longer able to restrain his tears, he went back to the parlor. There on the floor lay Strozzi stark and dead, his glazed eyes staring, as if in defiance, to heaven. Doctor Franzi had the corpse removed, and threw himself wearily upon a sofa. Presently he saw Laura's Italian greyhound, with a piece of paper between its teeth, with which it seemed to be playing. He was watching its motions, as people whose minds are preoccupied with a great sorrow, are apt to watch some particular object within view, when suddenly it howled, made a leap into the air, and fell panting on the floor. The doctor stooped to examine it. It was dying.

---

* This attempt to poison Prince Eugene is historical.

"Why, the poor little brute has been poisoned !" said he to Conrad.

Conrad shook his head. "Impossible !" replied he. "It has been with me this whole day, and came with me hither not half an hour since."

"Stay," replied the doctor, picking up the bits of paper that lay scattered over the carpet. He took them to the light, and held them above it. In a few moments a white vapor mingled with green was seen to rise in the air, and an odor of garlic pervaded the apartment.

"Come, Conrad," exclaimed the doctor ; "leave the room quickly ! Happy it is for us that all these doors and windows are open, or my curiosity would have cost me my life."

"And the marchioness ?" asked Conrad, sadly.

The little French clock on the mantel struck the hour. "You hear," said the doctor. "She has not a half an hour to live."

Not half an hour to live ! And Eugene knew it ! For above the breaking waves, above the tumultuous beating of his bleeding heart, even above the tones of her dear voice, he heard the striking of that clock.

But one half hour !—He was on his knees, her little hand locked in his, and her eyes fixed upon his face, with a look of love such as no human tongue had power to speak. But he could not bear to see her so motionless ; he feared that she was about to expire.

"Speak to me, my angel ; say thou lovest me," sobbed he.

"I love thee !" said she, with a joyful smile. "Ah, Eugene, I have spoken these words so often that earth and air, sky and sea, will echo them forever."

"But thou—thou goest from me !"

"God has willed it thus. But, beloved, how beautiful to me is the death that giveth life to thee ! Ah, my sovereign ! lord of my heart ! weep not for her who dies as woman loves to die !"

"Weep not for thee ! Alas ! shall I have courage to bear the burden of the life thou hast purchased with thine own ?"

"Yes, God will give thee strength to fulfil thy heroic destiny, my Eugene. We have been very happy on earth, and in heaven He will perfect our imperfect union. " Farewell, beloved, farewell ! "

"Oh, look at me once more ! " cried Eugene. " Laura, Laura, speak to me ! O God ! it cannot be that thou must die ! "

She made no answer, but her fast-closing eyes were fixed upon his. He bent closer and closer, and opened his arms, with a vain longing to fold her to his heart. But he durst not ! His embrace might extinguish the feeble spark of life that glimmered yet for his momentary consolation.

But his tears fell upon her face, and awakened her failing senses. She spoke again, and the melody of her voice was like the faint notes of an Æolian harp.

"Do not weep," murmured she. " I was happy. I will be near to thee in spirit. I—"

A last sigh fluttered from her lips, and the Æolian harp was silenced forever !

---

## CHAPTER VIII.

### THE BETROTHAL.

THE Duchess of Orleans sat weeping in her cabinet, and yet she had been several times reminded by her tire-women that monsieur awaited her in the drawing-room. She held in her hand a letter—the apparent cause of her unwillingness to move.

"It has terminated as I feared," thought she ; "her short-lived happiness has been purchased with her life. To think that her relentless foe should have had no mercy upon her youth and beauty ! And so it is—to the good are apportioned tribulation and trials—to the wicked, prosperity and long life ! God is merciful, and allows to those who are destined to burn in hell their short season of triumph on earth. But I, who am no saint, will avenge my dear child's murder, by exposing its instigators to public scorn. My poor, darling Laura ! God only knows how I am to bring it about, but He will surely prompt the right words at the right moment. And now to discharge the tiresome duties of the sacrifice I made to the shameless exaction of Louis XIV. ! Now for the act that befouls the escutcheon of France with the blood of De Montespan's bastard !"

She folded her letter, and, putting it in her bosom, called with her stentorian lungs, for Katharina.

The tire-woman, who had been anxiously awaiting the summons, appeared immediately, and approached her mistress, in great haste to commence.

"Katharina," began the duchess, "do not be provoked if I reject the magnificent attire you have prepared for me to-night. I cannot wear it."

Katharina drew back in terror. "So your royal highness does not intend to appear at court to-night?"

"I intend to appear there, because I am compelled to do so," returned the duchess; "but I do not know that it is incumbent upon me to be as gay as a peacock, on the occasion of my poor Philip's betrothal to that girl of De Montespan's. To me it is more like a funeral than a festival, so you may get out my suit of court mourning. The skirt of black velvet, the train and head-dress of purple."

"Is the Empress of Austria dead, that your royal highness should wear purple?" asked Katharina.*

"A personage of more consequence to me than the Empress of Austria is dead—an angel has taken her flight to heaven, and no royal princess can replace her here below. Hush, Kathi—you need not open your mouth to remonstrate, for my purple mourning I will wear, and nobody in France shall hinder me."

Katharina knew this so well, that she inclined her head, and went off in search of the costume, which, as Elizabeth-Charlotte never lingered before her looking-glass, was donned in less than a quarter of an hour. She returned to her cabinet, and gave a quick glance at her image, as she passed before a large Venetian mirror, that reached from floor to ceiling. She smiled, and began an apostrophe to herself, after the following manner:

* At the court of Louis XIV., purple velvet was worn in the deepest mourning only.

"You are unquestionably a homely woman ; and, in the
finery that decks royalty, you look somewhat like the scare-
crows I have seen in gardens at home. But, soberly clad as
you are at this moment, you are not an unsightly or undignified woman, nor would my poor murdered darling despise
me, were she to see me now. Ah, Laura ! would that the
battle of life were over for me, as it is for thee ! For
the world has apportioned to me much vexation, but little
happiness."

She turned away from the mirror, with a sigh. "Well, I
may not mourn any longer. I must put on my court-face, and
sing with old Luther :

> 'It must be so,
> That pain and woe
> Will ever follow sin;
> Then go your ways'—"

The duchess was singing out this doggerel in a rough, loud
contralto, when her chamberlain appeared at the door, and announced that his royal highness was waiting for her to descend.

"Tell monsieur not to let me detain him," replied she. "I
will be escorted to the Louvre by the Duke de Chartres. Hey,
Kathi ! come with my wrappings !"

Kathi had just enveloped her highness's stout, robust form
in a cloak of purple velvet, when the little duke came skipping
into the room.

"Here I am, chère maman," cried he ; "here is Cupid,
ready to attend on Venus."

The duchess replied with a glance of displeasure, and took
his arm. As they were crossing the corridor, she said : "Cupid was a fractious and rebellious boy, and I remember that
Venus had many a time to box his ears for his misbehavior.
You are quite right to liken yourself to Cupid, for you are just
as contrary as he—"

"And just as handsome ?" asked the duke, coaxingly.

The duchess tried to suppress a smile. "You are a little
puppy," said she ; "and if I resemble Venus in no other way,
I shall imitate her maternal corrections, and let you feel the

weight of my hand, if you provoke me, sir." And so saying, she tumbled herself into the coach.

"I have already felt its weight," sighed the young duke, "and a right heavy hand it is, when it is lifted to chastise."

"Then take care not to deserve its chastisements. But now, Philip, listen to me, and be serious. It is understood between us, that you refuse to sign the contract—that you avow loudly your aversion to marriage in general, and to Mademoiselle de Blois in particular ; and that you throw yourself at the feet of the king, and ask for two years' delay."

"Oh, yes, maman, yes, of course," replied Philip, hurriedly. "I understand it all perfectly. Ah, here we are at the Louvre ! Allow me to assist you to alight."

And the duke, vastly pleased that the maternal lecture was at an end, leaped from the coach, and escorted his mother to the palace.

The royal family, with the nobles and dignitaries that were to witness the signing of the contract, were in the king's cabinet. The court awaited them in one of the magnificent rooms of state.

On a marble slab, supported by three gilded dolphins, lay a long roll of parchment, and close by was an inkstand of gold, set with sapphires and diamonds. The king was in an adjoining apartment, anxiously waiting the arrival of the Duchess of Orleans and the bridegroom-elect.

" Methinks," said Louis to monsieur, " that madame makes me wait."

As these words were uttered with great severity, the duke was abashed, and scarcely knew what he way saying. " Your majesty," stammered he, " you know how—may I entreat of you—"

" Her royal highness the Duchess of Orleans, and the Duke de Chartres," cried the gentleman usher.

Louis rose from his arm-chair, and advanced to greet his eccentric sister-in-law. Suddenly he drew back, and looked like a Jupiter Tonans.

" Madame," said he, eying the duchess from head to foot— from her purple feathers to the very edge of her long purple-velvet train—" madame, what means this extraordinary attire ?

Have you forgotten, in one of your fits of absence, that you were invited, not to a funeral, but to a betrothal ? "

"Sire," replied the undismayed duchess, "I am not subject to fits of absence ; but I beg to apologize for my dress. It is appropriate to my feelings, for I have just experienced a most painful loss."

"What member of your family is dead ?" asked his majesty.

"Not a member of my family, but a beloved friend, has been foully murdered."

"Murdered !" echoed Louis. "Who has been murdered ? "

"Sire, I will tell you, but Monsieur Louvois must be by to hear the recital."

Monsieur Louvois was summoned, and while awaiting his arrival, Louis expressed a wish that the duchess would make her story as short as possible ; he was anxious to have this ceremony over.

"Sire, I shall do my best," was the reply.—" Ah," continued Elizabeth-Charlotte, " here is Monsieur Louvois. Perhaps he can tell your majesty why I am in mourning."

"I !" said Louvois, with a defiant stare at his enemy. " I have not the honor of being in the secrets of madame."

"But *she* has the misfortune to be in yours," cried the duchess.

"Sire, a few years ago, there appeared at your majesty's court a young girl of extraordinary beauty and worth. She was one of my maids of honor, and was as dear to me as my own child. Lovely, innocent, and virtuous, as she was, she was an object of aversion to her own kindred. She became ardently attached to a youth of rank equal—I mean to say, superior to hers, against whom her relatives entertained a prejudice that manifested itself by every species of persecution. There could be no reasonable objection to the alliance, but the lovers knowing that, for very hatred of them both, the maiden's father would oppose their union, agreed to be married in secret. They were betrayed, and you will scarcely believe me, your majesty, when I tell you that the poor girl's own father and brother deceived her by forged letters, and so arranged matters that they came by night, and, substituting a man whom she detested, for her lover, they obtained her signature to a fraudulent marriage."

"Her father did his duty," interrupted Louvois. "He had a right to select her husband, and exercised his right. I hope that his majesty is of the same opinion."

"Madame," said the king, taking no notice of Louvois' remark, "pray continue your narrative."

"Your majesty, the miserable girl refused ever to acknowledge the marriage. The man they had forced upon her imprisoned her for years, giving out to the world that she was insane, but holding out to her a promise of release, whenever she would recognize him as her husband. She never would—she never did."

"But her lover—what was he about all this time?" asked Louis.

"He believed himself forgotten, nor could he discover whither his betrothed had been conveyed by her tyrant. Finally by means that seem almost miraculous, she effected her escape, and joined him; and, believing herself to be his spouse before God, they lived together as husband and wife."

"I should have regarded them as such," was the remark of the king. "I hope that her unprincipled relatives did not seek to repeat their sacrilege by any attempt to part her from him to whom she had veritably plighted her faith."

Louvois could not contain himself. "Your majesty," cried he, "the sacrilege was hers and not her father's. She was legally married, and the tie that bound her to her lover was a crime!"

Louis contemplated his own illegitimate children, there present, and Louvois' words roused his ire. "Sir," said he, "you mistake human prejudices for principles. How can you presume to contend for the sanctity of an infamous falsehood like that of a marriage ceremony fraudulently performed?"

"Thanks, your majesty, thanks for those generous words," exclaimed the duchess, joyfully. "They rehabilitate the memory of my darling, who was as pure and chaste as she was constant and loving. In her case, endurance of the world's contumely was heroism. She felt it to be unjust, but bore it for the sake of her lover, and was happy. Her relatives, how-

35

ever, urged by their hatred of the poor child, made use of her demented husband to avenge what they pleased to term their outraged honor. They armed him with dagger and poison, and her own brother brought him to the town where she was living, and led him to her villa."

"What an unnatural and wicked brother," exclaimed the young Duke of Maine, who had edged himself in to listen.

The duchess gave him a grateful smile, and continued her story :

"The murderer made an attempt to poison his rival. He was recognized under his disguise by his wife, who darted forward to save her lover's life. As she did so, the assassin drew from his bosom a poniard and stabbed her to the heart."

"Horrible !" was the exclamation of all the bystanders.

"Sire," resumed the duchess, "the woman so foully murdered by the tool of her father and her brother,—she, whom I loved so dearly, and whom your majesty's self honored by your attention, was Laura Bonaletta—the daughter of Monsieur Louvois, and the sister of his depraved son—Barbesieur."

"The Marchioness Strozzi !" cried the king, turning his indignant eyes upon Louvois, who was vainly trying to effect a retreat.

"Sir," said Louis, "I hope you will be able to disprove this dreadful charge, and convince her royal highness that she has been misinformed."

"Sire, I am not aware that any guilt attaches to my actions as a father. I married my daughter to the man whom I chose should be her husband, and I hastened the marriage that I might save her from the artful snare which Prince Eugene was laying for her large fortune."

"Sire," cried the duchess, "the whole world knows Prince Eugene to be above mercenary considerations, and it also knows that had Monsieur Louvois not driven him away from France, he would not now be the most distinguished officer in the army of a foreign prince."

"Very true," returned the king.—"Louvois never showed himself to have less penetration than when he undervalued the genius of Prince Eugene. But this blunder we can pardon, so he but clear himself of participation in the assassination of his daughter."

"That I can easily do, your majesty," replied Louvois. "I knew nothing whatever of the attempt on Prince Eugene's life."

"Then how comes it that this intercepted letter from your own hand speaks so knowingly of it to your son?—Sire," continued the duchess, "this letter was sent to me by Victor Amadeus. The courier to whom it had been confided was arrested by a vidette of the duke's, and the letter forwarded to his highness. From my step-daughter, the Duchess of Savoy, I hold my information; and it was imparted to me at her husband's desire, that I might transmit it to your majesty, and Louis XIV. might hear how Louvois vanquishes the heroes that are opposed to him in war. Sire, not only your friends, but your enemies, know that you hold such warfare in abhorrence."

"I do, indeed," cried Louis, "and I thank not only Victor Amadeus, madame, but yourself, who have not shrunk from the ungrateful duty of accusing a man whom many another would have feared, because he was high in my estimation. I thank you that you have given me occasion to vindicate my honor from the foul blot which this man would have cast upon it. I say nothing of his cruelty to his unhappy daughter, for that I leave to his Maker. But, as regards the attempt on the life of Prince Eugene, it shall be investigated;—and woe to him, should he be inculpated by the examination of these papers!—Go, sir, and until your fame is cleared, consider yourself a prisoner in your own house."

Pale and trembling, Louvois retreated from the royal presence. Around the door of the cabinet were groups of highborn dames and titled lords, who all drew back to let him pass. No one wished to breathe the atmosphere that was tainted by the presence of a suspected murderer; and the rumor of his disgrace spread so rapidly through the palace, that it reached the room where the court was assembled, and every man there turned his back upon the favorite who, an hour before, had been greeted with courtesy and respect by the proudest nobles in the land.

The king's eyes followed the bowed figure of his fallen minister until it passed out of sight; then, as if nothing had happened, he smilingly addressed the Duchess of Orleans:

"Madame, will you take the bride by the hand? I, myself, will escort the bridegroom."

Elizabeth-Charlotte, who, in her sorrow for the tragical death of Laura, had forgotten the occasion of her coming, gave a sudden start, and her heart died within her. She turned her sharp eyes with a searching look upon the Duke de Chartres, hoping for some significant glance that would reassure her as to his intentions. But the young duke's eyes were turned another way: he was following the master of ceremonies, and making a profound inclination before the king.

Madame dared no longer hesitate: she gave her hand to Mademoiselle de Blois, and led her forward to the table where lay the dreaded document.

At a signal from the king, the keeper of the seal advanced, and, taking up the parchment, read the marriage contract of his royal highness the Duke de Chartres with Mademoiselle de Blois. The duke's marriage with the king's daughter entitled him to the *grandes entrées du cabinet*, and *the entrées de derrière*,—privileges highly prized by the members of the royal family. The contract also recognized Mademoiselle de Blois as a daughter of France, and gave her a dowry of two millions of livres, several large estates, and a complete *parure* of costly diamonds.

With the exception of madame, everybody was enraptured with the royal munificence. Again she tried to meet her son's eyes, but they were steadfastly fixed upon the hand of the king who had signed the contract, and was in the act of placing it before his daughter.

Mademoiselle de Blois scribbled her name under that of her father, and passed the pen over to the bridegroom. The decisive moment was at hand. With fast-throbbing heart, the duchess bent forward to hear her son's rejection of this insulting mésalliance, when lo! that son, with a placid smile, accepted the pen, and signed!

A cry had well-nigh burst from his mother's lips, as, with every show of respect, he presented her the pen. Speechless with anger, she advanced her hand, but it was not to take the instrument of her humiliation : it was to administer to her rebellious son a box on the ear which resounded like a pistol-shot through the apartment, and created considerable astonishment among the aristocratic guests therein assembled.*

The young duke uttered a howl, and, rubbing his cheek, jumped behind the hooped dress of his bride-elect.

"Madame !" exclaimed the king, "what means this violence ?"

"Your majesty, I was killing a fly that had lit upon Philip's cheek."

"It must be a robust fly, if it is not crushed to atoms," replied the king, much amused.

The court, unable to withstand their merriment, burst into one simultaneous shout of laughter, under cover of which Elizabeth-Charlotte, with tearful eyes, signed the fatal document which mingled the noble blood of Orleans with the muddy stream of illegitimacy.

## CHAPTER IX.

### VENGEANCE.

So great had been the haste of the courtiers to spread the news of Louvois' disgrace, that the very usher who opened the door that led into the vestibule, performed his office with a superciliousness which proved him to have heard it as well as his betters.

Louvois felt as if his grave were yawning before him. He had forgotten that his carriage could not possibly have returned so soon ; and now he stood alone on the perron of the palace, staring up and down the street in the vain hope of concealing himself in a fiacre from the gaze of the curious. No sentinel saluted him, no soldier presented arms, as, ashamed of his rich dress and sparkling orders, which rendered him

* Historical.—See " Letters of the Duchess of Orleans to the Princess of Wales."

conspicuous, he walked on and on, an object of curiosity to every passer-by. At length, on the Pont Neuf, he met a dilapidated old hackney-coach, amid whose threadbare cushions he was glad to retreat from observation.

On his arrival home, nobody came out to assist him to alight ; for how could the lackeys who were idling around the porte-cochère surmise that the occupant of that shabby vehicle was their haughty master ?

He entered the hôtel, and, without vouchsafing a word to the astounded valets, ascended the staircase that led to his own private apartments. But they came after him to ask whether he was indisposed, and whether they could be of service.

Their offers were rejected with scorn ; but Louvois thought it politic to inform his own valet that, having been attacked with sudden indisposition, he had been forced to leave the court-ball, and return in a fiacre. While he was being divested of his rich dress and long curled wig, the valet went on to announce that Count Barbesieur had arrived from Italy, and was desirous of seeing his father as soon as possible. A lady also had called to see his excellency ; and, having been told that he was at the great court-festival, she had replied that he would be apt to return home early, and she would await his arrival, for she had important business to transact with him.

"Where is the lady ?" asked Louvois.

"She is in her carriage at the side door of the hôtel. Shall I ask her in the drawing-room, your excellency ?"

"Later," said Louvois. "I must first speak with my son."

"I am here," cried Barbesieur, who had silently entered the room.

"Leave us," said Louvois to the valet, "and when Count Barbesieur has retired, admit the lady. I—"

He paused, and caught at the arm-chair for support. He had become suddenly dizzy, his face grew scarlet, his eyes blood-shot, and his breathing oppressed.

The valet hastened to his assistance, and offered him a glass of water. He emptied it at a draught, but his hands shook so, that he could scarcely hold the goblet. Barbesieur had thrown himself full length on a sofa, whence he contemplated his father with the most consummate indifference.

"You ought to be bled," said he, carelessly.

"I will do so. It may relieve me," replied he, panting. "Go," added he to the valet, "go for Fagot."

The valet hurried off, and the father and son were left alone together. The former lay gasping with his head flung back on a cushion ; the latter watched him closely, but without the merest appearance of sympathy or interest.

After a pause, he spoke : "Father, have you forgotten my presence ? "

Louvois opened his eyes wearily. "No ; I have not forgotten it."

"You do not ask me about the result of my expedition," said Barbesieur.

"Nor do you seem to think it incumbent upon you to ask wherefore I suffer, or why I am here instead of being where I ought to be, at the *fiançailles* of Mademoiselle de Blois," replied Louvois, whom his son's indifference had stung to returning energy.

"What care I for the *fiançailles* of Mademoiselle de Blois ? " answered Barbesieur. "And as regards your indisposition, it is not the first time that I have seen you similarly affected. These congestions invariably leave you stronger than they find you ; so let us pass on to affairs more momentous. I have to inform you that my expedition to Italy has resulted in a disastrous failure. Have you seen my courier ? "

"No, I have not seen him, but I know that you were guilty of sending me written dispatches on a subject which pen should never have recorded."

"Oh ! " sneered the dutiful son, "you are better, I see, for you grow abusive. Then I suppose my courier has been arrested ? "

"Ay, and your letters are in the hands of Louis XIV."

"Can it be possible ? " cried Barbesieur, anxiously. "How came he in possession of them ? "

"They were given him by the Duchess of Orleans."

"But she—"

"She received them from her step-daughter, the Duchess of

Savoy. Not only them, but your imbecile-written promise to Strozzi that his wife would return to him as soon as Prince Eugene was dead."

"It was a blunder, I admit," returned Barbesieur. "But the idiot had so set his heart upon it that I was forced to yield to his whims ; there was no other way of controlling him. I had no sooner given him this paper, than he became as plastic as clay."

"Nevertheless, Laura is dead, and Eugene of Savoy lives."

"Oh, yes—the thing miscarried, but how, I cannot conceive. I was close at hand, waiting with horses for Strozzi, who was to seize Laura, and make all speed for Italy. I waited so long, that at last I ventured to creep up to the house, and there I learned how Strozzi had stabbed Laura, and Eugene had shot Strozzi. As soon as I found out that all had gone awry, I galloped off to Bonaletta, to get my share of Strozzi's and Laura's property. But the covetous relations would not let me lay a finger on Laura's estates, without your written authorization. That brought me hurriedly to Paris. I want it at once, that I may return to Bonaletta to-day."

"You must remain for a while longer," said Louvois.

"And why, pray ?"

"Because you must at least wait until my funeral is over," replied the unhappy father.

Barbesieur began to laugh. "Oh, papa ! pray don't get sentimental. People are not apt to die of these little vexations. I suppose the king was rude, as he has been many a day before this—was he ?"

"He was more than rude ; in presence of all his nobles he accused me of participation in Laura's murder, and banished me from court until I returned with proofs of my innocence."

"H'm—" muttered Barbesieur. "The affair looks ugly."

"Insulted before the whole court," murmured Louvois.

"Pshaw ! Don't take it so much to heart. It is not your first affront. You know full well that if old women get the better of you to-day, you will outwit them to-morrow. Witness your feud of years with De Maintenon."

"I shall not outwit them this time, Barbesieur. The duchess has played her cards too dexterously for me to escape.

Nor would the king befriend me ; he is under too many ob-ligations to me not to desire my humiliation and my ruin. Moreover, he is anxious to propitiate the Duke of Savoy, and will give him full satisfaction for the attempt on the life of his kinsman. I am lost—irretrievably lost ! "

"Then so much the more imperative is it for us to lay the foundation of some new structure of fortune elsewhere.— Luckily, Laura's large estates in Italy are all-sufficient to make you a very rich man yet. So give me authority to act for you ; I will go at once and take possession, while you ar-range your affairs at home, and then follow me to Italy."

"He thinks of nothing but wealth," murmured Louvois ; "he has no shame for loss of reputation or good name."

"Nonsense !" said Barbesieur, with a coarse laugh ; "no man that has money loses reputation. Poverty is the only crime that the world cannot pardon, and you, thanks to the Marchioness Bonaletta, have just inherited a fortune."

Louvois shuddered. "A fortune through the murder of my child ! "

"For which we are not accountable," said Barbesieur, care-lessly. "We owe that obligation to Strozzi, and I must say it was the only sensible thing I ever knew him to do."

"Silence !" cried Louvois, incensed. "If you have no re-spect for the living, have some reverence for the dead ! "

Barbesieur rose with a yawn. "I see that my honored father is not in a mood for reasonable conversation. Here comes the surgeon with his lancet. Perhaps, when you have lost a few quarts of your bad blood, you may see things in a better light." So saying, he sauntered out of the room. With scorn and hatred in his eye, Louvois watched him until he disappeared from sight ; then turning to the surgeon, who had entered by another door—

"Be quick, and take some blood from my veins, or I shall suffocate ! "

A half an hour later, the operation was over, and Louvois felt much relieved. His face was pale, his eyes no longer bloodshot, and the surgeon having prescribed rest, the dis-graced favorite was left alone.

He sat propped up in his arm-chair, staring at vacancy—

his solitude embittered by the recollection of what he was, and
what he had been. The stately edifice of greatness, which he
had spent a lifetime in erecting, had fallen like a *château de
cartes*, leaving nothing behind but the stinging recollection of
a glorious past. He could not outlive it—he could not retire
to obscurity—he—

Suddenly he shivered, and gazed with eyes distended at the
figure of a woman that now stood against the portière opposite. Great God ! had delirium seized upon his senses ?
Were the memories of his youth about to take shape and form,
and mingle their shadowy images with the tangible realities
of life ! He knew her—tall, beautiful, pale as she was—and
the recognition filled him with terror indefinable.

He knew her well ! In her youth he had loved her, but
she had scorned his love, because she was cherishing the hope
of becoming Queen of France ! This triumph had been denied
her, and she had hidden her disappointment by a marriage
with another. And fearfully had Louvois avenged her rejection of his love ! He had cited her as a criminal, before the
highest tribunal in France, and had driven her into exile.
Destiny had also given him power to crush her son—to blast
his life as a lover, and his good name as a man. But ah ! that
daughter whom Eugene had loved ! He had blasted her life
also, and had given her over to a monster that had murdered
her ! So young, so lovely, so attractive ! She had died to
gratify the malice of her own father !

Like a lightning-flash these thoughts glanced athwart
his brain, while, breathless and terror-stricken, he gazed upon
the spectre that stood against the portière !

Was it a spectre, or some delusion of his disordered mind ?
She stood motionless as a marble statue of Nemesis ; but those
eyes—those glowing eyes—there was life and hate in their
fiery depths !

Louvois had not the power to look away ; he was as spell-
bound as a bird under the glance of the basilisk.

"Olympia ! " cried he, at last, with a supreme effort to dis-
solve the spell.

She threw back her proud head, and came directly in front
of his chair. "You recognize me," said she, in tones of icy

*hauteur.* "I was waiting before I spoke, to see whether you had forgotten me."

"What brings you hither?" stammered he, confusedly.

"Destiny," replied she, sternly. "Louvois, God is just, for He has chosen me to be the instrument of your destruction. I was travelling through Turin to nurse my son, who was not expected to live. I learned that his illness was of the heart—not of the body. His Laura had been murdered before his eyes, and, for love of her, he was in danger of dying. Ah, Louvois! it was the second time you had almost robbed me of my child! But God is just! To my hands were confided the proofs of your participation in the crime of your daughter's assassination, and it was I that delivered them to the Duchess of Orleans. She had her Laura's death to avenge, I—great God! what had I not? The humiliation of my flight from France—my persecution by strangers in a foreign land—my son's lifelong sorrow!—But ah! you, that drove him from his native country, have fallen, to rise no more, while Eugene's name is but another word throughout the world for genius and valor."

Louvois' teeth chattered with fear. He raised his hand, as if to implore forbearance. She gave him, in return, a look of scorn.

"All Paris rings with your disgrace. The populace are before your windows, ready, at a signal, to assault your palace, as, at your son's instigation, they once assailed mine. Your servants are stealing away, and you are forsaken! Poor, fallen, powerless Louvois!"

"Not so," screamed Louvois, "not so! If I am powerless it is because I am dying!" And, with a passionate gesture, he tore the bandages from his arm.

The blood gushed out like water from a fountain, and Olympia looked on for a while in cruel enjoyment of her enemy's mortal agony. But her hatred was unclouded by passion.

"It were a kindness to suffer you to die now," said she; and her words fell like sharp icicles upon his poor, lacerated heart. "But you shall live to endure the contumely you forced upon me and mine! Farewell! I go to call for help."

She crossed the room, and, as she entered the antechamber, Louvois swooned, and fell upon the floor.

"Go to your lord," said Olympia to the valets who were waiting. "The bandage has become loosened, and he will bleed to death if you are not prompt."

Crossing the antechamber, she opened the door that led to a corridor where her own valet was awaiting her return.

"Can you tell me where I may find Count Barbesieur?" asked she.

"Yes, my lady. He is in his own room, to which I was directed by his valet."

"Show me the way," said the countess, following the man to the farther end of the long corridor.

"Here, my lady," said he, pausing, "is his anteroom."

"Go in and announce me."

The valet opened the door and crossed the antechamber. It was empty; for Barbesieur's valet was, with the other servants, in the vestibule, discussing the mysteries of the evening. Seeing that no one was there to announce the countess, the lackey knocked until he heard a voice from within. He then threw the door wide open, and cried out—

"The Countess de Soissons!"

Barbesieur, who was seated before a table, deep in the examination of the title-deeds of the Bonaletta estates, started up in amazement at the unceremonious interruption. As he turned around to chastise the insolence of the servant, he encountered the stately figure of the Countess de Soissons.

"It is long since we met," said she. "Do you remember the occasion of our meeting?"

"No, countess," replied he, awed by her queenly bearing into momentary courtesy.

"I will refresh your memory. When last I saw you, you were at the head of the rabble that mobbed the Palace de Soissons, and had just received a wound in your arm from the pistol of my son, Prince Eugene. I had not the satisfaction of being present at the horsewhipping he administered to you at Long Champs, for I was obliged to fly from your persecutions, and I have never set foot in France until now."

Barbesieur laughed. "I have had my revenge. I owe him

nothing. The very grief that is sapping his life at this moment is the work of my hand."

"I know it, and I, in my turn, have avenged *his* woes."

"You must have done it secretly, then, for I have never felt any inconvenience from your vengeance."

"You will experience it before long. Did one of your servants bring you a fine peach on a salver, about half an hour ago?"

Barbesieur turned very pale, and stammered, "Yes."

"Did you eat it?"

"Yes," murmured he, "I did."

"Then, Barbesieur, that peach avenged Eugene and Laura both. I sent it to you."

"You!" cried Barbesieur, with a shudder.

"Yes," replied Olympia, her black eyes darting fire as she spoke. "I sent you the peach, and if you have eaten it (it will be very slow in its effects), you have just four years longer to live!"

As he heard these terrible words, Barbesieur dropped, like a felled ox, to the floor.

"Count Barbesieur," cried a voice in the antechamber, "your father is dying of apoplexy."

Barbesieur started up with an oath, and darted from the room. The Countess de Soissons followed him to the corridor. No one was there, for the servants had all congregated, as near as possible, to the chamber of the dying statesman. Olympia passed on, unchallenged, reached her carriage, and set off at full gallop for Nice.

She found Eugene improved, and sitting up. He was in his arm-chair, gazing with tearful eyes at a portrait opposite— a portrait of Laura, as Sister Angelica. His thoughts were so far, far away from the weary present, that the door had opened, and his mother had put her arms around his neck, before he became aware of her entrance.

"Eugene, my beloved son," said she, "I have avenged you."

"Avenged? Dear mother, what can you mean?"

"I mean that Louvois is dead—dead of humiliation. And that Barbesieur lives; but lives in the knowledge that, in four years, he must die. His life, then, unto the bitter end, will be

one long agony. Eugene, you avenged my wrongs. I have
now paid the debt."

Eugene sighed heavily. "You have erred, mother. You
should have left further vengeance to God. What does it
profit me that Barbesieur suffers—his sufferings cannot recall
my Laura."

"Ah," said Olympia, disappointed, "if you were in health,
you would not be so pusillanimous, my child. 'Tis easy to see
that you are sick."

"No, mother, I am no longer sick. At Laura's command,
I have wrestled with bodily weakness, and have overcome it."

"I do not understand you, my son."

Eugene pointed to the figure of Doctor Franzi, who just
then entered the room. "Listen, mother, and you will understand."

The doctor advanced, and, taking Eugene's extended hand,
repeated Laura's dying words. Eugene looked at his mother,
and smiled.

"This message has been the medicine that has restored me
to health. My Laura speaks from beyond the grave, and I
must obey."

"Who but a hero could have obeyed a mandate at once so
loving and so cruel !" exclaimed Doctor Franzi. "Countess,
I am rejoiced to see you, but more especially rejoice that you
should have arrived to-day."

"I travelled night and day to return in time," said Olympia, looking fondly at her son.

"Is it a festival ?" asked he.

"Yes, dear child," replied his mother, kissing him. "It is
your thirtieth birth-day."

"My thirtieth birth-day !" murmured Eugene. "My
youth is no more ; I enter upon the stern epoch of mature
manhood."

"Youth, with its sweet visions of love, has passed away ;
but manhood will indemnify you, prince, for the sorrows of
the past. Before you lies a future of usefulness and heroism.
—Congratulate your son, countess, for he yesterday received
from the Emperor Leopold the chief command of his armies
in Italy. The troops are on their way now, to greet their gen-

eral. Hark! Do you not hear the drums? Every brave heart in the army is beating with joy at the prospect of seeing him again."

"And I, too, am joyful at the anticipation," replied Eugene, rising from his chair. "You are right, Franzi. I have been sorely grieved, 'tis true; but I bear about my heart the knowledge of my Laura's love—as veritable now as when I saw and felt her mortal presence. This blessing shall make me a hero. So help me God! I will strive hereafter to do my duty as a man, a soldier, and a Christian."

The drums rolled, the trumpets sounded, and thousands of voices responded without:

"Long live our general! Long live Prince Eugene!"

(5)

THE END.

23232